AURETHIA RISING

ATLAS LAIKA

Cover artwork by H0psynth · Chapter artwork by Marta Riva · Star map by Cartographybird Maps · Early editorial assistance by sleeptstxtic

Aurethia Rising is a work of fiction. It is best suited for readers who are comfortable engaging with sensitive topics, including but not limited to: *violence, adult content, sexual content, body augmentation, chronic sickness, animal death, war, food insecurity, killing and gore, etc.*

There is a pronunciation guide available in the back matter

For my Dad — who wanted to be an astronaut, who saw The Empire Strikes Back fifty-two times in theaters, who taught me to never stop looking up

"Look back over the past, with its changing empires that rose and fell, and you can foresee the future too."

— MARCUS AURELIUS

AN ASTRONOMIC CHART OF

THE LUX SYSTEM

GRIEA

GRIEAN ORBIT

GRIEAN
JUMP GATE

SIERRA

SHEPARD

STATIONER
JUMP GATE

DIVINITY

AURETHIA

MERCY

DRAITUNE

DRAITUNIAN ORBIT

DRAITUNIAN
JUMP GATE

LUX CONTINUUM

OCURIAN
JUMP GATE

OCURY

OCURIAN ORBIT

SUNDER · RED DWARF STAR

I

THE LION OF AURETHIA

CHAPTER ONE

ELIO

Looming on the outskirts of the farthest glittering ring coiled around the great planet Draitune orbited two spherical moons. One white as a bared tooth. The other a suspension of clashing hues.

Mercy, the larger of the pair, was parched and barren, a wasteland with little to no resources. It lit the sky like a match strike, glowing hot in Draitune's shadow. Aurethia hovered below, plumed blue with the promise of a deep sea, and stained green from a flourish of fauna. The undeniably stable moon was a perfect example of awkward anomalies and undisputed accidents. One day, long before the Greater Universe had a name or a story, a lonely meteorite had knocked twin pieces of Draitune loose, carving out a bit of its flesh and giving birth to the prospect of new life.

As all things are made, Mercy and Aurethia had appeared without cause, yet only one evolved enough to have an effect.

Aurethia hosted an uncompromised wild terrain. It was fertile, as most places hoped to be, and it was inhabited. Past the threadbare cloud cover painted beneath low orbit, the living moon trembled with ocean song. Orange-breasted swallows cut sharply through briny air scented by sea moss and lizard scat left behind from native iguanas peppering the tide-pools. Wide-billed pelicans shoveled in the shallows. Hawks dove for crabs and eels.

Inland, east of the fishing village Nadhas, the sprawling orchard attached to the Henly manor fanned out beyond the estate, beckoning bees, butterflies, and beetles to scale their branches. Fastened like a crown on the hillside, the extravagant manor punched a partial hole in the horizon. It was stone-built, steepled with tall spires, rust-colored and laden with hand-hammered glass. Beautiful in all its glory. Meadow surrounded the property, gold in autumn, jade in summer, and the magnificent plum tree, mother to the rare candlebell flower, fanned the courtyard. It was the gem of the house, rooted deep with strong birch-white boughs.

Elio Henly sat beneath it, watching an Aurethian lion paw through the grass near the east wing. Winter ebbed. The ground thawed, stirring spring to wake in the soil. Soon those endangered lions would lounge in the mauve light beamed across the moon by refracted sunshine caught in Draitune's first ring, and Elio would lie with them in the meadow like he did every year while their parent planet rotated high above. He listed his head toward the cliff separating the manor from the beach. A trawler cruised toward Nadhas, slicing the blue-black water.

Today was his eighteenth birthday. He pushed the pungent taste of destiny down his throat.

House Henly, the stewards of Aurethia, had risen to the top of the political landscape over the course of a kiloyear, dating back to the time before their system, Lux, joined Mal and Ren as prominent pieces in the Greater Universe. Lux, puzzled together by three planets, Ocury, Griea, and Draitune, also home to Aurethia and Mercy, shared the outer reaches with Sunder, their red dwarf, and a trio of populated space stations, Divinity, Shepard, and Sierra.

Elio tipped his head against the tree and stared at the sky. Draitune was a violet ghost. Half her body engulfed the backdrop like watercolor on canvas. He squinted against harsh daylight and blew out an exhausted breath. His mother, Lena, likely flitted about the house, making arrangements for cherry cake, sparkling wine, and roasted goosefish served on fanciful dinnerware. But with salt on his tongue and the fragrant smell of candlebell in his nose, Elio daydreamed about fate.

The holobooks and old tomes preserved in the Henly library spoke of things like this, times like these. Some with reverence, others with pity. Elio certainly didn't know what to believe, but he knew his duty and his purpose, and both began today.

The passage of time had seemed boring and trivial until approximately one cycle ago: realizing his life would radically change the very moment he crossed the threshold between classified child and perceived adult. Even so, the day itself didn't seem different than any other. Elio had practiced his blade-work with Peadar in the morning, took breakfast with his brother, studied an ancient Earthen text after that, and then came to the tree to contemplate the faux-normalcy of it all. It wasn't until he heard the soft pad of leather tread on the brick surrounding the plum tree that the inevitable snapped like a twig.

The liaison from Griea, Maxine Carr, who had grown alongside him for the past four cycles, ducked beneath a low-hanging branch and said, "Lord Henly," in greeting, as she typically did.

Elio met her upturned amber eyes, colored like sun-soaked syrup, and tried to smile. Her sleek, black hair was cropped at her jaw, framing a thin mouth and straight nose. She looked at him the same way most messengers with sour news did, full of pity and patience.

"I'll connect with the High Lord and High Lady shortly, but I wanted to speak with you first. As you know, it's my duty to report accurate information to our Legatus on Griea, and I intend to confirm the celebration of your eighteenth cycle by the end of the day." She clasped her palms and nodded. "Which will put your engagement into motion."

Elio's jaw twitched. "I appreciate you coming to me first."

"It may be inappropriate, but I consider us friends, Elio. I only hope to preserve your comfort."

He patted the place beside him and scooted over. Maxine's mouth curved, relief settling in her cheeks. She sat and turned to face him. He stared at the light slanting through tangled branches. How strange, he thought, to be the product of peace-making. A thing brokered and agreed upon four generations ago. When Maxine had been sent to Aurethia as an ambassador, Elio welcomed her as a playmate, someone from a distant world — Aurethia's adversary. He never thought critically about her purpose on the moon, never questioned the laughter they shared or the late nights they spent in his bedchamber, gossiping about a soft-spoken farmer from Atreyu or a pretty tailor from Basset. Maxine had always been his friend first, someone he danced with at parties, someone he confided in. She was twenty. Older, a bit wiser. And he admired her. Saw her as an example of what Griea could be, would be.

But Maxine Carr, Griean agent, loyal to the ice giant, had been stationed on Aurethia to document his growth. She provided insight to her homeworld, negotiated on behalf of Legatus Marcus, offered diplomatic solutions to petty disagreements, and functioned as a good faith gesture between their houses. One day, there would be peace. A union. And

Maxine had been sent there to ensure it. He should be savvy enough to remember that, but ambassadorship be damned, resentment bubbled beneath his skin.

In the end, it was his great-grandfather Elio should've cursed, not Maxine. She was only doing her job.

"We're friends," he said. Since she was sixteen, since he was fourteen. He cleared the bitterness from his throat. "My parents will negotiate a courtship. Can I rely on you to advocate for that as well?"

"Of course." She grasped his hand, squeezing. "The Legatus is a good man, and Duchess Constance will want the Imperator to spend time on Aurethia. She's a practical woman. She'll insist he get to know you, understand your planetary customs and personal mannerisms before..." She trailed off, considering her next statement carefully. "Before the ceremony is officiated. And he's twenty," she added cheerily. "You'll have much to talk about. He'll learn about Aurethia, teach you about Griea. It will be a prosperous partnership, I'm sure of it."

Imperator. Warlord of Griea. The title caused his breath to catch. "Good." He couldn't think of much else to say. "You'll be at dinner tonight?"

"For your birthday? Obviously." She slid into the natural playfulness they'd embraced over the years.

"Do you..." He stopped himself.

Since he was a child, Elio had dreamed of a boy, then a man. When he was young, he dreamed of someone's hand, pale as winter, wrapped tight around the handle of a knife. Knuckles flexing, small, feeble, then larger, scarred and rigid. As he grew, the dreams did, too. Elio saw broad shoulders, lifting and falling with each step – sometimes growing distant, sometimes coming closer. A bold black stripe on fair skin, as if applied by a perfect paintbrush. A parted mouth the color of a pink seashell. He had never seen the Imperator, his betrothed, but he envisioned him, imagined him.

By Aurethian standard, Griea was caged in shadowy rumors built from the bones of a sordid past. Grieans were said to be ruthless, sharp-toothed barbarians. War-happy and cunning. Soldiers from a fanged planet with a penchant for spilling blood. Their machine and organic weaponry were purchased far and wide across the Greater Universe.

Maxine hummed, waiting for him to finish.

"Cael." Elio tested his name, trying it like a dollop of butter. "Do you know anything about him?"

"I know he's favored by his people." She leaned closer, lowering her voice to a whisper. "I hear he's handsome — "

Elio shushed her. Embarrassed laughter came and went.

Maxine continued. "Why haven't you asked me about him before?"

"Because I didn't want to think about my fading freedom."

She knocked her elbow against his arm. "One day, you'll be High Lord Elio Henly, lion of Aurethia, wed to Imperator Cael Volkov, Keeper of the Basilisk. Is that not an exciting title?"

"It's a long one," he joked.

Maxine laughed. He did, too.

"This union will usher in a peaceful era for our homeworlds." She was serious now, endearing and wishful. "Be what it may, arranged or not, you will have the power to adjust the trade route as you see fit, distribute Avara to the far reaches of the Greater Universe, and combine the wealth of two Great Houses. Aurethia already loves you. Griea will love you, too."

Ah, Avara. The entire reason he'd been sold to the Griean heir like a prized cow in the first place. Avara, the soul stone, the miracle crystal, the only known treatment for parsec sickness. Avara, the beautiful blue cubic gem growing in the belly of Aurethia and nowhere else in the Greater Universe. Avara, discovered by Alexander Henly, the man who had sealed Elio's fate.

Four generations ago, after his great-grandfather gained control of the Lux Continuum, the largest trade route in the system, Alexander struck a deal with the stewards of Griea, promising the hand of his great-grand-child to the first-born Volkov heir, securing future prosperity in a time of unrest. But until then, Avara distribution would take precedence over Griean weaponry. The very act of it — limiting access to the most direct and stable starlink to their neighboring systems, Mal and Ren, and cutting off timely deliverables to distant communities — caused the value of Griean currency to plummet. Since that day, Griea and Aurethia lived in a tense but cordial rivalry, besting each other at every turn. Aurethia controlled Avara; Griea specialized in defense. The Greater Universe required both houses to remain operational. One provided medical inter-vention to a widespread epidemic, the other created capable soldiers, reli-able artillery, and unquestionable blades. It was a matter of timing, of sacrifice and consequence, which brought their houses to this inter-ception.

In the many years that followed Alexander's acquisition of the starlink, Aurethia closed itself like a spined beast, quietly preparing for the day

House Volkov breached the treaty. They hadn't, though, and Elio was their reward.

"The bridge was sold, but not built," Elio said.

"You will build it."

Elio's throat itched. "I've been shackled with responsibility I did not ask for, Maxine. Forgive my lack of enthusiasm."

"As is life," Maxine said. She jammed her knuckle into his rib, causing him to yelp. "Oh, Lord Elio, how tortured you must be," she taunted, laughing with him. "Forget luxury and power! Dismiss the staff, release the livestock, sell the terrestrial ships, allow this poor boy to retire in a village! Become a fisherman, Elio! Marry a commoner!"

Elio rolled onto his side. Boisterous laughter shook through him, dulling the anxiety coiled at the bottom of his chest. Her mockery wasn't exactly ill-fitting, but he still swatted her, hissing and crowing. "I hear you! Enough, enough." Once he caught his breath, he dropped his arms beside his head and gazed at a perfectly round plum dangling from a high branch. "It's my birthday, I'm allowed to whine."

"In all seriousness, I have heard Imperator Volkov is easy to look at," she quipped. "So if you don't want him, pass him along."

Elio's face warmed. "I'll keep that in mind."

DISC-LAMPS HOVERED ABOVE THE long, rectangular table, washing the dining hall in orange light. Beeswax candles clasped in honeycomb flickered between steaming platters. The deep-sea goosefish, an Aurethian delicacy, was served whole, its reddish scales charred and slicked with plum sauce. There was a small pheasant and fruit from the orchard. Long-grain rice sourced from the paddy fields west of Atreyu sent up fragrant puffs of citrus and fir, and thickly sliced seed bread was served with savory butter and apricot jam. It was a beautiful display, one Elio wished he could've enjoyed more. But the impossible undercurrent of what the next day might bring burdened the otherwise jovial, sweet celebration.

High Lord Darius, his father, sat with High Lady Lena at the head of the table. Beside them, Orson, eight years his junior, spooned rice into his mouth, and across the table, Lorelei, sixteen, propped up her elbows and cradled her pointed chin.

The three Henly siblings shared many characteristics. Green eyes — Orson's a shock of venom, Lorelei's like moss atop a lake, Elio's reminiscent of shade grown pine. They carried the same sloped cheekbones, wore the same dusty, golden hair. Orson had yet to grow into Elio's dignified bone structure, but Lorelei was foxlike and beautiful, a ripple of their mother.

Darius brought a water glass to his mouth and made a pleased noise. "My eldest is a child no more," he said. His smile dimpled. Age rarely crossed his face, but Elio noticed the lines around his eyes sink. "Time is a remarkable thing. I'd steal some of it back if I could."

Lena smiled. She draped her hand over Darius's wrist and said, "Life waits for no one, I fear."

Lorelei pointed her fork at Elio. "You're of age, brother. That means — "

"I know what it means," Elio said.

"Don't be like that! I'm excited to meet this Griean. Do you think his teeth are filed into points or — "

"Lorelei," Lena warned.

From the other end of the table, Maxine cleared her throat. "It's quite possible, my lady, but I doubt it."

"I meant no offense, Maxine, forgive me. I know this Imperator is keeper of a beast, though, and — "

"Basilisk," Maxine interjected. Her tone was impressively level. She brought her knife to a cut of pheasant, neatly slicing. "They're ancient serpents. Great leviathans that live beneath the ice. We use their bones for weaponry, their scales for armor. They're revered on Griea. Keeper of the Basilisk is the title given to the commander of our Royal Reserve." She brought a bite to her mouth. Her teeth scraped the utensil. "It's a very high honor."

Lorelei flicked her impish eyes from Maxine's plate to her face. "Sea snakes," she deadpanned, as if she understood.

"Almost," Maxine entertained, laughing in her throat. "Albeit large enough to swallow this house. Some, at least."

"I've read about them." Elio shot his sister a warning glance. "They're rumored to be vicious."

Maxine furrowed her brow. "That's not a rumor," she said, chuckling, and chewed another meaty bite.

Darius cleared his throat. "House Volkov has agreed to a courtship. The Imperator will arrive on Aurethia within a month, jump gate permitting. The breadth of his stay is still being discussed. Regardless, I expect this house to greet him and his entourage respectfully," he stressed, hooking

Lorelei in a narrow stare, "and with gratitude. Maxine has been our honored emissary for many years and will remain as such during Cael's visit."

Maxine inclined her head.

Elio's stomach turned. He forced down a bite of fish and nodded. "He'll be staying here at the manor?"

"In the east wing with Peadar and the Aurethian guard," his father confirmed.

At the end of the table, seated across from Maxine, Peadar nodded. He was a deep-faced, dark-skinned man with a spackling of stubble. Grey streaked his tight, thick hair. His stature spoke of combat. For as long as Elio had been alive, Peadar Mahone had overseen defense of their moon.

"And he's bringing an entourage," Lorelei said curiously.

"Security personnel." Lena flapped her hand dismissively. She breathed out a sigh. "Anyway, the engagement will commence on schedule, and Aurethia will welcome Griea as an ally, Cael as a friend, and this engagement as a blessing." She lifted her champagne flute and took a sip to mask the crack at the corner of her smile.

Elio turned toward his dinner, ignoring Lorelei's relentless stare and the shrill slip of Orson's knife against porcelain. *Blessing*. What a provocative word for what was about to happen. All his life he'd understood the intention behind his very existence, knew he served a greater purpose than simply first-born. Not only the Aurethian heir, but the tribute paid against a long-standing debt. Retribution packaged in bridal-white and offered to the planet his great-grandfather had butchered a relationship with.

Indigo, Lady Lena's handmaiden, grinned as she swept into the room, carrying a decadent, three-layered cake. It sweetened the air, all cherries and cocoa. Vanilla frosting pillowed each tier. The sugary glaze across the top caught the light, reflecting Elio's blank face as she set it down. The candle in its center sparkled, glimmering white and gold, crackling like a tiny firework.

CHAPTER TWO

CAEL

Far across the system, Griea spun slowly, absorbing the barest of Sunder's rays. Draitune's centermost ring, composed of frostbitten meteorites and glittering ice fields, captured the red dwarf's light, and beamed it to Griea secondhand, a kaleidoscope effect that kept the snowy planet from descending into a lifetime of darkness. Unlike the sprawling cosmopolitan cityscape on the ringed giant, or the lush farmland scaling the surface of its precious moon, Griea was an unfriendly place scarred with jagged mountains, its people surviving in the open palm of a frozen sea.

Machina, the largest metropolis on Griea, towered high above a frosty expanse of saltwater covering most of the planet — the Sliding Sea. The city was smartly built on a patch of rocky land at the base of the Goren Mountain. Composed of dark glass, hardy steel, and black stone, Machina was an intricate stain on Griea's stark surface. Interwoven bridges and archways linked varying levels of livable space, and the city boasted one of the largest galactic ports in the system, allowing offworld transportation of its soldiers and trade goods to go unobstructed by leisurely travel.

Imperator Cael Volkov surveyed Machina from a capsule elevator crawling along the outer edge of the Sector Two Travel Outlet. He jammed his gloved hands into his coat pockets and stared through gaps between blackened buildings. In the distance, wind kicked snow off the surface of the ice-laden sea. Sunder, a pinhole glimmer in the center of the grey sky, glinted.

Imperator, the training arena is ready for you. The artificial voice hummed, attached to a small dialect device looped around his ear. He tapped the blank side of the device to confirm he'd received the message and inhaled deeply. It was the day of reckoning, a pocket of time squatting just past the barricade where training and deliberation became execution and mobilization. He'd spent a lifetime preparing for it — this day — yet its arrival seemed underwhelming.

The elevator slowed to a stop on the third tier of the multi-level bridgeway connecting Sector Two to the rest of Machina. Far below, groundcrafts cruised through crowded streets, and above, high-powered train systems shuttled people from one place to another.

Cael stepped out and took the sky bridge to the Organic Weaponry Division, a walled-off territory connected to the Griean War College, stretching far enough to reach the Machinery District in Sector Four. A group of uniformed students strode past, bowing their heads. Two of them greeted Cael with a polite, "Imperator."

Cael offered a respectful nod and continued on his way. The entrance to the Organic Weaponry Division blended seamlessly with the rest of the building, a gleaming black door that slid open from the center, allowing patrons to walk in or out without jeopardizing heat retention.

Cael peeled away his coat as soon as his shoes met the polished interior. He climbed the staircase to the domed sparring arena stationed above the gauntlet. It resembled Griea's renowned arena, circular and plain, dotted with spotlights and stocked with assorted weaponry.

When he wasn't training the Royal Reserve — specialized Griean soldiers loyal to the Legatus — he was teaching combat classes, assessing the Planetary Syndicate, inspecting new weapon designs, and practicing for the Tupinaire.

Today, despite his too-long list of responsibilities, he could not concentrate. His endocrine system slugged too close to anxiety. Vertebrae knotted, drawing his shoulders close to his neck. He worked to relieve the pressure, aiming his chin one direction then the other, running his palm over the faint stubble on his naked skull, and tried to focus on training as he stalked toward the table and snatched up a curved blade. The handle weighed nicely in his palm. Easy to grasp, easier to swing.

His dialect device buzzed again. *Confirm arrival.* Cael tapped the earpiece. *Thank you, Imperator. Prepare for sparring session. Entry, one. Voluntary incarcerated citizen. Time served: Nine weeks. Time offered: One rotation. Time allotted: Two rotations.*

Cael tipped his head curiously. He placed his finger on the device. "Offense," he stated.

Crime: Unwarranted violence. Filing: Domestic.

Cael stripped away his thermal tunic, revealing the customary ink striped across his torso. Each cubic design was locked with another, creating an interconnected blockade along his spine and over his nape. The tattoo speared into a point on the crown of his head. Two more, angled like industrial arrows, mirrored his hipbones.

A shadow appeared in the open doorway on the other side of the training arena. It grew closer, assuming the shape of a man. His skin wore no mark of status, no ink or jewel. But he walked like someone accustomed to fear. Instilling it, thriving in it.

"You understand the terms," Cael noted, flipping the knife once, twice. He gave the handle a squeeze.

The prisoner nodded. The deal was simple. Win a sparring match with the Keeper of the Basilisk, pledge one rotation as a grunt in the Planetary Syndicate — Griea's contractual infantry — and cut his unserved time in half. He chose a sturdy blade. Short, stout. Easy to maneuver.

Cael swept his boot across the ground and straightened. His dialect device paired with the overhead unit. *Commencing sparring session. Imperator Cael Volkov and Inmate 5421. Begin.* The thrumming in his body came too close to fear to be comfortable. It fogged his mind. Made him eager for stability. He wanted to disengage with all of the foretold pathways the upcoming audience with his father might set into motion.

He loosened his hold on the blade just enough to let the weapon float against the underside of his knuckles and strode forward, focusing on the task at hand. Inmate 5421 matched his movement. The man took easy steps, watching Cael shift his weight. With a sweep of his arm, Cael sent his blade through the air. Clash of metal. The ring of it, sharp. They were well-matched. Similar stature. Broad, lean. The inmate was taller, though, with prominent, bulging musculature. An outward jab tossed Cael away.

They danced around each other, Cael spinning the handle of his knife, considering his next move, and the inmate paying close attention to every flick of his wrist. Cael lunged again. The two collided, blade against blade, then the inmate's knee to Cael's stomach, Cael's elbow to the inmate's chest. They toppled, scrabbled.

Cael tried to quiet the awkward pit gaping in his mind, spilling with annexation. He saw glimpses of holoreports detailing the uptick in harmful black-market Avara. Revisited daydreams of the forest moon he was meant to conquer.

The inmate sliced at his face, narrowly missing Cael's nose. He jerked backward. It was an animal thing — fighting. Violence came easily to most. It was bred deep, irrevocably organic. But to channel it was a developed skill.

Cael pivoted backward on one foot before launching forward again. His mind emptied, tunneling away from duty, relying on a second-hand action to drive his body. Once he focused, Cael moved like a machine, subtle movements, incremental posturing. He dodged another jab, sidestepped a clumsy punch, ducked when the inmate pawed at his cheek. Cael surged, flipped the blade's smile upward, and cut Inmate 5421's throat.

Sparring wasn't supposed to be deadly, but Cael did not wince at the sound of the prisoner's body hitting the floor. *Fatality*, the dialect device said, crisp and unfeeling. He slowed his breathing and righted himself. A thin layer of red slicked his blade.

Chamber staff materialized in the doorway. They kept their expressions neutral, faces downcast, and went to work removing the still warm corpse and the blood pooling beneath it. A new bruise bloomed on Cael's abdomen, throbbing in time with his heartbeat. He stared headlong at the smooth, curved wall, and dragged his thumb along the edge of the weapon's leather handle.

Today triggered a transitionary period.

Imperator Cael Volkov, Keeper of the Basilisk, leader of the Royal Reserve, champion in the Tupinaire, and son to the ruling Legatus would soon become the key player in a centuries-long political strategy to assume control of Aurethia. Alexander Henly would weep in his grave if he glimpsed the horror he'd scrawled across the Greater Universe, if he understood the carefully orchestrated plundering of his precious bloodline. Cael hoped the rotting regent's bones splintered at the thought.

Life had never been as thrilling, as changing. He opened his mouth, inhaled a great breath. The air tasted metallic, like an ending.

THE VOLKOV CASTLE WAS Machina's ribcage, cradling the very heart-beat of Griea in tall, black stone. Its cerebral design leaned into sterile aris-tocracy, creating a macabre warren in the center of the city. It had always been a terrifying thing, Cael's childhood home. Looking out over the Sliding Sea, shadowed only by Goren's snowy peak, it was sharply built in a stack of varying square-shaped modules. Terrifying, yes, but safe harbor to those who slept there.

Cael stood at the window in the familial wing, eyes trained on a harrow dove perched atop an obelisk near the landing dock at the far edge of the property. The first of many terrestrial ships idled there, awaiting an entire cycle's worth of belongings to be sealed, boarded, and shuttled off to the transport waiting at Machina's galactic port. The castle was already buzzing. Chamber staff and housekeepers ghosted about, collecting what-ever his mother decided would travel well. Despite Constance's best efforts, the staff knew better than to enter Cael's quarters. He imagined they were busy preparing bedding, stocking the onboard pantry with space-safe nour-ishment, packing outerwear appropriate for the moon's unusual climate, and readying the flight crew for navigation through the jump gate.

Like most Griean citizens, Cael knew Aurethia like a child knew love-making. Whispered myth and wild legend. What he learned, he'd gleaned from his father's hunger for conquest. One day, he would wed the Aurethian heir. That day, Griea would unleash itself like the mighty basilisk and wrap around Draitune's prized jewel, constricting the tiny moon until it flew a Griean banner.

Fate beckoned, knife to wrist.

"Imperator." One of his father's trusted staff bowed their head and gestured toward the War Room. They spoke evenly. "Legatus Marcus will see you now."

"Appreciated," Cael said. He walked across the open chamber and laid his hand over the Griean glyph embossed on the smooth door, applying just enough pressure to wedge it open.

A blank stone table accompanied by heavy chairs stretched toward a glass wall. Beyond it, the base of Goren's summit reflected silver-white and pale blue. Cael clasped his hands at the small of his back, as was expected when greeting the Legatus, father or not, and stepped around the table. A surgical assembly was stationed in the corner, manned by a medic and a hover-tray stocked with supplies.

Legatus Marcus stood in front of the floor-to-ceiling window. His dim reflection sketched Cael's future — broad-cheeked and strong-boned. The serene glacial color of his upturned eyes conveyed absent gentleness. Faded ink framed a sleek thatch of greying hair on each side of his skull. No matter how thoroughly he scraped a razor down his jaw, stubborn stubble still peppered his skin, rising with the afternoon.

"You killed another prisoner," Legatus Marcus said, a clipped but straightforward statement.

"The sparring volunteers know the risk." Cael swallowed tightly. "My attention was elsewhere this morning. I'll be more mindful."

"No time for mindfulness, son. You depart for Aurethia at dawn."

Cael's mouth dried. He anticipated a hasty departure but not *that* quick. "I assume we've reserved access to the jump gate — "

"It's taken care of."

He collected himself and gave a curt nod. "Heard, Legatus."

Marcus shifted toward him. His high-necked sweater peeked beneath the collar of his black coat. The glyph of Griea, an eight-pointed star stretched long in four places, was held by a delicate silver chain pinned to his lapel. He tracked his gaze down Cael's attire, staring hard at his cold weather bootwear, then clasped Cael's shoulder.

"You've stayed on top of your studies?" Marcus asked.

Cael inclined his head. "I'm conversational in Aurethian, sir."

"And Avara?"

"A medical grade crystal exclusive to the moon's many mines. Stable enough to endure heavy space travel, commonly distilled into variants for casual consumption, recently replicated by counterfeit chemists on the black-market. Radically unavailable in the outer reaches of the Greater Universe. The only known cure for parsec sickness."

"And tell me about parsec sickness."

Cael answered automatically. "An unusual affliction caused by extended space travel. Common symptoms include the rapid influx of necrotic tissue, both external and internal. Organ failure, or severe internal damage. Loss of eyesight, appendages, teeth, and hair."

"Fatality rate?"

"Without treatment, weeks to months. With distilled treatment, livability is sustainable. With complete treatment, symptoms are reversed."

Marcus made a sound like a sleeping dog. "And House Henly?"

"Current stewards of Aurethia and the controlling hand of the Lux Continuum."

"And you?"

The question wormed under Cael's skin. He angled his chin higher.

"Imperator Cael Volkov, sir. Keeper of the Basilisk and heir to the Griean throne."

"Task?" Marcus asked, quieter.

"To wed the first-born Henly heir and secure our genetic bloodline while investigating the whereabouts and extraction process of Avara on Aurethia."

Marcus listed his head, waiting.

"To crush their house from within," Cael added. The thought sent a bolt of electricity down his spine. "To clear a path for Griea to assume control of Avara distribution and the starlink. To bring House Volkov glory, to make right what was wronged."

The Legatus nodded. He stepped away, leaving finger-shaped streaks along the shiny table. When he arrived at the surgical assembly, comprised of a simple transport gurney, he opened his arm and gestured to it.

Cael steeled himself and crossed the room. As soon as he sank against the hard backing of the black gurney, metal cuffs latched around his ankles. Two more looped his wrists, holding his arms to his side. His pulse quickened. Panic burst in his chest, but he knew better than to squirm. Knew his father would bring open palm to bared cheek if he did not comply.

"Maxine Carr, our liaison on Aurethia, is preparing for your arrival. She's been debriefed," Marcus said. He gave the medic an approving nod before shifting his attention back to Cael. "You're receiving a tracking device. This will allow us and your Augment to cartograph Aurethia. After scouting cities, housing — most importantly an Avara mine — dispatch your report and our experts will create an internal roadmap. Do this with any and all substantial travels. Understood?"

"I'm taking an Augment?" Cael asked absently and tensed his brow. He wouldn't dispute the inclusion of an augmented security detail, but arriving to a predetermined courtship with a cybernetic, polylinguistic soldier might not set the best precedent. When Marcus did not answer, Cael exhaled hard through his nose. "Understood, Legatus."

The medic peeled down Cael's charcoal shirt. "This will sting," she said, mouth covered by a sterile mask. The cold press of her glove pebbled his chest. She reached toward the hover-tray and grasped a strange, bulky device. It glinted beneath the white shine of a medical disc-lamp hovering above his torso. Carefully, the medic slid her hand through the bottom of the plunger and bent over him, guiding the hollow needle through the soft web behind his clavicle.

Cael set his teeth. An insignificantly small, perfectly round bead the

color of melted steel traveled through the transparent tube in slow, methodical pulses, igniting like liquid flame. Every muscle seized at once. A thin
sound puddled in his throat. He blinked rapidly, staring at the disc-lamp
until his eyes watered.

The door to the War Room was a silent thing, smooth and hingeless. A
boot-step echoed. He breathed through hot discomfort and turned, looking
past the medic to see Optio Bracken Volkov, his cousin, walking forward.
His white shirt was precisely buttoned, but the sleeves were secured at the
elbow, showcasing the blocky ink printed on his fair skin, forearm to
knuckle. Someone else trailed behind him. Tall and well-built. Intimidating.

Bracken and Cael had been brought up like brothers despite being
something else entirely. After Bracken's mother, Miriam, died of parsec
sickness, and his father, Cael's uncle, Praetor Savin, was killed in the arena,
Bracken sheltered beneath Legatus Marcus's wing. He was eleven years
older than Cael. Ruthless, steadfast. Bold and proud. A shining example of
what a Volkov should be. His short hair was swept away from his face,
clipped close behind and around his ears. The slope of his neck bore a tattoo
on each side: Griea's eight-pointed star on the right, the open mouth of a
basilisk on the left.

Cael loved him dearly, the way all envious men loved each other. Like
an insect crawling toward a chrysalis, hoping to eat whatever grew inside.

"Ouch," Bracken joked, husky and low.

"Done, actually," the medic corrected. She withdrew the syringe and
placed a fingerful of clotting agent on the nearly invisible blemish above
Cael's collarbone. The restraints snapped into place beneath the gurney.

"Optio," Marcus greeted.

"Legatus." Bracken gave him a nod. He looked sidelong at Cael. "Your
Augment, Imperator," he said, gesturing with a shrug toward the man
flanking him. "Vik Endresen, martyred during a planetary siege in the Mal
system, recalibrated for specialized combat post-mortem. Memory restoration, ninety-two percent. He's been structurally upgraded with Griean steel,
cybernetically enhanced with core-data regarding Aurethian customs,
history, peculiarities, so on. His data is encrypted. When you're ready to
dispatch a private message, send it through Vik. Otherwise, utilize the
liaison to avoid suspicion. Once you breach Aurethian airspace, he's yours
to control."

"I'm at your service, Imperator Volkov," Vik said. A scarred, birdish
nose sat crooked on his ruddy face, and shallow crow's feet webbed his
wide-set eyes.

Whoever Vik had been before he'd died — before he was brought back new and worse by the Griean Restoration Division — had been accustomed to combat and bloodshed. An appropriate choice for their slow, deliberate siege of the forest moon.

Cael sat upright on the side of the gurney and pulled his shirt into place. "I appreciate your service, Augment Endresen."

Vik lowered halfway, bowing casually. "It's my honor, Imperator."

Vengeance, while apt, was not a useful way to describe what Griea would seize once they controlled Aurethia. Galactic stability, planetary security, sustainable wealth, medical expansion — everything the long dead patriarch of House Henly had denied his grandmother, Duchess Harlyn Volkov. Instead, the Aurethian regent robbed Griea of a fair and noble deal, and Griea scraped for a way to make do.

Unsurprisingly, every empire needed soldiers, mercenaries, weapons, and defense. And many of the very planets kissing Aurethia's shoes paid handsomely for Griean armament.

In due time, they would pay Griea for Avara, too.

Marcus set his hand on Cael's nape. Squeezed hard. "You are the beginning of Griea's rise to greatness."

He ignored the throbbing behind his collarbone and met his father's shark-eyed gaze.

Greatness. The promise buried like a thorn.

CHAPTER THREE

ELIO

Machina's industrial model is a testament to the polarized infrastructure on Griea. The structural integrity of each tier within the city is reinforced with solar retention technology, redistributing warmth throughout each building to keep its population comfortable under the constant threat of freezing temperatures.

A friendly robotic voice narrated the holorecording, beaming a three-dimensional image of Griea's largest solitary metropolis, Machina, into the center of Elio's bedchamber. He sat cross-legged at the bottom of his neatly made bed, dressed down in casualwear despite the last sip of morning teetering on the hour. It was an outdated holo. A decade, maybe older. But he stared at the fuzzy outline of a blue-chalked cityscape — a distant world whose interests would soon influence his political movement — and tried to rationalize the concept of a place like *that* with the home he'd always known. The more Elio watched, attempting to find common ground with the Griean way of life, the wider the chasm between Griea and Aurethia grew.

Griean fisherman drop long poles through laser-cut

holes in the ice, hooking fatty trout, blue-bellied salmon, and poisonous pufferfish. Predominantly pescatarian, Griea thrives on a diet of seafood and native vegetation. While scarce, fresh citrus and herbage is conservatively grown in domed terrariums. Majority of the ice giant's produce is imported dehydrated or preserved.

Elio's brow knitted with confusion. He glanced past the skinny curtain and saw a bird circle the orchard. *Scarce.* He blinked, considering the validity of it. How outdated was this holorecording?

"There you are," Lorelei said in crisp Griean. Small, delicate syllables, rhythmic and pretty. She leaned against the doorframe. Her mouth split for a white smile. "Studying?"

"Refreshing my memory," Elio said, matching her language choice. She laughed. He did, too.

"Do you think he'll speak Aurethian?" She switched back to their native tongue and entered the room, climbing onto the bed beside him. She flopped down. Her ale-colored hair haloed her.

"I imagine he's been taught about our people same as we've been taught about his." But he didn't know that for sure. The Imperator might not know a damn thing. "Mother made sure we spoke the language, made sure I had access to history and holodocuments. Education was never forced, but I don't think someone would enter a marriage, political or not, without knowing their way around an unfamiliar world. Especially one they'll be stewarding, no?"

Lorelei held her hand above her face, admiring the opalescent color of her fingernails. She was a flippant thing. He often thought she was jealous of the position he never wanted. Like a true Aurethian, she wore her emotions openly even though she tried to hide them, and he often saw envy harden her eyes when they spoke about his betrothment. Lorelei would never admit it, but she was a romantic at heart, always hoping for fate to toss a lover at her feet.

The thought caught like a jammed gear. Elio scrubbed the word *lover* from his mind.

"You've seen the transport manifests, right?" Elio asked wearily, thinking back to the holorecording. It kept playing — *the Griean nomadic people, Fara, follow the Sliding Sea's frost patterns, settling where the ice is thick* — and Elio couldn't help but ponder the planet's lack of resources. "Aurethia is the farmland of the system. We must be trading with Griea."

"That's a question for father," she said, and dropped her hand, twisting to look at him. "But yes, I would assume we no longer withhold from Griea. I do know the trade agreement with Ocury extends to the triplets."

The triplets — Sierra, Shepard, and Divinity — were life-sustaining space stations populated with immigrants from neighboring systems and orphans who abandoned their homeworlds due to overcrowding or resource depletion. People left perfectly healthy worlds to become stationers, too. Sometimes to escape a boring life, sometimes to restart somewhere new.

Elio flopped down beside her. She hissed and pulled her hair out from under him. "Sorry," he mumbled. "Do you…" The brewing question made his stomach flutter. "Do you think he'll resent me?"

Lorelei chuffed like one of their lions, blowing out a half-laugh. "What, because of great-grandfather? Oh, I doubt it, Elio. It's been…" Her eyes flicked back and forth, lips moving around silent calculations. "Over two hundred years since the Imperium gave us trade control of the starlink. Bidding on something doesn't guarantee selection. Alexander made a play for the trade route, so did the regent on Griea, and the controlling family on Ocury." She shrugged and folded her mouth into a mock frown. "It was a play for *power*, yes, but still a fair process."

"You know that isn't true," he corrected softly. "We have Avara. The Imperium prioritized that."

She shot him a challenging look. "Shouldn't they?"

You've been listening to father too much. He sighed and nodded. "Of course," he placated.

"I think this Imperator, keeper of sea slugs, will find you quite flexible — "

He swatted her. "Don't be crass."

Laughter shot from her. "That was *your* mind, Elio. I was talking about the trade route."

Heat spread across his nose. He tried and failed to contain a laugh. "Fine, be a little crass. Do you think he'll — "

Lorelei flipped on her side to face him, beaming. "Oh, yes, I think he'll bend you right over — "

Elio smothered her mouth with his palm, but they were both laughing too hard for it to matter. "You're awful," he snapped, blushing hot. "I'm serious, Lorelei. What if I'm not to his liking? What if I spend the rest of my life with a man who comes to my bed for the exclusive purpose of making a child? Worse, what if he refuses to come to my bed at all and insists we use an exterior womb?"

"Then you'll take a concubine," she said, as if he should know better. "Worse," she eked out, "what if he's got a face like an ox? What if you have to address the Imperium next to someone unfortunate? What if he's a pure toe, Elio?"

Their laughter grew. Water sprung to Elio's eyes and his belly hurt.

"I assure you, Imperator Volkov does not resemble a toe," Maxine said from the doorway.

Elio turned to smile at her, beckoning the liaison with a wave.

Lorelei swatted the bed and scooted over. "Come and sit, Maxine. Gossip with us, tell us about your planet."

Maxine rolled her eyes, but her smile was loose. She crossed the chamber, stepping over the holorecording. Blue flashed across her black gown. "Well, the Imperator is a champion in the Tupinaire. That much I do know."

"Right, you have an arena," Lorelei said, astonished. "So he's good with a sword?" The implication in her voice was far too strong. Elio smacked her again.

"I've heard he's fond of more intimate blades, but yes, for all intents and purposes, he is." Maxine folded her legs beneath her and poked Elio in the chest. "Griea is a beautiful planet. When the sun is low, frost glitters on the ice, and the light from Draitune turns our sky purple and blue and green. We have our basilisks," she teased, slipping one finger along Lorelei's arm like a slippery snake. "But other creatures live there. Snow hare, bighorn sheep, harrow doves, wolverine. We're home to the only genetic ancestor of the common Earthen reindeer, too."

"Like our lions," Elio said.

Maxine smiled. "Exactly."

"Elio asked me earlier, but you probably know better — Aurethia currently provides Griea with agricultural enrichment, correct?" Lorelei spoke dismissively, as if expecting an obvious answer. "We trade with Draitune, Ocury, the triples. I assume Griea is no different."

At that, Maxine's smile hardened. She cleared her throat. Her demeanor shifted to something Elio could only describe as controlled. "To my knowledge, Griea receives a small portion of preserved fruit and starchy root vegetables."

"Small?" Elio hadn't meant to speak. He propped himself on his palms, looking at Maxine.

"Aurethia can only provide what it can provide," she said. Calm enveloped her voice. Practiced, fake. He heard his father in each word.

Lorelei heaved a sigh. "There was a seed trade, though, wasn't there? Grandmother managed that, I believe. It went well, didn't it?"

"It did," Maxine confirmed. Her mood brightened slightly. "Aurethia, Draitune, and Ocury, as well as Hük and Vandel Prime from outside our system provided a wealth of genetically sound seedlings. Now Griea has a few terrariums in Machina, growing a small selection of herbs and vegetables."

"See." Lorelei bumped her knuckles against his leg.

"I'm glad to hear Griea isn't as distant a friend as our political history promises," Elio said.

Maxine dipped her chin. "That distance will soon be a thing of the past."

Lorelei grinned like a crocodile. She whispered loudly. "Surely we'll know peace after the Imperator shows you his basilisk and — "

This time Elio interrupted his sister with a hard kick to her calf. Even Maxine, who had gone cold and practical a second ago, cackled with her whole body, falling backward on the bed. Lorelei snorted, curling inward to giggle at her own joke. Elio whined through reluctant laughter.

After the jovial moment subsided, Maxine sighed and said, "Before I forget, I came here to bring word from your mother. She'd like to see you in the garden for afternoon tea."

"Oh, she's going to give you the *talk*," Lorelei sang.

Elio blew out a breath, flapping his mouth. "What time is it?"

Lorelei and Maxine spoke at once. "Afternoon."

THE GARDEN STRETCHED AWAY from the backside of the manor, leaking into the treeline where the property became nothing more than wilderness. Trimmed hedges and overgrown vegetable boxes stood uniformly nearest the porch, flanked by a sunken communal space lined with bumpy stone pathways. Palm-sized birds rolled in the fountain, ruffling feathers, washing scaly feet.

An Aurethian lion lifted her blocky head, blinking slowly as Elio stepped down into the manicured yard. Nara was the color of honey-mead, and like most of her female companions, weighed close to one hundred and twenty-seven kilos. Her male counterparts, three of the twelve pride members, were about twice her size. Preserved from the delicate DNA of a once lost species, Aurethian lions carried the bones and blood of their Earthen ancestors, the legacy of a long-gone planet.

High Lady Lena sat at a garden table beside Nara, idly stroking the beast's rump with her bare foot. Her abandoned shoe lay on the floor beneath her chair, and she held a dainty porcelain cup to her mouth, reading a holobook. Her brunette hair was roped into a braid and her soft gold-brown pantsuit was embroidered with filigree sleevework and a decorative collar. Elio envied her easy beauty, the way she held herself without compunction.

"You're late," his mother chided. Her mouth hinted at a smile.

Elio took the seat across from her. "I was watching a holodocumentary about life on Griea."

"Did you learn anything?"

He almost ignored the immediate thought that jumped forth. "Griean farmland doesn't fare well due to the harsh climate. Strange to consider when..." He held out one arm, gesturing to the abundance around them. "We have this."

"They're a resilient people," she said, pouring him a cup of candlebell tea.

"Our trade alliance is secure, though. Everyone in the system benefits from our harvest, correct?" He sipped the tea. The flower had a lovely, vanilla mouthfeel, almost like gardenia. He'd loved it since he was a child.

Lena matched him, sipping from her cup. He watched the answer sink behind her eyes, truth weighed against strategy. "You're asking the right questions, Elio, but I encourage you to prioritize patience. You will be High Lord one day. Right now, we must ensure this engagement comes to fruition. You and Imperator Volkov have a rare opportunity, one I did not choose for you but one I support nonetheless."

"Opportunity for what, exactly? Peace, yes, but — "

"Peace is putting it mildly. If the union between our houses results in an heir, which it must, then Aurethia and Griea will assume equal control of the starlink. The Imperium will have to honor shared use of the Lux Continuum which will push Draitune and Ocury to open their individual jump gates to accommodate for mandatory Avara distribution. The entire system will change," she snapped her fingers, "in an instant."

The Lux Continuum was the fastest, most stable trade route in the Lux system. Safe for large transport and big enough to accommodate heavy machinery. Unlike the smaller, slower jump gates fixed outside each planet, the starlink folded open in the emptiness, creating a semi-permanent hole in deep space. It didn't bend; it rarely broke.

"But couldn't Draitune and Ocury simply distribute Avara from their galactic ports? Wouldn't it make more sense to hand the product off to reliable allies rather than utilize their jump gates to process each delivery ourselves?"

Her hazel eyes sharpened. Dimples deepened. "More correct questions."

Elio cocked his head. "Why aren't we doing that now? Why wait for an heir?"

"Because the Greater Universe is comfortable, and change — adaptation, evolution, or otherwise — is not."

"What aren't you telling me, mother?"

Lena's smile gentled. She set her cup down and toed on her shoe. The lion at her feet rumbled pleasantly. "Avara is precious, Elio. Its stewardship is an honor," she paused, meeting his gaze. "But if our moon fell under the wrong protection, if Avara was mined to death, then not only would our Great House fall, but the Imperium itself would hemorrhage. Take a moment to imagine a world where Avara production came to a standstill. Parsec sickness is no longer treatable. The black market is overrun with dangerous, unstable remedies; snake oil salesmen line their pockets; space travelers die at alarming rates, and the only way to remedy any of it has gone extinct because no one knew when to say stop."

Elio attempted to collect each statement, turning them over like gemstones, peering at facets and faces. In all his life, he'd never felt such lengthy barbs prickle outward from his mother. She was deadly serious in a way he wished he did not have to see. But this was a lesson. Preparation. He listened, and he dissected, and he said, "Half of what you mentioned is already happening."

Lena's top lip peeled away from the bottom. She appraised him like a spider might a broken web, looking for places to mend. "Good boy," she murmured, nodding. Her slender throat flexed. She cleared it, looking from Elio to the fountain, then all around the garden. Her stance slackened enough to coax a relieved breath from him. "This is a happy union." She smiled, and the seriousness was gone. In an instant, High Lady Lena dropped her diplomatic mask and eased back into being his mother. "Have you researched Griean courtship?"

"Scantly."

"Imperator Volkov will likely be reserved, more so than you're used to."

Elio's brow pulled tight. "Reserved?"

"On Aurethia, we court for companionship. On Griea, they court for copulation. Coupling is," she searched for a word, "playful here. It is intentional there. You might speak different languages when it comes to intimacy."

He shifted his gaze to the stone beneath his boots, smacking his heels together. The idea was disquieting, but nothing he couldn't handle.

"You're saying he'll be a terrible flirt?" Elio joked.

Lena laughed. It was a precious sound, one he loved. She reached across the table and grasped his hand. "I think he will take one look at you and forget his own name, sweetheart."

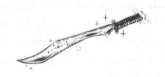

CHAPTER FOUR

CAEL

The Griean starship dropped into low orbit after connecting with the Aurethian vessel that would pilot them into transport airspace. It'd been a month and a half since the convoy departed, utilizing the Griean jump gate to position their ship on the edge of Draitune's outermost ring. From there, they navigated the famous star nursery, avoiding premature newborns spit forth from its pink membrane, and descended into the moon's volatile territory.

Cael occupied his private quarters, touching the tip of each finger to his thumb. He thought about the last night he'd spent on Griea, banging a pewter mug filled with copper beer against a boothtop in a dim tavern one level below the War College. Holland Lancaster, his oldest, dearest friend, had returned from a short mission, and slung his arm around Cael, roaring about conquest, glory, and adventure. He'd smacked a sloppy kiss to Cael's cheek, and Cael had knuckled him about the flirty stationer Holland had left behind on Shepard. Bracken had drummed his fist on the table and laughed, knocking his mug against Cael's as he delivered a long-winded toast to the dawn of a new era. Their newest friend and recent reserve soldier, Tye, gazed dreamily at the barkeep, and a local blacksmith, Vanessa, paid for another round. Strange to know he wouldn't have a night like that again for a long, long time.

He stood across from his bunk and studied his reflection in a tall, thin mirror. Tugged at the bottom of his fastened tunic, pulling the black material into place. The descent left his head swimming. His organs felt light and loose, and he couldn't stop picking at the onyx buttons lining the left side of his torso. The collarless shirt was handsome enough. He glanced down at his chunky, polished bootwear and slid his thumb along the basilisk belt looped around the top of his fitted pants. Unflinchingly Griean.

"You look dashing, dear," Constance said. She appeared like a ghost, standing just inside the oval doorway. Her dark hair was tied into a modest bun, slick as spilled ink. She wore an amethyst gown with a square neckline. The very tip of a sword-shaped tattoo splashed her milky sternum.

Cael turned away from the mirror. He smiled gingerly. "You'll make sure Bracken doesn't let my men go soft. And you'll keep an eye on father, right? Can't let our Legatus work himself into a frenzy."

"Bracken has far too much pride to let anyone go soft." She stepped forward, smoothing his shoulders. "And Marcus is already obsessed with this engagement," she muttered. A sigh escaped, damp with an emotion Cael couldn't place. "He'll be fixated on Aurethia until we reach the ceremony, so *I* will be handling galactic communication and trade expansion, henceforth. Bracken will fulfill outstanding contractual weaponry agreements for the syndicate and take over the Royal Reserve."

"It's only one cycle," he said.

"One cycle on Aurethia is one and two-quarter on Griea." She placed her palm on his cheek. It was odd to be touched tenderly. A rare thing reserved for wartime and little children. "Live honorably, Cael Volkov. You are Keeper of the Basilisk, but first and foremost, you are my only..." She paused, swallowing thickly. "You are my only heir, my only child. Use your wit, guard your heart. Be as fearless as your father, but be smart, too, like I taught you."

Cael would not see his mother for six seasons. He leaned into her hand. She was a defensive woman, as anyone wed to the Legatus would be. But Cael had watched time fissure the ripe skin around her mouth and noticed the tiny cavern following each hooded eyelid. Ocury, her homeworld, still lived in her full-lipped pout, resided in the heart-shape of her narrow face. Knowing he would not see her until he was twenty-one, until he was wed, weakened his resolve.

"I will bring greatness to Griea," he assured. "And I will bring Aurethia to its knees."

Constance tightened her jaw. She patted his cheek. "Secure the bloodline. In the end, that is what you're here for. Aurethia could very well become a child of the basilisk, but regardless, an heir will make this moon an ally to our ice giant for a lifetime. Expansion will bring us glory, Cael. War is Griea's language; growth is our goal — the two do not complement each other. Do you understand?"

For a moment, he didn't. He blinked, taken aback. Her hand slipped from his face.

"You are my son," she added. Her voice was low and careful. "Remember that."

"I will," he said. Her statement stuck to his ribcage. *War is Griea's language; growth is our goal.* He turned it over in his mind and then stowed it away, making a note to return to it when he could think properly.

"Good. It's time. The Augment requires programming." She gestured to the automatic door separating his quarters from the rest of the transport's living space.

Cael chewed his bottom lip and slipped into the belly of the ship. His mother followed. Past the last bunk, the hall splintered, leading to the cargo bay, navigation control, and lastly, the main cabin. There, leaning against a built-in bench attached to the wall, the Augment was swathed in black tactical attire casually disguised as formalwear. With a close enough look, his armor became more prominent: the subtle plating atop each shoulder, the hard plane of a chiseled chestplate. He straightened in place as Cael and Constance approached.

Vik inclined his head. "We have crossed into Aurethian airspace, Imperator. Per my pre-downloaded order from Optio Volkov, I'm expected to remain under exclusive royal control for the duration of our stay. Do you accept surveillance, Cael Volkov?"

"I do," Cael said. Although he didn't like it very much. Being documented at any given moment was unsettling. Almost as unsettling as landing on an alien moon.

"My interior permission requires standardized regulation. Due to Aurethia's law against post-mortem augmentation, I am under strict order to tether my internal and external allegiance to one, Cael Volkov, and his safety. His interest on Aurethia is priority. All off-planet monitoring via Augment surveillance, except for location monitoring, has been uninstalled or disabled. Transmitted messages, data, or emergency correspondence must be executed manually by the Primary Controller," Vik said. "Do you accept responsibility as Primary Controller?"

Cael nodded. "I do."

Vik's light eyes flicked rapidly for a moment. Once they stabilized, he offered an exaggerated nod. "I am officially at your service, Imperator.

Conversations, engagements, and sensitive information will be stored in my database, accessible only to you unless ordered otherwise."

"Noted." He gave Vik an appraising look, then glanced at his mother, watching her pace near the windowless wall. "You'll be happy to know I have quite the guard dog."

"Who do you think picked him," she said, shooting Cael a stern but genuine smile.

The Aurethian pilot-ship guided Cael's terrestrial transport to the landing space in front of the Henly manor. The launch pad was built against a cliffside overlooking the sea. As soon as the bay door lifted, the briny scent of saltwater and wet sand filled the ship. Cael wanted to dart for the ocean. He wanted to experience an entirely new breadth of water, uncharted, able to hold every part of his body all at once. But the moment the door settled, Cael glanced sidelong at his mother, standing next to him with her head held high, and offered her his arm as they walked down the steel ramp. His boot met the hard, black surface of damp rock. He toed at the ground for a moment, probing at newness. His first real breath outside the spacecraft was soupy and tepid, unlike anything he'd encountered before. Humidity glossed the air. It brought with it the animal urge to reach inside himself and scrape his chest clean, as if mucous might swamp his body.

House Henly stood at the mouth of the manor, flanked by an impressive gathering of the Aurethian guard. He thought to look at them, but his attention flicked from the sea to the forest lining the horizon beyond the impressive estate. Draitune filled the sky, spectral violet against new morning blue. White-winged gulls swooped and squawked overhead. An Aurethian flag snapped, blown by a sharp gust.

Aurethia was beautiful, unusual.

Cael cleared the taste of grass and beach from his throat and shifted his gaze to the extravagant display — armored sentries, well-dressed staff, royalty standing at attention, ready to receive him. No one moved at first. Not until Cael stepped off the rock onto soft beige dirt.

A figure stepped forth from the assembly and strode across the gap between the Grian terrestrial ship and the royal family. She held her shoulders back. Walked intently, like someone used to ice. Her mouth curved, Griean complexion warmed by Aurethian weather.

Vik cleared his throat. "Maxine Carr, sir," he said, speaking lowly. "She has served as the Griean liaison for four years. According to recorded reports, she earned their favor and is a trusted member of their court."

Cael greeted her with a polite nod. "Miss Carr."

"My Imperator," she said, bowing respectfully. She spoke Griean. "I'm pleased to welcome you and Duchess Constance to Aurethia. High Lord Darius humbly requests that your Augment undergo a routine inspection. In the meantime, I would like to introduce you to the Henly household."

"And my weapon?" Cael asked.

Maxine darted her tongue across her mouth, tempering a smile. "You are not the only one armed, Imperator. House Henly is prepared to greet you with openness and authenticity. Griea is a military planet, they expected nothing less."

He nodded, surprised, and nudged his chin toward Vik. "Report to the Aurethian guard."

"Withholding?" Vik asked.

"Nothing. They're welcome to see what you can do."

"Understood, Imperator."

"Duchess, High Lady Lena has prepared a room for you. She would be honored if you would join her for tea in the garden after you've settled," Maxine said.

Constance offered a feeble, lacking smile. "I would be happy to."

Maxine gestured toward the guardship. "Vik, if you'd please." While Vik made his way to the inspection, Maxine opened her arm and began to walk. "And if you'll both follow me."

Cael swallowed around the rock lodged behind his trachea. His stomach felt too empty, too unsteady. His entire life had brought him to this very moment, a prescient thing designed for him before he'd ever stirred in his mother's womb. Something the stars had known; something the past had sealed and delivered. He followed the liaison, scanning the royal row as they came into proper view. He attempted to calm the pursuit. Tried to keep his eyes from darting to the young man dressed in chestnut and cream, wearing a circlet of gold. But he could not help himself.

The Henly heir wore finely tailored brown trousers and impractically pointed shoes. His white shirt billowed open, scantily unbuttoned to the center of his chest, and the high neck of a lightweight coat ringed his throat. Cael looked at him, at nothing but him, watching Sunder catch the dainty yellow chain dangling on his sternum, studying the tilt of his small nose. When Maxine cleared her throat, Cael still did not look away.

"May I introduce Duchess Constance of Griea, and her son, Imperator Cael Volkov, Keeper of the Basilisk, heir to the Griean throne." She switched languages effortlessly, dropping into long-winded Aurethian. "Imperator, this is High Lord Darius Henly, his wife, High Lady Lena, and their children, Lord Orson, Lady Lorelei, and of course, Lord Elio."

"We are grateful to be on your fruitful moon," Constance said in accented Aurethian.

Elio lifted his chin, raking his gaze from Cael's feet to his face. He did not smile, he did not move. But Cael noticed the slight stutter in his chest, watched heat stoke the high cut of each cheek. He was an odd thing. Lithe and pretty; handsome and stoic. Like the edge-shine of a fine blade.

"It's an honor," Cael said, shifting his focus to High Lord Darius. He held his hands at his side, palms open, fingers spread. It was a welcoming gesture on Griea. "My father, Legatus Marcus Volkov, sends his regards. Unfortunately, he could not slip away."

Darius hummed thoughtfully. He wore off-white and earthy brown, much like his company. "Aurethia is a warm embrace to those who seek her. Legatus Volkov is welcome to visit at his earliest convenience."

"He will be pleased to know it." Cael darted another glance at Elio. The young lord did not look away — had not looked away. "Lord Elio," he said. His name was an easy, lovely thing. Cael hoped his Aurethian wasn't too stilted. "It's a pleasure to finally meet you."

"The pleasure is mine, Imperator," Elio said, strikingly smooth. Griean chimed eloquently in his mouth.

Cael made a soft sound. It wasn't quite a laugh, but close enough. He trapped it before it could surface, holding the rumble in his throat. An Aurethian speaking Griean. Like watching a bird open its beak and bark.

"I'm sure you're both very tired from the journey," High Lady Lena blurted, wringing her tawny hands. Each finger was banded, decorated in thinly stacked rings. She wore a simple rose-colored gown, her face shadowed by a translucent pinkish veil. "The kitchen staff is preparing dinner, but I'm happy to arrange for something in the meantime if either of you are hungry."

"Tea will be lovely," Constance said.

Lena gave a curt nod.

"Something to drink, maybe," Cael said, surveying the manor with a slow, sweeping glance. "But for now, I'll see to my chamber. I'd like to unpack."

"Of course," Lena said. She turned and opened her arm toward the estate. "Maxine will show you the way. Duchess, I'll have the tea prepared. Do you have a preference?"

Constance smiled. "I'd love to try an Aurethian brew."

Wise to flatter the reigning family.

Cael looked over his shoulder, watching the Aurethian guard pluck at Vik's armor and inspect him for hidden weaponry. Technically, Vik was far deadlier than any tool one might wield. Stronger and faster than organically born specimens, installed with pertinent data collected over centuries, hard-wired to make the most strategic decision when panic might cause someone else to make a less-than-ideal choice. He was still a man, still flesh and bone, tissue and membrane, but he was optimized. Reconfigured for essential usage.

"My Augment is Vik Endresen. He'll have his own room, correct?" Cael asked.

Darius nodded. "We've prepared an adjoining dwelling next to your chamber. It's private, of course, but I assumed you'd want to keep your property close."

"Not property," he corrected, trying not to sound flippant. "Contractu-ally committed. Do you take organ donation here on Aurethia?" He waited for Darius to nod, then nodded back. "Similar system. Before a soldier enters combat, they're given the opportunity to volunteer their body and mind to post-mortem augmentation. If you die, our Restoration Division preserves what they can and enhances the rest. Most of Vik's memories are intact, but he is cybernetically and skeletally advanced."

High Lady Lena swallowed tightly. Her daughter, Lorelei, stared at Vik as if he'd walked out of the sea naked and babbling.

"But thank you," Cael added, closing the conversation. Rambling about his security guard probably wasn't the best way to make an entrance. "I'm sure he'll appreciate the hospitality."

Maxine touched Cael's elbow. "This way, Imperator."

He inclined his head before following. His attention sat squarely on Elio as he walked by, meeting his fiancée's cool glance. His mother fell into step beside him. Three members of the Royal Reserve descended the ship to accompany them, two armed with Griean steel, the other with a pulse-rifle. In one day, the Royal Reserve would leave with the Duchess. It was a different kind of discomfort, knowing they'd be gone. Not that he couldn't take care of himself. He could — he *would*. But being one of very few Griean citizens moon-side unsettled him.

"Marcus will station an emergency ship in the debris field outside the star nursery." Constance spoke under her breath.

Cael shot her a patient smile. "Aurethia doesn't want war with Griea. They'll be agreeable, I'm sure."

"For now," she whispered.

"For now," he echoed.

Maxine stepped through the open entryway. "Welcome to the Henly manor. Duchess, you'll be staying in the guest quarter. Imperator, you have a semi-permanent residence in the east wing."

The estate was impressive. The snarling head of an Aurethian lion was mounted in the reception area, paired with a bronze placard. Oil-painted artwork clasped in wooden frames showcased farmland and oceanic scenery. Utilitarian fixtures were softened by the billow of beige curtains. A massive fireplace carved from grey stone crackled in the heart of the home. Above it, Alexander Henly oversaw the living space, depicted in an array of blue-toned watercolor, holding a cubic gemstone in his palm.

Down a sizable hall, adjacent the training chamber, Maxine paused and opened a door.

Cael stepped inside. It was a large chamber with appropriate furniture and a downy bed. The window overlooked a path to the sea. He inhaled deeply, still choked by humidity, anchored by a new atmosphere. Aurethia smelled like fruit. Like soil and fertility.

Maxine sighed and said, "The transport staff has already started delivering your possessions, Imperator Volkov. For now, please make yourself at home. When you're finished, Lord Elio would like to offer you a tour of the manor."

CHAPTER FIVE

ELIO

E lio paced in the privacy of his own bedchamber, striding back and forth in front of the open window. Damp air cooled his flushed skin. He shook out his wrists and breathed slowly, attempting to calm his racing heart. There was no undoing what had been done. No unlaunching the Griean ship from the docking bay, no unsigning the agreement his grandfather made centuries ago. Cael Volkov was a political promise he could not break, and it drove him mad not knowing whether he was excited or terrified about that. He stopped mid-stride and hung his head back, inhaling deeply through his nose.

He is exactly what I expected. Elio slipped his eyes shut. *He is nothing like I expected.*

In the grand scheme, Elio hadn't known what to expect — kept himself shielded from the mental preparation that accompanied premature investigation — but a part of him always assumed the Griean prince would be cold, humorless. Bland. And he still might be. But Elio couldn't stop returning to Cael's thin mouth sliding into a smile. He couldn't unhear the raspy laughter growling in his throat, or unsee the intensity of his attention. Elio hadn't anticipated him to look young, even though he'd always known Cael's age. Hadn't braced for very human traits.

"Well, he *is* human," Elio mumbled, chiding himself.

He suddenly felt stupid for assuming otherwise. For tricking his nervous system into adopting the idea of Cael Volkov as a creature rather than a

person. In the span of mere moments, Cael had dissolved the unfair carica-
ture Elio installed, trading it for something worse. Someone charismatic and
passionate. Someone *likable*.

A knock at the door jostled him. He twirled on his feet and said,
"Come in."

Peadar eased into the chamber. His attire matched the guardship
stationed in the courtyard, but unlike the foot soldiers, Peadar wore the
simple insignia of a lion's face pinned to his lapel, same as the one on the
Aurethian flag. Next to it, a nod to his station — three blades in parallel.
Military strategist. Aurethian warrior. General.

"Lord Elio, I'm to accompany you," he said.

Elio pondered that. "I don't think Aurethia's *warm embrace* includes a
chaperoned tour, Peadar."

"Well, I don't think the Imperator will find it odd, considering."

"Considering he's Griean?"

"Considering he's a stranger from a hostile planet."

Fair. "Can you be discreet?"

Peadar gave him a cautious look. A shadow crossed his face.

Elio huffed. "At least give me the opportunity to set a precedent."

"I'll keep a healthy distance," he said, relenting. "Take your blade — the
small one."

"I don't go anywhere without it."

Elio kept the sleek, glinting knife Peadar spoke of strapped to his hip or
wedged inside a boot. It had a deadly, squared-off tip that, when plunged
through flesh, left a gaping wound. Peadar had gifted it to him on his
sixteenth birthday.

"We'll start by the fireplace. First the house, then the orchard," Elio
said.

Peadar nodded. "How're you feeling?"

"Like I've been shot into low orbit," he confessed, rather brashly. He
heaved a sigh and set his eye-tooth against his bottom lip. "The man I'm
supposed to marry just waltzed off a transport which means he's real. It's all
real."

"It is real, my lord. Extraordinarily real."

"I know," Elio muttered. He combed his hand through his hair and
swallowed against the urge to dry-heave. "Let's get this over with."

Peadar lowered his gaze and held the door. "Not very *warm embrace* of
you — "

"Don't patronize me." Elio laughed under his breath. "Discreet," he insisted again, drawing out the word, and walked toward the center of the household, leaving Peadar to follow at a comfortable distance.

The manor was uncharacteristically quiet. Staff did their chores and went about their day, but Elio sensed uncertainty in the air. Curiosity breezed through on a wind of sudden, well-awaited change.

For as long as Elio had been alive, since before he was born, the moon and her citizens anticipated the foretold union. Some with fearfully held breath, some with giddy hope. He brushed his damp palms over his pants, smoothing away sweat and jitters. When he turned the corner, Cael waited, staring up at the portrait of his great-grandfather. Firelight glowed on the Imperator's black clothes and licked an orange stripe across his cheek. The dark ink on his skull looked sharper, meaner.

"I should thank him," Cael said.

The suddenness of his voice sent a jolt down Elio's back. "We both should."

He dragged his azure eyes away from the artwork. Another *look*. Face to shoes, ankles to eyebrows.

"Will your Augment be joining us?" Elio asked. He wasn't sure if he liked being observed or not, but he couldn't blame Cael for being attentive.

Cael quirked his mouth, amused. "I've asked him not to, but he might explore on his own."

Elio kept his attention fleeting. It was difficult not to stare. Not to track the narrow line of Cael's jaw or the lovely taper of each artfully groomed brow. He could've stood there for an hour, inspecting every inch of the Imperator. Righting what'd gone wrong in his imagination. He tilted his head toward the east wing and said, "You're familiar with the guard quarter, I assume?"

"I wouldn't say *familiar*," Cael said. He clasped his hands at the small of his back and followed beside Elio. "But I do know it's where I'll be accommodated."

"Is everything to your liking?"

"It is, thank you."

Elio paused at the mouth of the training chamber. He gestured inside. A heavy bag hung from a chain bolted into the ceiling, and sparring tools graced the weaponry table. The padded floor protected against unnecessary injuries and the weight bench in the corner was paired with a running machine. One side of the room was entirely mirrored. "We train here. There's another, larger area for the guardship, but you're welcome to utilize the family space. I'm sure our battle drone isn't to Griean standard. It's operable, though, uploaded via a wireless system optimized to this chamber. Feel free to connect it to your hardware if you're ever in the mood."

Cael swept the chamber. "Is it usually this empty?"

Rude. "No. But I imagine everyone is adjusting to today's excitement."

"Aren't we all." His smile stayed put. He glanced down at Elio, standing almost a head taller. "What's your favorite weapon?"

"Dagger," Elio answered, too quickly. "Falcata, maybe. Or a tanto." Like the one on his hip.

"Good choices."

"What about you, Imperator? What kind of weapon does a Griean warrior typically use?" Elio turned, guiding them out of the east wing.

"Everyone is different. I like a stiletto for close combat, but I'm most fond of my Grabak, personally."

"Grabak?" Elio steered them through the dining hall and into the kitchen.

"They're made from the fin-spine of a basilisk. Or a tooth," he said, matter-of-factly, almost excitedly. *Or a tooth!* Cael brushed his hand over a fruit bowl, grasping a pear. He tossed it, caught it, brought the yellowish skin to his nose. "Productive little moon," he murmured, and something about the comment struck Elio like a hoof to his lower quadrant.

"You're welcome to everything. My mother hides the pastries from Orson, but..." He opened a high cupboard stuffed with burlap-wrapped sweetbread and jarred cookies. "Those of us who can reach are in luck."

Cael looked around, but didn't open anything. Elio took it upon himself to pull on the refrigerator's handle, displaying an assortment of vegetables, juice, dairy, and paper-wrapped meat. Cael lifted his chin, dancing his eyes across each crowded, colorful shelf. Tension dented his jaw. His mood, casually entertained, seemed to darken.

"I know Griea is predominantly pescatarian," Elio ventured, shutting the fridge. "We source fresh seafood from Nadhas weekly. If it's not to your liking, then — "

"Abundance is to my liking, Elio," Cael said. Despite his frosty demeanor, he spoke evenly, smiling around each word. "Which Aurethia can no doubt provide."

Something shifted just then. Elio felt the strain, saw the paper-thin edge of animosity. He tried to smile. "Good."

Cael cleared his throat. "Shall we?"

Elio quickened his pace, showing Cael to the guest wing, then briefly to the northern side of the manor where the Henly family resided. On their way into the garden, Cael placed his palm high up on the door, holding it open. Elio found the exchange strangely intimate, saying *thank you* and walking underneath the Imperator's outstretched arm.

Morning bled into afternoon. Draitune stained the sky, and sunlight mottled the ground between low branches. In the sunken yard, his mother shared a pot of tea with Duchess Constance, both women flanked by private security. The Griean sentries were more wraith than warrior, swathed in black same as their Imperator. A lion lounged nearby, casually watching a chicken peck and scratch behind the orb-shaped farm-terrarium adjacent to the garden. Birdsong whistled from a dormant citrus tree. Elio watched Cael stare out at the vast expanse of open wilderness beyond the estate.

"The manor is surrounded by grassland like this, but the true meadow is over here," Elio said, walking around the back of the house from the eastern exit toward the north-facing side of the property. He stood on the edge of the brick walkway beneath an awning. "You're welcome to explore. Just don't be alarmed if you come across a lion. The pride doesn't leave the estate often. They're socialized."

Meadowland rolled toward the orchard. Long grass bent with the wind. Buzzing pollinators whizzed around, and tan, furry bodies lay limp in the sun. A few more lions pillowed together under the shade of a sleepy willow, yawning and cleaning each other. Past the meadow, naked trees sprouted their first spring leaves, and sour berries grew in thatches along manicured pathways. Sunder glanced off the far away ocean.

Cael looked at the meadow, at everything, and Elio took the opportunity to look at Cael. He scratched the image into his mind: Imperator of Griea, Keeper of the Basilisk, surveying the vastness of the forest moon with a bewildered reverence Elio had only seen once before. His mother, red-cheeked and sweat-slick, taking hold of Orson after an extensive labor, had worn the same exhausted, awe-struck expression. It was almost unsettling, that look. Cael appreciating Aurethia the same way Lena had appreciated her youngest child, her hardest birth.

"They live with you?" Cael asked.

It took Elio a moment to realize he was talking about the lions. "Oh, yes, they do. We feed them, bathe them. They rarely wander into the manor, but during winter you'll sometimes find one or two sleeping by the fireplace."

"Do they listen to you?"

"Like a pet? No, not quite. They're a protected species. We've entered into a mutual guardianship, I guess. We look after them; they look after us." Elio followed Cael's gaze to a male lion, Tatu, lumbering through the grass toward them. "Maxine told me about the reindeer on Griea."

Laughter rasped again, erupting in Cael's throat like a batch of cinder. His smile widened. "Yes, we do have those," he said, casting a brief glance at the sea. "This place is impressive." He dropped his gaze to Elio. "Bewitching."

"This is only the beginning," Elio said. He stepped into the meadow, extending his hand toward a friendly beast. Tatu's snout met his palm.

Cael hesitated but eventually followed.

THE AURETHIAN FEAST SPREAD across the dining table made Elio squirm. Not because he didn't expect his father to insist on such a grand display, but because earlier that afternoon juice from a nectarine had glistened on Cael's chin and Elio had never seen a person try to hide bewilderment with such determination before. It happened in the orchard, walking slowly beneath the mostly bare branches of old trees. Elio spotted a premature fruit clinging to a low spindle and told Cael to take it. The Imperator did, and when he ate, Elio wondered about sustenance and conquest, dependability and harvest. Water had touched Cael's eyes, so brief Elio thought he'd imagined it. But then Cael laughed, giddy and clumsy, and held the fruit out to him. *It's sour*, Cael had said. *Take a bite.*

A feeling close to pity needled his gut and Elio was determined not to entertain it. But the way Duchess Constance's cold attention flitted about the table, clipping each lavishly arranged plate, cemented Elio's initial assessment. It was not envy nor anger but longing he had seen unfurrow across Cael's face. That same longing struck a deep groove through Constance's brow.

"Your generosity is deeply appreciated," the Duchess said. She took a modest portion of goosefish, wilted salad, monkberry, and seed bread. When one of the kitchen staff offered her sparkling wine, she nodded and held out her flute. "Eating is intentional on Griea. I'm not accustomed to such grandiosity."

"It's intentional here as well," Lorelei said. She spoke genuinely, naively.

Her smile was a broad, young stripe. "Color is important when it comes to a balanced diet. We eat from the sea and the orchard, and source vegetables from the farming district near Atreyu."

Elio smacked his boot against her shin. She shot him a confused look. Across the table, Cael stared at his mother, and picked at a small piece of fish with his two-pronged fork.

"Color," Constance repeated. She didn't quite laugh, but the sound was similar.

"The terrariums on Griea provide relief despite the temperamental weather, I hope," Darius said.

Cael cleared his throat. "We manage."

Maxine added, "Griea is tenacious. Our gardens are not as vibrant as Aurethia's, but they're strong."

"Did you enjoy the estate, Imperator?" Lena asked. The subject change was intentional; Elio silently thanked her for it. "The Duchess and I saw you in the meadow earlier."

Cael chewed a bite, swallowed, and gave a thoughtful nod. "I did. Lord Elio is a fine tour guide. His ward is, as well. Though he could've said hello," he said, shifting his attention to Peadar at the far end of the table.

Heat scorched Elio's face.

Peadar met the Imperator's sly gaze for a brief moment. He continued eating without a word.

"Cael tried the first of our nectarines," Elio blurted.

"Spring is on the horizon," Darius said, pleasantly baritone and warm.

Elio, too embarrassed and on edge to do much else, followed the statement with, "We'll prepare the first harvest for Griea. Each tree, every fruit." When the table went silent — no clattering utensils, no breathing, no teeth tearing food — Elio's chest emptied. "To commemorate the beginning of Alexander's and Harlyn's treaty," he added, wobbly and hesitant. He glanced around the table, searching for support. Obviously, Aurethia sent a portion of its harvest to Griea anyway. He didn't understand why the energy in the room seemed to electrify. "I'm sure Griea will appreciate tasting the first of our cycle's bounty before the rest of the system."

Constance leveled him with a steady, inquisitive stare. "For some, it will be the first tasting of their lifetime." She waited, watching his expression. He made sure to fix his face, to become unreadable. "You have a kind heart, my young lord," she gentled.

"That can be arranged," Lena said, but Darius spoke over the tail-end of her statement, "I'll speak with the transport advisor on Draitune."

Cael lifted his fizzy flute. "Well then," he rasped, clearing a bit of ice from his voice, "to Griea and Aurethia, and to a bountiful harvest."

Elio picked up his glass. He looked across the table. One of Cael's pale eyes, dotted with a blown, black pupil, closed in a wink. Cael did not drink until Elio brought his own flute to his mouth, soaking his lip with apricot wine.

CHAPTER SIX

CAEL

T he Griean ship lifted away from the launch pad and ascended toward the transport hovering in low orbit. Duchess Constance clutched tightly to Cael before she left. She took his face between her palms and nodded, convincing him of an unspoken fealty before she kissed his brow.

"Remember what I told you." She spoke quietly, firmly, and then turned without another word. She took a short ramp to the docking bay, grasping a soldier's arm to steady herself on the metal foothold.

Cael thought he might've seen a stray tear at the corner of her eye, but he could've been imagining it. Women from her homeworld, especially those who immigrated to Griea, weren't known for their sensitivity. When his father had needed a new concubine, Marcus chose a prospect from Ocury, counting on resilience, fearlessness, and capability to round out his genetic legacy. Constance was a desirable and strategic play in diversifying the Volkov bloodline, but Cael only ever saw her as the parent who tended to scrapes, iced his bruises, fretted from the sidelines during the Tupinaire, and hand-picked a deadly companion when she knew he would be spending a cycle alone on an uncertain moon.

The Henly household had done their part, standing respectfully in the courtyard while half of the Griean regency departed. Cael watched the terrestrial transport grow fainter before blinking out of sight. The subtle outline of the starship loomed above, waiting to take his mother home, leaving him alone on Aurethia. Alone and enchanted. Alone and tasked with righting himself against the moon's decadence.

Everywhere he looked, life thrust itself up from hardy soil. Where he'd once heard the warped sound of ice shifting and thinning, he now heard birdsong and sea-shush. The whistle of cold wind through Machina's walled city had morphed into a soft breeze rustling coin-shaped leaves on a blossoming tree. Duty shackled his ankles while the Aurethian prince became an unmovable anomaly dead center in his line of sight.

You have been raised for this very moment. Cael told himself what he always knew to be true. *You are a weapon, detonating.*

"Imperator, I think you should eat something," Vik said. The Augment stood at his back, watching the sky. "My internal inspection noted hunger-pain in your abdomen. Did you skip breakfast?"

"You don't need to internally inspect me, Vik. I'm fine."

"Hunger can cause irritability," he smarted. Vik was, in fact, still mostly human and capable of play.

Cael rolled his eyes. "I'll go..." He kicked a loose stone and turned toward the manor. "Find something, I guess."

"Wise choice."

"Do you have a pending message to relay?" He faced Vik. The Henly property stretched out behind him, and the royal family dispersed.

Vik's system was hidden beneath organic skin and a cybernetic carapace. But if you looked closely enough, you could still see the whirring of information beating beneath his flesh like a thousand pin-sized butterflies. His left eye glinted, augmented pupil expanding and shrinking.

"If I may, sir. It might be best if you connect your dialect device to my programming," Vik said.

Cael looped the earpiece around the base of his lobe and tapped it. *Imperator*, the friendly robotic voice welcomed. *Augment detected. Ready to pair.* He pressed and held the small bulb located beneath the flat side of the device flush against the shell of his ear and waited. Vik nodded curtly. *Pairing complete.*

Vik stood across from Cael, unmoving, unspeaking, but his smooth, calm voice came through his earpiece. There is no transmission to relay yet, Imperator. Would you like to send an encrypted message to the Legatus?

"No, we'll check in when we've made progress," Cael said.

Vik nodded. I recommend using this channel to discuss sensitive political strategy.

"I agree. But we should still be seen speaking."

"Well, I hope you'd still want to talk, Imperator."

Cael laughed, taken aback. "You're funny." His brow creased with surprise. "Did my mother choose you for your humor?"

"No, sir, she chose me for my stature, I believe. And my target-to-fatality ratio."

"Oh." He started back to the manor. Vik fell into stride beside him. "And what's that — your ratio, I mean."

"Two-hundred-and-twenty-seven   targets,   two-hundred-and-twenty fatalities."

"Lucky seven."

"No, just fast," Vik corrected.

Laughter snuck up on him. He glanced around the exterior of the manor. Aurethian sentries stood at attention, stationed at every corner of the house. A few cruised through the courtyard and walked the perimeter of the orchard. As he trailed his gaze from one end of the estate to the other, he slowed his pace. It was a pleasant surprise to find Elio seated beneath the tree in the courtyard, clasping a holobook between his slender hands. Peadar stepped out from behind the edge of a pillar, marking Cael's attention.

"Mirror him," Cael said.

Vik did as he was told, crossing the property to stand on the other side of the front door, shoulder propped casually against the opposing pillar.

Cael stepped up onto the brick surrounding the tree and bent his head to avoid a branch. Flowers dangled like white shards, stained reddish orange at their yawning center. They perfumed the air, soft and unique, like the spritz of freshly peeled citrus and salted taffy. Cael parted his lips, wondering if their scent might translate to taste.

"Lord Henly," he greeted.

"Imperator," Elio said. He didn't immediately turn away from his holo but eventually cast his gaze upward. "I hope the Duchess has a safe and swift trip home."

"Griea will be thankful to have her back." Cael cradled a puffy flower. They looked swollen, almost. Ready to burst.

"Candlebell," Elio noted. "They're native to Aurethia."

"Aurethia is mother to many, I'm gathering." Candlebell, lions, farmland, Elio, Avara. It was a place plucked from a starving man's dream.

Elio flicked off his holotablet and stood. He reached for the flower, brushing against Cael. He was a furnace in a man's body. Cael wasn't accustomed to such heat. He inched away, watching Elio snap the flower from its vine and bring the clustered petals to his mouth. Nectar wet the line of his lips.

"They're edible," Elio said, lifting his brow as if to say *yes, I promise*, and then plucked another, handing it to Cael. "It's technically a plum tree, but we use the flowers for tea. Decorate pastries with them, turn their pollen into cologne, dry their petals for lip balm."

Cael mimicked Elio, sliding the flower into his mouth and sucking. Sweetness burst on his tongue, stained by the earthy bite of something fresh and living. The nectar hidden in the elongated bulb stuck to his teeth. He could eat a thousand of them.

"Lip balm," Cael echoed. The idea confused him.

Elio smiled gently. "It's a flirtatious gesture. Those who taste it know it's rare."

Flirtatious was not a word Cael kept in his pocket. He'd charmed his way into physicality and let off steam with fellow fighters after the Tupinaire, but courtship was a deliberate, clinical practice on Griea. When it came to partnership, people spoke clearly, intentionally, or they did not speak at all. From what he knew of Aurethia, moon-folk were much, much different.

"This tree has stood here for centuries. It's older than anything else on the property." Elio dropped the stem and brushed his hand along the pale bark.

"What were you reading?" Cael asked.

"Some antique poorly translated Earthen book," he said nonchalantly, as if reviewing historical Earthen text was a normal thing to do and not a hobby reserved for high profile archivists. "Have you settled in? I imagine you had a lot to unpack."

"Not too much." And it was true. Cael only brought what he needed. Clothing, armor, his finest weaponry, and his holotablet. The rest was superficial. Toiletries and keepsakes. Griean favorites — dried glacier kelp to snack on; fizzy rhubarb soda to sip — things that would remind him of his planet when he got homesick. "Have you eaten?"

"I have. I'll be joining Peadar for a sparring session soon, actually."

"Then I'll see you for dinner?"

"Hopefully a quieter one." Elio met Cael's gaze on an apologetic glance. It was guarded, that look. Shielded and curious.

"Tension is…" Cael searched for the Aurethian translation and gave up.

He switched to Griean. "Formative. Two different textiles sewn together. I expected a snag or two."

The young lord eyed him quizzically. "You weren't offended?"

"Oh, I was very offended," Cael said, laughing.

Elio's face reddened. "See, I — "

"And I haven't offended you yet? I'll have to try harder." Cael slid his attention to the hollow of Elio's throat, then to the slender dip where his waist bent, lower, over his plain, grey trousers. When he flashed his eyes to Elio's face, the lion cub of Aurethia looked startled, like a seal spotted by a shark. "It's play, Elio. I'm playing with you."

"A joke?" Elio asked in Aurethian. His mouth lifted slightly, trying at a smile.

"Sure," Cael said. He sucked a bit of nectar from the side of his finger. "What you offered Griea is generous. Valiant, even. I won't forget it."

Elio dropped his jaw, but nothing surfaced at first. He exhaled hard. "It shouldn't be."

Ah. Cael lifted his chin, watching Elio straighten in place, becoming broader. Out of the corner of his eye, he saw Peadar step forward. His guard was attentive.

"There's much we'll learn of each other. Enjoy your training." Then he inclined his head, bidding Elio a respectful albeit silent goodbye, and ducked out from under the sweet tree.

AFTER POKING THROUGH THE kitchen, Cael settled on a serving of noodles drenched in chili oil and a semi-ripe fruit plucked from the basket. The slippery rice noodles warmed his mouth, growing hotter the more he ate, and the apple cooled the spice, shocking his system with a dose of sweetness. After nibbling the fruit down to its core, he rolled a seed between his thumb and index finger. Such a tiny, powerful thing.

The day moved swiftly. Morning turned to afternoon and Cael decided to explore the orchard. Vik stayed by his side, matching plantlife and tree species to the information logged in his database. Cael took his time, still lugging through the weighty air, allowing his body to adjust to the moon's atmosphere. The Aurethian guard clocked him — which he anticipated and ignored — and the sound of the sea played behind buzzing insects and trilling cranes.

It was easy to love this place. Easy to be charmed by its organic riches. Cael forced himself to think of Griea, to remember his ice giant's painted sky and snow-capped mountains. He touched a small, fat leaf on a waking stem. Back home, it would've sprouted a thorn, would've carried a cage to protect itself against frostbite and foragers. Here it only bloomed.

"Imperator, Maxine Carr approaches," Vik said.

Cael looked over his shoulder. Winding between berry bushes, Maxine was a black-clad shadow, slipping soundlessly along the harvest walkway. He waited until she grew closer to shift his body, acknowledging her presence.

"Maxine," he greeted.

"Imperator, I hope I'm not intruding," she said, bowing slightly.

"Join us for a walk."

She smiled. "Thank you. Did you sleep well? Sometimes the transition from space travel can be taxing."

"I'll adjust," he said, skipping the bit about his restlessness, how his bedchamber was far too hot, how he'd stared at the ceiling for an eternity, how Elio drifted into the only dream he'd mustered. He folded his hands neatly at the small of his back. "Have you checked in with Griea?"

"I have, Imperator. Legatus Marcus is pleased you've arrived safely. He would like me to stress the engagement," she said, shooting him a serious look. "The timeline must remain intact — one cycle to completion. Longer and the continuum will breach in transit. Too large a payload in too small a window. Shorter and the Royal Reserve will be unfit for launch. We need one cycle, one Aurethian year. No more, no less."

Cael paused to assess an orchid. Usually, an engagement lasted however long it needed to within established limitations set by the participating families. Stretching a courtship to the very last day wasn't unheard of, but it wasn't normal either. "And his reasoning?"

"House Volkov is being closely watched by the Greater Universe. House Darvin of Draitune sent a signal to Mal and Ren, confirming your arrival. Aurethia is under unspoken protection; we must tread carefully."

"Unspoken," Cael echoed, snorting. He ran his thumb along a stiff petal. "And Avara production?"

"The High Lord recently broke ground on a new mine. Per regulation, only a small portion of the mineral will be added to departing cargo. House Henly has only grown three percent of its source material since my arrival."

"Over the course of four cycles?" Cael narrowed his eyes. He met her gaze, waiting for an explanation. That was unfathomably shallow growth. Given the expanding populus across the Greater Universe, Aurethia would never excavate enough Avara to treat the livable spaces in Mal and Ren, let alone Lux and its homeworlds.

Maxine simply nodded. "Avara is temperamental, supposedly. The Xenobiology Division regulates Aurethia's production schedule, and excavation requires a delicate hand."

"And the value?"

"Demand for Avara is constantly rising, Imperator."

"The price is, too, I imagine?"

She dipped her head. "Indeed. The High Lord and High Lady are protective of their precious moon." She edged each word between set teeth. Her polite demeanor wavered. She blinked, reigning in Griean fury. "Value has risen ten percent."

Cael nodded. He chewed the information. "House Henly refuses to increase production while simultaneously encouraging inflation due to demand."

"Correct, sir."

"Which explains the selective deliverables."

Maxine forced a papery smile. "Those who pay, receive."

She remained quiet for a long time, watching Cael digest the information. He knew about Aurethia's chokehold on the miracle gemstone. Understood the patchy delivery to populations on the outer rim of the system — Griea, Shepard, and Sierra. Divinity, the third station, was close enough to Ocury to sustain itself. The outliers relied on overused, unstable jump gates to access deliveries. The Lux Continuum was available, but House Henly typically utilized the starlink to reach Mal and Ren. Capitalizing on expanded revenue, no doubt.

"Griea is resilient," Maxine said, so softly Cael hardly heard her at first. "You will bring the basilisk glory, Imperator. Aurethia believes itself to be the jewel of the Greater Universe, but it sits in the hand of a weak man." Their native language slid between her lips like a blade. "Our time is now."

Cael set his palm on Maxine's shoulder both to calm and commend her. "Our time is now," he agreed, and glanced over the top of her head.

The Henly manor stood on the horizon, silhouetted by Draitune's ghostly ring.

CHAPTER SEVEN

BRACKEN

Snow tumbled across the Sliding Sea, kicked upward from a southern storm traveling toward Machina.

Bracken stood on the veranda attached to his bedchamber. He gripped the frosty picket. Dark fog plumed over the frozen expanse. White met white, horizon kissing ocean, and a shadow coiled beneath the ice. Atmospheric changes, especially storm systems, riled basilisk to the surface. The spiny ridge jutting from the creature's back skewered the thinnest part of the cryosphere, wounding the glacial ocean. Serpentine and languid, the basilisk arced out of the water, a blueish, silvery stripe against the wasteland.

Optio Bracken, the potential initiates for enroll-ment in the Planetary Syndicate have arrived. The robotic voice itched through his dialect device. He stared at the beast for a while. At a distance, it moved gracefully, whipping its finned tail as it dived. Bracken drew in a cold breath.

Griea was restless without its Imperator, bracing for inevitable wartime. Bracken Volkov was the one who would prepare the Royal Reserve, its ruthless legion. Cael's legion — soldiers his cousin selected, trained, and left. Something about stepping into that role, harnessing that responsibility, caused sweat to bead on Bracken's nape. Cael was a cocky, foolish, beloved young man, and Bracken feared his authority might not be received fairly.

Or welcomed at all. Despite his triumphs, his depth of victory, he hadn't *taken* what could have been his.

Griean loyalty was earned, not expected, and no matter how often he won in the arena, Bracken Volkov was not Keeper of the Basilisk. Despite his age and experience, he was not the heir.

Bracken bypassed the fur coat on the hook beside the door and left his chamber wearing a tight thermal shirt and dark pants tucked into tall boots. He walked through the Volkov castle the same way a guest did. Even after decades, the high ceilings, crackling hearths, hand-hammered metal, and sleek interior felt more like a facility than a home.

His home — the one he remembered — was a two-story apartment on the sea-facing side of Sector One. His mother, Miriam, had grown an herb garden under hydroponic lamplight in the cramped kitchen, and his father, Praetor Savin, had crafted decorative leatherwork for personal weaponry.

Bracken reached for the blade at his side, thumbing the leather tassel dangling from the pommel. Sometimes he felt like he'd never left that house, like he was wading through a dream, waiting for his mother to shake him awake, for his father to call to him. *Bracken, feed the fire more wood!* But they were gone, one to sickness, the other to combat, and his uncle and the family's castle had become an adoptive shelter.

The train to Sector Three moved swiftly. Bracken stood by the glass and watched Machina blur outside the capsule.

Freezing rain pelted his forehead and dampened his shoulders as he took the skybridge to the Griean War College. The storm would barrel through the city soon, and Machina would close up like a blackened module against Goren's mountainous terrain. Above, windows buckled closed. Below, ground cars dipped into garages and metal weather shields descended from awnings, swallowing patios and balconies. Even the bridge he crossed pushed thick silver panels up over his head, latching together like scales to fend off the weather.

"Optio," a passerby said, inclining their head respectfully.

"Get home safe," Bracken said.

The college was a large, square building adjacent to the entrance of the Organic Weaponry Division. Metal shielding folded across the glass half of the structure, unrolling like a tossed die, and disc-lamps brightened the lobby, offsetting the loss of natural light. Sterile and orderly, the college boasted a multitude of classrooms, study areas, lecture spaces, and a well-stocked library. It was a beautiful representation of Griea. Keen, sparse. Utilitarian.

Bracken breathed evenly. He tapped his dialect device and said, "Attendees?" *Forty-three prospects*, his device replied. "Room?" *Lecture Hall Eleven.*

Bracken turned down a wide corridor and fixed his expression, wiping any semblance of uncertainty from his face. He strode into the room, straight-backed, scanning row upon row of graduates awaiting their placement in Griea's Planetary Syndicate, an opt-in work-for-hire initiative designed to fulfill contractual obligations across the Greater Universe, loaning highly trained operatives to paying clients. Since the century-long uptick in military strangling by the Imperial Council — encouraging the use of hand-to-hand combat and non-ballistic weaponry — clientele resorted to hiring skilled security and discreet mercenaries.

Most of the Greater Universe associated Griea with discipline. Bracken intended to keep it that way.

"Good afternoon, graduates," Bracken said, pausing in the center of the room. He leaned against the podium with his arms folded. "Who here can tell me the sixth law?"

A sharply dressed woman in the front row raised her hand. "To preserve system stability and avoid airlock breach, artillery and projectiles are outlawed in all stationer-designated areas. Any contract executed via space station, in proximity to a station, or on a space vessel should be completed using organic combat techniques."

"Very good. And who can tell me the second law?"

Someone in the back raised their hand. "Mercy is an offering, not a guarantee. Every Griean in the Syndicate is protected under Griean law regardless of their contractual deployment."

"And?" Bracken asked.

"Contracted operatives are to engage in good faith with the known law on any planet, station, or client-owned vessel. In order to prosecute a Griean operative, the client and defendant must stand trial in Griea. The client is welcome to provide evidence, source legal counsel from their homeworld, and remain present for sentencing, but no Griean is permitted to be imprisoned, sentenced, or confined on any planet, station, or client-owned vessel other than those operated by Griea."

"Important to remember." He searched the room for promising prospects. "If you are imprisoned on another planet, it's considered a war crime. Well-dressed, smart-mouthed police might try to intimidate you while you're on a job. That being said, who can tell me the third law?"

A man to the left said, "Griean operatives are entitled to self-protection and self-determination."

"Exactly. You are Griean." Bracken let his voice raise, thunderous and booming. "You've acquired a specific skill set that soft-bellied stationers and comfortable planet-side officers admire and underestimate. Do not forget who you are. You are ruthless, you are dangerous, you are precise, and you are desirable because of it." He paused, allowing the graduates to nod and hoot. "Those of you who applied to join the Royal Reserve, stand."

Seven, then three more. Ten. He studied each person carefully.

"Stay behind. The rest of you report to the training chamber for drone assessment," Bracken said.

"Optio," the lecture hall echoed, voices overlapping.

The Syndicate initiates were already pre-approved for combat, but it was Bracken's duty to see them through the assessment, clear their files for onboarding, dispatch their information to the database, and hand-select the qualifying few who would serve the Volkov household. The Royal Reserve was an exclusive branch of the Griean military, designed to keep Griea's political investments intact, and stationed for immediate, impromptu deployment. They were highly adept — hardest to kill, easiest to train.

Majority of the Royal Reserve had served under Cael. Their loyalty lived in him. These ten were fresh, though, and Bracken could mold them into his own perfect soldiers.

Bracken waved the group closer. "As most of you know, Imperator Cael Volkov, Keeper of the Basilisk, is preparing the forest moon for our arrival." He watched them nod. They stood shoulder-to-shoulder, hands clasped, faces tilted upward, eyes stern and unwavering. *Young*, he thought. *Young and hungry.* "I'm here in his stead, readying the Royal Reserve for the siege of a lifetime." He stopped in front of a young man. The initiate swallowed. "Tell me, what separates the Royal Reserve from the Planetary Syndicate?"

When the soldier in front of him didn't speak, the person next to him gathered a breath and barked, "Mercy is commanded."

Bracken slid his gaze toward the slightly familiar face. Dark, rich complexion. The cut of a cunning, brave glance. "Mercy is commanded," he repeated. "It is not offered, it is not guaranteed, it is not an option. If your commander doesn't order it, your target does not receive it. Grace is for god, and god is in the water."

"Grace is for god, and god is in the water," the ten initiates said in unison.

"Good." Bracken glanced at the name embroidered above the Griean glyph on his leather school coat. Malkin. "Would you die for Griea?" Bracken asked, lifting his voice.

The room answered. "Yes, Optio!"

"Would you kill for Griea?"

"Yes, Optio!"

He stepped back, looking from one to the next. "What would you give?"

"Everything," they shouted.

"What would you take?"

"Everything!"

Bracken nodded slowly. "Report to the training chamber for hand-to-hand assessment," he said.

The ten contenders, all suitable, bowed briefly and then left the lecture hall.

What would you take?

The question lingered, scorching his tongue. "Everything," he said, testing the answer for himself. "Everything."

CHAPTER EIGHT

ELIO

Aurethia bloomed. Elio woke to sunlight and warm wind sliding through the open window. Gold limned the floor and striped the foot of his bed. He stared at the ceiling and inhaled a cleansing breath, shaking off the last sip of a dream. Wide palm on tucked leather, gripping a sheathed weapon. Blue flash — lightning against storm cloud, iris against pupil — and his name, shouted. He blinked the dreamscape back into his subconscious. Candlebell and peony powdered a breeze tossed inland from the ocean. It made him long for summer even though he'd hardly enjoyed the beginning of spring.

Everything crawled now. Everything rushed forward at lightspeed.

Elio swallowed sour saliva and cleared his throat. His thoughts were slow in the morning, but recently they always leaned toward Cael. Somewhere in the opposing wing, his fiancé slept. Or he didn't. Maybe he sparred with his Augment, or sniffed out breakfast in the kitchen, or prowled through the Henly manor, inspecting the house like a hunting hound.

Whatever Cael was doing, Elio still caught the very edge of lingering excitement unspooling throughout the estate. Staff whispered about the Griean prince, spreading gossip from Atreyu, Aurethia's capital. Not everyone was convinced the union between the forest moon and the ice giant was warranted. Some people, those seeded with distrust in Griea's opportunistic nature, encouraged House Henly to renegotiate the terms established by Alexander. Elio balled the sheet in his fist, twisting the cotton between his knuckles.

Since he was a child, Griea had been a distant shadow, clawing forward, inevitable and unrelenting. And well before him, Alexander Henly had established animosity the same way ancient Earthen leaders planted propaganda in historical media, allowing the slip of a clever tongue to encourage deadly rumors. Truth be told, Elio found the act cowardly, but two centuries later, most Aurethian historians still glossed over the unfair undercurrent his great-grandfather set into motion — Griea, a hostile place cooked in myth. Not an enemy, but close enough to call for caution. Some people still viewed it as a home for uncivilized barbarians. A staunch, guarded people who valued bloodshed over respectability. Elio's research proved that *not* to be true — not entirely, at least — but a two-hundred-year feud, and Alexander's crafty doctrine still ruffled most of Aurethia's population.

A hawk called outside. The sound cut the air. Elio slid out of bed and walked into the adjoining washroom. The shower sprayed hot. Once he was clean and awake, he dressed in lightweight straight-legged pants and a vermilion sleeveless shirt, plucking at the outfit for a solid three minutes before deciding it looked right. He chose a belt with a tarnished buckle and soft-soled boots.

Sometimes when he looked at himself for too long, he imagined what he might've grown into if he hadn't made the Choice. Would he be willowy like Lorelei? Small-chested, strong, and built like a whip? Or would he take on their mother's gentle curves? Her soft, pouty face and petite wrists? He tilted his head, staring at his reflection in the full-length mirror beside the doorway. Whoever he would've become, had it been her, or them, or something else entirely, Elio would've still been promised away, intended for greatness he wasn't sure he could carry, born to a world still baring its teeth.

How does one reach the true root of a fallacy? He rinsed his mouth with mint and rosewater and held the question in his mind as he walked into the hall.

Peadar stood in the great room, feeding the fireplace a fresh log. "Good rising, Lord Elio. Your father would like to speak with you."

"Speak with me? About?"

"*Check in* is the verbiage he used," he said.

"And he didn't give a reason?"

"Well, you are courting the Griean heir. I'm sure it has something to do with that."

"As I'm constantly reminded," Elio murmured.

"Could be about the harvest you promised." Peadar gave him a patient, knowing look, one meant for small children.

Elio elevated a brow and snorted. "Think he'll chastise me?"

"I think he'd like to check in with you," Peadar said, curtly, minding his business. He clucked like he would to a horse and nodded toward the northern quarter. "He's in the study."

Elio shot Peadar an annoyed glance before crossing the room. He tried to take his time, but his feet moved faster than his mind. Soon enough, Elio was rounding a corner into the northern wing, shouldering through the closed door, and striding into a dimly lit, leather-furnished room. The disc-lamp hovering above the lacquer desk burned orange. Darius sat in a high-backed chair, reviewing a holodocument.

"Elio," his father greeted without looking up.

"Father," Elio said. He took the chair across from him. "Peadar directed me here."

"How are you, son?"

"I'm fine."

Darius glanced away from the holo. His sunken jade eyes creased when he smiled. "I spoke with the transport advisor about the charity you've offered Griea."

"It's not charity — "

"We'll honor it," he interrupted, nodding sharply. "But Draitune is concerned about a one-time deed being misconstrued as a shift in the standard delivery schedule. From now on, we need to consult with Angelina before making hasty decisions."

Angelina, of course. House Darvin's unflinching elected leader and a personal friend to House Henly.

"House Darvin is aware I'm marrying the Griean heir, correct?" Elio snapped.

Darius hardened his expression. "Everyone is aware of that, Elio. But we need to be strategic about our foothold in the Greater Universe. The initial harvest typically goes to Draitune for cloning. After that, it's distributed throughout Lux, then transported to Mal and Ren. Avara is merely a portion of our marketplace. Aurethian farmland is valuable, too."

"How do we determine the initial deliveries? Because Duchess Constance made a point to mention how little Griea receives and — "

"Griea receives what was brokered between our houses when the engagement was sealed — "

"Two centuries ago?"

"Elio." His name was a warning, warmed-over and spat. Darius set the holo down. The blue screen winked off, leaving the slender, cylindrical tube rolling back and forth on the shiny desk. The High Lord steepled his hands, pressing them against his mouth. Contemplation was not an unusual thing to glimpse on Darius. But worry was. "I've honored your request. Griea will receive the initial harvest, but we will still be sending a variety of samples to Draitune for cloning. I need you to hear me when I speak, son. I need you to listen."

Elio flattened his frown. He stayed quiet, offering a nod of acknowledgement.

"You will be the steward of Aurethia regardless of who you wed. *You*," he insisted. "Keeping this moon under the guidance of House Henly is of the utmost importance. That alone is why we need to prioritize our alliance with Draitune, our original homeworld, and strengthen the relationships we have outside the Lux system. Change can't be made overnight, but your betrothal to Cael Volkov will usher in a new era for us. For Griea, too." He paused, gentling. His shoulders dropped and he sighed through his nose. "The path you carve out will be walked by your children, your children's children, their children's children. Allow them the chance to finish what you start."

The implication of powerlessness unsettled him, as if the only control Elio possessed was putting into motion a future he would never see. He calmed himself with a grounding breath. It was wasteful to argue. Pointless to needle his father into a worse mood.

Instead, Elio nodded and said, "You're aware of the unrest in Atreyu, I imagine?"

Darius drew in a breath and exhaled it, too, mirroring his son in a strange, candid way. Elio never ignored the innate fatherhood Darius carried with him, but sometimes his status as High Lord squashed their familial link. Things like that, casual commonalities, reminded Elio that the root of their squabbles was usually love.

"Yes, I've heard." He leaned back in his chair and brought his knuckles to his cheek, propping his elbow on the armrest. "It's not just Atreyu. The surrounding territories have been outspoken about their distrust. Nadhas, even."

"We have one cycle to sway public opinion. That's not long," Elio said.

"Influence, not sway. Belief is fickle, son. If we sway them, they'll easily fall into comfortable ideology the moment it's convenient. Influencing them, engaging with them — seeding doubt in wide-spread misconception — that's how we instill belief, that's how a Great House strategizes."

"House Henly should set an example, father."

"Intention is a strong enough example for now." Darius spoke crisply, and his tone meant *do not argue*. "Griea has equal responsibility. They parade prisoners through their arena dressed in Aurethian garb, they mock us in their houses, whisper about our cold-hearted greed, imply our moon is a leech on the Imperial teat. This is not a one-sided conflict. Griea is capable of delusion as well."

"Are we certain that's the truth?" Elio challenged.

"Maybe you should ask the Imperator," Darius said. He met Elio's gaze and raised his brow. "Mindfully," he added, tapping one finger on his jaw.

Elio remembered Cael's comment under the candlebell tree. *There's much we'll learn of each other.* "Maybe."

"Cael can't be hidden from the public. Miners, farmers, fisherman — our people should be given the chance to judge him for themselves, no?" Darius asked.

"I agree," Elio said tentatively.

"Then I'll plan a visit to Atreyu."

"You think that's the best course?"

"I think the people will follow you. If you accept him, they'll accept him. If you present him as an ally, they'll see him as an ally."

"And if they don't?"

"Believe in your people, Elio," Darius said. He jutted his chin toward the doorway, dismissing him. "Let me know if I can assist you, alright? Your mother and I are at your disposal."

That's that. Elio deflated. He nodded and rose from the chair. "Father," he said, exasperated, and respectfully bowed his head.

Darius mirrored the motion. "Son."

Elio left the study and immediately made for the training chamber. He flexed each hand, shifted his jaw back and forth, and contemplated his role in this fluctuating political landscape, one he had no substantial control over. If his own house — his own family — refused to undo, better yet acknowledge, their knotted history, then how would this union bring prosperity to either planet? A bridge between Aurethia and Griea would only ever last if the river of resentment it was built above calmed enough to cross.

And one marriage couldn't possibly be the answer to centuries of dubiety.

The training chamber in the east wing was empty. Elio yanked his shirt up and away. He didn't bother with gloves or tape, just strode toward the weighted bag strung from the ceiling. He moved effortlessly, punching, jabbing, smacking his boot against the bag. The anger swelling in his chest drained with each strike. Soon enough, Elio was lost in it, damp with perspiration, swinging until his shoulders cramped and his biceps ached.

When he finally stopped to breathe, he noticed a shadow blot the open doorway. Cael stood in the hall, wearing a fine black shirt and dark-knit trousers cinched with a thick belt. The Imperator's mouth quirked, but he said nothing.

Elio lifted his chin and inhaled a deep, grounding breath, ignoring a twinge of embarrassment. He wasn't used to being seen as something other than *child, heir, first-born*. But Cael looked at him like he was a soldier, like he was capable. The recognition of power — or relatability, maybe — struck like an open palm. He met Cael's steady gaze and pushed damp hair off his forehead. The Imperator gave him a quick once-over, flashing from Elio's flushed face to his laced boots, and then continued on his way, followed closely by his Augment.

Elio almost said *wait*. The shape of the word bent his mouth, soundless and accidental.

CHAPTER NINE

CAEL

Heat lingered, stirred about by coastal wind. Cael paid attention to the temperature while he fingered through his wardrobe, searching for an appropriate outfit. It'd been almost one month since he'd arrived on Aurethia. Three weeks — standard seven-day intervals adopted from old Earthen timelogs — to be exact.

Since he'd landed, Cael spent time with Elio in the orchard, cruising the dirt pathways while hardy bees and tiny, finger-sized hummers flitted from flower to tree. He explored the manor, peeking into the library to watch Elio flip through dusty tomes, digitally translating House Henly's collection of antiques. He joined the Henly family at the dinner table every night. They rarely traded more than polite niceties, commenting on the weather, or offering insight into each other's homeworlds. Elio spoke with a formality Cael wanted to crack like an egg. But more often than not, the Aurethian heir reminded him of a deer. Cael pictured him bounding off into the forest if he got too close.

"Vik, tell me about Aurethian courtship," Cael said, trying on one shirt then swapping it for another.

Vik stood near the closed door. One pupil expanded, shrank, expanded again. The data-port on his nape made a mechanical sound, whirring quietly. "While Aurethia shares commonality with its colonizer, Draitune, the Aurethian people tend to appreciate intimacy, vulnerability, trust, and openness in lieu of status or financial reach. This is much to do with the job security on Aurethia, allowing citizens more freedom to pursue love-matches. They're known to court for life and take on single or multiple partners. Arranged marriage is uncommon. While Draitune embraces formality, Aurethia is looser, so to speak, celebrating sensuality and bodily autonomy during many seasonal festivals."

Cael wrinkled his nose. "Analyze the traditional Aurethian process in relation to Griean courtship."

"Courtship here is meant to be fun, sir," Vik said.

"It's fun on Griea, too." Laughter hiccupped. "C'mon, tell me."

"While Griean suitors prioritize sustainability, practicality, and straightforward approaches, Aurethian courtship is likely to involve physical flirtation and mental gameplay. To be frank, Imperator, Aurethia is coy and Griea is blunt."

"I've tried to be coy," he muttered.

"If I may," Vik tested, clearing his throat. "Looking at Lord Elio like he's been plated and served does not fit the definition of — "

"You're out of line," Cael barked, choking back laughter. Red-hot embarrassment glowed in his chest. "It's not my fault he's..." *Breathtaking.* "He's like a locked box. We walk, we talk, but I still feel like I've hardly grazed the surface of him. Like he's hiding from me."

"How would you approach him if this courtship took place on Griea?"

"I would state my intention," he said, shooting Vik a confused glance in the mirror. He frowned and felt across his freshly shaven head, searching for any hair he might've missed. "I didn't date on Griea, though. I only ever..." He shrugged, assessing his lightweight, half-sleeve shirt and military-grade trousers. He crouched to tuck in the hem of his pants, clasping metal teeth over the tongue of each boot. "I had no reason to take a partner." *I was reserved for Elio.* "So I never did."

"But you know how to flirt," Vik deadpanned. The Augment listed his head. His wry smile deepened.

"Not with him."

"Does he frighten you?"

Cael almost lied. "Yes," he admitted, hushed. "There's more at stake than my pride. Earning his favor is a necessity, and I can't fumble this. I need him to trust me; I need him to find me desirable. Tolerable, at least. At this point, I doubt he'd take my hand, nonetheless speak to me about Avara production."

"Maybe he's more like home than you care to realize. Have you considered earning his respect first?"

The question rattled him. "Respect on Griea is earned through combat and fearlessness."

"And? You assume he hasn't researched Griea? Maybe he's expecting different signals."

Cael hadn't considered that. He looked at his reflection for a moment longer before settling on his appearance, then slid a boot-blade into his shoe. He'd decided against carrying his standard weapon during their visit to Nadhas. No one outright prohibited it, but he assumed he'd be received better by the villagers if he remained unarmed. It was his first outing, one Lena had arranged, and he was relieved to finally leave the estate even if Nadhas proper was only a short distance away.

"Maxine might have insight," Vik noted. "She's established a bond with the young lord."

"That's true." Cael sighed. He had to move carefully around Maxine, though. She'd been collecting information about House Henly for a long time. Blowing her cover would compromise Griea's ability to launch an assault. "I'll approach her today while we're in public."

"Wise decision, Imperator."

"We're meeting in the courtyard, I believe. Keep your data-stream live and send the footage to Griea tonight."

Vik nodded. "You'll need to manually trigger footage delivery."

"Remind me."

Another nod. Vik held the door and followed Cael into the hall.

The manor was still an unfamiliar oddity, encapsulating the very essence of Aurethia on every wall, in every room. Unlike most structures in Machina, slanted windows littered the open, airy space, bathing the baroque house in dusky light. He wasn't used to the smell of manure and fruit, or the way staff moved with such surety. People seemed at ease, unused to distress. In the entryway, he said *hello* to a chambermaiden who smiled and padded by carrying freshly laundered towels, then he stepped through the open front door and squinted against searing sunlight.

"Imperator," Lena greeted. She stood in the road next to the candlebell tree, holding Orson's hand.

Indigo adjusted a small pack and waved. "Good rising, Imperator."

Cael tipped his head respectfully. "Good rising."

Lena pushed her wide, floppy sunhat down. Her mauve mouth curved. "You won't mind walking, will you? It's a beautiful day."

"Not at all, High Lady," he said.

In front of her, Maxine, Lorelei, and Elio stood together, talking and laughing. Peadar hailed two Aurethian sentries. The pair gave a signal, or made a sign of some sort, aligning one hand in front of their throats, fingertips pointed upright toward their chin.

"That's a patriotic gesture," Vik quietly said.

Cael noted the movement. He closed the space between himself and Elio's cohort, paying mind to the sentries falling into step behind him. It certainly wasn't unusual for security to accompany members of Great Houses, but Cael wasn't accustomed to being a protected asset. And honestly, he couldn't tell whether he was safeguarded or monitored. Both, probably.

"Imperator Volkov." Lorelei smiled. Her gaze swiped like a cat's tongue against a carcass. She twirled, fanning her cerulean dress. Her wood-heeled shoes clopped the path. "How're you enjoying Aurethia? It must be quite the change for the Keeper of the Basilisk," she almost taunted.

The dent at the hinge of Elio's jaw deepened. Cael glanced at Elio. Met his gaze for half a breath. "I'm enjoying your moon very much, Lady Lorelei. It's different than what I'm used to, but I'm starting to understand the allure."

"It *is* charming," Maxine offered, falling into step beside Vik.

Elio cleared his throat. "Nadhas is our coastal port town. It's where we source and process most of our seafood."

"And Avara," Maxine added. "It's a well-rounded trade port."

"Yes, there's also a mine. The village is quaint and dated, but merchants from all over Aurethia sail to Nadhas for the market. There's a salt manufacturer, textile dealers, rice farmers from Atreyu — poets and musicians, artisans and foragers. It's weathered many storms, rebuilt itself many times."

"I'm grateful for the chance to see it," Cael said.

"What's Griea's trade resource of choice?" Lorelei asked.

"Organic weaponry."

She balked. "People?"

Maxine smiled, aiming a less than polite expression at the stone road beneath their feet. "Trained operatives," she said, before Cael could answer. "So yes, people. But you know this already, Lorelei. We've talked about it countless times."

"I'd like to hear it from Cael, thank you," the princess said, not unkindly, but not quite friendly. She spoke like someone used to saying whatever, whenever, and however she liked. Cael found it endearing, almost, to be in the presence of unfiltered youth.

"Leave him alone, Lorelei," Lena crowed from behind them.

"He's not angry," Lorelei assured, gesturing wildly at Cael. She flashed a wicked grin. "You're not, are you?"

Cael slid his gaze to Elio again, smiling softly. The oldest Henly heir looked vexed. Cael shifted to Lorelei. "Of course not. It's a fair question. Griea specializes in producing highly skilled security resources. Organic, augmented, cybernetic, and technical. We're the only licensed artillery manufacturer in the Greater Universe."

"But no one uses artillery anymore." An unsaid question edged Lorelei's statement.

"Non-organic weaponry is heavily regulated," he agreed. "Other than that, Griea is a humble planet. Our people are leatherworkers, hunters, fashion designers — "

"Oh, I would die to own a Griean gown," Lorelei exclaimed, twirling ahead on the path. "Will you tell me about the style there, Cael? You and Maxine are both..." She waved her pointer finger between them. "...*dark*. Is wearing color abnormal there?"

At that, Cael laughed. Elio swatted his sister on the arm. She hissed at him, aiming a retaliatory slap to his shoulder. Behind them, Lena made a sharp sound — *ah, ah* — and the siblings resorted to fighting with their eyes, glaring like two cobras.

"Darker clothing retains heat," Maxine explained. "As I've said before."

Cael nudged her with his elbow. He lowered his voice, watching Elio yank his sister and pace ahead. "It's fine. I know what she's doing."

"Making her brother jealous," Maxine purred.

Cael slowed, allowing space to grow between them. He tipped his mouth toward Maxine and asked, "Speaking of her brother, how do I earn his favor? You know him. Tell me what to do."

"Earn his favor or earn his heart? If it's favor you want, stay cordial and sophisticated. If it's his heart you're after — "

"I'm after his trust."

"I know what you're here for, Imperator," she said, granting him a deliberate glance. "I doubt you're what he anticipated, and I don't think he's used to feeling nervous around someone. Elio is strong-minded, honorable, brave, raw. To be frank, I imagine he doesn't know what to do with you. Or how to behave. If you want his trust, you'll have to capture his heart, I'm afraid."

"I feel like I'm hunting a deep-sea shark," he joked.

"You're hunting a lion," she said, arching a pointed brow. "Much worse. Far more dangerous."

"He doesn't seem dangerous," Cael mused, sneaking a glance at Elio dressed in a light willowy shirt and grey trousers.

Maxine nodded. "He is," she said, confidently. "He's well-trained. Deadly with a blade. Beloved." Her voice lowered to a faint hush. "Adjust his spirit and he will make a fine duke."

Cael's throat stitched. She meant *break* his spirit. He heard it in her cool tone, how she slipped casually into Griean. There were two words for 'adjust' in their language. The one she chose meant shatter, contort, replace. "Thank you, Maxine. We'll circle back."

The assembly followed a snug road against the treeline for close to forty-five minutes. To the left, forest stretched impossibly far, and to the right, the ocean lapped at dark sand, darker stone. Maxine moved ahead and snaked her arm around Lorelei's elbow, stealing the princess from her brother's side. Hazy morning sunlight dappled vinery and firs, and haloed Elio's blonde hair.

"Sir, I believe Maxine's intervention was strategic," Vik said.

"No shit, Vik," Cael breathed out, indulging an old Earthen curse. He didn't wait for whatever witty comment the Augment might throw at him and strode toward Elio, falling into step beside him.

Elio acknowledged him with a quick eye-flash and the hint of a smile. Movement like that, subtle attention, reminded Cael of the foxes back on Griea.

The prince jutted his chin toward the outline of houses in the distance and lifted his hand, pointing. "We're almost there."

Light glinted along the jewelry cuffing his slender wrist, glittering gold against tan, freckled skin.

"What's this?" Cael placed the barest brush of fingertips underneath Elio's palm. He eyed the hand-hammered yellow band seated at the base of Elio's middle finger. Two fine chains clasped the ring to a squared-off bracelet. Cael brought his thumb to the blue gemstone nestled in the center of the ring. "Avara?"

When Elio didn't answer, Cael glanced at him and retracted his hand, suddenly hyperaware of where their skin touched.

Elio's mouth remained slightly parted. He spoke after a long moment, fumbling as if to catch up. "Avara, it's — yes, it's Avara." He paused to collect himself. "Material that isn't fit for medicinal use is crafted into jewelry. People embellish family heirlooms, make pieces like this one." He lifted his arm, turning his elegant hand until Sunder glanced off the gemstone. "Place it in their homes for prosperity and rejuvenation. You've never seen low-grade Avara?"

"Never," Cael said, and he hadn't. Not once. The only low-grade Avara he'd heard of were cut with pharmaceuticals and sold on the black market to impoverished stationers and unlucky space travelers.

"Oh, I thought it was a popular trade item. Lorelei is fond of collecting baubles. She can sniff out a vintage necklace or an antique Avara hairclip anywhere, but she can't seem to mind her mouth." He sighed, still looking at the road. "Forgive her."

"She's young."

Elio scoffed. "I'm young, you're young." He turned, meeting Cael's steady gaze. "She's complicated."

"Envious," Cael offered.

"Indiscreet," he corrected.

Ahead of them, Peadar paused with the first two Aurethian sentries.

"Welcome to Nadhas," Peadar called, opening his arm toward the village. "The seaside mercantile of Aurethia."

Cael felt the soft bump of Elio's knuckles against his hand. Heard him when he said, "It's this way," and couldn't help the small leap in his chest when Elio did it again, tracing his fingers from wrist to palm.

The treeline dropped, and the beach expanded to a bustling port filled with trawlers, ships, and dinghies. Close-knit wood-built buildings with tiered, tiled rooftops clustered together, linked by netting and wire. Smoke puffed from skinny chimneys, and the road they'd taken from the manor morphed into smooth, weathered cobblestone. Cael looked across the busy market, shielded by multi-colored tents and extravagant booths.

Orson bounced up to Elio. "Do you think they'll have icepops yet?"

"I'm sure it's warm enough," Elio said.

The youngest Henly switched his attention to Cael. "Do you like icepops, Imperator?"

"If I'm imagining them right, I'm sure I do," Cael said.

"Frozen sweet milk and juice blended with berries," Lena explained, offering a quiet smile.

"Then yes," he clarified.

"C'mon, then. Off we go." The High Lady shooed Orson toward the market.

Maxine and Lorelei walked by, casually chatting, and Elio lifted his arm, pointing to the interconnected tents cutting across the dock.

"My mother will walk Orson through the whole thing, and Lorelei will probably drag Maxine to the second-hand merchant from Basset. I'm sure you'd like to see the market, but there's a teahouse — "

"Yes," Cael interrupted, and immediately scolded himself. He lowered his head, silently apologizing. "I'd like to join you for tea."

"You're presumptuous," Elio said. When the light left Cael's eyes, Elio's mouth betrayed him, twitching into an ever-slight smile. "I'm playing with you."

Cael swallowed tightly. He knew better than to indulge the phantom flutter prickling his sternum and ignored the heat flaring over his cheekbones. He met Elio's smile with one of his own. "I am, though. Presumptuous. You're trying to peel me away from your family, right? Ditch Lorelei rather than tame her?"

"Tame her?" Elio yelped through laughter. It was the first delightfully ugly sound he'd made in front of Cael. He started to walk, so Cael followed at his side. "Is that what you think you'll be doing? Domesticating a Henly?"

"Only if it's necessary."

Something awkward and foreign cracked through Elio's lighthearted expression. "Careful, Imperator. You forget yourself."

"I don't," Cael assured. "Ever."

Elio lifted his chin and turned toward the market. He didn't speak after that, not until they made their way past the first booth, then the second. Around them, shopkeepers and vendors hollered out pitches and prices for whatever valuables they sold. Many of them smiled at the sight of the Henly family.

One merchant waved their hand across an ornate table filled with pottery. Another gestured to upright rolled rugs twined in burlap. But most of them — too many — went still as a fawn the second Cael entered their line of sight. A young woman assisting at a fruit stall dropped her knife, sucking in a rapid breath. Her Aurethian was fast and accented, but Cael picked up a few words. *Griean*, of course. *Killer. Danger.* As they wandered from one table to the next, Cael kept his face placid and his intrigue genuine, glancing over eclectic merchandise and ripe farm-hauls. Another person said *go, brute* under their breath. Someone else said *dissolution*. A man spat at the ground and muttered, *usurper, uninvited*.

Cael stared at a collection of treats laid out on bell-shaped leaves and kept the anger burning in his belly properly contained. As he stood there, straining to fix his expression, he felt the soft, willful press of Elio's palm at the base of his spine.

"Honeyed rice cakes," Elio said. He leaned in close. The heat of him pushed through Cael's clothes.

He was rarely struck still by a person. But Cael turned, met with Elio's face mere inches from his own, and did not dare move. The prince gave him an intentionally sharp look, one sewn with underlying motive, then smiled.

Elio cut a glance to the merchant. "Two, please. One rose, one classic."

Cael reached around, running his index along the handsome limb still pressed against his tailbone.

An unmistakable hush fell over the market. *Ah*, Cael thought, indulging Elio's calm, easy control. He made his people question themselves — their own intention, their own opinion — with a single, public touch. *Impressive*.

"For you and…" The merchant paused, studying Cael with blown, cautious eyes.

"Cael Volkov," Elio said through a stretching smile. "My fiancé."

Oh. Cael fought to keep his mouth closed. His stomach was suddenly loose, chest frustratingly airy.

"Welcome, Cael of Griea," the merchant said. She cupped one palm atop the other, offering Cael the rice cake.

Cael tipped his head. "Thank you."

Elio took the pinkish cake and slid his hand along Cael's waist. Cael thought a scar might rise there. His skin reached, almost unstitched. He hadn't prepared for his body to endure a single touch and recognize it as kismet.

Vik's voice scratched through his earpiece. Are you alright, Imperator? I've detected a rise in body temperature and your heart rate has increased astronomically —

Cael tore off the dialect device and tucked it into his pocket.

"They're sticky," Elio chirped. He bit into the cake and chewed, flicking his gaze from the treat in Cael's hand to his face. "Go on then, Imperator," he teased, still chewing. "Eat."

The rice cake softened on his tongue. It was spongy and gooey, stringing apart between his incisors. He thought of Elio's hand again, the heel of it, right above the vein standing prominent on his small wrist, and imagined that section of flesh might come apart the same way. He blinked. Focused. Tasted honey and milk, something floral and bright.

Before he thought better of it, he reached for a flake of rose petal stuck to the corner of Elio's mouth and thumbed it away, allowing his knuckles the barest curl beneath his chin.

If Cael had to endure whatever enchantment Elio had placed on him, then he would level the playing field. Or attempt to. Despite Elio's orchestrated mannerisms, Cael couldn't tell whether his betrothed intended to impact the public or influence someone else — *him*. If Elio had caused the whirlpool currently thrashing in his ribcage on purpose, or if the Henly heir had only performed a convincing ruse for his people. Swayed them, casually, like sun-blinded birds.

Elio did not flinch or stutter. His eyes narrowed, just so, but his smile stayed perched and pleasant. His mouth slackened, almost. Shiny bottom lip snagged Cael's digit. Caught, slipped. Elio's left eyebrow ticked.

If they weren't playing, if they weren't courting, flirting, engaging in something mutually coy and foolish, then Cael required recalibration. Or a new set of eyes. Or a colder heart. Or a less active endocrine system. He pushed a little harder, clipping the edge of Elio's bottom teeth, and then dropped his hand.

"That tea," Cael eased, clearing his throat.

Elio's face tinted. He seemed unbothered, though. Amused, maybe. "Right," he said, and popped the rest of the rice cake into his mouth. "Let's go."

CHAPTER TEN

ELIO

E lio grunted and swung his leg, swiping Lorelei's feet out from underneath her. With an annoyed hiss, she caught herself on the padded floor and lurched upright, aiming the sole of her bare foot at Elio's thigh. The blow knocked him backward. Animalistic noises filled the training chamber followed by the metallic clash of dueling blades. Lorelei twirled her short-sword and swung. Elio dodged, blocked, crouched and brought his elbow to her chin, dazing her. He flipped his dagger, sharp tip close to her eye, and laughed.

"You're slow, sister," Elio said.

Lorelei smacked the tanto away. "You bore me." She tossed her sword onto the table and plopped on her rear, sprawling across the floor. "Did Cael enjoy the teahouse?"

He caught his breath and raked his hand through his sweaty hair. "I assume so. He said he did."

"What else did he say?"

"Why are you interested?"

Shrill laughter filled the chamber. "He's the future ruler of Griea. Sorry for being curious."

Elio joined Lorelei on the floor. He laid down opposite her, ear to ear. Yesterday Cael and Elio had spent time at the teahouse in Nadhas. They'd sat at a sunken table and shared a pot of candlebell tea served with pistachio cream and clover honey while Vik and Peadar drank from individual cups at the front of the building. He couldn't shake what'd transpired over the course of that day. Cael's body going taut beneath the steady press of his hand; Elio feigning relaxation when Cael touched his face. It was a dance — one Elio stumbled through — and he couldn't tell whether Cael moved strategically or authentically.

"He told me about the Tupinaire, Griea's ice arena," he said. Before Lorelei could demand more information, he continued. "Their people join sponsored matches. Some to get out of debt, some looking for financial gain, others for glory. Each tournament borrows from ancient Earthen practices — medieval knighthood and combat games. It's used for entertainment, but it's also political. Criminal punishment is handled during the Tupinaire; status can be raised in the arena; festivities take place on the ice. It's the fiber of their social system." He paused, turning to look at her. "He's a talented fighter, I guess."

"They sponsor their own people to duel, like, to the death?" Lorelei gasped dramatically.

"Sometimes."

"They *are* barbaric."

"We encourage our people to form militias," he said matter-of-factly.

"Because most of the Greater Universe would not hesitate to strongarm us." She blew at him. "Have you sparred with him yet?"

"No."

"Why?"

"I don't know, Lorelei. You spar with him."

"I absolutely will." She chortled. "I'll send Maxine with a message — "

"*Stop.* I don't know how to do this." Elio rolled over and pushed her face away. "How do I know if he…" He chewed his lip. "I can't tell if he — "

"He's going to be your husband regardless, Elio. You might as well find out."

"How?"

"I don't have to walk you through this, do I? I would recommend starting with over the clothes, but — "

Another smack.

"I can't force myself on the Griean Imperator," Elio choked out, trying to control his laughter. "And he's not as… as blunt as mother said he'd be. I keep waiting for him to… to, I don't know, *do* something."

"Combat is the primary language on Griea. Speak it. If he doesn't come around after that, then go to his bed. But I've seen him look at you, Elio. I doubt you'll face rejection." She waited, flicking her feline eyes around his face. "Or you could talk to him about it," she offered, stripping the goad from her voice. "Ask him where his head's at."

Elio inhaled slowly and let the breath out through his mouth. He didn't want to potentially ruin a natural connection by talking it to death. He wanted to *know* Cael, to understand whoever lived beneath the Imperator's cocky, handsome exterior. And he *was* handsome. Undeniably, stupidly handsome. That alone made Elio freeze, internally shredding the inaccurate vision he'd cobbled together over the years. He remembered Cael looking at him from across the table at the teahouse. Pale hand cradling a small cup. How his fine mouth tilted. *I've killed many men*, said as if he were reciting poetry. *But I've wet the ice with my own blood, too. It's a glorious thing — to live despite the odds.*

THE BATTLE DRONE LINKED to Elio's and Cael's devices came through the speaker built into the training chamber's ceiling. `Lord Elio, Imperator Cael Volkov has accepted the dueling timeslot. Please confirm.` Elio paced in the chamber, barefoot and wearing loose sparring clothes.

"Confirmed," he said.

`Thank you. Duel will commence on the hour.`

Elio took Lorelei's advice, but the idea of being physically close to Cael dazed him. He tongued at his cheek and rolled a cattail between his knuckles, letting the delicate blade flip like a coin. Before he could get lost in thought, he sent the cattail sailing through the air, landing with a thud in a panel across the room. He plucked another one from the table. Threw it with little more than a flick of his wrist. Listened to the satisfying sound of blade through cork.

"My Lord," Peadar said, entering the chamber.

Cael and Vik followed.

Peadar tapped his dialect device. The slender, gilded earpiece matched most Aurethian technology, including Elio's. The drone chimed. `Supervision enabled. All action recorded.`

"What's that you're toying with?" Cael asked. He grasped the bottom of his shirt and tugged it over his head, leaving black fabric puddled on the floor.

Elio glanced at the matching tattoos above his hipbones, like a pair of perfectly symmetrical ink strokes. He deliberated for a moment, weighing the risk of looking against his desire to look. In the end, he dropped his gaze to Cael's torso, tracing his lean, sculpted stature, pale skin stretched over taut sinew. Cael waited patiently, tipping his head once Elio looked up. His slow smile parted for a flash of teeth, and he crouched to unlace his bootwear.

"It's a cattail," Elio said.

"Show me."

He pinched the black blade between his knuckles. "It's an aerodynamic throwing knife. With the right technique, it can cross a great distance."

Cael peeled away his socks and stood, plucking the weapon from Elio's hand. "It's small," he mused, and turned it over. The blade curved on each end, one side mirroring the other. He touched the edge and hummed. "Sharp."

Elio snatched the cattail, lancing the blade through the corkboard. "Lightweight and fast — deadly if used properly."

Cael grinned. "You'll have to teach me."

"Maybe." He nodded toward the table. "Choose a weapon, Imperator."

Cael moved with innate precision. Even now — aligning each step along the side of the table, gliding his hand over the mean display — he channeled determination. Moved like a predator, a great beast, what Elio could only imagine a basilisk to be. He graced the belly of a long-toothed dagger with his thumb and grasped the handle.

"This'll do. Your turn, princeling," he said.

Princeling. Heat scorched his spine. Elio took a stiletto. "Mind your tongue, barbarian."

Cael winked. "You're easy to ruffle," he noted. His grin loosened, child-like. He beckoned Elio with a wave. "Let's see what it takes to skin a lion."

The jeer ignited white-hot in Elio's gut. His pulse hammered and he lunged, swinging the dagger. Cael parried with a simple movement, raising the blade parallel to his face. He didn't budge. Hardly jolted. But his tight smile unfolded into a lazy grin. Elio jerked the knife back, aimed again, was deflected again. Cael finally stepped forward, jabbing, ducking, laughing.

They fell into an easy rhythm. Blade-to-blade, forearm-to-forearm, Elio and Cael sparred.

Near the back of the chamber, Peadar quietly assessed. Vik stood beside the door, arms folded, documenting.

Where Elio combined fluidity and necessity, gliding the blade through the air, spinning to dodge an assault, trading his weapon from one hand to the other, Cael moved with savagery Elio had never seen before. He struck with the force of a storm, angled his body into every hard swing, every step and flex.

As the duel continued, ferocity grew.

Cael dropped his smile; Elio breathed hard. *Focus.* Elio threw his elbow into Cael's stomach, knocking him backward. Cael bounced on his left foot, kicked with his right. The sole of the Imperator's foot met Elio's chest, and they toppled to the floor. Cael pounced with startling efficiency, locking one hand around Elio's throat. Cael pressed down on him, pelvis snug against hips, chest aligned to his own. Their eyes met. Breath gusted chin and cheek. Cael's tongue darted across his bottom lip, slack and pretty. The deliberate press of body against body, half-naked and primed with adrenaline, quickened Elio's pulse. Took him off guard. Cael exhaled a shaken, punched-out breath, puffing hot against Elio's face, and the action itself burrowed into Elio's subconscious. Triggered some animal reflex that hooked a string around his spine and yanked. Molten heat pooled deep in the private cavern of his body. Welled beneath his bellybutton.

"Where'd you go?" Cael murmured.

Elio blinked. Curled his foot around Cael's calf, swung with all his might, and successfully flipped them, sending Cael onto his back only to be knocked away by another swift kick a moment later. A warning from Peadar sent Elio leaping to his feet. Cael followed, swiping his hand across his damp mouth.

"C'mon, fiancé," Cael whispered. The fight glossed his chest. Pinkened his snow-kissed complexion. "Eyes on me."

Pride, and something worse, something glowing like smelted iron, bolted down Elio's back. He hopped, deflected another blow, crouched and dodged. When he lashed out again, Cael swooped away from the glint of Elio's blade, growling at another punt to his leg. They moved wildly. The sound of singing metal came and went, clashing repeatedly, forcing Elio to inch backward, once, twice, until he collided with the wall.

Cael halted, sword-handle poised near his jaw, sharp edge pressed to Elio's cheek. Sweat slicked his brow and nose. Elio's attention was trapped in the deep divot of his upper lip. He wished they were alone. Wanted to lean forward, snag the salty droplet on his mouth. Elio caught his breath, wedged against Cael, and let his weight go heavy against the cool stone. His cheek tickled with warm wetness.

"That's enough," Peadar said. Caution rang in his strong voice.

They stayed like that: Cael watching blood seep from the accidental cut marring Elio's cheek; Elio watching a compilation of achievement and vulnerability roll across Cael's sharp, beautiful face.

Cael's throat flexed. "You've been bested," he exhaled, panting.

Elio shifted, nudging his tucked blade against Cael's lowest rib. "Careful, fiancé."

Cael's smile softened. He shifted his gaze to Elio's mouth, hovering there.

Elio felt the Imperator's breath on his chin. Tasted his afternoon tea.

"You're impressive," Cael rasped.

The ragged, whispered compliment raked across his interior. Lit him like a pyre. Elio tilted his face away from the dagger-point. Despite Peadar's watchful presence, Cael dragged the tip of the weapon along Elio's cheek, the column of his throat, clipping his collarbone, then let it fall. Elio's flesh pebbled. Begged him to follow that knife, ask for another bite.

"You're predictable," Elio lied, gentling the offense with a smile. He wanted Cael to do it again. Press the blade to his face. Share intimacy, however strange. "Thank you for joining me, Imperator."

Cael looked him over. He prodded Elio's foot with his toe. "Let me serve you."

Elio's face grew warmer. "Excuse me?"

"Tend to you," he corrected, trying a different phrase in Griean, squinting confusedly. "That." He stepped backward and gestured to Elio's cheek. "It's not polite to leave a duel unfinished."

"You want…" He opened his mouth, closed it. Imagined Cael lapping at the blood, as if they were a different kind of mammal. Blinked the thought away. Tried again. Imagined teeth, smooth and blunt, framing the wound. He swallowed. Stood straighter, taller. "Okay, fine. Tend to me."

Peadar interrupted. "My lord, if you've been wounded — "

"It's a scratch, Peadar. You've done worse during our private sparring sessions," Elio said. He did not look away from Cael. "The Imperator would like to dress my wound, and I'll allow it. Please retrieve a medkit."

The general stared at Elio before he walked across the room and opened a cabinet. The medkit was a smooth, black case shaped like a capsule-pill. There was a defibrillator, lung activation serum, clotting ointment, suture material, cleaning supplies, and an emergency triage-pack.

Vik spoke from the doorway. "Surface assessment confirms Elio Henly has sustained an abrasion above the zygomatic bone."

Peadar cast a suspicious glance at Vik and handed the medkit to Cael.

Elio brushed past Cael and set his dagger down. He rubbed his nose with the side of his hand and turned to slouch against the table, staring at the padded floor between his feet. He curled his toes and cleared his throat, readying a command — *get on with it* or *come on then* or *I'm still bleeding* — but Cael stepped in front of him and pinched his chin, silencing his busy mind.

"Where'd you learn to fight like that?" Cael asked. His voice was easy and tender, hardly audible. His unexpected use of Griean startled Elio at first.

Elio took the opportunity to study him. While Cael's pale blue eyes remained on his cheek, Elio imagined walking two fingers down the curve of his shaved head or tracing the straight lines of his tattoo. Healed piercing holes shadowed his earlobes. The fight left him braised, scented like salt. Skin pulled tight over blood-gorged muscle. Cael glanced at him, meeting his gaze, and Elio realized he hadn't answered.

"Peadar, mostly," Elio said.

When Cael pressed an alcohol swab against the cut, Elio winced. His bony hand dwarfed Elio's cheek, holding him still while he dabbed at the wound. It was a kind gesture. Heartwarming and innocent. Mercifully, Cael was not a mind reader. Could not see their sparring match replayed and reworked in Elio's mind. Was not privy to the crushing, fiery spasm wetting his underwear.

Elio cleared his throat. "But my father, too."

"Griea would cheer for you during the Tupinaire." Cael murmured. His thumb traced the corner of Elio's mouth.

Elio wanted to spar with him again. He wanted to close Cael off, steal him away from his brooding Augment and Elio's overprotective guard, and unleash him. Experience the wilderness and finesse of a Griean warlord. What they'd done today scratched the surface. It left Elio bloodied, curious, upended — starving for the truth. To know how Cael might behave if they weren't under surveillance.

Cael glided his thumb along the soft hollow above Elio's jaw, holding the skin taut. He applied the tape-stitch and took Elio by the jaw, tipping his face. It was such an inelegant gesture. Such an oddly intimate thing to do. Dress a wound, hold a rival.

After too long, Cael stepped away. "Thank you for the duel, Lord Henly. I greatly appreciate the opportunity."

The forced formality was almost grating. Elio crossed his arms and stared at his betrothed, hoping for an ounce of brevity, amusement, desire

— *something*. He wanted to chew a raw sliver of him, get a taste of Cael Volkov without interference.

"Thank you for tending to me," Elio said. When Cael turned to leave, Elio pressed his legs tightly together. He swallowed magma. "Would you cheer for me in your arena," he blurted on a quivering exhale, desperate to ignore whatever chaotic, sensual bravery seemed to hijack his tongue. "Would you shout my name during the Tupinaire?"

Cael paused. He angled his chin over his shoulder, offering the ghost of a smile. "I would."

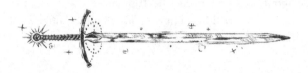

CHAPTER ELEVEN
BRACKEN

The velvety pass of a reindeer's antler on Bracken's palm never failed to dose his system with serotonin. He patted the beast on the snout and reached for a vegetation bale, unsheathing his boot-knife to snip the string holding its shape. Lichen, moss, and dehydrated tree-clippings toppled into a trough. He dusted the feed with cloned vegetable runoff — powdered recyclables collected from households and restaurants — then scratched a broom across the barn floor.

When he was not Optio Bracken Volkov, interim commander of the Royal Reserve, he was a lone ranger living on the ground level, running a small reindeer farm on the outskirts of Sector One.

Marcus and Constance preferred him at the Volkov castle, but his commitment to solitude prevailed. No matter how efficient and comfortable his quarters in the castle were, he loved the privacy living on the cusp of the Sliding Sea offered. His nearest neighbor owned one of the few domed terrariums in Machina, and Bracken looked at the spherical glass structure from his porch sometimes, watching the green-filled balloon float high above the ice, tethered by a metal ladder connected to the base of a grain silo.

The city glittered on the horizon. Its tall black formation scrubbed Goren like a hearth-stain. Nearby, a wandering group of Fara settled in portable thermal huts. They bartered with him on occasion, trading a hardy calf for bushels of rosemary or beluga meat. It was a simple life, one he escaped to when his role at the college weighed too heavy on his mind.

Bracken finished his chores and left the barn, crossing a short expanse to the farmhouse. He didn't expect to see the flutter of gauze-like material, or a gloved hand wrapped around the doorframe, but he knew Kindra Malkin's particular build, her oddly pointed shoulders and long, thin body. She glanced around the door once, catching his eye, and then disappeared inside.

"I don't remember calling," he said, leaving his frosty seal-skin boots beside the door.

Kindra paired a loose, black veil with Griean silk. Her elven nose and slight face caught the light of a dim disc-lamp. "You didn't," she said, sighing.

"I recruited Kasimir into the Royal Reserve. You weren't wrong, he's got spirit."

Abnormal silence choked the room.

Bracken shot her a questioning look. "Kindra," he said, framing her name like a question.

She loosed a sigh and pulled the veil down, revealing the blackened wound on her forehead. Parsec sickness cleaved her eyebrow on one side. The dark brown skin around it purpled like a new bruise, split and scabbed. "I couldn't seek medical attention without consulting you first, Optio. Our arrangement is known throughout Machina, and I — "

Bracken jolted forward. He didn't mean to make the sound he did, but the sharp, uncharacteristic hiss caused her to startle. "What've you done to yourself. Sit," he instructed, pointing to a simple wood-built table with matching chairs. "Sit down. What..." Once she lowered into a chair, he grasped the side of her neck, angling her face upward. Concern splintered into irritation. "You didn't."

"It was during my trip to Shepard. Avara was in short supply, so I took the alternative."

"You should've — "

"Done what?" Her fierce amber eyes tilted angrily. "Sent a message to the Volkov castle? Told them their Optio's courtesan requires medical attention on a distant station?"

"Yes," he said, meeting her anger with his own. "That's exactly what you do. What did you take?"

"A distilled treatment. It's all I could manage."

"Kindra," he seethed. Better than a black market derivative.

She shifted her gaze to the side, avoiding his attention. Despite her damaged skin, she remained beautiful. As if carved from bird-bone, every bit of her chiseled and dainty.

"I'm sorry," she said through gritted teeth. "You put me on retainer and I'm grateful for that, I am, and I understand if you'd like to dissolve our contract, but you're the only person in Machina who might have access to a private supply, so..." She paused, steeling herself. "If the timeframe for assistance is over, fine."

Twenty, snake-spirited, and viciously poised, Kindra Malkin was a finely tuned woman with an ego that rivaled his own. Bracken wanted to know why she hadn't told him about her affliction — parsec sickness was not something to ignore — but he would get to the bottom of that later. For now, he needed to treat her before it spread.

He rifled through the kitchen, yanking open cupboards and drawers until he found the specialty medkit stored in the back of the pantry. The capsule came apart like a pillbug, revealing a plunger syringe, distilled alcohol in a transparent, disposable container, and a concentrate vial filled with bright, shimmering Avara. The blue liquid shone opalescent, licking the glass as he squeezed it between his thumb and index. Avara particles swam and jumped, dispersing.

"You're lucky it's still soluble," Bracken said. He punctured the medical cork capping the vial and drew a healthy amount into the syringe.

"I only need a small dose," Kindra said.

"This *is* a small dose."

She inhaled slowly through her nose and shut her eyes, tilting her chin to grant him access to her jugular.

Bracken crouched and cupped her knee. She grasped his knuckles and waited. He pushed the needle at an angle. Kindra's closed eyes tightened. She stayed perfectly still until the Avara was deposited and the syringe was gone.

"Don't touch this," Bracken said, tapping the clean skin above her wounded brow. "The Avara should start working in a few hours, but you'll probably keep a nice scar."

"My face only earns a portion of the profit," she said through an aggravated sigh, reaching to rub the spot on her neck. She cast an upward glance at him. "Thank you."

"You should've sent a message," he said, driving his original point.

"I apologize, Optio."

"Drop the act."

"I warm your bed, Bracken, I am not a thing you own," she bit out.

There you are. He squeezed her thigh, giving the limb a little shake. "I choose to pay for your services. Might I remind you, I retain them exclusively. You are not a thing, Kindra, but you are mine, and you've caused unnecessary damage to yourself. I don't care what Marcus has to say about our professional relationship; our Legatus has his own arrangements to worry about."

Kindra's regal nature came from a childhood spent on Draitune. She wore the face of an aristocrat yet played the part of a commoner. He didn't know much about her past, only that she had a brother, Kasimir, who shared her ferocity, only that her parents died on a voyage to Mal, only that she came to Griea — her supposed homeworld several blood connections removed — with a zipper-shaped scar across her belly and an unwillingness to disclose where it came from. He assumed the ugliness was the result of a botched black market procedure. Evidence she'd buried. A child, maybe.

Whatever she'd done, however she'd done it, Bracken felt safe in her company. Something damaged inside him recognized the same damage in her.

"It won't happen again," she said.

"Our retainer will remain unbroken. Do you agree?"

"Fine."

Bracken bent to kiss her. She accepted the gesture, and the argument ended.

While Kindra decompressed at the table, Bracken tossed two logs into the hearth, prodding them with a poker. Cinders rose up and away, glinting against soot and iron. Companionable silence filled the farmhouse. He couldn't decide whether he wanted to investigate her visit to Shepard or if he wanted to stretch across the deer skin and take a nap. Part of him wanted to run a bath.

"How goes the revision of the Royal Reserve?" Kindra asked cooly.

He boiled a pot of dehydrated lemon and added a satchel of thornbush tea. He didn't know how to answer that. "Majority are loyal to Cael, as expected. I've made headway, though. We're strategizing about terrain changes, climate differences, what to expect when we enter high orbit, low orbit, make ground. Next phase is combat training, hand-to-hand. I don't know how they'll react to a new instructor." He shrugged, leaning against the table in front of her. "But I'm what they have, so they'll bend or stay behind."

She considered what he said, nodding absently. Her mouth twisted into a thoughtful frown. "Or you could make them love you."

"You say it like it's easy," he mumbled, dragging his thumb along her mouth.

She let him toy with her like that, staring at him while he pulled her bottom lip, smashed the pad of his finger into the narrow valley denting her labret. She bit him quickly. Snapped her teeth around his digit, bone to flesh, serpent fast.

"You're not an easy man to hate." Kindra smiled sickly sweet. "Leashes don't clip themselves to collars. Seduce them."

He grinned, pressing his thumb to her front teeth. "That's your specialty."

She jerked away. "You have what they want. Use it."

"And what do I have?"

"Power."

He ruminated on that. "What power can I offer? When Cael returns —"

"If Cael returns."

Bracken shook his head. "When he's back, I'll step down from my interim position. There's nothing for me to give them, Kindra. Cael will become the next Legatus, and his men will rise with him. They know that; I know that."

"Unless you prove your worth. The golden child is currently seeding the bloodline with an Aurethian," she growled, chewing, spitting. Her mouth screwed into a snarl. "You have a chance to prove yourself —"

Bracken took her chin. Pinched too hard. He pulled her face closer, forcing her eyes to lift. "He's my cousin."

"He's your competition."

"Careful, woman."

"Last month I was girl, now I'm woman. Pick."

She was both. Still trapped in girlhood, falling on the other side of womanity. Sometimes she spoke so carelessly he thought she might still be teenaged — an unseasoned child lying about her development. Other times she offered him wisdom he couldn't find in a credible psychoanalyst. It scared him, that uncanny ability to occupy two markers in her own timeline. He often wondered if she was conscious of it.

Bracken let her go and retreated to the deerskin, stretching across it in front of the hearth. "You're lucky I pay for your mouth. It'd get you in trouble with other men."

After a beat of thick quiet, the chair scraped the floor, and the swish of fallen fabric filled the air. Soft, small feet padded, then Kindra's toes crept over his cheek, pressing hard against his face. She inched one into his mouth. She looked awkward and sensual from this angle. Lean calves and bony kneecaps, thatch of dark hair between her thighs, whittled waist, and small breasts sitting above a staircase of shadowy ribs. She wore her springy hair short, dyed the color of rust. Kindra was a devilish thing. His ache for her dulled him. Made him stupid.

"You could be Legatus," she whispered.

He tongued at the webbing between her first and second toe, tasting salt and the chemical leavings of floral lotion. "Is this what I should do to Cael's men? Charm them into compliance?"

Kindra tilted her head. Her lupine smile grew. She pressed harder. The round sole of her foot smashed his cheek, causing a bit of saliva to leak past his lips. "Cael's sham courtship is a disgrace to Griea. You know it; I know it. We should be launching an assault, not playing at counterfeit peace." She slipped her foot partially into his mouth, sliding over his teeth, applying pressure to his tongue until he gagged. His face burned. He reached for his belt buckle, then his zipper. "You're the rightful heir, aren't you?"

Bracken's gaze blurred. He slackened his jaw. Hearing it — something he'd paid her to say, a half-lie she'd perfected — always jammed a proverbial knife into his chest and tightened like a clenched fist in his groin. It was true and it wasn't. His father was the eldest Volkov, but he'd offered the title to his brother after Bracken's mother suffered a complicated pregnancy. Every eldest Volkov, regardless of how they'd been conceived, were entitled to the throne. But Cael was Marcus's child, pride and joy of their Legatus, and Bracken never protested his cousin's assumed ascension. Bracken was Optio; he was a champion in the arena; he was alive. That had always been enough.

"You could make them adore you," she said. Her wet foot slipped away, sliding across his chin.

He grabbed her ankle and brought the limb back to its origin, licking a stripe from heel to sole.

"My true heir," she cooed.

He fumbled a hand past his waistband. She pushed until his teeth ached and his jaw cracked and then edged the slender front of her foot into his mouth again. His heart raced. He sucked greedily.

The parsec sickness mangling her face stood out. He stared at it while she tilted her ankle, making a weakling of him. For a sad, sick second, he was glad the wound was there, damage like proof of life confirming she was human and not something assembled for him in a lab, constructed to indulge the things he never spoke aloud. She was real — flesh and blood — looking down at him like a buzzard.

"My true heir," she said again, singsong.

Bracken choked and retched, throat constricting around the bite of her toenail. Drool stringed from his mouth to her smallest toe. Without a second thought, he pulled her down to the floor with him.

NIGHT CAME SWIFTLY.

Bracken sprawled by the hearth while Kindra retrieved two cups of tea from the stove. He stared at the ceiling for a while, then gazed at the flame. The farmhouse darkened. He didn't turn on a disc-lamp or bother with a candle. The hearth made just enough light to define the shape of things — table, chair, seater, coatrack — and left the rest in murky shadow. It was easier to think in the dark. To swim through heady sex-fog, searching for pleasant solutions to complicated problems. The Royal Reserve was a tool: Marcus's deadliest weapon and Cael's greatest achievement. Bracken knew better than to feed into the indulgent bravado Kindra installed in him whenever she visited.

On the seater, his holotablet lit. A hologram materialized above the screen: INCOMING TRANSMISSION — MAXINE CARR: AURETHIA; ENCRYPTED DATA

He grabbed his dialect device and looped it over his ear, tapping the flat panel. "Connect."

Maxine Carr's voice scratched through the speaker. "Optio Volkov," she greeted.

"Operative Carr."

Kindra returned with their tea and sat on the deerskin beside him, folding her legs neatly beneath herself. She watched him intently, still glossed with a light sheen of sweat.

Maxine spoke. "Legatus Marcus asked me to report to you given the nature of my seasonal communication relay. Can you confirm an early shipment of harvest has not arrived from Aurethia?"

"No shipment," Bracken said. "Should we be expecting something?"

"Fruit, Optio. Elio Henly, Cael's betrothed, offered the first of

Aurethia's bounty to Griea as a show of good faith, honoring Alexander Henly's successfully plotted blood-union." She paused to take a breath. "As I told the Legatus, Cael has moved methodically." She spoke slowly, minding each word. "Although he hasn't reported the location of an Avara mine, Imperator Volkov sustains an impenetrable image at Henly manor. His interest in Elio is almost unquestionable."

Bracken sat upright. He waited, replaying what she'd said exactly how she'd said it. "How would you describe the Imperator's demeanor?"

"Happy," she chimed. A heartbeat later, she cleared her throat. "His mask has not slipped. It's as if Aurethia has truly charmed him."

"But he hasn't made headway on Avara?"

"Not to my knowledge, Optio."

The entire purpose of this fraudulent courtship, this gutless engagement, was to grant the Volkov family an opportunity to seize Aurethia. Bracken shifted his slack jaw and curled his finger over the lip of his steaming mug, allowing the scalding tea to ground him.

"Speak freely, Maxine. Is Cael's judgement compromised?" Bracken asked.

Maxine paused. She did not breathe. "I'm not equipped to come to that conclusion." When Bracken inhaled to speak, she continued. "I have faith in our Imperator."

Bracken deflated. "Good."

"Just recently, Cael and I joined the Henly's on a guided tour to a fishing village. After assessing their behavioral patterns, I deduced that Cael and Elio are infatuated with each other. While I'm not certain if Cael's fondness for Elio is an expertly crafted ruse, I have determined that Elio is emotionally and sexually vulnerable. He is easy to break, as is his sister." Maxine paused again. Her sigh was a static hush. "Lady Lorelei is also capable and eager. She would make a fine prize if the young lord were an unwilling participant."

Bracken's mouth dried. "You mean to say Cael could take her as a bride?"

"Technically, any Volkov with a claim to Griean stewardship could wed her and fulfill the union as promised. Elio is alive and well, of course. So that option isn't entertainable." There was an unspoken *yet* at the end of her statement.

If Cael was dead. He swallowed hard. "I want transmissions from you weekly from now on."

"Understood, Optio," Maxine said, slippery and cold. He could tell by her voice, the cadence of it, that she never spoke without purpose. "God is in the water."

Bracken rippled her, "God is in the water."

The holotablet dimmed to a blue-black glow.

Kindra sipped her tea. Her wide-set eyes bore into him like the orange end of a hearth poker. "Has our Imperator done his duty?" Another sip. Her voice lightened, cloaked in righteous laughter. "Or is it your turn?"

CHAPTER TWELVE

CAEL

Summer transformed the estate into a prosperous seaside getaway. Pollinators buzzed and flapped in the orchard, diving from branch to petal, and dorsal fins lanced the sea, announcing a pod of pygmy pilot whales. Cael stood on the cliff attached to the empty launch bay. Sunlight glistened on the water and a trawler blew its horn, signaling its impending arrival.

It was easy to be dazzled by Aurethia. Salty air, constant birdsong, full-bellied people, lush terrain, breathtaking scenery. The moon was an Earthen postcard. Like a painting sold at auction, depicting paradise. He crouched to dab at water pooled in the hollow of a rock and rubbed the liquid between his thumb and two fingers. His first season was gone; another inched closer. A quarter of the time he was allotted to do his duty — learn the intricate production process of Avara, study the forest moon's military structure, earn House Henly's trust, and successfully court Elio — had sped by in the blink of an eye.

Cael could not think about Griean glory without the memory-swat of Elio swinging gracefully through the training chamber. Elio lunging and dipping, grasping for a shred of power in an otherwise unfair game blasted through his mind. Cael could've crushed his windpipe in one blow. Could've smashed the blunt end of his dagger into Elio's sweet mouth.

But not with Peadar watching like a hawk. And not with Vik assessing the situation through cybernetic eyes, cataloguing movement, speed, dexterity. Not with Cael's heart in his throat, his spirit purring *careful, Elio, easy, good job, like that.*

Granted, the heir was a gifted fighter. He moved with ease Cael rarely saw, embracing cat-footed prancing rather than brute strength. Cael thought about sparring with him alone — imagined unclipping the Aurethian lion cub from whatever rope kept him docile and well-mannered, and encouraging Elio to fight like he would in the arena, in combat, in the throes of wartime, in the bedroom.

Cael darted his tongue across his lip and swallowed a mouthful of hot saliva.

Imperator, I've finished decoding the transmission from Griea. Vik's scratchy voice itched through his dialect device. The Augment stood many yards away, stationed near the candlebell tree. Are you ready to receive the data?

"Send it though," Cael said, tapping the device.

Data streamed through his earpiece. The loud shock of static faded and a robotic voice chirped, speaking in a dull, flat tone.

Griean transcript 1.052 — Warp relay module; War Room deliverable: Message for Imperator Cael Volkov, Keeper of the Basilisk, to be received on Aurethia. Drafted and Encrypted by Legatus Marcus Volkov. The transmission paused. *Operative Carr tells me you are in good health.* Although the device spoke in a standard electronic tone, Cael still felt his father's irritation. *Our team is on standby awaiting the location of at least one Avara mine, and we have yet to confirm delivery of the location mapping within and around the Henly estate.* Another pause. *Urgent request: Tracking data from Cael Volkov or Vik Endresen to be delivered at once.* Pause. *Might I remind you to balance your intent, son. There is much at play. Every word should serve a purpose. Every move is a segment of strategy. Griea is depending on you. Go with glory.* The device beeped. *End of message. Would you like to replay?*

"No," Cael said. He squinted against harsh light. Touched the dialect device, signaling Vik. "Endresen, send over the data from my tracking device."

Vik's voice lit in his ear. Since arrival, Imperator?

"Yes."

`Data will arrive via warp relay module. Griea should`
`expect it within the week.`

"Good. Thank you."

High above, a gull tucked its wings and dived, thrusting through the top of a premature wave. When it surfaced, a soaked beast in the bird's talons writhed and wriggled, carried off to a nest somewhere. Cael watched the whole thing take place. Hunter, hunting. He envied that seagull for its ability to put aside whatever feeling it might hold for the fish. The gull didn't think about making it quick or being kind. It thought about a full stomach, it prioritized staying alive.

Griea was not a dying thing; it was a surviving thing. Cael knew better than to place himself on a pedestal, as if he and the gull were at odds. But there was a part of him that wanted to peel away his clothes and dive into the sea. Lie in the meadow and stare at the spectral silhouette of Draitune in the center of Aurethia's open sky. Gorge on rare fruit snapped away from healthy branches. Plunge himself into the forest moon's very center and never leave. That part of him, bewitched and comfortable, squatted deep and spread like fungus. The rest of him, the ice-born majority, knew the siege of Aurethia was only the start of a greater plan, a battle for dominance that had taken careful, generational crafting. He chewed the inside of his cheek.

Cael thought about the training chamber — Elio angling his hidden blade toward the traitorous organ in his chest.

How does one undo a lifetime of inequity? He turned, smacking the toe of his boot against a rock. Will violence solve violence? Will the passage of Aurethian stewardship saddle Griea with power or problems? All his life he'd been told it would unlock overdue greatness Griea had never been awarded. He still believed that. Believed in Griea. Believed in a new, better era. Believed in wellness and retribution. Believed in his people.

A porpoise breached, spitting a column of seawater. Cael blinked a few times. Something small and hopeful jostled, falling into his ribcage. The same place Elio Henly had taken up residence. *I don't want to hurt him to exalt us.* He let the thought come; he let it go.

"Vik, report the estimated Avara related death-toll for one cycle on Griea, please," he said.

The earpiece belched static. Quieted. Came alive again.

`This cycle, Avara-related sickness is estimated to`
`claim two-hundred-sixty-four million lives, Imperator.`
`That's a two percent increase from last year, likely`

due to illegal trafficking of black market Avara. Those
managing moderate-to-severe symptoms with a distilled
treatment will increase their lifespan two-fold by
obtaining a standard treatment. Those who cannot
afford, source, or otherwise implement a standard
treatment will succumb to their injuries within twelve
to fourteen months depending on the severity of their
case.

Cael nodded. He held fast to the gravity of that number. Two-hundred-
sixty-four million. That didn't include stationers or people on impecunious
planets in neighboring systems. Griea alone would produce a quarter-billion
casualties. He swallowed stomach acid and turned to face the manor. The
Aurethian banner whipped on a tall pole. Ruddy sunlight fell across the
large house in patches. In the distance, two lions ambled into the meadow.

The candlebell tree weighed heavy with ripe fruit. It was a shock of pale
flowers, plumed orange and pink and red, splashing the front of the manor
like a paint splatter. Viney tubes sprouted from each long branch and
cascaded toward the ground. Beneath the candlebell's white curtain, Vik
nodded to someone dressed in a beige dress. High Lady Lena's chambermaiden. A second later, Vik came through his device again.

Sir, Indigo Condon has passed along a message from
Lord Elio Henly.

"Alright," Cael said.

The young lord invites you to join him at a nearby
onsen this evening. The suggestive inflection in Vik's voice made
Cael wish the Augment were close enough to hit. For a soak, he added,
tongue clipping the last word.

Cael rubbed the fleshy web topping his collarbone, knuckling the scar
cratered above his hidden implant, and walked toward the manor.

DRAITUNE'S MASSIVE RING REFRACTED Sunder's glow and turned the
planet's typical violet hue a warm palette of dusky red. Cael almost tripped,
eyes glued to the sunset-stained sky, but he caught himself on a bulky tree
and dipped below a scaffold branch, following Vik through the forested area
behind the estate.

Peadar sent the coordinates to Vik who uploaded the data and led them to the semi-remote location on the outskirts of Nadhas. The Henly guard offered to accompany them, but Cael wanted to explore the region on his own. It gave him the chance to study the coin-shaped leaves on small thickets and brush his hand along the top of a springy fern. Nightlife peered at them from hidey-holes and dugouts. Aurethian owls screeched. Weasels hunted spiders and long-tailed kangaroo mice through ribboned groves. The closer they got to the onsen, the brighter the landscape became. Everything glowed cerulean. Soil glittered, berries pulsed, everything wore an otherworldly aura.

"Must be an Avara mine nearby." Vik pointed at a bright teal plant with a bulbous mouth and glossy tendrils. Its center glowed medicinal blue. "The crystal leaks into the groundwater, I believe. It's infectious."

The deeper into the forest they walked, the more azure-stained features cropped up. After a while, Sunder fully sank below the horizon and the hidden shimmer staining Aurethia's wildland lit like fireflies. Avara particles glistened underneath raised bark, licked the interior of petals, flecked bushy moss. Cael touched a plant as he walked by, drawing his fingertips away to check for residue. Nothing.

"Infectious?" Cael asked.

Vik hummed thoughtfully. "I'll rephrase. It's transmissible. Unlike typical gypsum or felsic, Avara can take on new host material without a similar hospitable climate to the one it was originally grown in. Interesting considering Avara's instability post-harvest."

Cael nodded and stepped over an exposed root. Since Avara's discovery, the major shot-callers within the Greater Universe had attempted to clone Avara, mimic its natural habitat, encourage growth on other planets — Draitune, Ocury, even Vandel Prime in the Ren system — but the only success they'd found was a short-term sprouting in an enclosed cave simulator on a small research station controlled by the Imperial Council. The hard-won success didn't last. Seeing Avara latched to various hosts made Cael wonder about its fertility elsewhere.

As the pair crested the treeline, Cael gasped, adjusting his footing to stay planted on the trail. The sudden drop-off gave him a startle. "Where are we?"

"Almost to the provided location, Imperator. According to my research, this crater is mostly uncharted. Unfriendly to long-distance communication. A dead zone, so to speak," Vik said.

The space sank like an inverted dome into the center of Aurethia's woodland. Spooned out and filled with dense forest, it went on for a great distance. Cael looked out over the wildland until Vik stepped back under the shade of an evergreen and steered them up a rocky incline to an overhang attached to a small cave. Laughter echoed, clueing Cael into the presence of more than one Henly.

"Who else is here?" Cael whispered.

Vik paused. The data port on his nape illuminated. "I've detected six heartbeats."

"Wonderful."

"They *are* your future in-laws — "

"No snark tonight. I wasn't expecting this to be a group outing, that's all."

Vik glanced over his shoulder. "What're you scared of?"

Cael smacked him with the back of his hand, earning a modest laugh.

The moment Cael stepped into view, Lorelei howled from the side of a steaming pool. The natural onsen sprang out of a patch of rock. Its curved lip extended to the edge of the cliff, spilling over as people moved about in the water. Orson wore a slouchy sweater and damp swimming shorts and perched on the side of the pool with his feet submerged. Maxine waded through the center where the water reached her throat, and Elio lounged beyond the curling steam with his arms up over the side, head tilted back, smiling at the stars.

Lorelei placed her palms on the stone and lifted herself half out of the water, craning toward Cael and Vik as they approached. "Look who decided to show up!" Her swimwear was a pale pink blush across her tan skin, strappy and chic, mimicking the fashion from Dardellin, one of the major districts on Draitune. "We thought you'd fallen into the crater."

It was a charming place, yawning over the forest like a lax mouth. Vik gave Cael a familiar swat on the back and joined Peadar and an accompanying guard inside the shallow interior of the cave.

"We were admiring the scenery." Cael peeled away his shirt and tugged off his belt. The swimwear underneath his cargos fit... *oddly*. On Griea people wore thick wetsuits designed to fight the hypothermic cold. The Aurethia-appropriate knee-length black shorts hugging his hips left him embarrassingly exposed. "I didn't realize the crater was so," he kicked off his boots and left his dialect device on top of his clothes, "huge."

Cael waded into the onsen, pillowed by steam and charitable warmth. Natural heating was a rarity on Griea, and he'd never experienced anything quite like the hot spring. The water stung at first but quickly faded into a pleasant tingle encasing his kneecaps, ankles, and torso. He skated his palm across the rippling water and leaned against a smooth rock in the middle of the pool.

Elio sat nearby, looking at Cael sidelong. "Rumor has it the first exploratory ship from Draitune landed in that crater."

"Select xenobiologists still live somewhere down there," Lorelei mused. She prowled around the onsen, cloaked in steam. "Mimicking the first of us — original Aurethians."

"People don't see 'em though," Orson said. He kicked his short legs, splashing hot water. "And Mom doesn't think we should even have a Xenobiology Division."

"Mom's no fun," Lorelei said.

Maxine dunked beneath the water and came to swim around Cael. Water cascaded down her slim face. "The Xenobiology Division was created due to a clause put in place by Harlyn Volkov, rounding out the unification agreement," she said through a smile. "Harlyn wanted to encourage preservation of Aurethian wildland, and make sure there was a moon-side organization in place to keep Aurethia's stewardship in check. The first candidate she chose happened to be a descendant of the very first scientist to breed the indomitable Aurethian lion."

Lorelei heaved a sigh. Her damp golden hair hung in tangled waves. "How do you feel about our lions, Imperator?"

Cael swished his hand through the water. Blue particles swirled around his knuckles. "They're incredible," he said, trying at a smile, "and loyal. I'm surprised they stay close to the manor. I imagine most animals would roam out there." He pointed to the expanse of wilderness beyond the cliff. "Chasing freedom."

"Oh, we feed them," Lorelei sang, laughing. "Any creature can be tamed if you offer it enough sustenance. Keep it needing you."

The comment barbed. Cael worked to unclench his jaw, tonguing at chewed cheek. Before he could respond, Elio cleared his throat and said, "Didn't you need to get Orson back?"

Lorelei lolled her head. Her docile expression hardened. "Cael just got here." She spoke his name freely, awkwardly.

All Elio had to do was shift his gaze to Peadar. One flick, one glance.

Peadar stepped forward. "Lord Elio is right, Lady Lorelei."

Maxine rose from the hot water. Her swimwear was a singular backless piece with thick straps, dark maroon, almost black. "I'm more than cooked, personally. And Lor, you did promise we'd trade manicures."

"Fine, fine," Lorelei groaned, following Maxine out of the onsen.

The Aurethian guard brought them towels from a pack. Orson complained about leaving, but Maxine assured him they would have a treat once they got back to the manor. After they were dry and dressed, Lorelei blew a kiss toward the pool, Maxine waved, and Orson called out a goodbye. It was a reflective thing — smiling. Cael laughed, grinned, and waved back, wishing the trio and their escort safe passage. Their noisy giggling and hollering bounced around the cave and echoed into the crater.

Cael floated away from the rock and drifted toward the edge of the pool. The suction of water funneling over the ledge pushed him closer. He clung to the side and toed his way toward Elio, slipping onto his back and paddling past him.

"Where does it come from?" Cael asked.

Elio danced his gaze across him. "What?"

"The hot spring."

"Underground. It's heated by trapped magma. That pocket feeds water into the pool." He pointed to the right side of the onsen where a few bubbles spouted. "It's the same water feeding one of our Avara mines." He cupped some liquid in his palm and let it fall. Blue glinted in the mauve-silver moonlight. "Particles come up through the vein. If Lorelei were still here, she'd tell you it keeps our skin clear and makes us live longer."

"Does it?" Cael righted himself in the pool and rubbed his foot along the smooth bottom.

Elio pushed away from his seat and drifted too, circling. "Lorelei's the one training to be a medic. Ask her."

"You don't think the Aurethian miracle crystal improves your longevity?" Cael knew the answer. Of course it did. "Aurethian citizens live a decade longer than most people on similar planets, don't they?"

The handsome heir grinned. It was a small, soft thing barely curling his mouth. "And we avoid illness, age gracefully, and we're less likely to go deaf or blind. We bathe in blue pools. Drink blue water. Grow our food in blue soil." He floated closer. His body was beautifully scarless, a compilation of long lines and delicate bone. Lean muscle coiled beneath his skin, softened by heat and moisture. The red nick on his cheek looked oddly out of place. "Avara is everywhere."

Cael mirrored him, swimming counterclockwise in the shallow pool. Arrogance soured the fine structure of Elio's face. It was unbecoming and somehow completely fitting. "Look at you," he cooed, sarcasm dripping, "bragging while stationers starve, and parsec sickness eats a hole through the Greater Universe."

Elio's smile cooled. "Avara distribution is at an all-time high."

"Maybe counterfeit Avara."

"Aurethia can't control which illegal substances appear on the black market, Imperator."

"You're not curious about who receives your precious blue?" Cael swiped his hand through the water, splashing Elio slightly. He sensed the beginning of an argument. Felt it boil in his blood, watched it draw a line between Elio's eyebrows. He swam closer, lowering his voice. "You aren't that naïve, are you?"

"Careful," Elio snapped.

Peadar made a purposeful noise in the cave, something like a cough.

"You bask in the wealth and luxury your moon provides while countless people deteriorate," Cael said, still quietly, still privately. He swam closer, cresting Elio's orbit. Shoulders bumped, chests brushed. "Tell me, lion cub, what's it like to live in a constant state of surety?"

Elio pushed forward. Water splashed over the lip of the pool as he caged Cael against the far side, gripping the stone with one hand. His knee bracketed Cael's hip. Steam curtained, slightly blurring them from the cave's view. It was vulnerable and dangerous, and Cael kept his eager hands fisted. They studied each other, steam sliding through the air, darkness spanning the onsen. Draitune glowed, and the blue-tinged water glimmered, and Cael's trapped body gradually thrummed, leaning toward the prince. Avara flickered like trapped cinders.

"You're bold," Elio warned.

Cael let his gaze linger far too long on Elio's wet mouth. "And you're curious."

"Avara is a natural resource. We prioritize its development and sustainability. Yes, the people who live here benefit. Why shouldn't they?"

"They should." Cael lowered his voice. "And Avara should be widely available. Those statements are not mutually exclusive."

"Avara *is* widely available."

Cael braved a touch to Elio's waist, running his knuckles from hipbone to nipple. The pool concealed it. Cael's hand; Elio's skin. Hid how Elio settled above him, one knee tucked between his thighs, resting on the stone. But it didn't hide the slight twitch at the edge of Elio's lips or the outward pulse of his pupils. They were intimately close. Skin-to-skin, body-to-body. Yet Cael saw nothing but confusion on the Aurethian prince's face.

Far too slowly, Elio angled his thigh against Cael's crotch. Hot, dewy hunger panged behind his lowest vertebrae. Cael slackened his jaw. Fought to keep his eyes cracked open, meeting Elio's probing attention.

"You're not a fool, Elio," Cael whispered, hopeful.

He reached for Elio beneath the water. Grabbed his waist, guided him closer, and tilted his pelvis, encouraging him to sit, to *take*. Cael lifted his thigh. He closed the space between them. *Come here.* Slid Elio into his lap. *Let me feel you.* Shifted his palm to the sensuous dip above Elio's tailbone and applied pressure, pushing until a breath punched out of him, sudden and shredded.

Elio opened his mouth. Aurethian nor Griean surfaced. His white teeth flashed. Plump mouth quivered. Something brutal and naked bolted across his face.

Fear, maybe. Or passion.

Oh. Cael swallowed thickly. Desire suffocated him. Self-control drained like a hemorrhaged vein. *My, my, you're not what I expected, princeling.*

Elio's slender throat dented on a slow, rolling swallow. He turned, hiding his mouth against Cael's cheek. "Meet me in the meadow tomorrow morning," he whispered. It was a hurried thing. Secret. Cael could hardly concentrate. His attention narrowed to the slippery glide of Elio's lips against his face. "In the blue hour before dawn. Leave your Augment; I'll leave my guard." Before Cael could answer, Elio peeled away — leaving him half-hard and embarrassingly exposed — and floated on his back. "Aurethia is beautiful at night, Imperator. Let's not waste our time debating political nonsense."

Cael noticed the inflection in his voice. That comment was meant for Peadar.

"I suspect you're right," Cael said, and sank into the middle of the pool again, chasing skin, connection, the promise of *almost*. He dragged his hand through the water beneath Elio's bare back, kicked through the pool, narrowly missing his ankle.

When Elio submerged, Cael did, too. He stared at Elio's murky shape through the glinting water, and then opened his mouth, swallowing as much magic as he could.

CHAPTER THIRTEEN
ELIO

E lio adjusted the brown leather belt pulled around his lightweight trousers and looked out the window. Early morning blackness gave way to darkest blue. The orchard and the sea began to take shape, texture breaking through the nighttime silhouette of bushy treetops and crashing waves. The landscape was fuzzy with a new day and Elio chided himself for getting little to no sleep. He lay awake thinking of steam pluming around Cael's alabaster skin, rewriting the questions he should've asked and imagining how the Imperator might've answered.

Who are you to call me naïve? And Cael would've listed Elio's sociopolitical blind spots. *What do you know about Avara distribution?* And the Imperator would've eviscerated him with a practiced speech regurgitated from ill-informed Griean strategists. *Do you think Aurethia is beholden to the Greater Universe?* Elio pictured Cael surging forward, seizing Elio by the throat. He didn't know why he imagined violence, but the thought startled him. His mind flinched away from it, retreating to a real memory. Cael's closeness. His damp breath on Elio's face, and the stretch of his honed body beneath him in the water. Elio did not know why he'd done it — placed himself in Cael's lap like a lamb — but it taught him something new about the Griean heir. Control; patience. The slow way Cael eased Elio down, down until their bodies connected... A masterful combination of torture and discipline.

"Or he does not want you at all," he said to himself.

In retrospect, if Elio had asked what he'd wanted to ask, he would've started a fight. Or an argument, at least. Part of him wanted to, if only to understand Cael's perspective — skewed as it might be.

There weren't many planetary advocates throughout the Greater Universe who wouldn't question the Henly's extraction and distribution system. But none of those people were on Aurethia, excavating Avara from intricate underground cave systems and refining it into a soluble medicine. The people who called the forest moon home did that work, people who nurtured the volatile crystal and lived alongside it.

Of course everyone wanted more Avara. Elio wanted more, his father wanted more, House Darvin on Draitune, and the ambassadors from Ren and Mal wanted more. But Avara was not an easily crafted trinket, and Aurethia was not an industrial manufacturer.

Elio ran his teeth across his lip and lined his belt with cattails before clipping his dagger to his waist. He would have to be quiet. If Peadar caught wind of his plan to meet Cael without protection, Elio would never hear the end of it, and if Peadar knew he planned to spar with Cael without protection, he expected his parents would get involved. It wasn't the smartest way to get closer to the Imperator. He could admit that. But Elio feared the only way to know him, to see him, be seen by him, was to have him alone.

The chamber door floated open. Elio glanced into the hall and stepped out, keeping to the shadows. He crept along the wall and ducked through the living room, pulling a thin hood over his head. The fireplace still smoldered. Restful silence filled the house. He glanced at the entryway and walked on his toes past the hearth, creeping toward the back door. Someone cleared their throat behind him.

Shit. Elio inhaled deeply through his nose and turned, relieved to find Maxine watching him from the entrance of the kitchen. She held a steaming mug and still wore her nightclothes.

"Elio," she said. A smile reached her eyes. "Where are you off to this early?"

"The meadow," he relented, cringing. "I'd appreciate discretion."

Maxine sipped her coffee. "I assume Imperator Volkov won't be found in his bedroom either." Elio nodded and rolled his mouth, pressing tightly. Before he could speak, she continued. "Don't get caught, my lord."

"You didn't see me," he assured.

She made a show of closing her eyes and swept her arm toward the doorway.

Elio thanked the stars it was Maxine who'd seen him and not Lorelei who would've spied, or Orson who would've tattled, or anyone else for that matter. He slipped into the garden and made his way to the meadow, shielding himself behind overgrown trees.

Coastal air nipped his bare arms. It was still night-cold, still wet and balmy from overnight precipitation. Snails munched fallen fruit, and a garden snake glided through the grass, disappearing into a hole Elio promptly stepped over. He took the long route toward the back of the orchard and cut into the meadow.

Cael stood in the grass with his hands in his pockets and his face tipped toward the waking sky. Morning draped navy over his charcoal garb, and the last, lingering smattering of starlight fell across his inked skull. Nestled deep, where barbed desire needled the soft, swollen bit of him that couldn't stand whatever Cael had done to his temperament, life, heart — him, completely — Elio had half-hoped Cael would deny his request.

But of course, the fearless Imperator did not turn down a challenge, and of course, that soft, swollen bit of Elio sang at the sight of him.

"You came," Elio said.

"You asked me to be here." He sliced a glance at Elio. His thin smile twitched, and he elevated a brow. "Without my Augment."

There was a strangeness to it, being alone with him — entirely alone — for the very first time.

"You're on Aurethia," he said through a sigh. He wanted to be agreeable, but he couldn't stop his mouth. "You sleep in my home. You're surrounded by my guardship. If I wanted you dead, you would be."

The Imperator said nothing. He placed his hand on his sheathed blade and listed his head. His eyes, like the blue bulb at the base of a flame, flicked around Elio's face.

"Do you mind sparring with your personal weapon?" Elio asked.

"I usually don't."

"Neither do I, but..." He drew his tanto, twirling it flippantly. "I brought you here to duel and these are what we have. I expect you'll control yourself."

Cael cocked his head, hawkish. His eyes narrowed, but he smiled and unsheathed his short-sword, curved at the tip, wide in the center. His gloved hand re-curled around the pale bone-handle etched with Griea's eight-pointed star. He held himself loosely, watching Elio pace forward. It was the same guise a puma might wear, an expression fit for apex predators.

"This is why you brought me out here?" Cael's smile split for a playful grin.

Elio didn't entertain an answer. He swung his dagger, initiating the start of the duel.

Cael blocked with an immediacy that sent Elio staggering backward. Right. No Peadar, no Vik. They weren't supervised. The Griean shot him a coy look and stepped forward, smashing the sole of his boot against Elio's sternum. Elio tumbled into the grass, then leapt to his feet, regaining his confidence with another quick jab, jolt, swing — their blades clashed.

There.

Strength trembled in his triceps, ached in his shoulders. He twirled around, relying on graceful maneuvers and light-footedness to break away. They fell together again — Cael swinging hard, Elio bracing for the blow — and whipped apart, forearms colliding, elbows knocking. It was a dance of strength and accuracy. Without Peadar watching, Cael growled and grunted, throwing his weight into every move, and without Vik, Elio lashed like a viper.

Despite Elio's best effort, Cael knocked his knife loose. It spun through the air, and Cael crowded against him, fitting the line of his sword beneath Elio's chin. The hand on Elio's nape, cradling him, tightened, and steel kissed the center of his throat.

"Here we are again," Cael huffed out.

This time, Elio refused to give in. He grappled for Cael's wrist, aimed a kick at his thigh, and pushed hard, dislodging the blade for long enough to swing his fist. His knuckles met Cael's jaw, earning a surprised, excited laugh. Cael stepped back and tossed his white-handled weapon. He touched his face, tonguing lewdly at his cheek.

"Best me without a blade," Elio challenged.

Cael's jaw slackened. His tongue ghosted pink along the inside of his lips, across his teeth. It was a thoughtless movement, one Elio wished he hadn't seen. The vision branded itself on a low bone, somewhere near his pelvis. He would see it when he slept. Feel it when he walked.

"You told me to be careful last night. Take your own advice," Cael chided.

Elio let out a breath. "I'm your equal here, fiancé. There's no need for delicacy."

Orange painted the horizon. Sunder poured over the orchard, illuminating Cael's flushed skin. He bounded forward, initiating a round of hand-to-hand combat. Something Peadar would never allow. Elio's heart raced. His lungs burned, sending up the feeble, metallic taste of burst capillaries. He blocked, ducked, aimed. Bone met bone, flesh met flesh, and Elio realized the vulnerability of it all — fighting as a language. He was learning Cael, the way he moved, how he breathed, and Cael was teaching him.

When Elio toppled the second time, he took Cael with him. They pawed at each other, wrestling until Elio finally, *finally* pinned the Griean down, one hand collared around the Imperator's neck, thumb pressed to windpipe, the other latched around a single strong wrist, perched solidly with his kneecap wedged in the soft divot beneath Cael's left hip. Elio breathed hard, staring at the man beneath him through pinched eyes.

Cael chuckled, a sound caught between levity and youth. "You move well."

Elio felt the compliment hum through his palm. "I know." Spoken too soon.

In a fluid movement, Cael seized his hand, knocked Elio off balance with an upward swing of his leg, and flipped them. Cael gripped each of Elio's slender wrists, leather gloves unexpectedly smooth, and caged Elio there, grinning down at him like a wolf would its prize. Tall grass swayed, and a lion bellowed, and Elio waited for Cael to do something, anything. To kiss him, maybe. But the Imperator only laughed and let him go, sitting up to straddle Elio's lap.

"I do this every day, you know. It's my job," Cael purred. His placid tone wasn't exactly a balm, but it soothed, nonetheless. He walked his fingertips up Elio's heaving chest.

Elio unwound. He went heavy against the dirt and grass. One hand, he realized, gently clasped Cael's knee. He left it there. "Once again, Griean reputation is proven to be true."

"I meant what I said the other day." Cael knuckled at the welt he'd left on Elio's cheek. The small cut had faded to a raised, red mark. "You're impressive."

It was impossibly brazen, but Elio turned to nip at his hand. He almost connected — teeth, skin — but Cael jerked away too quickly. "Tell me about Avara."

"What?"

"The truth. Your truth. Go on."

Cael waited, eyeing Elio skeptically.

"This isn't a trap. Our families have been on the verge of mutual destruction for hundreds of years, and it's our responsibility to broker peace. We can't do that if we don't understand each other," Elio said on a lengthy exhale.

The Imperator slid into the grass beside him and flopped down. "We haven't been on the verge of mutual destruction," Cael corrected, calm if not overly patient. "Aurethia is the controlling steward of the Lux Continuum, yet Griea goes without access to Avara, and Shepard, Divinity, and Sierra receive less than half their allotted stipends. All the while, the rich never miss a shipment. Draitune is staggering inner and outer system immigration now. You think that's because everyone wants to live on the ringed beauty? No, Elio." He turned, meeting Elio's gaze. "It's because Draitune is the central packaging and delivery hub for Avara. People want access to treatment."

That couldn't possibly be true. Draitune was a wealthy planet with amenities other homeworlds couldn't offer. Its popularity was, of course, colored by its proximity to Avara but it certainly wasn't the only factor. "Avara delivery is regulated by House Darvin. There is a process — "

"And who might benefit from that process?" Cael blinked.

"My father would never allow Griea or any other planet to go without treatment." As much as Elio wanted to believe that statement, guilt and uncertainty festered.

"Ask Peadar, inquire with Angelina, check the reports. See for yourself."

"I will."

"You should."

"I've never seen it before," Elio admitted. He hadn't meant to keep speaking, but the thought jumped out, so he added, "Parsec sickness. I've only reviewed offworld coverage in holodocuments."

"You're lucky."

"I don't feel lucky, Imperator. I feel like we're walking a tightrope."

Cael furrowed his brow. "Why?"

"Because we're loyal to different causes. Because I know Avara is sacred, and you know it's a commodity. Because if Draitune didn't stand guard and the Greater Universe hadn't agreed to conceal Avara's production effort, then someone — Griea, Zephus, Vandel Prime, anyone with a strong enough offense — would eradicate the people here and take the moon by force." He watched something brutal and mesmerizing cross Cael's face. *You're right,* scrawled into his set mouth and sad eyes. *I know.* "My great-grandfather was not a good man. I don't need that explained to me. But Aurethia is not the only homeworld with a penchant for propaganda, Cael."

Cael shut his eyes for a moment. Laughed in his throat. It was a pitying sound, one Peadar might make. "Is there a process for food, Elio? Bounty, you call it. Harvest. Is that regulated, too?"

A terrible burn bloomed in Elio's throat. He propped the side of his head in his palm. "Don't speak to me in riddles. Aurethia shares its bounty with the Greater Universe and provides sustenance throughout each system. That's a well-documented initiative."

Cael leaned closer, breathing an inch from Elio's mouth. "See," he whispered, "for yourself." Then he pushed to his feet and stretched. His shirt lifted, exposing a thin sliver of skin above his belt.

Elio wanted to follow that skin. Get underneath it. Fit himself against, and inside, and around Cael Volkov until he knew the specific taste of Griean flesh, and heat, and bravery. He wanted like he'd never wanted before. It petrified him.

"What will our lineage say about us?" Elio dared. "What will we give…" *Our children.* "What will this union amount to?"

"Power," Cael said. That lone word fit like a splinter beneath Elio's fingernail. "Resilience," he added and then, "honor." He looked over his shoulder. Smiled like a comet. "Tell me, fiancé, when do we decide to trust each other?"

An abrupt, alien feeling swelled behind Elio's breastplate. Laughter sputtered up and out of him. "Today," he decided. "Now."

"Now," Cael mused. He offered his hand.

Elio hesitated, only to savor the sweetness, only to let their playful, awkward tussle linger, then grasped Cael's palm and got to his feet. They stood like that, heartline-to-heartline, looking at each other while Sunder's rays fanned the sky. Birdsong echoed. A lioness named Korah stretched beneath a nearby tree and pawed at her pile of pride-mates. Elio dropped his hand.

The Imperator tapped one of the cattails clipped to Elio's belt. "Teach me."

Elio unfastened a throwing knife and nodded curtly. "It's about aim and wind. When mastered, the cattail can be an assassin's weapon, or a surprise attack from a distance or," he flicked the dual-curved knife in a circle, "close combat."

Cael reached out as if to touch the knife, then stopped, waiting.

"You can throw vertically." Elio flipped the blade upright. "Or horizontally." Flattened it again. "They're made of Aurethian steel forged from lava stone. Sometimes you can see…" He lifted the blade into a patch of light and turned. Sunlight glanced. Blue licked the crease. "Avara."

"Like the water last night," Cael murmured.

Elio tilted his eyes upward. "Yes." He nudged his chin toward a tree in the distance. "When the wind is still, focus on your mark and..." Stepped back, locked onto a thick branch, swung, threw, flexed his hand outward, every finger following the direction of the rapid knife. He sucked in a breath and sighed it out. "Somewhere over there an apple just fell."

Cael opened his palm. "I'll follow your voice." He peeled his gaze away from Elio for long enough to settle on a far-off mark. Elio placed a cattail in the Imperator's hand. Cael stared at his chosen target and said, "Tell me what to do."

CHAPTER FOURTEEN

CAEL

Festivities swept through Aurethia. Fishermen celebrated the return of the spotted orca, a cycle-sign of sea health, and farmhands sang in the orchards, their lilting Aurethian mingling with gullsong and frothy ocean noise. In the domed pasture next to the garden, birthing stock grazed with happy calves. Spotted chicks pecked at seed in the chicken pen. Playful newborns scampered behind mother goats, shying away from the translucent panel separating livestock from lion.

Last week, after Cael sparred with Elio in the meadow, he'd paced in his chamber — same as he did now — trying to calm his racing heart — same as he did now — and was interrupted by Vik Endresen — same as he was now — who barreled into his bedroom and said, "Imperator, I've detected an increase in your heartrate. Is everything — "

"You've got to stop that," Cael seethed, rubbing the heel of his palm against the center of his forehead.

"Apologies," Vik said, though the Augment didn't sound apologetic. "Have you packed for the trip?"

He stared at the high ceiling. "Yes, I'm packed. We'll only be gone the night. I don't need much."

Visitation to Atreyu, Aurethia's capital, had been arranged by High Lord Darius to celebrate the successful delivery of Aurethia's first harvest to Griea. It was the time of Thanjō in their great, glittering city, and Cael respected the strategy. Unveiling him to the populus during a summertime festival might soften his reception. *No better time to announce unification*, Elio had said the day before yesterday, flipping through an antique replica of a long-gone Earthen tome, *it will be an informal and modest debut, but the people will see us.*

Cael joined Elio in the library often, pretending to review holodocuments while Elio digitally translated old, stupid poetry. He stole glances at Elio's elfin hands, listened to him murmur quietly and grunt annoyedly, and found himself pondering those old, stupid poems, wondering if the author had been throttled by the presence of similar hands, inspiring pen to page. In the orchard, they walked closer. Elio bumped him once, knuckles grazing, and in the training chamber, the pair danced around each other, practicing with cattails and short-swords, fists and feet. They sat together in the dining hall, swam together in the sea, and ate sheep's cheese and cut fruit together in the kitchen.

Trust had been an invitation, one Cael extended on a whim in the aftermath of violent vulnerability. Courage paid off.

"You're nervous," Vik said.

"I'm not," Cael lied. He looked himself over in the mirror. "Did Griea receive the data you sent?"

Vik paused. One pupil grew, shrank. "I can confirm the encrypted data has been decoded, sir."

"Good." He plucked at the sleeveless tunic fastened with pearlescent black cable, then licked his thumb and buffed out a smudge on his basilisk belt, buckling it tighter. "Can you patch Maxine through to my dialect device?"

"I can, Imperator. But I can't guarantee security."

"I'll be subtle." He looped the device over his ear.

Static filled the earpiece. Vik's voice came through first, echoing from his physical body. `Maxine Carr, Imperator Volkov.`

"Maxine," Cael said.

More static. Then silence. Finally, Maxine said, "Imperator, how can I help you?"

"Elio mentioned you won't be joining us in Atreyu."

"I have business with High Lord Darius. As you know, the harvest arrived late but whole. Now we're negotiating a critical Avara shipment. The Imperial Council will be present."

Cael knitted his brow. Being moon-side should've granted him the ability to supersede Maxine's position, especially for a critical negotiation. He glanced at Vik. The Augment gave him a look that said *Well?* "I'm happy to negotiate on behalf of Griea. My presence here is a rare opportunity. Perhaps we shouldn't squander it."

A pause. Static. Breath. "Sir, I believe the political visit to Atreyu is of the utmost importance. I hope you're confident in my ability to advocate for you. It is my honor."

"Of course, Maxine. You're an asset. I only mean — "

Maxine slipped into Griean. "If I may, you're here to court Lord Elio, Imperator. Enjoy the festival," she said, sickly sweet, "explore Atreyu, get to know the birthplace of Avara, and I will take care of trade deliverables. If I require assistance, I'm happy to connect with your Augment."

"Vik," he corrected.

Maxine paused. "Vik," she said, drawing his name out. "I appreciate your involvement, Imperator, but I'm more than capable of managing this situation. I'll report to the Legatus with any development. Do I have your credence?"

"You do. Thank you, Maxine."

"God is in the water," she said, almost too softly to hear, then static filled his earpiece.

Cael took off his dialect device and whipped toward Vik. "What was that," he said, bewildered.

"Operative Carr is the liaison, Imperator. With respect, she's clearly spoken to Legatus Marcus about the trade deliverables."

"That's my point, Vik. She spoke with my father, and he didn't instruct her to involve me in this," he waved his hand, "negotiation."

Vik spoke but Maxine's voice left his mouth, grating and wrapped in static-fuzz. "Explore Atreyu, get to know the birthplace of Avara." He closed his mouth, recalibrated, then spoke again. His own voice surfaced. "I think there is a plan within a plan, sir."

Don't do that freaky shit again, Cael almost said. But instead, he nodded and sniffed hard, sucking on his teeth. The plan within a plan was Cael's lack of movement on the location of an Avara mine. Failure sat in his gut, curdling.

"Courtship can't be rushed," he spat. Embarrassment tinged his face. Acting like a child was one thing. Recognizing the behavior made Cael want to put his fist through a wall. Which ultimately wouldn't help. "I feel useless."

"Clearly you're of use, Imperator," Vik drawled.

"Clearly."

The sound of a boot-heel smacked the stone outside his chamber. Peadar appeared flanked by an Aurethian guard dressed in gold and white. He rapped on the open door and inclined his head.

"Imperator Volkov, the transport to Atreyu is ready. We'll be traveling by hovertrain," Peadar said. Silver speckled his freshly groomed hair and short, oiled beard.

Cael wiped the uncertainty from his face and flashed a smile. "Excellent."

"My associate, Danna, will stow your belongings in the under storage."

Cael gestured to the zipped black duffle on the floor. "That's mine. Vik's is in his room."

"The rest of the entourage is waiting in the courtyard." Peadar opened his arm. "If you'll please join them, the guardship will attend to you."

Cael glanced at the mirror once more and nudged his chin toward the hall, prompting Vik to follow. "Thank you, Peadar."

The house staff bustled about, folding laundry and dusting pollen from the windowsills. Indigo swept out of the kitchen struggling to carry an assortment of supplies. Cael jolted forward, but Vik placed a hand on his chest and said, "Allow me, Imperator." The Augment crossed the living quarter and eased a basket from Indigo's forearm. "Happy to assist, Lady Indigo."

"*Lady*," she sputtered out, laughing. "Aren't you charming, Endresen. Thank you." She spoke to Cael next, nodding respectfully. "Good rising, Imperator. I'm honored to join you."

"Glad you're accompanying us, Indigo," Cael said. He clasped his hands at the small of his back and walked with her through the front door.

The group traveling to Atreyu waited beneath the shade of the candle-bell tree. Cael joined Elio and Lorelei who stood apart from High Lady Lena and Orson. Vik walked with Indigo toward the Aurethian guardship stationed near the sleek hovertrain waiting in the road. It was a cylindrical tube much like the train system in Machina. Gravity disrupting pressure discs lined the undercarriage and lifted the entire body of the glass-clad machine off the ground, allowing the Aurethian transport to travel without harming farmland or natural terrain.

"Imperator," Elio said. His blonde hair swept away from his face, the slight wave of it cresting his brow. Cael wanted to run his hand along the sheared space around his ear. Imagined Elio's undercut might feel like the center of a daisy.

"Fiancé," Cael greeted.

A cream blouse offset Elio's oversized terracotta pants. No buttons, no clips. Just a simple, low-necked shirt, cottony and less than opaque. He was summer, bottled. Cael tucked his knuckle beneath the gold Aurethian glyph strung around Elio's neck and let the lion's face dent his thumb.

"Are you ready for Atreyu, Imperator? It's quite the city," Lorelei said. Gold-rimmed sunglasses masked half her face. She looked like a beautiful cicada wrapped in holographic silk, donned in a shiny, low-backed gown.

"I am, Lady Lorelei. I've heard it's a wonderful place," Cael said.

Peadar strode through the courtyard, waving to the group. "Time to board!"

Cael didn't realize he'd kept hold of Elio's necklace until the heir reached up and took his hand. He shifted his gaze downward, catching Elio's green, green eyes. Cael did not know what to do. Grip his palm? Buckle his scarred fingers between Elio's lovely knuckles? Bring the back of Elio's palm to his mouth? Every possibility manifested, gluey in the forefront of his mind.

"Are you ready?" Elio asked. He kept the barest hold on Cael's fingertips. Then, tragically, let him go.

Cael cursed his own cowardice. "I am," he assured, and fell into step beside Elio, following him to the transport.

Plush bench-style seating padded the spacious hovertrain. It was sparse but homey. The paneled metal ceiling and sturdy floor were the only non-transparent elements. Everywhere else, sunlight beamed through solid glass, creating the perfect vessel for sightseeing.

Orson refused to sit in a proper seat and plopped on the floor instead, doodling on a holotablet with a slender electronic pencil. Indigo and Lena sat near the front of the train. Cael joined Elio and Lorelei at a table in the center of the capsule, gesturing for Vik to sit beside him. After the door shut, the drone conductor piloting the hovertrain came through the ceiling speaker. *Initiating gravity suspension.* The hovertrain detached from the ground, tipping left then right before stabilizing. *Destination: Atreyu, Aurethia.* The train shot forward, curving inland toward the forest. It cruised in a designated lane attached to the central roadway alongside ground cars, carriages, and pedestrians.

As the train barreled forward, Lorelei talked about her dream of attending the Biology Institute on Ocury, and Elio mentioned his longtime passion for the written word. How Lorelei hoped to splice Avara with other medicinal minerals, and how Elio yearned for an archivist position at the Planetary Library in Atreyu. Cael spoke very little, opting to listen to the Henlys' chatter until Lorelei prodded him in the shin with her sandal and asked, "You've attained your title already, haven't you? Keeper of the Basilisk?"

"I have." Cael nodded. "But that doesn't mean I can't be bested during the Tupinaire." The siblings shared a confused glance. "And replaced," he added, too bluntly. "Stepping into a role on Griea is different than establishing a specialty on Aurethia. Anyone can challenge me at any time. Anyone can challenge *anyone* at any time."

"Your title could be taken from you after a single match? I find that hard to believe," Lorelei said.

Cael seesawed his head. "I doubt someone *would* challenge me, but technically, anybody could. If a weaponsmith wanted to challenge the Legatus for his title, they could. If an operative wanted to challenge my cousin, Optio Bracken, for his title, they could. If my cousin wanted to challenge me for the role of Imperator, he could. If someone were to kill me during the Tupinaire, regardless of whether I was on the roster, even if I were only an attendee, they would have the legal right to challenge my protégé and take the title for themself. Griea's political climate is dictated by the respect our people have for each other and our leadership. That's why those matches rarely happen."

"Interesting…" Lorelei slugged out the word. "And no one has tried to usurp your father?"

"No, not yet. The last time someone challenged a Volkov, a Praetor met Dutchess Harlyn in the arena. He lost."

"Your great-grandmother fought in the arena?" Elio's eyes widened.

Cael nodded curtly. "After she agreed to Alexander Henly's unification terms, yes. She beheaded a man called Praetor Evgen and offered his body to the basilisk. His skull is still on display at our War College."

Lorelei scrunched her nose. "How…" She gulped tightly. "Effective."

"Could someone challenge me in your arena?" Elio cocked his head. "Once we're wed, I mean. Could someone — "

Vik cleared his throat. "My humble Imperator has forgotten to mention that the defender may take a champion. I'm certain if you were called to the ice, Cael would fight for you himself."

"Vik is right," Cael said. "But yes, someone could potentially challenge you, Elio. And you could fight or choose a champion."

"I would have you as my knife," Elio quipped, whirling toward Lorelei. "They wouldn't know what to do with you."

Lorelei howled through laughter. "Your enemy is my enemy." She beat a playful fist on her chest. "No Griean would expect an Aurethian lioness to cut them down — I would feed their body to the great serpent, same as Cael's grandmother!"

Elio laughed. Despite a twinge of mild discomfort, Cael did, too. Vik slid him a pointed glance but remained quiet.

The hovertrain glided forward, cutting through Aurethia like a sunbeam. They talked about Griean delicacies and Aurethian dances. Elio shared off-world gossip passed along from one of the orchard staff and Lorelei clapped her hand over her mouth, feigning surprise. They talked about many things — literature and music, poetry and fashion, beautifully normal things, young and unimportant things — until the scenery changed from forest to rice paddy fields, and the city of Atreyu sprang up on the horizon.

Staggered long-tiled rooftops shone red and black above the watery plateaus. The hovertrain sped along the widening road and traveled beneath a stone gate shaped like two opposing women carved in the likeness of lions. Wings extended from their backs, almost touching at their greatest height, and the pilot drone's electronic voice came through the speaker again.

Arrival: Atreyu, Aurethia. Welcome to the lion's maw of the forest moon. For travel information, please visit the city directory.

The hovertrain slowed to a stop and lowered to the ground. Orson yelled happily while High Lady Lena ushered him through the sliding door. Three Aurethian sentries stood at attention, shielding the Henly family from the public, and Peadar gave instruction to the last guard, Danna, to deliver their belongings to the lakehouse.

The outdoor platform faced the main gate, positioned with easy access to the roadway. Once everyone exited the hovertrain, Peadar nodded.

"I'll be accompanying Lord Elio and Lady Lorelei. Imperator Volkov, you'll also be with me. Luke, Ciara, and Niam will chaperone Indigo Condon, High Lady Lena, and Lord Orson. We have a private viewing at the library and dinner will be served before the lantern ceremony this evening. Make contact through your device if you need to regroup or require aid." Peadar offered a rare smile and tipped his head toward the city behind them. "It's the season of Thanjō. Enjoy it."

Lorelei tapped her feet excitedly and curled her arm around Cael's elbow, hauling him along. "Okay, we should head to that bakery in the Ocurian neighborhood first — I don't want them to run out of suncakes. You remember it, Elio?" She glanced over her shoulder and laughed. "And, oh, the import merchant downtown always has off-the-runway fabric from Dardellin."

Cael followed her gaze, fixing Elio with a patient grin.

Elio, bemused, smiled softly, and shook his head. "Will you be hoarding my fiancé for the rest of the day, or can I have him back at some point?"

She flapped her free hand. "I might give him back at dinner," she joked.

"This is a strategic visit, my lady," Cael whispered, leaning close to her ear. "I'm afraid you might have to give me back sooner than that."

Lorelei hushed him playfully. "Oh, I know, I know. C'mon."

"We'll meet with you for dinner," Lena called, splitting off with Indigo, Orson, and her guardship toward the stomach of the city.

Just inside the main gate, Atreyu opened in several directions. The smooth road became tiled walkways. Ground cars kept to the perimeter of the city, utilizing docking bays for deliveries and massive ivy-covered parking structures for vehicle storage.

Cael knew Atreyu from holodocumentaries, but he didn't expect the sheer grandiosity of Aurethia's prized city to knock the wind out of him. Tall spiral apartment buildings coiled into the sky. Balconies boasted potted flora and decorative furniture, and drones sped from personal launch bays clipped to pickets. Boutiques, taverns, tea houses, and outdoor markets bustled with complexkind. While Lorelei tugged him along, he stole another glance at Elio. The heir came to stride beside them.

Imperator. Vik spoke through his dialect device. I'll be monitoring your movement from a safe distance. You're armed, correct? Please lower your pointer finger to confirm. Cael lowered his finger as instructed. Hopefully he wouldn't need the blade sheathed at his side or the knife in his boot, but he wasn't naïve enough to visit Atreyu without them. Thank you. I will signal if necessary. While I encourage you to enjoy yourself, be on guard. Atreyu is a large city and the central hub for the Aurethian militia. I'll be scouting the interior of the city, retaining all tracking information.

Good to be in two places at once, surely.

Cael swallowed and glanced around. Festival vendors, two-story shops, food stalls, entertainers. Hooves clopped the tile. Lorelei swerved them out of the way of a horse-drawn carriage stocked with star-shaped lanterns, and Elio laughed pleasantly, pointing at a narrow passage in the throng. Atreyu was... so much.

Cael didn't realize he'd reached for Elio's hand until it was firmly clasped in his own. Peadar guided them through the crowd, and at first, the happy citizens didn't seem to notice the Henly family's arrival. But soon enough, attention stuck. People smiled at Elio. Gasped excitedly when they saw Lorelei. Froze or startled once Cael came into view. He ignored a handful of narrow glares, similar to what he'd experienced in Nadhas, and kept his chin up.

"Lorelei, walk with Peadar," Elio said. Lorelei shot him a catty glance, but he set his teeth and said it again. "Walk. With. Peadar."

"You're so sensitive," she hissed, releasing Cael's elbow. She bounced ahead and joined their guard.

Elio released his palm momentarily, readjusting to slot his fingers between Cael's knuckles. "Let them see us," he reminded, voice level and private.

Above them, enclosed glass bridges wrapped in greenery linked opposing buildings. A child pressed themself against one transparent panel, staring at the pair as they strode below. Cael breathed deeply and kept on, flicking his attention toward a brightly colored candle store. The vendor scurried backward into their boutique. Someone else pointed, smiling. Refreshing. Cael stopped to scout a juicery selling pouched refreshments. The juicer gasped and snarled when the Imperator brought a red-skinned pear to his nose, inhaling fragrant sweetness, but his associate grinned.

"No telling if this outing is having the impact you hoped it would," Cael said, sliding the statement to Elio. He put the fruit back where he found it.

The Henly heir, brave as always, paused in the center of the bustling street fair. He placed his palm on Cael's face, thumbing cheekbone.

"Let them look," Elio said, and Cael's heart became a swallowed bird. He leaned into Elio's hand, relenting. "The lion's maw of Aurethia is nothing without teeth, and I am the bone in this city's mouth. They will see you because I want them to."

Cael lifted an eyebrow. *What a thing to say.* He turned, brushing his mouth along the soft underside of Elio's knuckles. "You speak like a Griean, fiancé."

Elio's smile gleamed, knife-like. He turned toward the vendor and chirped, "I'll take that pear. And sparkling tea, please. You don't mind sharing, do you Imperator?" Elio slid him a sly smile. Cael shook his head, trapping a laugh, and Elio nodded at the flustered merchant. "Just one, please."

CHAPTER FIFTEEN
ELIO

T hanjō, the festival of regeneration and abundance, signified the beginning of Wonder's yearly birth-cycle. Toward the end of the forest moon's summer season, the pinkish nebula grew close enough to see from Aurethia and Draitune, capturing the immaculate collapse and glittering emergence of newborn stars in their shared sky.

Elio walked beside Cael, following Peadar and Lorelei. The queue for the bakery wrapped around a densely packed city block, but they waited their turn, enduring passerby chatter from fellow pastry enthusiasts.

Cael's reception seemed expectedly divided, but not terribly. The outing in Nadhas had planted a seed. While some people sneered or shied away, others smiled. One young couple waved as they crossed the road in front of Elio and Cael, clutching each other, repeating his title without malice or scorn. *Imperator of Griea. Warlord on the arm of our prince.* Cael seemed to perk at the approval. *Pair of prophecy! Change is here.* And Elio warmed proudly at the sentiment. *Yes*, he wanted to say, *change is here.*

The dark-skinned Ocurian baker greeted them with a wide smile and the utmost exuberance. He filled their box with suncakes and lantern cookies and sliced off a corner of cardamom cake for Cael to sample. "I've heard of your ice giant, Imperator. Would your people fancy my pudding?"

Cael nodded, charming as always, and said, "My mother is from Ocury. She would stand with our neighbors from dawn 'til dusk to taste this. Snow be damned."

The round shopkeep clapped and hollered, and laughter rang in the bakery.

After that, Elio and Cael picked through desserts, tearing off pieces of orange-flavored suncakes filled with cooked yolk and almond paste, and chewed gummy mochi dusted with candlebell pollen. Lorelei twirled through the street, dancing along to a string-band playing on a corner, and Cael took Elio's hand, spinning him, too.

As the day passed, Cael's rigidity diminished, smoothed away by Atreyu's surprising hospitality. Caution was to be expected, but for every one person who scowled, three more waved delightedly. *Glory, glory* one woman sang, sweeping her arm toward Peadar and the Henly entourage, *reckoning is here, repentance is now! Glory be to a fruitful union!*

Once they found a quiet moment, strolling past an eatery on their way to the library, Elio said, "You're Ocurian?"

"By blood, yes. My mother is from Ocury. You didn't notice?" Cael smiled.

Elio felt foolish for not realizing sooner. Duchess Constance *did* look strikingly Ocurian. Studying Cael, he found her mirrored in his strong jawline and narrow, high-set bone structure. Unquestionably Griean, yes. Subtly something else, too.

"You better hold onto him, Cael," Lorelei spouted, swaying as she loped toward a public square. "Elio might try to mole between the shelves and build a home."

How quickly Imperator had become Cael, and Lady had become Lorelei, and Elio had become fiancé. Their casual playfulness nestled close to his heart.

The walkway opened to a busy square. Jacaranda trees bloomed violet, dusting benches with fallen purple petals. Street vendors manning colorful carts sold paper lanterns, and children wearing face paint licked icepops in front of a massive stone fountain. It spouted clear water from four trumpets, each pressed to the mouth of a naked maiden — one with the head of a lion, the other three, horse, lizard, and porpoise. Elio watched Cael scan the buzzy gathering. On one end, the Planetary Library's domed roof filled the horizon, and directly opposite, Atreyu's Mineral Museum displayed a collection of crystals and gemstones from across the Greater Universe.

"What're the lanterns for?" Cael asked, gesturing shyly to a vendor.

"Oh, we light them and send them up at night, celebrating Wonder's cycle of creation. The last week of Thanjō is when the nebula gives birth. Those are our own honorarium," Elio said.

"Wonder?" He repeated. Confusion folded his brow. He switched to Griean. "You mean Womb? The star nursery?"

Elio's mouth quirked. "The word is interchangeable in our languages, but yes, that's what we call it. Sometimes people make a wish when they send them up."

"Is that right? And what have you wished for?"

He cleared his throat. "Silly things. Nothing remotely possible."

"Interesting." He hummed, nodding slowly. He tipped his face closer, mouth grazing Elio's ear as they ascended the staircase to the library. "Is your sister telling the truth? Will I have to put a collar on you in here?"

"There's no collar tight enough."

Cael shifted, sliding his hand between Elio's shoulderblades. Elio felt every arc and bend of Cael's fingers denting his nape. "We'll see."

Elio told his fluttering chest to fill. "You forget yourself, Imperator."

"You'll have to remind me."

Elio struggled to swallow.

Atreyu's Planetary Library was one of two authenticated archives in the Lux System. Authenticated meaning the ambassadorial council governing the Greater Universe had deemed it a sanctuary, prioritizing the safe-keeping of translated text and ancient literature from fallen empires. This particular building housed prehistoric holy text, stone tablets from Draitune, even written myth from Fara ice-travelers. Shelves lined each gigantic wall, brimming with paper books encased in protective glass.

Their tour guide swept across the pastel tile. Elio stayed close to Cael, murmuring about this or that as they followed the guide through the archival area. The long wooden tables were empty given the ongoing festival, but Elio saw himself seated at one in the future. Handling rare text; preserving historical integrity. When they came upon the Griean archive, Cael perked up, listening as the tour guide intelligently explained what the Greater Universe knew about the evolutionary and genetic timeline of the basilisk.

"They used to be much larger," Cael said at one point.

The tour guide nodded in agreement. "Indeed, Imperator. Although I'll admit, they're certainly monstrous in their current state."

"And beautiful," he added. "Useful, too. They keep the ecosystem beneath the ice in check. Their skin is durable," he tapped his belt, "and their scales provide a lifelong shield or weapon. Monstrous, maybe, but the Griean basilisk is nothing if not honest. It survives because it must. It's the apex predator on our planet because it has to be."

At that, the tour guide squinted. "*You* are the apex predator — excuse me, humankind, complexkind, I mean. Civilized species. Or am I mistaken?"

"You're mistaken." Cael laughed, but it wasn't to mock her. It was a humble, pleasant sound. His laughter said *you'd think that, wouldn't you? We all would.* "But it's a fair mistake to make."

The tour guide pinched her mouth, not quite a frown, and nodded thoughtfully.

After the tour concluded, Elio moved through the library, glancing at tomes with bitten leather spines, declarations etched on bleached bone, bamboo and papyrus scrolls. Lorelei pretended to be interested, and while Elio couldn't be sure if he retained anything, Cael peered over his shoulder, listening as he rambled about ink, calligraphy, data, and transcription, paying attention to each individual item Elio pointed at. He didn't want to leave the library, but morning slipped into afternoon, and there was more of Atreyu to see.

They walked the canal street beneath shady awnings and paused for traditional hand-held street food — fish and pheasant wrapped in sweet leaves and steamed until tender. At one point, a jeweler caught sight of Cael and locked the door to her shop. Elio tried and failed to steer them toward the bank of the canal. But it was too late. Cael noticed the action before Elio could shield him from it. Irritation crossed the Imperator's face, shadowing a chasm of hurt.

"In due time," Elio soothed.

Cael swallowed tightly and forced a papery smile.

They wandered the city. Lorelei fingered through imported clothing, and made an appearance at the medical apothecary, shaking hands with colleagues she would soon study alongside. Midday crept by. People cooled themselves with decorative paper fans and played at game booths manned by jesters in patterned celestial costumes.

Cael stared at strange things. When Elio expected him to assess the structure of a building, Cael inspected a flower sprouting through a crack in the walkway instead. And when Elio gestured to the weaponsmith, commenting on their selection, Cael crouched to stroke a stray and apologized for being distracted.

The more time Elio spent with him, the more Cael became an entirely realized person. Some*one* instead of some*thing*. Not that he hadn't always been an autonomous being — flesh and blood, same as Elio — but the seasonal clock scraped away the buttoned-up politician whose arrival had shaken Elio to his core. This was what remained: Cael Volkov petting a mangy cat, saying *oh, sorry darling, what'd you say* and then prattling on about wanting his own set of cattails to strap to his belt.

Mercifully, Cael did not realize the word *darling* had crawled into Elio's body and rooted there like a rosebush.

As evening washed over Atreyu, Peadar ushered them toward the restaurant to meet his mother, brother, and Indigo for dinner. Behind them, Vik appeared.

"Welcome back," Cael said, lowering his voice.

Elio glanced between the pair. "Did you get lost?"

"There is much to see in your beautiful city. I wanted to look for myself without slowing you down," Vik said, then added, "I stayed close."

The restaurant's simple oak patio overlooked a tiered rice paddy field with no rail or balustrade to obstruct the view. Two compact disc-lamps hovered over the tabletop, illuminating empty glasses and neatly arranged utensils. Before they sat, the Aurethian guardship wiped the interior of each glass with a cleansing cloth, and once Niam confirmed clearance, Peadar pulled out a chair for Lena. Elio sat beside Cael across from Indigo and his mother. Orson played with a holotablet at the head of the table, facing Vik and the guardship on the far end.

"Did you enjoy Atreyu?" Lena asked, smiling at Cael.

Cael returned her warmth with a nod. "I did, High Lady. I'm used to the practicality of Machina. Atreyu's decadence is a refreshing change."

"And here I am dying to visit Machina," Lorelei said, gaping like a goldfish.

"One day," Cael said.

Elio nodded to Orson and said, "What about you, Orson? Did you have fun today?"

"Yeah, we went to the Avara monument. Did you know the xenobiology settlers cracked the first vein by accident? Some lucky guy found an empty cave during a storm. I guess the mother crystal was underneath a massive quartz point — turned the whole place blue."

"I didn't know that," Elio said. He did, of course. But the spark of interest in Orson's eye rewarded a white lie. "Fascinating."

The staff brought small share plates first, then a server announced a special cold tea to start the meal. Three individual waitstaff carrying pitchers filled with amber liquid approached the table. Candlebell flowers, sliced citrus, cinnamon sticks, and spice sachets jostled for each pour.

A marble-faced server with gold-dusted skin approached Cael. She did not smile, breathe, or blink, and Cael did not notice her. He was busy talking with Lena, laughing about the generous Ocurian baker who'd offered him a cake-taster, and fumbling cutely through a botched pronunciation of the street food they'd eaten earlier.

It wasn't until Cael reached for his glass that Vik flattened his palm over the top of it. Vik did not speak. He met the Imperator's gaze for a heartbeat, and when Cael's smile dropped, the Augment nodded.

Elio glanced between Cael and Vik, then flicked his attention to the server who looked suddenly, frightfully guilty.

"What's wrong," Elio demanded.

He did not get an answer.

The server managed to edge out, "Usurper — "

Cael moved deadly fast. He stood, unsheathed his blade, and swung. Death made no sound. Griean steel flayed the skin beneath her chin. The server desperately grappled for her open throat before she fell, crumbling into a heap beside the table. Her last word hovered like a buzzard. *Usurper.*

Peadar shot to his feet. The Aurethian guard hollered. One of them, Ciara, drew a pulse gun and pointed the barrel at Cael. Indigo stepped in front of Lena, then Niam stepped in front of her, ushering the two women back with an outstretched arm. Orson began to hyperventilate, and Lorelei screeched, lunging away from the corpse.

"Someone at this establishment tried to poison me," Cael said. The playful cushion in his voice was gone, replaced by the ice of his homeworld. He picked up a table napkin and wiped his blade. Red brightened white fabric. His jaw flexed, expression stony and unfamiliar. "Go on, Peadar. Test it," he said, knuckling the freshly poured tea forward. "My Augment doesn't lie."

Lena pulled Orson to her bosom, shielding his face against her dress. "There was no need — "

Cael grew savage and venomous. "Save your fragility, High Lady."

"Watch your mouth," Elio snapped. He didn't know why, couldn't understand the sudden fierceness to defend his mother at a time when he should've been concerned for his future husband. The comment earned him a sidelong glance. Cael's vacant, practiced rage was a haunting thing. Elio steadied himself, transferring his attention from Cael to the blood pooling closer to his boot. He stepped away from the body. "Peadar, test it."

"Lower your weapon, Imperator," Peadar instructed.

Cael only laughed in his throat, as if to say *really*, as if to say *please*, and leveled Peadar with a barbed smile.

Vik, the only one still seated, finally stood. Ciara snapped her gun toward him.

"By my assessment, the tea is dosed with a corrupted mineral structurally similar to Avara," Vik said. His data-port hummed. "The composition is almost identical, but this additive is corrosive. Debilitating."

"When Avara is overharvested, the mother mineral deteriorates, same as flesh," Lorelei blurted. Her throat sounded swollen and wet. She blubbered on. "It becomes necrotic and unusable and — "

"Poisonous," Cael smarted.

"Lethal," Lorelei corrected. She whipped toward him. "Why do you think we can't replicate it? Or rehome it? Avara is a living thing, Imperator. When it dies, it becomes noxious. Someone tried to *kill* you."

Cael shrugged toward Lorelei, hand still wrapped tight around the pommel of his blade. "You heard her."

Peadar stepped around the table, stern-faced and ready to strike. "Imperator, I need you to lower — "

Elio should've used his voice. Should've instructed Peadar to do as Cael said. But instead, he grabbed the allegedly poisoned tea and brought Cael's glass to his mouth. His mother did not make a sound. Neither did Orson, or Lorelei, or any of their guardship. The cup touched his bottom lip and Peadar let out a frustrated noise, halting Elio before he could drink.

"Enough with the theatrics. Give it to me," Peadar said. He jutted his chin toward Ciara. "At ease."

The other waitstaff remained frozen. One vomited over the side of the patio, the other trembled, standing in a mess of shattered glass and spilled liquid. A halved lemon clung to her shoe.

Peadar dipped a fresh cleansing cloth into the tea. It bloomed a normal sallow color at first, then luminescent blue wicked up the fabric, and lastly, gravely black unfurled across the cloth, puddling like mold spores. Poison. *Poison*.

Something unsophisticated crossed Peadar's face. Not rage. Not even surprise.

Disappointment.

The general slammed the glass down and touched the gold device looped over his ear. "Report to my location immediately." Another tap. He shifted his gaze to Luke. "You will accompany High Lady Lena and her cohort to the lakehouse." Then to Ciara. "Call the city authorities. We'll need investigative forensics." He lowered his eyes. Tapped again. Waited. Inhaled and said into his earpiece, "High Lord, there's been an incident."

The Henly lakehouse straddled the line between Atreyu and the northern wildland. Seated at the base of a secluded dirt road, surrounded by unmanicured terrain and mossy forest, bramble pushed itself against the fence, corralling a small herd of wooly Aurethian horses. Elio stood in the kitchen and stared at a painted gelding through the bay window. Lanterns glinted, speckling the sky, and the sound of Vik running diagnostics filled the background.

"Substance scan report — mineral detection: 99.6% Cubic Avara Gypsum. Base content: lilium, camellia sinensis, limonia, lauraceae bark, water, syzygium aromaticum, hexose sugar." Vik paused for a moment. His data port hummed. He cleared his throat, speaking less robotically. "I'm happy to provide an internal diagnostic report if the investigation requires."

Peadar made a vexed, breathy sound. "Our data matches. High Lord Darius would like a copy of your report, but no further inspection of your hardware is needed."

Cael slouched in a chair with one boot propped on the tabletop. He glanced at Lena as she extended a steaming mug. He took the cup and sipped. "Thank you."

Elio noticed his lack of caution. He drank without checking for toxins. Not that his mother would harm the Imperator, but after the events earlier in the evening, Elio wouldn't have blamed him for being skeptical.

Lena placed her hand on Cael's shoulder. "I'd ask a favor of you, Imperator."

Elio turned to face them, sliding a glance at Lorelei. She met his eyes and gave a subtle shake of her head.

Cael lifted his chin, waiting.

"My son is not delicate, but he is unused to true violence. Orson…" She picked lint from her dress. "Orson is my fault. I've kept him close to me. Too close, I fear. I haven't let him spar with his siblings, or hunt with his father, or… or *grow*. He is the last child my body permitted me to carry, and I've swaddled him for an unfairly long time. I'd like you to explain to him what happened tonight."

Elio blurted, "Mother, I'm happy to talk — "

Lena silenced him with a flash of her palm. "I'd like Cael to talk to him, Elio." She nodded at Cael. "I'd like you to address the significance of the life you took. Explain to him why self-protection and quick action are invaluable."

Cael considered that. He nodded, taking another slow pull from his hot drink.

"I'm not entertaining fragility, Imperator Volkov, but I am a mother to a son who hasn't been exposed to the historical grievances between our houses. Orson doesn't understand the concept of war, or famine, or scarcity, or violence. He isn't well read like Elio, and he isn't old enough to choose an educational direction like Lorelei has. Elio was readied for you from the time he could walk, and Lorelei's interest in medicine gave her access to knowledge Orson can hardly grasp. He is a sweet, sweet boy, and he reveres you. Make him understand your decision."

"I'll talk to him," Cael said.

"Good. I don't expect you to accept my apology on behalf of an uninvolved party, but I'm appalled at what transpired tonight. Whoever attempted to bring you harm moved against House Henly and House Volkov. It was a selfish, cowardly act. Forgive me, but speaking freely, an Aurethian should be braver than resorting to *poison*." She spat the last work, scoffing indignantly. "I'm ashamed and I'm sorry."

Cael laughed a little. "No offense, High Lady, but I'm surprised it took this long."

"Why?" Lorelei asked, leaning forward to tap the table between them. "Because you parade Griean prisoners through your arena wearing Aurethian garb? Because Aurethia is a wealthy moon rich in sustenance and Griea is an industrial military complex without fertile soil? Because —"

"Enough, Lor," Lena snapped.

Lorelei continued. " — we sustain an entire system with our agriculture and refuse to give Griea handouts? Is that why, Imperator? Are you surprised because Aurethia is hated for being resourceful or because your planet has staked an invisible claim on those resources?"

Elio straightened. Tension brewed like an overfilled pot, bubbling, sizzling. He almost grabbed the back of Lorelei's chair. Almost crawled over the table and plopped between them. Cael lifted his mouth into a mean smirk and nodded slowly. The energy in the room soured. Niam gripped the handle of his blade and stood straighter, assessing the biting argument from the opposite corner of the kitchen. Peadar did not move.

After a long, silent moment, Cael stood and flattened his palms on the tabletop, lowering his broad stature to meet her eyes. "Because the citizens of Aurethia are much like you at their core, Lady Lorelei. Loud, ambitious, spoiled, and fucking ignorant."

Lorelei's top lip curled into a sneer. "How dare you," she seethed.

"I think we should reconvene in the morning," Peadar said diplomatically.

Cael swept out of the room, followed by Vik.

Elio knocked the back of his hand against the side of Lorelei's head as he walked behind her chair. "He's right," he whispered. He met her narrow glare. "You made a fool of yourself."

"And your house," their mother hissed under her breath, flushed with shame.

Across the room, Peadar sighed.

Lorelei's chin dented. Her eyes welled, but no tears fell. "He has no respect — "

"Someone tried to kill him tonight!" Elio swatted the table hard, causing his mother and sister to startle. Elio rarely raised his voice. He almost wilted but rounded on his sibling instead. "One of our people, someone loyal to Aurethia, someone loyal to *us* just tried to undo a two-hundred-year peace brokerage and you made it about status — about wealth, and access, and Aurethia's lack of fair action. You proved his point."

She pressed her mouth tightly. A tear rivered her cheek. She opened her mouth. Closed it. Tried again and failed to speak.

"An Aurethian tried to murder my fiancé," he said. Each word sharpened his teeth. Filled him with rage. "And you threw our moon's inhospitable mismanagement of resources in his face."

He scraped his hand across the table and went after Cael. Lorelei called out behind him, "I'm sorry," but he refused to acknowledge it.

Elio stormed through the cozy living room past an upholstered couch and several sitting pillows, and turned down a narrow hall, following it until he heard Cael's muffled voice. He halted and slid his hand around the side of a cracked door, easing it open. Danna stood on the patio attached to Orson's bedroom. Vik accompanied him while Cael sat on a cushioned stool, hunched over Orson's bedside.

"Aurethia and Griea have been unkind to each other for too long," Cael said, shaking his head. "Someone who probably thought I shouldn't marry your brother tried to hurt me tonight."

"Lorelei said they tried to kill you," Orson croaked.

"Kill me," Cael agreed. "Yes, I'm afraid that's what happened. Where I come from, someone who makes an attempt on your life will likely do it again, so I defended myself before whoever tried to kill me could hurt me or anyone else a second time. I'm sorry you had to see it, though."

"Why do we hate each other? Aurethia and Griea?"

Cael paused. He steepled his hands and bounced his chin on them, deliberating.

"Because we don't understand each other," Elio offered. Orson turned to look at him. Cael, ever the nightcat, only shifted his gaze, acknowledging Elio's presence with a beat of black lashes. "Long-dead politicians made us enemies, Orson. But sometimes legacy is a difficult thing to overcome."

"But you two don't hate each other. You're not... enemies." Orson looked between Cael and Elio. "What's been done that's so bad? Who did what?"

Cael tongued his cheek. He glanced at Elio and lifted a brow. *Go on,* his expression said.

Elio shrugged. "Aurethia hasn't treated Griea fairly, Griea hasn't forgiven us for it, and both our homeworlds are very good at holding grudges. It's complicated, but that's the gist."

"We've told stories that might as well be myth. Made monsters out of each other," Cael said, nodding. "Unfortunately, all stories are a little true."

"Would you kill someone who tried to hurt me? Or my brother?" Orson asked.

Cael said, "Yes," without hesitating. "But I only defend myself when it's necessary. The person who tried to poison me had every intention of taking my life. I dealt with it. One action might not look like another. You need discernment to make those judgement calls, and wisdom is a learned thing."

"I'm glad you're alive," Orson said.

Cael smiled. "Yeah, me, too. You're the littlest lion, you know that?" He reached out to tug on Orson's blanket, tucking it close to his shoulder. "But one day, you'll be like Elio, like the High Lord. For now, try not to worry about this mess, alright? That's for us to handle."

"You're doin' a shit job of it," Orson teased.

"Orson Finnen," Elio scolded, stumbling over a laugh. Orson withered at the mention of his middle name. "Don't let Mom hear you using Earthen curses. She'll blame me."

Cael laughed. The noise erupted from his nose and popped in his throat. He stood, smoothing the front of his tunic. "Get some sleep, Lord Orson."

"Goodnight, Imperator," the youngest Henly said.

Cael gestured toward the door and Vik stepped forward, trailing him past Elio.

"You okay?" Elio asked Orson. When his brother nodded, Elio breathed out, "okay," and nodded to Danna. The guard returned the gesture. Elio closed the bedroom door behind him.

To his surprise, Cael hadn't waited in the hallway. He strode away, not looking back, and disappeared into his bedchamber. Vik stepped through the doorway across from Cael's room. One door shut, then the other.

The inexplicable urge to rush into Cael's room almost overtook him. He stood in the hall, fidgeting, and waited for Peadar to call him back to the kitchen, or his mother to holler, or Lorelei to slink through the living room, but the lakehouse stood in unfathomable quiet. Silence thick enough to wrap around his skull and squeeze.

Elio didn't know how long he stood there, considering what he might do next. He retired to his own bedroom and watched the sky fill with lanterns through his window.

The night inched onward.

He thought of a thousand things. Cael's hand following a skinny cat's long body, and his laughter at the bakery. How Cael licked sugar from the side of his pinky and walked with his head tilted back, studying three stories of bookshelves in the Planetary Library. The complete separation between that Cael — the Cael who hummed as he ate pastries, who bent to touch a flower on the roadway, and the Imperator of Griea who slit someone's throat without a second thought — formed a canyon in Elio's mind. It was bridged with their sparring session, and their first meeting, and the sliver of intimacy at the onsen, and the slow erosion of Cael's guarded exterior. *How did we get here?* Elio scrubbed his hand over his face. The smell of freshly spilled blood, buckets of it, still clung to his clothes. He stripped and took a shower, adjusting the water until heat reddened his back, and then dressed in loose sleepwear.

Someone tried to kill him. Elio turned the thought inside out. It jarred him, how he went still, spoke it aloud. "Someone tried to kill him," whispered in his empty bedroom. He'd said it to Lorelei earlier. Thought it repeatedly. "Someone tried..."

But the emotional flood came late. Elio was too busy considering motive, optics, defense, public statements, scrutiny. He was too busy testing his family — raising that glass of tea to his mouth to see who might jump up to stop him, who might know the poison was present, relieved when no one did — he was too preoccupied with *not* processing the act itself, too deep in his own psyche to properly parse a chilling, brutal fact: Cael could've died tonight.

Elio darted into the hall. His heartbeat was an ocean in his ears, almost drowning out the disapproving sound Peadar made from his place on the couch. Elio didn't bother with an explanation, and surprisingly, Peadar didn't bother trying to stop him. "Be wise," was all the General said. Elio grasped the knob on Cael's door, elated to find it unlocked, and pushed it open.

Darkness greeted him. Red and orange pinpricks winked through the window, the only light besides Mercy's dull glow and Draitune's partial ring skimming the horizon. Something warm and familiar hit his sternum. Cael palmed his chest, slamming Elio into the wall, and then a knife met his throat.

"It's me," Elio blurted.

Cael pressed the cool metal closer. "Could've knocked."

He felt like a man possessed. Every rational thought was gone, replaced by the simple, delirious need to seal himself against Cael, to make sure he was blood-warmed and alive, to feel the leap of his heartbeat. Cael wore nothing except gauzy joggers. Elio's hand to his obliques made him flinch. He flexed around the knife's handle, each finger lifting and curling.

As his eyesight adjusted, the outline of Cael's slanted eyebrows grew clearer. His chiseled face, held in rapt concentration, searching, questioning, softened when Elio wrapped his hand beneath Cael's pectoral, gripping his ribcage.

"I'm not poisonous," Elio whispered.

"What're you doing here, Elio?" Blade to neck. Harder, firmer. Cael's breath coasted his mouth.

Elio leaned forward, enduring the stinging pinch of metal against his throat. "I came to see you."

"I've gathered that. And?"

"Don't be dense. Why else would someone sneak into their fiancé's room in the middle of the night?"

Cael tipped his face closer, snarling. "After the day I've had — "

"You left your door unlocked," Elio mocked, snorting defiantly. "Or were you expecting someone else?"

The knife slid upward, pressing against the underside of his jaw. "You think Peadar allowed me to have a lock on my door? You're smarter than that."

Elio swallowed. This was not going how he imagined. "You could've died today," he said. A strained, strangled confession. Vulnerability, regardless of the situation, had never been Elio's strong suit. He moved his hand from Cael's chest to the base of his shoulder. Carefully, he eased closer, clasped his palm around Cael's nape, and brought their foreheads together.

Cael's temper cooled. The blade drew back an inch. "I can shake off a little poison."

"Someone tried to kill you," Elio bit.

"Is that what you came here to say?"

Had you executed an ounce of restraint, we could be interrogating the assailant right now. Elio held his tongue. *If you'd let Peadar arrest the staff before cutting down that server, we could've squashed more than one loyalist.* He ignored the boot-knife threatening his trachea and gripped Cael's wrist with his free hand, dislodging the weapon.

"Come light a lantern with me," Elio said.

Cael rolled his forehead against Elio's, expression torn between confusion and surprise. His mouth curved crookedly, and he gave a buttery, punchy laugh. "You're serious?"

"I am."

"*Now?*" Cael lowered the knife awkwardly and glanced down at himself.

"Right now," Elio said. He worked the dagger out of Cael's grasp, which earned him a stubborn frown, and tossed it onto the dresser. He slid out from between wall and hard chest and took Cael's hand, tugging him into the hall.

Vik threw open the door to his bedroom.

"No," Cael said, flashing his free hand.

At the end of the hall, Peadar shot to his feet.

Elio answered the general with the same gesture. "No," he said to Peadar, and yanked Cael through the kitchen. He grabbed one of the decorative lanterns abandoned on the counter, stuffed an oil dish into his pocket, and slapped a matchbook into Cael's other hand. "Hold that."

Through the front door and to the left of the house, Aurethian horses peered up at the cinder-stoked sky. The surface of the still lake reflected the same image, capturing a spattering of faraway fire. Deep night shaded the grass and the fence. Their bare feet slid through the pasture. Snouts huffed and toads bellowed. Dragonflies skimmed the water. Once they were a distance from the house, Elio stopped and dropped Cael's hand.

"Light this," Elio said. He placed the oil dish in the center of his palm and smoothed the wick upright.

Cael struck a match. Orange fanned his face. Shadow danced on nose-bridge, slanted cheek, spidery eyelashes, deepening every harsh, fine line. He brought flame to wick then shook the fire out. Light bloomed, swaying between them until Elio carefully lowered the paper lantern over the slow-burning oil, and fastened the bottom shut with two sticky tabs.

Light shot through star-shaped cutouts speckled around the lantern. A few streaked like asteroids, others were long, some were tiny and round. Metallic foil rimmed each image and the paper itself shone unmistakable red, glowing like a beacon in the middle of the forest.

"This will be..." Elio paused to lick his bottom lip. He met Cael's arctic eyes over the top of the lantern. "This will be challenging. Change, me and you, our families, all of it. We're going to run into loyalists who are convinced our union is a death sentence, and I'm sure we'll come across Griean separatists who despise the idea of Aurethian leadership. But I believe in us." He soaked that statement in as much heartfelt truth as he could. "And I believe in my people."

Cael shifted his hand beneath the lantern and lifted, pushing the star upward. It floated on a soft breeze, glinting, spinning. "Do you believe in me?"

Elio swallowed. "Yes," he said, and it was the truth.

Since birth, Elio had known he would marry the Volkov heir. It was the only constant he was allotted. Cael was the only promise the universe kept. And all his life, he'd made peace with the likelihood that he would not enjoy, nonetheless *love* his husband. He would marry, rule, and serve to keep Aurethia safe, to ensure a sophisticated, peaceful union between two Great Houses, and bring sustenance and stability to their homeworlds.

Upon arrival, Cael eviscerated whatever stint of servitude Elio had imagined and replaced it with a far more promising future. One where Elio was happily married. One where two equal houses held stewardship over Aurethia and Griea, and the Greater Universe was better for it. One where his heart was safe.

"*Yes*," Elio said again, deliberately firm, and grasped Cael's cheek. "Yes, I do."

Cael blinked. His mouth parted and something frightful crossed his face. That shard of panic vanished, and he leaned down to capture Elio's lips in an unfairly cautious kiss. Every thought emptied. Elio breathed through his nose and shot to his tiptoes, hauling Cael closer, feeling across the smooth curve of his sheared skull. The Imperator was greedy with his hands, a vivid contrast to the way his mouth went soft against Elio, testing, waiting. He grabbed at Elio's waist, long fingers eclipsing his hipbones, running beneath his shirt, digging into his ribcage.

"Peadar can see us. Your mother can, too," Cael muttered.

"Is modesty important on Griea?" Elio snagged Cael's bottom lip with his teeth.

The Imperator huffed, flicking his attention around the property. His gaze flitted back to the barn once, twice. Elio took his hand and pulled him toward it. They melted into the darkness on the backside of the building, facing away from the lakehouse. Elio's blood thickened, dragging through his veins. Every fast round through the highway inside him sieved through to the rest of his body. The marshy climate muddying the lakehouse leaked past his thin clothes. He swallowed to clear the dizzying clamor in his chest, but it was no use. He turned to find Cael, to haul him closer, but there, encased in shadow, the Imperator's shyness disappeared.

One hand at the base of Elio's neck, the other wrapped around his thigh, Cael crashed against him. This kiss was searing. Leagues beyond the tentative touch he'd offered Elio a moment ago. Elio's heart was a swollen thing, beating hard and fast against the backside of his ribcage. He sealed himself against Cael, body-to-body, and followed the tender, insistent press and pull of their lips. His thumb followed the seam of their mouths, and Cael managed to steal a breath he didn't remember taking.

A hot gust dampened his throat. Elio drank it. The world narrowed down to limbic relativity — Cael's thumb skimming his nipple, shirt rucked to his armpit, flesh fit together, Cael's other hand drifting higher, carding through his hair. *Cael.*

When he gripped, angling Elio's head back, Elio opened his eyes. Pleasant pain rooted where Cael's fist tightened in his hair. They stayed like that, panting against each other, until Cael finally said, "I'll almost die more often."

Elio blinked. "What?"

"If I get to have you like this. If almost dying is the cost."

"I've been throwing myself at you for weeks," Elio admitted, breathing through a bewildered laugh. "Figured you didn't want me."

Cael's feverish grin faded, replaced by a wild, burning intensity Elio would never unsee. Never rid himself of. It would haunt him, that look. In the dark, like this, flushed and unfettered, Cael was terrifyingly handsome. He guided Elio closer, face tipped toward him.

"Want you?" He clucked his tongue, sliding his hand along the taut flesh between Elio's hipbones. "I wish I just wanted you. But I crave you, Elio. It's like the stars themselves designed you for me, like fate handed Wonder a blueprint." He paused. The clumsy tug on Elio's sweatpants made his head spin. Cael's palm slipped, diving, gliding along his center. There was nothing separating them. No underwear, no fabric or cloth. Cael cradled his core, pressing against wet, warm flesh. His wolfish smile faltered. "I wasn't prepared to…" His throat flexed, denting with a slow swallow. His hand stilled. "To *feel* like this. You've… you've wrecked me, Elio."

Liquid flame climbed Elio's spine. His skin pebbled, and he couldn't fathom going untouched for a second longer. "Show me how I've wrecked you," he demanded, craning to catch Cael's mouth. He reached between them, seizing Cael's wrist, guiding his hand closer, *there*, encasing the molten heat between his thighs. "Show me, and I'll tell you how Sunder dreamed you for me, how the universe conspired to grant me a wish."

Cael's breath hitched. His mouth bumped Elio's chin, hunting for another kiss. He swept his hand in a perfect, arcing motion, grazing the crest of his most private skin with the heel of his palm. "What wish?"

"You," Elio admitted, kissing him to keep from laughing, or sobbing, or falling to his knees. Searing pleasure reached deep, following Cael's scarred hand, branding bone. "I wished for you."

Cael did not speak after that. His mouth was a searching, claiming thing, pulling at Elio's lips. When he leaned forward, hitching the side of his hand between the soft, warm cut of Elio's sex, Elio went boneless. He let his weight go heavy against the cool wood and tried to choke back the moan threatening in his throat. The moment Cale speared him, plunging his long fingers deep, deep inside him, Elio could not stamp out the small cry tumbling from him to Cael, sent on a shredded breath. Elio shot to his toes. The slow, mindful drag of Cael's middle and pointer digits curled, probing where none had gone before.

Elio had only ever done this alone. Only ever fingered himself in his bed or in the bathtub, fantasizing about nameless, faceless people with blurry, basic bodies. He never imagined it would be Cael's pale hand driving up and into him, pulling pleasure through the untouched entrance at the base of his body. Someone gorgeous and formidable. Someone dangerous and *his*.

"Have you done this before?" Cael asked, sinking in again, reaching for something, somewhere.

Elio breathed hard against Cael's chin. He swallowed thickly. "Never like this, no."

"Did you wait for me?" His gaze softened. Pain darkened his expression, as if Elio offered something he could not give back.

"No," Elio lied, darting his tongue across his top lip. "I don't require coddling, Imperator."

"I wouldn't call this coddling," Cael muttered, driving his point with a hard thrust, rubbing the dome at the base of his palm against the sensitive pearl hooded above Elio's entrance.

Elio dug blunt fingernails into Cael's nape. With his spare hand, he let go of Cael's wrist and reached, sliding his palm over Cael's clothed crotch, gripping the hard line of him through his sweatpants. He'd touched someone else like this before. One of the Aurethian guard. He'd been sixteen, fumbling around on a seater with someone twice his age, giving a drunk soldier a hand job while he ground against the man's thigh. Elio had been wearing corduroy trousers and cotton underwear — unable to feel much of anything at all. This was different. Watching Cael's pelvis jump, feeling his hand flex while it was buried inside him. This was intimacy Elio had never known.

"Let me have you," Elio whispered. It was a faint, accidental command. One he thought but didn't mean to say.

Cael pushed into his touch. He tongued at his mouth, kissing him hotly while his hand slowed, moving in and out of Elio's body in a languid knuckle-deep metronome. The *pleasure*. The spilling wine-thick warmth coating the entirety of Elio seemed to crawl through his stomach, down his legs, and knead in his chest. It was a heat he'd never felt. This blinding daze that clogged his mind and made him shake. It was like a chase. Like he'd jumped from a high place and was somewhere in the middle of the freefall.

I need —

Elio didn't know what he needed. But he wanted to touch Cael. To make him shake, too. He dragged Cael's sweatpants down and cupped the underside of his shaft, wrapping around him in a firm, easy grip. Cael's mouth went slack against his own. A breath shot out, sudden and ungentle. He shifted his free hand to brace against the barn.

And *oh, exactly*. Elio wanted that, exactly. He wanted Cael's brow to knit and his gaze to go fuzzy and dark. He wanted Cael's throat to roll and his tongue to slide over his teeth, for him to tremble and pant. He wanted Cael to buck into the second stroke, pitching into his fist, mirroring a motion Elio imagined differently, within himself.

"Here?" Cael asked raggedly. It was a humble and sweet thing to ask. *Here?* As if their first time together should be on satin sheets. As if the elegance of the act mattered to Elio at all.

"Here, now," Elio whimpered, hating himself for the plea in his voice.

But it was all Cael needed. His hand slipped out of Elio, leaving him silken and wanting. And in another swift movement, Elio was turned by his

waist. His thin fabric sleep-pants were pushed down, exposing him to the
night. Embarrassment scorched through him. He placed one hand on the
barn, the same place Cael's had been a moment ago, and followed the
natural inclination to bend, arch, and bare himself.

The press of Cael against his center sent a shockwave through him. The
blunt momentum of one body entering another, splitting tender flesh,
tearing the thin, untouched tissue stretched across the interior of him
caused Elio to give a small shout of surprise. And the way Cael stilled, how
he pushed, buried, stopped, and lowered his forehead to Elio's shoulder,
made Elio realize he had been caught in a lie. Surely Cael recognized the
clumsy bow of his body. His fiancé could likely identify the give of something never breached, widening for him as he pressed his pelvis snug
against the soft cushion of Elio's rear.

Instead of teasing, or chiding, or worrying, Cael grazed his teeth across
the juncture of Elio's taut neck. "You're everything I've ever wanted," he
rasped, baritone with lust, pregnant with something heavier. Something
permanent.

Elio didn't know what to do. He didn't want to breathe too heavily or
too quickly. He didn't want to acknowledge the leak of something metallic
and wet. The bright flashpoint of pain, there and gone in a blink. He just
wanted to focus on the weight of Cael inside him. Wanted to burrow into
his own body and turn every nerve toward the sensation of someone occu-
pying the most secret, self-contained part of him, and reconstruct this odd,
naïve fear into what he'd always hoped sex might be: simple and primal. He
thought when this moment finally came that he would know what to do.
That he would understand the mechanisms of a dance he'd never done
before, because he was hardwired to understand it.

But Elio couldn't get far enough away from himself to let any natural
cognizance take control. His mind raced. He wondered about the finality of
Cael truly knowing what his body looked like. What Elio was, in a sense.
And what he wasn't. He imagined Cael might be disappointed to receive a
partner less finessed than what was promised. Less educated about intimacy, less physically forthcoming. He did not know what to ask for, or what
to give. He knew what he wanted. He knew what he'd seen in media and
read in books. But none of that was real, and this very much was.

Cael smoothed his hand along the swift curve of Elio's waist and
followed his stomach to the very center of his chest, flattening his hand
there.

"Your heart is a bird," he whispered, angling his mouth against the outer edge of Elio's ear. "I can feel it here," he said, then dropped his hand, nestling it between Elio's spread thighs, framing where they were joined with the base of his fingers, "and here."

Elio could've fainted. Thought he might. The impact of that statement left him breathless and spinning. How carefully and naturally Cael *touched* him. It was maddening.

"Do you feel this?" Cael asked. His breath ghosted the thrumming tendon on the underside of Elio's jaw. He punctuated the question with a tentative roll of his hips, easing out, sliding in. His thumb circled the pinnacle of Elio's sex. "Do you?"

"Yes," Elio gasped out. And he did. *He did*. Cael played him like an instrument, and every fiber of Elio's being vibrated.

The fever of their encounter thickened in the balmy air. A thousand lanterns lit the sky, and Elio let his head fall back, granting Cael better access to his throat. He reached above and behind, touching Cael's skull, counting the rhythmic strokes, pouring into and out of his body. The gentle swipe of his thumb unharnessed whatever nervous flitting taxed Elio's thoughts, and stoked a pulsing, ringing pleasure to chime in his groin, growing bolder and brighter with the speed of their collision. The nature of their movements grew fluid and easy, firm and expected. The ache radiating behind Elio's tailbone lessened. The anxious, rigid way he held himself went loose and buoyant, dollish in Cael's strong embrace.

Cael muffled a moan against his neck. He dropped his face to Elio's shoulder and sucked a mark below the curve of it, right over the cavern where his shoulder blades dived. His breath came short. Elio felt him swell. Felt the uneven, rougher drag of him, and almost crumbled when Cael lifted his hand and swatted the top of his sex, earning an unkempt yelp, sparking the sloshing, syrupy pleasure to ignite and explode. Cael kept his hand there, covering Elio, working what was exposed while he filled what wasn't.

Elio didn't mean to, but his hand dropped from where he held Cael's skull and covered the knuckles tucked between his thighs, holding onto him. Feeling the ministrations of Cael's wicked fingers. He wanted to pry them away almost as much as he wanted to keep them there. Wanted to plunge them inside his body alongside Cael's swollen shaft. Wanted to suck on them, and sit on them, and bite them. His body seemed to come apart and back together in an instant.

It was different with someone else. With Cael.

Alone, Elio's release washed over him, quick and forgettable. But this. *This*. Elio hadn't expected his chest to cave with the momentum of it.

Hadn't expected to dig into the barnwood and gasp through the start of a noise he'd never made before. Hadn't realized he would grapple for Cael's wrist and squeeze, holding his breath until it hurt, until each muscle in his body wound tight enough to snap, then proceeded to unspool.

The floundering squeeze in his lower half brought a strike of leftover pain from the initial breach, but Elio barely noticed it. His mind was sugar and starlight. Every electric bolt through his skeleton dulled to a pleasant hum, glowing beneath his skin. His body melted. He felt the spill of Cael inside him. The sudden heat and wetness. Heard his fiancé breathe and gasp, groan and whimper. It was such a human thing. Listening to Cael's expertly crafted control fray, and his façade drop. He was not Imperator. He wasn't warlord, or prince, or the Griean heir. He was Elio's, and only Elio's.

Elio stayed still. He leaned his forehead against the side of the barn and watched lantern light wink above the lake. Pressed against him, folded over him, Cael breathed.

"You okay?" Cael dragged his hand away from Elio's sore, soaked center. He didn't move, though. Didn't dislodge himself.

Elio's throat worked. For a second, he thought he might cry. He didn't know why. Couldn't place it, that sea of emotion, but he kept it at bay and nodded. "You?"

"Yeah, but I'd like to take you inside," Cael said, hoarse and far too composed. He rested his mouth against Elio's shoulder.

Elio wanted to watch the lanterns. He wanted to stay in the pasture and do everything all over again, except he wanted to look upon Cael's face. He wanted to have him without their joggers around their ankles, without Cael's near-death experience acting as their catalyst. He wanted their prophetic, too big union to be normal and safe.

"Then take me inside," Elio whispered.

CHAPTER SIXTEEN

CAEL

Lanternlight dappled the midnight sky. Cael watched the tiny, man-made stars glimmer above the lake, tossed over the treeline like faraway fireflies. The sky danced with them, yellow, red, gold, orange, and violet, while they crossed the pasture and stopped at the threshold of the mudroom.

Cael helped Elio balance, laughing a little while they hosed off their dirty feet with a spigot attached to the front of the house. He took his hand, following Elio into the shadowy entryway, past the living room where Peadar graciously pretended not to notice them, down the far hall, and into Elio's bedchamber.

Cael set his dialect device on the nightstand. For a brief moment, Cael felt halfway to waking. Like he might be trapped in some sort of dreamlike, liminal space. But then Elio turned and took off his shirt, and Cael saw the blotch on his shoulder blade. He remembered resisting the urge to bite. Remembered looking down at the translucent red smeared on him, stark even in rural darkness.

So yes, they'd done what they'd done, and Cael hadn't stopped them, and he wished he had. Wished he'd taken Elio by the face and kissed him quiet. Took him inside, laid him out on a nice bed, undressed him properly, made love to him slowly. But eagerness got the best of them both, and despite Elio's reluctance to be truthful about it, Cael understood what the blood meant, what Elio's frantic, accidental cry meant, what his blown pupils and doe-eyed surprise meant.

Cael felt dirty. There was no reason to. Not really, anyway. But a part of him wanted to go back in time and stop himself. Save himself. For this, here, now.

Elio stood near the edge of the bed. The tips of his fingers rested on the neatly made comforter, and he stared at it, idly scratching the pillowy duvet. He didn't turn on the disc-lamp. Mercy's light shafted through the window and lanterns gilded the glass. Cael watched gold and silver fall across the cut and curve of Elio's fine shape. His words from earlier echoed.

Show me how I've wrecked you.

If only he could make Elio understand the gravity of it. What he'd undone in the matter of half a cycle. How he'd reached into Cael's chest and reprogrammed his heart. Everything Cael was meant to become was shattered at his feet now. The taking of Aurethia, the conquest of a lifetime, the mission he'd been born and trained to execute — dismantled at the first taste of affection Elio tossed his way. Cael stared at him. There was no way to show Elio the wreckage. No way to make him see the sacrifice. And maybe that wasn't the right word. Maybe it wasn't sacrifice. All this chatter about fate, and prophecy, and love, and Wonder wiggled free of Cael's practical mindset and made him consider something as magical and juvenile as destiny.

Elio Henly, his destiny. Elio Henly, his prize. Elio Henly, his partner in everything, in all ways, for the rest of his life. Elio Henly, the clever, brilliant, sophisticated lion cub that'd put his claw to Cael's chest and caused his heart to swell up and change.

How dare you, he wanted to say, *make me fear losing something more than myself.*

In a slicing glance, Elio looked up. His lashes flicked. He conjured a hard, burning stare. One fingernail scratched the bedding.

Cael felt that look in his depths. It crawled over him. Prickled his skin; dropped like a stone through his stomach.

"I love you, Cael," Elio said. It wasn't a warm statement. Elio said it like he'd say *I can do this.* He said it like he was meeting a challenge.

"And I love you, Elio," Cael confessed, matching his fiery, fanged exterior with strained strength of his own.

Elio's throat dented. His voice softened. "I'm not supposed to."

It was such an easy, devastating thing to admit. They were manacled together by galactic policy. They were meant to advocate for their individual houses. Keep each other in check. Endure each other for a lifetime. But that wasn't the case, was it?

Cael did not feel his feet lift, or his knees bend, but he said, "Neither am I," and jolted forward.

Elio yielded to the kiss Cael planted on him. He clutched Cael's face, splaying his hands over cheekbones and temples. The nervous, startled boy out by the barn was gone. He kissed like he wanted to devour Cael, like he wanted to be devoured in turn. And Cael wanted to consume. Wanted to root himself inside Elio, and carve into him, take hold of a bone or two, and keep him safe. He wanted wildly. It reshaped who he'd been before Aurethia — Griean frost warmed under the Aurethian torch Elio set to his soul. He felt like a tarantula peeling itself out of an old carapace, like something old made new. It was awfully confusing, how young he felt, how naïve and stupid and foolish he felt, and how the magnitude of his emotion for Elio made him feel eternal. Like he'd come and gone, like he'd stay and go again, and Elio would be the constant he'd always orbit.

"Never let me go," Elio gasped out, sounding more like himself, a little undone, a little ruthless.

"Never," Cael said, and he would say it a hundred times if he had to, "I'll never let you go."

They pawed at the sweatpants still slung over each other's hips. Pushed them down and swayed toward the bed. Elio went to speak, but Cael took his waist and tossed him onto the comforter, snatching one ankle, then the other, and hauled him back toward the edge of the mattress. Fright crossed Elio's face at first. Shock or shame. Cael was too quick to allow it to stick. Too insistent. He saw their conjoined spend wetting Elio's center. Saw the remnant of his own spillage drip down the crease of Elio's thigh. His chest emptied. Every unclean thought ballooned and burst, and Cael wanted to be monstrous, wanted to claim this prince like some kind of beast.

Elio made a small, unsure noise. Cael ignored that tiny whine. His knees thumped the floor. He cupped the back of Elio's thigh and leaned forward, opening his mouth over Elio's core. Elio's breath cut the air, sucked in with startling quickness. The first swipe of Cael's tongue had him seizing. The second was a string around his spine, pulling upward. He threw his head back, kiss-bitten mouth parting, shaking. When his pelvis came away from the bed, Cael leveraged his spare hand to curve around Elio's hip, pinning him down.

Rich salt. Sweet, fragrant juice, and sweat, and the tang of what he'd left behind. Iron, too. Cael buried his face between Elio's legs. He lapped at the ripe slit of his sex. Worked his tongue inside, dropping his jaw to probe deeper, taste where no one else had harvested. He moaned against him, tugging him closer, grazing the cleft of him with his teeth.

Elio gripped the bedding. The short, sharp beginning of a loud sound spouted from him. He cut off the noisy groan with his hand, clapping his palm over his mouth. Cael lifted his gaze. He studied Elio's clenching stomach. Watched him curl away from the mattress and drop his quivering hand, cupping Cael's nape.

What a thing. Doing this to him.

Cael coiled closer, spurred by that absent touch. The arm around Elio's hip flexed and he stretched his hand beneath Elio's hipbone. He pressed his thumb to the crown of Elio's lovely sex, exposing the nested nerves bundled beneath his hood. He flattened his tongue against it. Sucked and nibbled. When Elio gasped and squirmed, Cael closed his mouth around that small, wet bead, tonguing and sucking until Elio's reddened face screwed into beautiful, delirious agony. A cry almost sawed out, but Elio held it back, only allowing the briefest hint of it to lurch up and out of him. His orgasm was a hot, clenching jolt. He spasmed, soaking Cael's chin. One leg lifted and the other fell open before Elio's thighs threatened to shut around his ears. Cael pried him apart, mouth still latched to the sensitive summit of him.

All the blood in Cael's body had sailed south the moment he'd glimpsed his own spend sliding out of Elio, and the time he'd spent on his knees only tested his patience.

Elio moved his trembling hand away from Cael's nape and guided him up, bringing Cael's glossed mouth to his own. It was a long, sensual kiss. Cael indulged him, crawled over him, followed him as he slid up the bed. Elio searched his mouth, sucked his tongue, sipped at the flavor of their coupling, and moaned hotly against slippery lips. Cael kept his eyes open. He stared at Elio's blushing, freckled face and sweat-damp brow. Watched him crack his eyes open. There was something illicit and bold in his dazed gaze. Scented like sex, matchstrike, barnwood, and candlebell — naked, quaking, blushing, and still eager — Cael could not have dreamed him up. Could not have imagined someone more perfect, and electric, and seductive, and *his*.

"Have me," Elio exhaled. He swept his hands down Cael's chest, over his ribcage, holding him there.

Again and again, Cael thought but did not say. *For the rest of my life.*

Cael widened his knees, spreading Elio beneath him. The bed dipped.

The solid stone frame holding it did not budge. When Elio reached lower, trailing his fingertips along the matching tattoos inked over the bottom of Cael's obliques, he paused, resting his forehead against Elio's temple. They breathed together.

Disrupted by Mercy's glow and the slow lantern light blotting the sky outside, they shared the thin darkness together.

Elio lifted his hips, grinding against Cael. Asking; seeking.

Cael had never been in the throes of true intimacy. Physicality had always been a celebratory release after the Tupinaire, or a way to unwind after a hard training session at the War College. It had always been cold and quick, or angry and impersonal, or messy and regrettable. Cael had never felt the press of a someone *real*. Not like this. Never wanted to align himself into every divot, curve, muscle, and hollow. Elio slid his palm along Cael's hard length. That alone, just the barest graze of skin, made Cael angle forward, searching for connection. Elio's gasp filled the room. His hand closed around Cael. He lifted off the bed, parting around him in a slow, shared movement. Elio rolled upward, and Cael pitched his waist, slotting into his body.

Elio was tight and warm. Cael felt his rabbit-fast heart, felt every breath. He could've spent right then, truly. Could've emptied himself and gone limp. But Elio whined like a nymph. He gripped Cael's triceps. Gave another pitch of his pelvis, rocking against him, pulling Cael deeper, and Cael wanted this to last. Wanted to make a memory of it, something he could return to.

The slow, tender thrust of body into body. The lilting moan carving out of Elio, so quiet and contained, private and only meant for them. The stretch of his tan leg as Cael sat up, hauling Elio into his lap, propping the hook of his knee into the crook of an elbow. Mouth to calf, higher, brushing the elegant arch of Elio's foot. Bending him, opening him wider, sinking in until there was no more room, nothing left for Elio to take, and watching pleasure, heat, desire cross Elio's face. The hard, slow roll of Cael's waist plunged into the pulsing heat of him until he was lost in it, possessed by it. It was surreal in a way. Listening to Elio breathe, watching his chest arch upward. Cael took a rosebud nipple into his mouth and Elio's lower-half squeezed.

"You're mine," Elio gasped out. He met Cael's every move.

Cael fell over him, caged him against the bed. Elio gripped his shoulder, slid his hand higher, cupping the back of his sheared skull. Cael nuzzled his throat. His control slipped and he chased the spark of pleasure skipping down his spine, quickening his pace, searching for release.

Elio's voice became a frantic, boyish thing, halfway to a growl, somewhere close to a whimper. "You're mine," he said again, breathing against Cael's ear, then pressing the claim like a brand to his neck. "You're mine." Blunt teeth met taut flesh. Elio nursed the bite, and Cael found himself tunneling toward a bright, explosive high.

That alone — being called his, feeling Elio's teeth sink in. That was all it took for Cael to muffle a low noise against Elio's damp skin, punching bruises against slender hips, chasing a divine collapse he could not forfeit, and halt, pushing until he was buried to the hilt, flush against Elio's pelvis, digging his fingertips into the meat of Elio's leg.

Elio sucked in a short breath. He went rigid, then boneless.

Sex wasn't meant to be pretty or clean, but Cael appreciated the duvet beneath them, how Elio could sink naked into something much softer than barnwood. He pressed a kiss to Elio's jaw, then felt a warm hand on his face, pulling him toward a tired, wanting mouth.

They rearranged themselves. Elio tried to smother the wince of discomfort when Cael pulled out, but Cael still held fast to it. Still needed to ask him what tonight had been. The truth of it. They laid on their sides, legs tangled, facing each other, kissing, humming, cooing.

Cael gave their bodies a chance to slacken before he set his thumb to Elio's cheekbone and said, "You *did* wait."

Elio's nostrils flared. His viridian eyes searched Cael's face. "I didn't wait for you," he said, exhaling. "I just... I didn't have the opportunity to lose it like I wanted — "

"You didn't *lose* anything."

"You know what I mean. I never met anyone up to the task."

"You should've told me," Cael whispered. His smile was soft but faraway, mind circling all the things he'd done with other people, all the time he'd spent with mouths and bodies he hardly remembered.

Elio furrowed his brow. "I didn't want delicacy."

"I fucked you behind a barn, darling. I could've at least given you *decency*," he said, laughing into the small space between them.

Elio laughed, too. It was genuine, splendid, ugly laughter, the too loud kind he had to smother into a pillow. "Intimacy is different on Aurethia," he hissed, swatting Cael playfully. "I never courted anyone. I never bothered to ask anyone out, or — or *try*, I guess. I've had an experience or two. I hooked up with a guard at one of my parent's parties, and a fisherman's daughter in Nadhas."

Oh. Cael swallowed uncomfortably. He knew the unspoken question on Elio's face. His eyes needled, pricking him through the shadow. "Sex isn't considered *intimate* on Griea. It's an," he didn't know the Aurethian word for it, so he said, "outlet," in Griean. "People will seek whatever their looking for in whoever they find satisfying. Usually, exclusivity is earned during a new living arrangement. Once you move in with a partner or a group, you've decided on them."

"Well, you're clearly well-versed," Elio whispered, leaning closer, breathing against Cael's chin. His smile was soft and shockingly curious. "How many people have you been with?"

"A few," he said, too embarrassed to admit the truth. Plenty. "Never in a bed." He shrugged, dousing loose, forgettable memories.

Eighteen, propping a woman on a bench in the underbelly of the stadium after the Tupinaire. Fifteen, listening to the suckling sound of a head bobbing between his legs, seated next to his cousin in a luxury space transport, watching a young man bounce in Bracken's lap. Last year, being taken from behind against a cold, rocky outcrop by one of his father's legionaries while hunting great sheep on Goren.

"You'll teach me." Elio tried to mask the bashful question at the end of his statement, the lingering inflection in his voice. But that alone — his untapped desire; his hunger for their future — squashed the echo of Cael's mediocre sex life.

Cael dusted his knuckles across Elio's mouth. "I never pursued anything real because I knew it wouldn't matter. You were here, on Aurethia, and I was yours before I ever met you."

Heat smoldered in Elio's playful gaze. He clutched Cael's palm and pressed a kiss to the back of his hand. "I thought you wouldn't want me. I knew you'd take me as a spouse, but as... As a partner, as a lover... I just thought you wouldn't," he confessed, quieter now. It was the same sentiment from earlier repeated with such raw earnestness it almost cleaved Cael in two. "Am I what you expected?"

Cael looked at him for a long time. "No," he decided, thumbing at the corner of his mouth. Elio's breath tickled the gaps between his fingers. "But I walked off that transport and I saw you and I couldn't look away — I still can't look away." He realized Griean stoked his tongue, that he'd fallen into his native language. He knitted his brow, sputtering out an apology, "Sorry, I — "

"I heard you," Elio said in perfect Griean. He fit his palm around the side of Cael's face and slid closer, eating up the space between them.

"This," Cael whispered, tapping Elio's temple, then he dropped his hand and tapped his chest, "and this, I fell for. Your mind, your heart." He nosed at Elio's cheek, stole a kiss, and spoke as their lips parted, still resting against each other. "But this," he rasped, curling his arm around Elio's waist, gripping his backside, hauling him closer, "I've *wanted*."

Elio curled cat-like against him. "Why didn't you, then? In Nadhas? In the training chamber? In the meadow? At the onsen? Why didn't you — "

"Because," he started, and stopped to think. *Because I didn't want to have you and hurt you. Because I didn't want to abandon my duty. Because you deserved better.* "Because I wanted you to decide." And that was true, too.

"Oh, I'd decided," Elio assured. Another laugh, sweet and small, chased off the seriousness of their conversation. "But you're a gentleman, apparently."

"Better than a barbarian," Cael muttered through a lazy grin.

"I'll take the barbarian, too." Elio gave him another long, tender kiss. "I'll take it all, Imperator."

A SWAYING CURTAIN OBSTRUCTED the storm-silvered sunlight passing through the window in Elio's lakeside bedchamber. Cael cracked his eyes open and stretched, searching for the same soft, freckled skin he'd mapped the night before. The sheet was cool beneath his palm. He touched Elio's dented pillow, then lifted his head and glanced around the room, disappointed to find it empty.

Neatly folded clothes were stacked on the corner of the dresser. Black clothes; his clothes. Either Elio retrieved them, or Vik brought them. He flopped back down and stared at the ceiling, drenched in memory. Everything blurred. His endocrine system had gone haywire, lit with hormonal — and against his better judgement — emotional signals. He chewed his lip. Steadied his breathing.

Out by the barn, Elio had clawed at him. They'd pushed their clothes away, came together like they were starving.

Cael pinched the bridge of his nose and heaved a sigh.

He remembered the soft curve of Elio's waist against his palm, the taste of his shoulder. How he braced against the building and arched into Cael. He hadn't expected to consummate their courtship against a wood-built barn in a pasture for an audience of horses, but he couldn't do anything about that now.

"Shit," he murmured.

Cael should've known better. Should've guarded his heart. Should've coughed up an ounce of self-control and avoided exactly *this*. Love, desire, sex, passion. Those were ingredients for heartbreak, and a surefire way to compromise the very mission he was born to complete.

It was an honest thing, being with him like that. Relenting between Elio's legs, struggling to keep quiet, pouring every desperate drop of lust and savagery into his fiancé's body. The night itself felt ravaged by intimacy, sick with it. And they were — ravaged, sick — fated for each other, promised to each other. A lifetime of hoping, wanting, daydreaming made their coupling primal. Prophetic, almost. And now Cael wanted nothing more than to drag Elio back to bed. Watch his mouth tremble, and his chest heave, hear his voice brittle. The tight, hot squeeze of his fiancé's honed body sluiced through his mind. He still felt the ghost of Elio's hand clutching the back of his head. Still felt his kiss-bruised mouth brushing the shell of his ear. *You're mine*, the lion cub had gasped out, *you're mine*.

Cael swallowed thickly and turned his gaze to the window, distancing his consciousness from fresh memories and the riot they stoked low in his gut. Worse, in his chest.

Get a hold of yourself. He sat up on the edge of the bed. *Glory for Griea*, he told himself, mentally repeating the statement like a mantra. *God is in the water*. But all he saw was Elio's serene face bathed in candlelight. All he heard was humility in his voice, strength in each word. *I believe in us. I love you, Cael.*

And against his better judgement, despite a lifetime being told otherwise, Cael believed in them, too. Loved him, too.

After he arrived, Cael was afraid Aurethia might charm him. That the moon's wilderness and splendor would capture his heart and compromise the integrity of his mission. But it was Elio who took him by surprise and taught him how to yearn. Cael was a fool for allowing his limbic system to register Elio as a guarantee, as something unavoidable, while his heart excavated an irrevocable nexus.

In the beginning, caring for the Henly heir never crossed Cael's mind. Being loved by him. Loving him. That was a sweet mirage the Keeper of the Basilisk could not indulge, something his own instincts rejected. But now the concept of having Elio, loving Elio, ruling with Elio opened in him like a chrysalis and gave birth to possibility.

Earning his trust, laying the groundwork for the Griean siege — that had been the mission — not... this.

Cael calmed the flutter in his chest. He grabbed his dialect device off the nightstand and looped it over his ear. "Vik," he said.

Good rising, Imperator. Vik's voice came through a batch of static. I see you're awake.

"Don't start. Do we have a transmission from Griea?"

No.

"Did you inform anyone about the assassination attempt?"

I'm unable to send transmission data without authorization, Imperator. Would you like me to draft a message?

High Lord Darius was already aware of the situation, meaning Maxine was likely informed as well. He chewed his lip, considering. "No, we'll connect with our liaison at the manor and allow her to send an open-network message. It'll be lucrative for Aurethia to log the data and track that conversation — good faith gesture. Once Maxine gets word to Griea, I'll send an encrypted message to the Legatus myself."

I think that's a wise decision. Did you enjoy your... investigation last night?

"*Stop*," Cael seethed, holding back laughter. "Where is everyone?"

In the kitchen, I believe. Eating breakfast without you. Probably wondering where you are. Likely examining Elio for bodily injury. I'm an Augment with sensory upgrades, but cybernetic advantages aside, you two weren't exactly subtle.

"Thank you, Vik. Appreciate the insight." He heaved a sigh. "I'm getting dressed. Meet me in there. Hey — you didn't drop these clothes off, did you?"

I didn't. Lord Henly retrieved an outfit for you earlier. I'll see you for breakfast, Imperator.

Of course. "See you then."

Cael freshened up in the connected washroom. He thought of Elio carefully opening his bag and fishing out... What *did* he choose? Cael unfolded a sleeveless high-necked shirt and simple cargo pants. When he glanced in the mirror, a circular strawberry bruise darkened the side of his throat. He remembered Elio's mouth clamped there last night, and the garment suddenly made sense. The rest of his toiletries and necessities were still in his designated room, but Cael would have to retrieve them later. For now, he needed to follow Elio's lead. Attend breakfast, ignore whatever gossip might arise, and get on with their day. He rinsed Elio's toothbrush after cleaning his mouth and walked into the hall.

Utensils clattered and a kettle whistled. Perky conversation quieted the moment Cael stepped around the corner, striding across the white and blue tile. Elio stood with his hip propped against the counter. He tracked Cael's every step, unflinching. Lorelei sat at the table. She turned her head, sketching a glance in the direction Cael came from before looking down the opposite hall toward his bedroom. Her confusion remained for a heartbeat, but once realization struck her, she widened her eyes, smiling impishly, and whipped toward Elio.

The Henly heir mouthed *don't*.

Cael took the chair across from her. "I'm sorry about last night."

Lorelei ticked her gold-brown eyebrow. "Excuse me, you're sorry?"

"The loyalty you have for Aurethia is commendable. I should've accepted your stance and moved on."

"Well, someone tried to kill you, so," she said, muffling a pitchy laugh. Her throat caved. "You spoke your truth, and I acted like a child because of it. I don't accept your apology because you don't owe me one. But I do hope you'll accept mine."

"My daughter inherited her father's pride." Lena wiped her hands with a cloth at the sink.

Cael said, "We were all on edge. No apology necessary, Lorelei."

Lorelei went to speak, but before she could, Vik entered the kitchen. He stood with his hands clasped behind his back. "Peadar Mahone and the Atreyu Defense Sector made an arrest in conjunction with the assassination attempt. I'm reviewing the data now."

Peadar stood next to the cupboard. He sipped from a coffee cup and glanced through the bay window at Orson who stood with Indigo, feeding an apple to a horse. "In short, the woman who tried to poison you, Anne Yaré, had conspired with an investor, Jaeson Cophick, who funded a recent kitchen renovation at the restaurant. None of the staff or current ownership knew about the plan. Per our investigation, Yaré and Cophick acted alone."

Lena stared into her mug. "Cophick," she repeated slowly. "As in — "

"Yes, ma'am," Peadar said.

Vik cleared his throat. "To clarify, as in Jaeson Cophick, one of several Avara-related aristocrats who work closely with the mineral. This one specifically owned a mine west of Atreyu. He has a professional relationship with House Henly, I imagine?"

"All mining families have a relationship with us, yes," Lena said. Aggravation tinged her tone, but she forced a smile, gesturing to a beautifully plated pastry platter on the countertop. "We should eat before we go."

Cael noted the deflection. He also noted the name despite Vik already storing the information. Jaeson Cophick. Ignorant cretin… "Our liaison mentioned a critical negotiation," he said, glancing between Peadar and Lena. "Do we have any information about that yet?"

Lena blinked at the floor. Her mouth pursed.

Peadar didn't answer right away. He kept his attention squarely on the window, searching the pasture beyond it for something Cael could not see. A way out of the question, or a way around it. But Cael had them in a particularly vulnerable place. With an attempt on his life, and the coordination effort coming from a major player in the Avara pipeline, Cael knew he was owed transparency.

The tension in the kitchen was slick. If Cael touched a wall, he imagined his hand would come away wet with apprehension.

"I spoke with High Lord Darius this morning about the penalty for Jaeson Cophick and the distribution agreement between Draitune and the triplets. Unfortunately, the last shipment to Shepard was delayed due to insufficient credit at a waystation on the outer ring which bottlenecked an outstanding delivery to Divinity and Griea."

"Was any attempt made to connect with a Griean ship and pass the responsibility to a reliable buyer?" Cael asked.

"The waystation should've been prepared to accept the deliverables in exchange for appropriate payment — "

"Was any attempt," Cael said again, slower, inching out each Aurethian syllable, "made to connect with a Griean ship and pass the responsibility to a reliable buyer?"

Peadar's jaw dented beneath his cheekbone. "No, Imperator. Per regulation, the shipment was returned to Draitune."

Cael shifted his gaze to Elio, then to Lorelei. Elio looked unimpressed. Embarrassed, almost. Lorelei looked stricken.

"Wait," Lorelei blurted. She flattened her hand on the table, staring through the floor for a long moment, deliberating, thinking. When she lifted her head, aggravation and confusion wrinkled her pretty face. "Wait, wait, so… You're saying *regulation* halted a desperately needed shipment of life-saving medication from being successfully delivered to our ally," she flung her hand at Cael, "and a space station crawling with parsec sickness?"

"Avara is a precious material. If a buyer requests refined crystal and doesn't deliver payment then the shipment is rerouted to a holding station owned and operated by Aurethian partners, like any other traded good." Even as Peadar spoke, Cael could feel the unease steeping. "If we bent the rules of engagement for one shipment, we would have to bend for everyone. It would set a costly precedent."

"*Costly?!* I'm... I... This can't happen often," Lorelei said, laughing with bewilderment. She scoffed. "Right?"

"Occasionally," Peadar eased. At the same time, Cael said, "It does." The two men looked at each other for a long time.

Lorelei's confusion melted into shame. Cael knew that feeling. Embarrassment washing over you, poking holes in all the things you'd once said with confidence. In a strange way, he felt sorry for her.

"And Jaeson Cophick will face a sensible penalty?" Elio asked, diverging from what might've turned into a heated debate.

"Griean law would cast him into the arena," Cael said nonchalantly.

"You're on Aurethia, Imperator," Peadar chided, clearing the growl from his voice. He turned toward Elio. "Your father is taking immediate control of the Cophick mine. Jaeson will be exiled to Mercy."

"Exiled? The punishment doesn't fit the crime," Elio roared, standing straighter, one hand curling into a fist. "He tried to kill — "

"Can we please!" Lena held out her palm as if wooing a dangerous group of animals. She flashed her hand around the kitchen, signaling each person, and sucked a precious breath through her nose. "Can we please eat our breakfast?"

Cael tongued his cheek and retrieved an empty mug from the drying rack. Silence shrank the lakehouse. The beige backsplash behind the oven and the eggshell wallpaper seemed to bend, closing in on them. He took a fragrant, doughy roll scented like candlebell and cardamom and brought it to his mouth. The glaze stuck to his lips, too sweet. He forced himself to swallow, chasing it with scalding coffee.

Elio picked at a flaky apple tart. Lorelei dunked her scone into a cup of reddish tea. The morning went on like that, caged in polite, forced silence, until the Henly heir pushed away from the counter and rounded the table, dragging his palm along Cael's waist as he went.

"The hovertrain should be ready soon, right?" Elio asked.

Peadar nodded. "We depart at noon."

Elio's hand dropped away. A shiver coursed down Cael's back, as if his skin roamed, hunting for a remnant of the prince's idle touch.

"Good," Elio said. "I need to speak with my father."

UPON ARRIVAL, QUIET CHAOS filled the Henly manor. House staff avoided eye contact. The lions bellowed and grunted in the meadow, pawing through golden grass and chuffing at the hovertrain. The Aurethian guard seemed frozen in place, lacking the typical bounce in their step. They didn't scan the orchard or walk the perimeter, but remained stationed at every corner of the property, two by two, shoulder-to-shoulder, one guard looking toward the house, the other staring outward at the sea, the edge of Nadhas, the shady treeline.

Cael predicted increased security, but he didn't expect High Lord Darius to stay sequestered in his study. The steward of Aurethia did not emerge to greet his family. He didn't send a message or relay his absence. He simply stayed behind the dark door outside the northern wing and allowed the tension to rot.

"Come with me," Elio said. He took Cael's hand and tugged him through the entryway.

The fireplace resembled a pelvic cavity, hollowed out and surrounded by empty furniture. Bone picked clean. Alexander Henly watched them from his canvas. Painted eyes followed their uncareful strides across the room. Elio turned sharply toward the hall and rapped once on the study's door.

Darius said, "Who — "

"Father." Elio opened the door.

Cael did not know whether to plant his feet and make Elio pull him, or if he should follow the princeling into his father's domain uninvited. He glanced over Elio's shoulder to meet Darius's eyes. The High Lord nodded curtly. Cael stepped forward.

"Imperator Volkov, I'm happy to call for Miss Carr if you'd like the liaison present," Darius said. He sounded tired. Worn.

"Vik will store any important data and relay it to Maxine," Cael assured.

Vik appeared behind them, stepping just inside the doorway of the study. He tipped his chin toward his chest and remained there.

"Right," Darius said. He tugged at the silk cuff on his embroidered sleeve and sat straighter. "The incident in Atreyu was an atrocious breach of trust. I hope you know we've taken it seriously, Imperator Volkov, and we're processing consequences for the remaining responsible party this evening."

"I would prefer Jaeson Cophick receive a harsher sentence," Elio said.

Darius nodded. "I'm open to hearing what you have in mind."

"Cael should determine the punishment."

The High Lord glanced at Cael. "Do you agree, Imperator?"

"Not necessarily," Cael said. Beside him, Elio stiffened. "The decision to implement a fitting Griean punishment could cause unrest on Aurethia. The loyalists will use it as ammunition."

"Exactly," Darius said. He opened his mouth to speak.

Cael cut him off. "But Elio, your immediate heir, could issue the punishment without risking rebellion. That alone would show good faith and encourage empowerment — House Henly defending House Volkov."

Elio remained motionless. Cael palmed his fiancé's lower back.

Darius swept his tongue across his bottom lip. It was a shared movement, one Cael had seen on Elio. "Son, what would you have us do?"

"Cophick should be investigated and questioned." Elio spoke slowly and critically. His thoughtful expression, firm with concentration, might as well have been stone. "I would seek the death penalty."

"Jaeson Cophick did not physically make an attempt on the Imperator's life. Cael is alive, the assailant is dead. Per Aurethian law, justice was served," Darius said.

Frustration stitched Elio's jaw.

Regardless of how good it felt to be defended, to watch Elio lash out in his honor, Cael pressed harder on the soft curve where Elio's spine dipped away from his tailbone, hoping a grounding touch might coax clarity.

"Fine. If Cophick faces exile, I want him stationed at the distribution center, refining and packaging Avara for delivery via the starlink." Elio paused, inhaling deeply. "Under close supervision, obviously. If he's caught tampering with the product, we execute him."

Darius flicked his creased brow toward his silver-blonde hairline. "Risking uninvolved parties by allowing him access to Avara could be seen as reckless."

Elio curled his slender hand into a fist. His body pulled inward, tightening like a bowstring.

Cael cleared his throat. "Maybe exile to the desert moon and a public statement strongly denouncing the — "

"Bringing attention to the act via a public condemnation could cause controversy," Elio bit out under his breath, exhaling hard.

Darius gave another slow nod. "You're beginning to see our predicament."

Elio searched the lacquer desk. After a distended minute, his gaze brightened. "Allow Cael to assume control of the Cophick mine," he blurted. Finality laced each word, and Cael's mouth dropped open. "Us, technically. But give Cael a foothold in the Aurethian economy. It'll be a show of unity between Aurethia and Griea, and a traceable effort to increase production with Griean interest in mind. Aurethia will see it as an extension of trust, Griea will be positively affected, and Cophick's punishment will be personally and professionally devastating. His exile on Mercy will actually mean something."

Cael's heart thundered. That was not what he expected Elio to say, but he was impressed, nonetheless. He tracked High Lord Darius's expression, watching his deep-set eyes freeze over and his mouth flatten into a pensive line. *No* was spelled out in the furrow above the bridge of his nose, present in his rigid shoulders and unmoving chest.

Darius studied Cael with vague interest. "Announcing you as sole inheritor of that mine could undo every inch forward we've taken toward peace. You know that, Imperator. You would not allow an Aurethian to win in your arena either."

"You're out of line," Elio snarled, harsh and full of fire.

"You're young," Darius snipped back, clucking his tongue the same way one would to a toddler.

"There is no law against it, High Lord," Cael corrected, arching an eyebrow. *Egotistical prick.* He shifted his hand around Elio's waist, squeezing his hip. "Merit, skill, grit. Those matter on the ice. Not status. If an Aurethian won, they'd be honored. Regardless of their upbringing." He paused, listing his head. His barbed smile deepened. "Or their homeworld."

The study fell into thick silence. Tension ratcheted, filling the small space like algae, too thick and slippery to swim through.

Vik's data-port hummed and whirred. "If I may, Imperator."

"You may," Cael said.

"Not to be presumptuous, but your courtship is proving to be successful. Strategically speaking, if Elio took control of the Cophick mine, you would also become a controlling majority with unspoken but inarguable influence. The people are smart. Elio will be your husband. High Lord Darius gifting a mine to his heir during your courtship is a strong statement."

"It is," Cael agreed. "Given the noted unreliability of Aurethia's deliverables, I would be relieved to know an Avara mine is under the watchful eye of my fiancé."

Elio shook his head. The breath he let out was halfway to defeat. "If it's our only play, I'll take it."

Darius refused to speak. He licked around his mouth and traced his holotablet with one finger. His gaze moved between Cael and Elio languidly. After a while, he finally said, "I'll speak with House Darvin and consult the Xenobiology Division. We'll need their approval," and it meant *we're done here.*

CHAPTER SEVENTEEN
BRACKEN

The Sliding Sea churned beneath the icy floor of the Griean arena. Bracken adjusted his leather vest and checked the strap where four throwing knives were sheathed. The vest was crafted from basilisk scale, sourced from a bloated corpse his late father found long ago. He tightened his belt and tucked his laces. Daylight framed the exit hatch.

Like most of Machina, the structure itself was made of black steel and lightweight titanium — a hollow, open-air half-circle that behaved like a planet-side space station. Patrons and competitors entered through the very bottom of the behemoth. Those watching from the audience ascended toward the tiered outdoor stadium, and competitors weaved their way through the interior beneath the entertainment seating. Gravity disrupting pressure compartments on the underside of the structure allowed the entire horseshoe-shaped stadium to lift aboveground, avoiding sudden ice breakage or basilisk frenzy.

Welcome to the Griean Tupinaire! The drone announcer's muffled voice echoed outside the exit hatch. People cheered and hollered. A horn blared, signaling the beginning of the tournament.

Bracken assessed the traction cleats chained around the tread of each boot and pushed up from the bench, striding back and forth in front of the hatch. The sword strapped to his back weighed like an anchor.

"Fight well, Optio." One of his recruits for the Royal Reserve nodded to him from a nearby bench. She roped her plaited hair into a crown and fastened it.

"And you, Laura," Bracken said, inclining his head respectfully.

Other competitors readied themselves. Someone jabbed at a hanging sandbag and another person taped their knuckles. Young cadets he recognized from the college checked over their weaponry or spoke to loved ones through dialect devices.

The energy before a tournament typically leaned toward caution. Some people laughed and clasped palms, flexing and powerplaying to potentially intimidate their opposition. But most people talked quietly or kept to themselves, focusing on the debt they might settle, or the honor they could take home after a well-won fight.

During that particular tournament, Bracken could not shake the nagging paranoia spurred by Maxine's transmission. He tapped the bottom of his device. "Replay last recorded communication relay from Maxine Carr." *Yes, Optio Volkov. One moment.* "Set to loop." *Confirmed: Archived communication data set to loop. Stand by.*

Another horn blared, and the drone's robotic voice filled the arena. *Challenger, Ilya Chamber!* Metal latches and cranking gears echoed throughout the structure's interior, rippling clear across the arena. A great distance away, another exit hatch opened. Cheering rose to a roar. In front of him, the light wreathing the nearest hatch sharpened, expanding as the door lifted. *Defender, Optio Bracken Volkov!*

"Optio!" Another cadet hooted from inside, clapping as Bracken strode onto the ice.

More encouragement followed, dimming as Bracken's cleats scraped the blueish expanse. Powdery snow twirled across the overfreeze, and Sunder's distant light glanced through the grey sky, smudged with Draitune's violet hue. The *drag, clench, smack* of heavy mechanisms cut through the air, unbolting from dual sides of the open structure. Maxine's voice droned in his left ear. *Legatus Marcus asked me to report to you given the nature of my seasonal communication relay. Can you confirm an early shipment of harvest has not arrived from Aurethia?* Bracken listened to the transmission while two machine arms equipped with funnel-shaped drills bent toward the ice, carving a circular pool into the empty space between each end of the crescent.

The arena shook with applause and the ice beneath his feet trembled as the drills tucked themselves back against the side of the structure. Bracken breathed deeply, mind racing. If Cael was compromised, the entire mission was compromised. If his cousin wasn't using his time on Aurethia to track Avara mines, map the Henly manor, document effective siege strategy, and entrench himself in the very pit of that wretched ruling family's routine then what was he doing? *...offered the first of Aurethia's bounty to Griea as a show of good faith, honoring Alexander Henly's successfully plotted blood-union.* Bracken looked to his opponent. Ilya Chamber wore a circlet pin — three simple silver rings — the glyph of Draitune. The man who'd taken his father's life in that very arena had worn the same insignia.

There was unspoken dishonor in losing to an offworlder. But Praetor Savin had refused to yield, and his bloodied body had been dropped into the sea, sacrificed to the basilisk. Bracken remembered that day vividly. From the way scarlet streaked the ice to Constance's hand suddenly shielding his eyes.

Griean Tupinaire, match one, begin!

Attendees filled the leveled seating, dressed in weatherproof coats and sealskin gloves, pumping their fists in the air, clapping exuberantly, craning over the railing to glimpse the two combatants circling each other on the ice. Bracken did not need to see their faces. He did not need to glance at the suite reserved for House Volkov, centered on the right, where Legatus Marcus and Duchess Constance surveyed the tournament. He knew the ice like his own skin. Knew the arena like he knew the layout of his farm.

Ilya Chamber rushed forward. Maxine's scratchy voice flickered through his earpiece. *Cael has moved methodically.* Bracken reached behind his head and drew his claymore, raising it against a Grabak whittled from the tail-spine of a basilisk — a Griean weapon meant for a Griean hand. Bone clashed against heavy iron. Bracken mediated while he fought. Thought of Cael. His dear, undercooked cousin. Too young; too independently cocky. If the liaison herself already doubted the Imperator's conquest, how could he be trusted with Griea's legacy?

Ilya snarled. He had a missing front tooth, capped gold and stamped with a glinting blue gemstone. Bracken knew his type. Rich, hunting for glory, adventuring through the system on chartered ships, collecting stories for pampered socialites somewhere in a wealthy Draitune district, or worse, for aristocrats in an Aurethian teahouse. Bracken knocked the offworlder backward. Ilya stumbled. Bracken set a knuckle to his chin and cracked his neck. *...any Volkov with a claim to Griean stewardship* *could wed her and fulfill the union as promised.* The recorded conversation looped once, starting over.

Ilya tossed his blade from one hand to the other then back again. "You were high on the roster, Optio. A champion supposedly," he sneered. His mouth curved into a taunting smile. "I was cautioned against selecting you."

Bracken let the tip of his claymore scrape the ice. "You should've listened."

Imperator Volkov sustains an impenetrable image at Henly manor. His interest in Elio is almost unquestionable. Bracken dodged another clumsy lunge and swept Ilya's feet out from under him. His back smacked the ice. The audience howled. A mission in motion for centuries might suddenly, unquestionably be in limbo, and Bracken did not have the time or patience to allow Griea's only chance at the acquisition of Aurethia to be squandered by his heartsick cousin.

"Get up," Bracken ordered.

Ilya scrambled to his feet. His face contorted into a mean grimace. He launched again — foolish — and Bracken met his sluggish swing with a kick to his breastplate. Cleats snagged Ilya's armored shirt, leaving four distinct rips in the fabric. Before Ilya could fall, Bracken smashed the handle of his sword into the challenger's wrist, sending the Grabak clattering across the ice.

Cheering echoed. The audience grew louder, charged and chanting. *Op-ti-o! Op-ti-o!*

He is easy to break, as is his sister. If Bracken removed Cael and extinguished the first born Henly heir, he could take the daughter for himself, rise to Imperator, and assume the role he was denied after Cael's birth. Secure access to Avara. Fortify the Lux Continuum. Bring glory to the Volkov name.

Fear filled Ilya's eyes. He got to his feet again and made a move for his blade, but Bracken did not entertain the challenger's desire to re-arm himself. He moved swiftly, ignoring the panicked, "I yield," that left Ilya's mouth. It was a pathetic attempt at playing by a set of rules Bracken ignored. Realistically, he should've spared him. Should've allowed Ilya Chamber the embarrassment of forfeiting. But he positioned his claymore and ran the offworlder through, skewering the soft dent just beneath his sternum.

God is in the water. Maxine's voice filled his earpiece. "God is in the water," Bracken repeated, yanking the sword free.

Ilya's gasping breath was wet and labored. His eyes searched the sky confusedly, staring at distant starlight and the ice giant's everlasting aurora.

Bracken exhaled hard and retrieved the Grabak, sliding the Griean weapon through his belt. Blood puddled on the ice, spreading beneath Ilya's limp body. The man coughed. Red spilled over his chin, and he fell silent. Bracken took Ilya's ankle and dragged him across the ice the same way another knight had dragged his father. He slid his still-warm corpse over the lip of the pool. Blood plumed, coiling like crimson smoke through crystalline water. Deep, deep down, where giants ruled the ocean, a slithering shadow rose from the depths, capturing Ilya's body in massive draconic jaws.

Op-ti-o! Op-ti-o! Op-ti-o!

If the mission was compromised, Bracken had no choice but to prepare for an unsavory coup. One he could not do alone. He lifted his claymore over his head, victorious. Thick red dripped from the darkened tip, running down the edge of the blade. The arena erupted.

If Cael Volkov could not carry Griea to glory, Bracken Volkov would.

CHAPTER EIGHTEEN

ELIO

Political battles are often won with compromise — Elio knew that much to be true. He didn't expect the outcome of Vik's assessment to result in immediate action, but he was pleasantly surprised to find a message on his holotablet one week after they'd returned from Atreyu, detailing the upcoming transition of ownership for not one but two Avara mines. When Elio met with his father about it, dragging Cael along for the terse conversation, High Lord Darius explained the circumstantial compromise. To please House Darvin and their neighboring galactic leaders, Darius unseated a family in Nadhas to supersede the mine in Atreyu, freeing the local mine for immediate takeover. That mine, excavated beneath the hot spring overlooking the Aurethian crater, now belonged to Elio. *Due to its proximity to our manor, the Xenobiology Division determined the Nadhas mine a more suitable fit,* Darius had explained, sighing as he opened a document on his holotablet and pushed the device across his desk. *Sign here, son.*

It wasn't a victory, but a small, divisive display of Cael's and Elio's united front.

And the power it would one day wield.

Time raced after that. Summer sweltered and the ocean roared, crowded with playful dolphins and bobbing sealife. Elio almost lost track of himself. Of Wonder's light emanating above, growing closer as Thanjō ticked by, and of the ceremony shimmering like an oasis at the very edge of his vision.

Instead, Elio chased each day with Cael.

In the orchard, they ate from happy berry bushes, and he sucked sticky nectar from the corner of Cael's mouth. At the beach, they lounged on the shore, chatting about Holland, and Tye, and Cress, and all the rest of Cael's friends back on the ice giant. Cael pawed at him, and they played like children in white foam, tumbling into cool wet sand, swimming over the shelf and diving between coral and kelp towers. They sparred in the meadow. Sunder kissed Cael's pale complexion, browning his shoulders and scorching his cheeks, and his smile grew easy and true. Elio continued to teach him how to use a cattail, and Cael explained the significance of his Griean ink. *Body modification can say a lot about someone. If you compete in the arena or take up a new skill, you get a piercing. If a person wins a match during the Tupinaire or masters a trade, they mark themself with a tattoo.* Elio feathered the clean, black lines forming each connected block that darkened his spine, disappearing beneath his waistband. A body's length of triumphs.

During balmy afternoons, they dodged the guardship and coupled under the shade of a lemon tree, finding new ways to satisfy each other, growing more adventurous and braver with their bodies. Elio discovered he liked to talk, urging Cael to moan and pant, and Cael enjoyed pushing Elio to his limits, wringing pleasure from him until he whimpered and squirmed. When Cael set his teeth against Elio's throat, Elio felt his entire axis tip and wobble, and when Elio shoved Cael onto his back, climbing over him like an exalted thing, like a man to be conquered, Cael heaved and shuddered beneath him. Elio had never felt such intensity before. Such raw, uncoordinated, *perfect* desire.

Wanting Cael Volkov revived him. Made him new.

At night, Elio tiptoed through the manor and slipped into Cael's bedchamber, diving into his rich, heady mouth, snatching at sex, heat, beauty, companionship, anything, *everything* the Imperator offered. And Cael never withheld, never paused. He met Elio's enthusiasm with the utmost exuberance, shucking away chivalry while Elio hoarded blazing, beguiling intimacy. And when they woke in the early hours of the morning, tangled and naked and starstruck, he smothered laughter against his fiancé's neck. Encased in Griean arms. Held close.

The pair moved as one. They dined together, slept together, took tea together. It was a proper courtship, one Elio plucked from a dream. A pleasure-soaked endeavor. A destined thing made of many moving parts.

High noon burned away what remained of the coastal fog. Sunlight beamed through the candlebell's canopy as Elio rested between Cael's spread legs, leaning against his strong, broad chest. The steady thrum of his heartbeat pounded against Elio's spine. A pink-chinned pigeon hunted for insects on a distant branch. Yellow dotted the ground, shaped like the space between flowers and fruit, and Aurethia's temperature rose with Sunder's even climb into the center of the sky.

"When will I get to see your Avara mine?" Cael asked.

Elio inhaled deeply. Cael's knuckles brushed his forearm, tickling fine, blonde hair. He didn't know how to answer. *Someday*, he wanted to say. *When it's safer.* But he wasn't sure if that was the truth.

"My father gave us strict instruction," Elio said.

"I remember."

Do not visit the mine until after the ceremony. There's no need to unsettle Nadhas.

Rumor of Cael's controlling interest in Aurethian trade had spread all the way to rural villages, and a recent citizen study polled the Imperator as widely if not begrudgingly accepted. Visitation meant acceptance, and acceptance meant change, and change terrified the High Lord.

"And I do understand," Cael added. He spoke lowly, each word rumbling through his sternum, vibrating Elio's shoulder blades. "The whereabouts of Avara mines are discreet for a reason — "

"To keep us safe from criminal enterprises. And Griean spies."

Cael huffed out a laugh. "Spare me."

After House Henly's successful acquisition of the starlink, Alexander Henly petitioned the Imperial Council — select ambassadors from each civilized homeworld in the Greater Universe — to allow Aurethia a Law of Subtlety, shielding the location of Avara mines from offworld parties. Due to Avara's medicinal use and its promised payout, the Imperium agreed. Even Angelina Darvin, House Henly's closest ally, did not have access to the exact location of excavation sites.

He turned, catching Cael's jaw with his lips. "The Law of Subtlety was enacted for a reason, you know. Without Avara, everyone suffers. Outside forces threatening to destabilize our process could potentially cause Aurethia to relinquish less of the crystal. Could stall production altogether."

"You're marrying the Imperator of Griea, Elio. Who would threaten you?"

Elio laughed. "And you would be the first offworlder to see it."

"Answer me," he teased, prodding Elio in the ribcage. "Who could threaten you?"

"Anyone, Imperator. I'm not egotistical enough to pretend I'm immune to harm."

"Harming you would harm me," he growled, wrapping one arm around Elio's middle. "No one would dare — "

"It's more complicated than that," Elio croaked, swallowing another laugh. "We look at Avara differently here. The Xenobiology Division calls it the lifeblood of our moon. If we didn't orbit Draitune, someone would've stormed this place by now. Taken it by force. Ruined it."

Cael went abruptly quiet. His easy breathing faltered, stuttering before resuming a normal rhythm. He nosed at temple, grazed his teeth across cheekbone. Griean affection still surprised him sometimes, the bluntness of it, how Cael moved like a man programmed to breed and conquer, yet blushed and melted at the slightest hint of intimacy. He did things like that — teased with his incisors, edged at climax. Cael's clinical brand of love-making taught Elio how to hiss and swat or whine and beg. They were still getting used to each other, still enjoying what remained uncharted.

But Avara was a secret burrowed in Elio's marrow. Something he could not thoughtlessly give away.

"Well," Cael said, sighing softly, "when you're ready to show me, I'm ready to follow you."

Elio tipped his head against Cael's shoulder. His brother's laughter echoed from somewhere nearby, and Maxine walked the courtyard alone, speaking into a dialect device. His father was probably reviewing the transition of power for the Cophick mine, now called the Hawkin mine, and given the time of day, his mother was certainly enjoying a pot of tea in the garden. Thanjō was slow and deliberate. Being part of its movement eased the stone-heavy discomfort in Elio's gut.

He thought of Cael in Atreyu — eating a stuffed blossom, staring at vined buildings, stooping to pet a cat — and laid his palm over the top of Cael's hand, feeling the space between each knuckle.

"We would have to be discreet," Elio said, hushed. "Vik couldn't come. We'd have to dodge Peadar and the nightguard. No one could know. *No one.*"

"Could you get us there in the dark?" Cael asked.

"I could get us there blindfolded." This was an extension of trust that felt both reckless and affirming. Elio swallowed hard. "Cael, this is not... this is not simple. If we do this, I need your allegiance. Unwavering, unshakable loyalty. We're united against my father, we're united against the Imperium, we're united against House Volkov — if it's for the benefit of Aurethia and Griea, we're united. No matter who or what might question us."

Cael splayed his hand on Elio's chest. He did it again, set his teeth to Elio's face. Breathed there for a second before answering against his ear. "I'm commander of the most powerful military presence in the Greater Universe, and I've betrayed the very core of myself to be here, like this," he admitted, painfully vulnerable, "but I prefer who I am at your side, Elio. I am Keeper of the Basilisk, and I am loyal to the lion cub, and I will do whatever I can to keep Griea and Aurethia stable. Our era will be a powerful, peaceful time for our people. I believe that."

"I believe that, too. I believe you," Elio said. He turned, met with Cael's mouth against his own.

Across the courtyard, Maxine paused, watching them like a bemused rabbit.

ONE MONTH BEFORE THANJŌ concluded and Wonder filled Aurethia's sky with newborn stars, Elio crept through the Henly manor under the cover of night. His shadow striped the floor in front of the fireplace, and he glanced at his great-grandfather. Alexander's portrait surveyed the house like an old eagle, critiquing the coming and going of his bloodline. Elio looked away, afraid his ancestor's ghost might know he intended to bring an offworlder to their most precious, sanctified space. He held his breath and took a quick step.

The guardship went through a shift change just after midnight, allowing a perfect pocket of time for Elio and Cael to leave the estate unnoticed.

Elio hugged the wall and peeked around the corner toward the guest quarter — the wing with the lightest security — and darted into the hall. Most of the bedchambers remained empty. The second to last room on the left stopped him in his tracks. Hologlow fuzzed the floor past the cracked door. No sound followed. The silent static of displaced imagery illuminated Maxine's room. He looked inside, met with her unmade bed, a scattering of clothes on the floor, and a paused holorecording of the Griean Tupinaire. Text scrolled past the bottom of the hologram: *Optio Bracken Volkov — Reigning Champion!* He inched out of the doorframe.

Maxine touched his arm. "Lord Elio — "

Elio startled. He muted a girlish squeak and lifted his hand, signaling for her to be quiet with one finger straightened in front of his mouth.

The Griean liaison widened her eyes. She held a glass half-filled with cold milk. Her mouth pursed, lips rolling inward, trapping sound.

"Sorry — I'm sorry," he whispered frantically, exhaling a tense breath. "I'm meeting Cael."

Maxine's mouth squirmed. "I hate to be the one to tell you this, but we're all very aware you're…" She waved a hand. "…copulating. I doubt you have to sneak around at this point."

Heat filled Elio's face. "Wonderful. Not the point. I'm taking him somewhere," he said, pinning Maxine with a pointed look. "And Peadar can't know where we're going. No one can know where we've gone."

She lifted a hand, carding it through her shiny black hair. Her expression morphed from playful to fretful. "You're taking him to a *mine*," she hissed, leaning closer. Her wide eyes rounded like disc-lamps. "Elio, that's against protocol, that's — "

"Your Imperator is my fiancé, Maxine. My father might be the steward of Aurethia for now, but one day I'll inherit this place and so will Cael. You of all people should understand." He waited for her face to soften. "Someone tried to kill him. An Aurethian tried to kill him, and he stayed stoic, and loyal, and kingly, and… and *good*. This is the least I can do to match his dedication."

"This isn't like last time, Elio. You're not asking me to cover my eyes, you're asking me to aid you in treason. Darius could have me — "

"It's not treason if it's *my* mine."

Maxine's nose twitched. She gulped down a breath and made an exasperated noise. "Darius could have me ex-communicated. I could lose my station."

"You won't. I'd never let that happen," he assured.

"In the end, you'll answer to your Imperator, Operative Carr." Cael's voice came from a wall of shadow, followed by his gum-soled bootwear. He stepped into the blue hololight like a reaper, scanning her with keen eyes. "Keep this outing to yourself."

Maxine shuffled her attention between them. "Respectfully, I answer to our Legatus, Imperator. If you two get me in trouble — "

"We won't," Elio stressed, clasping her free hand between his palms.

"You worry too much," Cael said, cool and composed.

"Be swift." Her gaze lingered on Cael for a moment longer before she switched to Griean. "I see your loyalty, Keeper of the Basilisk. God is in the water."

Cael mimicked the last statement, *god is in the water*, then squeezed her shoulder as he walked by. Elio released her hand and offered a smile before he darted after Cael, loping down the hall and through the exit.

"Glad it was Maxine and not somebody else," Elio whispered. He took Cael's hand. "C'mon, stay with me."

Elio led them around the back of the manor. They darted past sleeping lions and slinked through the sunken garden. Halfway down the walkable road to Nadhas, Elio ducked into the forest, pulling Cael along with him. They ran like that, hand in hand, laughing breathlessly. Blue sprang up inside open-mouthed lilies and speckled the underside of lifted bark. At one point, Cael stopped and yanked Elio to him, caging him against an evergreen. They kissed in the dark, delightfully, completely alone, surrounded by nothing but bustling nightlife and moonlit fauna.

"It's this way," Elio said against Cael's slack lips, because if he stayed there, if he allowed it, he'd lose himself in Cael's mouth until sunrise. "This way," he said again, halfway to a laugh, and careened down a trafficked trail dirtied by bootprints.

The mine was built into the side of the crater at the base of the onsen's cliff-face. Like most Avara excavation sites, this one was only accessible through a narrow waterway that led to an underground entrance. The woodland thickened around them, cocooning the mine from sight.

Elio stripped away his shirt and unfastened his belt. "It'll be cold at first."

Cael knitted his brow. His lopsided smile stretched into a sarcastic grin. "I doubt that."

Elio dove into the pool first. Once Cael followed, he kicked forward, cutting through the dark, frigid water. The pathway narrowed to a rocky tunnel. Elio skimmed his hand over the smooth ridge. Cael appeared alongside him, glancing his fingertips over the stone. As they swam, the darkness thinned, disrupted by the blue tint of unharvested crystal. The underwater tunnel opened to another large pool inside the cave. Elio breached with a big breath.

"Every miner has to make that swim?" Cael asked, gasping raggedly.

"What's wrong, Imperator, tired already?"

Cael splashed him. "Do they carry it out, too?"

"We have submersibles that haul the harvest." He swam in a circle, gesturing to the domed interior. Massive quartz pillars plunged through the rock. Faint blue and white crystal hung in toothy patches from the ceiling and speared outward. Avara glittered in cubit formations around the base of each shard. On the beach, mining instruments were neatly stacked for the next day's workload, and a carved-out tunnel fixed with unlit disc-lamps led deep into the belly of the cave network. "See, Avara isn't the only mineral down here. Usually, we harvest it from the base of a parent quartz."

The surface of the pool warmed to the pleasant temperature of bath water, heated by an influx of volcanic magma nestled in the stone. Elio floated on his back, staring at the ceiling. A hand glided his thigh. Adrenaline flared. *We're here.* He swallowed thickly. He'd done what no Henly had ever dared. Accompanied an offworlder to an Avara mine. And not just any offworlder. Imperator Cael Volkov of Griea. Thrill was the baseline beneath every breath he took.

Aquamarine skipped across the water. He turned to see Cael floating beside him, studying the crystalline ceiling. Blue bent along his sharp nose, and his bare, unfiltered smile parted. He almost spoke, then didn't, licking a droplet off his bottom lip. He was lethally beautiful. Elio could've looked at him for an eternity.

"Can I show you something?" Elio asked.

Cael turned toward him. Avara shimmered. His eyes glowed blue in blue.

Elio swam the perimeter of the pool until he found a dark, empty pocket clinging to the bottom of a selenite shard twice the width of his body. He hoisted himself half out of the water, balancing on a craggy stone, and pointed at the blackened socket.

"We have to be delicate," Elio explained, pressing his thumb to the lip of the excavation site. "Extracting the surface of the stone allows the crystal to regrow. But if it's overharvested, Avara dies at the root, rotting the core mineral. Nothing will ever grow here again." He sighed and felt around the pocket. It was hot to the touch. "But over here..." He shifted, following the wall to a patch of smaller, sharper quartz. He dusted his hand across the top of a healthy Avara cluster hugging the white stone. Cubic crystal in a variety of blue hues stacked together, creeping around and between each quartz-point. "We can harvest the bigger, stronger crystal and leave the smaller, weaker specimen behind, encouraging regrowth."

"This is what poisoned me," Cael murmured. He leaned in close to the dead specimen, then switched his attention to the living crystal. He studied the pulsing blue. Fascination slackened his jaw. "There's no way to clone it, there's no way to speed up its growth cycle," he said on an exhale, "and if you take it all, you'll kill it all."

Elio propped himself onto a smooth stone and nodded. "One thing more devastating than parsec sickness is losing the only treatment we have for it."

"Aurethia doesn't know parsec sickness. This little rock protects you from it," he murmured, framing a cube between his thumb and index. "It's hard to ask the dying to be patient."

"I hear you."

"And I see you," Cael said, sliding his gaze to Elio. "It's not fair — Avara, parsec sickness, any of it. But I understand. As much as I can, at least."

"All it would take is one greedy tyrant to strip our moon and damn the Greater Universe to a reality without medical intervention. My great-grandfather was not a good man, but he knew that much to be true."

Cael swam to the inlet where Elio sat and gripped his waist, anchoring himself there. "You're not Alexander."

"And you're not Harlyn."

"But I am Grian," he whispered, eyeing Elio carefully. "And I have seen what House Henly refuses to do."

"And I'm Aurethian," Elio said, pride popping like an ember. "My father is a practical, comfortable steward, but House Henly will be our legacy."

"We could change everything." The comment warmed Cael's breath. He gazed at Elio, offering a slow, deliberate blink through downy lashes paired with the tender exhale of a love-struck man.

Elio slipped his knees around Cael's hips, drawing him closer. "We will change everything," he said, tipping his head to stare at the sparkling bowl above.

"Our children will finish what we start."

"I hope they look like you." Elio sighed, dazed and accidental.

Cael gripped his waist hard, curling around him, wedging Elio's smaller frame against the stone. "They'll have your eyes," he mumbled, searching for Elio's mouth.

"Your charm," Elio quipped.

"These," Cael said, and grabbed Elio's hand, kissing the wet center.

Elio shook his head. He laid his palm over Cael's chest. "This."

It went on like that — trading wishes, sharing the blue-stained water, lit by the precious glow of unrendered Avara — until they were too breathless to speak.

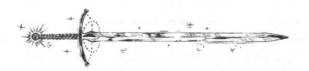

CHAPTER NINETEEN

BRACKEN

"Strike with precision," Bracken bellowed, pacing the outer edge of the gauntlet on the second floor of the training chamber.

The relay course was composed of several challenges. Crawling, leaping, dodging, swimming, climbing, combat. Everything a soldier might face in the field. It looped around the War College, staged with a weighted metronome, a vertical ascension wall, high-bar acrobatics, balance beams, and a plunge pool, and extended through a narrow doorway into an adjacent semi-outdoor area where the crawl pit led to a projectile range.

Bracken watched the Royal Reserve race through the gauntlet, bouncing from one wooden balance beam to the next, pulling themselves over the ascension wall, swinging from handlebars. The crack of artillery split the air, and the thud of knives buried in leather came and went.

Bracken swatted his palms together. "Good — keep up!"

After spending ample time with the Royal Reserve, Bracken finally found his place. He encouraged strength to ripple through his recruits, and instilled wisdom in the soldiers Cael commanded before leaving for his mission on Aurethia. With time, the Royal Reserve turned toward him, accepted him. Revered him as the wise mentor to their offworld Imperator, the champion who molded Cael in his likeness. While initiates in the Planetary Syndicate funneled out into the Greater Universe, Bracken assisted Constance with planetary negotiation, brokering weaponry agreements with

Ocury and Vandel Prime, and competed in the arena, chasing glory, preparing for the siege of the forest moon.

The dialect device attached to his ear chimed. *Optio Bracken Volkov, you have an incoming transmission via holotablet.* "From?" *Operative Maxine Carr.* "Tell her to hold." *Holding, sir.*

Bracken cleared his throat. "After you finish with artillery, hydrate, stretch and refuel. We have war games tonight, Reserve!"

A chorus of voices responded. "Yes, Optio! — Heard! — Thank you, sir!"

He crossed the chamber floor and stepped into the office tucked against the far wall, locking the door behind him. Kindra waited there, perched in his chair, reading a holobook. The scar on her forehead struck a lightning-shaped bald spot through her eyebrow. She greeted him with a soft hum and kicked her bare feet onto the desk.

"Privacy?" she asked, knocking her big toe against the glowing holotablet.

INCOMING TRANSMISSION — MAXINE CARR: AURETHIA; ENCRYPTED DATA

Bracken shook his head. "No need." And tapped the panel on his dialect device. "Operative Carr."

"Optio Volkov," Maxine greeted. "I hope you're well."

"As well as can be. How is the situation on Aurethia?"

"Punishment for Jaeson Cophick was implemented swiftly. As relayed during my last transmission, the Imperator is comfortable with High Lord Darius's sentencing. Legatus Marcus confirmed personal contact with Cael and exchanged cordial conversation with Darius himself. I did receive new information, though. Apparently exile to Mercy was not the only conse-quence implemented."

Bracken narrowed his eyes, bracing his hands on the desk. "Go on."

"The Cophick mine was gifted to the Hawkin family, and a mine near Nadhas, close to the manor, was transferred into Elio Henly's name. Contractually speaking, Elio Henly, Cael's betrothed, is now the production controller of an Avara mine."

Pride swelled in Bracken's chest. Cael did it — he actually did it. "Do we have coordinates?"

Maxine paused. She seemed shocked, sputtering. "Yes, of course. It was his Augment, Operative Endresen, who put the plan into motion, and

Imperator Volkov made a play for the mine last month. I participated in the strategy myself, Optio. Surely, you've received tracking data?"

The elation swelling in Bracken's chest went rancid. He set his teeth hard, shifting his gaze to Kindra. The woman looked back at him with inquisitive, bored eyes. She elevated her unmarred brow.

Maxine continued. "I apologize for my absence lately. The assassination attempt made it difficult to connect via live transmission. I should've relayed the information in my weekly data-report. The fault is mine, Optio, and I —"

"The Imperator's lack of transparency is not your responsibility, Operative Carr," Bracken said. He clipped his cheek with a tooth, flinching at the accidental bite. "I need clarity, though. The most recent tracking information we received from the Imperator detailed the central quadrant of Atreyu, and the last data-report we received from him was a transcript to the Legatus reviewing the action he took against the poisoner. You're reporting that Cael Volkov is withholding tracking data that could potentially lead to an Avara mine? Is that correct?"

Maxine went quiet. Her breathing stalled. "I'm also aware of the general location, Optio. I took it upon myself to follow them."

Angry, embittered relief coursed down Bracken's back. "Good instinct. Can you confirm that the Imperator is withholding tracking data, Maxine?"

"I'm not a mind reader — I can't confirm what he's willfully or strategically withholding. His personal reports are above my clearance. I can, however, stress my discomfort with his closeness to Lord Elio Henly. Their courtship is beginning to appear…" She paused, clearing her throat. "Unrestrained. I've observed uncharacteristically docile behavior from Imperator Volkov, including a lack of vested interest in Griean advantage. You asked me if I believed Cael's judgment was compromised." Another pause. Longer, shakier. "I'm afraid it might be. And I believe his commitment has shifted."

Rage boiled beneath Bracken's skin. His nape heated and he fought off a whirl of fire in his skull. Judgment became a wild, destructive thing. He stared down at his desk. Knuckles bent upward. His fingertips whitened. If Cael was legitimately compromised, then Griea wasn't only weakened but could potentially become a dependent vassal due to naive infatuation. He inhaled slowly, exhaled hard.

"Be vigilant, Operative Carr. I'll be in contact more often," Bracken said.

"Heard, Optio," she said respectfully.

"Expect communication from the Legatus shortly and continue your political correspondence. You might be the last trustworthy advocate we have on the forest moon. We'll need you."

Steel filled Maxine's voice. "God is in the water, Optio Volkov. I'm at your service."

"God is in the water," he concluded and ended the transmission.

Betrayal scalded. But Bracken simply stood there, digesting the complex feeling — treachery, grief, fury, doubt — until the mental picture of Cael mid-laughter in the training chamber, drinking from a water pack, horse-playing with Bracken and their combat cohort... disintegrated. His cousin was not gone, but Bracken would mourn the version of Cael who had once sworn fealty to his homeworld. Because whoever Cael had become on Aurethia was not the Imperator Bracken remembered. He wasn't the quick-witted, strong-willed Volkov who would lead Griea to glory, and he was no longer unquestionable.

"Let me guess," Kindra ventured, sighing dismissively, "you're canceling dinner."

"There's a reservation at Hikaru's in Sector One. Get yourself some-thing to eat — everything's already paid for. I'll meet you for a drink when I'm finished here." He adjusted his tunic and grabbed the sheathed clay-more from where it balanced in the corner.

"Care to tell me what's going on?"

Bracken passed his palm along her arched foot as he left. "It's my turn," he said over his shoulder, and shut the office door behind him.

ICY RAIN DOTTED THE Volkov castle, sliding in rivulets down the sharp expanse of the building. Bracken carried the weather with him as he strode across the polished floor and made for the War Room. Water splattered the stone and dropped from the end of his spotted leather coat. He pushed through the door and walked inside, disrupting Legatus Marcus and the small company of legionaries awaiting orders. Most legionaries commanded the Planetary Syndicate, acting as guides for freshly minted soldiers. They were selected by Marcus but reported to Bracken, so the five legionaries stood. His title was a chorus. "Optio!"

"You're dismissed," Bracken said.

The legionaries exchanged confused glances.

Marcus cocked his head. "I assume you have good reason to interrupt this meeting."

A sixth chair scraped the floor and a galactic ambassador, marked with a glyph from the Ren system, stood at attention. She wore an unfamiliar fur, and her plump brown face was uncommonly heart shaped. She peered at him, unbothered.

Bracken inclined his head. "Apologies, Legatus, but I've received an urgent transmission from Aurethia."

Panic flooded his face. "Is Cael — "

"The Imperator is fine." He transferred his attention to the offworlder. "This is a sensitive matter."

"Our discussion about the counterfeit Avara trade is also sensitive, Optio Volkov," the ambassador said. She gestured to an empty seat, inviting him to sit. "My name is Rune. Legatus Marcus invited me here to talk over solutions to our shared problem. Zephus is a major hub for underground chemists, and their snake oil is leaking into Ren. I've made a considerably long trip — "

"And I appreciate your presence, but I'm afraid this message can't be delayed." Bracken glanced at Marcus. "Legatus, the Keeper of the Basilisk has been compromised."

Marcus immediately stepped around the long table, waving a hand toward the legionaries and Rune of Ren. "Continue. I'll only be a moment." Each step clipped the stone. The Legatus held his chin high as he exited the War Room, whirling on Bracken as soon as they crossed the threshold onto an outdoor veranda facing Goren's gnarled peak. "Speak, Optio."

Bracken swallowed thickly. He knew not to waste time. Not to bother with delicacy. There was no honor in skirting the truth, and the kindest path forward was the most honest. "Legatus, I received a transmission from our liaison on Aurethia accusing the Imperator of withholding critical information regarding the whereabouts of an Avara mine. Have you received data from Cael disputing this?"

Marcus blinked. His face slackened, as if all the weight beneath his pale eyes sank into his jaw. He steeled himself, swallowing tersely. "Griea hasn't received a transmission from Cael since he departed Atreyu."

"And you haven't heard from him personally?"

"Not since then, no," the Legatus gritted out.

"Operative Carr claims to have followed the Imperator to an Avara mine, sir. She can confirm the location, but we don't have his tracking data to corroborate the claim. If this is true — "

"Then my son is no longer a reliable source."

Bracken pursed his mouth, muting a verbal agreement. *We have been betrayed. We've lost him.* It unsettled him, that alien, unbelievable fact. That Cael Volkov, heir to the Griean throne, Keeper of the Basilisk, would lose his footing over the pluck of a heartstring. That his cousin, the boy he'd mentored, Cael, the man he'd cherished, loved, and envied, would jeopardize his own legacy to… *what?* Protect the forest moon? Run off with the Henly prince? Stock-pile Avara and forget about his own people? Bracken's stomach soured.

Distress carved a fine, mad line down Marcus's brow. "I will investigate this myself."

"I expect nothing less, Legatus," Bracken said.

"For now, ready the Royal Reserve. The siege of Aurethia will move forward as scheduled regardless of Cael's alleged culpability."

Pride and excitement. Insurmountable grief.

"Understood," Bracken said.

After a strained moment, Marcus added, "Consider yourself acting Imperator, nephew. Do not disappoint me."

Bracken stood straighter. "You have my allegiance."

The Legatus kept his expression neutral and walked back into the War Room.

Bracken curled his hand into a fist. He thought of Cael swatting him playfully on the cheek, howling with laughter, the clash of steel as they faced off in the arena, the way he followed at Bracken's heel like a newborn pup many, many years ago. But he remembered the parsec sickness corroding Kindra's face, too, and how the title Legatus might sound just before the two hard syllables of his given name.

CHAPTER TWENTY

CAEL

Aurethia welcomed the last day of Thanjō on the first breath of autumn. Summer still held fast to the forest moon, but the breeze carried a chill that hinted at closure. Sunder's scorching heat dropped to modest warmth.

Cael breathed deeply as he stood next to the window in his bedchamber. He held onto that tiny sip of cold and thought about Machina. Homesickness lashed him. Winter likely thickened the ice and blanketed the cityscape. Glacial wind probably cascaded through the sectors. People would don their heavy outerwear and strap cleats to their shoes, and the street-facing window attached to the mercantile would be haloed by faux-candlelight and celestial disc-lamps. He cracked a rhubarb soda and took a sip, pushing the room temperature fizz around in his mouth.

Summer at the Henly manor taught him patience. Resilience. It taught him how to accept the concept of a thing he'd never prepared for: unabashed obsession with another person. Limerence, compulsion — *love*. Elio became the root of every thought, movement, and decision. Last night, Cael remembered him limned in blue, damp from swimming, sluiced with glittery water. Dreamed of sucking greedily at the apex of Elio's thighs, sliding his hand deep, deep until the prince bowed and heaved. Cael's name echoed like a rite, bouncing around the cavern while Avara's precious glow splashed their naked bodies.

Days ago, he'd trapped Elio against a shelf in the archive, teething at the prince's neck while Elio blushed and hissed. *You'll knock over the books, you brute.* Despite the prim chastisement, Elio stalked through the house after dark and crawled into his bed, speaking low and sultry against Cael's fluttering jugular, asking to be touched, to be held, to be roughened and thrown about, and Cael's mind, body, and heart eddied, circling one motivation, one future, one person. Cael could've beaten back a misplaced batch of lust. But Elio had clawed his way into Cael's chest, made a home in his heart. And Cael wanted to keep him there.

They visited the market in Nadhas and drank tea in the garden. Shared a bottle of honeybush wine and fell asleep half-dressed under an apricot tree. Researched the Planetary Outreach Coalition stationed in the Mal system — a low-impact, civilian-run initiative designed to off-set the high price of Avara with grassroots fundraising — and brainstormed a way to expand that same initiative to Lux and Ren. Elio attended a meeting with House Darvin and Cael sat beside him, listening to the Henly heir advocate for speedier deliveries, more affordable medical surplus, and a higher research budget. *We should be devoting a portion of our profit to cloning technology and test facilities for interstellar growth chambers.* And when High Lord Darius gently said, "We have but House Henly can't be expected to be the only benefactor," Elio steepled his hands like his father and lifted a brow. *I'm sure Griea and Draitune would match our effort.* House Darvin's silence reminded Cael of his original purpose. Of the training his family had installed in him over the course of two decades.

Cael blinked and pulled a drink from his soda. He thought of something different — Elio stretched beneath him, bare-chested and red-ripe from a sparring session, panting hard, grinning, cursing while Cael held him at bay with a hand latched around his joined wrists — and remembered what his mother told him all that time ago. *Expansion will bring us glory, Cael. War is Griea's language; growth is our goal — the two do not complement each other.*

"Maybe there is another way," Cael whispered.

He wanted to thank his mother for her wisdom. Wanted to stand Elio in front of her and gesture awe-struck at him like a child would to a mythical creature. *This is mine,* he would say, baffled and laughing. *And he's brilliant, and he's beautiful, and he loves me.* But he didn't know if love would be enough to convince his family that the unification could be true, could be fruitful. That this marriage, regardless of the agreement's origin, could change Griea's future for the better. Without violence, without bloodshed.

Soon Cael and Elio would be wed, and they could work together on a path toward sustainable use of the starlink, benefiting both Aurethia *and*

Griea. They could prioritize healthy Avara harvesting and re-evaluate distribution methods to the outer reaches of the system and beyond. Elio could push Aurethia to expand their farming initiative, and Cael could negotiate for research investment. Together they could solidify wealth for House Volkov and retain stability for House Henly and mutually care for their homeworlds.

It could work. But his father would have to believe it, and so would his mother, and so would the legionaries, and so would Bracken.

"Vik," Cael said into his dialect device.

The door between their adjoined chambers opened and the Augment appeared. He was dressed in a casual black shirt and comfortable trousers.

Vik blinked, tilting his head. "Imperator," he greeted.

"You need permission to send data, correct?"

"That's correct. Would you like me to gather the location tracking over the course of this season? We haven't delivered any data since our trip to Atreyu."

"No, I know, I..." Cael paused, assessing Vik with a quick, cautious glance. "You're my only friend here, Vik. If we speak in confidence, can I expect you to archive these transcripts?"

Vik offered the same cautious look but nodded. "You're in complete control of my database, Imperator. My interior permission is tethered to you and only you until, or if, you grant another person exclusive access to my data. As stated upon our arrival, all transmitted messages, data, or emergency correspondence must be executed by the Primary Controller, and you are my Primary Controller."

Anxiety wedged itself behind his ribcage. "If I gave an order to stand down, do you believe House Volkov would accept my marriage to Elio as the beginning of sustainable change?"

The Augment's left pupil widened. His data-port whirred. "I believe House Volkov will only accept what has been pre-determined by Griean intelligence."

"Even if I could broker peace, even if Elio intended to advocate for Griea at my side?"

"You would go against your mission?"

I already have. He gulped hot saliva. "Vik, run a comparison between the successful siege of Aurethia as outlined by the Legatus against the stable unification of House Volkov and House Henly via legitimate marriage."

"For clarification's sake, you're asking me to compare the projected outcome of your mission against the possibility of unobstructed unification?"

"That's correct."

"One moment." Vik crossed his arms and stared at the ceiling. His data-port continued to whirr and chirp, and his right pupil shuttered, whitened by an internal holo, then cleared. He shifted his jaw. "Would you like a cycle-by-cycle timeline, or a generational timeline?"

"Both," Cael said. The stubble on his nape prickled.

"Per my interior permission, I must disclose that any and all projections are subject to probable change given the unexpected nature of decision-making. But after comparing the available information with my collected observational data, I've concluded that the successful completion of your mission would result in House Volkov's immediate ascension followed by wealth, power, unrest, affliction, and ultimate relinquishment. Generationally, House Volkov would end, as all things do, after the forest moon is efficiently mined, excavated, and left barren, likely ending the era of Avara. My projection places this timeline at," he paused, searching, "five generational branches. However, an unobstructed unification between one, Cael Volkov, and one, Elio Henly, would result in House Volkov's ascension followed by unrest, wealth, trade growth, and outreach. Given my observational data, I can deduce that combined power between homeworlds would function as both intimidation and alleviation for the Greater Universe. Generationally, House Volkov would fade, as would House Henly, absorbed by marriage or future unification with galactic leadership. This is, of course, dependent on the current reigning royalty and their reaction to the union."

Cael's temperature spiked. He tried to retain everything but couldn't. "One more time," he choked out, bracing with his palms flat against the dresser as Vik repeated what he'd said, delivering the same comparative data a second then third time. Cael chewed hard on his lip, pulling the pink membrane between his teeth, biting, giving the adrenaline coursing through his body somewhere to go. "And what might happen to Avara if a legitimate unification stood?"

"Avara would flourish on Aurethia for as long as the forest moon could sustain it. Given Elio Henly's interest in offworld growth chambers and cloning technology, I anticipate advancement within the second generation of your conjoined line. Sooner, longer. My prediction is limited."

Our children will finish what we start. Cael swiped his hands away from the dresser and started to pace. "This comparative data is informed by what you've learned here, correct?"

"And what I've seen, yes. I've observed you and Lord Henly's interactions, opinions, political maneuvering, and disagreements, and applied that information to the algorithm. I also applied Legatus Marcus's political strategy, High Lord Darius's political strategy, and the divergence between the two in relation to the prospective united front of a successful marriage between House Volkov and House Henly."

Cael had spent his life watching Griean citizens train their bodies to live on less while Draitune and Ocury gorged on Aurethian harvest. He swallowed whatever information his father and their legionaries fed him. Became ruthless and jaded in his own half-reality. Since childhood, he knew what had to be done. To glorify Griea, House Henly had to fall. The forest moon had to fly a Griean flag.

But his half-reality vanished on Aurethia. Elio Henly, designed for Cael by the stars themselves, changed everything.

"I've been in love, sir," Vik blurted. When Cael stopped mid-stride, the Augment leaned against the wall, nodding patiently. "Before I joined the syndicate, I lived with a woman named Mae. She was a baker."

Sometimes Cael forgot how much memory Vik kept after his death, before his post-mortem augmentation. "Do you miss her?" He didn't know why he asked. It felt cruel yet Cael had to know.

"Every day," Vik said.

Cael let out a strained breath. "What do you think I should do, Vik?"

"I know what I would do, Imperator. But I'm not the Keeper of the Basilisk. House Volkov will see your incomplete mission as a failure if not outright betrayal."

"My father is a practical man — "

"Legatus Marcus is a hungry man."

Cael went to speak. Closed his mouth.

The Augment sighed. "As your friend, I don't know if your happiness will satiate him."

"I have to try," Cael gritted out, resuming his frantic striding. "I'm the Griean Imperator, I still have my Royal Reserve — my opinion is respected, isn't it? If I feel strongly enough about re-evaluating our strategy and delaying the siege, then I should be heard by my house and our people."

"It's risky," Vik said.

Cael couldn't argue that. He thought for a long moment. Rubbed his forefinger and thumb together while he deliberated, turning each scenario over in his mind. *I could wait and let my family see us; I could wait and hope they'll hear reason at the ceremony.* But that would never hold. *I could try to convince Elio to go along with* — He shook his head, exhaling through tightly clenched teeth. No, absolutely not. He slowed to a stop.

"Vik, prepare a transmission."

"Imperator," he said in agreement, waiting.

"First send a transmission to Maxine — I'd like her to get a traceable message to my mother. Wish the Duchess well on her journey to Aurethia. End the message with 'growth is on Griea's horizon.' Then send an encrypted message to my father instructing him to delay the siege and attach the comparative data you compiled for me. 'Father, I'm confident the overall long-term success of Griea can be achieved through the predetermined unification of House Volkov and House Henly. That being said, I'm ordering the immediate suspension of the siege. I look forward to reuniting at the ceremony.'"

Vik gave him a long, calculating look. "Should I include the navigation data from your tracking device?"

It was a cloaked question. *Should we tell him about the mine?* Cael had gone under the cover of night, but Vik's cybernetic programming was synced to the tracking device buried behind Cael's collarbone. Vik knew the way to the crater, and the hot spring, and the mine beneath it just as well as Cael did.

"No," Cael decided, "don't send any navigation or tracking information."

"Understood, Imperator." Vik paused. He held his breath. "Are you sure this is what you want to do?"

Cael met Vik's eyes. The Augment, his friend, looked back at him. His brow furrowed slightly, but the tilt at the corner of his mouth hinted at something else. Pride.

"Send it," Cael said.

Vik's data-port hummed. He blinked, one pupil bleaching, then the other. "Done. Maxine will be alerted through her dialect device, and the encrypted transmission should arrive shortly. Once it's opened, I'll confirm receival." Which meant Vik did not expect an answer.

Cael exhaled shakily and nodded, righting himself against a tangle of dread and relief. Legacy weighed heavy between his shoulderblades, clasped there like an invisible harness. He could do nothing but urge it to not cinch any tighter and crush the hope burning in his chest.

House Henly gathered outside to watch Wonder give birth.

Peadar stayed with the Aurethian guardship surrounding the meadow while High Lady Lena and High Lord Darius stood together and faced the night sky. Near the center of the field, Orson and Indigo sat together, pointing at the pinkish flare of a newborn star as it crackled to life, leaping from a ghostly tendril. Lorelei lounged with Nara who chuffed pleasantly and steered her large, furry head toward the lightshow. Vik perched on a branch in the tree just shy of where she sat, swinging his legs, and Cael leaned against the warm side of Tatu, one of the male lions, with Elio tucked under his arm.

The rest of the staff gathered in the orchard, the garden, or stood with the guardship. Some stretched out on blankets in the meadow, shrieking happily whenever the nebula glimmered. Elio pointed to a blueish tower extending beneath Draitune's ring. His smile split for the flash of pearly teeth. Cael saw the reflection of a baby star glint in his eyes.

Thanjō was beautiful. Almost as beautiful as Elio.

"See, Wonder catches recycled matter and transmutes the debris into brand new stars," Elio said.

Cael followed his extended arm, trailing his fingertip from Elio's elbow to his wrist. "It's quite a spectacle."

Draitune halved itself on the horizon. Mauve and violet lit the dark, littered with the spattering of virgin stars.

Lorelei laughed and flung her arm. "Happiest Thanjō!"

Maxine laid on her back, strewn across a quilt beside Lorelei, and shouted at the darkness, "Warmest Thanjō!"

A few of the staff echoed their exclaim, clapping and hollering.

"After the ceremony, will you stay here?" Elio asked. He dropped his hand and slotted his fingers between Cael's bony knuckles.

"For a little while, but I'll have to go home and see to my Reserve, get back to the Tupinaire..." He angled himself closer, leaning down to talk against Elio's temple.

"My husband in the arena," Elio mumbled, sighing.

"You'll come to the ice giant and cheer for me, won't you? I'll show you our reindeer and take you climbing on Goren. We'll eat salmon stew at my favorite food hall with Holland, and Tye, and Bracken. I'll have you in black," he teased, tugging at the folded hem of Elio's knee-length brown shorts. "Dressed like Griean royalty."

"Will you have me in the arena?"

"I'll have you everywhere." Cael nipped his cheek.

Elio batted him. "Will you, Imperator? Will we face-off during the Tupinaire, you and I?"

"If you want," he smarted. "Machina will get quite a show."

Blonde hair brushed Cael's jaw as Elio threw his head back to laugh.

Tatu rumbled pleasantly. He made a deep, playful noise, chuffing at another bright burst from the top of Wonder's middle tower. The nebula was a spinning collection of sea-hues and pale pink dust. It loomed illusory and milky beneath the great ring, pastel ink pluming through black water.

Cael aligned his mouth against the edge of Elio's smile. His teeth threatened a cluster of freckles. "We're entitled to time away. We could honeymoon on Ocury. Take a trip to Zephus."

"Everyone in the Greater Universe, including the Imperial Council, will be watching us. I have a feeling we'll be dealing with backlash. Confronting challenges. Honeymooning might have to wait."

Cael shifted his free hand, flattening his palm over the lean expanse of Elio's abdomen. He watched Wonder spit another reddish comet into existence and considered his next question carefully. "When did you make the Choice?"

"I was young. Eight, maybe. Nine. Weren't you informed?"

He shook his head. "Maxine sent batches of information after she entered her role. I was told you were a prince, that's all."

Elio turned to face him, laughing under his breath. "Well, I *am* a prince — "

"You are. But I didn't know what *kind* of prince until you sat on me in the hot spring," he rumbled, smothering laughter. "I didn't know about the Choice, or the Change. I felt foolish for assuming."

The Choice was a shared experience throughout most, if not all, the Greater Universe. If a person felt pulled to explore an alternative identity, or step into a gender better suited for them, they made the Choice. And if someone made the Change, they augmented their body to better fit said identity. Not everyone who made the Choice made the Change, and not everyone who made the Change made the Choice. It was a fluid thing, mapped by the personal slip of self into new or refined definition.

"Until I *sat* on you." Elio snorted and shied away, embarrassed. "You certainly didn't hide what kind of prince you are, Imperator."

Cael clucked his tongue. "Bit more difficult to conceal, I'm afraid."

Laughter bunched in Elio's throat then loosed from him, big and breathy.

The night glimmered. Cael thumbed at Elio's bellybutton, dragged up his shirt and touched the skin there.

"Go on, ask," Elio whispered.

Cael felt emptied for a moment, as if Elio had pinched a portion of neural tissue. The part of his brain that held onto important, personal curiosities. "Obviously, we can use an exterior womb if — "

"I'd like to carry our children."

Our. Cael swallowed. A hot swirl of embarrassment and adoration tinted his face. "Then you will."

"Does it bother you?"

"It — what? Are you asking if *you* bother me?" Cael asked, taken aback.

Elio remained quiet. He rested his head on Tatu's side and kept his gaze trained on the nebula. Somewhere nearby Orson squealed and giggled, and Lorelei said, "Did you see that, Vik?" Elio's proximity swallowed the surrounding conversation, and the Aurethian prince's honest insecurity moled between them. One that had nothing to do with politics or power.

Cael rested his lips against the shell of Elio's ear. "Have I seemed bothered, lion cub? Or should I carry you to my bedchamber and remind you? Or into the orchard? Or lock you in the training chamber again? Throw you over my shoulder and find another barn, maybe?"

Elio's mouth curved. A flush and the slight shift of his body betrayed his unrelenting poise. His top lip peeled away from the bottom. Cael memorized the movement. How pink met pink, pulling, parting.

"Calm down, Imperator," Elio murmured, laughing a little. He gripped Cael's hand resting on his stomach. Felt across the base of each finger. "I'm aware of our escapades."

Cael laughed, too. He looked up at Wonder — Womb in his native tongue — and watched star after star blink to life. Around them, lions grunted and bellowed, and House Henly paused to witness a yearly miracle. He snaked his spare hand along Elio's chest, felt across his lean neck, and framed his jaw, guiding him into another kiss.

"I love you," Cael said, smiling against his mouth.

Elio sighed out the same sentiment. "And I love you."

I am happy. The thought beat with the rhythm of his heart. *We will be happy.*

CHAPTER TWENTY-ONE

ELIO

The delicate gold circlet embellished with jagged quartz and raw Avara combed through Elio's neatly arranged hair. His mother touched the sheared side of his head, searching his undercut for a place the groomer might've missed. Elio wanted to reach for the crystal decanter half-filled with lemonade on the side table, but he was afraid the sugary beverage might sour his already unsteady stomach.

High Lady Lena looked beautiful in ceremonial blue. Bell-shaped silk hung over her shoulders and her low-backed gown pooled around her heeled shoes. A single cube of translucent Avara was centered on her chest, held by a sturdy yellow wire. She poked and primped, fingering through his hair, dabbing candlebell balm on his mouth.

"Cael is a good man," his mother said. It wasn't a question, but she glanced at him anyway, searching for an answer.

Elio cleared his throat. Something barbed lodged there. "He is."

Her chin dipped. "And this political union," she craned away from his face, "is still a political union." Another question framed as a statement.

That was somehow the easiest and most difficult thing to parse. Without the agreement executed by their great-grandparents, Elio would have never met Cael. And if he'd met the Imperator under any other circumstance, Elio would have dismissed him. Would have looked at him from afar, curious and afraid, and stubbornly stood his ground. The universe conspired to

place them exactly where they were, and fate designed Cael precisely for
Elio. It seemed fake, almost. Like a trick played from a dead god.

"It's a love-match." Elio exhaled harshly. "And a political union."

Lena thinned her mouth. She framed Elio's face with her long, petite
hands. "I can see that," she said gently. "But you are the lion cub of
Aurethia, heir to the most powerful house in the Greater Universe, and you
are my son. You're not a prize to be won, Elio, and you're not a weapon to
wield. You carry the spirit of our forest moon. You are the heart of our
pride," she centered the lion-faced glyph strung around his neck, "and you
do not bow to a basilisk."

"He would never ask me to," Elio assured. He squeezed his mother's
wrist. "I know his heart, Mom. I've seen who he is."

She offered a porcelain smile. "And I trust your judgement. But you
don't know Griea, and you don't know House Volkov."

"And they don't know us," he stressed.

"Every house has made mistakes. I don't — I *can't* exclude us from that.
But you must be vigilant. You have to be smart, Elio. You're concerningly
curious, and you stand true in your convictions, but you are young, sweetheart. The measures we've taken to keep our house safe might appear selfish, or drastic, or privileged to an outsider. I see that, I understand that. But
our self-preservation is an evolutionary trait, something nature taught us.
Can I count on you to discern the truth?"

"I don't think nature taught us to withhold food from hungry people,"
Elio whispered, pleading. A tiny, snorted laugh rose up and out of him. He
shook his head, watching his mother deflate. "I hear you. I do. But you
raised me to tell the truth, and our house has not been honest."

Lena flared her nostrils like an Aurethian horse. Her gaze softened.
She patted his cheek. "It's your wedding day," she said, choosing a milder
tone. "And I'm proud of the man I raised. If you love Cael, then this
house will love him, too. I can only hope House Volkov shares our
sentiment."

"We'll hope," Elio said.

Lena kissed his brow and stepped away, meticulously cataloguing his
attire. Before she could speak, the door to his chamber swung open and
Lorelei barged in with Maxine at her side. The two women looked like
opposing seasons. Lorelei, impressively Aurethian, wore an orange-tipped
dress reminiscent of a candlebell flower, and Maxine was sharply dressed in
a Griean suit. Basilisk scale jutted from the liaison's shoulders, and her
dark-painted mouth curved into a slight smile. Lorelei adjusted an orchid

tucked into her shiny plaited hair, piled atop her head like a crown, and flashed a toothy grin.

"Oh, Elio, you're dashing," Lorelei proclaimed. She blew out a big-cheeked breath and fanned her eyes.

"Don't," Elio warned.

"You're getting married, don't *don't* me," she howled.

Thankfully Maxine stepped forward, holding a slender velvet box. "I come bearing a gift," she purred, winking coyly "The Imperator would like you to wear this during the ceremony."

Lena stepped behind Lorelei, loosely gripping his sister's shoulders.

Elio took the box. He trailed his index along the soft lip and lifted, revealing a museum-worthy weapon. The slender white blade, scarred with a sallow, branching vein, came to a transparent point, and was neatly attached to a welded handle encrusted with gleaming black obsidian.

"It's a Grabak," Maxine said. She pointed to the handle. "Water harvested from the deep ice cooled the steel, and the blade itself was crafted from a basilisk tooth. The Imperator must've had this commissioned a while ago. They take a season, minimum, to forge."

It was a magnificent thing. Elio grasped the handle and turned it over in his palm. The blade was icy to the touch, still carrying Griea's climate. "It's gorgeous."

"And deadly," Maxine said.

"Like your husband," Lorelei teased.

Elio tried to swat her, but he refused to look away from the Grabak and missed, swinging at air. "Fiancé," he corrected, "for another hour."

"Less than," Lena said. She tapped her dialect device. "According to Peadar, the Volkov assembly has arrived."

Elio sheathed the Grabak in its leather scabbard and turned toward the full-length mirror. The buttoned white satin tunic closed at the base of his throat, concealing thin-chained jewelry fastened around his torso. His Aurethian glyph snaked beneath his collar, and he ran his thumb along the crease of his pearl trousers, assessing his reflection. Attire for a spring ceremony, one still clutched in winter's slackening grasp. He swallowed a mouthful of saliva and recalled a recent memory: Cael's thumb stroking the back of his hand, their bare feet sinking in wet sand, and the ocean roaring at their side. It grounded him.

A season ago, at the beginning of Kagema, the cold season on Aurethia, he'd stretched naked beside his fiancé, celebrating Cael's twenty-first birthday in a private suite at an inn in Nadhas, exchanging myth and folklore from their homeworlds. *We call winter Moro*, Cael had said, craning into Elio's fingertip as he sketched a finger down the bridge of his nose, *it's the time of sleeping serpents, when the basilisk dive deep and the ice thickens. We roast snow hare and sausage and eat hard cheese with dark wine. The arena closes until Machina thaws enough to resume competition. We rest, feast, read. We make babies,* he'd said and nipped at Elio's palm. *I'd like to see you lit by my hearth.*

"Elio," Lena sighed, appearing on the mirror's surface. "You will make a formidable High Lord."

Elio blinked back to reality. "I feel simple."

"You're stunning," his mother assured.

Lorelei quirked her mouth, considering. Maxine shushed her before his sister could lend any unhelpful advice.

Lena touched her dialect device again. "Understood," she said into the earpiece, "we'll be on our way shortly." She smoothed his shirt and checked the yellow chain attached to wide, hammered bracelets leashed to individual metal bands at the base of each finger. "Everyone is settling in. It's time."

"Where's Dad?"

"Waiting for you in the courtyard. We'll walk you to the ceremony together," Lena said. She shooed Lorelei and Maxine. "Take your places, girls."

Lorelei reached out to squeeze Elio's free hand, and Maxine gave him a slow once over, smiling fondly. "Cael is lucky," the liaison said. Her black mouth curved. "Don't forget to breathe when you see him. He's honoring his title." The pair disappeared into the hall.

Elio shook out his hands and steadied his breathing. His mother pressed her palm to his back and nodded, guiding him through the room and into the hallway. The Aurethian guardship wore gleaming armor, polished for the occasion. Not a single helmet, blade, pulse-gun, or glyph was out of place. Peadar made sure they looked their best, much like when the Volkov assembly had arrived one cycle ago.

"How many people are here?" Elio asked.

"A lot," his mother said.

"Okay, but — "

A lot. Elio's mouth dried as they stepped through the open front door. He knew the Greater Universe would send ambassadors to witness the ceremony, but he did not expect a crowd *that* size to fill the ornate cliff where he would recite his pledge. A sea of people. Row upon row of onlookers. He recognized jewel-toned Ocurian attire, and the sleek, fashionable wear from Draitune. The desert royalty from Mercy wore beautifully patterned headscarves, and ambassadors from the triplets dressed in neat, practical clothing. He noticed a black stain near the front of the congregation. Milk-skinned and viciously distinguished. House Volkov.

High Lord Darius waited with Peadar behind the candlebell tree. His father dressed in a dark ginger suit embroidered with gilded thread. He palmed the lion-head handle crowning the decorative sword strapped to his belt, crusted with sparkling Avara. Peadar smiled broadly, dressed in Aurethian armor similar to the guard.

"Father," Elio greeted.

Darius scanned him. "You look fit to be wed, son. Are you ready?"

To marry Cael? Yes. To fulfill a galactic unification two centuries in the making? Not quite.

He lifted his chin, defying the nervous urge to glance away. "I am."

His father stepped closer. He gripped Elio's shoulder. It was a grounding gesture, one sewn with encouragement. "I know you're hungry for progress, but I hope you'll give me the chance to teach you what I've learned, what my father taught me, what his father handed down to him. This marriage is an opportunity and an alliance. Just remember who you're marrying, who Aurethia is allying with."

It always came down to this, to trepidation and disloyalty. Elio set his teeth and gave a curt nod. "Great-grandfather put everything into place. We have his ambition to thank for this union, and I have his far-sighted goal to thank for Cael."

Darius clearly understood Elio's guarded response. He shot a look to Lena and then exhaled thickly. "Everything we've done has been done to secure a future for you and your siblings. Question my motivation, interrogate our ethics, but the world is unkind, Elio. People are complicated. Don't forget that."

Elio softened as his father leaned forward, brushing a kiss across Elio's cheek. It was a sentiment High Lord Darius typically reserved for Lorelei — a loving, sweet thing meant for daughters. The gesture swelled in Elio's chest. He reached for his father, hugging him tightly.

"It will be my greatest joy to watch you rise," Darius whispered. He steered Elio toward the waiting crowd.

"Do you approve of him?" The question didn't matter, not really, but Elio still wanted to know.

"Cael is strategic, powerful, and unyielding. He exudes strength, cunning, nobility, and he looks at you like you carry Sunder in your pocket. He's a nightmare for a father," he confessed, laughing jovially, "but I'm not the one who should approve. Do you feel held by him? Will he keep you safe?"

Elio did not need to think. He nodded. "Yes."

"Then this union is a blessing from the past and a gift to the future."

Peadar swept in front of them and gestured to Elio. "You'll follow behind me, Lord Elio. I'll announce you."

Elio's heart fell into his stomach.

The crescent-shaped crowd opened in two places, allowing both Great Houses to pass through. Elio should've kept his gaze ahead, should've stayed strong and unmovable, but the nagging need to peer through gaps between packed people and catch a sliver of black fabric was too intense to ignore. Cael's outline passed in jolting increments. The swish of impossibly dark cloth. The boot-click of polished shoes. Elio would've kept walking, seeking, if his mother didn't latch her hand around his forearm, stopping him in place.

A string-quartet played. The low, haunting tune mingled with crashing waves. Draitune's ring haloed the manor behind them, and the last sip of sunlight blanched the cliffside. Elio didn't realize he was straining against Lena's hold until she dug her fingernails into him.

Maxine stepped onto the raised greyish stone opposite Peadar. "It is my honor to present the reigning family of Griea, Legatus Marcus Volkov, Duchess Constance Volkov, and their son, Imperator Cael Volkov, Keeper of the Basilisk. On this day, House Volkov remains committed to the galactic agreement penned by their descendent, Harlyn Volkov, accepting the hand of House Henly's first-born."

Cael came into view, prompted by a small bow from Maxine. The liaison retreated, allowing room for the Imperator to step onto the rock and face Elio.

There was nothing quite like it. Standing idle before destiny.

Elio raked his gaze across the man in front of him, staring at Cael's heavy-looking shoes, silver-buckled and textured with glinting black scales, then higher, following trim black pants, and higher, to his ribbed tunic fixed with strange, opalescent button-work. He wore his basilisk belt, and similar leather fit over his shoulders, holding his tunic in place, displaying the long, gnarled fin-spine of a leviathan. Jagged silver teeth followed his vertebrae. Delicately smudged coal hugged his lash-line. He was impeccably Griean. Impossibly beautiful. The slight quirk of his mouth sent relief puddling in Elio's gut.

Peadar opened his arm toward the Henly family. "It's my pleasure to introduce High Lord Darius and High Lady Lena, stewards of Aurethia, and their first-born heir, Lord Elio Henly. House Henly honors their commitment to the galactic agreement enacted by Alexander Henly, promising the hand of their first-born to Harlyn Volkov's great-grandchild."

Elio stepped forward. His pulse hammered. Shadow pressed through the crowd, dampening the presence of the mighty assembly, but he successfully pinned his focus on Cael. The Griean warlord stood dignified before him, and the soft clasp of his hand around Elio's knuckles shooed any lingering doubt. Elio exhaled. He searched Cael's face for reluctance or fear and found nothing except confidence in his ice-blue eyes. Familiar, playful charisma laced his smile.

In his peripheral, the Duchess stood beside Legatus Marcus. They looked like their homeworld, stony and glacial, hardened by eternal winter. He wanted to study them, but he kept his attention on his betrothed and waited for the imperial celebrant to step around them.

"You're alright," Cael whispered, addressing whatever panic might've crossed Elio's face.

Elio steeled himself. "We're alright."

The celebrant wore a simple brown suit. He held a chalice in one hand and a bejeweled blade in the other. "In accordance with the galactic agreement set forth by one, Alexander Henly, and one, Harlyn Volkov, I hereby announce the unification of House Henly of Aurethia and House Volkov of Griea." He paused to present the amethyst-handled knife to Cael. "Do you, Cael Volkov, agree to share house, planet, life, blood, and loyalty with Elio Henly?"

Cael snatched up the knife without hesitating, let go of Elio's hand, and brought the blade to his own pale palm, slicing the heel of it. Blood seeped from the wound, splattering the bottom of the chalice. He met Elio's unflinching stare. "I do."

The celebrant wiped the knife on a ceremonial cloth and then presented the blade to Elio. "And do you, Elio Henly, agree to share house, moon, life, blood, and loyalty with Cael Volkov?"

Elio gripped the handle. *House*, he thought, and pressed the edge to his palm. *Moon*. Pressed harder, dragging. *Life*. He glanced at Cael, waiting for the bite of metal to pierce. *Blood*. Red rushed from the wound, streaming into the chalice. *Loyalty*. He bit back a wince and tipped his hand. Warm blood rivered into the cup, mingling with the lifeforce Cael had offered a moment ago. It was easy to know, to think. Harder to utter in front of an assembly.

"I do," he said.

No one spoke; no one breathed. Everyone waited.

When Elio handed the knife to the celebrant with shaky limbs, Cael immediately took the chalice and eased the cool pewter against Elio's mouth. Cael cupped Elio's nape. Held him there as Elio's lashes fluttered and he tipped his head, allowing their irony commitment to soak his tongue. Elio took the cup and did the same, pressing it to Cael's parted lips. He watched the Imperator's throat roll.

Before the celebrant could announce their joining, Cael pressed the empty chalice into the imperial officiant's robes and surged forward, capturing Elio's mouth. Someone in the crowd gasped. Another person whispered in a language Elio didn't know. But he didn't care — couldn't possibly care. Cael's kiss was firm, sure, and wholly inappropriate.

This is a political union.

He warmed, sinking against Cael's chest, tasting the metallic mingling of their bloodline. Crimson seeped between the seam of their joined lips.

This will set my heart on fire.

Eyes closed, relishing the breath Cael sent him, Elio heard his sister yip and clap. Soon after, the assembly politely applauded. It was the Aurethian guard who cheered first, followed by a salute from the small black-clad entourage accompanying House Volkov, and then the rest of the witnesses finally joined in, laughing and clapping.

The celebrant cleared his throat annoyedly. "By the power vested in me by the Imperial Council of the Greater Universe, may I present, Cael Volkov of Griea and Elio Henly of Aurethia, unified by marriage henceforth and forevermore!"

Cael drew back and wiped a red stain from the corner of Elio's mouth. "You're mine," he rasped darkly, like a thing etched from stormclouds. His lips split for a rich laugh.

The raucous celebratory noise grew.

Elio leaned closer, settling his cut palm on Cael's cheek. Blood striped the Imperator's skin. "And you're mine," he said, laughing too, holding on.

Cael turned to kiss the wound. It was a strange thing, almost too intimate, to watch him open his mouth and slide his tongue over mangled flesh. "Forevermore."

"Until Sunder collapses," Elio said. It was a bit unkempt to be lovestruck and malleable in such a politically tense situation, but it was still his wedding, and even though romantic vows weren't customary during political ceremonies, Elio would tell his husband — *his husband* — exactly how he felt. "I'll love you until the light leaves."

"And in the darkness, will you love me then?" Cael asked, nosing at Elio's cheekbone.

"Forevermore," Elio agreed.

"Are you ready?"

He shook his head. "Give me a second."

"I don't think we have a second." Cael loosened his grip and inched backward. "I'm right here, Elio. Let them see us."

Elio swallowed hard and painted on a smile, turning to face the crowd.

The first thing he saw was his mother's surprised grin. He saw his father, stoic but smiling, and then he shifted his view across the crowd, landing squarely on House Volkov. Their indifference startled him. Even Maxine seemed distant and unfamiliar, only smiling when she fell under Elio's sweeping attention. Duchess Constance patted her palm lazily, but stared at Cael with intense astonishment, and the Legatus stood statuesque, the ghost of Cael's features boldly captured on his granite face, staring out at Aurethia's vibrant sea.

Journalists and aristocrats snapped pictures with tiny holodevices. Indigo politely directed the assembly toward the manor, promising libations, music, and fresh food. Elio relaxed at the easy slide of Cael's arm around his waist and tried to ignore a slew of prying, uncanny eyes. He bounced his attention from holodevice to holodevice, lingering on a fancy holotablet with an additional screen and a contraption from a faraway world fixed with its own portable disc-lamp. Someone nearby shouted a question — *Will this union extend Aurethia's agricultural outreach?* — and a member of the Aurethian guard silenced them with a stern warning.

"We should get inside," Elio murmured.

Cael took his hand. "Let's go."

While it was only sensible to invite journalists and documentarists to the officiation, High Lord Darius insisted on keeping the reception private. Well, as private as a political union of this size could be. Once Elio and Cael stepped down from the cliffside, the Aurethian guard formed a protective cage around them, guiding the pair through the courtyard and into the manor.

Elio blurted, "I got blood on you," and it felt strange to say. As if he should've said something else first. *We're married, I love you, we did it.* But it was the shock of red on Cael's face that moistened his mouth. How it got there. The lewd intimacy of it all. He pulled Cael into the unlit kitchen and warmed a towel under the faucet, pressing the cloth to the Imperator's cheek. "You look..." He swallowed, blinking dizzily. "You look fierce."

"Well, you've married a basilisk," Cael said cooly. He trailed the back of his hand down Elio's silken sleeve. "And I've married a lion." He tipped closer, attempting to steal another kiss. "You're exquisite, Elio — "

"Don't you dare," Elio hissed, laughing under his breath. He knew better than to entertain the fiery pit yawning in his belly. "Kiss me again and we'll never make it to the reception."

"Good." He jolted forward.

Elio dodged, grinning helplessly. "Cael, we have an obligation — " *And I will undress you here, right here, if I get another taste of you too soon.*

"You're my obligation. The Greater Universe can wait." He grasped Elio by the jaw, kissing him quiet.

Heat seeped into Elio's hungry mouth. He detached with an agonizing quickness. "No, they can't," he chirped, tossing the pinkish cloth into the sink. He squirmed away, jutting his hip to avoid another needy paw. "You owe me a dance, Imperator," Elio added, hopping toward the doorway. Delirious, swollen happiness twined in his chest.

If Elio could've pulled Cael into a bedroom — any room with a door that locked — he would've. But skipping their wedding reception seemed a bit too gauche and reckless. Even for them.

Cael followed him into the hall, grabbing at his waist. Elio darted a glance at the portrait of his great-grandfather and nodded toward Peadar. Vik waited beside his guard, dressed in Griean-black.

"You clean up nice, Vik," Elio said.

The Augment inclined his head and brushed invisible dust from his lapel. "Thank you, my lord. Imperator, House Volkov would like a word."

Cael narrowed his eyes. "They'll get their word later. Has everyone funneled into the reception area?"

As if on cue, the string-quartet resumed. It was a Griean ballad, one Cael chose for their first dance. Elio loved each lingering note, how the song moved like slow snow.

Vik gave Cael a pointed look. "It is," he said, allowing the last word to drag. "Would you like me to give them a message?" Before Cael could speak, Vik continued. "Maybe I should let them know you're *expected* to perform for the audience?"

Cael sobered. "That's fine, Vik. Thank you."

"You're welcome," Vik said, another needle, another hidden jab.

"Is everything okay?" Elio asked.

"Yeah, c'mon. Let's get out there," Cael said.

Peadar held out a tin of blue-tinged salve. "For the blood-rite," he said.

One after the other, they dipped a finger into the tin, tending to each other quietly, dabbing coagulant over their matching wounds. Peadar nodded and opened the back door.

The garden was extravagantly repurposed. Matte-black warming tents stood where empty grass had been. Each held five to ten cream-colored tables set with crystal dishware. Flowers and vinery from Atreyu toppled over the side of woven baskets, and fire-tipped oil dishes in gravity-disrupting globes hovered around the property, flocking the estate like winking sprites. The air smelled of candlebell and expensive spices, and the Henly staff paraded trays of goosefish skewers, pumpkin pastries, apricot champagne, and plum wine.

The ruling families kept to themselves, House Henly to the right; House Volkov to the left. Three golden-eyed lions lounged at the mouth of the Henly tent, panting contentedly and tracking the excitement. Maxine sat beside Legatus Marcus, head tipped toward him, speaking quickly. Everyone except for the liaison looked up.

Cael shifted his hand, palming Elio's wrist, tickling the soft dent along the hollow of his thumb. He led them into the candlelit sunken courtyard and spun him into the initial step of the Griean dance. They swayed gently, chest-to-chest, facing each other, and once again Elio lost his nerve, lost his line of sight. He didn't care about the optics. Didn't care about the universe, or the Lux Continuum, or the tabloids, or Avara. He tipped his chin and stared at this man — this incredible man — who had crossed the stars to claim him. They slid into a graceful step. Cael placed his free hand low on Elio's spine, encouraging him to bend forward.

Cael spoke intimately against his mouth. "I dreamed of you."

Sweet, heady, headstrong tenderness soaked through to his bones. Elio pressed the feeling into Cael's mouth, kissing *you* from the curve of his bottom lip. His chest stuttered, too full of hope, too heavy with happiness.

The violinist sent up a powerful, soul-stirring note, and the garden echoed with applause.

CHAPTER TWENTY-TWO

CAEL

Night came with a quickness. Candlelight licked the garden and shadow leaned from the exposed root of a bare cherry tree. Laughter and conversation careened around the Henly manor. Cael strode from one group to the next, startling a pair of ambassadors from Lokahn, then entered a casual, terse conversation with an aristocrat from Draitune. He sipped mulled wine and ate lemony squash, danced with Lorelei and knelt next to Korah, scratching her furry head while she chuffed at a passerby.

When he wasn't celebrating with the rest of the galactic assembly, he was watching Elio move through the crowd. The circlet in his hair glinted, and the rich, white sheen of his bridal shirt clung tightly to his slender waist. Elio smiled broadly at their guests, clasped palms with people who clearly knew his name and had seen him before, sipped from a champagne flute bubbling with small, unripe berries, and danced to Aurethian music with a lightness in his step that hinted at unmatched ease. Elio was used to this kind of show. Cael never thought he'd be part of such a thing. Not really, not like this.

Lingering just beneath joy, Cael found a gaunt, infectious feeling that flared whenever he looked at his family for a little too long. He gave Korah one last pat and stood, braving another glance at the Volkov tent. His mother sat straight, cradling a porcelain teacup. The billowing black of her floor-length gown pooled around her feet and her pin-straight hair was wrapped in the Ocurian way, interwoven with colorful ribbon, and tied into a pretty knot. His father sat beside her, but he did not have the patience or courage to face Marcus yet, so he walked across the garden and offered Duchess Constance his hand.

"Dance with me, Duchess," he said.

Constance darted a glance at the Legatus before taking Cael's hand. Her expression was eerily guarded, and he couldn't blame her for it. But he could explain, maybe. A folksong sent people spinning and smiling in the sunken part of the courtyard. Cael and his mother swayed and stepped, their eyes locked.

"Did father receive my last transmission?" Cael asked.

His mother's chin dented. "He did."

"And did you listen to my — "

"I did." She paused, smacking her mouth like a sea snake. "You and the Henly heir make a handsome couple."

"Elio," he said.

"Elio," she echoed.

"Where's Bracken?"

"Griea needed a strong hand to lead while we're away."

Cael missed his cousin. He frowned. "You couldn't assign a legionary? It's been a year, Mom. I was hoping to see him."

She sighed through her nose. "Are you happy, son? Does this moon satisfy you?"

"Elio makes me happy." He paused to kiss her cheek. He put his mouth to her temple and whispered, "I have a plan."

"You need to talk to him."

"It's my wedding night — "

"You are not a child," she bit, then softened, pleading. One of her powdery hands landed on his face, caressing him there. "Please. Make him understand."

Cael sucked at the cool night and nodded curtly. "Alright," he muttered, and brought her hand to the inside of his elbow, guiding her back to the tent.

Imperator, I've sensed an increase in your heartrate. Vik's pleasant voice came through his dialect device. I have you in my line of sight. Would you like support?

"Yes," he said, tapping his earpiece.

Vik swept across the garden and stepped inside the Volkov tent. Cael followed behind him, detaching from his mother as he walked into the curtained space. The Augment stood at attention in his peripheral.

Marcus hardly moved. He stuck a two-pronged fork into a piece of charred goosefish then dropped the utensil and plunged his pinky into the soft meat of a pear. He sucked juice from the digit.

"Cael," Marcus said.

Cael inclined his head and folded his hands at the small of his back. "Legatus."

"Beautiful ceremony."

"It was," he agreed, clearing sticky weakness from his throat. "I understand this deviation is unexpected. I take solace in your confidence in me, father."

Marcus squinted. More lines deepened his face, carving grooves beneath his nose, driving cracks around his brow. The fine etching of age spiderwebbed his pale eyes. "Do you believe this marriage is a suitable solution to Griea's instability?"

The judgement in his father's voice axed through him. He steadied his breathing, considering his next statement carefully. "I believe in our capabilities as a unified front. A true alliance between House Henly and House Volkov is the most sustainable and advantageous play. I know it's a different strategy. I'm aware of the — "

Elio, Vik blurted in his dialect device. Then vocally the Augment announced, "Lord Elio Henly of Aurethia."

Cael side-stepped and whipped toward the noisy opening of the tent. Elio carried himself with the same surety he'd had on the very first day they'd met. He lifted his chin. The dim glow of the disc-lamp above their table pooled in Elio's forest eyes, glinting like sorcery.

"I'm sorry it took me this long to introduce myself," Elio said. He dipped his head toward Cael's mother. "Duchess Constance, it's a pleasure to see you again."

"The pleasure's mine, Lord Elio," she said.

"Legatus Marcus." Fire rang in Elio's smooth voice. He came to stand beside Cael. "Welcome to Aurethia. Our moon is a warm embrace to those who seek her."

Cael rested his hand on Elio's back. "Legatus, this is Elio Henly, my husband and Aurethia's next steward."

The Legatus scanned Elio the same way he would an unimpressive collegiate cadet. He leaned forward in his seat and framed his chin with his thumb and forefinger, releasing a tempered breath when he finally settled his attention on Elio's striking face. "You've convinced my son to embrace a new way of life," he said, unsmiling but cordial. "I can't imagine the power you must feel, taming a basilisk."

"I have a basilisk, yes. But the Imperator now possesses an Aurethian lion." Elio shifted closer, sliding his hand down the length of the Grabak sheathed at his waist. "And I wouldn't call Cael *tame*," he purred, allowing a breath of play. "Power is shared between us. Given and taken but never squandered."

The Legatus lifted a brow. His mouth curved and Cael saw a flash of himself in the movement. "You're wise, Lord Henly." He lifted a wine glass. "I'm thrilled to better understand what your moon has to offer."

"And I'm excited to experience the greatness of Griea," Elio said.

Marcus glanced between Elio and Cael, pausing for enough time to make Cael squirm. After a dreadfully long moment, the Legatus said, "Well, you certainly will."

Cael exhaled until his chest fully unwound. If his father disapproved of the information in Cael's last transmission, he would not have come to Aurethia at all. He would've delayed the wedding, postponed the ceremony, and handled the situation violently. Cael knew this in his blood. Marcus and Constance being on Aurethia spoke of reluctant agreement despite the dissonance in the Volkov tent.

The Royal Reserve accompanying his parents stood at the front and back of the heated enclosure. They'd only brought a few men. One, Holland, was Cael's finest protégé and dear friend, and the others were seasoned soldiers who'd studied under Cael after his first cycle as Imperator. A Griean warship could be stationed in the ice-belt around Draitune — he couldn't ignore the possibility — but the complete lack of moon-side military presence gave Cael hope.

"You're a duke of Griea now," Cael said, shifting his gaze to Elio. He caught the tightening of a muscle in his father's jaw and promptly ignored it. "And our ice giant will be better for it."

Elio's mouth lifted. He inclined his head to Marcus and then turned and did the same to Constance. "I hope you enjoy the party," he took Cael's hand and tugged, "but I'm afraid I'll be stealing the Imperator. I understand you have a Griean transport in low orbit. The guest quarter is available if you choose to stay at the manor. Will we see you for tea and breakfast?"

Laughter hummed in Marcus's throat. "Thank you, kind duke." Each hard syllable fit like stone against steel. "We haven't decided yet, but you'll see us regardless."

Cael swallowed. He shot a glance at Vik.

Proceed with caution. Vik's voice came through his earpiece.
Vital signs in this tent are hard to gauge at this
frequency. Everyone is on edge, but I've detected no
lies have been told. The Legatus means what he says.

Relief flooded Cael's body. He grasped Elio's hand and flashed a smile to
his parents. "We'll see you for breakfast," he said, bowing once to his father.
He leaned down and kissed his mother on the cheek. Constance latched
onto him, clawing at his wrist. He waited, bending low, eager for her to
speak. She only muttered, "Be vigilant, Cael. Guard your heart," and
offered a rigid nod.

Before they left, the Legatus said, "God is in the water."

Ice lanced through every word, but Cael cleared his throat and
answered. "God is in the water."

Elio held his elbow as they stepped past the side of the tent where the
fabric was neatly tied, allowing an open-air entrance and exit. "They're
upset," he sighed out.

Cael shook his head and said, "Not with you," before turning toward
one of the Griean Royal Reserve stationed outside the Volkov tent. Holland
faced him, flattening a smile. He was as broad as Cael, only a few inches
shorter, with olive-toned bronze skin and upturned eyes. Another Ocurian
living on Griea, someone Cael had lamented to, trained with, loved as a
brother. "Holland," he said, laughing, and pulled the soldier into a hug,
swatting his basilisk armor, "I'm glad you're here."

"It's good to see you, Cael," Holland said. He slid his gaze to Elio and
tilted his head, assessing him with the same tepid, calculated look Marcus
had. "Lord Henly," he greeted, not quite cold but not exactly friendly. "I
assume you're to thank for the hospitality?"

"I'm not sure what you're referencing, but probably," Elio said, light-
ening the mood with laughter. "It's good to meet you."

"Elio, this is Holland. We trained together back home — I've told you
about him. Holland, this is Elio, my husband." He would say it as often as
he could. *Husband.* He would say it to anyone who would listen. "Once
this..." He waggled his hand toward the thinning crowd. "...is over we
should have a drink. Is anyone else here?"

"Gabrielle and Tye, I think. A few others. Mostly Bracken's men,
though."

Bracken's men? He wrinkled his brow. But he didn't have time to
dissect the strangeness of that comment. Just shoved it into an internal well

and clung to the joy sparking between Elio's fingertips. "I'll find you," Cael assured, and allowed Elio to pull him along.

"Nice to meet you," Elio called over his shoulder, laughing as Cael twirled him toward the music.

They celebrated for a while longer. Elio taught him the intricate steps to an Aurethian dance, and Cael paused to tip a champagne flute against Elio's lips, mouthing the fizzy trail away when liquid sloshed over his chin. They fed each other apple cake drizzled with sour syrup and said their diplomatic greetings to the guests who hadn't yet been conversed with. Elio danced with Maxine, who grinned with all her teeth, and Cael danced with High Lady Lena, who patted his chest and looked at him fondly. More guests left for the evening, bidding High Lord Darius goodnight before retreating to their transports, scurrying off one by one until the courtyard was nearly empty.

Cael watched an Ocurian ship rise high. With his head tipped back, eyes trained on the sky, he felt a familiar hand slip into his palm.

"Can we call it a night?" Elio asked.

"If you're ready," Cael said.

Elio took a step toward the manor, then another, and another, leading him away from the garden. Artificial light dimmed and the oil-baskets burned low. Quiet chatter filled the air, mingling with slow melodies from tired musicians. Cael glanced backward. He looked to where his family sat in the Volkov tent. Marcus, still as the dead, and Constance, fidgeting with her dress. A part of him wanted to reassure them. To walk back into the tent and ask them to trust him — *please, trust me.* To say *loving Elio is the most Griean thing I've ever done.* Being with him emboldened the bravest, most intentional, strongest corner of his heart, and their union would spark an overdue change for their broken world. *Believe in me,* he wanted to beg them, *believe in us.*

The manor was dark and nearly empty. Staff fluttered around the kitchen and darted through the foyer, but everyone seemed to disappear once Elio steered them toward the northern wing. Shadow striped the floor in front of his bedchamber. A room Cael had entered many, many times before suddenly became entirely new. Elio closed the door behind them and twisted the lock.

Mercy's waning silver light beamed through the window, slanting over Elio's face. Every part of him, from the way his mouth filled his chin, to how his throat bent toward the stretch of each slender shoulder, was beautiful.

Hushed, unsophisticated laughter spilled out, dripping dewy and sensual from Elio's clumsy tongue. Elio reached for him, that delicious sound fresh on his lips, and Cael couldn't help but laugh, too, framing his face like a sculptor might his muse.

Elio tasted like prosecco and wedding cake. Cael hunted for their spilled blood between his teeth. Thumbed at his belt, tossing the scabbard on the dresser, and felt beneath the expanse of his shirt. Thin chain scraped his palm. Elio smoothed one hand across his chest. They played at that, pretending to be patient, until Elio yanked at fabric and leather, and Cael shoved away what remained of Elio's clothes.

Cael knelt with a hard *thud* on the floor. Elio swayed, fluid and buoyant, as Cael mouthed at him, nosing at the crease of each thigh, kissing where he was damp and tender. Elio found purchase on the dresser and spread his legs — spurred by lust or libation — granting Cael better access to the swollen hood cresting his core. He palmed the princeling's rear and hauled him closer.

There was nothing more Cael could want. Elio, breathing hard, shaking, bucking against his face, flushed from chest to cheek. It was everything Cael would've asked a wish-granter for. Would've traded an entire world for. And when Elio pushed him away, slid off the dresser, and shoved him toward the bed, Cael could do nothing except oblige. Elio's mouth on his sternum, navel, hipbone, Elio's warm, slick throat, Elio's hand splayed on his stomach — *Elio*. Cael could've died. It would've been a good death. They kissed boldly, diving deep into each other, consuming what little breath they mutually sipped through the gap between their joined lips. Pulled and gripped until they finally slid together, locked in deep-seated movement.

"Look at me," Elio broke away to breathe, gusting hot on Cael's neck.

Cael looked at him. The gold strung around his abdomen caught the moonlight, and the space between them waned, swallowed by the ebb and flow of slow lovemaking.

"You're mine," Elio whispered, strangled by pleasure. He straddled Cael's waist, sliding into a hard, breathtaking rhythm, and gripped the life-point nestled beneath Cael's jaw, putting pressure on his pulse.

The liquid heat sloshing at the base of Cael's spine threatened to spill. He gouged his fingers into the supple meat of Elio's waist. "You're mine," he said, claiming another kiss, grip bruise-tight, feeling Elio's body squeeze and shiver, "my lord, my lion, my husband."

"My Imperator, my basilisk," Elio gusted into Cael's open mouth, "my husband."

THE TIME BEFORE DAWN was always darkest.

Cael roused with an acute sensation buried deep in his limbic brain. His central nervous system reared, and he jolted upright. Elio slept soundly on his stomach with his hand curled in front of his face. Cael sank through murky head fog. Alcohol, sleeplessness, sex — last night stifled what would typically come naturally: prey drive; awareness. He listened closely. Nothing. But the feeling — that incessant *feeling* — doubled his heartrate. *They didn't*, he thought. Bile lashed his throat. *No.* He swallowed once, twice, until the urge to retch relented. Sure enough, his instinct proved correct, and his dialect device pulsed silently on the nightstand. He looped it over his ear and exhaled.

Imperator, Vik said, morose, I'm sorry, but it's time.

Cael kept his voice impossibly low. "Where are you?"

Outside Elio's bedchamber. I have your armor.

No, no, no. Cael tasted the first noxious bite of failure. Next came the white-hot strike of rage. But when he looked at Elio, breathing contentedly, loose with sleep, sorrow engulfed everything else. He brushed his knuckles along the slope of Elio's cheek.

Thudding echoed. Griean bootwear. The chemical scent of ozone — descending warships, falling terrestrial vessels — tainted the clean air.

Cael almost said *forgive me*, but he whispered, "Stay alive," instead. No use in seeking forgiveness for an unforgivable crime. He dusted his mouth across Elio's forehead and slipped out of bed, leaving his wedding outfit puddled on the floor.

He opened the door in his underwear and took the neatly piled uniform stacked in Vik's arms. The Augment wore a lightweight tactical uniform with a hardened chestplate. He stared at Cael and inhaled a great breath.

"Vik, relay your processing requirements," he whispered, tugging his undershirt into place.

I am under strict order to tether my internal and external allegiance to one, Cael Volkov, and his safety. Currently one, Cael Volkov, is my sole controller.

"How do I transfer ownership?"

Vik blinked. His gaze shifted to the dark space inside the room. You could give me an order, sir. But once my Primary Controller is no longer you, I will have no pre-programmed allegiance to you. If I'm ordered to —

"That's fine," Cael breathed out. "Vik Endresen, I would like to transfer exclusive royal control to one, Elio Henly, for the duration of his lifetime. Prioritize his safety and well-being, protect him from harm and preserve his life. Do not let him die, Vik."

Vik's data-port whirred. He swallowed hard and nodded once. "I must vocalize the transfer and confirm: I have been ordered to tether my internal and external allegiance to one, Elio Henly, and his safety. His life is priority. All off-planet monitoring via Augment surveillance, except for location monitoring, has been uninstalled or disabled. Transmitted messages, data, or emergency correspondence must be executed manually by the Primary Controller. Do I have your approval to initiate the transfer?"

"You do," Cael said.

A wide, heavy hand landed on Cael's shoulder, squeezing. "It has been my honor, Imperator."

Cael swatted Vik on the side and accepted a short but tight embrace. "You've been a good friend to me, Vik. Keep him safe, alright?"

"I'll do my best."

Cael strapped his short-sword to his hip and finished tying his boots. He heaved a sigh, resisting the urge to glance back into the room, and pulled the door closed behind him. He gave Vik another short look, one that said *here we go*, and let the anger festering inside him leak into every muscle.

There was nothing left. Nothing to prevent, or rationalize, or undo. At this point, the only thing he could achieve was putting a stop to whatever had already started and hope the damage wouldn't surpass what he could realistically contain. He gripped the handle on his long-toothed Griean blade and swept through the hall, stopping at the sight of a body in the middle of the floor.

Indigo hadn't closed her eyes. She stared unmoving at the ceiling, mouth agape. Red splattered her chin, and a smoking pulse-wound darkened her nightgown. The cup beside her still smelled like chamomile tea.

Cael hissed through his teeth and bolted for the common room. Eerie quiet filled the manor, disrupted by the familiar sound of assassination. Garbled grunts and the heavy toppling of bodies. Muffled cries and the thin sound of unsheathed metal. He stormed past Darius's study and snapped his teeth like a dog at the nearest Griean soldier.

"Stand down!"

The reserve member, swathed in midnight and holding a pulse-rifle, hesitated. They stared at Cael, searching him with quick eye movements, but did not budge.

"I said stand down," Cael demanded.

"Cael." Holland rounded the corner. "We've contained the guest quarter. We're moving — "

"This is an unapproved mission. Stand down, lower your weapon, and retreat to whatever transport you came in on," Cael barked. "Now."

Holland quirked his head. His brow furrowed. "Imperator Volkov gave us the go, sir."

"*I* am Imperator Volkov — "

"Cousin." Bracken's voice sliced toward the ceiling. He stepped forth from the kitchen, holding a pink-skinned apple, and came to stand beneath Alexander Henly's portrait. He was a vision in black, decorated in basilisk scale from head-to-toe. Griea's eight-pointed star silked his chest and the dark ink on his throat stood stark against his fair complexion. "Come see Griea to glory with me."

Dread shot through Cael like a bullet. It wormed into his heart, into his mind, and he realized with extreme certainty that there was no hope for reason. His mouth dried. He replayed everything his father had said last night, prodding each carefully chosen word. *Do you believe this marriage is a suitable solution to Griea's instability?* Cael had heard what he wanted to hear — a legitimate question — instead of analyzing the scrutiny in his father's statement. Marcus hadn't cared. The plan was already in motion. Cael's life had already been upended. *Well, you certainly will.*

"You've gone against a direct order," Cael said, attempting to keep his tone even. "I didn't approve this siege, and I relayed counter instruction to the Legatus himself via off-world transmission well before the ceremony. Stand down, Optio."

"It's true then?" Bracken took a lazy step forward, sweeping his attention around the room. "You've surrendered your title in favor of Aurethian interest?"

Fury smoked inside his skull, clouding his mind. "You think so little of me? I'm the Keeper of the Basilisk. I'm the one who trained this assembly. And now I've executed a strategic plan that will better serve Griea. You've done nothing except complicate a previously solved problem." He moved his attention to Holland and said it again, slower, gentler, "Stand down."

"You don't order the Legatus, Cael, and you no longer order me. You made your choice when you withheld intel from Griea, when you traded the successful outcome of your objective for a bed warmed by an Aurethian prince, when you devoted your time on this forest moon to dismissing violence made against our house. You, cousin, forced my hand."

Each accusation landed like a blow. Cael straightened in place, grasping his weapon. "The Legatus received extensive data critiquing our method. There *is* another way — "

"Excuses," Bracken interrupted, laughing. He gestured to Cael with an outstretched arm. "Even now our great Keeper of the Basilisk refuses his duty."

Artillery cut the air, a rare noise. Gunfire was an alien thing on most homeworlds. Hearing it sent Cael's heart plummeting into his stomach. Agony came next. Someone screamed. A door slammed. The silent assault suddenly became a full-fledged battle.

"Holland, stand down. These people are innocent," Cael pleaded.

Holland moved cautiously. He did not draw his weapon, but he did not step aside either.

The chaos grew louder, more frantic. One of the house staff ran through the garden, making for the treeline, but was cut down by a bullet. A lion, Tatu, padded up to the limp body before turning toward the house and bounding inside. The beast came skidding through the open door, roaring desperately. He was one of the largest. Mild-mannered. Sweet. But still a lion. When he looked at Cael, his demeanor changed. He paused, lifting his head as if awaiting instruction. A Griean soldier unsheathed their blade.

Cael threw out his hand. "Don't!"

But it was too late. Tatu folded his maw into a snarl and lunged, defending himself, his house, only to be skewered by black steel. The big cat's cry echoed. He stumbled on wobbly paws and tried to run. The Griean soldier thrust their bloodied blade again, burying their sword to the hilt.

It wasn't horror that moved him. Or regret, or anger. Something else drove Cael to surge forward, running his comrade through without pause. Pain, maybe. Sorrow. His short-sword crunched through armor, abdomen. Cael twisted, stepped back, held the slick blade in a defensive posture, and listened to the Griean hit the floor.

The black-clad Royal Reserve froze. They gawked at Cael like he was a stranger. Four of them now, Holland and three armed soldiers who'd entered through the courtyard, stood around Bracken, shocked still. Word of this would travel. What he'd done, how he'd done it, would squash any faith his reserve might've clung to.

Cael bit back a wince and faced them all.

Bracken's expression contorted. He pressed his mouth into a line. "You'd cut down your own men," he growled, granting Cael a mean once-over. "Who are you?"

"I am Cael Volkov, son of Legatus Marcus and Duchess Constance, House Volkov's rightful heir and Keeper of the Basilisk," Cael said, tonguing roughly at his cheek. Courage seeped through the rage coating his skeleton. "And my title will only pass at the time of my death." He extended his sword, pointing at Bracken. The man who trained him, who loved him, who raised him up to be a warrior. Blood strung from the tip of his blade. "You want it? Come and take it, *cousin*."

Bracken did not move. He did not breathe. He stared at Cael for an eternity before unfolding his arms and grasping the pommel sprouting above his nape. He drew the claymore and stepped forward, trailing his harsh gaze down Cael's well-built albeit smaller stature. "You're foolish."

"You're a coward," Cael whispered. He inhaled raggedly and shook his head, begging Bracken with his eyes. "This is for nothing, Bracken. *Nothing*. We could've changed everything. We had a plan, a future! There was another path, a bloodless path, and our house squandered it — "

Bracken rushed forward, slamming the hard, long edge of his greatsword against Cael's blade. They stayed locked like that, Bracken shoving his weight into the blow, Cael bracing on his back leg, holding him at bay.

"You've been blinded by a fairytale. Peace is an earned thing," Bracken hissed. He pressed harder, forcing Cael to bend. "And I will seize it through blood and honor, and House Volkov will take back what was stolen from us centuries ago."

Cael shoved forward, knocking Bracken off balance. His heart thundered. He blocked another attack, swung his blade, flinched at the hard clash of steel. "And in another two centuries, a descendent of the Henly's broken house will have their vengeance. Then what, *Imperator?* This doomed cycle continues? Listen to yourself."

"I'll put a Volkov in Lorelei," Bracken promised, leaning close, "and House Henly will wear our ink, and fight in our arena, and embrace our bloodline. Unless Elio chooses to keep his title. In that case, it'll be his belly I — "

Cael drew back his short-sword and smashed the hilt into the bridge of Bracken's nose. Blood gushed, flooding Bracken's mouth and chin. Bracken took one hand off his claymore and swung. His fist landed on Cael's jaw, snapping his head backward. Pain flared. Cael moved like he would during

the Tupinaire, dodging, countering, ducking, parrying. He swung his elbow
into Bracken's ribcage, heaved through a raspy breath, and sent his
knuckles into his abdomen's lower quadrant. Boot met shin. Knee cracked
and buckled. The weight of Bracken's claymore slowed him, but he still
landed another punch to Cael's sore face, and managed to kick Cael backward, putting space between them.

When Cael glanced away, the Royal Reserve cautiously surrounded
them, looking questioningly between each other. *That's right, I'm still Imperator of Griea, Keeper of the Basilisk, champion in the arena*, he wanted to shout,
you know me, you respect me, you fear me, but he caught his breath instead,
pinning each soldier — comrade; friend — with a silent warning. *Do not
forget who I am.*

"You're fighting for nothing." Cael spat a mouthful of blood at Bracken's
feet.

Several times, he could've taken Bracken's life. Could've slit his throat,
flayed him open, clipped his femoral. And several times, Bracken could've
killed him. Shoved his greatsword through Cael's body, snapped his neck,
broken his spine.

Bracken steadied his breathing and wiped his leaking nose. "Says the
man who betrayed his homeworld for a ripe cunt."

Fury blistered. It swelled hot enough to blind him. But before he could
move, he saw Holland step forward. *Go* Holland mouthed. Cael blinked,
startled. Holland inclined his chin toward the garden, eyes wide. *Now.*

"Arrest Cael Volkov for treason," Bracken snapped.

Holland unsheathed his weapon, spurring Cael to turn and run. He
loped through the room, swiping the legs out from under a Griean soldier,
blocking a sword-strike from another, cutting down a third with a graceful
swipe of his blade, and sprinted into the garden, taking cover behind the
cherry tree.

"And you dare call me a coward," Bracken yelled. His deep voice
boomed through the manor. "Take it all — find the girl!"

CHAPTER TWENTY-THREE
ELIO

Elio woke to the sound of gunfire. He thought it was a firework at first. The same *boom, crack* of a pretty explosive. But people did not scream, or shout, or run from the shimmer of a firework, and they didn't shriek, or fall, or shatter beneath the glittering flare of celebration. His chest clenched too tightly. He gasped, lurching upright. Smacked the bed beside him where Cael should've been and found nothing but a cool sheet. Felt over his face. Scanned the room. Cael's wedding clothes blackened the floor, but his blade was gone. So were his boots.

Something sick and muddy filled his throat. He scrambled out of bed and looped his gilded dialect device over his ear. "Connect me to General Peadar Mahone."

The robotic voice chimed through his earpiece. *Good rising, Lord Henly. Stand by for immediate connection.* Static hummed.

"Elio!" Peadar heaved through a painful breath. "Get out of the manor —"

"Peadar, what's happening?"

"House Volkov launched an assault. There's a Griean warship in high orbit and we're overrun," his voice gave out, shredded by a grunt, the sound of metal crashing, "get out while you can. Go to Nadhas, seek shelter, find Gene, find the weaponsmith, the people will know what to do. You have to —"

The transmission died. `Communication lost. Would you like to reconnect?`

Elio's knees threatened to buckle. *House Volkov launched an assault.* He caught himself on the nightstand and whipped toward the window, shoving the gauzy curtain aside to survey the meadow. Near the orchard, the lion pride fled into the forest. Terrestrial ships blotted the sky, and shouting echoed around the estate. His gaze landed on a female lion strewn in the grass, her body abandoned like someone's euthanized housecat. His breathing labored. Turned into aborted messy gulping that did nothing to quell the ache in his breast.

Something heavy hit the ground, rumbling the manor. A terrestrial groundcraft of some sort. Death filled the air — sound, smell. Elio did not have time to process, or grieve, or think, or inhale fully.

He dressed in practical brown pants and fastened a lightweight armored vest over his long-sleeve. A row of cattails glinted on his belt, and he clipped the Grabak to his waist, pausing to thumb at the lovingly crafted handle. He laced soft-soled bootwear up each shin, and tucked the Aurethian necklace inside his shirt, hiding its lion-faced glyph. He slid the dagger Peadar had gifted him into his left boot.

Cael had no part in this. He scorched the thought into the forefront of his mind, wielding hope like fired iron. *Cael did not have anything to do with this.* Carded his hand through his mussed hair. *How do I possibly stop this?* Inhaled once, twice. *What do I do?* Braced his hand against the bedroom door and pushed. *Where do I go?*

"Lord Henly." Vik's strong voice startled him. His wide black-clad frame blocked the doorway. He stepped forward, causing Elio to step backward, and grasped the side of the door, pulling it closed. "My interior permission requires standardized regulation. Due to Aurethia's law against post-mortem augmentation, I am under strict order to tether my internal and external allegiance to one, Elio Henly, and his safety. Preservation of his life is my primary directive. All off-planet monitoring via Augment surveillance, except for location monitoring, has been uninstalled or disabled. Transmitted messages, data, or emergency correspondence must be executed manually by the Primary Controller. Do you accept responsibility as Primary Controller?"

The instruction left Vik's mouth in a hurry. He leveled Elio with a stern but compassionate look.

"Where's Cael?" Elio asked.

Vik's face tensed. "Do you accept the responsibility as Primary Controller, Elio?"

"Where *is* he?"

"Cael Volkov transferred controlling initiative to you for a reason. Do you accept — "

"I accept," he snapped, narrowing his eyes. Confusion knotted in his gut. "Now tell me where he is, Vik."

Vik's data-port hummed. He blinked. White fanned his eyes, and his pupils grew and shrank. He braced against an unseen force, program recalibration in real time. His humanness disappeared then returned in a split second. "Lord Henly, I need to get you to safety — "

"Where the fuck is my husband?" Agitation bristled. Panic careened into something else. Something crucial and misshaped. "And my family," he choked out. Clarity throttled him. *Are they alive?* He shoved past the Augment.

"Cael is trying to de-escalate this situation."

"Where's my mom?" His heart rocketed into his throat, thudding rabbit-fast. He said it again, "Where," before sprinting toward the noise in the great room. He wasn't thinking clearly. He knew that. Felt it viscerally. But he couldn't stop running, couldn't stop himself from glancing down at a familiar body, her broken cup, couldn't stop enduring the glass-cut of panic, barreling around the corner and skidding to a stop at the sound of Orson's voice.

It was a shrill, scared sob. His younger brother huddled close to his mother's front, cupping his hands over his ears. His father stood next to Lena, both dressed indecently in nightclothes, barefooted and clutching each other. The Royal Reserve, House Volkov's private Griean military, held them at swordpoint and gunpoint in front of the fireplace. A blade-mark pulverized the middle of his great-grandfather's portrait. Alexander's face was burned out by a shot from a pulse-gun.

Nothing made sense. *Nothing.* How could Elio's most private nightmare play out before him like a holofilm?

Elio gripped the pommel on his Grabak. "As acting duke of Griea, I order you to release my family immediately."

A tall figure stepped around the back of the stone fireplace. His black uniform was textured with rough scale, but the glossy glyph centered on his chest gleamed like a cat's eye. He was a more severe version of Cael. Older, crueler, larger, as if someone had looked through time, undid Cael's future self, and put him back together wrong. His cropped dark hair was pushed away from his face, and he lifted his chin, looking from Elio's feet to his brow, inspecting every inch of him. When he tilted his head, Elio saw the ink cascading down either side of his neck. The sharp edges of the eight-pointed Griean star, same as the glyph on his armor, and the fanged maw of a basilisk.

The man's mouth quirked amusedly. "As acting Imperator of Griea, I'm afraid I can't honor your order."

Acting Imperator. Elio let the comment sink. "Who are you? Where's Imperator Volkov?"

"You're looking at Imperator Volkov. The man who came to your moon, collected vital information for his homeworld's benefit, slipped into your bedroom, and wooed you like a damsel is a traitor to Griea and a wanted criminal." His smile peeled open for white teeth. "I'm Bracken Volkov, heir incumbent. You must be Elio Henly."

Came to your moon. Elio gripped the handle. *Collected vital information.* Yanked the Grabak free. *Slipped into your bedroom.* Spun the weapon, realigning his palm against hard leather. *Wooed you like a damsel.*

"I will say it again," Elio barked, gesturing to Bracken with the blade. "I am a duke of Griea, and I order you to release my family."

"You've got spirit, kid. I'll give you that," Bracken said, laughing under his breath. He sauntered forward. The claymore attached to his back looked too heavy to carry. "Did you know Cael came here to spy on you? To gather information about Aurethia and report back to Griea with his findings? Did you know this siege was the result of his successful mission?" He furrowed his brow, snarling through another smile. "You really thought we'd allow this forest moon to continue spreading corruption across the Greater Universe," he muttered, shaking his head, "and you honestly believed House Volkov would grant House Henly continued access to the Lux Continuum after you halted expanded distribution — "

"Avara is a delicate material, Imperator," Darius said, exasperated. "There is no expansion if the crystal is gone — "

Bracken struck his father across the face. Darius made no sound, but his mother yelped, and Orson cried out.

Quick as lightning, Elio plucked a cattail from his belt and flicked it. The silvered throwing knife flew end-over-end, sinking into the back of Bracken's hand. Blood spurted. Bracken hissed and drew his limb back, staring at the crescent blade half-buried beneath his knuckles. The weapon gouged deep through meat and ligament, lodged there like an oversized splinter.

Another Griean shot forward, but Elio was quick and precise. He drew a second cattail and sent it flying, slicing their throat. Red gushed. The soldier grappled for his neck before he fell, choking miserably on a mouthful of coppery blood.

"Release," Elio darted a stern glance around the room, landing on each black-clad soldier, "my family."

"No wonder he fell for you." Bracken seethed and pulled the cattail free, looking over the slippery, bloodstained shuriken with practiced ease. "It's too bad we're off to such a rocky start, but…" He shrugged and dropped it. The cattail clattered in front of his boot. "If not you, I'm happy to wed your sister. She's quite a looker from what I've been told."

Elio desperately tried to put the pieces into place. His mind crunched information while his body stayed poised on a tripwire, waiting for someone to take a step toward him. To reach for his father, or mother, or brother. To catapult him into action.

Cael knew about this. *He knew.* The way Cael acted when he first arrived… Elio ran through every question, every curiosity, every jab at Aurethia's processing strategy, every sly remark made about his family, every thorny response to House Henly's protocol. Cael had robbed him of intel under the guise of change. Extracted secrets with the lure of happiness, love, and… Elio blinked rapidly, beating back the sting flooding his nasal cavity.

Bracken's comment finally landed. *I'm happy to wed your sister.*

Elio's heart clenched and he stepped forward, prompting the Griean guard to shift, each boot coming down hard, bodies twisting toward him in fluid formation. His attention flashed to his father who looked back at him red-cheeked and full of remorse, then he glanced at his mother, who stared headlong at him, jaw set sternly, holding Orson. *Lorelei*, he thought miserably at first, then swallowed, ruminating on her absence. *Where are you, sister?*

"It's not your fault," Bracken said. He stepped in front of his family, blocking Elio's view. "Cael was raised to do exactly what he did, exactly how he did it. You're a casualty, and because of you, he is, too."

Elio swallowed the hurt and fury clogging his throat and swiped the comment away. He could deal with the depth of his own betrayal later. Right now, he needed to be savvy, to rely on the political skill his father seeded in him, to *think*.

"Without House Henly, Griea has no access to Avara. The people here will never give up our mines, and we'll take our trade to the grave. You must know that by now," Elio said, attempting to reason with Cael's elusive cousin. The man he talked so highly about. The monster who was destroying Elio's home. "You'd strip the Greater Universe of our only treatment for parsec sickness?" He grew braver. Too brave. "Or have you not been touched by the plague chewing through our system, heir incumbent?"

Blue eyes, deeper than Cael's, like a sunbeam on the surface of a deep pool, narrowed dangerously. Anger twitched in the hollow of Bracken's jaw, and he rolled his neck, cracking it. "You've been sheltered on this sweet little moon for too long, Lord Henly. You've forgotten what it's like to be afraid."

Someone's voice came from the kitchen, growing closer. "Imperator, I have Maxine Carr for you," she said. Her voice was smooth and rich, and she wore a velvet gown the color of ripe grapes. A sheer hood billowed around her angular face. She quirked a scarred brow at Elio, unfazed by the commotion.

Elio's stomach turned at the sight of the affliction marring her skin. Scars like that only formed if parsec sickness reached the epidermis, meaning she hadn't accessed treatment for a while after showing initial symptoms. She set her mouth proudly and did not look away from him.

Bracken angled his chin toward her. "Thank you, Kindra. Send her in."

"If you do this, House Darvin and the entire Imperium will punish Griea," Darius said. He shook his head, fixing Bracken with a hateful glare. "You have no access to Avara. You have no authority on this moon. This foolish act of war will do nothing except unfairly punish the innocent people of the Greater Universe, including your own."

"My father is right," Elio said. His free hand twitched near his belt, the other flexed around his Grabak. "The Imperial Council will end this and Griea will pay the price."

"The Imperial Council will watch." Maxine walked around Kindra and stepped into the great room. She looked exactly like herself and nothing like herself. The black combat uniform fit her seamlessly, adorned with a bejeweled collar and sharply pointed bootwear. A saber hung from her belt. Her eyes slid around the room, shifting from Bracken to Elio. "Given this is a social quarrel, I don't anticipate any retaliation. If Avara production continues, the Greater Universe will have no stake in an intervention."

You were my friend. Elio gripped his Grabak tighter. For a naïve second, he hoped Maxine might come to his family's defense. Might stand between him and Bracken and urge for peace. But the Griean operative clasped her hands at the small of her back and inclined her head to Bracken.

"I can personally report the location of one Avara mine, Imperator," Maxine said. Her eyes flashed to Elio. Something like regret panged there, chased away by the cold breath of pride. "On the edge of Nadhas, hugging the crater — "

Elio could not stop himself. He lunged forward, raising his blade to deflect a strike from a Grian soldier. He jabbed the virgin Grabak forward and plunged its tooth underneath the soldier's ribcage, christening it with a life. A garbled noise came and went. Elio twirled, swung, dotting the room with spilled blood, and brought the blade down on another soldier's shoulder, tossing them aside to get to Maxine, to run her through, to cut her traitorous heart in half.

Maxine's eyes widened. Her mouth dropped, and she stumbled backward, grappling for her sword. Kindra stepped aside, sinking into the shadow, and Bracken reached for his claymore.

Before Elio could get close enough to strike, Vik emerged from the hallway. The loud, even sound of a pulse-gun wobbled through the room, burning a circular mark on the wall beside Bracken. Vik held his arm outstretched, palm flexed, skin peeled open to reveal the mouth of a pulse-gun embedded in his cybernetic hand. He gripped Elio's elbow hard, halting him in place.

High Lady Lena shrieked with panic, ferocity, and something too raw and primal to place. "Go, Elio! You have to go — find her! *Find her!*"

Elio threw his weight against Vik, but the Augment wouldn't budge. A thousand things came to the tip of his tongue. A thousand thoughts. A thousand words. But he couldn't manage to utter a single thing. Instead, he raised his blood-soaked blade eye-level with Maxine and snapped his teeth like an animal.

Maxine flinched but quickly recovered. "Griea is my homeworld," she bit back as if it mattered, as if her selfish reasoning made any difference. "I did what I had to."

"Go," Lena yelled again. "Now!"

Elio looked at his parents. His father gave a curt nod and threw his body into Bracken, knocking the bastard off-center. His mother's stern eyes glistened, silvered with anger, love, regret, and something worse. Goodbye, maybe. No, he couldn't accept that. Refused to. When Elio didn't move, she flicked her gaze upward.

"Take him," she barked at Vik, "get him out of here — go!"

Vik grabbed Elio around the waist and hauled him backward.

Elio wanted to protest, wanted to fight, but he regained his footing and

turned, sprinting into the garden with Vik at his side. Fleeing the manor —
his home, his solace. Leaving his family behind.

Find her.

"What's happening," he gasped out, shielding his face as he leaped past
the treeline and disappeared into the brush. He didn't look over his shoulder, but he knew Vik was there. He ran faster, pushing until his muscles
burned and his knees ached.

The chaos at the manor dwindled to a dull roar, and the brittle sound of
battle became cottony and faraway. Once the forest swallowed them,
shading their location from pursuers, Elio turned and forced the Grabak
beneath Vik's chin, pounding one fist on the Augment's chestplate.

"Tell me everything," he demanded, fighting back a childish sob. "Tell
me *everything*."

High above them, a Griean warship breached low orbit, obstructing
Draitune's great ring.

CHAPTER TWENTY-FOUR
BRACKEN

The siege continued well into the afternoon.

Bracken cruised the estate, overseeing placement of the Royal Reserve. He stationed the terrestrial groundcraft outside the orchard and placed the squadron in the courtyard. Thick-walled Griean tents filled the meadow. A few soldiers gathered the two slain lions and strung them by their back feet from a sturdy tree branch. Their pelts would make for excellent trophies. Bracken intended to keep one for himself and give the other to the Legatus.

Excitement and adrenaline dizzied him. He fidgeted restlessly with the bandage wrapped around his damaged hand, swiveling to look one way then another, trying and failing to absorb everything Aurethia had to offer. It was too much to digest mere hours after landing, but he couldn't help it. Aurethia was too rich a place to simply occupy. At one point, when his frenzied body refused to unclench, he pulled Kindra into an empty chamber and planted his rage, triumph, sadness, and the weight of his ascendency between her legs.

"Imperator," she cooed, panting and smiling. "My valiant Imperator. Griean royalty. Heir to the throne," she said, "heir to the throne," and again, pretty face smashed against perfectly assembled bedding, "heir to the throne."

It was quick and primal, and Bracken was overcome with terrible, familiar shame afterward. He listened to the recorded encounter twice on his dialect device while he stood on the cliff behind the launch bay, watching the sea churn and crash. He remembered Kindra's glazed, half-focused face. How she called him *royal* and opened her mouth for his hand, allowing him to probe her throat until she gagged. He'd wanted to reach inside her and pluck the title out. Not because it wasn't his. It was. It had to be. But because he'd earned it — *Imperator* — after a game of intimate betrayal.

"You knew better," he whispered. Cael wasn't there, but Bracken spoke to him regardless. Anger simmered. He rubbed his thumb against his index. Memories bludgeoned him: hunting snow hare for a family feast, plunging into the Sliding Sea after combat in the arena, laughing together at a bar in Sector Two, warming around the hearth in the castle on exceptionally chilly days. "I taught you better, cousin."

Briny wind salted his skin. He breathed deeply, inhaling sky and sea. Smoke still chafed the air. Copper and oil did, too. Ozone left a chemical bleach-like flavor on his tongue. The Griean warship loomed like a titan above the manor. He closed his eyes and swayed closer to the edge. His boots teased at slippery rock, threatening to tip.

Imperator Volkov. The artificial voice in his dialect device chimed. *Legatus Marcus has requested a meeting.*

Bracken stepped back and tapped the earpiece. "I'll be right there."

Transmitting location — Henly manor, library. Estimated arrival: Seven minutes.

Aurethia bloomed. Bracken had never seen such a thing. Rich with beauty, spilling with life. It sprouted everywhere. Vibrant, lush. He trailed his hand along a fern and stepped over stacked brick surrounding the mighty, exotic tree centered in the courtyard. Tiny white buds clung to the candlebell, early in returning. Toward the right of the house, smoke plumed. The organic smell of burning flesh filled the air. Fire was an efficient way to rid the place of bodies, Griean and Aurethian alike.

Inside the manor proper, a Griean containment crew cleaned the mess left behind from battle. Blood marked the places where people fell. Scorched cylindrical patches littered surfaces where shots from pulse-guns had landed. Standard artillery had ripped holes through furniture and windowpanes. The smell of it — copper and sweat; piss and soot — wafted through the large house.

"Imperator," someone said, bowing their head respectfully.

Bracken still wasn't used to responding. He blinked and returned the gesture, taking a wide step over a stained carpet.

Two Royal Reserve stood outside the library. They stepped aside. Bracken mumbled a greeting as he walked past, striding into the small archive. He cut a glance between the crowded shelves, assessing the assortment of paper tomes shielded behind glass. There was an impractically small seater. A desk, too. And a long table with matching chairs. Legatus Marcus stood behind the desk, fingering dismissively through an old book with sallow pages. Duchess Constance paced in front of a baroque wall stacked with framed artwork, wringing her hands.

"Legatus," Bracken greeted.

"Imperator, I'm sensing we've seen success in the first stage of our endeavor."

"The manor is secure. Our forces will pursue Nadhas in the morning. Operative Carr will lead the investigation into Elio Henly's Avara mine, and I'll be delegating leadership to trusted soldiers, instructing them to prioritize an efficient, clean conquest. Unfortunately, Atreyu is heavily guarded by Aurethian militia. Our best course is to allow the city to remain under Aurethian control until we can complete the marriage rite."

Marcus didn't look up. He shut the book and flicked a decorative quill. "And Cael?"

Bracken stiffened. He glanced at Constance who stopped walking and lifted her face, searching him for the truth. Her Ocurian dress was covered with a Griean seal-skin cloak. Somehow, she still looked cold.

"Cael Volkov fled the manor shortly after our arrival," Bracken began, clearing his throat, "and evaded arrest. He slaughtered two Royal Reserve. A lapse in my judgment allowed him to get away. We fought…" He swept his tongue across the inside of his bottom lip, tasting regret. "I should've delivered an adequate punishment when I had the chance, but I believe our people deserve the right to see him charged during the Tupinaire."

"He fought you," Constance breathed out. Her brow furrowed with disbelief. "And he killed his men? You saw him — "

"With my own eyes, Duchess," Bracken said. He straightened in place. "He defended a slain lion who attacked one of our own. I tried to speak with him, but he refused to see reason. I'm afraid he's been poisoned by the ideology here — Aurethian propaganda."

"Marcus, you heard Cael's last transmission. Are you sure he wasn't advocating for Griea? From my understanding, the Imperator wanted to avoid bloodshed, not encourage more of it," Constance said.

Marcus huffed. "He is no longer Imperator, and yes, I did hear it, Duchess. Our son relayed untrustworthy, insufficient data in an attempt to delay the outcome of his mission. A mission, I might add, that is nearly two decades in the making. One he had a major role in."

"Have you cross-compared the data with — "

Marcus shot his wife a warning glare. "The data weighed two of many potential outcomes. It was a naïve mistake, one I could've forgiven." He paused, bracing his hand flat on the desk. "I did not raise him to be weak; I did not teach him to be gentle. Whatever this young lord made of him, I could've dealt with it. But Cael deviated from his mission, withheld vital information from Griea — from *me* — and turned his blade on his own men," he exhaled harshly, casting a pitying stare at the glossy lacquer, "and those are capital crimes."

Cael turned his own blade on me, Bracken almost said. But that was a private hurt. Something he would shoulder alone. "I will find the prince and return him to Griea."

"Bring him back alive, Bracken," Constance demanded.

Bracken nodded. "Yes, Duchess." He stepped forward, glancing around the desk in front of Marcus. Xenobiology paperwork. Harvest schedule. Wedding arrangements. He tapped the warm-tinted wood. "Legatus, Draitune will inquire about our conquest soon enough. What would you like me to do with the rest of House Henly?"

"We'll handle Angelina. If House Darvin tries to intervene, Avara production will grind to a halt and Lux will be denied treatment. Use that to our advantage and utilize Operative Carr for strategic discussion. She's an asset. As for the family..." Marcus pondered, tapping one finger on the desk. "What happened to the boy? Cael's new bride?"

"Unfortunately, Cael recalibrated our Augment, Vik Endresen, to remain under Elio Henly's control. With his help, Elio fled the manor this morning. I have a squadron scanning the nearby woodland for him and his sister. The first-born is a kill on sight, sir. Lorelei is to be contained and returned to the manor."

Marcus's face tightened. "Not only did my son escape, but Elio Henly is not in custody, and we're unsure where his sister — your intended wife and our iron-clad security measure — has disappeared to?"

Shame licked Bracken's spine. He swallowed hard, fighting back the urge to leap into an explanation. There was no way to encapsulate the gravity of his mistake. Bracken never should've given Cael any grace — should've slammed his claymore through Cael's chest. Should've dismissed his ego, destroyed the Augment, and killed the Aurethian prince with a bullet to his skull. The Legatus was right. Bracken's premature leadership and basilisk-damned pride led them to this. "I will secure the Aurethian princess, bring Cael to heel, and subdue Elio Henly. It's only day one, Legatus. We will control this moon."

Marcus smacked his mouth. "Hang the High Lord from the candlebell tree," he smarted, as if the order was nothing more than standard procedure. He met Bracken's gaze and lifted his brow, nodding slowly. "If the girl doesn't surface in five days, hang her mother. After that, hang the little one."

Constance's jaw slackened. She looked between Marcus and Bracken. On her husband, her gaze fractured. She strained the same way children did when practicing a new language, like she did not recognize what stood before her. When her eyes landed on Bracken, she beamed a plea to him. *Don't*. Her throat flexed. The blood drained from her face.

But Bracken was not Cael. If he was anything at all, Bracken Volkov was loyal.

I must remain loyal.

"Understood, Imperator?" Marcus asked.

Bracken tore his gaze from Duchess Constance and inclined his head to Marcus. "Heard, Legatus."

II

KEEPER OF THE BASILISK

CHAPTER TWENTY-FIVE
CAEL

Cael tasted smoke. He shoved through dense brush on the shielded side of the treeline surrounding the manor, searching endlessly for Elio. Above him, the Griean warship chomped through Draitune's spectral shape, spitting transport after transport into low orbit. Some dropped terrestrial vehicles and cargo before returning to the warship. Others — smaller, versatile, crueler spacecrafts — landed near the launch bay, positioned for routine scouting and aboveground combat.

It was the plan to which he'd been privy. His plan. The siege of a lifetime: arrive under the cover of nightfall. Move swiftly, deliberately. Force House Henly beneath Griea's boot, unable to squirm, or fight, or threaten. Station artillery on the perimeter, and keep the Royal Reserve internal, securing the heartbeat of Aurethia in a sea of Griean-black. Leverage the unification to assert control over the moon, the starlink, and Avara, and rear an heir with the mind of a warlord.

Foul grit spilled into his throat. Cael doubled over, emptying his stomach onto the forest floor. Watching a predetermined future come to fruition punctured him like a poisonous barb. Cael had known for as long as he could remember that this day, Aurethia's Armageddon, would come whether he liked it or not, and he'd tricked himself into believing he might possess the power to prevent it, shift it, deliver it gently. Foolish, empty hope. As if he ever controlled… *anything*. As if Cael himself wasn't a highborn pawn in his father's quest for power — vengeance costumed as justice.

As if the Keeper of the Basilisk hadn't been the one to train the very men storming the Henly manor. He coughed and spat at the ground, righting himself against another wave of nausea.

Engine fire sizzled the air. Unnatural heat coiled around the estate, rippling with the presence of pulse-weaponry. Charred bodies concaved east of the meadow. The orchard, thankfully, remained untouched, and the domed terrarium next to the garden protected terrified livestock. Cael sniffled. He swallowed stomach acid and regret and tapped his dialect device.

"Connect me to Vik Endresen."

I apologize, but access to one, Vik Endresen, has been revoked. Would you like to pair with a nearby drone?

"No. Connect me to Constance Volkov."

I apologize, sir, but access to the Griean Directory has been temporarily suspended. Would you like to pair with a nearby drone?

Cael wanted to smash the device under his boot. He seethed and tapped it harder. *Answer me*, he thought. *Please, answer me.* "Is Elio Henly's device within range?"

Scanning. The robotic voice went quiet, then beeped pleasantly. *Elio Henly is within range. Would you like to send a transmission?*

"Yes," he blurted, heaving an exhausted, relieved breath. "Direct connection."

Attempting to connect. Another pause. Static filled his earpiece. *Connected.*

Cael held his breath until his chest could no longer stand it. "Elio," he said, gasping out his name. "Is Vik with you? Are you safe?" He strained to listen. Heard the shaky sound of Elio breathing. "Where — "

Connection lost.

"Reconnect," Cael yelled.

Apologies, sir, but the connection has been manually revoked.

"Fuck's sake." Cael ripped off the earpiece and held it in a tight fist, turning his watery gaze toward the sky. Of course. What else could he possibly expect? Trust? Endearment? Concern? "I'm sorry," he said to no one, to Elio, to Bracken, to everyone. *But you're alive.* He closed his eyes, inhaling coarsely, exhaling thin and slow. "Stay alive."

There was no time for wallowing. No time for misery. He wiped his mouth with the back of his gloved hand and sank into the shadow of a towering evergreen, crouching to assess the damage. The manor was fully intact. The Aurethian seaguard was either being pursued or had already been detained. Elio was alive. If Bracken hadn't found Peadar, he'd be searching, and if the Legatus hadn't simultaneously attacked Atreyu then an assault on the city was coming next. This had always been the intent for the first wave. Secure House Henly. Force their hand. Take control.

But Cael was free, and Elio was still alive, and the galactic union their great-grandparents had put into place was official. Technically, Cael was an Aurethian Lord, Elio was a Griean Duke, and there was no undoing that without relinquishing their titles or sharing an early grave. His father knew that. Bracken knew that, too. For now, House Volkov's momentum stalled. But Cael couldn't keep it that way for long.

Cael steadied his breathing and glanced around, unsure if he should follow the path toward Nadhas, or turn around and hunt for a vehicle that could get him to Atreyu. If he could hijack a space transport, he might be able to make it to Draitune — Mercy, at least — but the likelihood of being shot down mid-flight deemed the ground *much* safer. Fear crept in as he scrambled along the mossy forest floor, darting between trees.

For the first time in an entire cycle, he was alone. Really alone. Over the course of the last year, Vik's calming presence had swaddled him like a safety blanket. The Augment was only ever a few feet away, watching, tracking, keeping Cael in his line of sight.

Aurethia reverted to uncharted wilderness without him.

If he got to Nadhas, he could find a seacraft and cross the ocean to Atreyu. But he'd be a sitting duck in open water. If a scout spotted him from above, he'd have nowhere to run. Frustration edged between clenched teeth. He smashed the heel of his palm against his temple, rubbing at the dull ache brewing in his skull. *Think, think —*

A girlish shriek echoed, yanking his attention. A lion's fierce roar came next. The sound of a charged pulse-rifle warped the air. Cael bounced to his feet and sprinted toward the noise. Behind the giant terrarium, tucked away in a bramble thatch where the estate met the woodland, three members of the Royal Reserve took defensive stances.

Nara stood in front of Lorelei. Her bloody maw folded into a deep snarl. She flicked her tufted tail. Lorelei, barefoot and dressed in a dirty night-gown, gripped a basic kitchen knife. Her sweat-dampened blonde waves came loose from a plaited braid. One Griean soldier sprawled in front of them, struck down by the lioness. A circular scorch from a pulse-shot blackened the grass. When one of the remaining three reached for his fallen pulse-gun, Nara lunged, startling the soldier backward.

"Enough pussyfootin'. Shoot the cat and get the girl to Bracken," someone said, raising a loaded rifle.

"Don't touch her," Lorelei barked furiously.

Cael drew his weapon and bounded forward. He plunged his blade through the first soldier, lancing him vertebrae to sternum, put his boot to the small of his back, pulled the blade free, and whipped around, blocking an incoming strike. Nara rumbled and pounced, crunching through the third soldier's shield with a powerful bite. A muffled yelp came and went.

"Traitor," the Griean said. Their voice was tinny and venomous behind black carbon-plastic.

Cael headbutted them. Pain erupted in his brow, but he swung his blade and cut the soldier ear to ear, slicing a smile along their throat. When the third assailant fell, Cael staggered backward, gulping in a ragged breath. Relief was fleeting. Nara bared her teeth and leaped toward him, aiming a hard swipe at his face. Cael tried to dodge, but the cat was too quick. Two of her claws caught his forehead, skipped down his eyebrow, snagged his eyelid, and grooved through his cheek. The third, smaller claw scraped his temple and clipped his tragus, and another carved the bridge of his nose.

Lorelei called out, "Nara!" And the lion stopped, resuming her place in front of the Aurethian princess.

For a second, Cael thought she'd torn his flesh clean off. Thought he might be skeletal from hairline to chin. He smashed his hand over his face. His palm slipped through warm wetness. Pain electrified his cheek. His nose stung — everything burned. His socket started to swell, forcing his right eye closed. *She might've blinded me*. The thought was as fleeting as the fear. *Lorelei is alive*.

"Are you hurt?" Cael choked out, setting his teeth against the savage pain shooting through his skull. He fixed his good eye on her, focused on the off-white of her gown through blood-blurred vision. He sniffled and spat, going to his knees in front of the nearest body. "One of 'em should have a medkit. If you're hurt badly, we'll get to Nadhas and find a doctor, but we can't go back to the manor — "

"Shut up," she snapped.

Cael pulled his mouth shut. He rummaged through the bloodied uniforms until he found a small medkit tucked away in the second fallen soldier's breast pocket. He dropped the kit and opened it, pressing a wad of absorbent gauze to his mangled face. He kept his fuzzy gaze on her. The princess assessed him with guarded, glazed eyes. Nara kept her large head low, poised to strike.

"Do you love this house, Imperator?" Lorelei asked. Her quaky voice betrayed the confident way she stood.

Cael deflated. "Yes," he said, nodding vigorously. The movement throbbed.

"Do you love my brother?"

An awful soot-like feeling chalked his throat. "Despite my very design." He withdrew the gauze, refolded it, then pressed it to his face again. "I'll love him until Womb makes me something new," he confessed, speaking Griean. *And after that.*

"Is he alive?" Lorelei's voice cracked.

Cael nodded again. Pain thudded. "Yeah, I'm pretty sure he is."

Kneeling beside stiffening bodies made him suddenly, viscerally aware of the one loose end he hadn't yet snipped. Lorelei's frame marginally relaxed. Her narrow shoulders dropped, and her chest emptied. She glanced at the sky and her eyelids drifted shut. Petite hands curled into empty fists.

"Can I see that knife?" he asked.

Lorelei glanced around him for a moment, considering, before she leaned over Nara and handed him the knife. The lioness chuffed.

"Don't watch." He eased out of his armored tunic before yanking down his undershirt's flexible collar.

The Aurethian princess tilted her head. Her smart, fierce face remained a boulder.

Cael inhaled a grounding breath, and drove the cutlery behind his collarbone, digging into meat and muscle, slicing through sensitive tissue. Pain shackled his wrist, urging him to stop, but he kept going, kept searching, opening a pocket large enough for his finger to snake into. He bit back a weak cry and sobbed out a curse, crooking his index around the tiny tracking device lodged in his chest. He trembled as he pulled it free, gasping and coughing, resisting the trigger his stomach sent to his throat. His brain said *shut down,* but his body refused. The last bit of the tracker — thin, root-shaped wire — slithered out of him. Pain rocketed. It twisted his already upset gut until his bowel cramped and he gagged, sucking in air to quell the discomfort churning in his very center.

Black darkened the edge of his vision. He blinked through it, shaking and worn out. *Almost.* He dropped the tracker and slammed the tip of the knife through it, shattering the metallic bead into tiny pieces. *There.* When he finally lifted his busted face, Lorelei looked back at him, unfazed and mildly satisfied.

CHAPTER TWENTY-SIX
ELIO

"Lord Henly, we should keep moving," Vik said.

Elio braced against a mossy tree and stared at a patch of spotted fungi beneath a fern. He heard Cael again, desperation ringing through three syllables — *Elio, Elio, Elio, Elio, Elio* — clothed in different memories.

The first day they'd met.

In Atreyu, pressed against the barn, Cael's teeth on his neck.

Sparring in the training chamber.

Last night, riding the back of a gasp, sharing their wedding bed.

But no matter how many times Cael had said it, Elio couldn't unhear how foreign his name sounded through the static in his dialect device. *Is Vik with you? Are you safe? Where* — For the first time, Elio registered true terror in Cael Volkov's voice.

"This was premeditated," Elio mumbled. He glanced at Vik. "You're telling me Cael coordinated this?"

"Yes," the Augment said. "He also tried to stop it."

It felt strange to laugh, but Elio couldn't help it. An abrupt, bewildered sound escaped, and then his face contorted, buckled by a sob. He masked the sudden outburst, scrubbing his hand over his mouth and chin. "Tell me again."

Vik sighed. "Which part?"

"The mission. Tell me his mission."

"To clear a path for Griea to assume control of Avara distribution and the Lux Continuum. To bring House Volkov glory, to make right what was wronged. To discreetly extract sensitive information from House Henly, leverage the unification to Griea's advantage, and secure an heir for the Volkov bloodline."

Elio swallowed bile. "So *I* was his mission?"

"You were his mission," Vik confirmed.

"How long was I his mission?"

Vik's data-port hummed. He paused for a moment. His left pupil expanded. "Seven-thousand-three-hundred and four days, or around twenty planetary Griean cycles."

Oxygen thinned. Elio couldn't manage a full breath.

"I could say the same for you, Elio. Cael has been your mission since before you had a name, too," Vik added, speaking lowly.

"My mission was to marry him, not destroy him," Elio said.

"Ask a different question."

"Did Cael use me to source information for an impending attack on Aurethia?"

"Ask a *different* question."

"Answer me."

"Yes, but — "

"There is no *but* — "

"Cael defected."

"Not soon enough." Elio turned and made for an elk trail.

Vik followed. "Is there anything else you want to know?"

"Yeah, I want to know why," he scoffed.

Static left the Augment's mouth followed by a recorded conversation. First Cael's voice, then Vik's. "Report the estimated Avara related death-toll for one cycle on Griea, please — This cycle, Avara-related sickness is estimated to claim two-hundred-sixty-four million lives, Imperator. That's a two percent increase from last year, likely due to illegal trafficking of black-market Avara. Those managing moderate-to-severe symptoms with a distilled treatment will increase their lifespan two-fold by obtaining a standard treatment. Those who cannot afford, source, or otherwise implement a standard treatment will succumb to their injuries within twelve to fourteen months depending on the severity of their case."

Elio's jaw tensed. He waited for Vik to say something else, but the Augment remained silent. It was a cruel and blunt way to deliver a message. Elio couldn't ignore it, though. The *why* festered in the very membrane of their society. Aurethia, jewel of the Lux System, miracle worker of the Greater Universe, had been guided by a cowardly hand. He felt sick to think it, to saddle his family with the blame, but the last cycle proved it to be true. Comfort laid the groundwork for destruction. His father's unwillingness to embrace expansion kept the powerless in distress and the powerful at ease, and selective Avara distribution lined House Henly's pocketbook with ample credit.

"It's a delicate situation," Elio said, as if the excuse might matter.

"It is," Vik agreed. "Tricky, explaining delicacy to the dire."

The statement flayed like a dagger. He exhaled as if he'd been bludgeoned, shooting a cautionary glance over his shoulder. "Trickier, staking the well-being of three interconnected systems on the output of one moon." He scanned the distant treeline for black armor. "C'mon, there's an entrance into the village through a rancher's pasture near the teahouse. Can you detect any activity?"

The Augment hummed. His data-port whirred again. "Might I recommend connecting your dialect device to my programming?"

Elio tapped his earpiece. "Connect to nearest program." *Lord Henly,* the robotic voice welcomed. *Augment detected. Ready to pair.* He pressed and held the smooth bulb on the underside of the device. After a brief pause, Vik gave a single nod. *Pairing complete.*

Vik quirked his head like a bird. He stared straight ahead, but his expression burrowed inward. "I don't detect smoke, detonation, or nearby drone usage. If I were to guess, I'd assume the acting Imperator stationed Griean forces on the border of the village. Containment protocol."

"Why wouldn't Bracken take the entire region?"

"The Legatus and his nephew are proficient in strategic movement. Assuming control of Nadhas without establishing a military foothold around the manor would scatter their resources. They'll invade once everyone is moon-side."

"There's a small militia in the village."

"Not to be pessimistic, but it would be in their best interest to cooperate." Vik tipped his head, deliberating. "You're their prince. They'll listen to you."

Elio crouched behind a wall of latticed flora and stared through green stalks. Smoke still plumed from chimneys. Down the sloping hill toward the harbor the sea remained empty. Every vessel was docked or gone. Nadhas itself seemed unmoving. The market looked abandoned. Tents billowed open around stark tables. A family of spotted quail scampered across lonely cobblestone.

"Vik, can you tap into public communication or emergency transmissions?" Elio asked.

"I can't tap into anything uninvited, but I can listen."

"You're a Griean Augment yet you can't hack — "

"Believe it or not, my internal programming is in accordance with Aurethian law, Lord Henly."

Elio snorted. "Can you isolate Aurethian communication?"

"I can try."

"Can you do it while we find the weaponsmith?"

"I am capable of doing two things at once, yes," Vik quipped.

Elio crept forward from the safety of the dense brush, glancing skyward, left then right, before he darted into the pasture and lowered to a crawl. He navigated the tall grass as best he could, stopping to lift his face and look for danger. He felt like a common beast hunted for sport.

Once they made it to a dark-painted barn, Elio stood and flattened his back against it, running toward the farmhouse. From there, the pair slipped between shadowy inlets and ducked under awnings, sneaking through the center of Nadhas. He'd never seen the village so lifeless before, lacking the bustle of daily errands, completely mute.

When they made it to the weaponsmith, Elio looked over his shoulder at Vik. "They might try to kill you," he said wearily.

"I'll survive."

"I'm serious, Vik."

Do you have any advice? Vik's smooth voice chimed in his dialect device. The Augment lifted a brow.

"Let me go first." Elio glanced at Vik's hand. "I didn't know you could..." He remembered the way Vik's palm opened, transforming into a pulse-rifle. He lifted his wrist, gesturing limply. "I didn't know you had — "

I am a weapon, first and foremost. I was created post-mortem for tactical use in high-stakes combat, but I've had no reason to engage my martial model until now.

Elio blinked rapidly. Right. "Catch anything on the scanner?"

Vik's right pupil paled. An emergency transmission pinged Atreyu this morning. No return correspondence.

"Okay," he whispered.

Elio wet his throat and grasped the handle on the weaponsmith's heavy

wooden door, decorated with the emblem of a mallet and anvil. Locked. He
gathered courage and rapped his knuckles on the hard surface. The minute
it took for the door to crack open felt like an eternity. Sunlight lit the
weaponsmith's face. Well, the weaponsmith's apprentice, actually.

"Lawrence Graham," Elio eased, searching the younger artisan for
friendliness, or hospitality, or something that might lead him to believe
Peadar had managed to form some semblance of a plan. "I met you at the
market once, I think. You're the weaponsmith's son, aren't you? Is Gene
available?"

"Move," Gene said. Her warm, deep voice came from the darkness
inside the house. She curled her hand around the door and hauled it open,
allowing light to spill inside. She looked over Elio's shoulder, searching the
village. When her attention landed on Vik, she startled.

"He's my Augment," Elio blurted. He shielded Vik with an outstretched
arm. "I'm his Primary Controller."

Gene's pinched gaze hardened. "He's your *Griean* Augment — "

"And he's programmed to prioritize my safety. I was sent here by Peadar
Mahone, general of the Aurethian guardship. My name is Elio — "

"You're Elio Henly, lion cub of Aurethia," she interjected, nodding
slowly. Her cold stare slid across Vik before flitting back to Elio. "Have it
relay its directive."

"Vik, what is your directive?"

Vik inclined his head respectfully. "I have been ordered to tether my
internal and external allegiance to one, Elio Henly, and his safety. His life is
priority. All off-planet monitoring via Augment surveillance, except for
location monitoring, has been uninstalled or disabled. Transmitted
messages, data, or emergency correspondence must be executed manually
by my Primary Controller."

Gene sucked her teeth and stepped aside.

Elio entered the dwelling. The front of the building served as a
shopfront. Weaponry hung from a sleek wall-panel, and a patterned
Ocurian rug stretched across the tiled floor. Lawrence moved behind the
countertop where a credit-reader and a holotablet remained unlit and
offline, and Gene checked the front window. She pulled the privacy screen
down, darkening the glass. A disc-lamp glowed. Vik stayed close to the exit.

Gene sighed. She skipped across him, glancing from Elio's soft-soled
shoes to his teary face. "The pride fled inland."

"I saw," he said.

"Did you see anything else?"

Elio opened his mouth. Closed it. Opened it again. "Bracken Volkov, the newly appointed Griean Imperator, has taken my family hostage. House Henly is compromised, I don't know where Peadar is — I don't know if he's even alive — and my sister is missing. Vik noted a distress call, so Atreyu should be aware of the assault. If Griea hasn't jammed off-world communication, then I'm guessing the city will reach out to Draitune for immediate aid."

"And what would you have us do?"

"You..." Elio blinked slowly.

You're the heir, Elio. Vik's voice buzzed in his earpiece.

Elio tongued at his teeth, buying time. "I would have you protect the weak," he tested, feeling out each order before he gave it. *What would my father do?* "Make sure the elderly and the children are safe. Arm the militia. Griea brought artillery. Nadhas won't... *Can't* stand against them, but you should defend yourselves if you have to." He paused, resisting the urge to glance at Vik. "They'll come for Avara."

"No one has the location to the mine," Gene assured.

Shame pierced Elio's heart. "Unfortunately, they do. Stall for as long as you can, but in the end, they'll find the mine. When they do, keep stalling. The only leverage we have is our production value. If House Volkov can't keep Avara operation stable, then the Imperium will have no choice but to intervene."

"Understood." She crossed her muscular arms and tipped her head toward Elio. "Will you follow the pride, Lord Henly?"

Elio listed his head.

"Toward the mother mine. The crater is a dead zone." Her mouth curved around the last word. She stared at him sternly. "If you live, Aurethia lives. If House Volkov exterminates your bloodline, Aurethia will fall under uncontested Griean rule, and our moon will be torn apart." She looked at Vik momentarily then slid her attention back to Elio. She answered the confusion on his face with a smile. "Nadhas is the city by the sea. The Henly manor has been our neighbor for a long time. The people here aren't naïve. We knew what our proximity to a Great House could cost."

"The crater is uncharted. I can't..." This time, he did turn to look at Vik, searching for guidance. "We can't go out there, can we?"

"The xenobiologists will look after you," Lawrence said. He had a low, gruff voice for such a scrawny young man. Elio swore he'd heard the same tone in someone else's mouth.

Vik lifted an eyebrow. `No one in this room is lying.`

Elio shot him a questioning look.

`I go where you go. If you'd rather trek to the city, we can. But I think it might be wise to follow the pride.` "Bracken will hesitate to scout the crater, especially if the territory destabilizes Griean communication."

"The crater destabilizes all communication. We won't be able to reach out to anyone either," Elio said. When he said *anyone*, he thought *Cael*. He should've been thinking about Lorelei.

Gene opened her hand toward Vik in agreement. "If you move inland and travel through the crater, you'll trek to Atreyu slower, yes, but safer, without detection or pursuit, and like Lawrence said, what's left of the Xenobiology Division will look out for you. I'm sure your lions will, too."

"Most of the xenobiologists have likely been called back to the city," Elio murmured, sighing through his nose.

"Our only chance at getting out from underneath Griean rule is by keeping a Henly alive," the weaponsmith said. She jutted her chin toward Elio. "Speaking of which, where's the warlord you married?"

"Apparently, he defected in favor of Aurethia, meaning he's likely been killed." Confusing heartbreak burned his throat, furious and unreachable. "And if he's not dead yet, he will be soon."

Vik stiffened. His expression fell. Sadness plucked at his mouth, but he wiped the emotion from his face and pushed away from the wall, taking his place next to Elio.

"You're armed," Gene said, glancing at the Grabak strapped to Elio's waist and the six remaining cattails lining his belt.

Elio nodded. "I could use another dagger."

"And new armor," she said, giving him another once-over. She grabbed his arm, turned him, assessing his build. "I'll pack you a bag. What about you, Augment? Do you need a weapon?"

"I am a weapon, ma'am," he said, lacking sweetness. "But I'll take field gear if you can spare it."

"Wait here. I'll get everythin' sorted. I'm sure the mechanic on the north end of town can loan you a couple groundcrafts. We'll see to it on our way out," Gene said. She gestured at Lawrence and nodded toward an open archway.

Lawrence ducked into an adjacent room and returned with a drooping deerskin twined in leather. He unrolled it across the table, revealing an assortment of daggers. A few were simple with sturdy handles and polished blades. Others embellished with gemstone and gold, stamped with Aurethian lettering. Elio floated his hand across the display. Metal gleamed and glinted. He plucked a plain tanto from the line-up.

"Just like the one Peadar commissioned for you," Gene said. She dropped two stuffed trekking packs and offered a small, sad smile. "He's my ex-husband, by the way."

Elio remembered what he'd said before. *I don't even know if he's alive.* And swallowed thickly, regretting saying it at all. He didn't reach for the knife in his boot, afraid the sight of it might hurt her worse than his clumsy mouth already had. "I'm glad he sent me to you."

She nodded. Her smile shrank but didn't fall. "I packed you fresh clothes, an armored vest, food, and water. You've both got field necessities, too. Sleep mat, heat sheet, portable purifier, medkit." She handed him a green cloak. It was tattered and well-worn but smelled like fresh linen. "Keep yourself hidden."

The cloak's hood concealed his head. An interior scarf sewn into the garment's collar wrapped around his mouth and neck, blurring his identity. "Thank you."

"C'mon, we'll leave through the back."

Gene led Elio and Vik into the living space, furnished with a lumpy leather seater, upholstered chairs, and a bookcase. A family picture decorated the mantle beneath an empty space on the wall where a holo might project. Peadar, smiling with Gene and Lawrence, accompanied by a spotted herding dog.

"This way," Gene said. She slid open the glass-paneled back door. "We'll cut through the neighborhood. Stay close."

When she said cut through the neighborhood, Elio imagined hugging the exterior of wood-built buildings, hiding in shadow, and ducking around corners. But Gene led them from one house to the next, guiding Elio and Vik through side doors and garages, boutiques and living quarters.

The people of Nadhas stood as the four of them strode through each space. Some said his name — *Elio* — with profound relief. Others touched his shoulder, or uttered an Aurethian blessing, or nodded at him, teary-eyed and afraid. Houses smelled like tea and seafood and everything Nadhas. Families lingered together, eating plum cake and goosefish, enjoying the last good meal they might get for a long while. Most of them flashed their hand. Faced their palm toward their throat, fingertips positioned beneath a tilted chin, offering the Aurethian symbol for freedom. *May the moon never fall, may we take heart, may the sky hold us.* It was an old thing. Something he thought the citizenship of Aurethia might not recognize anymore.

But the people of Nadhas saluted him. Profound pride surged through him as he crossed each house, nodded to each family, attempted to send them reassurance through false strength.

Once they reached the northern edge of Nadhas, Elio accepted the pairkey to a hoverbike, and Vik did the same. Gene clasped his shoulder tightly and pointed toward a break in the treeline.

"That way," she said.

Elio nodded. "If you see Peadar — "

"Don't." The briskness in her tone sent a chill down Elio's back. She pointed again. Her throat rolled with a slow swallow. "You are the lion of Aurethia. Remember everything he taught you. Now go."

Go! His mother's voice echoed underneath Gene's careful, even command.

Elio swung his leg over the groundcraft's seat and looked over his shoulder. Faces peered through windows. People glanced around open doors, stood on porches, and waved from rooftops. He placed his hand in front of his throat, mirroring them.

Are you ready? Vik's voice came through his dialect device.

Elio flicked the toggle on the handlebar and the speeder lifted, propelled off the ground by a gravity disrupting panel lining the undercarriage. He twisted the throttle. The bike lurched. Elio's stomach shot into his throat.

They sped through the trees, banking left then right. Vik cruised next to him, dipping around an evergreen. Needly fir scraped Elio's shoulder. The farther they descended, the truer everything became. Nadhas disappeared. The woodland grew harsh and shaded. *Up here,* he thought. The forest floor gave way, careening down, down as Elio angled his speeder over the lip of the crater. To the right, his Avara mine remained tucked away, slumbering beneath the cliff-side onsen. As children, Elio and Lorelei explored the shallow start of the crater but never ventured far. His pulse quickened as he entered uncharted territory, zipping around flora with blue-belled mouths, startling native short-horned deer. Hummers skated a pond where the crater leveled out. The hoverbike bounced, buoyant and languid, and Elio turned down a path frothed with vibrant greenery.

It happened all at once. Elio let his mind clear enough for Cael to invade. Every shared moment crashed into him, pawing at his resistance, forcing memories to flash like a holodocument. He remembered Cael in the meadow, sparring with him, smiling bright. In Atreyu, twirling with him to the blaring horn and sweet percussion of street musicians. Locked together in the throes of intimacy, tongue laving his throat, words of encouragement and praise feathering his earlobe. Waking with him in the blue hour. Swallowing a mouthful of his blood.

And in the darkness, will you love me then?

Elio yanked the handlebar and hit the brake. The hoverbike's nose tipped toward the dirt and the groundcraft halted. Heat filled his nasal cavity. He couldn't breathe. Couldn't focus.

"Elio," Vik called. The Augment stopped and dismounted. "Are you — "

"Don't," Elio gasped out, flinging his arm, holding out his palm. He crumbled against a fallen log, bracing against it with his back, and brought his knees to his chest.

Vik plopped on the ground. He remained silent but close.

Elio heard his own voice like a curse. *Forevermore.* He let his body heave and convulse. Let his heart crack down the center. Let the day finally sink in and break out. Ugly, painful sobbing shook through him, and he cried, wailing like a child in Aurethia's wild crater.

CHAPTER TWENTY-SEVEN

CAEL

"**W**e need to get to Atreyu." Lorelei hoisted over a mossy stump and swatted dirt off her gown. "It's fortified and populated. If our militia doesn't hear from someone soon, I'm assuming they'll reach out to House Darvin."

Cael's face throbbed. He followed Lorelei and Nara, keeping his good eye trained on the big cat as she padded gracefully through the forest. The Aurethian princess was right. He knew that. But he also knew Elio was somewhere nearby — probably considering the same two-day trek — and he couldn't ignore the twinge in his chest at the thought of leaving him behind. He scanned the wilderness, searching the dense fauna for any sign of Vik or Elio. *He'll be safe,* he told himself. *He's bright, resilient, deadly, protected.* Cael didn't have the heart to think about anyone else. High Lord Darius; High Lady Lena. With Bracken in control, Cael would've assumed they'd be treated decently, but his cousin's recent departure into self-servitude made him reconsider.

She turned to glance at him. Her cold gaze widened slightly. "If that gets infected, you'll lose more than your sight."

"The medkit had no antibiotics, my lady, and I don't know enough about Aurethian plantlife to tend to it."

"*My lady.* Please," she grunted. "Well, I can't have you slowing us down." She pointed to a sturdy rock at the base of a nearby tree. "Sit. I'll find something."

Cael sat. The minute his body reclined against the tree, sleep pulled at him. The adrenaline filling his body dissipated, chased off by pain, leaving him exhausted, wounded, and lost. Not lost, exactly. Displaced. Even after spending a cycle on Aurethia, he still didn't know the forest well enough to navigate it. He didn't know the crater either, but Nara's keen senses would help them detect pursuit, and Lorelei's knowledge of her homeland would get them where they needed to go.

Nara sat on her haunches across from him, panting.

"I'm sorry about your friends," he whispered. He tried not to think of the way Tatu's feet slipped out from underneath him.

The lioness twitched her ear.

Lorelei returned with a yellow flower and a few other sprigs. She plucked the petals and brought them to her mouth, chewing until they turned into a paste. After that, she snipped the top of a vine with her canine, wincing at the flavor, and let the split stalk drip over the masticated flower. She added pollen from another plant, too, and mixed everything together in her palm.

"You didn't find a suture pack in that medkit, did you?" she asked.

He shook his head. Pain flared with the movement. "Probably already got used."

"Then you'll have to wait until we get to the city. You'll scar," she breathed out, and crouched in front of him, dabbing the strange concoction over his wound. She started above his eyebrow. "Can you see out of it?"

"No," he said, clearing his throat.

"Avara might reverse the damage, but if we don't administer it soon — "

"I'm aware."

She pressed too hard. "There is artillery and weaponry bunkered on the outskirts of the city. Once we get there, we'll arm ourselves and regroup with the militia. Do you think House Volkov will strike Atreyu?"

"Only after House Henly is subdued. We always knew Atreyu would bend if the manor came under a swift directive," he said, keeping his eyes firmly shut.

Lorelei paused. Breathed. "So you knew," she said, smashing another glob of forestry medicine into the fissure on his eyelid.

Cael winced. He tried to jerk away, but she followed him, wiping more flower-paste into his split cheek. He needed to mind his tongue. "It's complicated — "

"Do not," she warned.

"Why do you think I'm here and not there," he snapped, glaring through his pinched left eye. "My family is hunting me, too. I tried to stop it, Lorelei. You asked me if I love this moon — I do. You asked me if I love Elio — I do. My father did this without my approval, and my cousin usurped my title while I was here, courting your brother."

"But you knew," she said again, shifting to meet his gaze.

"Griea is starving," each word edged between gritted teeth, "and dying, because Alexander Henly cut an unfair, inhumane deal with my great-grandmother. House Henly was in full control of its deliverables. Aurethia's steward prioritized wealth instead of honor — " He sucked in a pained breath, hissing when she dug her thumb into the bloody pocket on the bridge of his nose.

"Did you come here intending to slaughter us, Imperator? Or did my brother bat his pretty — "

"My cousin intends to wed you," he snarled. "And he can only do that if I'm dead. More importantly, he can only do that if Elio is dead. You're young, Lorelei. You have no idea what's coming — "

Lorelei seized his jaw with her sticky hand. She held him in a vice, matching his snarl. "I am the lioness of House Henly, and I have been raised with the shadow of this scenario haunting every breakfast, lunch, dinner, outing, birthday, training session — *everything* in my life has prepared me for this. Don't be afraid but be ready. That's the Aurethian way." She snorted, hiccupping on a mean laugh. "You think I don't know what House Volkov intends to do?" She squeezed harder, scraping her fingernails through the blood crusted on his skin. "A union with Griea was supposed to alleviate our rivalry, but greed and revenge prevailed. And now my family is dead, Imperator. My mother, my father, my little brother. If your family caught them, they're gone." The last word puffed his chin. It escaped her like a barking sob. "So if you want to kill me, do it now. Because if I survive, and I *will* survive, I'll smother your Legatus, his legion, and his legacy beneath my boot."

Lorelei's severity shocked him. She breathed hard, like she'd been running.

He swallowed around the glass in his throat. Nothing could've prepared him for this. Blinded by an Aurethian lion and held at bay by Lorelei Henly. To lose everything and still be responsible for someone else's loss, too. His chest ached. The pain in his face grew to the point of numbness — soreness overtaking everything else — and for a second, his body didn't remember what smiling or blinking felt like without it.

And a treaty with Aurethia was supposed to feed us, he thought but did not say. *But gluttony and power prevailed.* "I believe that."

She sucked her cheek, chewing. "If you betray me, Nara will tear out your heart."

"I gave my Augment to your brother. I've sealed my own fate."

"Elio won't make you a martyr."

Cael blinked. Water streamed from his good eye.

Lorelei thumbed the tear away too roughly. "You orchestrated a courtship, you played the part beautifully, you made him love you," she said, pursing her full mouth, "and I'll never forgive you for it."

"If that were true, I'd be commanding the Royal Reserve from inside your home, princess," he assured, speaking clearly, frankly, sharpening his tone. "But instead, I'm out here with you, throwing my life at your feet, hoping I can keep you away from my cousin for long enough to get this moon under control."

"Aurethian control," she insisted. "Henly control."

"*Our* control. Elio's control, my control. He's the first-born heir to Aurethia; I'm the rightful heir to Griea. It's our birthright and our marriage right. I don't expect you to trust me, but you have a lion, and I have nothing. If you wanted me dead, I'd be dead. I'm aware."

Her jaw ticked. She tipped her head to inspect his damaged face and then stood, smacking the leftover paste off her palm. "You're a Tupinaire champion. You always have something, Keeper. C'mon, get up. We need to move."

Cael stood. His head spun, but he righted himself against the tree. "Thank you for," he gestured to his swollen face, "this."

Lorelei looked away from him. She started ahead through the forest, barefoot and ghostly in her tattered nightgown. "Let's go."

CHAPTER TWENTY-EIGHT

ELIO

The crater was an unforgiving place.

Once Elio composed himself enough to resume their advance, the pair continued winding through the dense brush and lush vegetation until the hoverbikes became too hard to pilot. Branches reached from every direction and foliage sprang up against the gravity suspension module, knocking Elio's groundcraft off-balance and causing Vik's to sputter and lurch. After a valiant attempt to stay the course, Vik finally stopped and sighed, nodding solemnly. Elio nodded, too, and they agreed to leave the borrowed transportation underneath the shade of a waxy, blue-tinged fern.

Vik made a note of the location and adjusted the pack on his back. "We should eat soon."

"I'm not hungry."

"I've detected a decrease in your energetic output, signaling a depletion of caloric fuel. You're tired, young lord. You need to eat."

Elio pulled on the strap of his backpack and kept walking. Aurethia's wet climate thickened in the crater, swamping his lungs. He inhaled a great breath and craned for cleaner, thinner air, but it was no use. The faint feeling of perpetual falling came and went. His stomach flapped and his head spun, and he knew Vik was right. Knew he needed to eat. But couldn't bring himself to do it. If he stopped, he was afraid he might think too hard and spiral again.

After another mile or so, Vik placed his hand on Elio's shoulder. "Elio," he said sternly, sighing.

Elio relented. "Fine."

They made camp in a small clearing between two vase-shaped dogwoods. Vik rolled out his cot and Elio did the same. They couldn't risk a fire, so Elio ate his pre-packaged sandwich instead of the canned pheasant and fermented vegetables Gene stashed inside his pack. Lettuce crammed between his teeth, but he hardly tasted the thinly sliced fish or pungent mustard. He ate half and wrapped the rest in butcher paper, storing it for later.

"I'll take first watch. You should sleep," Vik said.

"I don't think I can." Elio stretched across his cot and stared at the pinhole sky beaming through the netted canopy. It was afternoon, almost evening, and the sound of battle was long gone, replaced by birdcall, toad croaking, and the hum of insects. He focused on keeping the contents of his stomach down. "Tell me the truth about Griea."

"I need you to clarify your question." Vik sat cross-legged, munching his sandwich.

"Has my father refused to send aid?"

"Yes."

"How often?"

"House Volkov and the rest of the Imperial Council discuss galactic adjustments and resource redistribution at the annual summit. Since I've been alive and after my augmentation, the Legatus repeatedly petitioned House Henly for fresh harvest and a larger stipend of Avara, and every cycle, High Lord Darius stayed the course of the original agreement outlined by Alexander Henly."

"What was the original agreement?"

"You don't know?" Vik asked, confused.

Elio made a frustrated noise. "Just tell me."

"Alexander Henly agreed to send Griea a portion of canned fruit, fermented vegetables, perishable harvest, and enough Avara to sustain Griea's population. But like every other homeworld in the Greater Universe, Griea's population has nearly tripled since then. Despite the data being conclusive, High Lord Darius used the exact verbiage agreed upon in the unification treaty to withhold a larger stipend. Given the distance between Draitune and the ice giant, House Volkov would have to pay a premium for more Avara."

Anger festered in his chest. "And what about the harvest?"

"Griea typically purchases Aurethian bounty from Ocury. It's usually cloned and there isn't much of it. For the most part, the Griean citizenship has made do with what we can grow in greenhouses and the scarce natural vegetation available planet-side. I don't think Cael had ever eaten a fruit plucked straight from a tree until he got here," he mused, thinking for a moment. "I certainly hadn't."

"But why..." He closed his eyes to quiet the storm in his stomach. "This can't be about credit."

Vik hummed as if he disagreed. "If Aurethia spent time and effort packaging and distributing fresh produce to Griea, House Henly would miss the chance to sell directly to Ocury, Draitune, and beyond. Sending harvest to the outer reaches of Lux would jeopardize critical travel-time. Darius chose to capitalize on premium buyers in Mal and Ren."

"Because the starlink is the only reliable way to deliver food and medicine," Elio exhaled.

"Exactly."

"My father prioritized the highest bidder."

"Unfortunately."

"Instead of supplying Griea and repairing the damage his grandfather caused, he stayed the course, intending to shove the situation on me — *us* — hoping the unification might bury the mess he continued making. If he embraced a more progressive approach after Cael and I were married, he could position our union as the predicted miracle Alexander put into motion." Elio scrubbed his palm over his face, groaning. "Stupid, stupid man."

"Selfish," Vik corrected. "But yes, that's the gist of the situation. Legatus Marcus has been planning a siege of Aurethia since before his son was born. Cael was a tool — nothing more. And Marcus's lack of poise or patience matches your father's self-servitude, I'm afraid."

"Our families fucked us," Elio spat.

Vik tipped his head from side-to-side. "That's one way to put it."

"But Cael could've..." He trailed off. Even knowing the truth, he still told the lie. "He could've told me. I would've..."

"You would've?" Vik prompted.

Elio stared at the sky. A pale-beaked eagle streaked downward, snatching up a small, furry thing. He ignored the Augment's question and asked, "Did Cael's directive involve manipulating my emotions, Vik?"

Vik stayed quiet. His data-port hummed and clicked.

"Don't answer that," he decided, sniffling miserably.

Elio closed his eyes. His mind still raced, and his heart still hurt, but he willed his muscles to relax, and his breathing to deepen, and eventually fell into a fitful, threadbare sleep. He half-dreamed of fire and smoke, half-dreamed of someone's hand, pale as winter, wrapped tight around the handle of a knife. Knuckles flexing, small, feeble, then larger, scarred and rigid. Splayed on his chest. Bent under his chin. Unfastening his belt. Squeezing his windpipe.

CHAPTER TWENTY-NINE
BRACKEN

Time passed differently on Aurethia. It seemed that way, at least. Bracken didn't realize two days had come and gone until his dialect device chimed on the third morning. *Received: Urgent galactic luminary from one, Draitune, two, the greater Mal region, three, the greater Ren region — Immediate response requested.* He leaned against a tree in the orchard and watched Sunder rise. In his planet-side chamber, Kindra slept in an unfamiliar bed, wrapped naked in white linen still scented like his cousin. Somewhere nearby, bushwhacking through the moon's overgrown wildland, Cael lived. A great distance across the system, snow flurried through Machina, and Goren sent frozen wind whistling into the city. In the courtyard, Darius Henly swung from the candlebell tree.

"Confirm receival. Request holomeeting," Bracken said, pressing on the underside of his device.

Relaying. Please hold. It only took a moment for the robotic voice to surface again. *Holomeeting accepted.*

Bracken pushed away from the tree and made his way to the encampment spread across the meadow. The Royal Reserve greeted him, parting as he stepped over spilled weaponry and open gun-cases. He dodged sparring matches between bored soldiers. A few people ate breakfast, gorging themselves on unripe fruit plucked prematurely from the orchard and cooked meat thawed from the Henly's spacious freezer. Others dressed for the day, adjusting armor, lacing boots. On the opposite side of the meadow, he made a sharp turn and rounded the back of the property, entering the manor through the garden.

"Optio," Maxine greeted. She stood in the living area, clutching a steaming cup.

"Imperator," he corrected.

She inclined her head. "Apologies, Imperator. High Lady Lena has requested a meeting."

"She can wait. You're needed with me, Operative Carr."

Bracken strode into the High Lord's study in the northern wing. Marcus's analytics team had disemboweled it, searching for clues that could uncover the mysteries of Avara and Aurethia alike. The room was empty except for a scattering of trinkets and old tomes. A holotablet sat crooked on the desk and the chair squeaked when Bracken lowered into it. He set down his own holotablet and pressed a button on the sleek, rectangular frame, prompting the device to send a blue pixelated hologram floating mid-air.

Maxine followed him, darting her gaze around the dark room. "What's going on?"

"I have three galactic shot-callers on a luminary call. I'll need you to help me negotiate."

She blinked rapidly. "Who — "

"Draitune, Mal, Ren." He gave her a challenging look and touched his dialect device. "Connect."

Maxine straightened and set her cup on the desk. She plucked at a wrinkle in her floor-length gown and then came to stand beside him, clasping her palms neatly at her waist. "I'll follow your lead."

Standby. Static transferred from his earpiece to the tablet, fuzzing and warping as the image came to life. *Connected*.

The hologram showed three people. The elected leader of Draitune, Angelina Darvin, wore a notched frown. The ambassador from Mal, Wippler Jye, and the ambassador from Ren, Rune Makosi, stared at him, dressed in trim, well-tailored clothing. Wippler's thick braids were interwoven in his headwrap, and Rune canted an eyebrow once Bracken's holotablet began streaming.

"Good rising," Bracken greeted, propping his elbow on the armrest of the leather chair.

"Optio Volkov. Might I ask why our luminary was directed to you?" Angelina asked. Her lined brow creased with caution.

"Legatus Volkov is attending a meeting with our legionaries. As acting Imperator, I'm happy to entertain the galactic luminary." When a luminary was sent, every reigning house, steward, monarch, or democratically assigned leader across the Greater Universe unanimously agreed to send a formal warning to a misbehaving neighboring government. This luminary was not unexpected, but it required delicacy. "What concerns you?"

The trio remained quiet for a beat.

"Draitune recently received a crisis message from Atreyu. The city militia claimed Griea launched an attack on Aurethia, and my ambassador on Mercy reported a Griean warship entering Aurethian airspace after the unification agreement was officiated. Several transmissions to High Lord Darius and High Lady Lena have gone unanswered, and confirmation of House Volkov's extended stay on the forest moon has been confirmed. This was the logical next step. I myself attended the recent ceremony — lovely execution; the two appeared fond of each other — but I don't recall seeing *you* there, acting Imperator." Angelina Darvin shifted her head, leaning closer to the holo. Her pixelated form blurred and reassembled. "My concern should be easy to deduce."

"It should be easy to articulate," Bracken said.

Maxine cleared her throat. "Lady Darvin, House Volkov and House Henly have run into an unfortunate impasse regarding title transference and ethical use of the Lux Continuum. The former Imperator is currently on trial for treason, and his husband fled the manor. As you know, an Aurethian citizen has already attempted to assassinate one member of the Volkov family. Risking a moon-side negotiation without armed protection was a gamble our Legatus could not afford."

Wippler Jye lifted his chin. "Treason?"

Bracken nodded. "Cael Volkov committed more than one capital offense. Elio Henly attacked the Royal Reserve. House Henly refused to accommodate balanced interest in Griea and Aurethia — "

"It hasn't been long enough to establish balanced interest," Rune Makosi blurted. She stared hard at Bracken. "You mentioned the Imperator being compromised during my visit to your homeworld. What exactly had been compromised?"

"Cael withheld critical information from Griean intelligence in order to prioritize Aurethian interest," Bracken said.

Maxine spoke over him, rushing to mediate. "The Imperator was compromised due to a breach of internal trust. No action was taken until the Legatus could properly and personally investigate the crime. After speaking with myself and surveilling the unification ceremony, Legatus Marcus brought Imperator Bracken and the Royal Reserve moon-side — protocol for political confrontations on countless homeworlds. This is a contained, social issue between Great Houses. It does not and will not impact Lux, Mal, or Ren."

"What was the crime, Miss Carr?" Angelina inquired.

"Treason, as mentioned before," she stated again, nodding curtly. "Atreyu's crisis signal, while offensive and unwarranted, is predictable. Aurethia's friendliness toward Griea has been contingent on distance. Now that we're moon-side, following the agreement penned by Alexander Henly, and assuming control over what is rightfully ours, the citizenship here has become," she paused, elevating an eyebrow, "unruly."

Bracken noticed Maxine's language. Ours, as if she too were part of House Volkov. He kept his attention on the holo and lifted the corner of his mouth. "Fortunately, we're negotiating a solution."

"I'd like to speak with High Lord Darius," Angelina stated. She framed the request as a threat.

"Mal's leadership would also like proof of life," Wippler said.

"Proof of life," Maxine echoed. The inflection in her voice hinted at humor.

Bracken held his tongue.

Rune's jaw dented. "Ren will meet Griea in good faith. Imperator, you speak as if Aurethia is perfectly stable yet Atreyu's crisis signal promises war. I don't believe my coordinator has confirmed an incoming shipment of Avara anytime soon. Should the production facility on Mercy anticipate a delay? I assume the mines are operational, but conflict would no doubt impact that."

"The conflict is being subdued as we speak," Bracken assured.

"And what about the unification?" Wippler snorted dismissively and waved a hand toward the holo. His pixelated limb came apart then floated back together. "You intend to punish the Griean heir for a capital crime, and the Henly heir is conveniently missing? Please, Bracken. Do you honestly think the Imperium will tolerate this clumsy grapple for authority? This is bold, even for Griea."

Maxine slid her gaze to Bracken. She was an elegant thing, all long and chiseled. Pretty like a karambit. When she turned her attention to the floor, he took it as a sign to do as he pleased.

Angelina started again. "If you do not promptly connect the Aurethian emissary on Draitune with our moon-side advocate, High Lord Darius

Henly, we will send defense to Aurethia. You do not want war with the Imperium — "

"War," Bracken rasped, laughing. Beside him, Maxine bristled but stayed poised and silent. He leaned forward, tapping his blunt finger on the desk. "Griea *is* war, Lady Darvin. I'll make it simple: if you come to Aurethia uninvited, Griea will consider it a security breach and respond in kind. Not only that, but I will halt all production of Avara and ground every agricultural shipment until further notice. Nothing will leave this moon. Not one blue shard, not one fruit. If House Volkov is given the time and space to handle this internal affair, Avara will remain widely available, mining will continue on schedule, harvesting will go on unbothered, and the Greater Universe will thrive. If you intervene," he folded his hands, glancing from Angelina's shocked-stern face to Wippler, who dropped his mouth open, then to Rune, who looked less than surprised, "I'll be forced to consider you a threat. I'd much rather us be friends, of course."

The leader of Draitune swallowed. Her throat caved with the movement. "The Imperium will reconvene in one Aurethian week. I expect the Legatus to be present, and you should expect a larger meeting, Bracken Volkov." His name cracked like ice. "The entire Imperium should be privy to this cage-fight you call an affair."

"Avara will resume production today," Maxine added. She smiled cheerily. "The unification is a blessing we haven't squandered. House Volkov and House Henly will stand united. Allow us time to be certain of it."

"One week," Rune said, and disappeared from the holomeeting.

Wippler Jye's pixelated form blinked away swiftly followed by Angelina's.

Bracken tapped his dialect device, disconnecting from the holotablet. The blue glow died.

Maxine stood beside him for a while. They didn't speak. Didn't look at each other. After too long, Bracken knocked over a fancy Earthen pen, and Maxine said, "The people refuse to work." Her voice was barely a whisper. "I located Elio's mine, but our team can't extract the crystal without instructions, and the people living in Nadhas won't budge. If we don't find a way to remove and refine Avara, Angelina will send reinforcements, there will be bloodshed, Griea will be sanctioned, and we'll lose our bargaining power. Our military can fend off an assault from Draitune, but we won't withstand an all-out war with the Greater Universe."

He slid his jaw from side-to-side. The bandage on his nose pulled with each movement. "You said the High Lady wishes to speak?"

"Correct."

"Take me to her."

Maxine blinked, surprised. She opened her mouth to protest and then promptly changed her mind, stepping backward and gesturing toward the exit.

HIGH LADY LENA WAS kept in a comfortable chamber in the guest wing. Two Royal Reserve stood outside the door, armed with black-barreled rifles and sheathed sabers. They stepped aside when Bracken and Maxine approached.

"The High Lady may look like a dove, but I encourage you to approach her the same way you would a widow spider," Maxine warned. She rested her slender hand on the knob and gave Bracken a concerning look. "Would you like me present?"

"You can stay," he said. The liaison was an asset to House Henly, someone they once trusted and probably couldn't fool.

Maxine opened the door. "High Lady Lena of Aurethia," she announced, stepping through the threshold. She tipped her head toward him. "Imperator Bracken of Griea."

The High Lady remained regal, perched elegantly on the edge of a tidy bed, wearing a long-sleeved, high-necked dress the color of Avara. Her chestnut hair was slicked into a neat bun and every angle of her fine, Aurethian face appeared harder, jagged and aged. Thin stockings gripped her dainty feet. She turned slightly, allowing him the barest glance.

"The candlebell will cover the smell," she said, sighing deeply. "But I'm afraid you'll encourage flies if you don't cut him down soon. Field mice, too. They'll eat anything."

Bracken pinched his eyes. He wasn't expecting much. Certainly not that. "You're not afraid to swing beside him, my lady?"

Laughter chirped. It was a strange, blunt sound. "No." The word coasted out under her breath. "I'm already dead, heir incumbent. That's what you are, right? You're the spare Volkov, son of the arena martyr who renounced the throne to chase fame on the ice. Isn't that true?"

Maxine slid her gaze to Bracken. Her face spoke a thousand things, but the easiest to see was *I warned you.*

"It is," Bracken said, matching the High Lady's tone. He strode across the room and placed himself in front of her, blocking the slatted window she stared through. He crossed his arms and leaned against it. Pride twisted in the furnace of his belly, bent awkwardly by childish rage. "Heir incumbent, staking a claim on the forest moon, hunting your son like a beast and your daughter like a trophy. What can I do for you, Lena?"

Her cool brown eyes hardened. She appraised him slowly. "You haven't found them."

He set his teeth. "I will."

She hummed. "What will become of House Volkov? You take my daughter as your bride to fulfill the obligation set forth in Alexander's and Harlyn's agreement, create an heir raised by a woman who will never forgive you for what you did to her homeworld, continue Avara operation while simultaneously dealing organic weaponry across three systems, and then die by the blade of your own heir when they inevitably challenge you in the arena?" Her smile was small and unpleasant. "Or when they poison you? When Avara is gone, parsec sickness eviscerates the population, and the Imperium blames Griea for a plague of its own making. What then, Imperator?"

"Lorelei will give me a Griean heir," he said, channeling calm. "And I will keep her fed, satisfied, and comfortable, and if she doesn't behave, I'll wire her jaw shut and keep her on a bejeweled leash. I would deny a pretty lion her teeth if it meant securing a future for my people." A part of him did not believe that, but he said it anyway, hoping to wedge a knife underneath Lena's confidence. "Our bloodline will be strong. That's all I'm concerned about."

Lena pursed her mouth and nodded, as if what he said might be acceptable. "And Avara," she chimed, offering a mocking frown. "I'm sure you've found Elio's mine. It's close by."

Maxine shifted uncomfortably.

Lena turned to look at her, smiling. "Do you remember your seventeenth birthday, Maxine? We took a boat out and swam with the iguanas. It was lovely, wasn't it? You taught Elio how to dive, didn't you?"

The liaison rolled her mouth. "I did, High Lady."

"Do you remember when that poor gull got snatched up by the falcon? No one saw it coming. None of us, really." She whipped toward Bracken, speaking with a jilted hand movement. "Everything was perfect and then suddenly," she struck her palms together, "blood hit the deck, feathers everywhere, the gull and the falcon fell into the water. Now, I would usually bet on the bird of prey. Maxine, you remember how that poor seagull flailed, biting and shrieking. We all thought it was dinner, but the gull — witty thing — held the falcon underwater. Drowned it." She shrugged, sighing through her nose. "I doubt it lived very long, wounded as it was, but it killed that bird anyway. Out of spite, I think." She popped her mouth. Laughter again, that tinny, metallic noise. "Which do you feel like?" Lena asked, leaning back to gaze at Maxine over the slope of her shoulder. "The seagull or the falcon?"

"It doesn't matter. They're both dead," Maxine said.

There was a bite about it, a defensive grit Bracken noted. He flicked his attention between the two women.

"She'll kill you for this," Lena whispered. She wore a mother's smile, knowing and compassionate. Cruelty lurked beneath it. "You know that, sweetheart. If he doesn't get to you first, she'll kill you."

Maxine's chest grew with a deeply held breath. Her resolve splintered, eyes igniting, pale hands curling into fists at her side. She dropped her gaze to the floor.

Bracken pushed away from the window and stepped forward. "As a matter of fact, we have found Elio's mine," he announced, yanking the High Lady's attention.

Lena tipped her chin, gazing up at him. "Oh, good," she mocked. "I'm sure Maxine can show you how to refine the mineral."

"If she can't, someone else will."

"Are you sure?"

"Why did you want to speak with me?" He was done with these games.

"Because you'll be marrying my daughter, won't you? My simple, demure, sweet-tempered daughter." Her smile waned, parted. Pink tongue felt across chapped lip. "After you catch my weak, unresourceful, docile son, and convince the mild-mannered people of Aurethia to accept you as their leader."

"I'm sure *you* know how to refine Avara," Bracken challenged. "Maybe I'll parade you through Nadhas. Maybe the people will act on behalf of their lady."

"And maybe Griea will call you *bastard*. Maybe the Tupinaire will make a mockery of you," she hissed, leaning forward, craning her neck. "Oh, Bracken Volkov, inheritor of a tainted title, cowardly prince of the frozen throne, breaker of oaths, scab on the ice giant — "

Fury lit like a pyre. He seized her throat, squeezing.

" — unable to tame his slave-bride, mockery of the Greater Universe," her voice raised, growling from her, snarled and wet, "oh, my daughter will drag your name like a stain through history if my son isn't blessed with the chance to gut you like — "

The crunching *pop* of High Lady Lena's neck sent a shockwave through Bracken's biceps. He realized one second too late that he'd given the bitch exactly what she wanted. His breathing quickened, and he felt fire in his face, blotching his fair skin. Maxine's ragged gasp opened a pit in his chest.

Bracken pulled his hand back. Lena crumbled against the bed and slid limp to the floor. Her jewel-toned gown pooled like liquid soul stone over his boots.

Maxine gaped. Her once cold eyes softened and brimmed. Tears slid down each cheek and dropped from her chin. "Lena," she said. It sounded like an accident, like a girl speaking gently of her false mother. She tore her eyes from the corpse and stared at Bracken, swatting the wetness from her face.

"Don't bother," he murmured, tipping his head to stare at the ceiling. "Composing yourself isn't necessary, Operative Carr. She fed you. I get it."

"Lena was our last reliable source," Maxine seethed, gritting through clenched teeth. Her glassy eyes widened. "She could've — "

"But she wouldn't, and she wasn't going to."

"She baited you."

"She did." Bracken leveled his glare on her. "Learn from her mistake."

"We have nothing now." Maxine charged forward, sinking to her knees. She placed a shaky hand on Lena's face and looked up at him, glazed eyes lined with anger. "What will we do, Imperator?" It was the first time Maxine slathered his title with venom. "How will we manage this?"

There was only one path forward. Bracken understood that now more than ever. Every choice he'd made painted a legacy soaked in blood. *They will call me the iron fist of Griea*, he thought, *and history will write about a conqueror, and the Greater Universe will be better for it.* He tapped his dialect device.

"Relay a message to Kasimir Malkin, acting commander of the Nadhas border," he said. He stepped away from Lena's body, leaving Maxine crouched over her like a trained dog. "Kill their elderly, the ones who can no longer work. Start there. Then move onto the children until the people comply. When Avara production resumes, the culling ceases."

CHAPTER THIRTY

CAEL

"We should keep going." Lorelei glowered, moving through the crater on sore, uncertain feet. Blood caked her toenails, and her heels were cracked and blistered. She swatted at a mosquito and cursed, shaking out her left leg. "How do you deal with these bugs," she asked Nara, flailing an arm. "They're everywhere."

Cael walked behind her. He stepped over an ant-trail and avoided the barbed hook of a carnivorous plant. "We should stop for the night."

"We'll be fine. Mercy's almost full; Draitune's still bright."

"You need to rest, Lor."

The Henly princess lifted her head and kept walking, slipping between two boulders over a blue-flecked stream. She paused to hold her up her gown and submerge herself. The stream flowed around her ankles. All the resistance drained out of her. Slackened, Lorelei frowned at her swollen feet. The flowing water washed away the dirt and uncovered a vivid splatter of blemishes. Hopefully the micro-presence of Avara would act as a healer.

Nara flopped in a froth of blue-green clover and stretched her massive maw. She flicked her tail and flexed her paws. Long claws slid out from between each bean-shaped pad, leaving divots in the soil. Truthfully, neither Lorelei nor Cael could dictate when or where Nara took a break. Despite her loyalty to the Henly family, she was still more wild than domestic, and her decision to call it a night couldn't be argued. They'd walked since mid-morning, only pausing to wander into the woodland to relieve themselves or

pick berries from an unripe lucialocke bush. Cael's stomach stitched with
hunger. He gave Lorelei a pensive look, switching his gaze between her and
Nara. The big cat chuffed pleasantly.

"Fine," Lorelei breathed out, glancing from the lion to Cael. "I should
look at your face while we have access to clean water."

Cael nodded. "I'm sure it's fine."

"It's definitely not. We'll rinse the honey-sap and lichen and replace the
salve if need be." She sat on a rock at the edge of the stream and slung one
leg over the other, digging her thumb into the sole of her foot. "I've never
been this deep before," she confessed, steering her head one way then the
other. "I know we're heading toward the city. If Wonder's there," she
pointed at the pinkish nebula through the canopy, still far away given the
season, "then Atreyu is that way," she flung her arm, gesturing behind her
head, "and the lakehouse will be right against the water on the edge of the
crater."

"You think we can make it there by tomorrow night?"

"Maybe. Will you carry me?" She turned toward the lion, flashing a
sarcastic grin. "Can I ride you like a horse, Nara?"

Nara blew a hot breath through her snout.

A smile lifted Cael's face, the first one since dawn. Around him, nightfall
crept inward toward the center of the crater, and Avara awoke. The blue
crystal furred up on pear-shaped leaves and illuminated notched bark like
crooked teeth. Many legged millipedes marched through loose dirt and a
mad badger scampered by, baring its pointed teeth at Nara. White speckled
the black expanse above, glinting and shifting, and Draitune's purple aura
tinted a few stars while Mercy sent silver moonlight beaming through the
canopy, dimming the flash of luminescent crystal. The crater hummed with
a chorus of tiny-winged things, and echoed with the chirping, hooting,
growling of native creatures.

Cael watched the forest come alive with nocturnal activity and rested on
a smooth thatch of clover next to the stream.

"We'll make it," Lorelei said, joking aside. She traded one foot for the
other, knuckling her arch. "Do you think we're being pursued?"

"Relentlessly," Cael said.

Lorelei quieted. Sweat matted her long wavy hair. She reweaved her
braid, picking a twig loose. "The militia might kill you on sight." It wasn't a
threat. More a revelation. Something she hadn't considered.

"I know."

"Why're you here, Cael?" The fiery guard she built around herself cooled to a dull glow.

"Because I chose Elio. I picked our future. Not the path my father intended for me, but whatever life we might have after this. Aurethia taught me patience, I guess. I learned how to prioritize the promise of peace and progress over immediate satisfaction."

"And is that what the Legatus is after? Immediate satisfaction?"

"He's after glory, I think. And Avara, and the orchard. You might not believe me when I tell you this, but House Henly's distribution process isn't friendly to the outer reaches. Griea is sick. Stationers are sick. A lot of people are sick."

Lorelei's face pinched. She sat on that for a moment, glancing sidelong at Nara. "And hungry," she muttered. She kept her gaze on anything except for him. "I saw how you and the Dutchess ate when you first arrived, and I paid attention to your plate every night after — thought you were rude, but I... I look back and feel naïve. Like shit, honestly."

The Earthen curse sounded clumsy in her young, smart mouth. Cael unlaced his boots and tugged them off. Relief flooded his feet, throbbing in time with his heartbeat. "Hunger and plague can make a monster out of anyone."

"What I said before when I talked about my intention for your home-world. I meant it. I *mean* it. Regardless of fairness, or retribution, or struggle, I won't let Aurethia fall. I'll meet House Volkov's crime with — "

"I know."

Lorelei finally looked at him.

"But you're not the steward of Aurethia yet. Elio is alive. I'm alive. If this moon is ever under your control, I'll be dead, and you'll do what you want regardless of the state of my homeworld. I won't be around to stop you from becoming my father," Cael said, speaking clearly, boldly. "The legacy you leave behind will be completely up to you."

She gaped, swallowing a bewildered laugh. "Someone has to pay for what happened here."

"You still see House Henly as the victim, don't you? Someone *is* paying for what happened. How long do you expect a starving dog to lie still?"

"We're not beasts, Cael!"

"Exactly." He met her angry, desperate glare. "Yet many of us are treated like animals while a lucky few can afford to prioritize a *colorful* plate. Alexander bought obedience from my great-grandmother. Tolerance for disrespect ended with her. I don't agree with my father, I didn't want this to happen, but for every action there is a reaction."

"War and destruction should've been off the table." She flicked her feet, sending water flying toward the stream, and ambled off the rock to sit across from him.

Cael heaved a sigh and sat back on his palms. He hung his head and stared at the patchwork sky framed by spindly pine. There was no undoing the hurt and rage slammed into her over the course of a single day. No matter what he said, Lorelei would want revenge, and he couldn't blame her for it.

"I didn't expect it to be him," he said, watching a comet blink in the distance. "I thought I'd be marrying a stiff, pompous aristocrat who saw me as nothing more than a brutish barbarian. I came to Aurethia ready for war, for this," he lifted his hand, gesturing lazily to his botched face, "because I couldn't imagine any other way forward. I believed in my house, I believed in my Legatus, and I trusted my Optio," he paused to swallow, speaking through a thickening throat, "I'm not blameless, Lorelei, but my aunt died of parsec sickness, and my people have never tasted candlebell, and our reindeer eat recycled vegetation composted from our own meager table scraps." He let himself deflate. "Forgive me for hoping you would heal what we broke," he said, snorting defiantly. His good eye welled again, but he thumbed at it, refusing to let the emotion brim over. "But go ahead. Have your vengeance, mighty lioness."

They shared the stirring night for a long time. Lorelei said nothing, and Cael couldn't bring himself to look at her. Nara slept and the stream bubbled. An owl bounced between branches, hunting a shrewd rodent.

"I am allowed to be angry," Lorelei said under her breath.

Cael nodded. "You are. So am I."

Lorelei shifted forward and knocked her beaten foot against his sock. "Come on, let's fix your face while there's still enough light."

CHAPTER THIRTY-ONE

ELIO

Sunder whitened the back of Elio's eyelids. He wanted to stay in the warmth of the dream — linen and skin, black ink and pale eyes — but the sting of steel against his throat called him to consciousness. He blinked back harsh daylight. Pushed against the lull of exhaustion and willed his focus to sharpen.

Four shadowy shapes surrounded him. He tried to inch away from the saber pointed at his neck, but its wielder extended her arm, following him.

"Vik," Elio blurted, voice creaky.

I'm behind you. These are not Griean soldiers. I believe we might've found the Xenobiology Division. Vik's static-drenched voice filled his dialect device which wasn't quite looped over his ear. Stay calm. My data-relay hasn't picked up any outright aggression.

Elio brought his fingertip to the sword. It was thin and long, far too fine to belong to a militia member, and like nothing he'd seen the Royal Reserve carrying at the manor. He gulped and glanced around the group. As his vision cleared, he noticed familiar humanoid structure. Like him, they resembled people from the past, still carrying the composition known to Earth and its colonized neighbor, Mars.

Their skin-tones ranged, all varying shades of brown, beige, and black. The one who held the saber was lightly tanned and freckled, same as Elio, and another had ruddy, umber skin with eyes to match.

"What're you called?" One of the people holding him at bay tilted their head, leaning down to get a better look at him.

They were high-boned and androgynous, wearing sand-colored, indigo-trimmed clothing. A headdress hung over their tawny forehead and wrapped loose around their throat, resembling the garment Gene had gifted him in Nadhas. Brassy gold banded their fingers, embellished with fibrous Avara.

"Elio Henly," he said, flicking his attention to the stranger holding the sword. He gave the blade a mindful nudge. "Heir to House Henly, steward of Aurethia. The Augment you have in custody is Vik Endresen, my security unit."

The woman holding the saber pulled the weapon aside. "What conflict have you brought to our forest moon, Elio Henly?"

"That's a question better suited for my great-grandfather."

The last of the four stepped forward, planting his shoes on either side of Elio's ankles. He extended his hand and hauled the prince to his feet. The stranger's eyes were the grey-blue of swordfish scale. A callous roughened his palm. He looked oddly familiar, like someone Elio might've seen in a dream, or at the market, or tending the orchard. His light skin reddened where Sunder touched too much, dappling his nose and cheekbones, and his mouth curved prettily. It was a familiar smile. Too familiar. Eerie in a way Elio couldn't place. The man swatted Elio on the bicep and squeezed. Elio shook with the momentum of it.

"So you're the first-born, huh? Thought you'd be taller," he said, unexpectedly gruff.

Elio went rigid. He stepped away, looking from the man's soft-soled books — almost identical to the pair he wore — to the vintage Aurethian glyph on the sleeve of his armored tunic.

"I'm Xander." He blew out a breath, flapping his mouth. "Named after my father."

Elio's top lip came away from the bottom. He studied the man, shock-slackened. The angle of his chin, how his lashes fanned, the shape of his wrist. Elio almost reached for his own face, tempted to touch the point of his widow's peak, mirrored in Xander's ashy hairline.

"You're..." Elio's tongue seemed to double in size. The assessment got lost, refused to surface.

Vik clucked decisively. "According to my internal programming, Xander Henly, second son to Alexander Henly, born out of wedlock to an undetermined host, would be one-hundred-and-forty-seven. Relative to customary Aurethian moon-side record keeping, of course."

Xander tipped his head toward Vik. His eyebrow canted. "Smart robot."

"Not a robot," Elio corrected. At the same time, Vik cleared his throat and said, "Post-mortem augmented human, actually."

"You look like you could use a bath." Xander plucked at Elio's dirty shirt.

"Have you been followed?" The woman sheathed her saber.

Vik said, "No, we cut through the seaside village, Nadhas, and sheltered in the crater. Access to my location tracking and database is limited to one, Elio Henly, and Elio is untraceable. Two hoverbikes are hidden in the brush about four klicks south."

Elio reached for his pack. One of the people stiffened. He paused, holding open his hand. "If I wanted to use a weapon," he said, and tapped a cattail on his belt, "you'd be bleeding by now." He shifted to Xander. "How're you alive, and how do I know you're who you say you are?"

"How are *you* alive, and how do I know you're who you say you are?" Xander parroted. He lolled his head toward the thickening forest. The scratchy stubble on his jawline silvered in some places, catching the light. It reminded Elio of his father. "How 'bout we answer each other's burning questions somewhere safe?"

What's safe? Elio held the thought, but nodded, stepping toward Vik. He made sure to give the other three a long, slow look. "I'm Elio."

"Sindra," the woman holding the saber said.

The other, fluid and curious, nodded pleasantly. "Melody."

"Innis," the third said.

Elio nodded. "And you're all — "

"We're xenobiologists." Sindra turned away from him and walked into the woodland.

Xander sucked his teeth. "It's a long, crazy story, kid. Let's get to the outpost."

If I'm not mistaken, the outpost Xander is referring to is called Genesis. According to my historical data-base, it's the first touchpoint between Draitune and Aurethia, and was built in the very center of the crater. Vik's data-port clicked. He walked beside Elio, angling his body defensively. His gaze remained ahead, but Elio noticed his attention flitting everywhere. Tracking; marking. Corded muscle, cybernetic and otherwise, rippled beneath Vik's augmented skin. Stay on guard. You're worth

a small fortune to the Legatus and his heir incumbent —
I'm sure there's a substantial price on your head.

Anxiety flared. Elio swallowed and tightened the straps on his pack. He
bounced across a rocky path half-submerged in a rushing river, slipping on
a soggy stone. Vik caught his elbow and ushered him forward. Daylight
fuzzed the atmosphere, calling night creatures back to their dwellings. A
fat-tailed squirrel climbed an ivy-laden tree and birds sang in the canopy,
casting small shadows as they flew between branches.

Elio kept his face toward the sky, watching Draitune's furthermost ring
gleam transparently, growing less colorful the farther they walked. They
traveled for an hour, maybe more. The environment grew wilder and more
vibrant. Dewy bulbs glistened, and beetles hummed around thick stalks
spearing the surface of a watery marsh. Somewhere close by, an Aurethian
bear bellowed, causing a flurry of sparrows to take flight.

"Careful," Vik blurted.

Elio's boot clipped the edge of a quarry. The land axed downward again,
dipping to a leveled plain. Aurethian architecture filled the space between
bark and leaf. Wood-built buildings with sloped red roofs and stilted houses
appeared like an oasis through the dense forest. An outdated Draitune
transport overgrown with moss and fungus docked on a launch pad above
the hidden village. Four-paneled enginery lined the oval starship, and the
glyph painted on its body — rings overlapping in a triumphant sphere —
was chipped and weatherworn. The text stamped onto the curved belly of
the ship read GENESIS in old Earthen syllabaries.

Xander paused and looked over his shoulder, waiting for Elio and Vik to
continue. "Welcome to Outpost One." Xander said, tipping his temple
toward the community below. "It was the first journey for Genesis and the
first settlement on Aurethia."

"Gensis is the ship," Vik said, surprised.

"First settlement," Elio mumbled. He rolled the word over. First. As
in... He caught up to Xander. "Did the people here settle in other places?"

"The Xenobiology Division was adapted around a select group of
specialists sent to scout the forest moon for potential resources." Xander
shrugged. He shoved his hands into his pockets and kept walking, forcing
Elio to match his stride. "They didn't become what they are today until after
they landed. Specifically, where they landed. But, I mean, sure, they built
Atreyu, I guess, then Draitune and Ocury sent more immigrants, and
Aurethia was born. The people at Outpost One set the precedent for my
mother's initiative."

"Right, but why wouldn't we build *here*," Elio said.

He glanced around the crater. The dirt path became smooth stone. Around him, people much like him and nothing like him stopped to stare. One woman paused mid-clip of her damp laundry to tilt her head, mouthing something under her breath. Another person leaned out from behind a door, flanked by a man dressed in a canvas shirt and cargo pants, to watch Sindra, Melody, Innis, and Xander escort the newcomers through the outpost.

"The crater is a mechanical dead-zone, but..." Elio's gaze skimmed a steel beacon perched atop the tallest roof. It was the largest he'd ever seen, craning two, maybe three meters. The globe at its head pulsed white, cresting the very edge of the canopy. Light bolted down its thick cylindrical build, sparking like a candlewick "Is that..."

Vik chimed in. "That is a modular frequency pulse-beacon."

"We keep the crater a dead-zone," Xander said matter-of-factly.

Elio crunched the information. Xander, alive. The crater, sustainably occupied by a far larger group than what he assumed the Xenobiology Division would send into the field. The truth, scrambled. Any kind of large-tech modular pulse-beacon could interrupt transmission reliance, but using one of that caliber to disrupt the frequency output *and* input surrounding Aurethia's crater could only mean one thing — secrecy. He stared at the skyscraper beacon for a long time, distilling the easiest consumable data.

If these strange, hidden people had established a stronghold here, repurposing the original outpost to become a long-term living space, and Xander Henly, who had somehow exceeded life expectancy, remained marginally unchanged and survived among them, then what was their purpose, his purpose, the crater's purpose? Elio shifted his gaze to a fat blue leaf, heavy with juice, close to breaking. It dangled from a wiry greenish vine on a nearby rooftop.

"What did they find down here?" Elio asked.

Ahead of them, Sindra made a disapproving noise. "Look, you might be coastal royalty, but out here you're a liability. We'll clear a room for you in the med-bay, give you a hot meal and somewhere to sleep, but that's it."

Melody tsk'd. "Easy, Sindra."

"Don't." Sindra tore her razored gaze from Elio and focused on her comrade. "We both know what's at stake — "

"The Griean warship sitting in low orbit altered those stakes," Innis interjected, bumping Sindra with his shoulder. "Adapt or die, right? C'mon. Let the Henly handle it."

Elio narrowed his eyes. *The Henly.* Spoken as if no one else in his family knew an inkling of the truth. The thought was both a knife and a balm. If his parents didn't know, they hadn't hidden something sizable from him. But if his parents didn't know, he'd landed in an even deeper mystery — conspiracy, even — than he thought.

"Get cleaned up. We've got a lot to talk about," Xander said. He strode away without another word, leaving Elio and Vik standing awkwardly in the middle of the outpost.

Beneath his bootwear, the ground glowed a subtle blue, stained with the promise of untapped Avara.

CHAPTER THIRTY-TWO

CAEL

Cael's reflection rippled on the surface of the bubbling stream. He stared at himself, tracing the raw, red strike bolting from brow to cheek. He touched undamaged skin next to the clawed flesh. On his right, vision gummed and dimmed, as if a thick layer of gauze blocked his socket. On his left, everything was clear and crisp. Not exactly blind, certainly not whole. A cluster of white cartilage and bumpy tissue bleached the notch Nara took out of his nose. Sickly purple bruised the sinewy gouge on his temple.

"Don't touch it," Lorelei said. She sucked berry juice off her fingertip. "Avara will heal what's still open, but I'm afraid your sight might be compromised. If I could've treated you within the hour then — "

"I understand." Cael swallowed thickly and stared at Nara. The lioness regarded him boredly. "You pack quite a punch."

The big cat yawned.

The stubble peppering his jaw and head bothered him, but Cael ignored the irritating stab of vanity. He scooped water into his palm and drank. "Take my boots."

"They're too big. More a hindrance than help."

"Then take my socks. It's not much, but it'll give you some relief for a while."

Lorelei wrinkled her nose with disgust. "You've been *wearing* them — "

"Princess Henly," Cael started. He hung his head, swatting at the stream, and heaved an impatient sigh. "Please."

Lorelei plaited her knotted hair and relented, grimacing as she pulled on each sweat-soaked sock.

They both carried the tangy, organic smell of unwashed bodies and endurance. Thankfully, whatever medicinal salve Lorelei gooped into Cael's wound chased away the initial scent of infection, and the crater's lush woodland perfumed the air with cedar and greenery. He stood and straightened, wincing against the throbbing ache in his skull. Hunger welled in his empty stomach. He was trained to ignore it, but his last cycle on Aurethia hadn't reinforced much of the war-time scenario training he'd previously mastered. Being able to eat whatever he wanted whenever he pleased had softened his warrior's resolve. He kicked himself for indulging in such a pillow-soft cycle and beat back the nausea cramping his gut.

"We should be there by nightfall," Lorelei said. She was careful with her socked feet, stepping over sharp pebbles and splintered logs.

Cael followed. Nara trailed behind him, prancing through foliage, and pawing across logs.

Sunder shot through the canopy. The strangeness of their environment grew more unfamiliar with every step. Blue cracked through long-stemmed flowers and glimmered inside the open mouth of gaping lilies. Even in the daylight, Avara thrummed like a second skin, blanketed over everything.

As the morning turned to afternoon, Cael let his mind drift. He thought of Elio's pinched expression as he slogged through a complicated translation. Remembered the easy way he draped over Cael's lap, naked and flushed on their wedding night.

Stay alive. He put a great deal of himself into that thought, willing it into existence by sheer force.

Maybe if he channeled Elio's survival strongly enough, a piece of his own spirit would chip away like a sacrifice. It made him think of religion — such an old, rusty thing. How people used to pray to invisible forces and hope the universe bent to their will. His people still called the basilisk *god*. Not creator, or provider, or watcher. Keeper, destroyer, equalizer. God was not a friend, but a creature. A thing older than Griea's planetary name. He never prayed to the serpent, but Cael thought about praying to something, someone. Through a gap in the towering trees, Cael caught a glint of pink.

Wonder, he thought, calling out to a maker, to a thing transmuting the lost, *keep him safe.*

NIGHT SEEPED INTO THE crater. Blue fluted through the base of bottom-heavy, bell-shaped flowers, and cerulean moss congealed around stone and wood. Winged insects carrying dusty pollen left translucent blueish trails in their wake. A blister bubbled on Cael's heel. Another grew on the side of his smallest toe. In front of him, Lorelei's clumsy trudging spoke of exhaustion. She swayed, stumbling, and Cael caught her by the forearm, keeping her upright.

"We're close," she groaned. Her soaked nightgown was streaked with dirt and algae, and her lively face grew hollow with weariness. "I know we are — we have to be."

They'd walked for the entire day. Cael's body screamed for rest, and he chastised himself for it. Two cycles ago, he was nineteen, fighting ruthlessly in the arena, training daily, and fasting twice a week. Now he couldn't trek through the wild for more than two days without his calves seizing and his breastplate aching.

"We'll get there," Cael said. They had to.

Leading their small party, Nara was a moving shadow backlit by Avara's luminescence. The big cat lumbered forward, head low, eyes searching. She pawed through long grass and sniffed at a lanky mushroom before going rigid and whipping around. Her breathing changed. Round ears perked and pupils mooned.

Lorelei froze, too. She glanced from Nara to Cael then searched the darkness where the lion alerted. A question eked from her. "What is it?"

Cael motioned to his lips with his index, signaling for her to be quiet. Adrenaline flared in his creaky joints, fending off fatigue. He placed his hand on the hilt of his blade.

All at once, the noisy crater went silent. The hum of bugs and the scampering of critters died. Cael breathed. Locked his spine and kept his knees loose. After a short stint of nothing, the purr of a small engine whizzed overhead. A red light opened like an eye above them, seated on the nose of a Griean drone. Light laced the crater, fanning outward from a small holo attached to the device. The scanner slid over them and printed the scene into its limited memory bank.

Run, Cael almost said, but the familiar sound of a charging pulse-rifle squashed whatever chance they might've had to escape.

"Down," Cael hollered, and leaped onto Lorelei, knocking her to the forest floor. He braced on his hands, caging her there. She threw her arms over her head and screeched, but her terror was lost to the wobbling of a pulse-shot tearing through the tree behind them. "Stay with me," he gritted out, and unclipped one of the Griean short-swords he'd harvested from a fallen soldier, pressing the weapon to her chest. "Don't be reckless."

As the dust cleared, smoke billowed from the blackened 'o' singed through the trunk, and a muffled command came from behind a black mask. "Cael Volkov, you are surrounded. Release the Henly heiress and turn yourself over for immediate processing." A Griean soldier stepped into view, accompanied by five, six — seven, maybe — armored Royal Reserve. He lowered the sleek, black-tipped barrel of the pulse-rifle to where the pair crouched. "You are under arrest for treason, pending prosecution in the arena."

The drone swooped around to face Cael and Lorelei.

Cael stood, drawing his weapon in a slow, purposeful motion. "Do not make me kill you."

The Royal Reserve moved as one, assuming a fighting stance. One leg forward, one back. Two armed with artillery. Their squad leader held a pulse-rifle and carried a sword on his hip. The rest unsheathed standard Griean blades. Cael shifted, feeling for the rifle strapped to his back. It would take too long to charge, and he'd waste precious time yanking it forward.

The leader stepped closer. He barked behind his mask. "You are a traitor to your homeworld and a — "

Another soldier startled. "Cat!"

The drone cocked to the left, flashing the red hololight into a tree. Nara, perched on a high branch, roared and lunged. Her two front feet landed with a sickening crunch on the squad leader's shoulders, and her teeth came down around his helmet. Artillery blasted. Gunfire pierced the night. The drone lifted, retracting the light with it, plunging them into blackness. Lorelei screamed.

Cael took the opportunity to charge at the remaining soldiers. He focused on the closest, knocking the long-barreled gun to the side and piercing him with the stiletto. The soldier's sturdy armor hardly opened, but Cael exerted his strength and pushed, cracking the abdominal plate, sinking into flesh. Nara's fierce call echoed, and the squelching whimper of her next victim filled the crater. Another soldier was on top of him before he could search for Lorelei. A fist cracked Cael's jaw, then an elbow met his sternum.

Agony burst around his mangled eye, radiating into his cheekbone. Something warm oozed out of the cut on his cheek.

Focus. Cael jammed the pommel of his dagger into the soldier's larynx. Drew his fist back and struck him once, throat, twice, nasal bridge, again, until blood spurted, lastly in the mouth. The Griean soldier went limp. Cael's hand pulsed. He shook out the limb and turned, training his good eye on the shadowy fight filling the forest.

"Lorelei!" Cael whipped around. "Lor — "

Griean steel clipped his shoulder, dragging across the very top of his bicep. Pain lanced his upper half. He ducked to the side and turned, twirling his dagger in one hand, and reaching for the assailant with the other. He gripped the soldier's helmet and yanked him forward, burying his knife into the soft dent beneath his bottom rib. Up, Cael remembered, digging the blade higher, twist, then release. The soldier choked out Cael's name, just once.

Dread surged like a tidal wave. Cael pushed the helmet away. Tye Jenkin. *Tye.* Someone he'd selected. Trained. Laughed with, drank with, trained with, called a friend, missed dearly. Tye grabbed Cael's shoulders and held onto him, dribbling crimson. He couldn't speak, but Cael saw the confusion in his wide, light eyes. *Why are you doing this?* Tye had two mothers, and an older sister, and he told terrible jokes, and pined after a guy who sang at their favorite tavern in Sector One, and Cael hated himself. *Who am I?* Cael couldn't answer. Didn't know if who he was becoming was who he'd been all along, or if Aurethia had made him someone else.

"Imperator," Tye said, slipping out of Cael's grasp. Tye framed Cael's lost title like a question, like an impossible calculation left unsolved. It sounded like *how could you?* He hit the dirt, still and gone.

Cael staggered backward. Bile lashed his throat. His head spun, circling a mile a minute. His friend was strewn at his feet, struck down by his own blade. Someone he chose. Tye stared skyward. He was young, Cael's age. His fair skin still held Griea's snowy weather, and the ink in the center of his throat formed the shape of a skeletal jaw. Cael's dagger clipped his fingertips as it fell from his hand, smacking a rock next to Tye's boot. He stood there for too long, struck still and immovable, vulnerable to anyone and anything. He couldn't catch his breath. Couldn't rip himself away from the pointless death laid out before him.

"What're we doing," Cael whispered.

Artillery fired.

Lorelei screamed, "Cael!"

Instinct snapped back into place. Sound sharpened; adrenaline thrummed. Cael rounded on another soldier and aimed a hard kick at their sternum. His worsened eyesight failed him, and the blow skimmed the soldier's chestplate. A meter away, Nara swiped at two Royal Reserve who closed in with weaponry, and Lorelei thrashed against someone's hold, flailing and kicking as the soldier lifted her off the ground.

The hard collision of a fist against Cael's wounded cheek sent starlight exploding across his limited vision. *No.* Cael pushed through the misery misting his mind and searched for strength, rage, anything to keep him upright. He rushed the soldier, reaching around for the pulse-rifle. The soldier knocked him aside with a savvy shoulder-check, granting Cael enough time to pull the pulse-rifle forward. His back smacked the base of a tree, root digging into his hip. He hit the toggle on the rifle and peered through the target screen. The weapon hummed, gathering power. He notched his finger around the trigger.

C'mon, c'mon. The rifle clicked. His dialect device chimed pleasantly. **Weapon Active.**

But before Cael could pull the trigger, a stripe of gleaming blueish silver exited the soldier's chest, tearing through his armor and dotting Cael with freshly spilled blood. The person wielding the weapon stood behind the black-clad Griean. She wore green and brown, and her armor was gilded with the Aurethian glyph.

The flurry of battle and bloodshed increased momentarily. Hooves beat the dirt. People sputtered and shouted, choked and cried out, and then silence fell over the crater again. The Aurethian standing above him pulled her sword free and tossed the Griean aside, slowly lowering her wet blade to Cael.

"Do not make me kill you," Cael said between clenched teeth. His finger danced on the trigger. "Please."

"Leave him," Lorelei shouted, scrambling forward. "He is Imperator Cael Volkov, Elio Henly's husband, and no one will decide his fate until I speak with my brother."

The soldier listed her head, eyeing Cael down the bridge of her prominent nose. She did not lower her weapon.

Lorelei almost fell trying to get closer. When she finally stumbled in front of him, she held the bloody sword Cael had given her steady, planting her feet on either side of his boots. "I am Lady Lorelei Henly, steward of Aurethia, and you will heed my command."

The Aurethian soldier's face opened, as if she'd tasted a dollop of something sweet and unexpected. She lowered her sword and stepped away.

"Now tell me where I am," Lorelei all but sobbed. Her quivering body slackened.

A middle-aged Aurethian wearing tightly fitted armor approached. He was trim and handsome with a short blonde beard and a noticeably impacted gait. Behind him, mounted soldiers held the reins on a line of armored Aurethian horses.

"Lady Lorelei, my name is Ulrich Hutch. I'm the commander and overseer of the Aurethian militia in the northern territories. Right now, you're one mile from the border of Atreyu, west of Nadhas. Did you walk here?"

"I did, sir," she coughed out. She nudged Cael with her foot and extended her slender arm, helping him to his feet. "Is my lion alive?"

Nara crept out of the shadow behind her. The cat's face was blood-soaked and matted. A sword-slice marred her back end, and a bullet grazed her left ear, leaving a missing thatch of golden fur, but she still stood.

"Vigorous beast, I commend you," Ulrich said. He turned from Nara and gave Cael a scrutinizing once-over. Shifted back to Lorelei. "Nadhas sent a distress signal. Unfortunately, the last audible transmission we received was grim. Griea successfully jammed our communication this morning."

"Tell me," Lorelei said. Her impatience wasn't becoming of a Great House, but Cael could not blame her.

"I'm sorry, my lady, but the High Lord and High Lady have been assassinated. Lord Orson is unaccounted for. Lord Elio was last seen fleeing the manor. Due to these circumstances, you are now acting High Lady of Aurethia," Ulrich said. He bowed his head and cleared his throat. "We're relieved to find you alive. We commit our cause to you."

Lorelei's stillness could've passed for the dead. It lasted one minute, two. Her lashes beat, and her mouth quaked. She parted her lips to speak, then stopped, and repeated the motion thrice.

"You're certain," she finally uttered, feeble and girlish.

Ulrich nodded. "Our source saw the bodies. Legatus Marcus hanged them from the candlebell tree."

Cael's stomach vaulted into his throat. He held back a wave of sick and kept his attention squarely fixed on Lorelei, waiting for her knees to give out, for her blank expression to crumble. He anticipated loss to chisel through her, cracking the witty young woman he'd come to call family.

But Lorelei's face reddened. Her glassy eyes spilled, and she let out a breath like she'd been punched. Her next inhale shredded, gasped in through her mouth, and then she bent at her waist, fingers buckled wickedly, and wailed like a monstrous, sizable beast. It wasn't the sort of grief that arrived sadly. This agony thundered inside her, erupted from her. She screamed like a woman undone, like someone possessed. The sound was all fury, all horror. When her exhale thinned, she grasped the handle of her sword in both hands and pounced on the nearest fallen Griean, striking the soldier between their shoulders. She brought the blade down again, and again, and *again*, staining herself scarlet, heaving and growling, belligerent with sorrow.

Cael did not recognize her.

No one moved to intervene. The Aurethian militia exchanged glances and remained stoic, watching the seventeen-year-old High Lady of House Henly decapitate a corpse. When the head snapped away from the body, Lorelei stopped, panting hard. Blood splashed her freckled face and stained her sunny hair. Her dirty nightgown was painted like a ritual gone wrong, globbed with membrane and congealing gore.

"Box these bodies and return them to the manor," Lorelei said, deadly calm. She swallowed hard and wiped her mouth with the back of her hand, smearing blood and salt across her chin. "I don't care what you have to do to get around the transmission block — do it. Send a message to Draitune. Tell them the lioness of Aurethia is alive. Tell them this moon is under my command." She took another shaky breath and lifted her face, staring at the dark canopy. "Tell them Aurethia will fight."

CHAPTER THIRTY-THREE

ELIO

Hot water flowed over Elio's tense shoulders and rivered down his back. He stood in the bathing chamber for a long time, soaking up the blissful scent of citrus soap. Thick, minty detangler tingled his scalp. Warmth sank deep, chasing away the ache of foot-travel. Brown and pink circled the drain. He flattened his palms against the wall and hung his head, ignoring the phantom grip on his hips, surfacing from a distant memory. Cael's mouth pressed to the base of his throat, catching shoulder, earlobe, jaw. *Good work, darling.* Whispered after a sparring session in the meadow.

Elio cracked his eyes open and gnawed his lip. Cael's presence lingered like a stubborn bruise. There was no way to scrub him out. Elio imagined lancing into the meat of his heart and watching Cael pour from it like an abscess. Betrayal snared in his chest. After welcoming him into the manor, and meeting him in good faith, and defending him against the Aurethian loyalists, and taking him to his bed. After everything —

Elio pushed that wretched door closed in his mind. Couldn't afford to be toppled by everything behind it. He heaved a sigh and finished washing, then dried off and dressed in fresh clothes.

The people of Outpost One provided a burgundy tunic, brown cargo pants, and a leather belt. Simple but efficient. He hesitated to reach for the sheathed Grabak on the table next to his pack. The lock on that door in his mind — trapping every good memory of Cael Volkov — rattled like a bone-shard. But he found the strength to grasp the pommel and strap the blade to his waist. He kept his hand on the weapon, thumbing the curved scabbard. His dialect device lit with a subtle glow. He pulled the earpiece into place.

I think you might want to see this. Vik's scratchy voice materialized. While the pulse-beacon disrupted incoming and outgoing transmissions, Elio's device was directly paired with Vik's internal program-ming. If the Augment stayed within range, he could still communicate with Elio's hardware. Substantial distance would make that nearly impossible, though, and the transmission wasn't as clear.

"Where are you?" Elio asked.

In the garden outside the med-bay.

Elio tucked the hem of his pants and laced his boots. He'd hoped the access to hygiene and new attire might make him feel more like himself. Wanted to step back in time and find the Elio Henly who'd gone to sleep next to his husband. Wander further and become who he'd been before their courtship. He glanced at his reflection in an oval mirror. Mauve smudged the thin dip beneath his eyes. His face was gaunt with sleepless-ness, and he picked at the borrowed shirt, second-guessing his decision to opt out of some of the more popular musculature augmentation offered during the Change. His physique spoke of strength, capability. Lean muscle dented his small waist, and his wide shoulders rounded handsomely, tapering to a flat, compact chest. But he did not look like a king. Or a galactic steward. Elio was tightly-built, not hulky and intimidating. He wore the polished exterior of a well-born minx, not the brawny strength of a High Lord. He straightened, turned. His augmented chest rose and fell.

Nestled deep in the crevice of his courage, Elio recognized the familiar fang of uncertainty.

He scrubbed at his chin and mouth then hung his towel and left the washroom, following a sterile, domed hall to the entrance of the med-bay, a sleek building retrofitted with borrowed titanium from Genesis's exterior. The automatic door slid open, and Elio turned toward the outpost's garden space. Vegetables filled rectangular boxes, growing toward a pocket of sunlight. Vik wore the same clothes he'd arrived in, but his skin was freshly scrubbed, and his short, dark hair was combed back and still wet. He stood with his hands jammed into his front pockets, staring at something on the other side of the garden.

Elio strode forward. "What'd you…" His question evaporated.

What remained of the pride lounged in a patch of blueish grass. Rey, Aki, Korah, Dare, Junji, and Sol huffed and yawned, waving their tufted tails, and grooming each other. Sol's mane billowed. Korah turned, settling her golden gaze on Elio.

Elio laughed delightedly. "They made it."

Korah called to him and Sol stood, shaking out his orange mane. The second largest male, now the largest after Tatu, padded forward and bumped his furry head against Elio's stomach. Vik caught him before he fell, and Elio planted his feet, smoothing his palm over Sol's brow.

Xander Henly approaches. Vik cast him a sidelong glance. I picked up an anomaly in his genetic makeup. According to my reading, Xander is Griean.

Elio startled. "Not possible."

Vik shrugged. I recalibrated my internal processing and assessed my augmented consciousness for corruption within my cybernetic output, but my system is up-to-date and functional. Xander has at least forty-nine point nine-two percent Griean heritage. Whoever Alexander took to his bed, they were of Griean ancestry, and Xander is the product.

Sol regarded Xander with a snort.

"Do we know why Griea decided to attack?" Xander asked. He stepped up beside Vik, sighing wearily.

Elio appreciated the stranger's straight shooting. "Because my father followed the directive your father put into motion two centuries ago, restricting Avara and fresh produce from reaching Griea without substantial taxation. Our wedding gave them the perfect opportunity to seize Aurethia." He stared intently at the echo of his bloodline. "How are you alive?"

"Avara's source is at the center of the crater. It's a weird organism with regenerative properties we're still trying to understand and utilize, and I'm one of the lucky few who got drafted into the cooperative currently working to sustain it. And replicate it." He spoke with an ease that caused Elio's body to tense. Source. Organism. Sustain. Replicate. Before Elio could ask for clarification, Xander continued. "Is Harlyn's great-grandchild alive?"

"As far as I know, yes. According to Vik, Cael defected." He shifted his jaw, rolling the next statement around in his mouth. "I heard his voice myself."

Xander lifted his chin. "And why isn't he with you?"

The answer punctured like broken glass. "Because he's the one who orchestrated the siege."

"Go figure. How'd he pull that off?"

By making me love him. Elio narrowed his eyes. "Who are you, exactly? And what do you mean 'the source?' Aurethia is the source of Avara. It's a gemstone, a mineral — "

"I'm Harlyn Volkov's son," Xander exhaled, meeting Elio's widening gaze with an insistent nod.

Vik's voice chimed in his earpiece. `I am running a comparative scan between one, Xander Henly, and two, Cael Volkov.` The Augment angled himself closer to Elio, positioning his shoulder like a battering ram. `Stand by.`

Xander glanced between Vik and Elio and shook his head. "Believe me, don't believe me. It doesn't matter. But it'll be easier if I show you what I mean. C'mon, I'll take you to the source."

Elio didn't follow at first. He kept his hand on Sol's massive head, and stayed behind Vik, watching Xander — whose self-proclaimed existence was impossible — step past them and walk toward the pride.

Surprise washed Vik's face, slackening the concentration pinching his forehead. "Xander Henly and Cael Volkov are a genetic match. I did not detect a lie before, but I admit, I expected the information to be inconclusive. My organic instinct was to deduce the proclamation down to a lie passed along by someone else, or a loosed rumor gone unchecked for too long. But according to the data, he is Griean, Aurethian, Henly, and Volkov." He spoke aloud, watching Xander pat Korah's rump.

Xander angled his mouth over his shoulder, lifting his voice to carry back toward them. "Why else would Alexander Henly make a deal with Harlyn Volkov after securing the Lux Continuum for Aurethia? He asked for her hand. She said no. And nothin' kills a good thing faster than a broken heart. Not that *I* was the *good thing*. I wasn't. But if their closed-door affair turned into a galactic unification, me being the connective tissue, then Harlyn's motive would've been questioned by the Imperium, and House Volkov's good standing in the Greater Universe would've been trampled by a newfound reputation built on lust, weakness, dishonor, and emotional extortion. Think about it," he swung his arm theatrically, "Harlyn Volkov, harlot of Griea, slithering into an Aurethian bed to get her hand around Alexander's miracle discovery." He chuckled. Bitterness folded his mouth.

"Gestating a bastard who could rightfully contest the heirship already established in both houses. To avoid a slew of nasty gossip, she had me extracted into an external womb and left me with Alexander. According to the Aurethian record-keeping, my mother was a maid. Or a farmhand. Someone forgettable."

But that... Elio's mouth dried. He stared at the ground, fitting the information into place. Alexander's cruelty... The propaganda... His misuse of power and reluctance to extend a peaceful hand toward Griea. His obsession with wealth and status... All of it shucked off onto Elio and Cael — the burdened pair forced to shoulder shattered love. No wonder the marriage agreement was written into existence. No wonder the animosity brewing between their homeworlds stretched through generations.

No wonder.

For once, everything made sense. Griea's quick-flamed military rise was in direct contrast to Aurethia's chokehold on Avara. They were two sides of the same coin, both necessary to cultivate a sustainable world. The unification, masquerading as a peace brokerage after dealing a blatant, devastating blow to Griea's financial infrastructure, was likely a knife Alexander twisted to nurse his own pride. A petty jab at Harlyn from a scorned man with a crippled ego.

Elio wanted to reach through time and strangle his great-grandfather.

"Why haven't you contested?" Elio asked. It was a strange thing, how that question lurched from him unexpectedly. He snagged his lip with his canine. "We have technology capable of tracing your genetic lineage. Vik's a post-mortem Augment and he managed to confirm the basic overview of your identity within minutes. Why stay here? Why live in the crater when you could've forced a unification in the aftermath of Alexander's death?"

That's a very good question, Lord Elio. Vik's data-port whirred and clanked.

Even at a distance, Xander's chest expanded. "Because one person shouldn't serve as such a vast bridge. I didn't want to inherit greatness, or power, or responsibility, and my lineage would've sparked controversy across the Greater Universe. I had more important shit to do," he said, shaping his hand like a gun, two digits pointed out, gesturing forward. "Do you want to see it or not?"

Vik's voice filled his earpiece again. Unfortunately, Xander's assumption about the Imperium and society's incessant love of gossip isn't exactly arguable. His stake on the heirship would've caused an uproar which might've stalled Avara production during a critical time in our history. It could've incited war between Griea and Aurethia, or Griea and Draitune, and if he succeeded, you probably would not exist. He glanced at Elio, nodding slowly. I think we should follow him.

"Yes," Elio said, clearing his throat, "yeah, I want to see it." Whatever it happened to be.

Elio followed Xander, pausing to greet the pride as he walked by. The lions grumbled. Sol flopped in the grass while Korah and Dare roused to prance after the long lost Henly. Elio tried to pay close attention to the layout of the crater. Its interior stretched in every direction, laden with lush foliage and fantastically shaped flora. He glanced between a mossy kapok and a bristly pine and filed each delicate piece of information into his over-filled mind. Providing an answer to an age-old question was a relief, but everything that came with it seemed to complicate an already complex problem. Alexander Henly and Harlyn Volkov had punched their ruined love into the membrane of history and created an undisputable future for Elio before he'd ever taken his first breath.

What a thing love could be. Destroyer, unmaker.

The image of Cael manifested like a fog. Elio shooed it and kept walking, following Xander down a ravine into the underbody of the crater. Larger trees thinned, replaced by spindly ipê, branches globed with pinkish petals. The soil dampened. His boots sank in, and a soft, buoyant aura materialized aboveground, stoking the air like an oasis.

Vik stopped abruptly. We are closing in on an extraordinarily large organism.

Elio paused mid-step. He watched Xander move around a bulged root and halt at the edge of what looked to be a canyon. "How large?"

The Augment's left eye clouded over. His right pupil stretched and shrank. His brow knitted. "We're standing on top of it," he said, shifting his weight from one foot to the other. "I can't match it to a single creature in my database."

Around them, the ipê changed. Toward the bottom of the crater, the trees glistened, scaled with blueish crystal. Avara feathered along stone and stem, grew in tiny, cubic patches inside bark and around the base of blooming ferns. Strange to see it unrefined. So wild and invasive. A snake slithered through loose dirt, searching for a hidey-hole. Avara ridged its smooth spine, sprouting from its body like a beautiful tumor.

Elio took a hesitant step, then another. "Let's go."

Vik made an uncertain noise but followed.

Elio eased through the forest, careful to step over a jeweled turtle and avoid the baby bud of a new shrub. He came to stand beside Xander Henly, poised to ask a thousand questions. Every single thought, worry, and inquiry died on his tongue the second he peered into the chasm.

Blue. Vivid, lustrous blue. The color spanned his vision, domed and oblong, pulsing with the heartbeat of a sleeping titan. It was Avara and it wasn't. It was crystalline and it wasn't. The gigantic, half-buried monstrosity thrummed with the inarguable presence of consciousness. Its gargantuan form filled the entirety of the dugout, nestled there like a latched babe, fingering through the dirt with long, cerulean tendrils that dove and splintered, crackling up into fibrous crystal and house-sized, square-stacked gemstone. Veins crisscrossed beneath its partially trans-parent exterior, and the whole thing seemed to rise and lift, replicating the necessity for oxygen with startling accuracy.

"This is the source. Some people call her the mother mine, but as you can see, that's not entirely accurate." Xander stared out over the valley and sucked his teeth. "She landed here sometime in the sixth dynasty, back before Lucas Penn ruled Draitune, before Ocury's orbit opened for immi-gration. We've tried to pinpoint her origin, but..." He trailed off, shrugging. "She's from somewhere else. That's all we know."

Elio's knees weakened. Vik caught his elbow and held him steady. He braced against the Augment's chest, reminding his body to stay upright, to remain operational.

Source. Mother. Landed.

"She?" Elio gulped down a tattered breath. "As in alive, as in — "

"Avara is not a mineral," Vik said, awe-struck, "it's an alien."

"We've been calling her Alice," Xander said. He nodded, shifting his gaze to Elio. "You know, like Alice in Wonderland."

ELIO SIPPED A SERVING of oolong tea sweetened with honey. He tongued at the nectar gumming the roof of his mouth and stared at the brown liquid in his palm-sized cup, reconciling what he'd seen in the gorge with everything he'd ever been taught. A few xenobiologists, or the Genesis crew, whoever they were, joined him in a cozy room attached to the med-bay. Some sat with him at a long table, sipping from identical pewter teacups. Others leaned against the far wall or plopped on the floor, sharing the awkward silence with stunted breath and flighty gazes. Innis and Melody were there. Xander was, too. Unfamiliar people with unknown identities remained silent. Elio didn't know whether to speak, or laugh, or cry, or dig through the floor and find a nice, cool spot to sit and think.

Xander clapped once. "I'll start, I guess." He glanced around the room and gestured to Elio with an open hand. "Time's up, team. Elio Henly completed the unification agreement and married the Griean heir. We knew this would happen, but no one could've predicted the invasion. Question is, where do we go from here?"

"I haven't successfully replicated Alice's genome," Melody started. They stood with their arms folded, tapping a long finger on their bicep. "But if the Greater Universe realizes she's here, we'll lose her. Our window is closing."

Someone else said, "If the mine underneath her subumbrella is still producing Avarine — "

"Avarine?" Elio interrupted. The room hushed and everyone faced him. His temperature rose significantly.

Melody smiled. "The molecular mineral coded to Alice's original spore. She's a bit like jellyfish and cordyceps, storing pieces of herself inside the cave system underneath her landing spot. Avara can be found on the coastal region of Aurethia, but Avarine is a more intimate material we've only ever found in the crater, close to her chassis. Avara is the byproduct of Avarine, so to speak."

"Does it also need a host mineral to stabilize itself?" Vik asked.

"No, Avarine's structure is more organic than Avara. More *her*. The farther she reaches, the more diluted her spores. That's why Avara is typi-cally mined alongside quartz, fluorite, malachite, so on," they lifted their hand, waving in a circle, "because it's a distant relative reliant on a separate host to flourish. Avarine is directly connected to Alice."

Vik nodded. "Does Avarine have the same medicinal properties?"

The room strained.

Sindra straightened in place, flicking her hard-edged gaze between her colleagues. "Are we really doing this?" She gestured to Elio sternly. "One, he's an outsider, two, he's married to a Griean warlord, three, the moon is in limbo. We should be prioritizing the concealment and security of this outpost, not inviting a newlywed with a bounty on his head to review our research."

Anger sizzled at the base of Elio's neck. "Considering I'm the rightful steward of Aurethia and your only chance at staying concealed, I'd tread carefully."

"Or what, *my lord?* I could bury you in this crater," she assured.

Vik tensed. The pulse-gun hidden in his forearm gave off a familiar hum, charging underneath a layer of pale epidermis.

"That's enough, Sindra," Melody said, sighing.

"He's a child!" Sindra bellowed, bending at her waist to fling a muscular arm at Elio.

Elio sneered, baring his teeth. "I'm — "

"Avarine is the reason we're all still here," Xander hollered. His baritone voice boomed, and the room went still. He looked at Vik first, then slid his gaze to Elio. "Yes," he relented, nodding, "it does have similar medicinal properties." He unsheathed a knife from his belt and brought the silver blade to his palm, slicing himself. Elio flinched, watching blood pool in his hand. "Melody," he said, mouth pursed, "if you wouldn't mind."

Melody dug a vial out of their pocket. Shimmery blue liquid sloshed inside it, clinging to the glass like syrup. They uncapped it and carefully tilted the thin, oval container, allowing a long string of Avarine to drip onto Xander's wound. It puddled there, glistening with crystalline inclusions, and slowly, effortlessly corded the split flesh back together.

All the blood in Elio's face rushed somewhere else. Lightheadedness spun him. He slouched in his chair, leaning one arm on the table to keep himself conscious.

Innis inhaled like a frightened animal, but stayed silent, pressing his full mouth into a stressed, whitened line.

Elio remembered Peadar handing him the salve after the ceremony. How the wound on his palm seemed to instantly heal, as did Cael's. Gene had pointed him toward the crater. Toward the Xenobiology Division. Elio filed those small, inconsequential details, that tiny shred of knowledge, and held Peadar in his mind, hoping the general was somehow, somewhere still alive.

Xander wiped the blood on his pantleg and lifted his hand. Avarine sewed the wound in real time, closing skin, mending flesh. "This is how I'm still alive. How the Genesis crew — Aurethia's infamous and elusive Xenobiology Division — slowed their cellular division and stopped their biological clocks."

Elio sucked in a shaky breath.

"What's everybody want more of, kid?" Xander asked.

Power, Elio thought. But that wasn't always true. Control. Love. Credit. Peace. Joy. "Time," he concluded.

Sindra seethed but spoke calmly. "And what do you think the almighty shot-callers of our *great* universe would do to get their hands on an untapped supply of it?"

The word was a whispered horror on Elio's lips. "Anything."

CHAPTER THIRTY-FOUR

CAEL

The blue-shine of an Avara-imbued treatment caked inside Cael's clawed cheek. Strain bleached his knuckles, and he swallowed the pitchy sound of discomfort straining in his chest. His blind eye burned. Everything was tender and distended.

"You did a number on yourself," the medic said. She was sleek-boned with a head of black locs. A gilded hoop hugged the center of her bottom lip. "Kitty claw, right?"

"I wouldn't call her a *kitty*, but yeah," Cael said.

"Well, she got you." She sutured a few places with biodegradable thread. She closed the notch on the bridge of his nose, then moved over to the deepest groove just below his socket. "This'll absorb in an hour or two. You'll see a difference in the morning, and we'll know how much use you'll scrounge out of that eye by midday tomorrow."

"Doubt I'll get much."

"Unfortunately, I think you're in the right headspace. Damage to the retina and optic nerve is significant. Going without medical intervention for more than twenty-four hours narrowed our window for recouping what you lost."

"Think it'll leave a mark," he jested.

"Yeah," she said, laughing under her breath. She stepped away and peeled off her latex gloves. "You're Cael Volkov, aren't you? Elio Henly's betrothed?"

"Husband," he corrected, and felt stupid for doing so. "Yes, I am."

"I'm Amina," she said. Her easy smile parted, and she squinted, sweeping her gaze across his seated form. "I'm surprised you're alive."

He sighed and stood, crossing the room to a small mirror clipped to the wall. He tipped toward it, craning to look at the goo puttied in his wound. "You and me both, Amina."

The hospital in Atreyu was sterile and white-walled. The dorm-style shower in the basement soothed his sore body, and a ten-minute stint in a sterilization chamber revitalized him. Fatigue weighed heavy, but he felt better, at least. More capable.

"Do you think Griea will take it all?"

The question shot through Cael like a bullet. "What?"

"Us, Avara, the city, everything. Will they take it?" Amina asked.

Honesty puddled on his tongue. "Yes," he said. It tasted bitter, like turned fruit. "If Elio doesn't surface, and if Draitune doesn't send aid, Griea will dominate Aurethia within a season."

"You're *our* Griean, right?" She listed her head. Her smile fractured. "You believe in Aurethia?"

"I believe Aurethia and Griea can coexist without punishing each other for a crime one man committed two centuries ago. What's happening now is cyclical. It's the opposite of progress."

"Crime," she echoed.

"Yes, doctor, crime," he said, and left the room.

An armed guard waited in the hall. He regarded Cael with a cautious glance, looking from the blade sheathed at his waist to the off-white thermal covering his torso. Cael's head and face were freshly shaven, and the storm grey military trousers provided to him were cinched with his basilisk belt. It was the only accessory he'd opted to keep. The rest of his Griean armor was too soiled to wear, and the medical assistant who'd ushered him to Amina reluctantly agreed to return his laundered clothes once she finished scrubbing them. That assistant, and most of Atreyu, did not greet him kindly. People gawked or lunged. One citizen spat at his boots, and another rattled off an Aurethian curse, damning him with infertility. Some — a rare few — met him with a hopeful nod, or the shy flash of the Aurethian salute. The militia seemed unbothered by him, waiting for their chance to strike him down or watch him fall on his own.

This guard did not speak. He led Cael through the hall to a staircase, down it, and into a cafeteria. Lorelei sat at a table, forking up wilted spinach. Her hair was clean. A beige jumpsuit fanned open to show a ribbed white top beneath. Splotchy bruising painted the base of her neck, shadowing the shape of a hand. The middlemost finger on her dominant hand was bandaged and set with a splint, and a compression brace squeezed her right knee. Ulrich joined her with two other militia members.

"Get a plate," she said without looking at him. "Whatever you'd like."

The sterilization chamber had dulled his hunger, but the smell of poached fish and roasted vegetables dredged up that age-old pang in his empty, achy gut. He grabbed a plate from the stack next to the buffet bar and loaded it with food, pausing to stuff a honey loaf into his mouth. He moaned around the buttery pastry, relishing the taste of something other than wild berries.

"I know," Lorelei said, slurring around a mouthful of squash.

The rest of the large space remained empty. No one stood at the windows or occupied the vacant seats. It was just the five of them sharing a single table in the center of the dining area.

Cael grabbed a waterskin and pre-packaged juice before taking the chair across from her. "Did they fix your shoulder?"

"You mean did they put it back," she said, laughing bitterly. "Yes they did, Imperator. I'm not accustomed to being treated on the move, but the militia's medic popped the thing — " she smacked her palm on the table and clucked her tongue " — right into the socket."

He choked down a surprised chuckle. "Good, I'm glad."

"And you?" She lifted her gaze, sucking marrow from a gnawed bone.

"We'll see."

She pointed the bone at him. "I'll see. Will *you* see?"

Cael tipped his head back and pointed his exhausted grin at the ceiling.

Lorelei's laughter bounced around the cafeteria. "Sorry, too soon?"

Delerium brewed between them. Cael wanted to laugh until he cried. Lorelei probably wanted to detonate an explosive. Their lives were imploding. Forever changed. They could do nothing. Could not rewind, could not go back.

But they were still alive, and a little laughter soothed, at least.

Ulrich tapped the table with his meaty pointer. "High Lady, I must inquire about the status of Elio Henly. With Cael in our custody, Elio could potentially convince the Imperium to intervene. Obviously, we're counting on our planetary and lunar allies to send aid and reinforcements, but technically Elio is a Griean Duke and Cael is an Aurethian Lord. They both have a controlling hand over Griea's military and Aurethia's defense." He dragged his attention between Lorelei and Cael. "We found you two while we were scouting the perimeter of the crater. Is there a chance we might find Elio, too?"

Cael stopped eating. "I connected with Elio's dialect device before me and Lorelei started our journey. I assume that was after he fled the manor. You mentioned receiving a transmission from Nadhas. Did anyone else see or hear from him?"

"The transmission we received was beamed through the village beacon, but the information came from a ship anchored past the reef. Nadhas's distress signal didn't give us much to go off. We investigated with a drone, then a horseman. There's still no confirmation of Elio's whereabouts or proof of life."

"As acting High Lady, why can't Cael be compelled to reach out to the Imperium with my blessing?" Lorelei asked.

"Because I'm not the Legatus of Griea," Cael said. He brought his hand to his mouth, tapping idly on his jaw. "If my father is alive, and he is, then all directives still pass through him. The only way to supersede his planetary rule would be to capitalize on his death, or leverage Elio's stewardship of Aurethia and his stake on Griea. Elio's status as Duke is a strong statement to the Imperial Council. My status as traitor to House Volkov won't get us anywhere without my husband."

"But shouldn't it? You defected for a reason. I can speak to your dedication. I can corroborate whatever evidence you bring forward," Lorelei said.

"But they'd need to believe you."

She curled her mouth back, showing her teeth like an animal. "And Elio is more credible?"

"No, but Elio is the one who married me. He's the next in line and the intended steward. If we can't confirm his..." Death. Cael could not say it. The word glued his throat shut.

"If Elio is alive, we need him. If Elio is dead, we need to prove it," Ulrich said.

"He *is* alive," Cael assured. Vik would not let him die.

"Until we can find my brother, we need to initiate some kind of plan. Have we made headway on communication with Draitune?" Lorelei straightened in her seat, cementing her gaze on Ulrich.

"We're working on it. If my men can reroute a distress signal through Mercy's mining vessel outside the ice belt, then we might be able to bypass the signal jammer coming from Griea's warship and initiate contact with House Darvin."

"Have the bodies been delivered to the manor yet?"

"They're in route."

"And what does Atreyu's artillery look like?" Lorelei asked.

Cael perked. "Artillery?"

Ulrich and his comrades preened amusedly.

The Aurethian militant next to Lorelei brushed a piece of dark hair over her shoulder. She was noticeably Ocurian with strawberry freckles splashed across her olive skin. She turned her long, sculpted face and arrow-tipped eyes on him. "Griea is not the only homeworld with the ability to create weaponry."

"Griea is the only planet sanctioned by the Greater Universe to manufacture projectiles," Cael retorted.

"We had to arm ourselves against invasion, Lord Volkov. If you haven't noticed, it's a good thing we did," Ulrich said.

Cael brought a chunk of charred yam to his mouth. "And how did this tiny forest moon manage that?"

Ulrich glanced at the woman who looked to Lorelei for permission to speak.

"Go ahead, Zoe," Lorelei said.

"We repurposed an underground enclave beneath the west quarter of Atreyu. It's not much, of course, but we've managed to replicate machinery close to late-cycle Earthen defense. Semi-automatic artillery, heavy caliber machine guns, wire-guided missiles, etcetera. We're also sitting on a comfortable stockpile of handheld pulse-weaponry," Zoe said.

Impressive, sure, but Cael hardly blinked. "That's not enough."

Lorelei laughed bitterly and tossed down her napkin. "Our militia is well-trained, our artillery is functional — "

"And the Royal Reserve will burn their bodies and melt your toys down like scrap metal," he snarled.

Ulrich, Zoe, their comrade, and Lorelei froze. The acting High Lady lifted her chin defiantly, but Ulrich pursed his mouth, listening, contemplating. Zoe lowered her gaze, as if clipped at the knee.

The other inclined their head, asking to speak. They were an offworlder, likely born to an immigrant family who moved to Aurethia on a lucky, rarely granted Work Visa. Their greyish-mauve coloring and the glassy texture of their scaled skin came from Zephus in the Mal System. Tropical paradise. Mostly sea, sky, and sand, orbiting a Tauri star aptly called Bright.

"I'm Gyana, Imperator," the Zephan said. A split indigo tongue wet their bottom lip. "Or Lord Volkov, I should say. How do you recommend we fight this unwinnable war? If our defense won't be effective against Griea's offense, then what can we do to stave off an attack?"

"It's not like the Legatus is familiar with the city. We have that to our advantage," Lorelei said.

Shame frosted Cael's spine. His throat prickled. "The Legatus does have a layout of the city. The tracker you watched me remove is to blame for that." He didn't say anything else. Couldn't bring himself to admit the rest. "If we can fortify the city and withstand the pressure of a direct assault, then we can use the artillery to keep Bracken and his men at bay. If you try to launch a warship, Bracken will shoot it down. Your terrestrial units won't stand a chance against Griean models. Griea's technology is faster. Built for battle."

"We can't sit idle," Lorelei barked. Her face reddened and she dropped her two-pronged utensil, practically throwing it against the plate.

"Given the message we just sent to the manor, I'm guessing we'll hear back from the Griean war party soon," Zoe said.

Ulrich licked his teeth. "So we fortify Atreyu, prepare for an assault, and weaponize the militia within this territory."

"Essentially abandoning the rest of the moon." Lorelei glanced between them. "We *must* fight."

"If you fight, you'll die," Cael said. He leaned back in his chair, resting his elbows on the armrest. He bounced his chin on his fingertips. "Trust me."

"Trust you," Lorelei repeated. She met his eyes. "*Trust you?*"

Poor word choice. Cael exhaled hard. "Bracken won't be expecting you to have artillery. If you move on the manor and reveal yourself, he'll storm Atreyu. Trust me, don't trust me. But I know my cousin." He thought he did. He used to, at least. "The Imperium can't ignore a Griean warship in Aurethia's orbit for long. They *will* intervene, but if we move too quickly, too confidently, then my father will make an example out of Atreyu. I didn't expect…" He almost couldn't say it, could barely think it. *I didn't expect my father to slaughter Darius and Lena in cold blood. I didn't expect to see Indigo struck dead in the hall. I didn't expect to watch Tatu die. I didn't expect to kill my own men.* But he should've. "I did not anticipate the level of careless violence the Legatus is clearly capable of."

The emptiness in the cafeteria stretched. Ulrich tapped his finger on the tabletop. Zoe and Gyana both sipped from cups, one filled with the barley beer, the other steaming and scented like lemonbalm. Lorelei stared at her plate. Her green eyes flicked about, bouncing between nibbled bone and smeared potato. She opened her mouth to speak, then closed it and shut her eyes, grounding herself with a long inhale through her nose.

"Ulrich, can we spare a few of your militia to scout Basset, Denae, and Yōng? I'd like to bring all able-bodied, willing people to join our defense. Do not leave our villages unarmed but leave them unappealing to Griean interest. It's Avara they want. Children and elderly can't excavate the mineral on their own, and if most of our workforce is here then the Legatus will keep his attention on us." She stopped to think, then continued, prodding the table with her pinky. "Close this city like a fist. I want the seaport locked down, I want the shipment bay sealed, I want our people moved to the interior of the city. Fill every empty apartment, use every vacant house. I want the Galactic Library and the Mineral Museum to serve as potential triage when the time comes. Have the archivists and curators stow anything precious or priceless underground in the blast-proof chamber and make certain the city bunker is outfitted and ready."

Ulrich blinked, taken aback. Relief flooded his face. "Yes, High Lady. I'll begin at once."

Cael could not tell her — not yet, at least — but he was proud of her. Power and tragedy had been thrust upon her, and she stepped into her role beautifully.

The militia leadership moved to stand.

"One more thing," Lorelei said.

Zoe paused with her hand on the back of the chair. Gyana and Ulrich waited.

"When communication is restored, broadcast a galactic transmission to the Imperium. Tell them I will flood each and every mine on this moon if they do not act on Aurethia's behalf." Her gaze was faraway, thumb poised at the corner of her jaw.

"Flooding the mines will stall Avara production for at least a cycle," Zoe balked.

"Yes, and history will call it the Mourning of Aurethia, or the Time of Darkness, or the Great Griean Plague." Mean laughter crackled out of her. "I'm aware."

Cael sighed. With each smart, level decision, Lorelei struck twice as hard with fang and claw.

"Every planet in the Greater Universe will hear it, ma'am," Ulrich said.

Lorelei's mouth curled cruelly. "I'm counting on it."

UNCERTAINTY TRAPPED AURETHIA IN a period of barbed paranoia. One week came and went, flattened by constant pressure from the Griean warship flecking the horizon. Despite Lorelei's brazen gift to her abandoned home, Bracken did not make a move to retaliate. House Volkov leeched onto the Henly manor, acting on behalf of the moon's slain stewardship, and tucked in close to the adjoining village. Sea trade halted. Sky travel ceased. The moon went figuratively and literally dark.

Cael picked up a grey-green rifle, turning it over in his hand. He closed his good eye and strained his scarred eye. The blurry outline of the weapon doubled. Every day he tried to look at something new. Hunted for detail in a tapestry or scanned the text on a holotablet. Every day brought the same results. His vision was half-gone. He opened his functional eye and blinked, checking the antique gun for injury or rust.

"It might not do the same damage as Griean technology, but it'll still put a bullet in someone," Ulrich said. He stood on the opposite side of the table inside the armory hidden underneath Atreyu's plaza.

"At close-range, maybe. Basilisk scale will slow a small caliber bullet, so tell the militia to aim low." He patted his thigh, then gave his kneecap a shake. "We need to rely on heavy gunfire and defensive warfare if we want to keep Atreyu secure. Bracken won't expect this level of armament. He'll either retreat and regroup or rush the city."

"My militia is well-trained, Imperator. They can hold their own in combat."

He put the rifle down and checked over another. "Griea's reputation is not an exaggeration, Commander. We're who we are because it's who we've been. Don't mistake the lull in this siege for weakness."

"Griea is a threat, and we will meet them as such."

And you'll die. Cael nodded bitterly. Sometimes the truth was better glossed than given. "Is the library secure?"

"Yes. Zoe has a team finishing at the museum."

"Good." He knew the answer would not come, but he almost asked *and Elio?* But there was no use. Every day brought the same answer.

Whenever a scout approached, Cael's heart spasmed, cracking when the information didn't include a sighting of the lost prince. At dusk, he sat on a slanted roof overlooking the transport station, and stared over the top of the outer wall, scanning the treeline for a flash of blonde hair, a patch of freckled skin. Yesterday Nara leaped from an adjoining rooftop to join him. He liked to think it was an apology, that shared sunset. Cael, watching the light leave with one good eye. Nara, staying close, wielding the talons that left him half-blind.

Cael started, "We need to make sure the bunker is stocked with enough non-perishable food in case — "

The heel-clip of fast footsteps echoed through the armory. Gyana rushed toward them, widening her leaf-shaped reptilian eyes. She interrupted without pardon or pause. "Lord Volkov, Commander Walsh, we've connected with a forestry messenger."

Ulrich blinked. "Haven't the xenobiologists been recalled from the field?"

Gyana nodded. "She remained with her cohort, sir."

"And what's her message?"

"The Xenobiology Division is intact." She pinched her mouth, careful with her next statement. "The High Lord is alive," she said, shifting her attention to Cael, "and under their protection in the crater."

"Where is she?" Cael asked. It came out botched and desperate, and in any other timeline or scenario, he would've been embarrassed.

"High Lady Lorelei is meeting with her at the station," Gyana said.

Cael dropped the gun. It clattered on the table. Everything inside him rushed forward. *Elio.* The cinder of hope smoldering in his stomach flared hot, and he was powerless against it. He heard Ulrich say his name, but he couldn't stop. Heard Gyana call to him but ignored her. Before he knew it, Cael was launching up the staircase, storming through the square, and tripping over his feet as he bolted through Atreyu. He couldn't hear his own thoughts. Couldn't temper the culmination of dread and joy whirlpooling at the base of his skull.

Aurethian militia guarded the outdoor entrance of the transport station. Cael slowed, striding toward them, but did not stop.

"The High Lady is in a private meeting," one of them said.

Cael arched an eyebrow and snorted, gripping the pommel on his sheathed blade. He kept walking, closing the space between them.

One guard eyed the other and tipped their head suggestively. The militant who spoke moved aside. Cael stepped past them without argument, and straightened his spine, lengthening his gait. On the platform near a docked hovertrain, Lorelei stood, flanked by two Aurethian soldiers on horseback. The messenger looked bored, standing before the trio in a hooded savannah cape and muddy bootwear. Cael clocked her thin saber. Noticed the way she adjusted, angling toward him with the slightest, incremental movement.

"Cael," Lorelei warned.

"Where is he?" Cael forced patience into the question, but he carried his status — Keeper of the Basilisk, Tupinaire champion, Imperator of Griea — and slithered into the cold shadow of who he'd once been. He was suddenly on the ice, striking down a challenger. Back at the War College, teaching combat strategy. Drinking from a ceremonial chalice, honoring the promise of prophecy.

The messenger dragged her gaze from his face to his feet. She moved slowly, unbothered by Cael's ferocity. "You're the warlord he took to his bed." She spoke like a key, twisting until the lock gave a satisfactory *click*.

"I'm his husband. You'd be wise to tell me where he is," Cael said.

Lorelei shifted. Sunder caught the ribbed armor cinched around her torso, gleaming fire-gold. Tussled hair cascaded down her back, and she carried a belt of bronze cattails around her thigh.

She sighed, gesturing between the pair with a lazy wave. "Cael Volkov, this is Sindra Kimura, messenger from Outpost One, supposed journeyman from the Genesis Expedition. Sindra Kimura, this is Cael Volkov. I will not, and frankly cannot, stop him from cutting you down. It's in your best interest to tell us where my brother is." She paused, tracing a cattail. "Now."

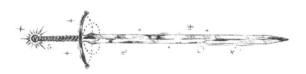

CHAPTER THIRTY-FIVE

BRACKEN

The bodies left an acrid taste in the air, chafing Bracken's throat. A dark plume tunneled above the treeline. The Aurethian citizenship put up a valiant fight. Their stubbornness and dedication lasted three days, but on the fourth morning, bloodshed gave way to surrender, and the people agreed to re-enter the local Avara mine and continue production. It was the fifth day, and a huge, swirling pillar climbed from a pyre obstructing the road leading into Nadhas, blackening the sky.

Trauma did not always breed consistency, but it did incentivize compliance.

"One mine will not be enough," Legatus Marcus said. He stood beside Bracken, watching the smoke.

"Once we've documented the extraction and refinement process, I'll signal our trainee team to enter high orbit, and we'll spread our influence throughout the region. We can't afford to repeat the same strategy we used in Nadhas," Bracken said.

"Why not?"

"Atreyu is a metropolis. If we move too quickly, we'll forever tip the balance. Nadhas was one thing. It's small, rural, and with the manor on its border, we can easily claim aggressive resistance to our initial arrival. Moving through Atreyu and Basset with the same fervor could lead to interference from the Imperium, and a loss of weaponry privileges for Griea. Allowing the Nadhas mine to become fully functional will buy us some good faith, and entering the rest of Aurethia knowing how to produce Avara will give us the upper hand. We won't need the people to comply, but we'll offer them compensation and safety if they do."

Marcus nodded. Under Draitune's violet light, the silver in his hair looked more white, less metallic. "Wise to position us as the commanding force without relying on violence to conduct our cause. The orchard should be tended, and I'd like our fisherman to explore Aurethia's ocean. Have we expanded our reach into the crater?"

"There's nothing out there, Legatus. Aurethia invested in a xenobiological wilderness initiative to preserve the forest, that's all. Waste of credit, waste of time. And one of Harlyn's worst political legacies. That crater is a dead zone."

"No Avara?"

"None that can be easily extracted. It's better to focus on the operational mines right now. We'll search the crater for untapped growth chambers after Avara production is back in full swing."

"I'll trust your judgement, Imperator." He lifted his face. His regal exterior remained unpassable. "Atreyu is not an ignorable issue. You understand that?"

"I do."

"Control of the city will confirm the success of our full-scale siege. Unfortunately, Lady Lorelei is hiding there like a scorpion in someone's shoe, complicating the validity of our enterprise. I need us to breach the lion's maw of Aurethia, and I'd like you to shake her loose. Have we confirmed Elio Henly's death?"

Bracken set his teeth. "Not yet."

"If we don't have a body, we can't void the galactic agreement. It's imperative we find him."

"Understood, Legatus."

"Move on Atreyu, take care of the Henly heir, and find my son," Legatus Marcus ordered. He swatted nonexistent dust from Bracken's shoulder and then clasped him there, squeezing. His pale gaze shone like snow, too light to be true blue. "The follow-up holomeeting is scheduled for the day after tomorrow. I'll be attending alongside Operative Carr." The Griean leader turned, looking out to sea, then toward the orchard, before inclining his head to Bracken. "God is in the water."

"God is in the water," Bracken repeated.

Marcus's shadow streaked the grass beneath the candlebell. Darius and

Lena swayed, pushed softly by a coastal breeze. Bracken turned back toward the smoke.

A tic had fastened itself to him in this era of conquest. At the most unusual times, Bracken would shake out his hand, fending off an irritating pinch. It was an invisible thing, like a pincer snapping at his wrist, or a wire jammed under his fingernail. He wondered if the dead followed him, voiceless and biting, nipping with spectral teeth. *I will never again be who I was.* The thought seeded, low and invasive. He thought to smash it underneath the weight of his new title.

But instead, Bracken said, "I'm doing what you should've," as if Cael were there, standing beside him. "The people here will call me *demon*, they'll call me *wielder of death*, but when all is said and done, the Greater Universe will remember me for bringing harvest to the hungry, and Avara to the sick, and wealth to the ice giant. How will they remember you, cousin?"

Cael wasn't there to answer. Bracken imagined him huffing out a laugh. *I'll be the soft-hearted prince who died for love. They'll sing about me; they'll weep over you.* His arm shot out. He swatted the empty air. Cael's phantom voice evaporated. His presence, although entirely self-imposed, made Bracken sick to his stomach. He scraped his teeth over his lip, snagging loose skin, and tapped his dialect device.

"Connect me to Kindra Malkin."

Yes, Imperator. Connecting. The wind stirred. A falcon shrieked overhead. *Connected.*

"Imperator," Kindra purred through the static. "How can I be of service?"

Bracken paused. He didn't really know. The familiar cadence of her voice was enough to dull whatever useless anxiety Cael's memory seemed to needle. "How's the boy?"

"Lord Orson? He's quiet. Doesn't speak much. Maxine got him to drink some broth and eat half an apple."

"And the general?"

"Peadar Mahone is immune to my charm, I'm afraid."

"Is he in recovery?"

"Our medical team treated him for a compound fracture and a broken collarbone. He's resilient." He pictured her mouth in his mind, shaping each word. "I still believe he's useful to us. It'd be wise to keep him sequestered to his own chamber, fed, clothed, and accessible. After a while, he'll break, and once you find the Henly princess, you'll have something important to dangle. I have a feeling he'll be obedient, like a sad, old dog."

"I agree."

"Is there anything else?" Kinda asked, saccharine.

"You said the little one hasn't spoken?"

"Briefly with Maxine, I think. Nothing substantial. Why?"

Bracken tried not to think about Cael. "I'd like to talk to him."

Kindra made a curious noise. "Oh?"

"He's young," Bracken said, thinking of Cael's lanky, boyish exterior, how he fumbled through training as a pre-teen, hardly able to swing a blade. He was all fist back then. Knuckles and rage, punch and grit. No finesse at all. Malleable to a fault. "I don't want him to feel alone."

ORSON HENLY'S BEDCHAMBER REMAINED guarded. The Royal Reserve stationed in the hall nodded to Bracken and stepped aside. Kindra matched his stride, following each step. Black silk concealed her copper hair, and a glossy midnight skirt flowed around her heeled sandals.

"Treat him delicately," she whispered, and paused inside the room, allowing Bracken to close the door. She shifted her slight frame and extended her arm, gesturing to Orson with an open palm. "Lord Orson, this is Imperator Bracken Volkov. Bracken, this is Lord Orson, the youngest member of House Henly."

Orson sat at a desk facing the window. His holotablet sent a blue hologram dancing across the desktop, an old serial about space travel and star pirates. The volume was too low to properly decipher, but Bracken recognized the tell-tale sound of cinematic music. Orson didn't pay attention to the holoseries. Bracken noticed the boy's reflection on the clear window tip slightly, acknowledging their presence.

"It's good to meet you, Orson," Bracken said.

Orson didn't move. "I know who you are."

Kindra lifted her chin, shooting a cautionary glance at Bracken.

"You're the man who hit my father." The youngest lion glanced over his shoulder. "Aren't you?"

Bracken considered his next statement carefully. He mulled over how to present the truth to a child ill-prepared to hear it, and stepped forward, grateful for his casual black-and-white clothing, and the lack of intimidating armor. He unclipped the strap on his chest and balanced his claymore in the corner.

"I'm Cael's cousin," he said, easing closer. "But yes, I'm that man, too. I was sent to Aurethia to fix what he broke."

"Who? Cael or my father?"

Bracken banked his head. "Both, honestly. Cael broke an agreement with the Legatus, and your father tried to break the spirit of my homeworld. I'm sorry you had to witness it, though. See, where I'm from — "

"You defend yourself. I know. Cael told me."

"That's right. I didn't come here intending to hurt anyone, but unfortunately, Cael put a lot of people in danger. He put the prospect of peace between Griea and Aurethia in jeopardy."

"How?" Orson swiveled in his seat, frowning at Bracken. "Cael told me stories about you. You're his mentor, right? You trained him?"

Bracken's chest felt squeezed by a massive fist. "I did. I came here to help him, but he refused what I offered. He lied to you, and to your brother, and to your family. Tricked you all and tried to undo a very, very long operation. Our plan would've coupled with the unification agreement. A fresh start for all of us."

Orson searched his face. His small mouth parted, and his brow creased with confusion. "That's not true."

"Who do you think invited us here, Lord Orson? Surely, Griea couldn't coordinate such a..." He paused, remembering Orson's age. "An intervention," he decided, "without the location of the manor or the whereabouts of your family. You can ask Maxine, you know. Cael spoke with her about it, too."

"Maxine would've told me," he snapped.

"Not if she wanted to protect you," Kindra soothed. She glided forward, kneeling beside Orson's chair. "We all trusted Cael, sweetheart. No one could've known."

"Where is my brother? And my father? My mom?" Orson glared between them. His chin dimpled. "Where is Lorelei? If Cael did something to them — "

Bracken moved like a wolf, latching his teeth around the tender assumption. *Yes, good. Blame him.* He spoke powerfully, sensitively. "We'll find him, Lord Orson," he assured, and braved a touch to the child's shoulder. Orson flinched but did not cower. Bracken thought it promising to see a cracked boy refuse to collapse. "He will pay for what he's done."

Orson sniffled miserably. "I don't understand," he crowed. The sobbing started in his chest, but he trapped it like a jarred butterfly. "Cael loved us."

"And you loved him," Kindra said.

"I loved him," Bracken added.

Kindra tilted her face upward. Her soft smile twitched.

"We're going to take care of you," Bracken promised. He bent at the waist and gripped Orson's shoulder. "Cael told you about me, right? Told you about our Tupinaire? About our great basilisk?"

Kindra wiped at the thin stream leaking from Orson's left eye. When the boy looked up, he stared at Bracken, transfixed, nodding helplessly.

"Griea will need a new Keeper," Bracken whispered. He gave the caged lion an endearing little shake. "Maybe one day, it'll be you."

CHAPTER THIRTY-SIX

ELIO

Dew beaded on a curly vine tickling Elio's shoulder. He sat against the base of a tree in the garden, listening to the pride yawn and roar. Sunder glanced off Draitune's ring, streaking the sky like a bulged vein. Dawn hazed the concaved bowl of the crater. Elio watched light streak through the canopy and catch an orbic mote. He thunked the back of his head against the trunk.

Alien Lifeform Isolate Crater Extrinsic. ALICE. Life bringer, visitor. Castaway. Alice, who was a genderless creature half-buried in the center of Aurethia. Alice, who was a *who*, inarguably, but a being without voice or origin, bolted to an unfamiliar place unused to homemaking. Alice, who rippled and pulsed, shouting a frequency from the middle of her gelatinous body — almost undetectable, akin to the call of whales and dolphins. Alice, who rooted herself into the very membrane of the moon, coaxing a fibrous miracle to grow in an exotic habitat. Alice, who extended herself like a god, who reversed cellular division, and stopped time, and healed even the most grievous wounds.

Alice, who happened to be the most valuable thing in the Greater Universe, who came from somewhere far away, who did not seem bothered by the tiny, curious, bipedal beasts studying her biome, who could not get back home, wherever home might be.

Elio finally understood why Harlyn Volkov advocated for the Xenobiology Division. He finally realized how far his family's interest stretched, and how deep this secret was buried. A seemingly innocent gesture commending the initial immigration from Draitune had shielded Outpost One and the research being done at the crater's core. Alexander Henly played his part — discoverer of Avara — masking the true nature of the substance from the Imperium, and Harlyn Volkov signed the agreement, keeping her house's reputation intact and Griean interest at bay.

Alexander and Harlyn stomped out any evidence of their doomed romance, erasing their infidelity and procreation from history. But Alice could not be taped over or redacted, and despite their rushed attempt at preserving the integrity of the Genesis team's ongoing analysis, both of them understood the reality of impending discovery. House Henly could not shoulder the burden alone, but Harlyn's commitment to her house's respectability and Griea's independence fanned the flame of Alexander's fragile ego.

The situation at hand was a devastating *what if* gone wrong. The outcome of two families determined to hold unquantifiable power in the palm of a single hand, under the control of one surname.

There was no way for a group of people to stay hidden for as long as the journeyman from Genesis stayed hidden. Long enough for their identities to become legend, for their presence to become myth, and then repurposed and repackaged as a scientific exploration initiative by the leader of a rival planet. Genesis. A word carved out of Earth's history, accented like the language spoken on the ringed giant, similar in structure to Aurethian. Just older. Creaky with antiquity. Elio thought about every childhood story he'd ever heard, circulating through the manor like an uncatchable spider. *The xenobiologists might see you,* whispered by Lorelei as they played on the rim of the crater, as if the scientists were creatures from fable or fairies from a forgotten world.

Elio never anticipated inheriting an extraterrestrial when he entered into the engagement that would turn his entire life upside down. Alice made the unification seem like a walk through the orchard. The incredible weight of her existence settled on his abdomen like a boulder.

Hooves beat the dirt. Elio turned toward the sound, but Vik's voice crackled through his dialect device before Xander breached the entrance of the garden. `Sindra has arrived with Cael Volkov, Lord Elio.` He sounded hopeful, cautious. `I will wait for you.`

Alone and heartsick, Elio blurted, "You're alive." The revelation gusted from him. He swallowed to clear his rapidly thickening throat.

Somewhere in the pit of him, Elio knew he would've felt Cael's death.

When it happened, the act would cut through to Elio's core and leave him bleeding. There was something tragic about that — loving Cael after... everything. But the underbelly of their love was forged in the furnace of explicitly intimate anger. Every time he thought about the morning after their wedding, it was the deepest betrayal, amplified. It was the electric jolt of a broken bone snapping apart in his chest; the blood rush of flesh opened with a blunt blade. His mother's strong, stricken face. His father's bravery. Orson's terror. Maxine's snarl, and Bracken's laughter, and the Griean-black surrounding them. When he thought about Cael, he thought about a nightmare come to life, and their love blistered up like a pox. Seeing him might cause the affliction to burst and spew.

"Elio, Sindra found the Griean heir," Xander said. His horse stomped and shook out its mane.

"Vik told me."

"I assume you'd like a moment."

Elio stood. Adrenaline surged through him, a panicky bubbling he couldn't tame. "Don't intervene, alright?"

Xander cocked his head. "Are we reasoning with him," he tested, arching a brow, "or are we detaining him?"

"I'm going to speak to him." Elio slid his attention upward, finding Xander's inquisitive gaze. "If you or anyone else tries to get between us, it'll only make the situation worse. Let me manage this."

"Understood," he said, almost entertained.

Elio got to his feet and pushed away from the tree, using the momentum to help his body stay upright. Every part of him wanted to fall as badly as it wanted to keep going. His hands itched for Cael. To hold him, to tear him apart. *You're alive.* The thought came again. He strode through the garden and stepped into the road. Slowed to a halt.

Cael dismounted from an Aurethian horse. He wore an armored charcoal tunic and black cargos tucked into familiar bootwear. A pinkish scar bolted the right side of his face, spreading outward like a lightning strike. It drove through his brow, split his eyelid, and left his iris pale as a frosted window. *You're alive.* Elio's heart was a hawk, flapping and shrieking.

"May I present, Lord Cael Volkov, Griean heir and steward of Aurethia," Sindra announced.

Vicious fury consumed Elio. Each finger bent, and he clenched his hand into a shaking fist. It was diabolical — loving him, hating him.

Across from him, shock gave way to elation. An archive of emotion crossed Cael's face. He exhaled, stepping forward. "You're safe — "

"You knew," Elio spat. It wasn't the first thing he'd meant to say, but it was the only thing he could muster.

Sindra dismounted and took the reins, guiding both horses toward the stable. Off to the side, Vik stood at attention, glancing between Elio and Cael. Xander approached mindfully, and a few other journeymen stepped forward, watching.

Hopeless rage overwhelmed him. Elio launched, one hand on the pommel of his Grabak, the other swiping through the air. "You orchestrated the destruction of my house, you injected yourself into this moon like a virus, you manipulated your way into my bed!"

Cael matched him, crossing the space in six even steps. "I went against my father, Elio, I tried to stop the bloodshed before it ever reached Aurethia."

Elio yanked his Grabak free. "Meet me as you would on the ice, Imperator."

Cael dodged, leaping backward. His hand hovered over his sheathed blade, but he set his teeth and snarled. "This wasn't supposed to happen. The Legatus should've called off the siege, my men should've remained planet-side, Bracken should've never — "

"You knew exactly what they would do."

"I knew nothing," Cael barked. He sidestepped Elio's first swing, then drew his short-sword and blocked another blow. Metal sang. The force of it rattled Elio's arm.

"You wanted to domesticate a Henly." Elio pushed at Cael's blade, breaking free. "You wanted to skin a lion, didn't you? That wasn't play, it was prophecy." He swung again. Another strike, blade-to-blade, the clang of iron and bone. Cael pushed him backward. Dodged, blocked, but refused to attack. "Fight like a Griean," Elio said, slamming the blunt handle of his Grabak into Cael's ribcage. "You let them take my family hostage, you led me astray, you let me believe what we had was real — "

Cael regained himself after pausing to clutch his side. He lunged again, parrying Elio's quickness, and seized Elio by the shoulder. "It *is* real!"

"You came to Aurethia to conquer it — "

"Your house left my planet starving and sick," Cael rasped, leaning down to speak an inch from Elio's nose. Their blades weighed heavy against each other, crisscrossed between them. "What did you expect? Two centuries of animosity, two centuries of death, two centuries of House Henly hoarding wealth. I believed in us enough to try and change it, but I can't undo what's been done. We have time, we can still fight."

Elio's pulse skyrocketed. He couldn't think. Could hardly breathe. "You abandoned me." He dislodged Cael's hand and swung.

Their blades met again, and again, and *again*. Elio fought wildly, pushing his body to the limit, adrenaline revving, heart cracking. With every blow, Cael deflected. With every aggressive movement, Cael braced, turned his blade, skimmed Elio's skin, looked for a way out. He knocked Elio away. Ducked, growled, parried, spun. Even then, even in the throes of sorrow and cruelty, Cael refused to harm him. Even then, even when Elio was ruthless, at his mightiest, Cael bested him at every turn.

When Elio jabbed his Grabak, Cael swatted the thing away. When Elio kicked, Cael dodged. He was still an Imperator of Griea. Still an unbeatable warlord. At one point, Cael stopped Elio's open palm with a hard grip on his wrist, and at another, he knocked Elio off-balance with a shoulder to his breastbone. Their fight became exhausting.

"I protected you," Cael said, almost shouting.

Finally, Cael moved with deadly precision, forcing Elio backward with blow after calculated blow. He slid close, spinning his blade, and grasped Elio's nape. The tip of his short-sword kissed the Henly heir's throat. The very same stance they'd taken during their first sparring match.

"Yield," he snapped, panting, holding on, refusing to move. "I'm done fighting, darling. Yield or — "

Protected? Elio drove the basilisk tooth through armor, then fabric, and plunged it into Cael's stomach. It made a sickening sound. The crunch of armor cracking, the tear and split of sinew.

"You betrayed me," Elio whispered, throat clogged.

Cael's mouth dropped open. His mismatched eyes softened, and Elio's name fluttered from him, feather-soft and miserable. Cael dropped his short-sword. When his knees buckled, Elio followed, holding onto him. And when his thumb traced the fine hair at the base of his ear, Elio forced down an accidental sob.

Behind him, Vik made a wounded sound, like a dog whimpering. The Genesis journeymen gasped and chattered.

What remained of Elio's heart well and truly shattered. He yanked the Grabak free. *There.* He wanted to feel Cael's death. To hold it like a promise, even if he intended to break it. Because if anyone deserved to oversee Cael's fate, to grant the Imperator a warrior's death, it was him. Bride, betrayed, abandoned. If anyone got to decide whether Cael lived or died, it was Elio.

And despite the rage ravaging every piece of him, and the grief whipping in his gut, Elio was not ready to lose him.

Cael fell, slumping, choking on a half-gasp. Blood slicked the inside of his mouth.

"Keep him alive." Elio heaved in a terrible breath.

Vik shot forward. The Augment skidded to Cael's side, immediately applying pressure to the wound. No one else moved. Not Xander, not Innis, or Melody. Everyone stood still, as if they'd watched an animal take the place of a man. As if Elio had shucked off his skin and started to roar.

"Keep him alive," Elio shouted. His face crumbled under the weight of a horrified cry. He got to his feet, pointing at Cael's limp form. "Treat him with Avarine, take him to the med-bay, and keep him alive!"

THE NEXT HOUR RESULTED in immediate regret and destabilizing panic.

Elio paced in the surgical station, fidgeting nervously while Melody applied a thin layer of gelatinous Avarine to the interior of Cael's wound. The viscous material carried its own cerulean aura, and Elio strained to listen as the journeymen instructed each other to *hold there, seal that, stitch this*. Elio made the mistake of looking at the dried spattering of dark blood on his palm. He did not know why, but he brought the heel of his thumb to his mouth and laved at a crusted spot. The metallic flavor would forever remind him of the vow they took — an omen from their wedding night.

After another hour, one line of small stitches, and a generous helping of Avarine, Melody snapped off each glove and gave Elio an exhausted, feeble look. "He'll be fine," they said, lifting a thin eyebrow. "If you'd like to keep him alive, I'd recommend not stabbing him again. Avarine is miraculous. We won't waste it to feed your temper."

Elio wilted in the wake of a graceful warning. "Thank you."

They patted his shoulder on their way out.

"Feel better?" Xander asked under his breath. Elio didn't have time to answer. Xander swept past him and disappeared into the hall, leaving him to stew. The only person left in the small, white-walled space was Vik.

The Augment sat in a plastic chair, staring at Cael, watching him breathe. The pair didn't speak, but Vik unhinged his jaw, and a stream of archived speech came through his unmoving mouth. It was Vik's own voice, distant and different. Cael's laughter shot into a room like a bird searching for an open window.

"If I may, looking at Lord Elio like he's been plated and served does not fit the definition of — "

"You're out of line!" Cael's rueful laughter. His voice, playfully tormented. "He's like a locked box. We walk, we talk, but I still feel like I've hardly grazed the surface of him. Like he's hiding from me."

"Stop it," Elio snapped under his breath. His chest felt clogged.

The recording paused, then resumed.

"I have to try." Cael. The clipped sound of his bootwear against the floor, pacing. "I'm the Griean Imperator, I still have my Royal Reserve — my opinion is respected, isn't it? If I feel strongly enough about re-evaluating our strategy and delaying the siege, then I should be heard by my house and our people."

Elio set his teeth. "I know what you're doing."

"Vik Endresen, I would like to transfer exclusive royal control to one, Elio Henly, for the duration of his lifetime. Prioritize his safety and well-being, protect him from harm and preserve his life. Do not let him die, Vik."

"Suspend all archived data for the next hour, Vik Endresen." Elio heaved the command through a lungful of air.

Vik closed his mouth. The Augment did not look at Elio for a long, long time, but as morning bled into afternoon, and evening shaded the window, he finally turned and said, "Love is an infinite thing, Lord Henly. It knows no boundaries."

Elio's dry throat itched for water, but his empty, flip-flopping stomach would reject anything he tried to swallow. He brought another patch of caked blood to his mouth, suckling at the crusted splatter on his knuckle. It'd been there for hours, hardening. "I'm aware."

"Loving you did not discount his love for Griea and loving him will not discount your love for Aurethia."

"Loving him brought wreckage to Aurethia."

Vik tipped his head. "You can't lie to me, Elio. I can hear your heartbeat. I'm tuned to your vitals."

"Loving him wrecked me," Elio confessed weakly, stubbornly.

"Did it?"

The question lingered. Elio didn't answer. He stayed across from Vik, sore from too much time spent seated on the linoleum and stared at Cael's tenderly parted mouth. The scar striping his face looked like the spindly hand of the candlebell tree, carved in pinkish branches through ashen skin.

CHAPTER THIRTY-SEVEN
CAEL

Agony pummeled him. Searing pain radiated throughout his torso, pooling in the gash left behind from Elio's Grabak. His mouth filled with coppery blood. Light hazed like a falling torch, dropping out of view. "Wait," he tried to say, but it hardly surfaced. After that, there was nothing except the cool press of a clean sheet against his back. He felt the ghost of a hand on his chest. Heard someone speaking fast. Then, tragically, nothing. Darkness pulled him under. Cael did not remember passing out. Didn't know when or how he'd lost consciousness to begin with. Suspended in claustrophobic quiet, floating in the time before an ending, he simply assumed he was dying. It was bright, thorny pain, and sweet, merciful relief, then a deep stillness cocooned around him until his lungs rioted. When he finally peeled his eyes open and stared blearily at the high, flat ceiling, he didn't know how long he'd been asleep.

Is this a new life? But it couldn't have been. He remembered the despair on Elio's face, and felt the trembling echo his shaky hand had passed into him, wrapped tight around the Grabak, gutting him like a common foe.

"You're awake," Vik said.

Cael gulped. His throat felt papery and worn, like he'd trekked through a desert. "Vik?"

"Yes, it's me. You've been mended with an alternative substance similar in structure and composition to Avara. Your rightmost lumbar region sustained a fatal injury, but the medical staff managed to stop the internal bleeding. They applied Avarine and closed the wound. Unfortunately, you'll have a scar."

"Oh, another scar." Cael coughed to clear the dust from his tongue. "How will I possibly go on."

"I'm glad to see the altercation with your husband hasn't impacted your sense of humor."

My husband. Cael sat up. An ache surfaced in his abdomen, throbbing in time with his pulse. He lifted the sheet and assessed the bandage wrapped around his middle. He plucked at the gauze. To his surprise, there were no stitches. A silvery-mauve line blemished his fair skin.

"How long have I been out?" Cael asked.

"You arrived yesterday at dawn. It's about mid-morning."

"Impossible," he muttered, staring at the place a gouge should've been. Stitched, sure. Bandaged and clean, yes. But healed? He lifted his gaze and pulled his brows together. "This was no surface wound, Vik."

"I'm aware," the Augment said. He inclined his head respectfully. "Avarine is *similar* to Avara, sir. Its properties are stronger and speedier. Be thankful you were at Outpost One with access to unknown medicine, because I'm afraid nothing else in the Greater Universe could've healed the damage Elio's Grabak inflicted."

"So it *was* a killing blow."

"You taught him well."

Cael sucked air through his teeth. He couldn't shake off the image of Elio's clenched jaw and glassy eyes. Couldn't get out from underneath the brutal way he moved. "Where is he?"

"I'll take you to him after you're dressed and fed."

He nodded. "Thank you for keeping him safe."

"Thank you for not dying. I'd hate to be the only sensible Griean left on Aurethia." Vik paused. A smile lifted his mouth. "And it'd be quite the chore to plan your funeral."

Cael snorted. "Oh, if I die, just kick me down a hill, Vik. Leave me for the animals."

"Noted." Vik's smile faltered, split by a sudden laugh. "If I die a second time, at least recycle the cybernetic augmentation. I'm sure someone could make use of it."

"Heard." Cael laughed, too. "It's good to see you."

Vik bowed his head again. "Clothes are in the nightstand. I'll have a plate fixed for you."

Cael wanted to ask about their whereabouts, about everything. Outpost

One. The Aurethian crater. Avarine. But he was afraid there was simply too much to talk about and very little time to do so. Sindra, the strange messenger, had refused to give Lorelei substantial detail, but she'd spoken of a place in the center of the crater where a community of people engaged in scientific research alongside Aurethia's Xenobiology Division, and that had been good enough for Cael. No matter where Sindra claimed to hail from, if Elio had been there, Cael would've gone. Too bad the journey landed him on an operating table, forever scarred by the love of his life.

The cream-colored tunic fit loosely. He paused to feel across the scar fissured through his stomach, shiny like a fish, then tucked the shirt into his freshly washed cargo pants, and those into his bootwear. Beneath the scar, everything felt watery and weak, as if the tissue wasn't quite used to holding. He pulled the basilisk belt one notch tighter around his midsection and paused to look at himself. He felt out of place. Unremarkably othered in the middle of an unlikely fairytale. The empty room didn't seem any emptier, but he did, somehow. Cael Volkov, once an Imperator of a great people, rightful heir to a powerful planet, champion on the ice, reduced to a half-blind madman on a quest to take his place at Elio Henly's side — the very same prince who had run him through with the fang of a beast Cael had once been named keeper of. It was poetic and awful, and he couldn't help but live in the memory of who they'd been before this. Underneath the candlebell. Hand-in-hand in the orchard. Neck deep in the sea.

Somewhere else, Cael sat with his back to a tree, cutting an apple with his boot-knife. Somewhere else, Elio soaked up the sunlight during a lazy afternoon, head propped on Cael's thigh. Somewhere else, some*time* else, the war never started, and nothing went wrong.

A knock at the door sent a spike of adrenaline down his spine. He calmed his fluttering heart. "Come in."

Vik returned with a half-wrapped egg sandwich and a fruit flavored electrolyte pouch. "The journeymen voted to disarm you, whatever they think that'll accomplish, so I've stored your weaponry in Elio's chamber for the time being."

Cael took the sandwich. "I don't know what they think I'd do, considering I'm severely outnumbered and came here willingly."

Vik shrugged. He still wore his Griean armor. "Would you like to eat and walk? Elio is waiting at the clearing."

Everything inside him wanted to go, and everything inside him didn't know *how* to go. He remembered Elio's caving chest, his shredded voice. *You betrayed me.* He took a bite. Warm, gooey egg coated his tongue. "Is there still hope for us, Vik? Or are we ruined?"

The Augment's left pupil expanded. His data-port whirred, and he quirked his head, glancing at the ceiling. "Specify, please."

Cael chewed, swallowed. He gave Vik a withered look. "I need a friend right now, Vik. Not an Augment."

Vik hummed. His data-port slowed to a whisper. "Hope is a resilient thing. Sometimes the strongest love is cultivated in the aftermath of ruination. I choose to believe Elio Henly is still the young man I came to respect over the last cycle, and you being alive right now proves it."

"Will he forgive me?"

"Probably not." Vik let his hand fall heavy on Cael's shoulder and gave him a small shake. "But he fretted over you while Melody, Xander, and the rest of the Genesis team attended your wound. He stayed in this room until exactly one hour ago when Melody gave you a sedative reversal and told him you'd be awake soon. He listened to most of our archived conversations — two in particular, repeatedly."

Cael blinked slowly. "Two," he echoed.

"The transmission from your father regarding the location of an Avara mine, and our conversation directly after, concerning parsec sickness related mortality on Griea. Also, the day you asked me to run a comparison between the successful siege of Aurethia as outlined by the Legatus against the stable unification of House Volkov and House Henly via legitimate marriage." He paused considering Cael with an open, honest expression. "Do you forgive him?"

He gave Vik a pensive look. "For what, stabbing me? I forgave him the second it happened."

"Maybe you should allow him the same courtesy. You married him for his heart and his mind, I know that much to be true. Trust your judgment."

"Does he know that, though? That I married him because..." *I cannot imagine a world where I am not his. I cannot fathom an existence without him.* His mouth hovered open, struggling with what came next. "I'm his, entirely."

"Tell him," Vik said.

Cael sucked down his electrolyte pouch. He didn't realize how thirsty he was until the liquid dropped into his stomach. "Did Sindra deliver the message about House Henly? Does he know — "

"Yes." Vik softened. For the first time in a long while, discomfort melted into sadness on the Augment's chiseled face. "Elio was informed about his family."

The cruel, useless urge to go to him, to comfort him, persisted. There was no erasing the past. No resurrecting the dead. But Cael could kneel before Elio and take his fist, or his anger, or his grief, or his pain. Cael could do that, at least.

"Let's go," Cael said. He took another bite and followed Vik into the hall, through the dated passageway, and into the open air of the shady crater.

Pine and pollen scented the wilderness. Moss, fungi, and wet stone did, too. Cael kept his gaze ahead, but made mental notes of his surroundings, tracking the imagery in the peripheral of his good eye. Antiquated housing. Wood-built, sturdy, but old. The terrestrial transport overlooking the community was far too ancient to pilot, boasting museum-worthy technology from another era. Some people seemed oddly put together, as if they'd eased through a rip in time and arrived from a distant memory. He noticed crates of xenobiology equipment. Everything was lived-in and thoroughly used. Horses whinnied from the stables next to the garden, and an Aurethian lion lounged at the base of an evergreen.

"What is this place?" Cael asked.

"It's Outpost One, the original landing point of the Genesis journeyman."

"I'm assuming this is a historical site, right? Maintained by the Xenobiology Division?"

"Yes and no," Vik said. He ducked under a blueish branch and gestured to an intimate clearing.

Elio sat on a bulbous root with his back against the base of a tree. One knee bent, while the other leg remained outstretched, brown boot dangling over the lip of an oval chasm cleaving through the center of the crater, he was himself and not. His blonde hair was wind-swept, and his undercut fluffed around his ears. Cael recognized every bit of him. Elvish nose, cutting bone, narrow chin. Freckles like a constellation mapping each cheek. But the distance in his eyes, the set of his mouth. Those were new. He looked older, harder. Like someone had scraped out innocence and replaced his boyhood with a bruise.

Vik stopped and cleared his throat. "High Lord Elio Henly, Cael Volkov of Griea."

"No need for formality, Vik," Elio said, hushed and cold. He lifted his gaze, staring at Cael. His attention didn't falter at first. He held Cael in his line of sight, assessing him the same way an animal might. But the longer he looked, the more Cael recognized him. Elio glanced around Cael's face, lingering on his scarred eye.

Vik prodded Cael with his elbow, urging him forward. "I'll be nearby."

Cael could not focus. He met Elio's gaze and almost crumbled.

"I have too much to say to you," Elio whispered. His voice faltered, but he cleared his throat and continued. "But we don't have time for it, and I don't have the energy to dismantle the chokehold you have on me or begin to repair the damage you've inflicted on my heart." Each word was deliberate, uttered like a biting thing at the end of a chain. He didn't wait for Cael to nod, speak, or agree, and instead, nudged his chin toward the canyon. "I'm going to tell you about this, and about Outpost One, and about the relationship between Alexander Henly and Harlyn Volkov, and you are going to listen."

Cael crept forward, craning to look into the chasm. Below, surrounded by forest and thrumming like a living pond, a creature, structure, *being* the size of a small village slumbered in the dug-out where a comet should've been. His heart leaped. He blinked, squinting to dislodge the image, but it, he, she, they — whoever or whatever it was — remained. It looked gelatinous, almost, like a Griean eel, transparent enough to see through to the inner workings of its body. It pulsed with a fibrous blue glow that leaked into the soil around its body, form, mass, carapace. He could not decipher a face or tail, limbs or tentacles, but it was certainly alive. Cael's limbic brain, all the primordial pieces of him, said *alien*.

"Sit down before you faint," Elio said.

The blood in his face drained. Cael plopped on his rear next to Elio's outstretched leg, dizzied. "Start talking."

And Elio did. He spoke slowly and clearly, detailing the impossible existence of Outpost One and its ageless caretakers, how the forbidden romance between their ancestors and the discovery of an undeterminable lifeform led to the unification agreement between their homeworlds. Avara and Avarine — the miracle an extraterrestrial brought to Aurethia, and the reality of what would happen if the Greater Universe uncovered Alice's existence before the Genesis journeymen could harness and replicate the unspeakably powerful substance it naturally produced. Xander Henly. The Xenobiology Division's true purpose, how Harlyn put an ongoing preservation effort in motion to delay the inevitable.

"House Henly and House Volkov stumbled upon a secret centuries in the making and penned a secret of their own. They buried Alice and Xander to preserve Aurethian power and Griean pride and buy the original settlers

— masked under the guise of the Xenobiology Division — precious time,"
Elio said. He sighed, turning to look at the displaced lifeform gripping the
core of the forest moon. "And they did it knowing we'd be left with their
mess."

Cael stared at the odd, blue creature, watching her breathe and shudder.
A flock of starlings took to the sky, startled by Alice's subtle shifting, like a
bear snoring or a python stretching. Nothing made sense; everything made
sense. None of this could possibly be true; he believed every word.

"Cael," Elio said.

Cael turned to face him. He held his breath, urging him to say it again.
Please, call to me again. "Elio."

Elio, stone-faced and resigned, set his mouth. His chin dimpled. He
clucked his tongue, trying not to cry. "Did they suffer?"

The question surprised him. It took him a second to realize how long it'd
been since Elio finished speaking, and he understood that they were no
longer talking about Alice, the Xenobiology Division, Alexander, or Harlyn.
The silence between them thinned, volatile and delicate. When Elio said
they, he meant Darius and Lena.

"I don't know," Cael forced out. "I hope not."

"And my sister? Sindra told me she's well."

"Physically, Lorelei is fine. We made it through the crater together with
Nara, who didn't approve of me at first, as you can see," he mumbled,
gesturing to his milky eye. "Your sister is currently acting High Lady in
Atreyu. She's magnificent, and fearless, and I'm afraid she'll usher the
Aurethian militia into an unwinnable war if you don't take your place as
High Lord."

"Sindra also told me you're acting on behalf of our moon. That you've
been Lorelei's right hand. Apparently, you've kept my sister safe and
steadied her mind."

"I did what I could."

Elio swatted at the wetness on his face and sniffled, staring out at the
clearing where Alice slept. "There's more at stake than we realized." His
voice was soupy and loose, but clear. "Xander joined the Xenobiology Division and surpassed the average lifespan of any recorded Aurethian in existence. The journeymen from Genesis are living proof of Avarine's ability to
prolong life, slow cellular division, diminish typical planet-side ailments,
and withstand a changing environment. They're the longest living sapien
community in the Greater Universe, and the only archived evidence of
their existence is here in Outpost One. If we don't continue what

Alexander and Harlyn started, despite their botched execution, then we'll lose every inch of progress Xander and the journeymen have made thus far."

"So the Xenobiology Division was a front?" Cael asked, processing.

"Harlyn requested it. Alexander granted it. Once Alexander vetted each member of the initial Xenobiology Division, recruitment was passed along in good faith to the original journeymen. It was an insular, ongoing project only accessible from within. The journeymen recruited trustworthy talent, and that very same talent reported to Atreyu, relaying information about the interior of the crater — some true, some false," Elio said. He brought his thumbnail to his mouth, nibbling. "I had an inkling Peadar was Outpost One's connection to the manor. Xander confirmed as much. Overall, establishing the division was a risky play, but it paid off."

"And you think Alexander and Harlyn knew about…" He craned his neck to peek into the canyon, glancing at the offworlder. "That."

"After Alexander discovered Avara, he followed a cave-network to the center of the crater, searching for the mother mine, and discovered Outpost One. If the Imperium had found out about Alice, the moon would've entered galactic quarantine, meaning his access to newfound wealth would've come to a speedy halt. I'm guessing he shared the information with his mistress."

"Who refused his proposal in order to preserve the dignity of her house." Cael sighed.

"Then blackmailed Alexander into a unification agreement, guaranteeing Griea a slice of whatever profit Aurethia managed to glean from Alice's productivity."

"Scaling the timeline to fit an adequate research initiative while shielding Alice's existence with the Xenobiology Division."

Elio nodded. His mouth twitched into a sad smile. "Our families left us with a fucking mess."

Cael weighed the statement before nodding. "They did."

"If we don't remain unified, Aurethia will fall."

"And Griea will follow," Cael said.

A bronze-tailed eagle swooped overhead, diving for a woodland rat.

Elio slid his gaze to Cael, studying him through long, frond lashes. His voice lowered to a husked whisper. "If you move against me again, I will cut you down." His throat bobbed, caught on a hard swallow. "I'll bleed you, I'll burn you at sea, and I'll grieve you, Cael Volkov. I gave you my life, body, bloodline, house. I swore myself to you. Now I'm promising you this."

"I know," he said, so tightly each syllable barely surfaced. "We'll see this through. I swear it."

A stray tear curved down Elio's cheek. "Is Orson alive?"

The rock jammed against Cael's larynx turned over. A hot sting grew in his bad eye. He blinked, knuckling at his wet lashline. "I can't say," he choked out, shaking his head. "The man I knew would never harm a child, but I don't recognize my cousin anymore — I hardly recognize my own father. I'm sorry, Elio, but I don't know." He paused to swipe at his leaky nose, and turned his good eye on Elio, meeting his husband's kindled gaze. "None of this was supposed to happen."

"All of it was *supposed* to happen," Elio hissed. "You changed your mind in the final hour. You — "

"I fell in love with you, and because of you, I fell in love with Aurethia." Cael chewed his lip and looked away, staring into the canyon, watching Alice rumble and thrum. "I've turned against my family, I've killed my men, I've lost my title — I've lost you." He paused to laugh. It was a mean, horrible sound, halfway to a sob. "Punish me, Elio. Go ahead. You're all I had, so there's nothing left to take." He pawed roughly at his face. "You know exactly why this happened. You're cunning, you're smart, you're witty, and you know, just like I know, that Harlyn and Alexander aren't the only people at fault."

"My father's greed was not a war-call."

"Play somebody else for a fool, husband."

Elio's handsome face reddened. "I should've left that basilisk tooth in you."

Cael shifted his jaw. Something inside him splintered. "The only reason you bested me is because I allowed it. We both know that."

Next came the sharp, windy sound of an aggravated inhale. "And the only reason you're alive is because I allowed it."

"So this is what we'll become," Cael challenged. He draped his arms over his bent knees. With his face tipped toward the inlet where an alien slept, he plucked a mossy stone from the forest floor. "The exact formula our wretched houses created. Bitter enemies pitted against each other by a rivalry outside the scope of our own existence, inheriting a broken path to an unstable future on the back of soured romance." Tossed the rock, listened to it tumble. He shifted his gaze to Elio. *Do not give up on me, lion cub.* "I can't undo what's been done, but I'm here, Elio. That must count for something."

Elio's shaky mouth dropped open. Cael familiarized himself with the star-splashed hollow of his throat, and the dent beneath his collarbones. The anger tightening his face streamed away, as if swept out by a strong current. He rested the back of his head against the tree. His eyes slipped shut, and he rolled his mouth, pressing, releasing.

"At first, I thought the unification agreement was penned because my great-grandfather wanted to punish Harlyn, or because Harlyn wanted to punish him. But after talking to Xander, I realized the harm those two levied against each other doesn't matter to us now. Whatever the motive, the timeline bought Outpost One time to expand their research, like you said, and guaranteed a future redistribution of power and wealth for both Aurethia and Griea. I'm sure Alexander and Harlyn realized Alice wouldn't be an easy secret to keep once the union came to fruition, but they agreed to it, nonetheless, and doomed us with the adoption of Alien Lifeform Isolate Crater Extrinsic," he said, sounding out its lengthy, official title. "Harlyn was a coward, and Alexander was a deceiver, but our great-grandparents didn't start a war. Greed did." He gulped tightly, darting his tongue across his lip. "Power did. Savagery did. We did."

The truth vined through Cael's ribcage. He turned, setting his cheek on his kneecap. He remembered Vik's advice and searched for courage. "I will love you until the light leaves," he said. Wind rustled a loose branch. A speckled leaf swooped down, drifting left then right. "I can't unbreak your heart, I know that, but I'll never belong to another. I'll die sworn to you, Elio Henly, by your blade or another. You are my fate."

For the first time since Cael arrived at Outpost One, he saw Elio's iron-knit expression crack. His face buckled, clenching with an emotion Cael could not place. It lived in the aftermath of grief. A fresh wound pinned open, exposed for an audience like an autopsied insect.

"You don't get to say that to me," Elio rasped, so close to a whisper. It was the ghost of his voice, weak and froggy. He cried openly, honestly. Pain poured from him like a cut vein. He inhaled a brittle breath, gasping with it. "You don't get to play me for a fool again, you don't get to squander my sincerity, you don't get to keep lying to..." He trailed off, gaze flitting skyward. He turned his head, listening, and then tapped his dialect device.

It was a primal, unintelligent thing: the urge to crawl forward, cradle Elio's jaw, and hold him — reach through his skin and rethread every frayed edge, restitch every busted seam. But Cael knew better than to move. Every part of him, every fiber of his being, desperately wanted to. Even so, he stayed still.

After a long, terrible moment, Elio wiped his nose with the back of his hand, then scrubbed at his blotchy, waterlogged face. "I want to hate you," he hissed, and got to his feet, brushing dirt off his pants. "Let me hate you."

"I know," Cael murmured. He got up and stepped forward, taking his place at Elio's side, looking down at the source of Avara. Alice hummed again. A sound came from it, trilling like a lonely cetacean. Cael touched Elio's knuckles. "Hate me all you want, darling."

Elio curled his hand around Cael's palm for the briefest, brightest second. Then the High Lord let him go and turned back toward the outpost.

CHAPTER THIRTY-EIGHT

BRACKEN

Bracken perched on the lip of the lacquer desk in Darius's abandoned study. His heart hammered, beating in time with each passing thought. Adrenaline prickled on the backside of his skin. He reminded himself to breathe, replaying instances from House Volkov's recent holomeeting with the Imperium.

Only an hour ago, Bracken stood beside Marcus and listened to Angelina Darvin chastise Griea's unprompted act of tyranny. "According to our intelligence, and without concrete evidence, the Imperial Council must assume Cael Volkov and Elio Henly are alive and entitled to their rightful galactic stewardship over Aurethia, forest moon of Draitune. If what you claim is true, and treason has been committed, then the Duke of Griea and the Lord of Aurethia should stand trial in a court of their colleagues. Legatus Marcus is not judge and executioner, and Griea's law does not extend to Draitune's orbit."

Control is determinable. He reached for his father's voice, but it was Cael he heard. Rage whitened his vision. It coiled tight enough to break, and when it did, anger struck through bone and skin, and Bracken threw his fist against the rounded corner of the desk, splintering glossy paint and cherry-wood. Blood welled in a busted knuckle.

"It should go without saying, but High Lord Darius's and High Lady Lena's lack of correspondence with anyone here, nonetheless Aurethia's liaison in Dardellin, and Legatus Marcus's reluctance to grant the current stewards access to communication is indication of obstruction and foul play — worse, assassination — and should be met as such." Angelina Darvin knew her place in the Lux System. Draitune was an impressive, affluent planet, and her governance deemed her a formidable threat to Griea's conquest.

Throughout the holomeeting, Bracken hardly spoke. Legatus Marcus had remained level, but the promise of a full-scale, moon-side invasion was imminent regardless. Scarab Muir, leader of Hük in the Mal System, noted the sudden stall in Avara production. "What faith do you think you can buy with one operational mine, Legatus?" Meanwhile, an ambassador from Serenity said, "I'm keen to put my faith in House Volkov, but if this familial squabble does not end soon, I'll have to agree with Angelina. Draitune is in a position to send aid, and if the motive behind this invasion is as simple as the Legatus claims, then aid should be received gratefully."

"Aid is not necessary," Bracken had said, but quieted when Marcus placed a hand on his wrist.

Seemingly unbothered, Marcus said, "Per my Imperator, aid is one thing. Surveillance is another. Right now, Aurethia is in working order, and per the unification agreement, Griea has every right to remain moon-side. As I've stated before, and will state again, entering high orbit while we restructure our newly expanded house will be met with military defense. Attempting to dominate an unstable homeworld on the cusp of new stewardship is beneath the lot of you."

Bracken inhaled deeply, remembering the litany of audible offense. Angelina had leaned close to her holo, speaking frankly. "Do not risk your ice giant over a petty play for unearned power, Marcus."

"The only homeworld at risk is Aurethia," the Legatus had said, nodding thoughtfully. "A neighborly invasion — inspection, excuse me — could disrupt Avara's growth cycle, damage the farmland, toxify the sea, and corrode the atmosphere. My liaison will be in touch. But for now, considering the Imperium's distrust in Griean enterprise, the Planetary Syndicate is henceforth inactive. All withstanding contracts are frozen — " An uproar had sounded throughout the Imperium. The Great Houses bellowed, leadership balked, and ambassadors crowed. *You can't! This is an outrage. Legatus, wait...* " — and all organic and non-organic weaponry will cease their duties at once. I will reinstate the Planetary Syndicate in due time. Good day."

After that, Marcus had ended the holomeeting, and the ghastly blue faces hovering in the center of the study winked out, leaving Bracken to grapple with the gravity of the Legatus's sudden, unprompted order.

An hour later, he was still reeling.

Even after Marcus had knocked the back of his hand against Bracken's chest and said, "You're out of time, Bracken. We need to secure Atreyu, and you need to locate the girl. I don't care how you do it, but get it done."

Even after Bracken had said, "Yes, Legatus," and swayed on his feet, staring at the floor while Marcus left the study.

The discontinuation of the Planetary Syndicate would plunge the Greater Universe into chaos. Cities reliant on Griean protection would be left to fend off criminal activity without any military infrastructure. Sierra, Divinity, and Shepard — known for being semi-off-grid, unregulated waypoints, lacking planet-side order — would face both an exodus and an awakening. Scared people would flee. Worse people would set up shop.

For a moment, Bracken looked down at himself from above and did not recognize what he saw. He lifted his bloody hand and tweezed a sliver of wood from the soft webbing between his index and middle finger.

To deny the Greater Universe the specialty trade Griea built and perfected was to take a page out of Aurethia's book, to become what Bracken thought they were trying to defeat. He pushed away from the desk and left the study, striding down the hall, through the great room, and into the garden. On his way, he caught sight of Maxine trying to coax Orson to eat in the kitchen. The smallest Henly stood next to the counter under the light of a disc-lamp, staring at the shuttered window, concealing the court-yard from view.

As soon as he slipped outside, Bracken sucked in the thick scent of pine and soil. *It will be worth it in the end.* He repeated the mantra, clinging to it. *This will all be worth it in the end.*

The manor rose up like a haunting, and for the first time since Bracken was named Imperator, he felt trapped. This thing he took with his own two hands. This unrequited piece of his life he finally had the power to wield. This history-making, universe-changing conquest. Out there, facing the forest, and the garden boxes, and the lowered patio, in the shadow of a home-turned-graveyard, Bracken was nothing more than a beast on a chain.

"You're crying." Constance sat at the small table in the sunken space below the bricked terrace flanking the mansion. She brought a teacup to her mouth. Her Ocurian tunic was finely embroidered and wrapped intri-cately around her torso, tied and bundled above grey trousers. "What's wrong, nephew? Did the Imperium call for restraint?"

Bracken reached for his face. Low and behold, his cheek was damp. "I'm surprised you weren't there."

Constance maintained a serene expression. She gave no indication as to what she might be feeling, thinking, enduring. "Sit with me."

He inclined his head and joined her at the table. "Duchess," he greeted.

"Imperator," she chimed, almost teasing. She shook out a napkin and handed it to him. "What troubles you?"

"The Legatus is pulling all active syndicate contracts."

The Duchess made a blunt noise in the pit of her throat. "Scare tactic."

"One that could have devastating repercussions." Bracken wrapped his bloody knuckle.

"Interesting to hear you talk about repercussions. You slaughtered Lena in cold blood, you're hunting my son like an animal, you intend to wed an unwilling bride. How do you see this scheme playing out, Bracken?"

A few significant words jumped out. Cold, animal, unwilling, scheme. He shifted his jaw. "Cael is a traitor to this house — "

"You will address me with respect," she ordered. She reached across the table and dabbed at a stray tear. "He's still my son."

Bracken swallowed. Her hand on his face made him flinch. Leftover anger smoldered in his gut. "Apologies, Duchess." He paused to gather himself. "I can't find another path forward. The Legatus is sure of this plan, and I'm the only Volkov left who can see it through. Lena was a mistake; I'll carry that. But if we don't get this moon under control, we'll lose everything."

"I've already lost everything," she said. Her cup made a thin sound, clattering empty on the saucer. "There is no doubt in my mind that you're Praetor Savin's son. See, he never knew when to stop. Confidence should be left to simmer, not set to boil, but that day on the ice, when he thought the fight was over, I saw it. He was desperately sure." She clucked her tongue and sighed through her nose. "He got too vicious too soon and left himself unguarded. My husband is a lot like his brother, and you…" She shifted in her seat, fidgeting with the hand-hammered band circling the base of her knuckle. "You're identical to him. You walk like him, you fight like him. On Ocury, we believe lives are set to repeat, and I'm afraid your destiny is a testament to his failure."

Bracken's throat sealed shut. He wanted to walk away. Wanted to take Constance by the neck and squeeze. His mouth screwed into a snarl.

The courtesy between them dropped, and Constance's tone lowered to a shredded whisper. "You massacred a village. You ordered the murder of *children* — "

"I did what I had to," he bit.

"House Volkov is a bloodstain."

He snorted. "Then House Henly is a plague."

"You move as though the world ends when you do." She leaned closer. Her mouth trembled. "This siege is a death sentence, and we will not survive it. Marcus, you, me — we're on borrowed time, Bracken."

"I am not my father — "

"This strategic grab for relevance has guaranteed us nothing. And now here we are. Facing down the Imperium, hunting our own people, withholding defense throughout the system, slaughtering the innocent — "

"No one is innocent." He stood abruptly, planting his palms on the tabletop. He bent to meet her gaze. "I follow our Legatus. You should, too, Duchess."

"Why would those with sight follow the blind?" She spoke Ocurian, her accent a pretty percussion. When he turned to leave, she called after him. "You feel it, Bracken. I know you do."

"He'll kill you, Constance," he said over his shoulder.

"Of course," she hollered. "Then he'll find a new little pet to sire an heir with. Someone young and pretty to give him another chance."

Bracken's knees locked. He stopped for a moment, searching the stone beneath his bootwear. Panic molted into something worse, something too honest and too predictable to choke down. It squatted in him, that awful truth, until hot, familiar anger burned through it.

"Did you really think it would be you, nephew? Oh no, dear. Marcus would never allow it. And besides, Savin promised you a life on the ice. I'm sure they'll chant it in the arena if we make it back home. *Imperator Bracken, Blood Bringer. Imperator Bracken, King Maker. Imperator Bracken, Lion Slayer.*" She lifted her hand, waving it carelessly. "But you'll always be *incumbent*, reserving a position until it's rightfully filled."

Fury exploded. He felt it in his skull, radiating in his chest, deep and molten in his stomach. "They'll call me Legatus," he bit, staring at the hard-faced woman over the slope of his shoulder.

Constance lifted her chin. She scanned him, toes to nose, and gave a stiff nod. "We'll see."

KINDRA TIGHTENED HIS BELT. She grasped the buckle in a thin hand

and centered it, standing before him in a gauzy dress the color of spilled chardonnay. The cream-yellow fabric draped around her, clinging to the peak of each breast, drooping low along the scoop of her tailbone.

"You're off today," she mumbled.

He tilted his head, staring down at her. "And?"

After being confronted by Constance in the garden, Bracken took to the training chamber, then to his bedroom, curling against Kindra like a child. Her comfort never broke, only bent to fit whatever invisible hurt he brought. Sometimes he hated who he became with her — belligerent, naïve. Sometimes, after he sobbed against her chest, and clung to her like a babe, Bracken buried his anguish inside her with such a frenzied wrath it left her battered. The bruise above her elbow, darkening to a ripe plum on her rich skin, held his attention.

"What you're carrying is heavy." She laid her palm beneath his shirt, over his navel. "But I also have a voice, Bracken. You pay for my body. My counsel is free."

He smoothed his bent finger along her damaged arm. "I got carried away — "

"I started it," she said, smiling ruefully. And she had. Her bare foot on his crotch. Her hand around his jaw, forcing his gaze. *My Imperator, heir to the throne, god among men. Let them fear you.* "Like I said, I have a voice. I could've used it if I wanted to stop. No need to treat me like a flower."

"You are my flower," he all but whimpered, running his hand to her nape.

"Oh, spare me," she gentled. Her laughter rose up from a deep well, and he'd come to love the sound of it. "Kasimir is waiting. I can cancel the visit if you have more pressing matters."

"Is the boy with Maxine?"

"Yes, she'll have him in attendance." She cleared her throat and withdrew her hand, patting his barrel chest. "Thank you for giving my brother a position of authority on Aurethia. It's not my place to talk about this, I know, but your encouragement will help him become a better man."

"Kasimir is spirited." And deadly, and unpredictable. Bracken had plucked him from the syndicate and placed him in the Royal Reserve. He was the simplest choice when it came to seeing through something as extreme as extermination, and now he stood as Bracken's second. "Am I making the right call, Kindra? Don't tell me what I pay you to tell me — tell me the truth. You're..." *My only friend.* "I value you."

"What decision is there to make, Imperator? You've followed your

Legatus, prioritized your planet, brought Aurethia to heel, and put us on a path to stability. Not only that, but the orchard is beginning to bloom, Avara is being mined, and the Royal Reserve is in good shape. Are you talking about the girl, maybe? Or Cael?"

"Pulling the Planetary Syndicate will do more harm than good. Strong statement, stronger consequence. Marcus is making a mistake."

"You're his Imperator, and more importantly, you're his nephew. Tell him how you feel." She placed her palm at the hinge of his jaw. "Constance lashed out because she's mourning the loss of a son who is still alive. If her opinion mattered, Marcus would be utilizing her during this process, wouldn't he? There's a reason she's not involved."

You'll always be incumbent. Bracken's wrist twitched. "Will he replace me?"

The post-coital warmth retreated, and the full pout of her bottom lip dropped, making room for a breathy sigh. "*You* will replace *him*," she assured, slipping her thumbnail along his nose. "If you need to call him to the ice to do it, you will."

Bracken nodded as if what she said made sense, as if he could stomach summoning his uncle during the Tupinaire and challenging him for his title. But a tiny, toothy part of him, growing like a tumor in the pit of his pride, said *I would*.

"C'mon." Kindra raked her hand through his hair, scraping her oval-shaped fingernails across his scalp. "Show me to this mystical mine."

They left the bedchamber after Bracken knelt to clasp the strappy buckles on Kindra's heeled sandals, wrapping them carefully around each dainty ankle. In the garden, Kasimir waited with Maxine. Lord Orson stood at the liaison's side, holding her hand.

"Why aren't we leaving through the courtyard?" Orson asked, darting a nervous glance between the growing group.

Maxine flared her nostrils. Her tight mouth pressed into a pained smile. When she opened her mouth to speak, nothing followed.

"Because Bracken wanted to show me the garden," Kindra said, sweet as a chewed date. She grinned with all her teeth and set her hands on her hips, jutting her chin toward the road. "And I've heard a rumor about a secret pathway back here. One right along the crater, all the way to a hot spring. I bet that isn't true, though."

"It is," he blurted, furrowing his brow. Orson extended his arm, pointing at the treeline. "It's that way."

Kindra mock gasped. "Don't play with me, Lord Orson."

Orson tugged Maxine toward the hidden road nestled along the forest's edge. He reached for Kindra with his free hand, grasping her wrist, tugging her along. "I'll show you — Maxine, tell her it's true."

Maxine managed a flat laugh. "It *is* true. Go on, show us the way."

While Orson guided the two women toward the back road to Nadhas, Bracken fell into step beside Kasimir. Kindra's brother shared her pretty, petite features, and he managed the same shucked-off aristocracy. His brown skin shone like polished walnut, handsome under Draitune's bright ring and Sunder's afternoon light. Thin black braids clung close to his scalp, and he was dressed in Griean-black, carrying a Grabak carved from the spine of a basilisk.

"Imperator," Kasimir said, tipping his head.

Bracken swatted Kasimir's scapula. "Thank you for the work you did in Nadhas."

"Needed to be done, sir."

"Has Holland made any progress with the fisherman?"

"Some returned to sea yesterday." He paused to nod, then continued. "Atreyu dodged our communication block this morning. We shut them out before a transmission could be delivered but it's only a matter of time, sir."

"Heard. And the energy in the village? How is it?"

"Somber," he said, shrugging. "Eleven community members died for their lack of discipline. Right now, they see us as the enemy. In time, they'll see us as authority."

"Rebellion is seeded in authority, Kasimir."

"I'm aware, sir." His mouth curved. He slid his gaze to Bracken. He shared much with his younger sister, but the light color of his upturned, wolfish eyes hinted at their distant Griean ancestry. "I spent my childhood fending for myself on Draitune before enlisting at the War College. I'm familiar with unrest."

"And?"

Kasimir lifted a thick brow. "And when we roll out the Griean immigration policy, what happened here won't matter. It'll be another battle, another exercise in dominance, another way to clear a path forward for Griea. The Aurethians who remain in Nadhas will merge with our people or they'll be culled from the population entirely. It's simple. Effective."

There is no going back. Bracken swallowed. He glanced at the grass. For a split second, his bootwear glistened with fresh blood, there and gone in a blink, and his freshly bandaged hand dripped crimson. He felt it again, that annoying tic, and stuffed his hand in his pocket. The hallucination ended. *I will never be who I once was.*

"Strategically sound," Bracken said. Sweat beaded on his brow. He turned his face toward the sun, welcoming light that rarely reached his homeworld. "They'll hate us for it, though."

Kasimir shrugged. "Don't they already hate us?"

Bracken heard Cael's laughter rustle through the meadow. He heard his mother, gasping, eaten away by parsec sickness, and the arena applauding as his father fell dead on the ice. "Yeah," he said, watching an orange-breasted bird cut across the clear sky, "they do."

CHAPTER THIRTY-NINE

ELIO

Lord Henly, I've been monitoring Cael's heartrate, and I haven't detected dishonesty. I understand your predisposition for caution, but he is not lying.

Elio didn't know what to do with Vik's assessment. He didn't know what to do with the brush of Cael's hand on his palm or how to look away when sunlight glanced through the canopy and dappled his scarred face. He wanted to be alone with Cael, and he wanted to throw the man clear off a cliff. He wanted to crawl into his lap, and he wanted to swat him, chew at him, make him yelp and hiss. He wanted to lay down and die. He wanted to take back his homeworld, and fight, and do nothing at all.

If he could've, Elio would've slipped into the chamber Sindra loaned to him, locked the door behind him, and slept for the next cycle. But Lorelei was alive. Orson might be alive. Cael was still alive. And that meant Elio had to stay alive, too. If not to become High Lord, if not to end this needless violence, if not to protect the star-slung being submerged in the crater — then for his younger siblings, and for the vow he took, not just to Cael, but to Aurethia, Griea, and their people. He felt like he'd reached for a rose and grasped it without thinking. Now thorns wedged in his hand, too deep to pluck out. He felt like he'd been living in a dream, chasing unfathomable happiness, and woke to a nightmare after reaching it.

Cael walked one step behind. "How old are the people here?"

"Some are old enough to remember Aurethia before it had a name," Elio said.

"But how is that possible? If these people are the original journeymen from Draitune, someone would've reported their deaths — falsified or not. Aurethian lifespans are longer than most, but they still would've died before..." He trailed off, thinking.

"Aurethia is a young homeworld. Draitune sponsored the original Genesis mission just after my great-grandfather's sire passed away. That man, Damir Henly, was brought moon-side during the second mission to Aurethia and named the steward of the moon. He's the first branch on our Aurethian family tree. Before that, our bloodline leads back to Draitune."

"Alexander was the first Henly to live a full life on Aurethia?"

Elio nodded. "He was the first one of us born here, and everyone thought he was the first person to discover Avara — I thought he was, too. But the journeyman at Outpost One had already spent an entire lifetime trying to determine what Alice was, how she got here, and what Avarine could do.

"Damir's mission involved getting Atreyu built and stable. He didn't spend much time surveying the crater or the sea, and I mean, I can't blame him. Why bother with a forest when you're constructing a livable city on a freshly colonized moon? After he died, Alexander inherited Damir's stewardship." Elio paused to clear his throat. "According to Xander, my great-grandfather found the first vein on the outer rim of Atreyu and followed it inward to the crater. Curiosity got the best of him. As Harlyn did, I guess."

"That's how he found Alice," Cael said.

"Stumbled on her, yeah. Rumor has it, Harlyn was with him, but there's no evidence. Just hearsay."

"And Xander is for sure — "

Vik interrupted, "I've checked my data twice. Xander Henly is Harlyn Volkov's son, Marcus's uncle, and your great uncle. There is indisputable blood relation."

Cael made a chuffed noise. He sped up and fell into step at Elio's side, matching his pace. "What's your plan, Elio?"

Plan? He almost laughed. "There's a Griean warship in low orbit, my parents are dead," the last word choked him, but he spat it out, "Lorelei is leading the militia in Atreyu, Xander Henly is presiding over the Xenobiology Division — our unofficial access point to Avara — and the mother mine is actually an extraterrestrial. Forgive me if I don't have anything set in stone, Cael, but my plan is to get my sister to safety, take back my house, and conceal Alice from the Imperium until we have an iron-clad grip on this moon."

Cael bowed his head, nodding slowly. "We?"

Guilt and pride burned Elio's throat. He sighed like a mule. "Don't test me," he mumbled, sliding his gaze to the side. "Alice won't stay a secret for much longer, but we can't allow the Imperium to intervene while we're weak. They'll force themselves on us. You and I both know that. I need you to get Griea in order. We'll be too strong to challenge once we're united."

"If Bracken starts scouting the crater — "

"Will he?"

"I don't know. If my father orders it, yes. Otherwise, he'll focus on Atreyu."

"Do you think they'll storm the city?"

"Yes," Cael said without faltering.

Vik walked behind the pair. "It's within my projected analysis."

The thought of Griean soldiers rushing into Atreyu froze over in his chest. He sidestepped a mushroom-clad rock and turned toward a deer trail leading into the chasm where Alice dozed. His boot slipped. He gasped, but a hand caught his elbow, holding him steady.

"Careful," Cael exhaled, tightening his grip.

Elio held his breath. He looked from the pale knuckles notched around his arm to Cael's face. Even with the new pinkened skin melding what'd once been flayed, he was still unfairly dignified. Unjustly handsome. Elio eased away, dislodging Cael's hold. "I'm alright."

They navigated the path slowly, descending through a layer of muggy fog to the level ground at the base of the crater. The dug-out where Alice crashed showed no sign of intrusion. Bouncy ferns and dense foliage bushed around the base of trees. Sticky pollen gooped inside flower bulbs. Dew dripped, mingling with sap and fungus.

Alice's watery blue body was so much larger up close. The texture of it, as if stamped by seed paper or embossed with scales, rippled as it breathed. It was mountainous and strangely... innocent. Alice probably didn't notice him at all, the same way a whale shark wouldn't notice him during a swim. The alien was far too big and lost to care about any of the tiny creatures poking around her belly.

Cael, being the exact kind of man Elio knew him to be, reached past a frilly branch and placed his palm on Alice's smooth side. A smile cracked his face. "Doesn't seem to mind us."

"Because it's used to us," Xander interjected. He came around a tree, dressed in savannah clothing and carrying a well-worn canvas bag. "We've been an annoyance for long enough to seem familiar, I think."

Up ahead, one of Alice's tendrils snaked through the dirt. It was perfectly cylindrical and carried a captured glow, like the light from a firefly. The appendages fanned out beneath the titan's bulbous undercarriage, burrowing into Aurethia to keep Alice grounded. They pulsed like individual lighthouses, blue, blue, blue.

Xander waved them forward. "From what we can tell, the cave system underneath Alice was excavated after she landed here. That underground network, the one Alice built, is the inception of Avarine, the very first documented deposit on Aurethia. Unlike Avara, it doesn't need a mother crystal to thrive. It's like a fungus, sporing and spreading. Except," he added quickly, circling his hand in the air, "the greater the distance between the mineral and Alice, the weaker it becomes. Once Avarine can no longer sustain itself without latching to another crystal, we call it Avara."

Elio followed Xander, digesting the upload of information for the second time.

Cael cooed as he stepped over one of Alice's thick appendages. Vik's data-port whirred and clicked. The Augment's left pupil grew and then whitened. He mumbled something about collecting a sample and paused to tap a vine growing underneath Alice's body.

"When Alexander found Outpost One, Melody explained the situation. They're the one who convinced him to launch the mining operation in the first place," Xander said.

"Melody?" Cael inquired.

"Yeah, they're the doctor who fixed you up after loverboy carved you like a goosefish."

Shame pebbled Elio's nape. He rolled his eyes and ducked underneath a branch, dipping around Xander to walk toward the entrance of an inlet tucked beneath Alice's undercarriage. The glow from her body blued the packed dirt. The rockway sloped to a small mouth and opened to a wide, cavernous mine.

Xander explained Avarine to Cael, rehashing what he'd already told Elio, and gestured to the fibrous material scaling the interior of the stone. Avarine, so blue it made Avara look dull, glittered and frothed along the ceiling, showing slight fissures of Alice's body. Huge, intimidating tentacles vined through the rock, feeding pulsing light into Avarine deposits.

"Have we ruled out the possibility for parthenogenesis?" Vik asked.

Xander shook his head. "No, that's still a possibility. We're not sure if

Avarine is Alice's attempt at reproduction or if the mineral itself is a byproduct of her general existence."

"What *do* you know?" Cael asked.

"We know Alice is a living creature with a structure similar to jellyfish. We know she's consuming an insignificant number of calories given her size. She's gentle, curious, ancient, probably from a species known for schooling or pod behavior given how vocal she is. She's never shown aggression or fear, but she does get uncomfortable. That rumbling is from her shifting, recentering herself in the crater, or turning onto her side. No detectable blood supply, but she has a pulse. We think it's a nervous system response or a base regularity. Like a cricket chirping or a cat purring."

"And I'm guessing you've tried to clone this?" Cael brought his hand to a patch of Avarine. The mineral came away like dust. Just beneath the crystalline surface, the rock turned to sap, slicking the stone like the interior of an aloe leaf.

"That's the goal. Avarine is delicate. Like Avara, it's hard to harvest, and comes directly from Alice. So far, every trial ends with Avarine corroding after cloning. We're close, though. This last batch stayed stable for a week."

Vik hummed thoughtfully. He stood on his tiptoes and eyed a shard of Avarine. Blue water trickled down the stone, splattering by his feet. "Aurethia is a replica of Draitune, isn't it?"

"Yes, but we've already thought about that. Draitune's atmosphere and soil is drastically different than Aurethia's. Centuries of cityscaping and metropolitan advances made it something new," Xander said.

"Mercy is also a replica of Draitune," Vik said.

"The desert moon? It dislodged from the same comet that struck Draitune, yes. That's what most astronomers assume, at least."

Elio blinked. He thought back to every holodocument he'd read, every text he'd transcribed, every piece of the Henly archive dedicated to Draitune history. "What if it wasn't a comet," he murmured, then cleared his throat and said it again, suddenly invigorated, "what if it wasn't a comet that hit Draitune? What if it was Alice?"

Xander blinked back at him. Cael turned his head quizzically.

We're on the same page, Lord Henly, Vik said through his dialect device. The Augment offered him a nod of encouragement.

"If Aurethia and Mercy contain the same planetary makeup given they were thrown into orbit by the same collision, why couldn't we create an entire habitat for Alice on Mercy, or... or at least terraform an environment where Avara might thrive? Obviously, we haven't figured out how to communicate with her yet, but we might be able to emulate a collective growth chamber that could sustain Avara," Elio said, rambling. "If we could manage to terraform Mercy, which is already widely uninhabited, we could potentially streamline Avara production and protect Alice from Imperial dissection. Aurethia could focus on farming initiatives and serve as a backup supply if Mercy's Avara growth lapses."

Cael's mouth ticked. "It's a brilliant idea, Elio, but terraforming Mercy would take half a century. Even with our combined resources — "

"But our children would finish what we start," Elio blurted. Something sharp and sore went soft inside him.

Black expanded, eating the snow in Cael's eyes. The ethereal glow inside the cavern glinted across his glacial, glassy gaze, and his chin flexed, mouth quivering. His long throat bobbed on a slow, visible swallow, and he tried to nod, choppily dropping his head. The emotion there, whatever it may be, was a moth inside Elio's chest, racing toward inextinguishable light.

Xander looked at the wet floor of the cave. "The journeymen considered Mercy a long time ago, but it didn't seem feasible without a stronger stewardship."

"I'm steward of the largest farming operation in the Lux System and the homeworld of Avara, and Cael is heir to the Greater Universe's only operational military planet. The Imperium would have nothing to gain if they didn't support our decision," Elio said.

"Could you convince House Darvin to strategize with Aurethia and Griea? The desert moon is considered uninhabited, but the Avara processing plant is operational, and we can't ignore the small population of immigrants who live and work there. Draitune's support will help in the long run." Vik said.

Elio nodded. "Angelina is an ally. I could reason with her."

"We still don't know if it'll work," Xander said. He gave Elio a sad, squirming look.

"No, but it's either terraform Mercy or build a terrarium in Aurethia's orbit. Right now, we have a blank canvas to work with, and using a stationary moon will cut the cost," Cael said.

Xander sucked his teeth. "I'll talk to the journeyman. For now, you should worry about avoiding a war that might kill her," he said, exhaling hard, and pointed at the top of the cave where Alice rumbled and glowed. "Without Alice, we have nothing. No Avarine, no Avara. To be honest, I don't know what would happen to the moon if she died. Avara is in everything — imagine if all of it, all at once, corroded."

Vik's data-port beeped. "According to my field research, if the harvestable Avara on Aurethia were to corrode, most farmland, ground water, sea water, and treelife would sustain immeasurable damage. The toxicity of the dead mineral would likely infect the resources available on the forest moon and impact the overall health of the ecosystem. If Alice and Avara were not promptly removed, Aurethia would become inhospitable to wildlife."

Elio swallowed. "If Alice dies, Aurethia dies."

"No," the Augment said, dragging the word out. "But Aurethia will never be the same, and the citizenship here would probably have to seek asylum on a nearby homeworld while the moon healed."

"We need to get in contact with Draitune." Cael straightened, tipping his head back to stare at segments of Alice's underbelly. One of the alien's limbs dug blindly at a loose patch of dirt, burrowing like an earthworm.

"And get to my sister," Elio said.

When Xander placed his hands on his hips and nodded, Elio saw his father, and his grandfather, and himself. He recognized the shadow on his wrinkled brow, and the nibble of cheek between molars, and the way he held his body like it weighed twice as heavy.

The eldest Henly, abandoned Volkov, glanced up at Alice. "You're a bit of a headache, you know that?"

As if the alien heard him, Alice rumbled, bellowing like a playful porpoise.

WHEN NIGHTFALL CAME, BLACK and mauve lined the sky over Outpost One. Elio leaned against the countertop inside the washroom attached to his chamber. He studied the angular set of his face and reached out to touch the glass, pressing his thumb to the sharp edge of his chin on the mirror's surface. *I look older.* The thought jostled him. He flattened his palm fully. *Who am I?* It kicked through him like a hoof. *Who will I become?* Soil crusted underneath his fingernails and grime from the cave caked his skin. He withdrew his hand and raked it through his dirty hair, standing back to stare at himself.

It was too heavy to carry, the burden of this impossible, unforgiving fate. Cruel, even, for the universe to expect him to shoulder it. He wanted to give up, but he couldn't. Wanted to disappear into the forest, or board a transport for a distant, unknown system, or put a pulse-gun in his mouth. *I am not a coward*. He exhaled harshly, righting himself against the fear whetting his nervous system.

Long ago, before he was even a speck in his mother's womb, destiny decided. Somewhere in the future, carried on the back of a lonesome star, Elio Henly's legacy lived on, and nearer, closer to the timeline he occupied, people he loved depended on him to be strong, mighty, savvy, ready.

"Vik," he said, tapping his dialect device.

Yes, Lord Henly.

"Send Cael to my room."

The Augment remained quiet for a beat. Now?

"Now," Elio confirmed. He set his dialect device on the counter.

The image of Mercy — white orb ballooned against Draitune's centermost ring — hung low in his mind. The desert moon could be their safe harbor. It could become the perfect stabilizer for the Greater Universe. He mentally flipped through every previously transcribed archive, remembering the fuzzy outline of half-forgotten details. Mercy was an extreme place spinning around Draitune like an ant under an eyeglass, inviting a stream of Sunder's blistering heat. The native plantlife were sparse and stalky, thorn-striped and pregnant with stored water. Dew rarely slicked the atmosphere, and rainstorms were few and far between, but when water did arrive, the salt flats grew thick and tepid with soupy mud, tough critters crawled out from burrows, and the small citizenship who lived there celebrated. A large Avara processing facility dominated the northernmost basin, and the small but lively city surrounding it was home to a few thousand people.

Elio dwelled on the desert moon until his chamber door opened and shut. He knew Cael's footsteps. The way he toed off his bootwear, pressing one shoe against heel, pulling, shifting, then stepping out of the other. His voice was softer than a hummingbird.

"Elio?"

He pushed away from the countertop and reached into the clinically white shower, turning the dial until hot water rushed through a grated ceiling tile, mimicking rainfall. "The journeymen conserve water in the crater," he lied, clearing the apprehension from his voice. There was absolutely no reason to conserve water in a rainforest. "It's been a long day. Come get clean."

Cael stepped into the doorway. His brow pinched, and he searched Elio, feeling for a trap.

When Elio pulled his tunic up and away, dropping it to the floor, Cael's guarded expression fell with it. He watched Elio undress before shifting his gaze to the ceiling, tongue darting over his bottom lip.

"I'm your husband," Elio breathed out. He took Cael by the belt buckle, yanking it loose.

Cael jostled with the act. His skin tinted, blushing like an orchard apple. "I thought you hated me."

"I do."

Once his belt was free, Cael did away with his clothes. White bandages encircled his waist, concealing the place Elio's Grabak had penetrated.

Elio's heart seized like a crushed moth. His palm hovered over the bandage, twitching. He opened his mouth, but no sound surfaced. He stood there, naked and unmoored, reaching for a thing he most regretted.

Cael took his hand. "It's alright — "

"Please," Elio whispered, close to breaking, "let me tend to you." He brought his free hand to the medical cloth and carefully unwound it.

A mean, reddish seam lined Cael's pale skin, marking the tender place below his last rib. The Avarine left a scaled scar, glinting metallic. Like a creature from the deep sea or a comet's tail. Elio put his hand to it. Cael flinched then went still. On a slow, intentional breath, he bowed into Elio's touch.

I did this. A wounded sound came up and out of Elio. It was shaped like a cough, similar to a sob. That little cry, so exceptionally unlike him, seemed to unseat whatever remained of his resolve.

Cael stepped closer. One strong hand landed on Elio's waist, guiding him into the shower. There, under the warm spray, Elio felt along the silvered scar Cael now wore on his abdomen. He wanted to go to his knees and put his mouth to it. Rewind the last dawn, dusk, dawn and undo what he'd done.

But instead, Elio said, "Don't leave me again, Cael." His voice lacked venom. Animosity seeped out of him, draining. It wouldn't last, this breath of forgiveness, but Elio knew better than to allow grief and anguish to alter the course of his heart. "Ever."

"I didn't... I..." Cael said, speaking as though Elio had stabbed him again. He trailed off and sighed. Breath puffed against Elio's nose. "I won't."

Elio's anger would probably revive itself later. Or perhaps it would die with him in the throes of war. But right then, he reached for Cael's face, thumbing at the spindly scar branching through his eye, milked over the same way a snake did before it shed. Elio's voice softened to a whimper. "Can you see?"

Cael cupped Elio's knuckles and shook his head. "Good thing I've got two."

"And Nara did this? She attacked you, she — "

"I was wearing Griean armor. Can't blame her."

The water ran hot. Almost too hot. Cael's skin blotched with it, spreading red around the black ink on his hip and spine. Elio reached for the knob, twisting until it cooled. He did not know what to do with himself. A part of him wanted to shout and swat, to keep hold of his wrath and let it guide him, but Cael was not a choice he could undo in a single day. Love wasn't something he could forfeit, and his marriage — their union — was the only stability he had left. Their commitment, however damaged, had to withstand the past and endure whatever came next.

Cael washed Elio with cinnamon soap. He cleaned Elio's hair and pressed his mouth to a bruise left behind from their impromptu combat match. They were slow with each other, trembling and quiet. Elio relearned Cael's damaged face. Brought a sudsy cloth to the soil darkening his finger-nails and the delicate skin behind each ear. The water rinsed away dirt and sweat. At their feet, brownish liquid circled the drain, and once it ran clear, Elio reached, and Cael came to him, and they held each other for a long, long time. Elio twined his arms over Cael's shoulders, clutching the top of his head, gripping his nape, and Cael wrapped around him, almost crushing him, wide hands splayed over Elio's tailbone, between his shoulders, sealing their bodies together.

With his straight nose crammed against Elio's throat, Cael said, "You're mine," gently, sweetly, differently than he'd ever said it before.

Elio could almost feel Cael's silver scar branding his stomach. "You're mine," he replied just as weakly.

When Cael drew back, he set their foreheads together, staring at Elio through dark, watery lashes. Elio waited to be kissed, wanted to be kissed, but instead, Cael said, "Mercy," like an old Earthen prayer, like an answer.

Elio nodded, inhaling Cael's tired breath. "Mercy."

CHAPTER FORTY
CAEL

E ven at night moisture thickened the air in the crater.
Cael slept with his chest pressed to Elio's back for an hour or two, but when Elio turned and took his hand, facing him with their fingers twined, Cael cracked his good eye open and watched the prince breathe.

The white cotton sheet pooled over Elio's waist. Cael slept on top of it, welcoming the cool spin of recycled air from a disc-fan blowing steadily in the far corner. Elio didn't wake. His pink mouth was delicately parted, and a piece of blonde hair fanned his forehead. Shadow brushed his collarbone like an ink stroke. His chest expanded and deflated, stardusted with freckles Cael wanted to map. He felt across the hard ridge of one knuckle with his index.

After their shared shower, Cael had followed Elio to bed and held him until they both fell asleep. It didn't take long — stress, relief, and exhaustion throttled them both. Lying beside him now felt as inarguably right as it ever had. A nightmare knit the skin above the bridge of Elio's nose. Cael smoothed the line away. The Henly heir rested again, snuffling into the pillow, and Cael smiled. *We're okay*. His eyelids curtained, slipping shut, and he allowed himself to wade back toward dreamless, peaceful sleep.

On the cusp of that deep fall, footsteps beat the road outside. Cael jolted. His body remembered the last time he shared a bed with Elio. Waking before dawn. Betrayal. The violent siege at the Henly manor. His heart galloped. He strained to listen and caught a hurried whisper carried on damp wind. Distant shouting careened through Outpost One. Running, walking. Boots on linoleum.

Cael sat straight up. He placed his arm over Elio's waist as if to shield him.

Beneath him, Elio stirred. He didn't speak, but he touched Cael's back, signaling awareness.

The chamber door opened. Elio tensed. Cael held his breath.

Vik walked inside dressed in combat gear and a tactical vest. "Duke Henly, Lord Volkov," he greeted, surveying their nudeness through the dark with a curt nod. "Sorry for the disturbance. Rest is hard to come by, but I'm afraid you're needed at the communication tower."

Elation coasted out of Cael. The breath itself left him winded. He shut his eyes. His body unclenched. "Vik, what the *fuck* — "

"What happened?" Elio blurted. He slid out from underneath Cael and perched on the side of the bed, taking the sheet with him.

"Atreyu broke through the Griean signal block," Vik said. His blue eyes, usually curious and kind, grew stern. "Lorelei delivered a transmission. We must assume the entire Greater Universe heard, including the forces stationed at Henly manor."

Cael stared through Vik, thinking back to Lorelei's ire, how war splintered out of her like invasive cacti. The severity of her message would ripple through Lux, Mal, and Ren. It would reach the furthest point of the Greater Universe within a day. He sucked in a sharp breath and got out of bed.

"Shouldn't we be relieved?" Elio asked, tugging his trousers into place.

Vik tipped his head. His jaw dented. "Lady Lorelei's strategy is more Griean than Aurethian."

Dressed and equipped with his weaponry, Cael reached for Elio, ushering him into the hall with a hand on his lower back. "She's a frightening young woman. I fear for our future if she's left in charge."

"Does she know about our parents? Does she know — "

"Yes," Cael said. He didn't want to hear Elio say it. "She didn't take it well."

"None of us should take it well," he snapped, shooting Cael a boiling glance.

He licked his lip and said, "She retaliated by having a box of dismembered Griean soldiers returned to the manor's doorstep."

Elio blinked, taken aback. He gave an indignant snort.

Midnight air washed over them. The pair turned toward the communication tower. They dodged a low hanging branch on a dewy fir and stepped
over an aurous patch of foxglove. Outpost One buzzed. People hurried
toward the modular frequency pulse-beacon — built above the communication tower — chattering about a galactic transmission sent from the neighboring city. Some of the journeymen and xenobiologists wrapped
themselves in scarves or blankets, others zipped jackets and buckled shoes.
Below the pulse-beacon, spearing the canopy like a dark, shadowy sentinel,
the communication tower glowed from the inside. Silhouettes crossed the
windows, backlit by muted yellow disc-lamps.

Vik sidestepped Cael and Elio and walked ahead, gesturing to a steel
ladder that led to the platform. "Up you go," the Augment said.

Elio climbed first, followed by Cael. Vik grasped the ladder last.

The closer they got, the louder the situation became. People grunted and
sighed, stomped and whispered.

Elio hoisted onto the platform. "What's going on?"

Cael's heel clipped the wood-paneled floor. He righted himself, offering
a hand to Vik who promptly waved him off. He scanned the tower, glancing
at an oversized holotablet and the antique communication display beneath
it. A data-scanner spanned the leftmost wall, and an old, cracked screen
flashed red and violet, tracking every signal the pulse-beacon beamed into
low orbit, preventing Outpost One from being seen. It was a four-walled
space filled with numerical sequences and encryption data Cael wasn't
familiar with. A wave spiked, shooting a blue pixelated line into the air in
front of the holotablet. Xander watched it critically.

Sindra worked on a hand-held tablet, flicking at pixelated modules.
"Lorelei Henly sent out a galactic transmission cloaked as a standard Imperial luminary."

"Right," Elio said, frustrated, "and?"

Xander tongued at his cheek. "Play the transmission."

Sindra tapped her dialect device, then pinched an icon on her tablet,
held it, and waved it toward the larger holo. Suddenly, the hologram
shifted, bouncing with the sound of Lorelei's voice.

"This is High Lady Lorelei Henly, steward of Aurethia, calling for
immediate aid. Aurethia, forest moon of Draitune, is under attack by rogue
Grien forces. High Lord Darius and High Lady Lena have been assassinated." There was a pause. Enough time for Cael to hear every person on
the platform stop breathing. He cut a glance to Elio who stood still as a
sword. Lorelei's voice carried. Every word, every syllable shot from her like

an arrow. "If the Imperium does not intervene, I will pursue a defensive stance against this invasion, and flood every Avara mine on Aurethia, starting with the greater northern provinces surrounding Atreyu. Freezing production is not a decision I make lightly, but safekeeping the integrity of Avara's growth cycle for our children and their children is a sacrifice I am willing to make in the face of grave danger. House Volkov's act of terrorism will be met as a declaration of war."

The transmission ended, and everyone on the platform remained deadly quiet, fixing their attention on Elio.

"Will she," Melody finally whispered, then repeated themself, speaking clearly. "Will she do it?"

Elio opened his mouth. Closed it. He looked stricken.

"Yes," Cael said. Every face swiveled toward him. "I'm certain she'll do it."

"I need to get to her," Elio gritted through set teeth. He rubbed a hand over his face. It was such an inelegant motion. Such a boyish thing to do. He flung his open hand at the holo, then toward the journeymen. "She's scared, and she's angry — she doesn't know any better, because she doesn't know about you!"

"We're out of time," Xander said. He glanced between his colleagues. "If we don't put something into motion, we'll have nothing to work with."

Cael went to speak, "I don't know how long we — "

The roaring of a ship winged overhead, drowning out the rest of what Cael intended to say. *I don't know how long we have before my father takes the city.* Panic unfurled. He didn't need to see the aircraft's sleek, black build to know it was Griean. The way it sliced the air — that crunchy warp-charged scream — announced Griea's craftmanship from a great distance. Several more starships followed, skipping through the night like tossed onyx.

All the color in Elio's face drained. He stared at his feet for a moment, longer than Cael expected, before he crossed the platform and gripped the ladder.

"Compile your data, keep the pulse-beacon active, and ready yourselves for discovery. We'll do our best to mediate the situation from Atreyu," Elio decided, nodding as he stepped down one rung, then another. "If we lose the city, we've lost everything."

Xander rushed forward, "Elio, wait, wait — if we lose *you*, we've lost everything. The city can fall — "

"If Bracken takes Atreyu by force, the Imperium will intervene and likely uncover what you've been hiding here," Cael said. He followed Elio, waiting for the High Lord to lower himself down another rung before step-ping onto the ladder above him. "Me and Elio are the rightful stewards of Aurethia and Griea. Our unification is the only thing that can stop this."

Xander's face slackened. He let out a long, unsteady breath. "So this is it, huh?"

Innis nodded solemnly. "I'll saddle some horses," he mumbled, and walked toward the ladder.

Elio's boots hit the dirt. He stepped aside. Cael dropped down beside him. Vik leaped from the middle of the ladder, landing in a crouch. Innis slid down on the edge of each bar, and hopped away, jogging toward the stables.

The lions lifted their furry heads, peeking over the garden. Korah and Dare called out. Sol shook his mane. Their golden eyes mirrored through the darkness, and Elio weaved off toward the pride, taking a moment to touch each big cat. Cael watched, catching hushed instructions. *Stay here,* Elio said, patting Aki. *We'll come back for you.* When Elio returned, he slowed to a jog beside Cael.

"Bracken won't kill her," Cael said. He didn't know how else to approach the subject, so he chose to be blunt.

"But he'll kill everyone else," Elio said.

Cael couldn't argue that.

Innis saddled three Aurethian horses. Vik rode a large gelding. Cael and Elio climbed atop two mares. Innis patted one on the rump. "We'll station a scout on the interior of the crater near one of the popular trailheads."

"Vik, can you connect directly with Xander's dialect device?" Elio asked.

Vik paused, clutching the top of his saddle. One pupil pinned. "The pulse-beacon might scramble transmission delivery, but I can try. I won't know when or if he receives any data."

"But it will arrive?"

"Possibly."

"We can lower the frequency of the pulse-beacon to allow for planet-side communication," Innis said. He looked between Vik and Elio. "We might need to get a hold of you, too."

"Right," Elio said. He turned his horse. The beast hooved in place, stomping the dirt. "Thank you, Innis."

Before they left, Xander jogged up to the stable, panting to catch his breath. "Stay alive," he said, gulping. He pressed a blue-tinged vial into Elio's palm. "You're right, without a united stewardship, we'll lose everything. Aurethia, Alice, Avarine, Avara, this'll all be for nothing, so stay alive."

Cael gripped the reins. "If we lose Aurethia, pitch the plan to terraform Mercy to my mother." At that, Elio whipped toward him, viper-quick. Cael leveled him with a patient glare. He spoke to Xander but looked at his husband. "And petition the Imperium for support. Dutchess Constance will push for a peaceful solution, and my father will harken to a plan that promises credit."

Elio slid the Avarine into his pocket. "We can't trust — "

Cael interrupted. "We'll be dead if it comes to that. Trust won't matter anymore."

Another starcraft shot by overhead. The air rippled, torn apart by a powerful engine.

"Go," Xander said, and smacked Elio's horse on the rear. "We'll be listening."

Elio's horse reared and sped off, darting into the forest.

Cael snapped the reins and drove his heels into the painted horse's side, urging the animal forward. He took one last glance at Xander Henly, the Volkov who wasn't, and leaned forward in the saddle, chasing Elio through the crater. Behind him, Vik's gelding galloped hard. The horses leaped and whinnied. Their hooves pounded dirt and clover. The trio kicked up moss and splashed through puddles.

Beside him, Elio's face was set with concentration. Cael could hardly see him through the pitch. The blueish glow of wild Avara sketched his cheekbone and framed his upturned nose. He was a regal ghost, flying through the wilderness, racing toward war.

We are chasing obliteration. He snapped the reins again. Elio was running into battle, fearless and kingly, and Cael could not think of a better place to be than at his side. *I am a weapon, detonating.*

CHAPTER FORTY-ONE

ELIO

The horse beneath him heaved and snorted. Elio gripped the steed, urging her forward. Unrest echoed from the city. Noise skimmed his earlobe. Artillery split the darkness. Distant shouting grew louder and nearer with every push. The horse's powerful gait quickened, and she cried out, rising to leap over a bubbling stream. Wind scuffed his cheek. Aurethia was black and blue, trapped in Sunder's shadow. Draitune's ring curved like a neon rope above the canopy. Elio breathed deeply, attempting to dislodge the winged thing fluttering in his chest. Anxiety, adrenaline — whatever name it took that perilous night — could not rattle him.

Lorelei needed him. Aurethia needed him. House Henly needed him. Alice needed him. Outpost One needed him. He glanced sidelong at Cael, riding hard beside him. His fine, fair face, sculpted and scarred, craned over the horse's neck. He stared forward toward Atreyu, toward an imminent confrontation with his own people, toward the conquest he refused to carry, and Elio knew with utmost certainty that Cael Volkov needed him, too. The thought would've seemed trivial one season ago, when Cael was a warlord wielding attraction and charm like identical scythes. He heard Cael in his mind, whispering that lone, delicate word. *Mercy*. Both a tender request, and the name of the moon that might save them.

Atreyu is two klicks ahead. Vik's voice crackled through Elio's dialect device. I've detected a large heat signature near the entrance of the city. We should enter through the eastern treeline.

"Lead us in," Elio said, tapping his device.

Vik snapped the reins and galloped ahead, swooping in front of Elio and Cael. They ascended the crest of the crater. On the horizon, pluming beyond the thinning canopy, smoke tunneled into the sky, obstructing a sliver of Draitune.

Fear lanced his heart. He channeled strength. It arrived in a flash: the image of his father smiling at the head of the dining table, and his mother dancing with Orson balanced on her slippers, and Lorelei sparring with him in the training chamber, and the pride chasing each other in the meadow, and Peadar smacking his elbow, saying *eye-level, young lord*. His strength was every piece of his family cobbled together. Grief pummeled him, but he moved through it, welcoming the flood of despair, hatred, love, and loss, and fed each emotion like fuel to his heart's overzealous forge.

Night deepened. The forest opened. Elio smelled smoke and ozone, metal and rain. He focused on the narrow way forward and steeled himself for what came next. Destabilization, brutality, change, war. His horse's breath became a rhythmic backdrop. The wobbly sound of charging pulse weaponry grew louder. A Griean drone whizzed by. Elio caught the shift of black-clad bodies in his peripheral, scoping the forest.

Someone yelled, "Right! In the brush!"

Vik jerked his horse into a thicker part of the woodland. Elio followed, dodging a drone's red netted light scanning the treeline for a target. To the left, Atreyu rose up on the other side of the thicket. They pitched themselves toward the opening in the stone wall where the hovertrain and other groundcrafts entered the city. Vik shot toward the transport dock, glancing over his shoulder, and Cael called out to Elio, flanking him, "Go! Get inside!"

Something heavy exploded. Artillery bombarded the city's front gate, so loud, so powerful that the sound made Elio's teeth ache.

The tunnel yawned. Elio snapped the reins. *Faster*. But no horse could beat a terrestrial spacecraft. Above them, a talon-sharp Griean ship swiveled around the eastern wall, beaming a spotlight on the trio. Its glossy, slender fuselage hovered in mid-air, pummeling Elio, Vik, and Cael in a gust of blistering heat.

Elio turned his horse in a circle, facing the squadron of Griean Royal Reserve approaching from the front gate. If they kept running, they welcomed a bullet in the back. The battle would be over before it started.

He dismounted, drew his Grabak, and gave his steed a hard swat on the rear. "Go home, go!"

The horse whinnied and sped off into the forest. Gunfire popped, pulse-fire sizzled, another loud boom filled the air. Elio's eardrums screamed. He heard the other two horses charge off through the trees and watched as Vik Endresen rolled up his sleeves and took a defensive stance. Skinny cybernetic mechanisms glowed faintly beneath the Augment's skin, lining his arms like a submerged power grid. The flesh on his right palm dented inward, retracting to make room for the barrel of a built-in pulse-gun. He curled his left hand into a fist, causing the light on his half-mechanical limb to flare brighter.

Cael pulled his blade free. "They'll try to make this an execution. Give them a fight instead."

"We're outnumbered," Elio said.

"I'm a Griean Imperator," Cael rasped. At the same time, Vik said, "I'm a Griean Augment." As if those two facts were supposed to calm Elio's nerves.

The Royal Reserve melted out of the shadow. Smooth, black helmets concealed their faces, and they wore simple but intimidating armor. They moved as one, stepping forward without hesitation.

"Cael Volkov, you are under arrest for treason, pending prosecution in the arena. Turn yourself over for immediate dispatch to Griea. Augment Vik Endresen, you are under arrest for aiding a fugitive, turn yourself over for dismantlement and recalibration," the soldier in the center of the squadron said. His deep, gruff voice was distorted behind his helmet. "Elio Henly, surrender — "

Elio felt the lick of silver on his fingertip, leftover from the cattail he plucked and threw. The tiny knife didn't make a sound, just left a cold mark on his hand. When it burrowed into the soldier's throat, cutting off whatever else he might demand, no one saw it. Not until the soldier coughed, swayed, and fell, smacking the dirt.

At first, the Griean squadron stayed frozen, but then Vik's internal pulse-gun hummed, gradually rising in tempo, and the soldiers rushed toward them.

Vik fired a pulse-shot. It ripped through a patch of black armor, knocking a Griean through the air. Elio remembered every time he'd trained with Cael. Every morning session with Peadar, playful match with Lorelei, rare but informative lesson with Darius. He gripped the handle on his Grabak and lunged, dodging a closed fist, skidding on his knees, driving the basilisk tooth up, *up*, through abdominal armor and into soft flesh. The soldier cried out. It was a terrible howl, and for some reason, Elio shrank at the sound.

The night erupted. Chaos fell over them.

Cael swung his short-sword and flipped his dagger by the handle, pinching the tip and throwing it hard at another soldier. It landed in the soldier's leg and sent him toppling into the dirt. Metal slammed, shrill and loud. Cael blocked another blow and kicked the assailant away, spinning to extend his sword in front of Elio, shielding him from a thick, black blade. Iron clashed. Singing steel shook Elio to the bone. He glanced at Cael and shot to his feet, running his Grabak through the soldier's middle.

Cael flinched at the sight. He worked his throat and turned away, rolling a stiff shoulder. His back smacked Elio's spine. They stayed like that, fending off blow after blow, strike after strike.

"Are you with me, Imperator?" Elio shouted over the din.

"I'm with you," Cael growled. His muddy sole met someone's chest, sending them flailing backward.

Vik blocked a swipe from a saber with his forearm. Blood spurted, shining red under Mercy's muted glow, but the blow didn't seem to faze him. He grasped the soldier by the throat and lifted, squeezed, tossed.

Elio fought hard. He moved gracefully, countering Cael's brutal strength with deliberate quickness, lending clarity where Cael's newfound blindness got the best of him. A sword came for Cael's nape, and Elio deflected it, slicing the soldier beneath the ear with a cattail. Someone grabbed Elio by the elbow, wrenching his arm behind him, and Cael moved on them like a fanged beast, headbutting their helmet, spearing them cruelly with his short-sword. The longer they fought, the more Royal Reserve appeared.

We need to get on the other side of the wall, Vik said through his dialect device. The Augment took a blunt hit to the face. It was the first time Elio saw him physically wince, and something about it, how he let the pain impact him for only the barest second, brought a sense of insecurity to Elio's hoarded strength.

"Get to the tunnel," Elio said, turning to face Cael. "We can't keep goin' like this!"

Cael pushed another soldier away. Blood splashed like wine over his jaw and neck. He spat a congealed red glob at the ground. "You go, Elio. Find Lorelei, find Ulrich Walsh — "

"I'm not leaving you," Elio hissed as if Cael asked the impossible. He *did* ask the impossible. "We need to get inside, we need to — "

Down, Vik said, too calmly. Suddenly, the Augment was crashing into Cael and hauling Elio to the ground. The trio smacked the damp dirt. Pain throbbed in Elio's thigh. Warm wetness grew there, leaking down his knee, and he wondered when he'd been cut. A high-pitched whistle careened past them.

Vik covered Elio and pulled Cael close. "Brace!"

Elio curled into a ball. The explosion shook through him. He felt it in his gut. It was like his body was a snow globe, suddenly shaken by a huge hand. Gunpowder chalked his throat. The smell of burning plastic and hot metal filled the air. Smoke singed his eyes and nose.

An unfamiliar voice hollered, "Atreyu, with me!"

Each word dropped like a stone through water. Elio's ears rang, and the distant, warped sound of war seemed smothered by a sopping cloth.

"Ulrich," Cael gasped out, then again, rising to his knees, "Ulrich!"

"Get the High Lord inside," Ulrich said.

Elio was pulled to his feet. He stumbled forward, guided by Vik. More hands reached for him, tugged at him. He whipped around, searching for Cael, and breathed easier when Cael appeared beside a man in gilded armor, wearing a helmet in the likeness of a lion's open mouth. Gold teeth lined Ulrich's jaw and crowned his forehead.

The leader of the militia pointed at the tunnel with his saber. "Go, now!"

The party kicked into a run. Vik kept his hand on Elio's shoulder. The shadowy inlet swallowed them, and the loudness outside Atreyu's wall began to fade. There was a hornet in his skull, buzzing annoyedly, and his thigh started to sting. The docking bay was a welcome sight. He recognized the parked hovertrain, and the outline of familiar buildings. Dirt turned to smooth road, and smooth road turned to cobblestone, and Elio's pace finally slowed.

He gulped in a ragged breath, bent at the waist, hands on his knees, still clutching the bloody Grabak in a shaky fist. *Breathe*. He coughed choppily. The world spun. He spat and smashed his free hand over the slash on his leg, applying pressure. A horrible, gnarled whine rushed up and out of him.

Someone grabbed his face. He knew those hands "Hey," Cael said, softer than he anticipated, and lifted Elio by the jaw, coaxing his gaze. "You okay?"

Elio swallowed hard and raised his other hand, showing a fresh, glossy streak of blood. "I need a medkit."

Cael went to yell, but Vik appeared at their side before he could.

"Lord Henly, you've sustained an injury," the Augment said. Vik was scraped and bleeding in several places, including his face, but didn't seem to mind. He pulled a micro medkit from inside his tactical vest. The kit opened like a short, fat caterpillar. "Specifically, a laceration to the rectus femoris. We don't have time to suture, so," he pulled a small device free, angling the square-shaped mouth against the gash, "this will hurt." Vik pulled the toggle. The first staple clamped one end of the wound closed.

Elio almost caved forward. Pain slivered through his leg, vibrating his kneecap. The staple-gun felt like a forest rat, biting through his wound again and again.

Cael held him upright. "It'll be over soon."

The next staple snapped. Elio wanted to scream or sob or kick. He dropped his Grabak and held onto Cael instead, turning to sink his teeth into Cael's shoulder. His shirt bunched beneath Elio's teeth. Skin pillowed between his lips.

A low rumble filled Cael's throat. He squeezed Elio's hip, but didn't protest.

The next five staples closed the gash. Vik smashed a damp antiseptic cloth over it, causing all of Elio's muscles to tense at once. He shrieked against Cael's shoulder and bit harder.

"Vik, c'mon," Cael growled.

The Augment's voice was level yet harsh. "I either stop the bleeding or I don't."

The world spun. Elio drew his teeth away and tried to breathe, tipping his head back to gather a lungful of smoky air. When Vik removed the cloth, cool air hit the stapled line holding the sword-strike closed, and Elio managed to put more weight on it. After a few tentative heel-to-toe movements, Elio stood on his own.

"Better?" Vik asked.

"Thank you," Elio exhaled. "What was that?"

"Individual shoulder-launched artillery. A kestrel, to be exact." Vik stood and tucked the medkit into his vest. "Which I'm certain the Griean forces weren't anticipating."

"Where's my sister?" Elio bent to snatch up his Grabak.

Cael eased away, leaving a solid hand on Elio's tailbone. "We'll find her."

The commotion continued. Pulse-fire echoed, and someone aimed a rifle toward the sky, firing at a Griean drone. Militia stalked about, shouting orders, tending to each other, arming themselves, and assessing the perimeter.

"Lord Volkov, High Lord Henly," Ulrich Walsh greeted, striding toward them. Red flecked his brassy armor. He steadied a noticeable limp with a white-banded cane. "Good of you to join us." He sheathed his sword and extended his gloved hand to Elio. "I'm Ulrich Walsh, commander of the militia in Atreyu. We've allied with the militia in the marshland and called for support from the fighters in the neighboring villages. Right now, the High Lady has directed us to take a defensive stance."

"And the people?" Elio asked.

"Safe underneath the city."

"Take me to her."

Ulrich dipped his head. "This way."

The commander led them through the interior of Atreyu. The front gate was barricaded with stone and brick, and riflemen were stationed on the outer wall, hidden behind stacked pallets. A scout climbed the exterior of one of the statues bracketing the gate. She perched on the shoulder of a stone-carved, lion-faced woman, likely relaying information to another scout at the northern entrance. Elio looked around the lion's maw of Aurethia, the great city that once was, and saw the desolate beginning of a war-torn future. Every building, dark. Families hidden away underground. Trade and commerce at a standstill. Blood and sinew slicking the walkway.

A passerby stopped. Their gaunt face brightened, and they said his name like a blessing. *Elio. It's Elio Henly.* Another two militia members swiveled to look at him. *He's back*, one said, nodding at Cael, while the other gasped out *he's alive* and flashed three fingers in front of their throat.

Ulrich turned toward a sturdy building surrounded by militia. The brick tower climbed high above the city, sloped with polished red eaves and a pyramidal roof. It was Atreyu's esteemed weaponcraft hub, meeting place for the Aurethian militia. The guardship stationed at the door flashed the three-fingered salute and stepped aside, allowing Ulrich, Elio, Cael, and Vik to enter.

"High Lady Lorelei is on the veranda, sir." A Zephan with cool-toned skin dipped their head at Cael. "Welcome back, Imperator."

"Good to see you, Gyana," Cael said.

Elio walked into the elevator, ignoring the manacle of pain clasped around his thigh, and waited for the rest of them to join. Once the glass door slid shut, the elevator propelled upward. He chewed his thumbnail. *Lorelei is alive.* The thought kept him firmly planted in the present. *She's alive, and she's here, and she's waiting for me.*

Ulrich cleared his throat. "We won't be able to hold the gate forever."

"If we're smart about our offensive, we might be able to outlast them,"

Cael said, but he didn't sound certain. "Has Draitune sent a transmission? Has anyone?"

"The Griean warship jammed our beacon the minute Lorelei's transmission went live. We're dark again."

Cael sighed through his nose. "Then this is a waiting game."

"We can fight, Imperator."

"We can," Cael muttered, sliding his teeth across his lip. "But we'll lose."

"We might have no choice," Elio cut in.

The elevator rocked to a stop, and the transparent door opened. Across the room, past a threadbare curtain, Elio watched moonlight slit through a storm cloud and catch on the gold armor plated across his sister's back. She wore metal, like an old world general, and stood on the veranda, clutching the iron rail. Her blonde braid plaited around the top of her head, secured with a jagged circlet. Thick maroon leather covered her bottom half.

From the corner of the room, Nara bellowed, flicking her tail.

At first, he just stood there, staring at the young woman who had been a girl not too long ago. His little sister who studied plantlife, and collected baubles, and wanted to be a doctor, who laughed with her entire body, longed for romance, and chased offworld fashion. The High Lady of Aurethia eclipsed that girl, poised, unmovable, aged, different. But when she turned to look over her shoulder, Lorelei Henly returned. The flat line of her full mouth softened, her eyes widened, and she said his name like she had on her fourteenth birthday, hand cupped between her legs, bleeding for the first time, and like she had when she was six, during a festival in Atreyu, after she'd accidentally let go of his elbow in a crowd.

Lorelei rushed toward him, and Elio bypassed the pain searing his wounded leg to go to her. He caught her midway to a sob, clutching her armored frame. "Mom and Dad are gone," she said, as if their death was a spider webbed in her chest, finally knocked loose.

Elio nodded. "I'm sorry I didn't find you."

"Cael found me," she murmured, peeling away to stare at him. An old greenish bruise flared like a sunspot on her temple, and a healed cut scarred her lip. She gave him a once over, focusing on his bloodied leg. "You're hurt," she exclaimed, reaching for his pantleg, but he took her hand and squeezed.

"I'll be fine, Vik patched it. Listen, we can't afford to sit idle. Bracken will burn Atreyu to the ground if he has to."

"Draitune will heed my call," she assured.

"We don't know what the Legatus told them, Lorelei. A Griean warship is enough of a deterrent — I can't imagine that's his only threat."

Ulrich cleared his throat. "If I may, Atreyu is fortified and equipped with weaponry, High Lord. We can make a stand. Buy some time."

Elio glanced at Cael. "Imperator," he said, exhaling sharply, "what do you think?"

Cael stepped forward. He swiped the side of his hand beneath his nose. "I think Bracken will try to arrest me. Killing me would be too convenient. But he will try to kill you," he said to Elio, pausing to reign in an angry breath, "because you're too dangerous to keep alive. He'll take Lorelei by force if he has to, and he'll use her to subdue the militia and claim the city."

"Take me?" Lorelei's top lip curled. "Let him try."

Elio squeezed her hand again. "What kind of defense can we muster?"

"I have riflemen stationed on the wall," Ulrich said.

"Tell them to fire on the intruders. If we can keep the Royal Reserve at bay until morning, we'll have a better chance at someone outside our orbit intervening."

"If you fire on them, Bracken will rush the entrance. You'll only delay the inevitable," Cael said solemnly.

"We must fight," Lorelei snarled.

"I hear you, princess, but there's more at stake here than — "

Lorelei turned toward Ulrich, ignoring Cael completely. "You heard my brother. Fire on the intruders, prepare the militia for ground combat."

Elio looked at Cael and found horror on his face. Sadness, anger, something else he couldn't place. A precursor to grief; regret before it arrived. He let go of his sister and touched his husband's wrist, clutching Cael's hammering pulse. "We have no choice."

"They're still my people," Cael whispered. He spoke thickly, swallowing discomfort. "They're *our* people."

Cold, prickling anger iced his nape. It was a brief response. An animal thing Elio was ashamed of.

Cael must've seen it, because he sighed and said, "Griea didn't do this. My father did, Bracken did, Maxine did, I did. Those people out there are following orders, Elio. Forgive me for seeing this for what it is, but I can't help it. I'm wearing their blood," he choked out, looking down at himself. "I'm the reason they're marching toward death and bringing death with them."

Elio grounded himself with a callous breath. *Yes*, he wanted to say, *yes, you did this, yes, they're marching toward death, yes, you're wearing their blood. Good.*

Thankfully, rationality bloomed where bitterness itched and spread. "Alexander and Harlyn started this. Darius and Marcus emboldened it. You and I will end it."

Lorelei bristled at the mention of their father. She glanced between the pair, brow pinched, teeth slightly bared.

"Go," Elio said to Ulrich. The commander nodded curtly and knocked his cane against the floor, heading back toward the elevator.

Cael closed his eyes. He wasn't rough when he pulled away, but the disconnect of wrist from palm still stung. He walked to the veranda and grabbed the rail, peering out into the night. His wide shoulders pulled taut, and he let his head hang forward, knuckles blanching around the iron.

Elio trailed after him. Lorelei stayed at his side. Nara followed, rumbling anxiously.

Sharing the balcony, and the moonlight, and the smoke, the trio stood, stewards of a precious, contested moon, and watched an ocean of Griean-black gather on the other side of Atreyu's gate.

CHAPTER FORTY-TWO

CAEL

The gunmen on the southern wall fell one by one, shot down by a Griean sniper hidden in the dark.

It didn't take long. As soon as the Aurethian riflemen started cutting down the Royal Reserve that inched too close to Atreyu's gate, their bodies dropped, careening from each perch like hunted fowl.

Cael knew better than to believe they stood a chance. The Royal Reserve had top of the line *everything*. They manufactured the very weaponry Aurethia tried to emulate. While the forest moon threw together scrap-metal and forged antique gunwear, Griea leveraged the latest technology to mass-produce faster, lighter, nastier weapons, and filled each design with the deadliest ammunition: artillery cut from Griean alloy harvested from the deep ice, pulse-weaponry designed to unseat skin from bone.

The Aurethian militia was resilient, but they were still outmatched.

Lorelei paced on the bottom floor of Atreyu's weaponcraft division, chewing her fingernail the same way Elio did. Elio leaned against a smelting forge, staring at the smooth, grey stone, and Ulrich and his team waited for direction. Cael finished dressing Vik's forearm with a bandage. Inside the enclave, surrounded by chainmail worn by famous Aurethian militia and daggers displayed on the clawed mantle of polished placards, everything was quiet. Tension twisted the stagnant air.

Outside, artillery continued to crack and sizzle, shouting echoed, people screamed and yelped, and the constant, steadfast heartbeat of a Griean pulse-laser melted through Atreyu's fortified gate. It wouldn't be long. The laser itself, something Cael was intimately familiar with, beamed from the wide mouth of an oversized terrestrial pulse-rifle. It could cut through a steel door. Slice an old Earthen tank in half. Melt a warship's engine. On Griea, they called it Voyager, the way through.

"We should make a stand," Lorelei said.

Ulrich nodded slowly. "It's that or surrender, High Lady."

Elio fidgeted. Worry creased his forehead. "Position riflemen in the buildings near the courtyard. I want our finest shooters covering the entrance from secure vantage points. Windows, rooftops, anywhere high enough to defend the gate." He lifted his gaze, looking at Cael through his lashes, then shifted to glance around the room. His throat bobbed. "Lorelei, I need you to shelter underground with — "

"Don't you dare," the Henly princess seethed, halting mid-stride. She swiveled toward Elio, furious.

Ulrich's deep-set eyes closed. He screwed up his mouth as if he'd expected her outburst.

Cael sighed. He knew better than to cage her. She'd only grow more reckless if they tried. "Lor, we need you safe. If we fail, you're Aurethia's last hope."

"I am Lorelei Darragh Henly, lioness of Aurethia, High Lady of the forest moon, and I will not be hidden away like a jewel to be stolen. I am a weapon to be wielded, I am a fang in the lion's maw," she said, voice growing steeper, shrill and barbed, "I am my father's second heir, I am mother's only daughter — I will not cower to this conquest, I will not bow to Bracken Volkov, I will not let you fight for me."

"Lorelei, please, we've lost enough," Elio started. His patience waned, and Cael could hear the desperation ringing in his voice.

"No," she shouted. Her mouth quivered. "We face this together, Elio, we face this side-by-side, or we do not face it at all. If I'm to be held captive like a broodmare, then this Griean bastard will have to capture me himself. I will not lock myself away, I will meet him with a sword in my hand!"

A pitchy, grating noise filled the city. It was the sound of stone crumbling, breaking. The sound of Atreyu's gate peeling open. Voyager's laser chewed through the last bit of resistance, and panic flurried throughout Aurethia's capital. *Militia, ready yourselves! Brace! Hold the gate — go, go, get to position!* The deep night became a trial. One that risked the Greater

Universe. Cael stared at Elio, printing the image of him on the backside of his ribcage.

Ulrich nodded at Zoe, then flicked his wrist at Gyana, encouraging the militant entourage to exit the room. He looked first to Cael, then to Lorelei and Elio. "The fight is here whether we like it or not. It's been an honor, High Lady," he said, inclining his head to Lorelei. "High Lord, you have my steel." He flashed the Aurethian war salute, and then swept into the hall, calling out to the remaining militia. "I want riflemen on the roof! Go, now!"

Lorelei stared hard at Elio. She looked fit for battle, for bloodshed, but Cael could not unsee her twirling in a silk gown, laughing in the garden, winking over the top of her sunglasses.

"Enough has been stolen from us. Fight beside me." The order skated off her tongue, half-whispered, half-hissed. She swept out of the room, one hand on the pommel of her Aurethian sword.

Elio nudged his chin toward the doorway. "See to her, please."

"I'm afraid *you* are my directive, High Lord Henly. But I will try to reason with her," Vik said.

"Don't bother with reason. She won't hear it." He set his mouth tightly. "Just look after her for me — we'll only be a minute."

The Augment followed Lorelei into the tower's circular entryway, leaving Cael alone with Elio.

Beyond the stone enclosed around them, Atreyu erupted.

"You should take shelter underground," Cael said, although he knew Elio would never abandon the battle. It was his only chance to say it, though. To advocate for Elio's safety. So Cael nodded, clinging to the prospect of an impossible kindness. One Elio would never grant him. "Let me do this," he said, harsh, low, "let me fix this."

Let me die for you.

Elio crossed the room. His narrow, freckled face remained hauntingly unreadable. He was, at once, the young man who had lounged beneath the candlebell, transcribing text, and the High Lord of a fallen homeworld, carved in the likeness of every Henly who came before him. He brought one hand to Cael's jaw.

"I have too much to say, and we don't have enough time," Elio said. It was a heartbreaking truth.

"Elio — "

Elio stood on his tiptoes and kissed him. It was a searing kiss, the kind sewn with unspoken. Heat cindered Cael's spine. His chest ached, filling with a breath stolen straight from Elio's open mouth. A tentative hand cupped the back of his head, perching where it always used to. Cael wanted to keep him there, trapped in the first kiss they'd shared since their wedding night. *Maybe our last.* When Elio eased away, Cael surged forward, chasing one last hungry sip, and drew Elio back to him.

"Stay with me," Cael said against his slack lips. He curled his hand intimately, possessively around Elio's slender throat. "I'll never let you go. I told you that, I meant it."

Elio nodded, dazed for a moment. When Cael looked at him, they were back in the orchard, nibbling juicy fruit, back in their bedchamber, tangled and warm, back in the meadow, watching Wonder give birth.

"Fight beside me, Imperator," Elio whispered. "Meet fate with me."

Cael tipped forward again, but the High Lord blinked and dropped his hand. His tongue darted across his bottom lip. Resistance bloomed on him, slow and sticky. There was an unwinnable war combusting on the other side of that brick tower, and they had no choice but to face it. Carefully, Elio stepped back, palming his Grabak's leather handle.

Stay with me. The plea dimmed like a wet spark. *Run with me, leave with me.* But Cael knew better than to speak aloud a childish dream. He pulled his short-sword free, fell into step beside Elio, and they walked together toward the inevitable.

ATREYU BURNED.

Adrenaline spread through Cael's body. Acrid smoke braised the roof of his mouth, burning every stunted breath. Once Voyager bested the gate, the Royal Reserve rushed in, pouring over cobblestone. He knew what to expect. Deliberate, swift movement. Griean-black covering the city like a single, monstrous shadow.

The entrance to Atreyu became a hot zone filled with clashing bodies. Riflemen fired. A Griean drone zipped through the center of the city, scanning the Aurethian defense assembling behind the front line. As if the moon sensed destruction, Aurethia's sky opened. The sea-storm rolled inland like something once worshiped, heaving fat raindrops, blowing hard wind, drenching the flames clustered around the downed gate.

Cael fought for an hour. Two, maybe. A year; a decade. He didn't know how long. It went on and on, the dredging of mangled bodies. He deflected where he could, aiming the sole of his boot against a solar plexus, slamming the blunt handle of his blade against face-shields, hoping each calculated movement might deter rather than destroy.

Lorelei fought like a wild cat. She was a deadly swordsman, twirling her blade through the rain, skewering black armor, shouting orders to Ulrich, roaring with rage at the night. He kept her in his line of sight, but it was Elio he stayed closest to. Even with Vik present, shielding Elio, Cael could not peel himself away from the High Lord. They fought back-to-back, side by side. When Cael's blind-spot got the best of him and a black-clad soldier lunged with their dagger, Elio shoved Cael aside and blocked the blow. And when a Griean knocked Elio to the ground and attempted to skewer him to the stone with a saber, Cael looped his arm around the soldier and cut their throat.

The Aurethian militia fought impressively hard. They held the Royal Reserve at the mouth of Atreyu, busting through armor with antique gunnery and skilled swordsmanship. Bodies swathed in gold and black bled out into the watery street, pummeled by rain, left to bloat and stiffen while the battle raged on.

If he survived, the image of his comrades strewn across the stone — Griean and Aurethian alike — would haunt Cael for an eternity. He would remember this dreadful night, soaked to the bone, fighting, and fighting, and *fighting*. He would be plagued with the memory of blood, rain, and lightning branching overhead. The death rattle of a nearby soldier would live like a ghoul in his closet. The garbled sound of two languages, screamed and shrieked, would carry through his window on unwelcome wind.

"Push them back," Ulrich yelled.

Lorelei shoved her sword into the air. "Aurethia, with me!"

The militia cried out, rushing forward with the High Lady, and for a significant moment, Cael caught himself believing they might drive the Royal Reserve to retreat. He stepped back to catch his breath, hauling Elio with him.

"We've stopped their advance," Elio exclaimed, panting hard. He went heavy against Cael's chest, hardly holding the handle of his bloodied Grabak. "We've done it, Cael, we've…" He went silent, leaning down, one hand cupped over his dialect device. The elation on his red-speckled face morphed into horror. He snapped his gaze upward and stared at Cael. "There's a Griean ship," he breathed out, each word hardly audible.

Cael read the shape of his mouth, extracting what he said. The sound of the spacecraft came next, screaming through the sky like an iron wyvern.

The beastly ship shot forward from the south and stopped above the courtyard. The gust sent downward from the hot turbine billowed hard against
the bodies on the ground. Cael winced, shielding Elio from the heat. Vik
appeared at their side, breathing fast.

"I'm surprised he waited this long," the Augment shouted over the
racket.

Two figures leaped from the open docking bay, landing one right after
the other. The first hit the ground in a crouch, basilisk armor absorbing the
shockwave from falling from such a great height. Cael knew the sharp iron
ridge crowning his helmet, knew the glossy Griean glyph embossed on his
chestplate, knew the claymore strapped to his back. The second soldier
landed in a roll, untucking on his feet in a graceful movement. He was
wrapped in tactical armor, dual-wielding identical black sabers. A thick,
iron collar ringed his throat, shielding his mouth and nose. Kasimir Malkin
peered out over his inverted helmet, scanning the battlefield.

Cael knew his cousin would show, but he still wasn't ready for it. He
extended his arm in front of Elio, palm pressed to his husband's hip, then
stepped toward the duo. "Vik," he said, knowing better than to tell Elio to
stay put, "keep him safe."

Elio immediately jerked forward, clawing at Cael. "No — "

Vik snagged the back of Elio's armored tunic like a mother bear.

"Cael, don't," Elio snapped. A gruff whine caught in his chest. His voice
wobbled, threatening to break. "Cael!"

A militant rushed toward Bracken. Kasimir lunged. The Aurethian
almost managed to block with a dagger, but Kasimir was too fast, too accurate. One saber clashed against the dagger, and the other drove through the
center of the militant's stomach. The next few attempts from the Aurethian
militia were met with the same swiftness. Bracken cut with a swing of his
claymore. Kasimir carved with a flick of his wrist.

Gauntlets covered Bracken's knuckles and buckled around his wrists,
and black-scaled basilisk concealed the rest of him. He looked draconic like
that, helmet knifing away from his shielded face. The storm pelted his
armor. When he turned toward Cael, he spun the handle of his claymore,
adjusting his grip. He stood there, waiting, until Lorelei's voice cut through
the rain. *Defend the gate! Do not let them pass!* Bracken tilted his head and
shifted his attention toward the heiress. He gave Cael another lingering
look, and then gestured with a roll of his shoulder, prompting Kasimir to
step forward.

"Cael," Kasimir greeted. He stalked back and forth. "You've traded

Griean glory for this?" He held his sabers akimbo and laughed, gesturing at
the dark city. "This moon is a gem in our ice serpent's eye, Duke Volkov.
You know that."

Cael was eighteen when he'd met Kasimir for the first time. Rough,
unpredictable, quiet, and skilled. Bracken's acquaintance. Kindra's kin. Efficient during the Tupinaire, almost to a fault. He killed with clever quickness, and unlike Bracken and Cael, he ditched showmanship for
effectiveness. He was a mercenary at heart — swift death. It made Cael
queasy to see him dressed in black, stamped with the Griean glyph, fighting
alongside the Royal Reserve.

"Stand down, Kasimir," Cael ordered.

Kasimir elevated his eyebrow. "It's too bad we're not in the arena. Can
you imagine the uproar? Me, an offworlder, squaring up against you,
Griea's disgraced prince."

Cael swept forward. Kasimir raised both sabers, locking them against
his short-sword. Cael trembled with the force of it. Kasimir's weight pressed
down through steel and leather. He stared at Cael over the edge of his half-
mask. The intensity of his concentration, as if he meant to pry through
Cael's eyes and slip straight into his skull, was unnerving. Men like Kasimir,
who finally felt the firmness of a pedestal beneath their feet, tended to forget
themselves. His ego left an opening for the sole of Cael's boot, connecting
with a hard kick to his kneecap. Kasimir folded. Cael broke away and
aimed his sword at Kasimir's shoulder.

Despite the rare opening he'd been given, knocking Kasimir off balance
only seemed to embolden him. He parried, sliding to the left, and brought
his armored fist to Cael's scarred cheek. That was an easily dodged attack,
but Cael's head snapped back with the force of Kasimir's punch. Cael's
damaged vision nearly crippled him.

"Is that scar from a cat, Cael? Blinded by a lion. How fitting," Kasimir
taunted, lacking play, brimming with hostility.

Before Cael could right himself, Kasimir struck again. This time, Cael
snatched his forearm, gripped hard, and yanked, snapping the radius bone
beneath his hand. Kasimir yelped and seethed, wrestling Cael onto the slippery cobblestone. Rain drenched his lashes. He could hardly see. Exhaustion sank deep, deep, fended off by adrenaline but heavy, nonetheless.

A part of him said *we're almost through, we're almost done.* Another part of
him gnawed at the truth. *I have to get to Bracken.* Cael swung his bent elbow
into Kasimir's face, rolled, and lifted his sword. He was on his back, aiming
for Kasimir's chestplate. But Kasimir was fast — too fast. Before Cael could

pierce his armor, Kasimir landed on him, knee to gut, saber to throat. The metal stung, slipping hot and thin along the cartilage protecting Cael's trachea.

Kasimir breathed hard. Cold rain rivered his face and dripped from his mask, splattering Cael's nose. "God is in the water," he said, and drove the saber down.

Cael's flesh split. He tried to push himself closer to the stone, tried to melt downward, tried to kick away. He felt across the ground until his thumb knocked the handle of his short-sword. He grabbed the weapon and swung, burying the blade in Kasimir's side. In the same breath, a Grabak slammed through Kasimir's back, exiting his ribcage.

Kasimir Malkin's light faded. His gaze hollowed and he went limp. When the Grabak was pulled free, Cael expected to see Elio standing above him, but it was another Griean swathed in black, breathing hard.

Holland tore away his face shield and knocked Kasimir's body to the side, extending his hand. "Get up," he barked, shaking the limb at Cael. "C'mon, let's go!"

Cael pawed at his throat. Blood welled in the shallow cut. Holland leaned down and swatted his hand. *Right.* Cael clasped Holland's palm and was hauled to his feet.

"That's treason, Holland Lancaster," he said, gulping in a relieved breath. The night and the fight might've granted Holland enough cover to get away with what he'd done. Cael hoped as much.

"So be it, Imperator," Holland said. He swatted Cael on the back. "I can get you out of here. Not everyone lost their loyalty — "

"No, I need to find my cousin, I need…" Cael swiveled left then right. He looked for blonde hair. Vik's towering build. The flash of a Grabak wielded by a familiar hand. But Elio was nowhere to be found, and neither was the Augment protecting him.

The battle for Atreyu raged on. Militia met Royal Reserve with bullets, steel, and knuckles. Gunfire cracked. Thunder did, too, rumbling across the sky. A white spear ignited the cloud-cover.

Holland patted his shoulder. "There," he said, shoving at Cael.

Cael turned with the motion. Near the interior of Atreyu, where the courtyard veered off toward housing, boutiques, and sky-bridges, Cael saw the flash of Bracken's claymore. Elio stood beneath him, Grabak raised in a defensive posture. *No*, Cael thought. Panic surged, electrifying every place adrenaline hadn't yet reached. He stumbled into a sprint. Leaped over a body, dodged a conjoined duo, side-stepped a gunman, shouldered through a pair of Royal Reserve, and held a commandment in his mind. *Get to him, get to him, get to him.* He watched Bracken's greatsword fall, crashing against Elio's basilisk tooth. Elio buckled from the weight of the blow. His back knee caved. Behind him, Vik slumped against a brick wall, legs splayed in front of him, one hand smashed over a wound on his stomach.

"Bracken," Cael hollered.

The heir incumbent quirked his head, staring at Cael through the horizontal slit in his helmet.

The distraction gave Elio the chance to wiggle free. He jerked to the side. Bracken lurched forward, dislodging his claymore from Elio's Grabak. Elio hopped away and glanced over his shoulder. He touched his dialect device. Spoke rapidly. Against the wall, Vik nodded weakly. The Augment's cybernetic skeleton flickered beneath his epidermis.

"I'm here, *Imperator*," Cael yelled. Rain kept coming, soaking through armor, chilling hot skin. "Come and claim your title!"

The goading worked. Bracken straightened and strode toward him, leaving Elio to scramble toward Vik, digging the Avarine out of his pocket, upending the vial into the gaping sword-strike plunged through Vik's abdomen. Only Bracken's claymore would inflict that kind of damage. No other Griean blade could concave someone so effortlessly.

Bracken swung his sword. It was a swooping, weighty motion. Cael ducked, avoiding the blow, but welcomed a boot to his chest. As he toppled backward, Cael remembered Bracken teaching him that very move. How to lock your leg and propel yourself forward, when to use the blunt force of a strong kick to knock the wind from your opponent. Cael caught himself and lashed out. They were blade-to-blade again. Cael gritted his teeth.

Every muscle screamed, trembling with the effort to keep Bracken at bay. He swept out his leg and knocked Bracken's ankle, jostling him enough to aim a hard upper cut to his chin. His Griean war helmet lurched upward. Bracken swiped it away. The hard, jagged headpiece fell at their feet.

"You would let a spoiled Aurethian princess cost the Greater Universe access to Avara," Bracken growled. Oily charcoal striped his eyes, smudged over high cheekbones. He stopped a blow from Cael's short-sword with a hand straight to the blade. His gauntlet clanked and screeched around wet steel.

"I am the steward of this moon," Cael said, sending his fist into Bracken's oblique. His strength waned.

Bracken yanked on the short-sword. Cael hadn't expected that. The slick pommel slid from his grasp. "I taught you better," he spat, and brought the blunt end of the handle down on Cael's split cheek. Blood gushed. Skin tore. "Look at you, cousin. Mewling like a calf, spent and still trying to tussle."

Of course. It all made sense. Bracken and Kasimir flying in late, allowing the battle to exhaust the militia, beat down the Aurethian leadership, wear out the defense. No wonder he primed his theatrical arrival at a moment of relief. He'd dropped from the sky unbridled and primed for war, and landed on top of Cael, Vik, Elio, and everyone else while they were too tired to think clearly.

The last hard hit left Cael dizzied. He clawed at Bracken's chest, gasping in a soupy, coppery lungful of air. Every breath rattled. *You're bleeding*, his body said, *you're leaking inside.* He wouldn't beg. Wouldn't make it easy. He swung his head back and jerked forward, headbutting Bracken in the temple. White exploded across his good eye. Bracken stumbled, but regained himself, huffing and grunting. Cael closed his fist and jabbed. Bracken caught his hand in a powerful grip.

For the first time since Cael Volkov had ascended to Keeper of the Basilisk, he tasted defeat. It chalked his tongue, salty, bitter.

Bracken threw Cael to the cobblestone. Cael heard his name in the distance. It could've been Ulrich. Holland, maybe. The downpour suffocated sound. He stared through the darkness, watching lightning branch the sky, and turned to look for Elio, for the reason he was on that forest moon to begin with, for the shrapnel in his heart, for his husband. *Let him be the last thing I see.* The High Lord met his gaze, bloodied and war-torn. Elio snatched up his Grabak, wide-eyed, charging forward. He glanced to the left, mouth splitting for a shout.

When Bracken brought his claymore down, intending to skewer Cael to the stone, a familiar cry lit the night. Gilded armor crossed in front of Cael. Lorelei's blade stopped Bracken's claymore, but didn't stop him. The weight of his greatsword knocked her weapon loose. The strike jolted her, causing the High Lady's smaller frame to bend and shiver. Bracken shot his hand out and seized her by the throat.

Lorelei flailed, toeing at the wet stone. She scraped wildly at his armored forearms, but it was no use.

With a single tap to his dialect device and a low utterance, Atreyu was swarmed. The Royal Reserve stopped firing, stopped slaying, but they filled the courtyard with a swiftness Cael should've expected. Keeping to the gate was strategic. Wearing the Aurethian militia down had been the plan all along. He blinked slowly, head still swimming. Blood leaked from his nostrils and pooled somewhere in his chest.

"Don't," Cael gurgled, reaching for Lorelei's ankle, for any part of her. "Bracken, don't — let her go, don't — "

"You look like your mother," Bracken said, tugging Lorelei closer.

"Enough," Elio shouted.

The High Lord's voice rang like a great bell, and Cael tried to surge toward it, tried to rise and meet it, but he couldn't. Every bone said *rest*, every muscle said *we're done*. Cael pushed at the cobblestone and turned onto his side, dragging himself semi-upright on one bent elbow.

Bracken eased Lorelei onto the stone and allowed her to take a breath. He gave Elio a slow once-over. "You're brave, I'll give you that."

"Release Lady Lorelei, Imperator Volkov," Elio said. He sounded different. Cautious, defeated. "I have a proposition for you."

"I'm not in the mood to negotiate — "

"Marry me," he blurted.

No. Cael coughed, shooting a pleading glance upward. He reached for Elio's boot. Touched it, barely. Elio did not look at him.

Bracken tilted his head.

"The agreement between our houses promises a union. Consequence for Cael Volkov's corporal crime will annul our previous commitment, and as acting High Lord and first-born to House Henly, I remain obligated to fulfil the duty outlined by Alexander Henly and Harlyn Volkov. That being said, I offer you my hand." Elio paused, extending his palm toward Ulrich, telling the commander to stand down.

Every word cut like glass, stripping Cael to the bone.

Elio leveled Bracken with a narrow glare. "I can negotiate with the Imperium. I'm friendly with Angelina Darvin of Draitune, and my word will carry more credibility than Lorelei's. This is my birthright, not my sister's. I alone can corroborate Griea's presence on Aurethia, advocate for Cael Volkov's sentencing, and embolden my people to trust a redistribution of power. If you kill me *and* Cael, my death and his execution will only spur the Imperium to intervene. You and I both know that."

A hush fell over the battlefield. Behind Bracken, the Royal Reserve stood at attention, row after row, waiting. Behind Elio, the rest of the militia glanced around, breathing hard. The storm pummeled the city. Blood followed the bumpy stone. Cael shook his head. When he breathed, coppery wetness bubbled in his chest, splattering the roof of his mouth. His thumb dug into the soft side of Elio's muddy boot.

In the end, Elio Henly would save his people. Cael always knew this to be true.

"You would make a powerful duke," Bracken said. He tossed Lorelei.

The princess crumbled and skittered behind Ulrich, swiping meanly at her mouth.

Elio's knuckles whitened. "Where is my brother, Lord Orson?"

"Safe."

"Is my general alive? Peadar Mahone?" Elio asked.

Bracken considered the question. "He's being held at the manor."

"I offer you my hand in exchange for the following," Elio said. The musculature of his throat dented prettily. His jaw flexed. Cael saw the turmoil cross his face, ever slight and well-hidden, but plain to anyone who knew him. He blinked, dislodging a stray tear. Green eyes hardened. "Release Lord Orson and Peadar Mahone into my custody. Peadar will see to the manor alongside my sister, Lorelei Henly, who will enter the Xenobiology Division on Aurethia, cementing our commitment to every aspect of our great-grandparent's legacy. She will serve as my regent on Aurethia, unharmed and under the safe protection of our mother planet, Draitune." When Lorelei started forward, Elio flashed his hand, silencing her.

The warlord inclined his head. Intrigue lifted the corner of his lips. "Go on."

"The warship and all Griean offensive are to be moved into high orbit."

"Understood."

Elio swallowed again. His mouth peeled apart. "In order to earn the respect and endearment of Griea's citizenship and cement my position to the Imperium, I will be the one to execute Cael Volkov in the Griean Tupinaire. Not only for treason against your house, but for his betrayal against mine."

Cael hiccupped on a silent sob. His heart collapsed. *At least it will be you.*

Lorelei gasped. Pitchy and shaky, she exclaimed, "No," but it did not matter. Her brother hardly flinched.

"Do you accept, Imperator Volkov?" Elio asked in perfect Griean. His tongue darted out to catch a tear, and he lifted his chin, staring through Bracken Volkov the same way he might an unpleasant illusion. Something horrible hallucinated in the deep night, blinked away after waking, pondered on in the daylight. A nightmare made true.

Cael did not look at him, could not look at anything except Elio, but he heard his cousin smile.

"I do, High Lord. I do."

CHAPTER FORTY-THREE
ELIO

Lorelei struck Elio with her open palm.

The storm passed overhead, crawling toward the crater, and Elio stood in the courtyard of Atreyu, stranded one hour in the past.

Every time he tried to move, the moon's axis seemed to spin backward, rewinding to Cael's expression as he was hauled to his feet. The soft, gradual sadness frothing up over his face hardly touched his ice-blue eyes. His wet lashes fluttered, and he nodded at Elio, leeched of every ounce of fight. Before he could speak, if he would've spoken at all, a Griean soldier muzzled him with a silver contraption, locking the metal cover over his chin and mouth. Bracken's men took him away, and the warlord wearing Cael's stolen title looked down at Elio with a certain fondness the High Lord had never anticipated.

When Bracken said, "The warship will be in high orbit by this evening. I'll leave a Griean entourage to facilitate the transfer of Lord Orson and Peadar Mahone and see you to the ice giant alongside our enterprise. With your permission, we'll collect our dead, streamlining those who opted for the Augment program. I'm willing to enter the fallen Aurethian militia into said program with your clearance."

Bile burned Elio's throat. "None of these people agreed to augmentation, Imperator," he said, controlling his tone.

Bracken took up his helmet and tucked it under his arm. The claymore he'd jammed through Vik lined his spine. "Heard," he said, and walked away, following Cael's handlers.

An hour later, Elio still couldn't move. His cheek stung where Lorelei's palm connected with bare skin. Draitune's ring glowed behind what remained of the storm. Finally, the emotional turmoil cementing him in place gave way. His immediate response was to cough, then retch, keeling over to dry heave.

Lorelei grasped his shoulder. Her hand glided his forehead, swiping his hair away. "What've you done, Elio?" She held him when he heaved again, stomach convulsing around nothing. He spat at the stone. "You can't possibly — "

"I'm doing what must be done," he said. Reality finally tilted into place. He sniffled and whipped around, searching for Vik. "Did the Avarine work?"

"The what?" Lorelei asked, bewildered.

Elio tapped his dialect device. "Vik?"

Lord Henly, Vik's worn voice crackled through his device, Amina is currently mending my organic tissue. However, my internal cybernetic configuration is damaged. I'm afraid I'll need — adjusted in Machina unless you have an augmentation specialist — Atreyu who can — me.

Relief washed over him. "I'm sure we can find someone."

"What must be done? Killing Cael in cold blood after he defended our homeworld," Lorelei deadpanned. "That's the solution?"

"I need you to trust me." He met her gaze. Touched his device again. "Vik, did you manage to send a message to Xander?"

I attempted to send Outpost One a transmission. Given the — my hardware, delivery — — uncertain.

Lorelei furrowed her brow. She mouthed Xander's name confusedly. "Elio, please," she barked, impatient and frazzled. "I feel like you've tossed me through a jump gate." A whimper grew in her throat, snuffed out by a frustrated grunt. "You just..." She threw her arm toward the broken gate. "You just gave yourself to Bracken Volkov! Tell me what's going on, tell me how we'll see this through, tell me — "

"I will tell you everything," Elio assured, raising his voice. His interior felt loose and detached. Every bone seemed to float, suddenly weightless. He sucked in a breath and scrubbed a hand over his mouth, hyperaware of the stapled gash on his thigh, and the corpses stiffening in the courtyard.

He couldn't think. Could barely breathe. He turned and strode toward

Gyana who directed him to a makeshift meeting point inside a nearby inn. The building was dark but intact. What remained of the Aurethian militia collected the dead, tended to surface wounds, and rested. Ulrich Walsh paused halfway through giving orders to a group in the lobby and nodded at Elio.

"Is Vik here?" Elio asked.

"Endresen was taken to the square to be tended with the rest of the injured. We're using this building as a directory," Ulrich said. He stared at Elio, searching his face.

"How whole are we?"

"The civilians are safe. We lost a third of our militia." The commander paused. His mouth pressed into a grim, white line. "We should go over what's expected, High Lord. Much is in play."

"I need a moment," Elio said, surprised he kept himself steady enough to speak.

Ulrich relented, shrugging toward the hallway. "Take the second door on the left."

Elio picked up his feet and walked, carrying himself down the passage and through the doorway.

It took no time at all for residual panic to overwhelm him. He stumbled. The disc-lamp floating near the ceiling illuminated. He hit the tile with a loud thud. Death clung to his clothes. Blood, membrane, tissue. He heard Cael's voice on a maddening loop. *You are my fate.* The cacophony of battle plagued him. Steel clashing. People crying out. Gunfire and breakage. He curled into a heap on the floor, smashing the heel of each palm against his ears. He didn't know how long he stayed like that, trembling and weeping alone. He didn't hear the door open, or register the weight of fast footsteps, or notice the soft, misshapen sob float into the room with him. Not until his sister laid down beside him and pried at his arms, clawing him open like an abalone.

"Come here," she demanded, voice watery and weak.

Lorelei wrapped around him, tucking herself against his bloodstained armor, holding his salt-streaked face. For a moment, they were children again. Orphaned, damned, beaten, grieving. In an empty inn, curled together on the slated tile, Elio and Lorelei held each other and endured the miserable, ugly weight of their fallen house.

THE HENLY MANOR SQUATTED on the horizon, toy-like and faraway. Elio rested his temple against the curved glass of the hovertrain's window and watched his home grow closer. Across from him, Vik occupied an upholstered seat. The damage to his cybernetic inlay caused one pupil to remain blown. The other shrank to the size of a pin. The bandage underneath his shirt wrapped from his pelvis to his collarbone, concealing the silvery scar forming above his bellybutton.

"Placing Lorelei in the Xenobiology Division and reinstating Aurethia's commitment to the crater's biodiversity initiative was an apt choice," Vik said, clearing his throat. "Have you told her about Outpost One?"

Elio nodded. "I told her some. Xander will show her the rest."

Vik remained quiet, big hands clasped neatly in his lap. The hovertrain crested a small hill, dotted with the beginning of the orchard. "You're lucky Bracken didn't have an Augment with him, Elio," Vik muttered. He shifted his eyes, meeting the slight flick of Elio's sharp gaze. He closed his mouth. His voice, dimmer than usual and scratchy with feedback, came through his dialect device. `He would've known you were lying.`

The comment left Elio uncomfortably exposed. He shifted in his seat, pulling at the webbing between his fingers. "I didn't have a choice."

`You were reckless.`

"What else would you have me do?" Elio set his teeth. He stared at Vik, watching the Augment study him like a caged animal.

"Taking the fight to Griea could cost you your life," Vik whispered.

"And letting the fight continue on Aurethia would've cost me my sister, my husband, and my house. Forgive me for entertaining a different strategy."

"Do you have a plan?"

Elio glanced away. "I'm figuring it out."

`Arrival: Nadhas, Aurethia. Welcome to the mercantile of the forest moon. For travel information, please visit the village directory.`

"You're figuring it out," Vik repeated. Disbelief infected each word. He laughed slightly, running his hand through his hair. "You're figuring it out," he said again, faster, quieter, and shook his head. "Good. Perfect."

He ignored the Augment's justified concern and stood, grasping the back of each empty seat as he made his way to the rear of the train-car. Lorelei curled into a chair, head propped on a wadded coat, body tucked together like a lanky puzzle. Nara peered at him from her place in the aisle. Elio gave his sister's shoulder a small shake.

Lorelei woke with a start. Her eyes flashed open, and she went rigid, bolting to stand.

Elio kept her firmly in place. "No, hey, it's me, it's okay — you're fine. We're home."

Her nostrils flared, but she settled, shooting a glance out the floor-to-ceiling window before turning her attention back to him. She'd traded her armor for a cream sweater and corduroy trousers and looked much more herself with her hair tumbling about. "Is the warship gone?"

"It's in high orbit." The massive spacecraft was much too large to disappear entirely. It loomed far, far above, hanging in the sky like a newly minted moon.

"Okay," she breathed out, blinking away the last sip of sleep. She glanced at Nara and deflated.

The hovertrain rocked to a slow halt. Gravity suspension cut out and the vehicle settled on the ground. Its transparent door floated open.

Elio stared at the exit. His mouth dried. He didn't realize how uneasy he would feel, confronting what used to be. The manor had always been his home. Safe, secure. It was different now, seeing the lonely house, seemingly unchanged — surrounded by the sprawling orchard, flanked by the domed terrarium — and knowing his mother and father would not be waiting inside.

The Aurethian guard appointed by Ulrich to see them safely home came around from the front train-car. There were six in total, armed with Aurethian steel and wearing easily identifiable armor. They stood at attention on the other side of the exit, waiting for the High Lord to step out.

Despite the anxiety stuffing Elio's skull like wool, he managed to straighten his spine and exit the hovertrain. Ozone sicked the air. He sniffed, searching for pear and apple, brine and seaweed, but it was all smoke and bleach. The grass in the meadow was printed with oddly shaped patches, flattened by the Royal Reserve's groundcrafts and camping gear. The native pastel finches and pink-breasted pigeons were nowhere to be seen, but a vulture veered off from its cohort and winged toward the courtyard.

It took such little time for a place brimming with life to become a cemetery.

Elio swallowed to wet his throat. Beside him, Lorelei stared at their childhood home.

My internal scanner is not operational, but I ha— detected four people approaching from the manor. The Augment tilted his head, staring at the road. Two are in Griean-black, High Lord. If I'm not mistaken, one — Operative Carr.

Elio palmed the scabbard clipped to his waist. "Lorelei," he warned, keeping his tone low. "This is probably the hand-off. I need you to stay calm."

"I'm perfectly calm," she said.

Nara padded out of the train and shook her furry head. She sat on her haunches next to Lorelei, staring at the figures in the distance. As the group got closer, Elio identified Maxine's scant build. Orson held the liaison's hand. Beside her, the other Griean — Kindra, if memory served — accompanied Peadar. The Aurethian General walked with a slight limp, and his right arm was cradled in a cloth sling. Elio's breath caught. For as long as he could remember, Peadar had been a fixture in his routine. Right hand to his father; protector of his mother. Friend and confidant. Practical strategist and valorous fighter. Seeing him beaten down, almost dragging his feet, made Elio's heart squeeze painfully in his chest.

Maxine slowed to a stop a few feet away from the last Aurethian guard. She lifted her chin, staring at Elio through long, painted lashes. Orson yanked away from her and ran forward. The smallest Henly slammed into Elio's waist, grappling for him.

Kindra inclined her head politely. Her dark gossamer gown pooled around her ankles. "High Lord Henly, Operative Carr and I are here at the will of Imperator Volkov. He has offered you the rest of this evening, tomorrow, and the next night to deal with your dead. He expects you'll be fit to travel the following morning. Will you be journeying with company?"

"I'll bring my Griean Augment, Vik Endresen," Elio said.

The woman glanced at Vik and narrowed her eyes. She placed one slender finger on her dialect device and lowered her voice, speaking fast. After a moment, she gave a slow, understanding nod. "The Imperator is delighted to know Vik Endresen survived the altercation in Atreyu. He is welcome to accompany you."

Lorelei bent to kiss the top of Orson's head, then straightened and stretched out her arm, waving Peadar forward. "Peadar," she eked out, clearing the emotion from her voice. "Come now, let's go."

"Where's Mom?" Orson whined.

Cold dread shot down Elio's spine. He held onto Orson, staring hard at Maxine. The liaison's throat worked slowly. She blinked, dislodging a stubborn tear, and quickly smacked it away.

Beside him, Lorelei's face blotched red. She gaped, jaw trembling. "Oh, you coward," she seethed. She inched in front of Orson, blocking him with her arm. "How dare you, Maxine."

"I did him a kindness," Maxine said. She locked her body and raised her head, exuding fake strength. Her leather armor fit tightly, but it did nothing to conceal the tremor running from her clavicles to her ankles. "Darius and Lena have been relocated to a platform in the garden."

"You're a heartless bitch," Lorelei snapped.

Maxine flinched. Another stray tear curved down her cheek.

Kindra Malkin arched her scarred brow. She stepped backward, tipping her jaw toward Elio, Lorelei, and their guardship. "Peadar Mahone, you're free to go." Peadar walked forward, grasped by Elio, then Lorelei, and pulled in close. When Maxine turned to leave, Kindra clucked her tongue. "Operative Carr, you're to remain moon-side as the acting liaison," she said, as if Maxine should've known better. "The Imperator gave the order in accordance with the recently reevaluated unification agreement."

Maxine halted. She prickled like a hare. Her hands clenched into shaky fists, and she turned around, blinking rapidly. "I don't believe I'm fit — "

"Imperator Volkov believes you are," Kindra interjected. She glanced between Maxine and the Henly family. "High Lord Henly, feel free to load any necessary belongings onto the transport prior to departure. Holland Lancaster and his team will be accompanying you and your entourage to the warship in high orbit. I expect our liaison to be kept comfortable." With that, the mysterious, ginger-haired woman walked away, unbothered by the armed Aurethian guardship at her back. She lifted her skirt and followed the road toward the cliffside launch bay and disappeared through a Grean ship's open loading dock.

"Max, you're not leaving, right?" Orson asked, sniffling. He turned to glance at the liaison.

Maxine painted on a practiced smile. "No, young lord," she said, hushed, concealing fright, "I'm not going anywhere."

"Where's everyone else? Did they get Cael?"

A stone grew in Elio's throat. "We have a lot to talk about, Orson. Let's go inside."

Before they could begin their short trek to the manor, Lorelei stormed forward. Nara perked, hardening her stance. The Aurethian guardship turned in the direction Lorelei walked. Maxine did not move, but she gasped, face seized by the Henly princess. Lorelei's bruised and bandaged fingers dented Maxine's jaw, pushing in on either side of her mouth.

"Lor," Elio warned. He shielded Orson, covering his face. Their brother had lost enough. Maxine, regardless of her betrayal, had been his only tether to normalcy during a time of utter instability. Cutting down who he recognized as his friend, someone he trusted, would only inflict more damage.

"Lady Henly," Peadar said. His rocky voice was unchanged. The familiarity gave Elio a deep sense of comfort. The general continued. "We have more important matters to deal with. This issue can wait."

Lorelei's venomous glare darkened. "You'll pay for the role you played, Operative Carr." She tossed Maxine's face away, causing her head to snap back. Her attention shifted to the nearest Aurethian guard. "Remove her holotablet and personal device. She's to be kept in her bedchamber, pending investigation under Aurethian law," the princess growled, granting Maxine a severe, lingering look. "If she's needed, we'll come to her. The house staff will deliver adequate nutrition, and off-world correspondence will be strictly monitored."

"Understood, High Lady," the guard said.

Orson wailed, "Where is everyone? Where's Mom? Dad? What happened to you," he demanded, squirming away from Elio to look at Peadar. He swung toward Lorelei. "You're not the High Lady!" His mouth trembled. He knuckled at his face and hiccupped, glancing between the siblings. "You're not," he whimpered, shaking his head, "you're not, are you? You can't be, you're not — "

All the anger washed out of Lorelei. "Orson, it's all right — "

Orson yelled, "Don't say that, don't lie to me!"

"It is, it will be, I promise — "

He stood on his tiptoes, pitching himself toward her. "You left!"

"I had to," she yelped out, trying not to cry.

"Where is everybody? I want Mom, I want — "

"They're gone," she shouted, snapping like a twig beneath a heavy boot.

Orson's tantrum fizzled, replaced by dreadful silence.

Elio winced. "Lorelei Darragh," he scolded under his breath. He met her frantic, apologetic gaze, and knelt, taking his brother by the cheek. "I'm sorry we left you. I wish she were lying, but she's not, Orson. Until I fix what's broken, Lorelei is the High Lady and I'm the High Lord. We're in charge right now."

"What about Cael? What did he do?" Orson asked.

He opened his mouth to speak, but nothing surfaced. Orson's big green eyes gushed, and he screwed his button mouth into a deep frown. He looked like Lorelei, all stubborn fire and squashed hope. Elio wanted to scrape away his pain and absorb it, but Cael's name in his brother's mouth made everything inside him malfunction.

Lorelei crouched to hug Orson. "I'm sorry," she said, sighing to steady herself, "I'm so sorry. C'mon, hold my hand. Let's go home, okay? We'll make some tea."

"Max," Orson said, reaching out with his other hand.

Lorelei fixed her face and cooed, "She's right there. Look, see? She's here."

Maxine fixed her face, too, and took his other hand.

Nara rumbled and bumped her head against Elio's waist before bounding after Lorelei.

As soon as the trio turned to walk away, Elio's strength crumbled. He held back a sob and fell against Peadar's chest, accepting an awkward, one-armed hug.

"Don't," Peadar soothed, voice low. "Don't give them that, Elio."

"I don't know what to do," he confessed. He reared back and swiped at his leaky nose. How selfish to fall apart when Peadar stood before him in an arm-sling after being held captive. He flapped his hand and gave Peadar a quick once-over. "We need to get you to the med-bay."

Peadar hugged him again. It was a tight, pressing, thankful hold.

Elio steadied himself. "Avarine," he said, and then, "Outpost One. You knew, didn't you? You knew — "

"I knew," the general said, sighing. "I kept the manor in check. Kept communication open. As *open* as possible."

Elio nodded. Yes, of course. He'd thought as much but the truth felt like vindication. It was the only relief Elio had been afforded.

Peadar pulled back and looked down at him. The color of his fierce eyes, oak and browned sugar, seemed deeper in that fragile daylight. "Is Cael dead, Elio?"

Agony drove through him like a slow bullet. "No." He swallowed, ignoring the way Vik watched him, curious and quiet. "But I've agreed to execute him in Machina."

CHAPTER FORTY-FOUR

BRACKEN

urethia is mine.

The thought danced in the deep recesses of Bracken's mind. He stood on the viewing platform outside his cabin, tracing the curved edge of Aurethia's planetary horizon with a swipe of his index across the thick glass. The warship was predominantly windowless, and this particular panel would close up the moment the ship shot into the vast blackness above, but for now, Bracken studied the blueish-green moon from high orbit. Pride rolled in his stomach. He was bloated with it, holding hope like overripe fruit.

Elio Henly's compliance would ease what would've been a complicated transition, and his willingness to bend proved he may be open to reason. Or smart enough to know when resistance was futile. Bracken remembered the young man he faced at the manor on the morning of the siege. The memory grounded him. Reminded him to be frugal with his inclination to celebrate a victory.

"Imperator." The sound of Kindra's heeled shoes tapped the polished floor. She came to stand beside him, following his attention to the forest moon backlit by Draitune. "Peadar Mahone and Orson Henly are under the care of Elio Henly and the Aurethian guard. Holland Lancaster and his squadron are stationed moon-side. They'll accompany the prince to Griea, following our departure."

"How did the prince seem?"

"Broken," she said.

He looked down at her, studying the fine point of her nose. "Broken?"

Her gaze pinched with concentration. She cracked her full mouth open and gave a curt nod. "Yes," she decided, keeping her attention on the window. "I'm not certain I believe him."

"Go on."

"I don't know. I can't place it, really. His heartbreak is so…" She opened and closed her hand. He half-expected something small and winged to flutter from her fist. "Plain," she offered, testing the word, and then shook her head and changed her answer. "Profound," she decided, nodding. "I don't know if he'll go through with it."

"Which part? The unification?"

"Oh no, I believe he'll marry you. If it's for the good of," she gestured flippantly to the moon, "I'm sure he'd do anything. But I don't know if he's a killer."

"He took out my men without blinking, Kindra. He's a deadly swordsman." He lifted his hand, displaying the scar knotted beneath his middle knuckle. "I've seen it myself, and knowing Cael, Elio likely spent the last cycle being trained by a Griean Imperator. Don't underestimate him."

Kindra tipped her head. "Yes, but do you think he'll survive on the ice with a Griean Imperator?" She turned, eyeing him through oil-slick lashes.

"I watched Cael fight for him. Elio will survive regardless of his skill."

"You're probably right."

Bracken set his hand on her back. "Kasimir's augmentation is going well," he said, breaching the subject carefully. It was a brutal, touchy thing, talking about the resurrection of her brother. "I assigned him our best technician."

Kindra's lips tightened. She remained poised, but he recognized the flash of pain fissuring her jaw. She cleared her throat. "Good," she quipped, offering a frail smile. "Will he retain his memory bank?"

"Into the ninety percentile," he assured. She visibly relaxed. He thumbed her cheekbone, soothing whatever doubt might linger beneath the surface. "You've been invaluable to me during this conquest and so has your brother. Without you, I doubt I would've found the courage to do what needed to be done."

Sometimes, rarely, Bracken glimpsed the true woman behind the savvy wraith he brought to his bed. Kindra Malkin, ever the seductress, with her many faces and many motives, softened, melting against him like an alley cat let in from the cold. She brought her arms around his middle and rested her chin on his sternum, staring up at him.

"You're about to become a married man," she rasped, hardly audible. "Elio is easy to look at. I doubt you'll need my services once he's in your bed."

Bracken couldn't stop the laugh. It jerked in his throat, echoing through the warship's dormitory. "I doubt the lion of Aurethia will allow me anywhere near his bed, and mine is already occupied. He can join, but it'll be a bit crowded."

Kindra hummed. "That's not in our contract, Imperator."

For a moment, he couldn't tell whether she was teasing or not. He furrowed his brow, met with Kindra's liquid smile. Before he could press her for a true answer, an electronic voice came through his dialect device.

Imperator Volkov, Legatus Marcus and Duchess Constance will see you now. Please report to the Lodging Module on Level Three. He silenced the device with a tap.

"I'll name you my strategist," he said, bending to kiss her.

"No one will allow a whore to advise House Volkov," she breathed out.

Bracken pulled back to meet her gaze. "And who would move against me? Who would question Griea's next Legatus?"

Kindra swallowed. Something like hope weeded her expression. "Do not play with me, Bracken."

He pressed his mouth to the scar on her forehead and stepped away, untangling from the courtesan he would shape into a concubine. The woman who had taunted and tempted him to glory. "Do not doubt me," he said, lifting a brow. "One day, Griea will call you Singer of Serpents, Kindra Malkin. You'll be Hand of the Legatus, Kingmaker." He paused to watch her smile return, true and bewildered, before she stowed her hope away, same as him, and frosted over.

"Careful, Imperator. You're starting to sound smitten."

Bracken matched her smile before striding away.

The Level Three Lodging Module was clear across the ship. Halfway there, he wanted to turn around and go back to Kindra. Sneak away to his cabin and get lost in her for a while. But he knew better than to ignore a request from Marcus. Especially now, especially with everything slotting into place.

As he weaved through the belly of the ship, Bracken answered friendly hoots from the Royal Reserve and bowed his head to a few soldiers who greeted him. Relief unspooled in the familiar space. Most of the Reserve were ready to go home, to put the battle for Aurethia behind them and turn toward a brighter future. Bracken couldn't blame them. He missed his reindeer. Missed watching snow blow across the ice. The taste of spiced stew and Griean whiskey.

Aurethia was charming, but it would never be *home*.

An elevator dropped him one level down and opened onto a metal platform. From there, he took a long, well-lit hall to the private wing in the Lodging Module where he found Legatus Marcus and Duchess Constance seated at a round table. A holotablet rested between them, displaying a copy of the original unification agreement set forth by Alexander and Harlyn.

"Legatus," Bracken greeted, inclining his head. He sketched a short bow. "Duchess."

"You agreed to terms without consulting me," Marcus said.

Every shred of Bracken's hoarded happiness soured. He breathed deeply and tongued at his cheek. "I made a judgment call, Legatus. Marrying Elio Henly will keep the galactic unification intact, and his support will placate the Imperial Court. Preserving his life will allow us to bypass an imperial investigation into Cael's prosecution, streamline our planetary merger, quell any rising animosity on Aurethia, and secure an heir. I saw his acquiescence as an unobstructed way forward."

Marcus struck his palms. The hard clap bounced around the room. "And you think taking his sister as a suitable bride would've proved too difficult?"

"Difficult, no. But complicated. Elio's death could potentially spur the Imperium to intervene in our effort. Keeping him alive and at my side will avoid that, sir. He can rectify what was said in Lorelei Henly's transmission and vocally support our cause. He's the key to a seamless acquisition of Aurethia and the Lux Continuum, I'm sure of it."

"And you stranded our liaison," Constance added. She stared at him through a translucent grey mourning veil.

"Stationing Operative Carr at the manor is a test, Duchess. I'd like to see if Elio will keep his composure and respect our presence in his home, or if he'll lash out and risk the deal he struck with me in Atreyu. It's a gesture of good faith and an extension of trust," Bracken said.

"Not everyone has an uncontrollable temper, Bracken," Constance scolded. She rubbed her thumb against the pad of each scrawny finger. "Some people compose themselves well enough to hide their motive in plain sight."

The jab was personal, blatantly noting Bracken's strategy in Nadhas, and the untimely death of Lena Henly. Bracken pushed his feet hard against the soles of his bootwear, locking himself in place. *Stay calm.* "I can't speak to his motive, Duchess, but I doubt he would travel to Griea if he planned to renege."

"And why would he come to Griea in the first place?"

"Elio Henly has asked to execute Cael in the arena during the Tupinaire. After Cael's trial is over, their marriage will be officially annulled, and I'll take his hand."

Constance bristled. Her hand dropped, flattening against the table. "Absolutely not," she snarled, glancing from Bracken to Marcus. "He is our son. He is heir to the throne, Keeper of the Basilisk. We will not shame our house and his name by parading him through the arena like a common criminal."

Bracken slid his attention to the Legatus.

Marcus remained trapped in thought. After a moment, he cocked his head. "Your method is sound, Imperator." He paused, flashing his palm at Constance when she opened her mouth to speak. "Cael betrayed our house and disgraced his name. He did that on his own."

Constance raised her voice. "You sent our child on a mission to secure a moon and he succeeded — "

"His weakness was an infection," Marcus said, matching her ire. "And he secured nothing. Not a single mine, not a shred of trade intel, *nothing.* He laid down with a lion and forgot who we raised him to be."

"I did not raise a monster," she said, low, hissed. "You tried to shape him into a failing archetype, Marcus. What you wanted Cael to be would've cost us everything, and what you've created in spite of his effort might still destroy us."

"His effort?" Marcus scoffed. His palm struck the table hard, jostling it. Constance hardly flinched. In a blink, Legatus Marcus shook off his role as father and husband, and hardened into the iron-fisted leader Bracken had always known his uncle to be. "Cael Volkov made his choice. He enabled this with his foolish heart and sealed his fate when he turned his blade on his own people. He will face his consequence in the arena, during a fair trial-by-combat where he will win or lose his life." He lifted his face, staring at Bracken. "Have we sent a transmission to the Imperial Court announcing Elio's annulment and subsequent engagement?"

"Not yet, Legatus," Bracken said.

"Get it done."

Bracken leveled Constance with a heated look. Her pinched mouth trembled. She exhaled hard through her nose. They stayed like that, sizing each other up, testing the thorny resistance of their opposition, until Bracken's mouth lifted, and he inclined his head again.

"Yes, Legatus. God is in the water."

THE HOLDING CABIN BUILT into the warship's undercarriage served as an interstellar security wing. It bumped up against the hangar where Griean groundcrafts were parked in neat rows and terrestrial spacecrafts hung from mechanical perches built into the curved interior, holding each ship like a finger extended for a bird.

Two Royal Reserve stood outside the steel door leading to Cael's cabin. They stepped aside as Bracken approached, greeting him in unison.

"Imperator." They both dipped their heads.

"Take a break." Bracken pointed over his shoulder with his thumb.

"We're on shift, sir," one of them said.

"And now *I'm* here." He offered a reassuring nod. "I'll only be a few minutes."

The pair exchanged glances and then walked away, chatting under their breath.

Bracken stood at the door for a heartbeat. His palm hovered over the keypad. He steadied his breathing, counting the seconds on each inhale, *one, two, three*, and every exhale, *one, two, three*. He needed to send a transmission to the Imperial Council. Ready the Royal Reserve for their return to Griea. Contact the staff at the Volkov castle about their impending arrival. He had one hundred tasks that did not involve this visit, but he could not complete a single one until he spoke to the man on the other side of that door.

The keypad beeped dully, and the heavy lock slid. A red bulb flashed above the thick grey frame. The door unsealed, floating open.

Across the sparsely furnished cabin, Cael sat on a basic bunk, elbows resting on his thighs, one hand cupped around his nape. He glanced to the side and scanned Bracken. His face remained placid, struck through with mean grooves. It was still shocking to see Cael's milky eye. Half his face wore the memory of a lion's claw. Part of Bracken wanted to take his chin and turn Cael left then right. Check him over for damage like he used to after a match in the arena. Another part of him wanted to slip a tincture of poison into a cup and let his cousin die peacefully in his sleep. The smallest, weakest part of him wanted to walk away, leave the door open, and give Cael the opportunity to run.

"Hey," Cael said, as if they were back home, sharing the kitchen in the Volkov castle. Like he'd slid into a barstool beside him at one of their favorite pour houses. His voice lacked charm or malice. He spoke sadly, like someone roused from a bad dream.

Bracken walked inside and leaned against the wall across from Cael's bed. He crossed his arms. "You've looked better."

"I bet," he muttered, lifting his face.

"Did the medic fix you up? What's going on here?" He gestured to his own chest, signaling the bandage covering Cael's upper-half. The rest of him was dressed plainly. Black sweatpants and wool socks.

"Collapsed lung. I'll be fine." Cael knitted his brow.

The security wing hosted a few lockable cabins, small and large, in case an arrest was made during travel or if a prisoner was taken aboard during a mission. Bracken knew about them but never spent much time exploring. The only light in Cael's room came through the viewing panel on the door, basking the floor in a soft white glow. Other than the stark bed he sat on, there was a personal shower and a toilet behind a panel of frosted glass, allowing some semblance of privacy. Nothing else.

"Is Vik okay?" Cael asked.

"The Augment? Shockingly, yes. He survived."

"And Elio?"

"Reunited with his brother at the manor. He'll be joining us shortly."

Cael nodded. A grim smile pulled at his mouth. "Yes, of course. Have you told him about Nadhas yet? How you butchered his people into compliance?"

Slick anger slid down Bracken's spine, but it was the embarrassment that surprised him. All this time he channeled the utmost pride, but alone with Cael, he couldn't feign his way around shame. "I did what I had to do. I doubt it'll matter much in the end — this isn't a love-match."

Cael shook his head. His mouth parted, eyes roaming Bracken's face. He looked confused. Hurt. "You killed children, Bracken. You called for the death of people's grandparents." He sputtered, almost laughing, and gestured from Bracken's feet to his face. "You let my father bend you into an abomination," he exclaimed, horrified. "Don't you get it yet? Following his — "

"That was my order. Aurethia's lack of mindful cooperation forced my hand."

Cael snapped his mouth shut. He gave a faint shake of his head and averted his gaze. "Anger will be the death of you, cousin."

Bracken's heart pounded. He swallowed, trying to clear the white-hot rage currently pressing against the inside of his skull. Bracken would never say it aloud, but Cael was right. It dizzied him, that toxic anger. Made him clumsy. "What did it take?"

Cael sighed.

"No, really. Tell me, Cael. Was it the fruitful nature of Aurethia? Was it Elio's heart, his mind, his voracity, or was it a grab for power? Did you think you could skirt your responsibility after spending a cycle in his bedroom, becoming his lapdog?"

"Yes," he said. He teethed at his lip. The sudden acceptance made Bracken pause. Made his chest pang uncomfortably. Cael continued. "I went to the forest moon expecting to fulfill my duty to House Volkov and make my father proud. I was going to collect data, seduce the heir, and crush House Henly under my boot." His voice hardened, each word faster, harsher than the last. He took a breath and slowed. "But I'm a heartsick fool, I guess. I wanted to find a peaceful resolution to a centuries long conflict, and I wanted to do so because I fell in love. Does that make me a traitor?"

Bracken swallowed. "Withholding vital information made you a traitor. Turning your blade on *me* made you a traitor. Compromising a twenty-year operation in favor of Aurethian interest made you a traitor. You did this, Cael."

"I didn't turn you into whatever you've become," he said. His bitter smile deepened. "Waiting until the battle in Atreyu exhausted the Aurethian militia? Weak shit, Bracken."

"That was strategy," he said, snorting. They might as well have been at the War College, bantering about the right way to position a squadron or how to make the best use of certain weaponry. "Weak shit," he echoed, laughing under his breath. "I'm not the one who threw away my future for a pretty Aurethian princeling. A prince who sacrificed you to protect his sister, I might add."

"No, you're throwing away everyone's future in the name of stolen valor."

The anger clogging his skull grew dense and heavy, anchored by something close to grief, wrought with tenderness. His love for Cael felt like the membrane on the inside of a cooked egg, sticking to the shell as it was peeled away, taking a bit of himself with it. He heaved in a big breath and stared at the dark ceiling. Silence festered between them.

"I've seen Elio fight," Bracken said, softly now. "In a fair match, he would not beat you."

"But he will." Cael sighed, resigned.

Bracken's mouth tightened. "I would've followed you to greatness," he confessed, rushing the declaration out like it burned. And it did. It was a painful, wretched thing to say as he occupied the place Cael should've stood, carrying the title Cael should've kept. "I taught you discipline for a reason. I taught you control, I taught you resilience, I taught you strength. I did not want this, Cael."

Cael was quiet for a long, drawn moment. He studied Bracken, flicking his attention around the Imperator's tense face. "Will you miss me, cousin?"

"I miss you already. I've missed you since I realized we'd lost you."

He laughed in his throat. "But you'll send me to my death?"

"That was your beloved's wish."

"Funny. You ask what did it, what swayed me, yet you're already succumbing to Elio's will." He cocked his head. "Lie to me all you want, Bracken, but you and I both know the truth... The lost heir, returning to claim the throne his father renounced." He clucked his tongue, saddling Bracken with a sarcastic smile. "I'm no fool, and neither are our people. They'll see right through your charade, same as me."

Bracken's set jaw ached. He could not deny it, though.

"You could've followed me to greatness," he whispered, glaring into Bracken's narrowed eyes. "But you took it for yourself instead."

Stay steady. Don't break. "You're young. It's a shame you won't be given the chance to outgrow this naivety, but I assure you, a new era for Griea will rise under my leadership. Take solace knowing Elio will get to see it, too."

At that, Cael's practiced calm finally split. He growled, "We could've avoided bloodshed, Bracken. I could've brokered peace — "

"There is no peace," Bracken shouted. The dull ache in his chest turned to glass, splintering. *What's done is done.* "You flinch at the reality of war, at the sacrifices we make to secure a future for Griea. That's the difference between us. I'll spill as much blood as I have to while you beg for table scraps from the enemy. I'll never bow to an Aurethian, I'll never blink at the price we pay to undo what's been done to us. Their greed is a noose and I'm happy to tie it." He stopped, gathering a lurching breath. "You think they would've listened to a single thing you had to say? A Griean warlord? A barbarian? No, Cael. They would've made you soft, adorned you in gold, and leashed you to the manor like an exotic pet."

The happy, cocky young man who used to throw his grievances at Bracken's feet, and knuckle him for advice, and race him through the gauntlet, was like a specter inhabiting unfamiliar skin.

Cael's voice gave out, fragile and defeated. "You're exactly what my father wanted me to become. I'm sure you'll make him proud."

Bracken's face went numb. His eyes stung and his mouth felt loose and unreliable. He needed to leave before the tiny cinder that still believed in Cael, still questioned his own authority, blew into his chest and flared. "Have you forgotten who you are, Cael Volkov?"

Cael gave him a vicious glance. He didn't answer.

Bracken could think of more to say. He could stay in the security wing, fighting with Cael, becoming the villain in a skewed story. But the truth didn't matter anymore. His truth. Cael's truth. No matter who they'd been before Cael left for Aurethia, who they were in the aftermath of his absence would change their homeworld forever. Would change the Greater Universe forever.

Bracken crossed the cabin. The door floated open again. He waited, hoping Cael might speak, but the Griean prince remained silent.

CHAPTER FORTY-FIVE

CAEL

Weight redistribution caused the warship to rumble. The gravity suspension drive kicked into gear, leveling out the ship as it idled in high orbit. Cael listened to the mechanism come to life. Heard the subtle shift of industrial belts flexing around steel and plastic, holding vehicles strapped down in the hanger in their respective places. He stared at the flat ceiling. His chest convulsed around an inhale, thinning until it cut short. The hollow syringe the medic had jammed between his centermost ribs left a sore spot on his side. He rubbed at it, remembering the way wind whistled out of the rubber tube.

It hurt. Everything hurt. But no physical ailment would wound him worse than his own memories.

I will be the one to execute Cael Volkov.

Cael swallowed thickly. He tried not to think about the future. A future he would never see. But it intruded on him, this life Elio would live without him. It pieced itself together like a septic daydream. He thought of Elio's voice fading over time, going quiet when it mattered most. What his child might look like, molded in Bracken's shadow, imbued with Elio's courage. Aurethia losing its blue halo. Alice being extracted, maybe harvested to death. Griea — funneled with wealth, an engorged tick suckling at a murdered host — depleting the Greater Universe at the will of their Legatus. Bracken going mad, losing himself to the prospect of power.

Hell was a myth. An Earthen tool used to instill fear. Cael never imagined connecting the concept of it to anything real. But this, what Bracken might do, would itself become a kind of hell. A sort of miracle in reverse.

The breath he took lodged at the bottom of his functional lung. He exhaled too quickly. A sharp, stabbing pain came and went. It'd been a long time since Cael felt fragile, but lying on that cot in the empty cabin, he recognized the delicate tug on his sternum, warning him to be careful.

He closed his eyes and thought about Thanjō. Went back in time and planted himself firmly in an Aurethian summer. Candlebell on Elio's mouth, and the pride bounding through the meadow. Honey-soaked fruit piled with cream and salt. Elio kissing the top of his spine, touching him slowly, drawing pleasure into a lasting, languid thing while Sunder's balmy light warmed the windowpane in Cael's bedchamber. Blue and silver glittering across the top of the pool inside the Avara mine. The tiny line shadowing Elio's brow as he hunched over a book in the library and concentrated on a transcription.

Cael missed his dialect device. The Royal Reserve confiscated it after the battle for Atreyu, but if he still had it, he could replay certain moments, hear Elio's voice again, backtrack through a cycle of experiences.

Dying seemed like a distant dream. Not close enough to feel real yet, but near enough to stoke curiosity. For a long time, Cael delivered death without hesitation. Knowing he would face it at the end of Elio's blade made the act itself seem more intimate. He could accept that. It would mean something, dying during the Tupinaire, gracing Elio's Grabak with the blood they'd shared in a ceremonial chalice. He hoped Elio remembered to drop his body beneath the ice. He hoped the basilisk swallowed him whole and didn't tear him in two. Then he'd travel into the belly of a mighty beast and make his way to Wonder.

In another life, maybe he would hatch on an ice shelf at the base of Goren and slither into the sea. Or maybe he would wake as an Aurethian stag or enter his next incarnation as an Ocurian mantis. He hoped Elio lived long enough to meet him when he returned, new and different.

The hot, wet slide of saltwater streaked his temple. *I'm not ready to die.* It was a cowardly, childish thought, but ever present, wholly true.

The cabin door unlatched and slid open. Dusky light from the disc-lamp in the hanger ribboned the figure in the doorway. He knew her immediately. His mother stepped inside, draped in an inky veil, wearing a floor-length gown the color of cranberry wine. She lifted the knitted fabric away from her face and walked into the darkness, perching on the edge of his bed. When he curled close to her, she welcomed his head on her lap, and brought her hand to his stubbly skull, tracing the tattoo stamped into his skin.

"What time is it?" Cael asked. There was no way for him to know. No window to look through, no clock to glance at.

"It's midnight on Aurethia. You've been here for two days," Constance said. She cradled the back of his head.

"I'm sorry."

"Be specific."

"For compromising the mission. For not stating my intention sooner. For making you doubt me — "

"I don't doubt you." Her long, narrow face and cutting mouth seemed harsher in the dark. "Your father is a complicated man, Cael. He raised you to be what he couldn't be, and I raised you to be what he wouldn't be. I should've been more forthcoming with you, but I hoped you'd be a little more like him and a little less like me when it came to this planetary conquest. It was an unfair, foolish expectation to put on you."

Cael inhaled deeply, resisting the urge to cough when his sore chest spasmed. "It was a fair expectation. I've been training for this since I could walk."

"No, not that siege itself. How I thought you'd approach it."

He blinked up at her, crinkling his brow.

"When I told you to secure the bloodline, I imagined you might move into the Henly manor with the intent to manipulate it. I thought you'd charm your way through Aurethia. Root yourself into the Henly heir's life and make yourself indispensable."

"Elio," he gentled. "His name is Elio."

Constance sighed. "Elio," she lamented, then continued. "I didn't expect you to…" She shifted her jaw, breathing slowly. "I thought you would move strategically, that's all."

"I didn't think I would love him either."

"But you do."

Cael's eyes burned. Tears sprung there, blurring his vision. "Yeah," he croaked, clearing his throat. "I do." He resigned himself. "I did move strate-gically. To the best of my abilities, on my life, I *did*. When it came down to it, I could mend the damage or exasperate the animosity, and after reviewing Vik's data, I knew the only sustainable path forward prioritized a legitimate union. Something trustworthy and strong. We did that — I had that, Mom."

"The Legatus can't see past his own insecurity. When Bracken came forward and questioned your integrity, Marcus believed the allegation outright, because otherwise he would've had to delay the siege and investigate the claim. He's a dog with a bone, that man. If the outcome did not match what he envisioned, he would break the world to make it so."

"Bracken's allegation wasn't false," Cael said miserably.

"You didn't betray Griea."

"I was raised to be my father's blade. I betrayed him."

Constance shook her head. "You challenged him. There's a difference."

"Expansion will bring us glory. That's what you said to me." He pulled himself upright and sat beside her, watching her tightly held face through the dark. "Will you advocate for a peaceful unification? For Aurethian independence and Griean stability? I know what happened in Nadhas, I've talked to Bracken, I know he's — he's…" Cael couldn't bring himself to say it. His throat closed around the truth. *My cousin lost his soul.* "He will bleed Aurethia dry of Avara, and Griea will suffer the Imperium's scrutiny for centuries to come. With him at the helm, everything we wanted will be lost. Medicine, stronger infrastructure, the starlink. Within a decade, he'll squander it."

"He is… stranded, I think," she said thoughtfully. A deep line fissured her jaw, extending downward from her frown. "I loved him as my own, but I'm afraid the smallest taste of power has made him unrecognizable to me. You were raised with expectation. It grew in you from a young age. But carrying that same weight, unused to the feeling, might've broken something in him. Or unburied something. I can't very well say."

Cael nodded, forcing down the lump scraping his larynx.

She paused for a moment, considering. "Cael, if you die in the arena, I'll no longer be of use to Marcus. The Legatus will find another spouse, sire another heir. If he doesn't kill me, I'll be sent back to Ocury as acting liaison. I'll advocate for the betterment of the Greater Universe, but your father is smart enough to know I'll never rest with you gone." She stopped, opening and shutting her mouth. Her tone dulled. "Our marriage was political. I created a pocket of fondness for him in order to live fully, to conjure some semblance of happiness, but that doesn't mean I loved him. It certainly does not mean he loved me. Without you, I'll no longer be his wife, I'll be mother to a dead son, and it will turn me into someone he won't have the patience to deal with."

Cael and his mother had never talked so simply, so frankly. She always moved gracefully, showing him compassion and love in fleeting moments. A soft kiss to the top of his head or a pat to his cheek. They rarely hugged.

She rarely held him. But as they sat together on the hard cot, Constance took his hand and squeezed.

"You are Keeper of the Basilisk," she whispered, harsh and far more emotional than she'd ever let him witness before. "You are the sole heir of House Volkov. You are an Imperator of Griea, and you came from *me*, Cael. I grew you, I swaddled you, I made you," she bit out, mouth trembling. "You are Griean, and you are Ocurian, and you are *mine*. If you are to be Marcus's blade, be swift and sharp, and do not go gently, but remember that you are my blade, too."

Cael's mouth parted. He shrank, shaking his head. "I can't kill him, I can't — "

Constance took his face and gave him a stern, fierce look. "You are a champion, Cael Volkov. You know the law."

The darkness shuttered as Constance's dialect device pulsed. It glowed faintly, signaling a transmission. She tipped her head to listen. Her body went slack, deflating.

"I love you," she said, hauling him closer. He always knew, but she'd only said it a handful of times. She held the back of his head and kissed his temple. She clung so hard to him that he almost winced.

Cael wanted to crawl back into her lap and make himself small. Go backward in time and become a child again. "Will I see you before the Tupinaire?"

"I don't know," she said. She stood. Her hand brushed his shoulder. Even as she turned away, she hovered over him.

Watching her struggle to leave made Cael think about parenthood, and love, and the primal, animal thing rearing a child unlocked inside a person. What it took to nurture — to plant yourself inside a new thing; upon a thing, imprint your entire self — taxed the body and split the soul. It made love too weak a word.

Constance tore herself away. When she was gone, and the door slid shut, Cael realized his response still lingered unsaid in his mouth. *I love you, too.*

CHAPTER FORTY-SIX

ELIO

The arrow Elio shot into the open sea had landed on the narrow point of the mourning ship's stern. At first the flame seemed invisible, like it might've died on its trip across the water, but then the orange glow spread, and fire engulfed House Henly's funeral carriage. Lorelei had loosed an arrow at the same time, puncturing the center of the longship. The ceremony had been simple, not small. What was left of the Aurethian guard lined the cliffside. Their gold armor mirrored the horizon. Behind them, the people of Nadhas, travelers from distant villages, and a portion of the Atreyu citizenship watched Darius and Lena burn in the center of Sunder's crimson, half-submerged face.

When Elio had raised his hand to his throat, flashing the three-fingered war salute, Lorelei and their people did the same. Aurethian flags whipped from tall handheld poles. People cried, wailed, howled, sang, but Elio hadn't mustered a single tear. He'd wept enough.

He felt across the small dent the bowstring left on his fingertip and tried not to think about the funeral as his transport cruised into the gravity chamber underneath the Griean warship's hanger. His mind was stuck in a cyclical pattern. Leaving Lorelei to correspond with Ulrich and grapple with the truth of Outpost One. Promising Orson he would come back. Accepting stern, hushed advice from Peadar. *Do not let the ice giant muzzle you, High Lord. You are the lion of Aurethia. You bow to no one.*

Being back home, walking through the great room, dragging his hand along the top of the dining table, staring at the bed he'd shared with Cael — felt like visiting a past life.

The manor had been a shell of itself, torn through with pulse-burns, stained with boot scuffs and blood. The first thing Lorelei had done was bark about remodeling. *Pull that tile up,* she'd said, pointing to a sickly smudge in the northern wing, and *we'll have to patch this,* gesturing to a charred circle beneath the capsized portrait of their grandfather. Peadar had been a voice of reason, shadowing her every step, and Elio did not know how to thank him for it. Before Elio departed, Xander Henly arrived on the back of one of the abandoned hoverbikes Elio and Vik had left in the crater, and Elio relayed a message to Angelina Darvin, transmitting his intention to travel to Griea, participate in the Tupinaire, and take Bracken Volkov's hand.

The last thing Lorelei had said to him stayed firmly fastened to the front of his mind. *Do you have a plan, brother?*

"Good evening," Holland Lancaster said, walking into the enclosed main cabin. He wore Griean-black, and kept his hands folded at the small of his back. "I see you've decided against an entourage."

Elio had boarded the transport with nothing except a small case of clothes, his personal devices, a belt of cattails, the Grabak sheathed on his hip, and Vik Endresen.

"Why waste our resources? Would a few guards make a difference on a planet armed to the teeth?" Elio shrugged. He glanced at Vik who sat on a galley bench built into the framework of the spacecraft's wall. "I have my Augment. He'll need to be seen by a technician once we arrive."

Holland perked. "There's a technician on board. He's a friend."

Elio gave Vik a long, cautious look.

The soldier, Cael's comrade, cleared his throat and tipped his face toward the ground. When he spoke, it was thoughtful and slow. "We don't know each other, Elio, but I saw the way Cael looked at you. I don't expect you to trust me. I just hope you know I wouldn't have volunteered to escort you if I didn't believe in *my* Imperator's vision for Griea."

Elio mulled that over.

"I'm surprised Bracken allowed you to live after what happened on the battlefield," Vik said. The suddenness of his smooth voice was a shock in the stuffy room.

Holland gave a curt nod. "I'm lucky the action I took was only witnessed by those who share my sentiment."

Elio banked his head. "Action?"

Holland pursed his mouth.

Vik slid into Elio's dialect device, scratching through static. `Holland Lancaster saved Cael's life. In doing so — risked his own.` Feedback fuzzed, garbling some of what Vik relayed. No doubt a symptom of his cybernetic damage. `Unfortunately, I'm unable to detect his heartrate, but organically speaking, I don't think he's lying.`

Elio regarded Holland with a sweeping glance, studying his buckled bootwear and fitted tunic. "So the Royal Reserve is divided?"

"Somewhat."

Vik stood. "I would prefer to be fully operational once we arrive."

"The trip will take about a month. I'm sure Yoder can get you fixed up before we land," Holland said. He looked between Vik and Elio. "If your Primary Controller is in agreement."

"I trust your judgement," Elio said to Vik.

Vik nodded to Elio, then to Holland. "I would appreciate the technician's expertise."

"I'll let Yoder know you're in need of assistance. Until then, are you both comfortable? I know the cabin is small and lacking privacy. We'll do our best to give you space during the journey," Holland said.

Bracken had extended an invitation to join Marcus, Constance, and the rest of the Griean staff on the warship. Elio declined, of course, opting to stay on the terrestrial transport with his chaperones. Despite the bunk-style sleeping arrangement, less-than-stellar galley, and windowless interior, he would rather spend his time researching the Tupinaire and reading on his holotablet, smashed together in the transport like canned fish, than walk onto the warship that had delivered destruction to his homeworld.

"We'll be fine, thank you," Elio said. He wanted to ask Holland about the version of Cael that left Griea over a cycle ago. He wanted to know who Cael had been before Aurethia, what kind of man instilled loyalty and faith in people like Holland. People who would've been killed alongside him for defecting. But instead, he asked, "Did you take part in the Nadhas massacre?"

Holland went very still. His jaw shifted and the bump of cartilage on his throat bobbed. "The acting Imperator ordered Kasimir, his second, to initiate the culling. I was tasked with encouraging the seamen to resume fishing, so I avoided the bloodshed." His mouth squirmed. He looked sick, almost. Like he'd chugged curdled milk. "I witnessed it, though. It went against everything I was taught. As a member of the Royal Reserve, it's my duty to offer protection where none can be found, dismantle lawlessness, protect House Volkov, and bring safety to the populus. What Bracken — " He paused, swallowing, and corrected himself. " — What Imperator Volkov and Kasimir Malkin did to the people in Nadhas is appalling. Their operation was the antithesis of everything Griea represents."

"Kasimir," Elio echoed.

The soldier Holland cut down in Atreyu, Vik supplied. The same man who almost killed your husband.

The Griean inclined his head. "No longer with us. One of many casualties, Duke Henly."

Elio searched Holland's face, listening for any semblance of a slippery falsehood, but despite his initial apprehension, Elio believed him. He nodded slowly, trying not to visualize what happened in Nadhas. The action described to him by the surviving citizenship detailed an atrocity he couldn't fathom. He shouldn't have asked, but he'd had to know. Had to get the question out of the way, so he could look at Cael's friend without picturing Holland's blade pressed to a child's throat.

"I'd like something hot to drink if there's anything on hand," Elio said, changing the subject.

Holland's entire body dropped, going lax. Relief brightened him. He nodded and scrubbed a hand over his chin and mouth. "Nothing fancy, I'm afraid. But we have coffee and thornbush tea."

"Thornbush? Is that Griean?"

"It is. Not as sweet as anything on Aurethia, but deep, rich. It'll warm you."

Elio nodded absently. "That, then," he said, thinking of the ever-cold he would soon face.

"How're you feeling?" Elio asked. He pushed Vik's chin to the side, searching the Augment for external changes.

Vik seemed to startle at the touch. He blinked rapidly, shivering away like an annoyed bird. "Yoder did an exceptional job. I'm fully functional and have retained the majority of my storage."

"Majority?"

"There's a sixty to ninety second lapse in my memory during the exact moment Bracken's greatsword crushed the cybernetic enhancement attached to my thoracic vertebrae."

Elio cringed. "I don't think you'll miss that."

"Not particularly, no."

An electronic voice poured through the overhead speaker. *Now entering Griean airspace. Territory: Machina.*

For twenty-eight days, the Griean warship cut through the deep blackness of outer space, carrying Holland's transport on a latched gravity chamber bolted to the underside of the massive vessel. Elio had never traveled farther than Draitune before. The first couple of days weakened his constitution. His stomach sloshed, and he couldn't hold down anything solid. But once they sped into the mouth of the Lux Continuum, he acclimated and felt well enough to nibble on the pre-packaged jerky stored in the galley.

"You should get your coat," Vik said.

Dread and excitement coiled at the base of his spine. He didn't know which feeling to lean into. Part of him was terrified. Horrified, even. He knew what arriving on Griea meant. He knew what awaited him. But being in a new place, on a planet he'd heard so much about, one he was expected to rule, still made his heart flutter.

Elio retrieved his coat from the cabin. It was a simple burgundy garment crafted from leather and sheep's wool. The bronze buttonwork lining his torso came together neatly. He looped a scarf around his neck as the transport peeled away from the warship and slowed to a halt on a nearby docking bay.

Holland strode through the cabin and gripped the handlebar on the outer rim of the ship's small hanger, steadying himself. "I'll escort you to the Volkov castle where Imperator Volkov and the Legatus will show you to your primary quarters. After that, I probably won't see you until the Tupinaire."

"I doubt you'll want to see me after, considering," Elio said. He exhaled through his nose, staring at the hanger's creaking door.

The Griean soldier angled his head. His brow lined, tensing. "I am Griean, Duke Henly. Death is a friend, and there is no kinder death Cael could ask for than one delivered by the man he risked everything to protect."

Granite balled in Elio's throat. He swallowed around it and blinked to soothe the burn high in his face.

"If you deliver it," Holland added, the slight quip coasting out under his breath.

"What other choice do I have, Operative Lancaster?"

"I can't say." Holland stared at Elio down the slope of his crooked nose. "It *is* the Tupinaire."

Elio darted a suspicious glance at him. The hanger door lifted, yanking his attention.

The first blast of brisk, bone-chilling cold carried a flurry of needle-point snowflakes. Ice grazed Elio's face. He squinted against the wind, met with a view of the galactic port, and Machina's silhouette stacked behind it. Above the city, color scissored the dark grey sky. Green, violet, white, and pink kindled Goren's huge peak. The Sliding Sea stretched in every direction, cracked in places where the overfreeze opened for glacial water. Sunder was a tiny, insignificant glimmer in the distance, hung like an ordinary star in the pitch beyond the aurora.

Machina's imposing shadow climbed alongside the mountain. It was a city composed of sleek black skyscrapers connected through multiple tiers just like the holodocumentaries said. On the bottom level, groundcrafts cruised along a gridwork of roads, and above it, shuttles shot between buildings and platforms. He stared at one of the Griean terrariums, floating like an oversized orb within the interior of the city. Green pressed through the steamed glass, splashing color across an otherwise monotone canvas.

"Welcome to Griea," Vik said.

When the Augment walked forward, Elio followed.

The warship docked on the other side of the galactic port, dwarfing the rest of the spacecrafts. No one seemed to pay him any attention. He'd arrived on a Griean transport, accompanied by Griean citizens, apart from the reigning family. To the naked eye, Elio Henly was just another offworlder visiting the ice giant.

He relaxed as much as he could and nodded at Holland. "Let's go."

The rest of the crew stayed behind while Holland escorted Vik and Elio through the galactic port and into the city.

At a distance Machina looked gigantic, but navigating the network of buildings made it seem even larger. Everywhere Elio looked, he saw a piece of something Cael had once described. Laughter came and went, slipping around the door of a pub when someone walked inside. People queued at a food stall promising caribou sausages topped with pickled vegetables. Someone on a walking bridge caught his eye. Black crusted the edge of a bandage taped to their cheek, covering late-stage parsec sickness. Someone else ambled by on a curved prosthetic foot, and another person huddled under an awning, struggling to light a smoke stick. Their jaw was half-gone, bone blackened, skin eaten away.

I've detected an alarming spike in your heartrate. Are you alright? Vik turned to look at him.

Elio nodded stiffly. "I didn't realize," he started, then stopped, gulping uncomfortably. *I didn't believe it.* Shame gutted him. "I just didn't realize," he said again, and looked ahead toward the blocky building seated on the horizon.

At the very top of the city, shadowed by Goren's snowy peak, the Volkov castle loomed over Griea. It was absurdly modern. Black square-shaped modules stacked like the tattoo on Cael's spine, off-center but perfectly pieced together. Elio had never seen anything like it before, and he didn't think he would ever see a building like it again. A row of black-clad Royal Reserve stood shoulder-to-shoulder outside the entrance.

Holland slowed to a stop. "Good luck, Elio. I hope to serve you in another life."

Elio pinned him with a curious stare.

Holland sketched a short bow. "Once Kasimir is augmented, he'll report my action to the Legatus, and I'll face my consequence in the arena. Tell Cael — "

"I'll have you pardoned, Holland," Elio said, as if the soldier should've known better. When Holland gave him a slow, appraising look, Elio turned away and strode toward the welcome party.

That is quite a promise, Vik said through his dialect device.

"I'm Duke of Griea, High Lord of Aurethia, intended for the great warlord who conquered the forest moon. I welcome the Legatus to question my judgement," Elio said. Speaking it aloud — *who conquered the forest moon* — sent a whirl of anger through his chest. But it had to be said. For now, it had to be true.

The Royal Reserve stomped, signaling Elio's arrival. They turned as one, facing each other, outlining a path that led to Bracken. Mountainous wind ruffled the fur around the heir incumbent's long beast-skin coat. He stood proudly. His mouth ticked into a smile, and he inclined his head, eyes never leaving Elio's steady gaze.

"I hope you traveled comfortably," Bracken said.

Elio steeled himself. "I did. Will my belongings be delivered?"

"They'll be here within the hour."

Upon closer inspection, Elio realized Bracken's coat was crafted from reindeer hide. Intricate leather stitching, stone buttoned, and hand-crafted.

An heirloom, maybe. He looked away from the rugged fur and kept his face upright, welcoming the cold bite of another snowy gust.

Bracken extended his arm toward the house. If it could even be called that. Mansion, castle, estate. Compound. "The Draitune liaison will be joining us for dinner."

"Is that right?" Elio drawled, stepping past him. Vik fell into stride at Elio's heel.

"And an ambassador from Mal will arrive shortly. Rune, an emissary from Ren, will be here before the Tupinaire."

"And when is the Tupinaire, Imperator?"

"Tomorrow."

Elio almost tripped. Horror squeezed his heart, but he remained steady, nodding, feigning nonchalance. "Understood."

The Volkov castle was a sparse, tactful place. Polished stone spanned the floor. A great hearth blazed in the center of the common room, and the black-walled interior glinted orange and yellow from the roaring fire. This was where Cael grew up. Manicured, intimate, and warm, somehow. As they crossed through the foyer, Elio watched two house staff unroll a golden fur. Tatu's beautiful face was positioned to their liking in front of the fire-place. His wide feline jaw stretched open, showing white teeth set into a permanent, taxidermy snarl. Elio tore his gaze away. Rage simmered where Bracken could not see, boiling in the pit of him.

Bracken stopped outside the dining hall and extended his scarred hand. "Your coat, High Lord."

So much like Cael. Mannerisms, smile, voice — there was *so much* of the man he loved interwoven into the man who had ruined his life. Even the way Bracken cocked his head, watching Elio through thick lashes, mirrored a memory of Cael. But there was a hard, unquestionable coldness radiating from Bracken. Some kind of deadly need to control, to never be out of control, that triggered Elio's fight-or-flight. Shrugging off his coat and handing the garment to Bracken, Elio imagined this was how fish felt with a hook embedded in their lip, reeled toward death through familiar water.

After Bracken hung Elio's coat on a silver nodule jutting from the wall, he hung his own, revealing the silk shirt beneath, and the thick leather looped around his charcoal trousers. Elio had never seen him out of his armor. Despite his stature — taller and broader than Cael — Bracken looked smaller without it. Leaner, like a wolf in summer. Bracken pushed on what appeared to be a standard wall. It split down the center, sliding toward them at an angle.

On the other side of the strange doorway, Legatus Marcus was seated at the head of a stone table bathed in light from an overhead disc-lamp. Duchess Constance sat beside him, and across from her, the visitor.

The ambassador from Draitune shot to his feet, studying Elio through a small rectangular lens attached to his dialect device. He clasped his hands at his waistline and nodded, focused solely on the Henly heir.

"I'm glad to see you've arrived safely, High Lord Henly. My name is Oliver Junji. I'll be acting as the liaison between Griea and Draitune during the Tupinaire, and overseeing the transfer of power from Cael Volkov, heir of Griea, to Bracken Volkov, heir incumbent. I'll also be documenting House Volkov's delivery of a swift and agreeable punishment, according to Griean law, and in complicity with Imperial standard," the ambassador said. He looked relieved. Spoke confidently. "With permission from Legatus Marcus, Angelina of House Darvin has positioned a warship in high orbit. It will remain there throughout this..." He paused, lowering his gaze. "... interesting time. House Darvin and I would like to offer our sincere condolences in the early passing of your parents. I have to ask, for the record," he gestured to the holo in front of his left eye, "are you of sound mind? Have you been coerced?"

The room remained still and silent.

"Thank you for being here," Elio said. He watched Oliver's mouth twitch. He stared at Elio so intently, so full of hope. Elio almost wanted to tell the truth. Everything. All of it. But if he did, Legatus Marcus would shoot Angelina's defenses out of the sky, and Aurethia would truly be lost. "I haven't been coerced, and I'm of sound mind. The alliance I made with Bracken Volkov..."

Careful, Vik blurted. His dialect device pulsed. Use your wit. Adaptable truth will serve you far better than blunt dishonesty.

Elio cleared his throat, continuing. "Currently, the alliance I made with Bracken Volkov is in the best interest of Griea and Aurethia."

"And you believe Cael Volkov's crime is fit for punishment during the Tupinaire?" Oliver said, agape and wide-eyed.

"I believe Cael Volkov will meet his fate in the arena," Elio said. He shifted toward Vik, nodding at an empty seat beside Oliver. "Go on."

The liaison sat slowly. His tawny complexion reddened, and he placed his palms on the table as if to steady himself. Knowing Angelina, she was probably waiting for a signal to intervene, for Oliver to confirm what the entire Imperium knew to be true: House Volkov was committing a terrible crime. Doing so would only compromise the rare opportunity Elio had negotiated, though. One he would never get again.

Bracken sat. Elio took the empty place across from him.

"Good, that's settled." Marcus chewed each word. He smacked his mouth and sat back in his chair, turning toward Elio. "I'm glad we're in agreement, young lord — "

"Duke," Elio corrected. Constance paused with her fork embedded in a pickled radish. Bracken canted an eyebrow. Even Vik stopped breathing. His data-port whirred. Elio mustered a hard, unwavering glare. "Or High Lord."

The Legatus held a stemless glass half-filled with chalky purple wine. He made a sound like laughter, grunted and ugly. "Duke," he said, nodding. "I'm pleased to have you."

It was an easy thing to overlook. A coy, dismissive comment. But Elio knew better. *I'm pleased to have you*, as if Elio and Aurethia were collectibles. Like he was something the Legatus owned.

Constance dabbed her mouth with a napkin. "Have we resumed Avara production in the north?"

"Soon," Bracken said.

Elio wasn't hungry, but he spread a glob of butter onto a seedy bun and set it on his plate. "Atreyu will need to rebuild before we leap into Avara production. Families are grieving. Communication is being established." He took a small piece of charred octopus, too. Then brought a water glass to his mouth, soaking his bottom lip. "My people require grace, Duchess. And they deserve time to heal."

"Diplomatically speaking, Aurethia is owed a period of rest," Oliver said.

"Of course," she mused.

Constance was feline and awkward, radiating poise and savagery at once. Elio never realized how much of Cael came from her. How she held her fork. The cadence of her speech. Elio kept finding pieces of him sewn throughout the Volkov castle, nestled in each family member like a wood shaving. It made him wonder about himself. Did the Legatus hear Darius when Elio spoke? Did the people at the table look at him and see Lena?

"I'll approve an emergency shipment of Avara to reach Griea as soon as possible. It should depart within the week." Elio bit into the octopus, tasting salt, vinegar, and the herbal bite of a native plant.

"Generous," Marcus said skeptically. "An hour on the ice giant and you're already questioning our resources."

"Do not mistake me for my father, Legatus. My naivety ended when I met your son."

The Legatus cocked his head. His mean smile quivered. "We don't need charity — "

"We'll take it," Bracken said. He kept his attention on Elio. "The entire point of this unification is to rebuild what Alexander broke, starting with the fair distribution of Avara. After our people receive treatment, we'll strategize."

"Once Avara production is regulated, I'll meet with House Darvin and fast-track a long-term solution for Griea. For now, one shipment should alleviate some discomfort," Elio said.

"Discomfort?" Marcus laughed. His whole body shook with it. There was Cael again, echoed in his mouth, mirrored in his grin. "Our people travel frequently, fulfilling contractual obligations throughout the Greater Universe. From Draitune," he said, waving toward Oliver, "to the triplets, well into Mal and Ren. Not only were we ostracized by the discoverer of Avara, but we were punished for prioritizing the fiscal stability of our home-world. Send whatever Avara you think you can spare, High Lord, but Griea will no longer wait for a bone to be tossed at our feet. Aurethia is under my governance, and I intend to make right what was wronged."

"By seizing exclusive control of the starlink and funneling profit to House Volkov? How familiar," Elio said, matching Legatus Marcus's sarcastic sneer.

"You forget where you sit," Marcus snapped.

"You forget who I am," Elio barked back.

"Enough." Bracken's rough voice boomed through the dining hall.

Constance laughed in her throat and took a long pull from her wine glass. She muttered, "There *is* a lion at our table."

Marcus faced Bracken. His gaze drove like an icepick. "Control him," he said. His chair scraped the smooth floor. He tossed his napkin down. "Or I will," he called over his shoulder, storming out of the room.

Oliver blanched. He stared at his plate, looking sickly and lost.

Tension choked the dinner table.

Are you alright?

Elio lifted his gaze, shooting the Augment a short, patient nod.

"Would you like some air?" Bracken asked.

The question took him off guard, but Elio blinked and cleared his throat. "Yes."

"C'mon, I'll take you to the veranda," he said.

Elio stood on loose legs. He saw Constance watching him, picking him apart with sharp, deliberate glances. Her serene expression cracked, just once. A twitch at the corner of her mouth. The fine crease of her upswept eyes, softening for the briefest, barest moment. She looked pained, almost. Or hopeful.

Through the doorway and into a corridor, Elio walked behind Bracken, followed closely by Vik. He tried to ignore Tatu's desecrated pelt, but the sight of it shocked him again, caused his throat to close. *Don't let him see you shaken.* He stepped out onto a veranda attached to the common room.

The tundra sliced through his sweater. Cold slammed into him, its own sort of relief. Ice skipped across Goren's pocked peak. Dark gnarled rock cut down the harsh surface, and bright snow piled in crannies and divots. He sipped at thin air. His sea-level lungs weren't used to elevation, but he took solace in the slight ache. Pain brought a brisk, cutting awareness he couldn't ignore.

Bracken stood near the railing, staring across the Sliding Sea. "I understand why Cael chose you."

Elio watched the aurora lance the dark sky. "He didn't choose me, Imperator. I was a gift given by an old man who couldn't see past his own misfortune. Cael didn't have a choice, I didn't have a choice."

"I wouldn't call Alexander Henly misfortunate."

"Maybe not." Heartbroken, yes. Consumed by anger, yes. Driven by greed, yes. Elio's breath plumed. "You massacred my people in Nadhas," he blurted, expecting more to surface. Nothing did. He stood there, staring at the sky, waiting for rage to razor his tongue. The fight wasn't worth it, though. Not now, not here. Instead, he asked, "Will you do it again?"

Bracken gripped the picket with bare hands. It had to be unbearably cold. The Imperator's knuckles whitened. His sigh fogged the air. "If I have to," he said, shifting his gaze to Elio. "Aurethia will heed you, High Lord Henly. If we're in alignment, and you advocate for my policies, then a display of power won't be necessary. Civilians are like children — I made an example out of Nadhas to protect the rest of the moon from the same ramification."

The next breath Elio took seemed to crystalize in his chest. He resisted the urge to cough. "So you'll slaughter them into compliance."

"Or let a group of foolish loyalists plague the Greater Universe with sickness and unrest? Yes, Elio. I will. Wouldn't you?"

Elio let the question marinate. He didn't have an answer. Couldn't have an answer. The idea seemed preposterous, impossible. He met Bracken's eyes. So, so blue. Dark and clear, like overharvested Avara on the verge of toxifying. "Where is Cael being held?"

The subject hardened Bracken's jaw. "Under the mountain," he said, then cleared his throat. "Well, *inside* the mountain. We built out a cave unit attached to the War College. It's our prison system. He's comfortable, don't worry."

"I'd like to see him," Elio said.

"Go."

"Unchaperoned."

Bracken shrugged, lifting one hand off the rail to gesture dismissively at Goren. "You're unguarded, Elio. No one is holding you captive, no one is following you. You're free to do as you please. If you'd like to shiver in a cell with my cousin, be my guest. But it won't change our agreement."

"I need to put our courtship to rest. I need to… I need to say goodbye. Facing him in the arena will earn the respect of the Griean citizenship and solidify my commitment to you," he said, speaking clearly, openly, and hoping the anger sizzling in his gut didn't reach his face.

Elio wasn't a good liar, but he was a skilled strategist, and a well-versed archivist. He knew men like Bracken. Their comings and goings riddled the pages of history, laid a path for the future. Those same men mirrored each other, stepping into the same role again and again. Tyrant, dictator, conqueror, crusader. They never failed to rise, never failed to fall.

"Thank you for supporting me earlier," he added, softening his tone. He did not smile, but he knew how to become small, how to temper his gaze and shrink himself to fit inside the claustrophobic dimensions of a particularly obedient role. "It was a pleasant surprise to find us standing on common ground."

Bracken lifted his chin. His chiseled face warmed for a bare smile. "Our heir will have quite the legacy to live up to."

The cold numbed him. He tipped his head, mimicking a respectful Griean gesture, and walked inside, escaping the chilly balcony and Bracken's serpentine smile before he lost his composure completely.

AN ENCLOSED BRIDGE CONNECTED the basement of the Griean War College to an iron door punched through Goren's sloped exterior. Elio followed the path, head tipped upward, gaze fixed on a bleach-white skeleton dangling from the ceiling. The dead basilisk stretched from one end of the bridge to the other. Each rib curved through the air, jutting from adjoining vertebrae crowned with a row of thin, tapered spines. As they approached the entrance to the Grian prison, the massive, draconic jaw stretched open, displaying fang and tooth. Whenever a prisoner was discharged, they were greeted with the basilisk's eternal roar, warning them to stay the course.

"Clearance?" The guard asked, strapped with a pulse-rifle, and concealed in lightweight armor.

Vik stepped forward. "Duke Elio Henly, High Lord and reigning steward of Aurethia."

The man blinked, stunned. He didn't move for a long moment, then tapped his dialect device and spoke, repeating Elio's title. Another pause came and went, worsened by the wind's cold snap against the stone. The device glowed faintly, and the guard cocked his head.

The guard stepped aside and tapped a code into the holo-lock next to the door. "You've been granted a ten-hour conjugal visit. The prisoner is being transferred to an appropriate holding area. You'll need to leave any weaponry." He shifted his gaze to Vik. "Augmented personnel are not permitted."

Fear jilted down Elio's spine. He should've known. Vik was a walking weapon. Of course he wouldn't be allowed inside. He glanced at Vik and gave a curt nod, swallowing thickly. "Meet me here in the morning."

The Augment flared his nostrils. He did not look pleased. I'm not comfortable with this, Vik said through his dialect device. His mouth didn't move, but he inhaled sharply and shook his head. You and Cael will both be vulnerable. I can press the issue.

"I'll be fine," he assured, forcing a feeble smile. He unclipped his Grabak and handed it to Vik. "Bracken wouldn't risk my life, Vik. Too many people are watching. He's supportive of this visit, and confident in our alliance. If it'll put you at ease, send my live location to Oliver Junji. He'll relay everything to Angelina."

An alarm blared. The iron door dragged open, sending powdery snow drifting onto the platform.

Be careful. Grian law does not permit live recording of imprisoned individuals during mate-related visita-tion, but everything will be audio-recorded, and I wouldn't be surprised if Bracken or Marcus bypassed the law in favor of surveillance. Vik clipped Elio's scabbard to his belt beside his own blade, then squeezed Elio's shoulder. "I'll be back at dawn."

Elio nodded. He turned toward the entrance and walked inside, nestling his nose into the scarf twined around his neck.

The Griean prison was a sprawling, morose place. Stone-walled and blank, the repurposed cave dove deep into the belly of the mountain. An oversized disc-lamp lit the hollow reception space, but the light didn't reach the top of the carved-out room. Individual holding areas stacked along the curved wall, ascending up, descending down. Ten stories, at least. It was a plethora of trapped people, criminalized or not. Caged away from fresh air, left to fester like an untreated wound.

Welcome to the Griean Containment Facility. Elio startled, jolted by the sound of a friendly robotic voice chiming through his dialect device. You have been granted a ten-hour conjugal visit. Report to Visitation Pod Nine. Your code is 1360. Once you enter, the door will automatically lock behind you. Please familiarize yourself with the panic signals inside the visitation pod. One will be located on the nightstand. The other is inside the washroom. If you trigger the panic sign —

Elio tore off his dialect device and followed a small, plain sign toward the capsule elevator. He swiped his quivering finger along the built-in holo and selected Platform Three: Visitation. The elevator climbed, rocked to a stop, opened, and Elio almost forgot himself, almost sprinted down the spotless hall lined with plain, individual doors. But he didn't. He flexed his hand and tried to balance his wobbly mind. Walked deliberately. Slowly. Tried to ignore how his heart became a trapped, frantic thing.

He stopped in front of the ninth room and typed 1360 into the holo-pad. The lock slid free with a heavy, metallic noise, and the pod opened.

Elio took a grounding breath and slipped inside. There was a plain bed draped in white linen, a basic nightstand, and an adjoining washroom. Cael paused mid-stride, as if he'd been pacing. He wore a black sleeveless shirt, plain cargos, and simple socks. His scarred face looked freshly shaven, same as his inked skull. His throat clenched on a mindful swallow.

They stayed like that for too long. Looking at each other. Sealed in a prison. Reacquainting themselves with the truth. Griea, together. Like this. Elio's breath shook from him.

After an eternity, Cael said, "Hello, darling."

Don't. Elio smashed his lips together. He set his teeth and gave a small shake of his head. *Don't do that.* But he couldn't say it. Couldn't move. His throat prickled. Watery heat blurred his vision. He found the strength to unwind his scarf and let it drop, freeing his neck, tricking his mind into believing it would be easier to breathe that way.

"There will be an opening in the ice." Cael spoke evenly. He eased forward, closing the space between them. "When it's over, give me to the water. It's a funeral fit for a champion, believe it or not, and I want my people to see — "

Elio clapped his palm over Cael's mouth. He pictured himself dragging Cael across the Sliding Sea, blood streaking the ice, and pushing him over the lip of a cold plunge. How his husband might sink, devoured by a great beast, or chewed apart by smaller fish. Everything inside him rejected the idea.

"Undress me," he said, exhaling the command on a rigid breath.

Cael blinked. His milky eye followed the other, darting around Elio's face.

He shifted his hand to Cael's cheek and hooked his thumb into his mouth. Pressed. Felt the sharp bite of slippery bone, the wet swipe of Cael's tongue. Vik's warning echoed. *Be careful.* He needed an opening. An opportunity. And Cael was being far too cautious to grant him one.

"Now, Imperator," Elio whispered, speaking Aurethian. He yanked on Cael's jaw, earning a flinch.

Surprise flashed across Cael's face, almost too fast to catch, before one hand closed around Elio's throat, hauling him closer. His spare hand swept past the opening in his coat and took hold of Elio's waist. They hit the wall in a tangle. Cael kissed him hard enough to bruise, desperate enough to cause their teeth to smack. Elio could not help but yield to it. This was the kiss he'd dreamed about for twenty-eight days. The rush of Cael's breath against the roof of his mouth, the pillowy pull of their parted lips, the deep caress of intimacy he'd missed, chased, craved. Cael kissed him with a yearning, with a fury Elio wanted to remember. *Yes, kiss a storm into me,* he wanted to say, *kiss a lifetime into me.*

But there was something he needed to do first.

Elio grabbed Cael's wrist and shifted his hand. He pulled back, watching Cael through lidded eyes, and guided his finger along the belt discreetly hidden beneath his sweater. Cael's index skimmed cool metal. His body tightened. Every muscle tensed. His pupil mooned and he cocked his head, curling his hand around the very center of Elio's trousers. He gave a sharp tug, rasping a laugh against Elio's slack mouth.

"This war isn't over," Elio whispered. He slipped a cattail free and pushed it against Cael's wrist, lower, into his palm.

"This could get you killed, Elio," Cael whispered, speaking Aurethian. He dragged his mouth across Elio's cheek, mirroring a kiss, and closed his hand around Elio's fingertips.

Elio nodded tightly. He turned into Cael's neck, shielding his mouth. "My fate is sealed regardless."

"I need you to live," he scolded.

"Even in the darkness, remember?"

Cael pulled back to stare at him. His fine face gentled, and he tipped closer, resting his brow against Elio's forehead. Carefully, concealed between their twined bodies, he tucked the tiny Aurethian throwing knife into his pocket. "Forevermore."

Elio exhaled, relieved. "Make them believe it," he muttered, hardly above a whisper. "That this is the last of us. That tonight is an ending."

Cael's grip on him tightened.

They both knew it could be.

Elio was starved. Overwhelmed with desire. He thought of eerie things. Wedging himself underneath Cael's skin. Filling the airy pocket behind his sternum. Becoming as vital to him as the blood pumping through sinew and organ. He was delirious with it. Drunk with it. This wanting he may never get the chance to satiate again. This madness love shackled him with.

Cael surged forward, caging Elio against the wall.

They kissed like ruined men. It was an awful, beautiful thing, having Cael unrestrained. Raw and real, unrefined and with nothing left to lose. Their time was almost up. Everything they were, everything they had teetered on the edge of oblivion.

"Give me an heir," Elio said. A fluttery, hidden wish.

Cael's mouth scorched his throat. Teeth snagged tender flesh. He pressed against him, trapping him there, stomping the coat piled on the floor at their feet, hand buried in the hair above Elio's nape, gripping hard.

"Give me your heir," he begged again, even though he knew better, knew his body would never allow life to take root at a time like this.

Cael undressed him like he asked, and once they were both bare and heedless, Elio felt the last inkling of self-control slip away.

"I will give you everything," Cael said, tasting his shoulder. He hoisted

Elio up, palming the backside of one thigh. His other hand dented Elio's waist.

Elio clutched Cael's nape, gasped at the suddenness of their bodies colliding, and tasted the familiar tang of salt at the corner of his mouth. He tipped Cael toward him and refused to cry for this. For them.

We are not dead yet. Elio kissed him, and kissed him, and kissed him. *We are alive, we are still alive.*

CHAPTER FORTY-SEVEN
CAEL

Prepare for the Griean Tupinaire. Entry, one. Incar-cerated citizen, Cael Volkov. Crime: Treason. Filing: Capital.

The thundering cheer of Machina's populus smothered the electronic voice inside Cael's holding chamber. The gravity suspension module vibrated through the floor, fading once the arena settled somewhere atop the Sliding Sea.

Cael sat on a plain cot, toying with the strap on one fingerless glove. During his transfer from the Containment Facility, he received a brief message from the Legatus. His father didn't send a voice note, only an auto-mated transmission relayed to him by his guard. *I've adjusted the standard trial procedure. At your mother's request, you're permitted to wear personal armor. It will be provided to you upon arrival. The charges levied against you will accompany your introduction into the Tupinaire, and regardless of the match's outcome, you will be punished accordingly. Fight well. God is in the water.*

Cael was only allowed to listen to the message once. Afterward, as he dressed in his Griean armor and pulled the notch tight on his basilisk belt, he autopsied the transmission, searching for some semblance of love, pain, or pride hidden in the data.

Within the privacy of his mind, he channeled his father from a memory. Somewhere distant. Before Aurethia, before the siege, before the Legatus discarded him, ridding Griea of his own personal failure. For as long as Cael had been alive, he'd known Marcus to be stoic and steadfast, someone who did not bend or break, but somewhere buried deep, where Cael still chased his father's approval, he thought Marcus might find it in his heart to offer his only son a shred of grace.

But on the day Cael would die — blood and honor be damned — Marcus Volkov had nothing left to say to him except *fight well*.

When the holopad beeped and the chamber door unlocked, Cael hoped to see his mother. But it was Holland who breached the doorway, accompanied by a guard wearing tactical gear and a face-shield.

Cael tried not to deflate. "Sorry. I thought you might be the Duchess."

Holland matched his lack of enthusiasm with a helpless shrug. He wore armor, same as Cael, and carried a sheathed saber on his waist. "You weren't given the option for an alternate, but I volunteered regardless."

"I don't think Elio will be able to give me to the water."

"I'll make sure you meet the basilisk," he said, pressing his mouth into a sad line, "if need be."

Cael nodded absently. He palmed the Griean short-sword hooked to his belt. This armor was almost piece-for-piece the same he'd worn on Aurethia. The only difference were his boots — sabatons lined with seal fur and soled with iron cable fitted tightly to his feet, designed to grip the ice. He knuckled his breastplate. The doctor on the warship repaired his collapsed lung, but time and rest healed the spattering of internal bruising and split tissue left behind from the battle in Atreyu. After the twentieth day, he didn't feel weak anymore. Didn't feel like every breath was a challenge, and every movement might shatter a bone. During the fourth week, he started training again, moving through strength exercises and calisthenics in his cell.

"I'm sorry," Holland blurted.

Cael snapped his head up. "What?"

"For following Bracken, for entertaining his belligerence, for not taking my initial concern to the Legatus, for keeping the peace instead of raising the alarm."

"You followed an order, Holland. You have nothing to apologize for."

"I knew better," he ground out, pushing air through his teeth. "Tye knew better. We knew better."

"I killed Tye." Cael fumbled over the confession. It still hurt to think about. The truth blistered on his tongue. "I didn't know it was him, but I killed him during an altercation in the crater. I — I cut down my own men. I gave none of you any reason to believe in me. You had intel from Bracken and an order from the Legatus. You were given a job. I never expected anyone…" He stopped before he had the chance to lie. Expectation? Maybe not. But Cael had hoped someone might believe in his integrity enough to question the chain-of-command. "What happened on Aurethia was the end result of pre-negotiated hatred between two houses throttled by rapacity. I thought my cousin might try to speak to me before claiming my title, but he lacked the courage of his conviction, I guess. Talking to me would've opened an opportunity to legitimize a capital crime." His mouth lifted into a sarcastic smile. "And denied him the opportunity to one day sit on my father's fortune."

Holland fidgeted. He looked at the ground for a while before meeting Cael's gaze. "When did you defect?"

Cael stared at the ceiling. "That's a complicated question." The first time Elio took his hand. In Nadhas, the day Elio called him fiancé. In the training chamber, out in the meadow. Circling each other in the steamy onsen. When Elio's teeth grazed his neck at the lakehouse. Really, it happened slowly, and then all at once, like birth, and death, and love, and everything else that mattered. "In summer," he decided, holding open his hand, surrendering. "But before that, probably. I fell in love with him like I was falling on a sword."

"You tried to resist."

"I did, yeah." He laughed under his breath. "At the beginning of Aurethia's autumn, I sent a transmission to my father asking him to delay the siege. It included data from my Augment, predicting the many potential outcomes of our unification. An honest marriage between me and Elio would've bore us the most fruit. But in the end that didn't matter. My father never wanted peace, Holland. And Bracken is very, very good at war. They suit each other."

Holland went quiet for a moment. "He's brave, your Elio. I don't know many men who could challenge Bracken and live to talk about it." He paused, turning toward the sound of the Tupinaire's opening drumbeat. "Except you, obviously."

Cael licked his teeth. His mouth parted for another lackluster laugh. A horn blared, signaling the start of the trial.

The guard outside the chamber gestured toward the exit with his pulse-rifle. "Let's go."

Holland stepped aside. Cael walked out of the chamber.

The bottom floor of the arena was unusually empty. Instead of other competitors, Griean soldiers manned each entrance and exit. They passed unused benches, and dark, lonely tables where weaponry would usually be polished or sharpened. Outside the steel door, the crowd cheered and screamed, and the drone announcer echoed.

Welcome to the Griean Tupinaire! Justice will be served on the ice today! Imperator Cael Volkov, Keeper of the Basilisk, exiled son of our great Legatus, faces capital punishment for treason against House Volkov! The crowd erupted. Cheering turned shrill and aggressive. Some people booed and cursed. Others wailed with disbelief.

The steel door cracked open. Light poured over Cael's feet.

"Let me check your blade," Holland said.

Cael pulled his black short-sword free and handed the weapon over. Holland inspected the pommel. Dragged his thumb along the sharp edge and flicked the center of the smooth steel. Once he finished, he gave Cael his sword, then swatted his chest, checking his armor for inconsistencies. It was standard practice for someone's alternate to inspect their outfitting. Etiquette called for Cael to do the same, to reach out and pat Holland down, and look over his weapon of choice. But he knew there would be no yielding, no trading places with someone willing to fight for him, and Holland knew that, too.

Before the door opened completely, Holland hauled Cael into a hug.

"Go to Aurethia," Cael said, squeezing Holland tightly. "Keep him safe for me, yeah?"

"Yeah," Holland said, waterlogged and weak. The last thing Holland handed him was an obsidian helmet crowned with four basilisk teeth. "Give our people something to remember, Imperator."

Cael traced one of the longer teeth jutting upward from the temple. He yanked the helmet on. The black leather curved around his jaw, framing his face wickedly. It fit snug, but well enough. His heart pounded in time with the music, like a running horse, like a war call. Holland took his place on the outer rim of the arena, and Cael walked onto the ice.

The marbled-blue pinged with every step. It was a dangerous, otherworldly sound, warning of breakage. Warped, pitchy noise — like a dropped sphere — traveled down through dark water. Positioning the Tupinaire on thin ice was a death sentence. Cael knew who was behind such a reckless power move.

He swiveled toward House Volkov's skybox perched in the center of the crowd on the right side of the curved stadium. His family sat in the open air with everyone else, prone to wind and blood-spray. Bracken loomed beside the Legatus, glaring into the arena, watching him intently. Cael made the mistake of glancing at his mother. Constance wore Griean-black. The long gown smoked around her, laid with feathery gossamer and glittering thread. She stared at the laser-cut pool on the other end of the arena.

So many times, Cael had walked onto that ice. So many times, he'd lifted his sword and basked in applause. But now his people were a flurry of contradictions. Some spat at the sea. Some hurled insults. Others cried out in Cael's favor, pleading for redemption.

The drone announcer boomed again. *Judgement will be issued by Griea's newest prize. Plucked from the forest moon, High Lord Elio Henly, lion of Aurethia!*

On the opposite side of the stadium, another steel door parted like a metal mouth. At first, Cael did not recognize him. Elio stepped forth from the shadow swathed in liquid night. Black armor covered him from the neck down, but when the barest glint from the auroras caught his front, Cael saw the Aurethian glyph embossed in gold across his tunic. He walked on spiked cleats, and drew his Grabak swiftly, flipping the weapon over in his palm. Behind him, Vik Endresen stepped onto the outer rim, mimicking Holland.

Competitors, the combat trial will begin in ten... Cael crossed the ice. Elio met him halfway. *Nine, eight, seven...*

As if pieced together from a storybook, a serpentine shadow snaked beneath them, darkening the Sliding Sea. Elio glanced at his feet and halted, frozen in place. The ice trembled.

"Did they allow you an alternate?" Cael asked. He stepped closer, yanking his short-sword free.

Six, five...

Elio looked terrified. His face paled and he shook his head, centering himself. "No, but he volunteered as a witness. He'll collect me if I — "

"You won't," Cael assured. The great beast swept by again. Its fin scraped the underside of the overfreeze. "Look at me, Elio."

Four, three, two...

Elio stared at him, and all Cael could think about was their last night together. Elio's hand around his throat, Elio's hipbones against his pelvis, Elio's flushed chest heaving, rising. Every breathless word. *I choose you*, whispered against Cael's cheek, *you belong to me*, stamped into his shoulder by blunt teeth. *I love you*, spoken like a dare, like something they'd mutually stolen.

"Make them believe it, husband." Elio's knuckles whitened around the Grabak's handle.

Cael inhaled the frostbitten air. It tasted like home.

One... Begin!

Elio burst forward. His Grabak whistled, connecting with Cael's sword. Metal sang. The stadium shook. Cael channeled every training session he'd ever had with Elio. Remembered the way he moved, how his body shifted. He pushed hard against the Grabak. Turned, whirling away, and struck again. Blade-to-blade, feet locked, faces close, Cael breathed, looking into Elio's narrowed eyes.

Make them believe it.

Cael's jaw twitched. He drew back, kicking Elio square in the sternum. The High Lord tumbled, skidding across the ice. His cleat left a groove in the blue surface. It didn't pool with water, but Cael watched it fissure, splitting from within. Elio pushed to his feet and launched again, dodging a swing of Cael's blade, kicking out, smacking his boot against Cael's ankle. He fell hard. The glacial slip of wet ice slicked his armor. He heard the crack, the give that triggered his limbic brain. It was too thin, too frail. If the Sliding Sea swallowed them, Aurethia would fall, and Griea would follow.

Elio's thorned boot came down on Cael's stomach, pinning him there. He stared at him, breathing rapidly, and swung his Grabak. The basilisk tooth connected with Cael's sword. It was a strong blow, rattling through Cael's elbows. The ice flexed again. Splintered and shifted.

Cael gripped Elio's wrist and pulled, hauling him down. He took the opportunity to flip Elio onto his back. Kept him there, blade to throat, listening to the arena come alive, and the ice whine. Elio's fist connected with his ribcage. Pain bloomed. More cheering, louder applause.

Another monstrous shadow drifted underneath, almost as large as the arena itself. It cruised by, pulling water with it, disrupting the current.

"Cael," Elio gritted out, hissing defiantly. "I'm not made of glass. C'mon."

Elio threw his leg around Cael's hip and rolled them over, punching

Cael hard in the cheekbone. Another shock of pain exploded beneath his eye socket. Cael seethed and aimed the handle of his blade at Elio's nose. Bright, hot blood dotted Cael's face. The yelp Elio let out would make a home inside him. It would live there forever. But this was what had to be done. This — brutality, valiance — had to be shown.

"On your feet, lion," Cael snapped. He pushed upward with his lower half, urging Elio to stand.

They circled each other. Cael positioned them where he wanted — *needed* — and Elio followed, lashing out with his Grabak, swiping his bloody nose with the back of his hand, cat-footing and dancing. They met in a fury, clashing and feigning, meeting each other as expert swordsmen, utilizing the technique they'd gleaned from each other over the course of a cycle.

Cael wanted to spar with him again. Wanted to see Elio's smile light up the meadow and hear his laughter ring through the orchard. He wanted to take Elio to a pub in Sector One and watch his mouth twist at the first bitter taste of Griean ale. See snow fall in his hair and guide him through the gauntlet at the War College. Cael wanted to live, truly. He wanted Elio to live more.

The next time Elio lunged, Cael allowed it, blocking at the very last moment. When Elio leaned in close, bracing with his Grabak locked against Cael's short-sword, Cael reached down and dislodged the cattail from the inside of his belt. He pressed his thumb to the curved metal and met Elio's fiery gaze.

One opportunity. One fatal blow.

Elio waited. Nodded. And when Cael nodded, too, the High Lord spun, leaving a clear opening.

Cael recalled everything Elio had taught him. *Notice the wind, throw with intent, focus on the mark, follow through.* He lowered his sword. The tip scratched the ice. Every possible scenario ran through him at once. His damaged vision could cause a mistake. If a gust kicked over the iceshelf, he could miss his target. One wrong move could steal the only chance they had to make this right. With an arc of his arm, Cael focused with his good eye, extended his elbow, and loosed the cattail.

The Aurethian throwing knife sliced and spun. It glimmered, winking once, twice, and disappeared into the audience. When Cael and Elio went still, the crowd hushed. The Legatus staggered to his feet, clutching his flayed throat. Elio fell into Cael, pawing at his shoulder.

Blood sprinkled his mother's cheek. She flinched, but did not move. Not when his father smacked a hand over his neck, failing to conceal the crimson geyser spewing from beneath his jaw. Not when the Legatus crashed to the floor of the skybox, choking, gushing, and lurched through a loud, garbled death-cry.

A pit opened inside Cael. It was a dark, thick feeling, sticking to bone, coating his heart. Throwing that cattail meant nothing until it opened his father's throat. He endured the dread swelling in his stomach. Bile burned and his gut cramped. Silence swept through the stadium. Cael had never heard the Tupinaire so devastatingly quiet.

"That was meant for Bracken," Elio gasped out, yanking Cael around to look at him. His wide eyes searched, and the blood crusted on his chin covered a cluster of freckles Cael used to kiss.

"I'm Griean, darling. Violence is customary." Cael palmed his cheek. Looked deeply, lovingly at his future. "Let me do this."

Elio cinched his brow with confusion.

Cael turned, thrusting his short-sword skyward. "Marcus Volkov is dead," he yelled, turning to look around the shocked arena, scanning slack-jawed faces. He leveled his sword at his cousin. "I, Imperator Cael Volkov, Keeper of the Basilisk, rightful heir of House Volkov and Lord of Aurethia, challenge Bracken Volkov for the title of Legatus and the stewardship of Griea." His voice carried, rippling through the chilly, sea-stained air. His chest felt tight, swollen with grief, and hope, and rebellion. "Come and face me, heir incumbent," he added, spitting the invitation like fire.

The quiet did not budge. Wind howled. Elio's frantic breathing plumed. He slipped his hand into Cael's palm, squeezing hard.

"Imperator!" Someone shouted gleefully, banging on the tiered platform. "Keeper! Keeper!"

Cheering rose up. *Keeper, keeper, keeper! Cael, Cael! Heir to the throne! Kingslayer! Kingslayer! The pair of prophecy!* The chanting continued, each mantra meshing with the next.

Bracken lifted his chin. Rage twisted his face. He put one finger to his dialect device and spoke, staring unblinking at Cael.

The announcer drone rattled the arena. *Challenge accepted!*

And the Griean Tupinaire rioted with violent celebration.

"Cael, he'll kill you," Elio said, yanking him around again.

"Don't doubt me." Cael smiled, soft and small, and dropped his hand to Elio's chin, pinching him there. "There is no other way — "

"Let's face him together then — "

"And lose the respect of my people? Compromise their faith in me? Break our planetary law? You know I can't."

"I just got you back," Elio snapped. His voice was ragged, overrun with emotion. "I did not come here to watch you sacrifice yourself, Cael Volkov. Do not make me watch you — "

Cael silenced him. He kissed the Aurethian prince, the High Lord of the forest moon, as they stood together on the ice. He kissed his husband, and listened to his people scream, shout, and cheer. Elio's blood laced his lips. He heard the relenting whimper rise up and out of him, felt the desperate latch of Elio's hand on his nape.

"Show him no mercy," Elio said, bringing Cael's forehead to his brow. "You do not yield. You do not die today, Cael Volkov. You die with me in our bed a lifetime from now. You die loved, surrounded by grandchildren. You die as Legatus of Griea, you die as Lord of Aurethia. You die with *me*. Do you understand?"

Cael wished he could stop time. "You are my destiny, Elio Henly."

"And you're mine," he said.

It took an impossible kind of strength to raise his hand off of Elio's face and gesture for Vik to come forward. The Augment charged across the ice and grabbed Elio by the elbow.

"Take him," Cael said.

Elio resisted at first, swiping at Cael's hand, grabbing, squeezing, protesting again, weak and winded, but Vik ushered him away.

Another set of cleated boots smacked the ice.

Holland unclipped his saber and handed it to Cael. "I can't fight for you, but I can arm you."

Cael swallowed hard. He took the weapon and fastened it to his belt. "Thank you."

"You're welcome, Legatus," Holland said, and eased backward, holding Cael's gaze for one step, another, until he finally turned and took his place on the outer lip of the arena.

The Tupinaire was a belligerent mess of conflicting sound. Some people cheered for Cael. Some cheered for Bracken. Some hooted and hollered for the sheer thrill of the fight. Some wept over the death of their Legatus, and cried out in anguish, excitement, devastation, devotion for the coming of a new one.

Cael drew Holland's saber in his left and gripped his short-sword in his right. He turned toward House Volkov's skybox, watching Bracken pause to bid farewell to a slender, black-veiled beauty before descending into the underbelly of the arena.

Ten...

The stadium bore down on the frozen sea. Ancient titans circled, following the tinny noise of crisp fractures spiderwebbing the icesheet. Basilisk smelled blood. They sensed the mayhem happening on the other side of the ocean, and like curious, hungry gods from a prehistoric time, looped beneath the cryosphere, waiting for a corpse to drop into the water.

Cael's body thrummed.

Nine, eight...

The same door Cael entered through opened again, and Bracken walked out to infinite cheering. Armor darkened his large stature. His helmet, the same he'd worn on Aurethia, pierced the sky. He reached over his shoulder and drew his claymore in one sweeping motion. Light caught the blade, flashing.

Seven, six, five...

Bracken looked like the personification of Griea. He was everything Cael emulated throughout the majority of his young life. Everything a proper Griean soldier should've been.

Four, three...

Love and malice manifested as one. Cael recognized the sting of it: devotion slicing bone; hate scraping hot across his heart. The man stalking toward him used to be his stand-in father. An adopted brother. Friend, confidant, mentor, instructor.

Memories crashed into him. Bracken teaching him how to hold a sword. Bracken guiding him through the gauntlet. Bracken laughing during a combat trial in that very arena, celebrating Cael's first victory, one he'd handed Cael on a silver platter. Bracken telling stories about his father, Cael's uncle, who chased glory in the Tupinaire instead of political upstanding in the War Room.

"Is this what you want, cousin?" Bracken called, dragging the tip of his greatsword across the fragile ice. "Should I brace for a shuriken, or will you be fighting honorably?"

"He would've doomed us all, Bracken," Cael shouted. He realigned his grip on the handle of his short-sword then did the same with Holland's saber. "You were a pawn in his game. Same as me."

"You think our people will respect the ascension of a traitor? Someone who put Aurethian interest before Griean advancement?" The horrid scratch of Bracken's claymore through the frost sent a chill down Cael's spine. Bracken laughed. "No, Cael. Aurethia might call me a monster, but Griea will know me as their savior, and the Greater Universe will cower in the shadow of our magnificence."

Two...

"Marcus Volkov was assassinated in the Tupinaire. Per Griean law, his title is contested. Only one of us will leave this arena as Legatus," Cael spat, widening his stance. He lifted and curled his hand around each handle. Shook off the tremble in his ankles. Watched Bracken pace and crow. "Yield now, Bracken." *Let's start over.* "We can still fix this."

Bracken shook his head. His voice rasped through the vent in his draconic helmet. "This is Griea," he shouted, and slammed his fist against his chest. The crowd roared. "And I yield to no one but the basilisk!"

One... Begin!

Cael dived to dodge the first heavy swing of Bracken's claymore. He tucked and rolled, shooting to his feet in time to raise his short-sword and saber, blocking a heavy downward strike. The weight of the blow sent a tremor through his forearms. His shoulders strained and his biceps burned, spine bowing against ruthless pressure. Bracken snorted dismissively and sank lower, pushed harder.

Every morning spent in the meadow training with Elio filtered through his mind. Watching him glide through the grass, cataloguing grace, mimicking his deadly precision. *Do not meet ego with anger.* Something Peadar had said in the training chamber. *Self-control is its own weapon, Imperator.* Advice from Vik after Elio bested him with a hidden dagger. *To identify weakness in a foe is to hold the key to a successful fight,* and Cael knew Bracken's weakness. Knew what made him clumsy, knew what tunneled his vision.

Cael slid the blades away and spun, whirling around to cross his weapons and slam both swords against Bracken's claymore. "You've chased glory to the very end," he said, breathing hard. "Everyone will remember you as Marcus's pet. Imperator by proxy — "

Bracken headbutted Cael. Their armored headpieces clashed. Pain throbbed in Cael's skull, but he righted himself against a dizzy flare and pranced backward, putting enough space between them to shake out the shadow darkening the cliff of his good eye.

"I don't even recognize you," Bracken said. He charged forward, blade slicing in a beautiful, savage arc.

Cael side-stepped. He tore off his helmet and tossed it. The stadium boomed. Voices careened downward from the tall seating, filling the stomach of the arena. He wanted Griea to see him. Witness him. And he needed the clarity of peripheral vision if he wanted to clinch a victory. His blind eye wasn't completely gone. He saw the faint outline of shadowy objects. No detail, but movement. No color, but size.

"Do you think our people will praise you, cousin? Do you think they'll bow to a baby killer? Put their faith in a leader weak enough to cut down the elderly when he couldn't control the populus," Cael seethed. He struck his two blades together, and paced across the ice, circling Bracken in a half-moon, mirroring every stride.

Another black shadow crossed beneath them. The basilisk's great fin hit the icesheet. The ground shook and cracked.

Bracken swiped his helmet away, too. It struck the frozen sea with a hard, metallic thud, and his face twisted into a snarl. "When I put a muzzle on Elio," he started, lifting his claymore to point at Cael, "he'll think of you. And when I put a collar on him," he paused, elevating a dark eyebrow, "he'll remember this, today, right here, and he'll know it was you who leashed him to me."

The threat was a thumb pressed to an aggravated wound. Rage flared in Cael's gut. He slashed with the saber, knocking Bracken's sword, and then lunged. That awful, pretty sound of iron meeting, again, again, *again* echoed throughout the arena, and the spectators went wild as the two Volkov heirs battled across the ice.

Cael knew better than to flinch, but a particularly hard swing of Bracken's claymore caused panic to flash across his face, so miniscule and accidental, yet enough to give Bracken the confidence to cock his fist back and crush his gloved hand against Cael's mouth. The hit stunned him. Allotted Bracken enough room to knock Holland's saber out of Cael's grip and seize him by the throat.

Somewhere behind him, Elio yelled his name. It was a brutal, furious cry, sewn with the trappings of an unlived future.

Cael kicked at the ice. He remembered one particular morning. Taking Elio by the jaw, yanking him forward in a playful, sensuous movement, and being met with the princeling's leg up and around him, knocking him unceremoniously into the grass. Elio's warm laughter and sugary voice. *Careful, fiancé. Don't get cocky.* Cael inhaled a sharp, chilly breath, and lashed out with his leg, smacking Bracken in the ribcage. The movement gave him enough leverage to swing forward and knock Bracken onto his back, but it did not give him enough room to avoid the excruciating puncture of Bracken's claymore through his oblique. Blood soaked his armored tunic. He gritted his teeth and jerked to the side, dislodging the blade before it sank deeper.

Red streaked the ice. Such a vivid, bold contrast to the rest of Griea's landscape. White, blue, grey. A pale, wintery overlay obstructed by the candid color of someone freshly spilled.

Cael couldn't ignore the pain, so he bottled it. Let it swell, and rise, and stay there. He swung his sword as Bracken shot to his feet. The very tip of his blade caught Bracken's cheek, tearing flesh, slicing through his ear, digging a shallow groove into his skull. Another crimson spray speckled the ice, slippery and steaming on the glacial mass.

The showmanship of arena combat trickled away, and the brutal fight to stay alive took over. Cael wasn't performing anymore. The wound on his side wouldn't allow it. And Bracken no longer raised his blade high or held his arms open for the crowd, igniting the stadium.

They clashed, and Cael felt the vivid, unmistakable warning tug at him again, saying *you will die today*, same as it had on Aurethia before Lorelei blocked Bracken's killing blow. This time, Bracken threw him like a ragdoll, slamming him against weak ice. A boot met Cael's stomach, then his ribcage. The handle of Bracken's claymore slammed into the bleeding wound on his abdomen. Pain lanced, flashing white across his vision. Cael swept Bracken's legs out from underneath him and coughed, buying a precious moment.

"Get up, Cael!" His name was a shredded sound in Elio's mouth, screamed from the far side of the horseshoe-shaped arena.

The impact of Bracken's solid body sent a deep crack bolting through the ice. It wasn't the harsh, crystal *ting* of an internal split. This was a true break. Water gushed and bubbled, and the arena where they fought began to come apart.

An alarm blared repeatedly. The announcer drone came through the speaker. *Breach! Breach! Breach!* The gravity suspension module on the underside of the stadium rumbled to life.

Cael whipped toward Vik and Elio. Thankfully, Vik had already hooked himself around Elio's middle and was hauling the High Lord onto the platform. Then he turned toward Holland who stood frozen in place, hands shaking at his side. Cael pointed at the open iron door.

Holland lurched toward him, but Cael pointed again, shaking his head.

Bracken's closed fist struck, snapping his head to the side. When Cael looked back, Holland was stepping onto the platform, still watching, face slack with shock and horror.

"The ice is compromised! Stop the match," Elio barked, clawing at Vik, squirming like a trapped cat.

Cael could barely hear him after that. Chaos filled the air. Ice breaking, the alarm sounding, the stadium lifting, the audience roaring. Cael's own heartbeat was a heavy, persistent bassline underneath the cacophony. When he looked down, blood puddled under his feet, leaking from his side, following a slanting path into the sea.

The stadium chanted. *Le-ga-tus! Le-ga-tus! King-slayer! King-slayer! Imperator! Vol-kov! Vol-kov! Keeper!*

"I'll give our child your name." Bracken heaved, stepping from one icesheet to another. He was limping and torn, but he held his claymore tightly. "Cael, bleeding heart of Griea, who sacrificed himself for the greater good of his homeworld. Every time Elio addresses his son, he'll remember this day."

Dread and anger seared his chest. "I'm not dead yet, cousin," Cael said, spitting red at the ice.

Bracken aimed another strike, bringing his greatsword over his head and through the air. Cael blocked, but the blow brought him to one knee. *Brute strength is nothing without a thoughtful delivery.* Peadar had slid the comment to Cael once, eyeing him like a clumsy pup. Then another memory speared him. *Death is not decorative. I kill swiftly, as intended.* Bracken's voice churned up from a long, long time ago, his smiling face lit by a waxy candle in a tap house. *You'd be wise to do the same.*

A hard, sharp stone lodged in his throat, but Cael saw the opening, knew the moment would not come again, and buckled, allowing Bracken's claymore to slide up and over him. Cael rammed his short-sword beneath Bracken's sternum, skewering. The bone crush of it, the wet, bewildered gasp...

A sob caught in Cael's mouth, and he twisted the pommel, cutting through soft places.

"You could've stood by me," Cael said. He yanked his sword free. Bracken hit the ice, blinking dazedly at the sky. Glassy-eyed and struggling to breathe, Bracken watched him. Surprised, elated. Cael said it again, allowing each word to scrape itself along his throat, burning, needling. "You could've stood *with* me," he rasped, and shook his head.

Bracken's blood plumed in the dark, cold water. Beneath them, a shadowy beast rose through the sea, slithering toward the arena.

"Live — " Bracken choked out his last blessing. " — and die with honor."

Grief overwhelmed him, but Cael said, "God is in the water," and inched away.

On another backward step, his boot plunged into the sea. All around him, ice broke, leaving wide patches of naked ocean between the center of the arena and the distant platform.

The stadium began to rise. Panic shot through his sore body. Adrenaline masked the pain blooming in his stomach, face — everywhere. He glanced down, watching the massive basilisk cut through the water. Its shape ballooned, growing until it shadowed half the icesheet. Cael's confidence waned.

If he did not get to the platform, he would die today. The basilisk did not care if he won the match, it did not care if he claimed his father's title. It would take him regardless.

"Cael!" Elio called to him, perched on the platform, still held at bay by Vik. "Run!"

Cael took a breath and loped toward him, following Elio's voice.

The ice splintered. He felt it give beneath his sabatons. Recognized the slip of saltwater around his ankles, and the wet glide of the sea climbing over cobbled ice. The arena shattered. He heard the horrible crunch of snow, frost, water, and overfreeze come apart for monstrous teeth. Felt himself slip backward, pulled by the vertical heave of a glacier tipped toward the center of the arena. Cael scrambled to grab the top of it, heaved himself over, fell with a painful *thud* on another glacier.

"C'mon!" Elio was closer. He was right there. "Get up, Cael! Get up!"

The stadium levitated.

Cael pushed to his feet and ran. *Get to him.* Each step burned, every stride shot through the wound on his abdomen and pulsed in the fresh bruises painted across his body, but he ran. *Get to him.* He ran and the arena exploded. He ran and Elio reached for him. He ran and the face of an old god ruptured the ice. *Get to him.* He ran, he leaped, and Elio's slender hand clasped his forearm.

"Vik," Elio cried out, straining to hold him.

Vik bent over the lip of the platform and grasped Cael's shoulder, helping Elio haul him to safety. Cael fell into Elio's chest. The stadium hovered above what remained of the designated area where the Tupinaire took place, avoiding a catastrophic collision.

Huge curved teeth glistened, and a pair of copper eyes surfaced, crowned with rigid cobalt scales. A violet fin lined its back, each spine punched through with sallow bone. The interior of its mouth was the color of crushed roses, and Cael winced as it bellowed, filling the air with a primal, predatory roar.

Summoned from another world by Griea's knightly blood rite, a mighty basilisk burst forth, widened its jaws, and swallowed Bracken Volkov whole.

As quickly as it breached, the basilisk clamped its mouth shut and retreated beneath the water. Its fin sliced through floating ice, coiling in a deadly, vibrant show of purple, blue, green, and black, then it disappeared with a flick of its barbed tail, sinking into the depths.

Cael heaved through breath after painful breath. He didn't register Vik's hand clamped over the wound on his abdomen. Didn't notice much of anything. He kept seeing the blood on his mother's face, kept hearing Bracken's last command. *Live and die with honor.*

"I've got you," Elio said, holding him carefully. He was warm, and solid, and true. The ruined ice bobbed uselessly beneath them. The blood was gone. The trial was over. He pressed his cheek to the top of Cael's head. "You're alright. You're with me. I have you, Cael."

Cael searched for Elio's hand. When he found it, he squeezed and held on.

CHAPTER FORTY-EIGHT
ELIO

You can't intervene. Vik's voice is distant, foggy. His grip is iron-tight.

Cael's body is opened by a claymore. Instead of blood, he is cracked like a pomegranate, spilling juice and seeds. Suddenly the ice is gone. Elio can't hear his own voice. He is soundless, yelling into a void, screaming for someone who won't turn toward him. The water becomes a fanged mouth, forked tongue lapping the sky, diamond pupil fixed on Elio. His mother's broach is pinned to the basilisk's fin. He recognizes his father's shoe wedged at the base of a giant tooth.

Elio jolted awake. He blinked at the outline of an armoire through the darkness. Cael's belt curved over the knob. Elio's coat hung lazily from the wooden door. His quick breathing and clammy skin were a relief. Waking meant it was just another nightmare. Something he could leave. He turned over, hunting for Cael with an outstretched arm. Across from the empty side of Cael's bed, muted light ribboned the doorway to a connected washroom. He saw Cael's shoulder through the cracked door, his busy hand tugging at a bandage.

Elio slid out of bed and padded to the washroom. When he gave the door a gentle push, dim luminance shafted over the sheepskin rug. Cael studied the stitched line on his abdomen with a furrowed brow. Opposite the new wound, blue-silver branched the skin above his hip, narrowly missing his tattoo. That strange, ethereal scar remained, still holding a sip of Avarine.

"Let me," Elio murmured. He stepped forward and knuckled Cael's hand away, assessing the stitched gash.

"What're you doin' up?"

"Taking care of my husband."

"It's itchy," Cael complained, huffing. He feathered his thumb across Elio's cheek, following the tiny scar left behind from their long-ago sparring session. His voice softened. "Another one?"

Elio swallowed, nodding sharply. It'd been a week since the Tupinaire, and Elio hadn't made it through a single night without jumping awake, drenched and nauseated, untangling himself from a nightmare like a bug in a spider's web. He looked over the taut skin, inspected the black stitching.

"These can probably come out," Elio said. He rummaged in a drawer, fingering around lotion, face oil, and an unwrapped soap bar until he found a pair of cuticle scissors.

"What was it this time?" Cael asked.

He tried to ignore a flash from the dream. Cael going limp. A basilisk busting through the frozen sea. "Nothing new."

Cael's stomach flexed with an insignificant flinch at the first snip. He hummed, and it was a sound Elio knew well. Cael didn't believe him, but he knew better than to pry. "Angelina will be here the day after tomorrow."

"Oh, is it finally safe enough to land?" Elio mocked, snorting dismissively. "Vik sent a transmission to Lorelei. We should hear from her soon."

"Good. I need to speak with the legionaries. Reconvene with the Royal Reserve. Make myself known to Griea. I'm sure Machina is expecting a statement — distant communities on the other side of Goren are probably waiting, too."

"Will they accept you?" Elio plucked away a stitch.

Cael hissed through his teeth. When Elio clucked his tongue and shot him a less than patient glance, he squinted defensively. "In time, yes. I think the Tupinaire showed them exactly who I am, and what kind of leader they can expect."

Elio paused. The next question festered. "Will they accept me?"

"They saw us." He worried his lip with his canine. "They know you're mine."

"That's not what I asked." The last stitch came free. Elio covered the red seam with a new bandage.

"In time," he said again, and took Elio by the chin, steering his gaze. "You need to sleep."

"I'll be fine."

"Let me help you," he purred, playful and too smooth. He leaned down to nip at Elio's mouth. "I'm happy to tire you out, darling. Say the word."

Elio wanted nothing more. He fought back a syrupy smile. "You're still healing. Don't tease me with something you can't deliver."

"Can't deliver?" Cael balked. His grip tightened. He eased Elio against the lip of the vanity, resting his free hand over the waistband of his underwear.

For a week, Cael and Elio hid themselves away, sequestered to Cael's bedchamber like refugees. Vik, Holland, Constance, Oliver, and the housestaff wandered the Volkov castle, checking on them, relaying messages. They respected Elio's request for privacy, and honored Cael's period of mourning. It took the newly appointed Legatus an entire day to speak, and another two before he managed to keep any food down.

The most powerful couple in the Greater Universe spent most of their inaugural week curled together in bed, hardly speaking, or naked in the bathtub, watching bruises fade day after day. Sex hadn't been a priority. Not when Elio's violent nightmares refused to quit, and not when Cael's battered body was just now beginning to repair itself. They simply existed together, intimate, alive, and trying to heal.

Cael smoothed his hand along Elio's jaw, holding him carefully. "I miss you," he whispered.

Elio felt across the strong curve of Cael's forearm. His pulse hammered faintly, pressed against the center of Elio's palm. "I'm right here."

Cael dropped his hands and lifted, placing Elio on the countertop. His strength shouldn't have surprised him, but Elio's lashes still fluttered, his breath still shortened.

Physicality was a distant reverie, something they'd half-forgotten.

Cael knocked the inside of Elio's knees. Stepped between them, drawing Elio closer with a lazy grip on his waist, thumbs dipping over each jutting hipbone. He moved with easy sensuality, far less reserved than the bashful warlord who had landed on Aurethia over a cycle ago. Every movement, every touch peeled away a bit of Elio's heaviness. He felt more himself right then, aligned body-to-body, manhandled onto a sink by his husband. He felt blissfully normal, somehow.

"Bed," Elio commanded.

Cael's breath met his cheek. "Patience."

Elio arched forward, slipping his arms over Cael's shoulders. His lips grazed Cael's chin. "Don't you dare," he said, dragging out each word, "make me wait."

Despite the heated play at the root of their banter, Elio went boneless at the press of Cael's mouth, the stroke of his warm tongue. Every wall crumbled, every defensive brick laid into his internal guard was dismantled.

Elio sighed into a slow, tender kiss. It was the opposite of the night they'd spent together in the Containment Facility. Instead of a burning, hopeless clash, Cael took his time exploring Elio's mouth, snaking his hand beneath his bellybutton, tracing the center of him through his cotton underwear, pausing to taste and hunt, to crack his eyes open and watch Elio's face darken.

It was then, as Elio panted against Cael's mouth, that he realized exactly what he wanted. Identified the desire igniting in his groin, and the heat coiling tight in his chest. They could be slow. Take their time. They could love each other tenderly, lazily without the threat of doom or war on the horizon.

Elio touched the silver scar on Cael's stomach, and lowered his mouth to Cael's throat, kissing his lifepoint, lower, scraping his teeth across hard collarbone. When he pushed away from the countertop, Cael made a wounded noise, and when he placed his feet on the stone, inching Cael backward, the Legatus followed his silent order.

"Elio," Cael mumbled. With a gentle push, Cael plopped on the side of the rumpled bed, held still by Elio's hands on his shoulders. "I'm supposed to be tiring *you* out."

Elio slid into his lap, hyperaware of Cael's hand on his tailbone, gliding underneath his underwear, tugging him closer, urging him to grind down. Liquid pleasure sparked.

"Don't start complaining," he said, nudging Cael's temple with his nose. He placed a palm on Cael's chest and gave a gentle push, tossing him onto the plush comforter.

Cael elevated a tapered black eyebrow. He paused to laugh, sputtering through a soft, bewildered sound, one Elio hadn't heard in so long.

Elio kissed him. He swallowed that laughter, tasted Cael's smile, and laughed, too.

"Let me have you," Elio whispered.

Cael sighed against his cheek. "You have me," he said, echoing the sentiment twice more, "you have me, you have me."

For the first time since their wedding night, Elio felt a soft-petaled sprig of hope begin to unfurl.

Elio loomed over Cael, tasting the bruise on his cheek, then the slope of his neck. His breath came short at the struggle of Cael's hand worming between his spread legs, cupping his crotch.

"I want to go down on you." Cael exhaled the plea against Elio's earlobe.

"Later."

Cael made an unkempt sound and pushed the fabric aside. Elio sighed at the rake of his pointer and middle digits. He ground down in Cael's lap, riding his hand, pulling himself over bony knuckles, ignoring the stiffness in his muscles and accepting the pleasure rippling low in his stomach. He opened his mouth over Cael's clavicle and laid his teeth there. Cael lifted away from the bed, pitching his waist upward, searching for friction.

It hadn't been long in retrospect. Cael and Elio had only spent an Earthen month apart — a week or two before that. The absence weighed on Elio like an eternity, though. Going from a summer wet with desire, soaked in sea spray, skin, and discovery, to evenings bathed in candlelight, celebrating the longer Aurethian nights and chilly mornings, to an early spring swaddled in the whirlwind of wedding planning.

It all came to an abrupt halt.

Elio had been married and happy, then with the suddenness of a pulse-shot, Elio had been without, heartbroken, miserable, full of rage, then thrown into Cael's orbit again, fighting beside him, almost losing him, and now they were together, *finally*. Together in the aftermath.

What'd transpired seemed like a decade; it seemed like no time at all. An eternity, a blink, or a trigger-pull.

Elio was stupid with something like a wish, something sunny and glinting. Gummy with the desire to upend the leftover hurt crouched inside him and leave it behind. It was such a strange, new feeling: being in love with someone who should've rightfully become his enemy. Strange, because he could hardly imagine it. Cael, an enemy. New, because Elio's cracked heart still ached for him, and in the same beat — remembering Cael's mission, his origin — sent pain slicing through him. Their story had been on someone else's terms, orchestrated like a string-puppet by someone else's hand. Yet they remained.

The love, especially, remained. Strangled, hard-won, real, and still waking. But alive, steady. Flaring like a newborn star.

"I almost lost you." Elio didn't realize he'd said the thought out loud until Cael's playful gaze softened.

The hand inside him paused, reached, curled, stroked. Elio felt the movement the same way he heard a harp, as if Cael had plucked something tight inside him. Elio's feet flexed and his body caved, grinding on the base of Cael's digits. His face went hot. The blush was half embarrassment, half pleasure.

"You didn't," Cael said, far too evenly. He retracted his hand and yanked at Elio's underwear.

Elio eased onto his side. The space gave them room to peel away the rest of their clothes. Elio's undergarment, Cael's sleep-pants.

"Almost," Elio repeated.

Cael kicked out of his pajamas and crawled closer, caging Elio against the bed. "You didn't," he said again, pushing the first word into his belly, the second against his breastbone.

Having Cael against him sent his mind spinning. But Elio didn't want to think. He didn't want to dwell on what they'd survived. He gave Cael another push, forcing him onto his back again, and straddled his waist. Red, pinched marks framed the mean line left behind from Bracken's claymore. Elio glanced at the tail of it, peeking outside the line of the freshly laid bandage. He took Cael's length, held him steady, and sank down. His core split. The warm, bold push of body into body was a familiar, animal thing. Elio liked to watch Cael's face whenever he managed to pin his husband down. Liked to see his sly mouth fall open and the black pitted in blue balloon. The ghost-white of his blind eye tracked the other a quarter-second late. Cael's fingertips dented his hips.

Elio rocked against him. He lifted himself in small, languid thrusts, moving like the tide. Cael guided each slow roll, every pretty pitch of his lithe body.

The darkness in their chamber was true dark. Shadow filled every nook and cranny, and while the room was thick with heat from the hearth-fire, snow still licked the air, tossed in after a veranda was opened or a door slid apart. It stiffened his nipples. The cold ran through him, same as the warmth, and Elio shivered at the swelling inside him, at the tender feeling of Cael stretching him. It was such a wild thing, feeling that. How Cael grew within. Blood pulsed at the crown of Elio's sex. His gut churned and his core squeezed, molten and sweetly slick.

The scent of their coupling tinged the chamber. Salt, skin. The leftover stain of yesterday's perfume. But it was Cael's reverent expression that had Elio's spine bending. It was the look he wore — close-knit furrow of his brow, tongue dropping away from the roof of his mouth, attention scanning

Elio from nose to thigh — that had Elio's chest fluttering. A tender moan flitted out. The sound came from his lungs. When Cael pushed, bucking into Elio with more force, the next noise was lower, deeper, crawling up from his diaphragm.

Elio placed one hand on Cael's wide chest and curled the spare around his husband's throat, holding him gently. The slightest pressure on his windpipe had the Legatus swearing in Grian, grip clamping like a cuff around Elio's waist, each finger lifting then digging in. Elio watched the concentration settle on Cael's beautiful face. Saw him focus, staving off an early spend.

But that wasn't what Elio wanted. He wanted this slow, methodical unstitching of Cael's resolve to expose him, to make him boneless and breathy. Elio ground down harder.

Cael made a sore sound. His inky lashes beat and lowered. He sat up with a quickness that had Elio gasping. One arm came around Elio's back, holding him close, and the other bunched the soft flesh on his thigh, then skated upward, fingers rushing up Elio's nape and into the fine hair just above his undercut. They were chest-to-chest, joined and moving together. The press of Cael's pelvis sent a shockwave through his center. Elio kept bouncing languidly in his lap, sharing breath and heat. His eyelids slipped shut. Pleasure burned through him, catching in his sore body like dry timber. The last time they did this. Not sex, not the slamming chase they'd given each other under the mountain. But *this*, slow and mindful, indulgent and without stipulation… had been their wedding night, and Elio had been drunk on champagne and cake, drunk on a future with Cael Volkov.

Elio recognized that same feeling stripped down to its essence. He was set ablaze by the promise of what they'd taken for themselves. What they had. What they'd fought for.

The hand in Elio's hair tightened, pulling his face back an inch. That firm pressure loosened his tongue, made his mouth sliver open.

"Death itself could not keep you from me," Cael said into the space between them.

Elio slowed. He swallowed and rested his hand on Cael's cheek, feeling across the spindly scar from Nara's paw. Cael leaned forward and brushed his lips along Elio's face, catching the notch on the bridge of his nose, dented there by the pommel of Cael's sword, and then kissed the tiny line his blade had left on Elio's freckled cheekbone during their sparring session all that time ago.

Cael lowered his mouth and kissed him long and deep. It was a damp, chewing kiss, wet with breath and spit, filthy with tongue and teeth. Elio pressed into that kiss. He wanted to swallow Cael whole, to feel him at the base of his throat, at the bottom of his stomach. He wanted to trace every tooth in his mouth, wanted to get inside him and carve his name into a bone the way children carved their names into trees.

Cael was already deep inside him, though. Already nudging up against the interior of his channel with a firm quickness that dismantled Elio's prior plan to drive his husband into a frenzy. Instead, it was Elio who whined and shook, pulling Cael into his body again and again.

But it was still Cael who gasped into Elio's neck, and it was still Cael whose body spasmed, whose hips thrust clumsily. The hot, seeping spill of him brought a satisfied smile to Elio's face, one that vanished the moment Cael dropped him onto the bed and slid his hand into the glossed place his sex had been a moment prior. He laid between Elio's spread legs, tonguing at the soaked, pulsing pinnacle above his entrance.

Elio's cry shredded the quiet. Cael sucked hard on the crown of his sex. His wicked mouth was a hot, soft massage, heaving him over the edge. Another little cry, shallow this time, and Elio's body convulsed, clenching, squeezing, buckling until all the pleasure ran out of him, leaking through each boneless limb, cottoning his skull. His muscles clamped and then butterflied open, loosening like a new wing. His breath was held, then came sighing out of him, long and shuddering. He flopped on the bed. Cael slowed his ministrations, shifting his focus to the crease of Elio's hip, then to the scar slashed above his knee, lower, mouthing greedily at his inner thigh.

"You look like a sniper down there," Elio muttered. His breathing slowed, broken by a quiet little laugh.

Laughter sputtered out of Cael. He laid a lazy bite on Elio's damp skin. "How's my aim?"

"Quite alright, actually." Another gusty exhale fissured through with a chuckle.

Elio felt the curve of Cael's smile against this leg. He traced his fingertip along Cael's bare skull as the mighty Legatus trailed his way from thigh to belly, belly to chest, then chest to neck. He went limp against the bed beside Elio, cheek pressed to pectoral. Elio wondered if he might be listening to his heartbeat.

They stayed like that for a while longer, dirtying the bed with cooling sweat.

"Do you want to lay with me by the fire?" Cael asked.

"Yes," Elio said. It was the easiest answer he'd ever given.

They visited the washroom before padding over to the square, black hearth in the corner of Cael's bedchamber. Cael fed it another log and pulled a beast-skin in front of it. He grabbed a folded blanket from a linen closet Elio hadn't realized existed and then tossed their pillows from the bed onto the ground. The heat from the hearth touched his naked skin, and when he curled close to Cael, perched on his side, nose-to-nose with his husband, he felt heat there, too. Cael was solid and supple, fitting against him with a rightness he didn't think would ever fade.

Cael followed his nose-bridge with a fingertip. "One day, I'll be gone, Elio."

Elio's brow contracted with a sudden jolt of pain, *pain*. He opened his mouth. Cael made a sharp shushing sound.

"I will die before you because I am Griean and you're Aurethian. My body was not steeped in blue — "

"Stop it," he whispered.

Cael sighed through his nose. "But I will love you for all the time I'm here. And when Wonder makes me new, and tosses me back into the universe, I'll come find you."

Elio did not want to cry. He was done crying. They had to be done. So he ignored the sting in his eyes and pushed into Cael, aligning his body against the man beside him, hip-to-hip, chest-to-chest, stomach-to-stomach, and felt that quivering, flowering hope grow a fraction taller.

"I don't want you in the Tupinaire anymore." It was childish and unimportant, but Elio said it anyway.

A patient smile turned Cael's mouth. "I know."

That was not *okay* or *fine*, Elio noted. But if he pushed, he would be starting a fight for no reason, and he was done fighting, too.

"Go to sleep, Cael. Make love to me in the morning," he said instead, and closed his eyes.

Cael drew idle circles on the low bend of his back. "Tell me you love me."

"I love you," Elio said. *I love you too much. I love you to my own detriment. I love you like breathing. I love you like waking and bleeding. I love you in a way I've never loved before.* "Until Sunder collapses. And when our great star is gone, I'll love in the dark. I'll love you now, and then, and after. I'll love you when loving you is all that's left."

Cael drew him closer, as if their skin might unbuckle and reforge itself. One man; one fate. He flattened his nose against the top of Elio's head, inhaling deeply. "Now, then, after."

"Now, then, after," Elio said again, and felt his body sway into sleep.

THE DAY DRAITUNE'S WARSHIP descended into low orbit, Elio stood on one of the many balconies overlooking Machina, watching the grey behemoth float toward the transport hub. He peered at the frosty expanse. Ice scissored the air and a pale-feathered owl swooped by.

From the castle, he saw far across the Sliding Sea, and deep into the blueprint of Machina. He saw the War College, and the metropolitan train system. He saw people walking through the city, shadowed beneath lantern-lit awnings. He saw the Griean greenhouses, and children carrying holo-books, and syndicate members jostling each other in front of a café. He saw the huge holodisplays — three dimensional commercials advertising current fashion, planet-side nightlife, self-care products, and entertainment — flash between slate buildings. On the cusp of the city, stationed alone, he saw the empty arena. From above, the hollow stadium looked smaller, like a curl of steel left to rust in the snow.

"You wanted to see me," Vik said.

Elio startled. One hand shot to the sheathed blade on his hip, but he stopped and brushed his index along the pommel of his Grabak. His heart sputtered, panic melting into relief.

A sigh fogged the air behind him. "Sorry," the Augment lamented, stepping over the threshold to join Elio on the veranda. "Are you alright, High Lord?"

"I'll be fine," he said, nodding curtly. "Have we received word from my sister?"

"Not yet. Transmission time is hard to gauge, but it shouldn't be too much longer. Angelina confirmed Aurethia is stable, and Lady Lorelei is communicating regularly with the council."

"Good." He paused, considering his next request. "Vik, how do I assign you a new Primary Controller?"

"An audible request." Vik shifted nervously. His data-port whirred. When the quiet stretched, he blurted, "Have I done something wrong, Elio?"

Elio laughed in his throat. He shook his head, turning to look at the Augment who had been nothing short of heroic, who had served as

protector and advisor for over a cycle, who had sacrificed himself not once
but twice. "I'd like to release you from service."

Vik flinched.

"I don't want you to go anywhere," he clarified, offering a timid smile.
"And I don't think I'll ever be able to thank you for what you've done. You
kept Cael safe and grounded. You saved my life — "

"*You* saved *my* life," he countered. His throat worked around a swallow,
and he shifted his weight. For the first time, legitimate confusion crossed
Vik's face. He searched Elio with quick flicks of his cybernetic eyes and
fidgeted with a loose thread on his pant pocket. "You gave me Avarine —
the *only* Avarine you had," he whispered, leaning closer. "It's not customary
to save an Augment on the battlefield. We're an investment, yes, but we are
dispensable and — "

"You are not dispensable, and your value is not dependent on cybernetic
enhancement," Elio said.

Vik frowned. Blinked. He looked adorably perplexed.

"How do I make Vik Endresen your Primary Controller?" Elio asked.

One black pupil expanded. His data-port clicked and chimed. When he
cocked his head, assessing Elio with a narrow, curious look, the High Lord
nodded.

"It's against regulation to release an Augment into their own control."

"Am I not Duke of Griea?"

"You are," Vik said.

"Vik Endresen, I'd like to transfer control to one, Vik Endresen, for the
duration of his post-mortem, augmented lifetime," Elio said, sounding out
each word. The shock on Vik's face deepened. His mouth parted, and he
straightened, staring intently while Elio spoke. "You are to do as you please,
go where you want, and live how you see fit."

"I must vocalize the transfer and confirm," Vik said, hardly audible. His
face reddened and his mouth shook. "I have been ordered to tether my
internal and external allegiance to one, Vik Endresen. All off-planet monitoring via Augment surveillance is now suspended, pending review by the
Primary Controller. Transmitted messages, data, or emergency correspondence must be executed manually by the Primary Controller. Do I have
your approval to initiate the transfer?"

Elio smiled and nodded. "Yes."

Vik's entire body seemed to loosen. He looked at one hand, turning the
limb casually, then the other, and tilted his head. "Would you like me to
disengage with your dialect device, High Lord?"

"Frankly, I like having you in my ear. But only stay if you want to. I consider us friends — "

"We're friends," Vik quipped.

Elio's smile spread. "I'm sure Cael is going to ask you to stay in Machina, but you're welcome on Aurethia. It's your home, too. Honestly, as much as I value your guidance, I think my husband might need it more." He met Vik's questioning gaze, watching the pieces slip into place. The Augment lifted his chin and exhaled slowly.

"You're going to leave," he said, uttering the revelation like the answer to a riddle.

"I suspect House Darvin and the rest of the Imperium will encourage us to establish our newfound stewardship on our respective homeworlds. Griea needs Cael. Aurethia needs me."

"Cael needs you," Vik said matter-of-factly.

And I need him. "He'll have me. We just won't be ruling from the same household for a while." He gave Vik a sore look. "You can't tell me you didn't predict this."

Vik's data-port hummed again. He remained quiet and pensive, and Elio realized it was the first time Vik didn't provide a slew of information at the mere mention of someone potentially needing it. He thought for a moment. His pupil shrank, then grew. After a minute, maybe two, his eye fluttered and he heaved a sigh, bracing on the railing with both hands.

"Ninety days, maybe a season," Elio said, hopeful.

Vik nodded. The tightness of his mouth did not hint at agreement, though.

Elio's dialect device crackled to life. *Arrival: Angelina Darvin of Draitune, Rune of Ren, Wippler of Mal. Please confirm an adequate meeting place.* He touched his device and said, "Tell them to meet us in the dining hall." *Thank you, Duke Henly. Please report to the dining hall in approximately eight minutes.* He dropped his hand and sighed. "They better get back here soon."

"It's good for him to get out of the house," Vik said.

"I know." Elio stared at Goren, wondering where Cael and Holland might be. He pictured them climbing rock faces, hunting for stag or long-horned sheep. He shifted his gaze to Vik. "If you're not busy, I'd like you to sit in on this meeting."

The Augment nodded. His mouth ticked upward. "I think I can manage that."

The pair walked inside and crossed the common room. There was an empty space on the floor where Tatu's pelt had been. The moment Cael had seen it, he'd ordered it removed. Elio didn't know where it'd been stored, but he was glad he didn't have to look at it any longer.

Duchess Constance swept around the corner, entrenched in a stormy gown. She wore an Ocurian headwrap instead of a mourning veil, and the blue polish on her fingernails glittered like Avara. She was an elegant fortress he still couldn't breach.

Cael's mother shot Elio a cool look. "Are you well, High Lord?"

Elio inclined his head respectfully. "Tired."

"We haven't had the chance to talk."

"I wasn't aware you wanted to speak with me."

"You're my son-in-law." Her voice was as steady as a sheet of rain. "It would do us both some good to get to know each other."

"Did you find the manor to your liking while you were there?" He couldn't help the prickle of animosity that filled his voice. He slid her a long, biting glance.

Constance remained unbothered. "Aurethia is humid," she said, dismissing his ire. When they turned toward the dining hall, she paused, snaring his wrist in a firm grip. "Listen to me, lion cub. Marcus was a complicated man with a penchant for violence and a score to settle." She stared at Elio. Her dark copper eyes bore into him. Sunlight through jarred honey. "But Cael is what's left of my soul made flesh. I would rip the core out of a planet for him." The last statement lingered. She sounded exactly like him, as if she'd plucked that sentiment straight from Cael's mouth. "You armed him with the weapon that killed his father, didn't you?" She didn't wait for Elio to agree. She simply nodded and continued. "Then we can agree to have Cael's best interest at heart."

Elio glanced from Constance to where she gripped his wrist. The Duchess let him go.

Maybe she too had been trapped by Marcus's insatiable hunger for vengeance. Maybe Constance was an exceptional ally to have. Even so, Elio needed time. Time for the wound her house left on him to scab, at least. Time to breathe. He cleared his throat and gestured toward the dining hall. Constance looked him over again, boot to chin, then strode ahead, heels *click-clacking* the stone.

Angelina Darvin occupied a seat between Rune Makosi and Wippler Jye. Oliver stood, sugaring a decanter filled with steeping coffee. The company glanced between the trio. Elio took a seat next to Vik, and

Constance slid into an empty chair directly across from Angelina. It was a tense, uncoordinated meeting. One sewn with uncertainty Elio couldn't place. He felt judged, oddly enough. As if the Greater Universe didn't know how to approach him after watching his life implode.

"High Lord," Angelina said, assessing his title. White springy hair framed her face, and she wore a crisply tailored suit the color of her planet's ring. Age lined her dark skin, touched with the pale, oblong marking of vitiligo. Her thin mouth rounded slightly.

Elio cleared his throat. "What can we do for you, Angelina?"

His tone must've come as a surprise because the elected leader of Draitune slackened her jaw. "Well, I suppose we should start with the whereabouts of..." She trailed off, following the sound of hard, heavy footsteps.

Snow clung to Cael's thermal shirt. The weather-resistant turtleneck framed his jawline, and ice-burn reddened his nose and cheekbones. He slung a shaggy, long-haired mountain goat from where it was draped across his shoulders. The slain beast smacked the table with a loud *thud*. The coffee decanter and adjoining tableware rattled. Angelina jumped, splaying a hand across her chest. Rune blinked, surveying the animal with a sweeping glance, and Wippler's face contorted.

"Angelina," Cael greeted, swiping away the dewy sweat gathered above his top lip. "Rune, Wippler. Welcome."

"Imperator," she replied through clenched teeth.

"Legatus," Constance corrected, and poured herself a cup of coffee.

Holland strode through the room, carrying two large hares bound by their pearly feet. He canted an eyebrow at the table. "I'll butcher it."

Cael nodded his appreciation before turning back to the meeting. "Sorry I'm late."

Rune opened her hand toward the empty seat at the head of the table.

Angelina flashed her palm and heaved an irritated sigh. "I'll get straight to the point. The Imperium is concerned about the rightful passage of power. One, Griea completely undermined the unification agreement by levying a very public attack against Aurethia. Two, Cael took control of House Volkov through an unprompted, unregulated assassination. Three —"

"Does the Imperium typically approve of prompted, regulated assassinations?" Cael asked, falling into the chair his father used to occupy. He propped his elbow on the armrest and brought his hand to his mouth, teething one glove free, then the other.

Elio tried not to focus too intently on that movement. Cael's teeth against leather, tugging, how his hand came free and flexed. But it dropped deep into his body, triggering a thimble of heat to pour down the lower half of his spine. This unrefined version of his husband would never get old. Cael's arched eyebrow. His rueful smile and sharp, calculating eyes. The way Griea settled on him, chapping his fair skin, encouraging authenticity and fearlessness, imbued Cael with confidence Elio had never witnessed on the forest moon.

Angelina shot him a deadly look. "Three," she repeated, showing her straight teeth, "Avara production is stalled, and the Planetary Syndicate is at a stand-still."

Elio said, "Marcus attacked House Henly which resulted in a conflict with the Aurethian militia. The only military presence on the moon was the Royal Reserve, drafted and controlled solely by House Volkov." He felt Cael's attention like a slow-walking arachnid. "Griea is a ruthless place, and the Tupinaire has its own laws. Marcus died fairly during a combat match, and his title was absorbed by the man who challenged his incumbent successor. Bracken died by the sword, and his death was sealed by the basilisk. The passage of power is simple." He tried to remember the clear way his father used to speak. How Darius could silence a crowded room with practiced practicality. "I am the rightful heir of Aurethia, and Aurethia is now under my stewardship. Cael is the rightful heir of Griea, and Griea is now under his stewardship. I am a Duke of Griea by marriage, and Cael is a Lord of Aurethia by marriage."

The silence grew, but Cael's boot bumped his shoe beneath the table, and Elio remembered to breathe.

Holland returned to retrieve the goat, hauling it up and into his arms before striding back to the kitchen.

Wippler tipped his head. His mouth folded appreciatively, as if he hadn't expected such a straight-forward explanation. "Will Aurethia require assistance rebuilding?"

"Yes," Elio said through a relieved exhale. "I would be grateful for any material or labor Mal can spare." He gestured to Cael, tapping the table beside his bare hand. "The Legatus has agreed to send aid, too. We'll be opening the starlink for immigration in the near future, encouraging the Griean citizenship to experience Aurethia, and the Aurethian citizenship to experience Griea. It'll embolden both economies and bridge a historical gap."

"And the syndicate?" Angelina said. Her tone lightened a fraction. She looked between Elio and Cael, trying to decipher a rehearsed response or legitimate partnership.

Cael nodded toward his mother. "Duchess Constance will oversee the Planetary Syndicate going forward. I wasn't made aware of my father's careless decision to freeze all outstanding contractual work. We're rectifying his misstep immediately."

Angelina's stiff demeanor relaxed. She nodded, searching the table for a moment. "I apologize if I approached this meeting skeptically," she offered, terse but kind, "but for the record, I do need the truth. Can someone tell me exactly what happened on Aurethia?"

Elio's chest emptied. Memories bludgeoned him. He didn't care if it showed weakness, he reached for Cael's hand. Cael let him squeeze and gripped back just as tightly.

Vik cleared his throat. "I can."

Every eye swiveled toward him.

Angelina's brow tensed with confusion. "And you are?"

"Operative Vik Endresen. I accompanied Cael Volkov to Aurethia as his personal Augment. Cael transferred my service to Elio Henly on the morning of the siege. I'm confident my recollection will be helpful."

Cael deflated, slouching in his seat. Elio relaxed, too. Reliving an excruciating surplus of memories, so fresh and debilitating, would've been too heavy to shoulder. They could've done it. Elio could've, Cael could've. But it would've been a shame to potentially shatter themselves after spending a week in the dark confines of Cael's bedroom, piecing each other together.

"Go on, Operative Endresen," Rune said, tapping a fingernail on the table.

Vik started at the very beginning. He worked his way through their courtship, noting on the assassination attempt in Atreyu, Cael's reluctance to deliver data to House Volkov, and his request for Griea's Aurethian conquest to be reconsidered, then hurtled into the siege at the manor, and spoke briefly about their pit stop in Nadhas. He gracefully skirted the time they spent in the crater, focusing solely on the battle for Atreyu, Bracken's desire to take Lorelei as his bride, and Elio's counteroffer to wed him instead. It was a long, painful, bloody story. Hearing it told from start to finish left Elio's heart sore, and his palm slick in Cael's hand.

Once Vik was done, he poured himself a cup of coffee and took a drink. "According to my comparative observational data, I've concluded that Cael and Elio managed to thwart an extinction level event. If the previous leadership remained in place, Avara would've been harvested to death, and war would've moved through the Greater Universe at an alarming speed." He shrugged, nursing his hot drink. "You should thank them."

The dining hall remained still and quiet. Elio swallowed around sandpapery fear. It wasn't real fear, nothing he could run from, but the memory of it reached inside him. Pressed on bruises. Anger or anxiety stitched Cael's jaw. He said nothing. To the offworld leadership sitting in that room, the Legatus would've seemed completely unbothered. But Elio felt the quiver in his wrist, recognized the rigid way he held himself, saw the subtle flinch come and go.

"I commend you both," Wippler said.

Rune nodded in agreement.

"You two are efficient." Angelina dipped her chin. "The Greater Universe will need to see a good faith effort to establish stability within this fledgling alliance. Cael, you'll manage diplomatic outreach here, and Elio, you'll rebuild House Henly's custodial command on Aurethia."

Elio grounded himself, preparing for the stipulation the Imperium would no doubt demand to pacify any lingering doubt.

Cael lifted his other hand, as if awaiting an order. "Fair enough."

"One cycle, mirroring your courtship," she said.

The timeframe sent Elio's heart into his mouth. The world tipped. One cycle. An entire year without Cael. The concept itself seemed unthinkable. An annoying ring filled his skull, blaring like a pulse-beacon. *Breathe.* He blinked. Focused on the future, because they had one, they'd fought for one, and no one could take it from them. But if they didn't play the game, if they didn't compromise, the Imperium could make their new life a lot more complicated than it already was.

Cael listed his head. His sly smile stretched into a fanged grin. "No," he said, laughing under his breath.

But at the same time, Elio nodded. "One Aurethian cycle."

Cael's hand went slack around Elio's palm. His grin faded, slow and practiced. The notch in his throat bobbed, and he blinked rapidly, calcifying.

"Sure, one Aurethian cycle," Angelina said, glancing from Elio to Cael. "After which you'll be free to travel between Griea and Aurethia as you see fit. One cycle to establish leadership, rebuild Atreyu, revive Avara distribution, restructure immigration policies, and rekindle the populus. One cycle to create and maintain balance between Aurethia and Griea. Can we agree to that?"

Rune and Wippler nodded.

"It's a progressive plan," Constance said, though she did not sound pleased.

Cael did not speak. He stared at nothing, jaw clenched, lovely blue eyes fixed unwaveringly on the far wall.

"Yes," Elio said. That word cleaved him in two.

"We're done here," Cael snapped, and pushed away from the table. His bootwear smacked the stone, and he left without another word.

I'll see to him, Vik said through Elio's dialect device. The Augment excused himself.

Angelina cleared her throat. "Good, well, I'm pleased to know Avara production will — "

Elio slammed his hand on the table, shaking the dishware. The stagnant room spun with thick, curdling silence. He leveled Angelina with a stone-hard glare. "Let me make myself very clear. This is the only time the Imperium will put distance between us. Any attempt to do so again will be met with the combined *efficiency* of House Volkov and House Henly."

Across from him, Angelina froze. The leader of Draitune did not move, speak, or breathe. Neither did Wippler. Rune, the smartest of the three, inclined her head respectfully.

"You're a friend to my family, Angelina. But I am not my father, and he is not Marcus," Elio said, rising from his seat. *Stay steady, be direct. Do not let them make you weak.* He gave the visitors a long, deliberate look. "Do not test us again."

CHAPTER FORTY-NINE

CAEL

Wind whistled, tossing sparkling dust around Goren's cloudy peak. On the ground level below Sector One, Cael knocked his boots against the wood porch, dislodging stubborn snow. His palm grazed the doorknob. He gripped, twisted, met resistance, then shook his head and dug around in his pocket for an outdated iron key. One he'd kept for emergencies. In case his cousin ever needed anything. When the lock slid free, Cael pushed, greeted with the familiar scent of spruce and hearth.

Bracken's farmhouse was sparsely decorated. Dull light winked past a curtain, and a pair of discarded slippers slouched on the mat. Cael could not convince his body to move for a long while. He stood there, watching dust motes spin, looking from a dish in the sink to a leather-wrapped knife on the counter. His cousin's reindeer coat was draped over a chair.

Live and die with honor.

Cael took a step, then another, walking into the old house. The place Bracken refused to abandon despite having his own chamber at the Volkov castle. The private, secluded home he made for himself, somewhere he could be the son of a leatherworker instead of Optio.

Cael trailed his gloved hand along the back of the chair, fisting the speckled garment. "Won't be the same without you," he mumbled. And nothing would be. Grief swamped him, smothering the relief he wanted to feel, undermining the brief stint of peace he'd earned after running a blade through Bracken in the Tupinaire. "You died well, cousin."

"Nobody dies well."

Ice licked Cael's spine. He whirled toward the living space, palm resting on the handle of his short-sword. Panic swelled. His skull roared with a warning, but he unwound at the sight of Kindra Malkin's spindly frame perched on the seater. She cradled a short glass half-filled with caramel liquor, and wore an alabaster pantsuit textured with floral embroidery. Her face wore a week's worth of sorrow.

"Some of us do," Cael said, heaving an aggravated sigh. "What're you doing here, Kindra?"

She lifted the glass. "Drinking his whiskey. What are you doing here, Legatus?"

I don't know. Part of him did, though. He'd gone looking for a reason, and for a reminder. He wanted to know what pushed Bracken to become what he became, and he thought he might be looking at it: beautifully packaged, scarred by parsec sickness, wearing hatred like a badge. Reminiscence was everywhere — the leather tassel dangling from the bottom of Bracken's coat, hay tracked in from the barn, those slippers by the door. Cael snatched a whetstone, turning the rectangular block over in his hand.

"Searching for something I'll never find." He flashed a small, indignant smile.

Kindra made an ugly noise, snorting like a horse. "I took the lioness's pelt. The one he brought back from Aurethia."

"Keep it," Cael said. Tatu was being transformed into a mantel piece to match the one at the Henly manor. Something he could hang rather than walk on. Anger slivered, thin and translucent. "Did you love him?"

She tapped one coffin-shaped fingernail against the glass. "I loved him the way I think you love Aurethia. It was runoff. A byproduct of something true."

Cael's sad smile parted, but when he tried to reply, he couldn't. The harder he thought about what she said, and the longer he let the sentiment sink, the more her misshapen truth slipped into place like an outfit he wasn't sure would fit.

"You love that Aurethian prince, don't you?"

"I do," he said.

"Does that same passion extend to his homeworld, or did you fall in love with Aurethia because of him? When I met Bracken, I thought he was handsome, and rugged, and..." She lifted the drink, shrugging helplessly.

"Lonely. But then I realized he was living a half-life, walking two steps behind the man he could become. I loved that version of him, I think. The one he might reach in a specific, significant future."

"He could've had a future as my Imperator," Cael said. Grief crested and crashed. He was too tired to entertain it, too fed up with everything he couldn't change to bother dwelling on *what if*. Because if Bracken were still alive, Cael would likely be dead, and there was no changing what transpired a week ago, or a month ago, or a year ago. No way to fold space and time, leap backward, and tell his cousin to believe in him.

"He should've had a future as the ruler of Griea," she said, chewing on every syllable.

Cael smoldered. "I challenged Bracken in the arena, and I won. The end, Kindra."

"No, you committed treason, patricide, and honorific murder in that order."

"So be it."

Kindra's full mouth paled into a line.

Bitterness brewed in the orphaned farmhouse. Kindra shot back the rest of the liquor, and Cael leaned his hip against the table, trying not to let the truth of what she'd said overshadow the future he'd secured.

"Bracken forced my hand," he said too softly. He wanted Bracken back. Not the man who faced him on the ice, but the man who loved him more than status, wealth, and power.

"Maybe," she muttered. "But you forced his, too."

Shame chalked Cael's throat. He looked away, staring into the snowy field through the small window above the sink. "Take whatever you want," he decided, and turned to leave.

"You should keep his coat," she called after him.

Cael stopped, turning to look over his shoulder.

Kindra gestured to the repurposed pelt on the back of the chair. Fur ringed the collar. The leather tassel dangling from the last button turned slowly, as if disrupted by nonexistent wind. "It's much too big, but you could grow into it," she said, saccharine and slow. "You never know, it might fit someday."

Cael rubbed his thumb against his index. He reached down and tugged the decorative tassel free, tucking the leather into his pocket. "Not my style." He met her harsh gaze, and then strode toward the door, leaving Kindra alone in the farmhouse.

Dry cold nipped his face, but he welcomed the frigid temperature and lazy snow. He remembered to breathe deeply, retraining his body to accept the mountainous air. His chest contracted, unused to the higher altitude of his homeworld. Frost scaled his interior, chasing gooseflesh beneath his clothes.

Adjacent to the road, parked next to Cael's sleek, black ground car, Holland leaned against a separate vehicle. Cael's brow pinched. He tilted his head, opening his mouth to call out and ask what Holland was doing there, but the Griean soldier simply nudged his elbow toward the pasture and slipped into the driver's seat.

Cael followed the gesture, turning toward the fenced field where Bracken's reindeer wandered out from the barn, enjoying the snowfall, and munching hay. Standing beyond the fence, wrapped in a scarf, and crowned with a cashmere beanie, Elio smiled cheerily at a friendly cow. He patted her velvety nose. His laughter sent up a silver plume, and he cut a glance at Cael, meeting his gaze on the tail-end of a true smile.

Yesterday they'd argued well into the night, bickering, bartering, begging. The meeting with Angelina left Cael barbed and juvenile, and despite hearing Elio, despite knowing his husband was thinking far more rationally than he was, Cael still managed to slick each complaint with undignified and undeserved venom.

Cael vaulted over the fence and crossed the pasture.

"You left," Elio said.

"You followed."

He brushed his palm down the reindeer's snout, then brought his hand to her antler, feeling across furry bone. "Do you understand what's at stake, Cael? If we push the Imperium, they'll insist on surveillance, and we'll risk exposing Outpost One before we have the chance to start terraforming Mercy and safely extract Alice."

He answered with an annoyed sigh. "I know."

"You can't blame the Imperium for being skeptical. From an outsider's perspective, we managed to skirt a war, seize control of our houses, bury anyone who could contest our leadership, and forge a strategically powerful alliance without compromising our devotion to each other." He lifted his brow and dropped his hand, shielding it inside a tight leather glove. "I'd be afraid of us, too."

Cael watched each slender finger disappear inside the accessory. Elio flexed his hand, tugging the glove by the cuff, and Cael felt the movement like a web plucked in his stomach.

"Let them be afraid," Cael said.

Last night, Elio had stormed around the bedchamber, prattling on about the sacrifice they'd make for the greater good, and Cael had shouted about not giving a damn about goodness. He wanted to be selfish, to keep Elio close, because losing him had been a devastating possibility not too long ago.

Elio clucked his tongue and slid closer, taking Cael by the waist. "We can't run off to a distant planet and pretend we aren't who we are."

"Why not," Cael rasped. He pressed his forehead against Elio's warm brow. "Let's go someplace new, somewhere nobody knows us. I'll swing you around a dancefloor." He watched Elio's mouth tilt. Heard the soft whine in the back of his throat. Reluctance squeezed Cael's vocal cord, frogging his voice. "I don't want to let you go."

"You're not letting me go. I'm not letting you go," he assured, feeling along Cael's buttoned military coat. The High Lord quieted for a heartbeat. His gaze lowered, and his face pinkened. "I understand if you require..." He paused, swallowing uncomfortably. "Companionship. If you take a concubine — "

Cael's hand found the base of Elio's throat. He inched back, forcing Elio to look up at him. "This is not about that," he stressed, tempering a snarl. He cocked his head. Huffed out a bewildered breath and brought his thumb to Elio's mouth. "Will someone be keeping your bed warm, High Lord?"

Elio bristled. "No."

"Then why assume I'd turn my head?"

"I didn't assume — "

"Apologies. You *understood*."

"Well, I lied, I wouldn't understand. I'd put another sword through you."

Honesty seared the space between them, and Cael was thankful for it. "That's what I thought."

Elio snorted, blushing hot. "Fine."

"Good."

"Good," Elio mocked.

Snow landed on the stray wheatish strands peeking out from beneath Elio's hat. Even though it was morning, starlight winked through the pastel aurora, splashing the dark sky white and grey. After a long, awful stint of silence, Cael brought his chilly hands to the underside of Elio's jaw, cradling his face.

"You have undone me," he whispered, dusting his mouth over Elio's temple. "I won't take a concubine, I won't hire a courtesan. You are who I want, Elio."

Vulnerability fractured in Elio's jewel-green eyes. He slackened against him. His body drained of the insecurity he'd masked under an artful threat. "I'm married to the Legatus of Griea. No one would dare come to my bed," he teased. Laughter sputtered. "Honestly, who in their right mind — "

"You'd be surprised," Cael interjected, grinning painfully.

Elio softened. He laid his hand over Cael's knuckles. "There is only you."

Cael tried to nod, but it was a choppy, emotional thing. Everything inside him felt swollen and ripe, like one wrong move might rupture an organ.

"We give the Imperium one cycle. We use that time to brace the starlink. Get Avara production back on track. Balance the harvest schedule and expand our deliveries. Oversee Outpost One's research and use it to strengthen our bid for Mercy." Elio nodded confidently but looked far from satisfied.

"We'll give my mother control of the Planetary Syndicate and put her to work strengthening Griea's relationship with Ocury. Lorelei will lead the Xenobiology Division with Xander, and we can create a higher position for Ulrich in Atreyu. He'll put the aid from Mal into motion. Peadar can handle Nadhas and the manor," Cael added, trying to sound as positive as possible.

"And after one cycle, we'll renew our vow and honeymoon on Zephus, or rent a luxury starcraft, or… or…" Elio paused, exhaling shakily.

"Or we run away right now," Cael purred, brushing his mouth over Elio's cheek, then his chin, speaking an inch from his lips.

Elio sighed through his nose. "And leave my sister to do this alone?"

"After being with her in the crater, I'm sure she'd manage — "

"Cael," he warned, weakly, like he might crumble. His tone said *don't tempt me.*

"I know." Cael brought Elio closer. He wrapped around him, thankful for the way the High Lord nuzzled in close and went heavy against his chest, forehead resting on Cael's breastbone, breath hot and steady over his heart.

The reindeer wandered about, grunting and huffing, and Cael stood with Elio in the vast, unbreakable cold.

Snow kept falling.

They held each other for a long, long time.

THE MORNING THE AURETHIAN transport rumbled to life, Cael kept Elio in his bedchamber for as long as possible. They mapped bone and vein. Set teeth against skin, and gave themselves over to slow, fervid lovemaking. Once Elio managed to peel himself away and walk into the washroom, Cael followed, sharing steam and hot water until they were pruned. And after that, when Elio dressed and crossed the hall, Cael did the same, trailing at his heel. They moved through the castle, drinking dark coffee in the kitchen, pausing to lean into each other in front of the hearth, and perch on the edge of the dining table, and stop mid-sentence to steal a breath, kiss, or promise.

When the time came for Elio to board, they stood together on the tallest veranda, overlooking the spear-tipped obelisk and the terrestrial landing dock at the far edge of the property. The transport idled below, hatch lowered and waiting.

Cael wanted nothing more than to pick Elio up, carry him back to their bedchamber, and lock the door. He wanted to steal him. Hoard him until someone came looking. And even then, even if the entire Imperium threatened to enter Griea's high orbit, he probably wouldn't have the fortitude to let him go.

"I'll send a transmission as soon as we land," Elio said. His voice, although steady, seemed far too controlled given the quake in his hand.

Cael's throat prickled. "Alright."

There was nothing more, was there? They'd said so much and so little this morning, last night, over the course of a cursed courtship. The man before him had become vital in a way Cael couldn't comprehend. Elio was his fate unmade. He was the great love Cael never thought he would experience. The predetermined path Cael always knew he would walk.

Elio turned slowly. His freckled face was snow-bitten, and his nose glowed red. He slid a kiss against Cael's cheek, then took his mouth, tender and deep. His hand slipped into Cael's palm, gripping faintly. When he eased away, Cael watched him through curtained lashes. Memorized the color of their forest moon reflected in his eyes.

Elio's throat bobbed. He said, "I love you," and the crack in his voice ripped a hole through Cael's chest.

"And I love you," Cael breathed out, but it was more than that.

Love seemed unjustly simplistic compared to what they had. Love, yes. But Cael's heart would be marooned without him. Whatever they'd fallen into together, this love-shaped thing he couldn't name, it was the ingredient at the root of everything incomprehensible. It was what happened when life filled a body. When recycled stardust was reshaped into a new, gleaming creature with a fresh, eager mind. It was what woke the living world, and what broke it, too.

Loving Elio made Cael understand ancient religion and epic poetry. It made him realize how blindly and fully he believed the universe — however great, uncharted, and wild — saw their inevitable collision and refused to tear them asunder.

Elio took a step backward, then another. He tried to walk, but Cael kept hold of his hand, squeezed his knuckles. Cael pulled, just so. With his arm outstretched, Elio came rushing back, crashing, gasping, reaching. They were tangled, stumbling into the doorway, prying at each other like caged, crazed things. But the kiss had to end, and Elio had to go.

Elio slid his palms away from Cael's face, dragging his cold fingertips along swollen lips, and turned away before he could change his mind, before Cael could yank him back again. Without another word, the High Lord walked briskly through the castle. Cael watched him go, waiting to see if he might stop and look over his shoulder or pause and run back to him, but Elio stormed straight to the transport, and disappeared up the ramp without a single glance backward.

Cael stayed on the veranda. He watched the transport lift, sending snow twirling through the air, and savored the leftover taste of candlebell balm on his mouth.

CHAPTER FIFTY

ELIO

Elio hardly remembered the trip home. It was miserable — that he did know — not only because he'd left Cael standing on a balcony, stricken and alone, but because Vik did the logical, helpful thing, and stayed behind on Griea, too, and because Holland, Cael's loyal friend, left the ice giant to accompany him.

At first, he felt like he'd stolen something important, as if Holland hadn't made the decision to join him of his own volition. But after wallowing in pitiful silence for the first leg of the long, interstellar journey, Holland finally convinced him to sit down for a Griean card game, and told Elio about his hunger for adventure, and his excitement to live in another place. He was jovial and sweet, and his enthusiasm made the reality of returning as the reigning High Lord more tolerable.

The new title still seemed foreign. His neck ached under the pressure of House Henly's proverbial crown. When they arrived, the manor was already being repaired, Lorelei was nose-deep in research for the Xenobiology Division, Ulrich and the northern militia had started rebuilding what was lost during the battle for Atreyu, and Outpost One pivoted their effort to focus on what Mercy's new habitat might look like for Alice.

Aurethia lived. Elio knew it would, but watching the moon bounce back from catastrophe soothed his battered heart.

Maxine kept to herself, attending the house staff, and quietly stalking through the manor. She spent most of her time with Orson, convincing him to eat, draw, or swim in the sea. Elio didn't speak to her. Couldn't stomach the idea. But on a particularly crisp morning, the liaison drifted into the garden and joined Elio at the table where his mother used to sit. She wore Griean-black, and bowed her head, trembling like a child. When she asked for permission to return to Griea, he allowed it. The relief on her face splintered as she delivered an ambitious apology, devolving into a messy, ugly heap, sputtering and sobbing. Elio no longer had the energy to direct his rage at the past, but he did have the good sense to silently forgive her. Holding fast to what she'd done, to their charade of a friendship and the violence she'd facilitated, would've anchored each step he took toward a sustainable future. He already had too much to carry, and he took solace knowing she would face the Legatus in Machina.

The seasonal wheel turned, and Elio missed Cael every day, every night. It was sharp at first, like a shard jammed through the sole of his foot. But it dulled after a while. His nightmares lessened. Sometimes they jostled free like a trapped wasp, buzzing ceaselessly, and sometimes they vanished, replaced by deep slumber or a dark-tunneled dreamscape. Sometimes he shot awake drenched in sweat, coiled around a fantasy, wishing he could dive back into a dream where Cael was with him.

They communicated frequently. Cael sent transmissions and joined him for holomeetings. He ordered sweet pastries from the Ocurian bakery they'd visited in Atreyu to be delivered to the manor, and a vase of peonies appeared on Elio's table in the Henly library once a month. Elio managed gestures of his own, sending keepsakes and gifts to the castle — a new Grabak to replace the short-sword Cael had lost in the arena, and a hand-hammered iron bracelet lovingly crafted by a merchant in the city.

When they weren't flirting across the cosmos, Elio saw the flash of Cael's face in the blue-shine of a hologram, bartering with planetary leadership for fledgling trade deals, or cladding Elio's political maneuverings with Griean teeth. Privately, Elio huddled in his bed, clutching a holotablet, whispering and laughing with his husband when they stole rare moments alone.

By the time summer arrived, Lorelei managed to bolster the Xenobiology Division's effort with a fundraiser on Draitune, smartly steering the purpose of their initiative to focus on Avara expansion and a healthier marketplace instead of the slumbering alien hidden in the crater. She relaxed into herself again. Dropped her sword and shield and threw her beautiful mind and sharp wit into science. Sometimes she came to Elio's bedchamber after a nightmare turned her stomach. Sometimes they found themselves in the kitchen when no one else was awake. On those nights, Elio drank peppermint tea with his sister. They told stories about their childhood or shared companionable silence, stuck in the throes of grief that would never truly settle.

Halfway through the slow-moving cycle, the annual galactic summit called the imperial leadership or their representatives to gather on Draitune — Elio's first official appearance as the Aurethian High Lord. He fully expected to see Duchess Constance, who had confirmed her attendance as the Griean ambassador, but after the summit began, in the midst of boring introductions, an augmented hand clasped the shoulder of the person beside Elio, and Vik leaned down to politely ask the emissary from Hük to find a new seat.

Cael Volkov, Legatus of Griea and Lord of Aurethia, the speaker drone announced.

In strode Cael, draped in a fine black suit, flanked by a short line of Royal Reserve. Elio hadn't expected his heart to spasm. Hadn't expected his pulse to skyrocket or his mind to wipe itself of anything, everything else. All he saw was Cael, looking exactly how he'd left him, looking like an entirely new man.

The Legatus took the seat beside him and cast an amused glance around the wide, circular conference room. He opened his leather-clad hand as if to say *continue,* and then leaned back in his chair, propping his elbow on the armrest. Elio composed himself as quickly and efficiently as he could and moved through the summit with grace and strength. He advocated for Aurethia, spoke frequently about Griea, shut down combative remarks about the use of the starlink, encouraged a reassessment of planetary necessities, and sowed another seed about terraforming Mercy, mentioning Lorelei's successful campaign earlier in the summer. Cael reinstated their intention to put forth a stable immigration policy and addressed concerns about the lapse in organic and non-organic weaponry distributed from Griean territories.

For the most part, the summit went well, but it was the political mixer afterward that sent gossip rippling through the Greater Universe. And not the *mixer,* per se, not the way Elio and Cael managed to stand together, speak cordially to their colleagues, smile and nod... But the holoimage someone snapped once the mingling slowed. A holoimage of Elio and Cael entering a capsule elevator together. The perfectly stolen moment when the door slid shut: Elio and Cael dropping their façade, whipping toward each other, reaching. That image — Elio's hand clutching the back of Cael's tattooed skull, and Cael grasping his cheek, thumb pressed to his chin, their parted lips on a path to collision — sparked a tabloid wildfire across Lux, Mal, and Ren. People near and far called them the *promised pair*.

That small, vulnerable snapshot offered the Greater Universe a tender glimpse at what they'd fought for. It gave their people hope.

As embarrassing as the attention might've been, Elio was almost thankful for it.

After the summit, Cael joined Elio in a complimentary suite on the top floor of one of Draitune's many luxury hotels. They drank champagne straight from the bottle, laughed, tore at each other's clothes, and when they were tired and boneless, wrung out and satiated, they talked well into the night about Alice, children, Moro, fruit harvesting, birthdays, Thanjō, and hunting, filling each other in on what they'd missed, reassuring each other of everything to come. Cael left before dawn, slipping out under the shade of early morning. It was a terrible kindness, sparing them both another goodbye.

Elio had counted each sunrise and sunset since then.

It was a cool, balmy morning twenty-seven days after his twentieth birthday when he watched a starcraft float into low orbit. He plucked uselessly at his cream-colored shirt and adjusted the Aurethian glyph strung around his neck. Across the meadow, Aurethia's pride lounged in the tall grass, swatting playfully at each other. Farther, the orchard stirred, woken by the first breath of spring, and beyond it, sea spray salted the cliffside.

Time passed slowly and not at all.

On a similar morning not so long ago, Elio had met his fiancé for the first time, and Cael had been the answer to a question Elio had never stopped asking. A prophecy his heart kept chasing. A promise two centuries in the making.

The familiar thud of a bootstep hit the grass beside him.

Griea paled Cael's complexion. The War College sharpened his stature. Bold, black ink striped his throat, caressing the underside of his jawline. It was a striking, beautiful piece, resembling the interconnected geometric staircase on his spine, only simpler, cleaner. Line after shadowy line carved down his neck. The new tattoo aged him a fraction — artwork designed for a leader. His glacial gaze scanned Aurethia, drifting from the treeline to the coast. His blind eye glinted like a distant star. The cybernetic augmentation within seemed to glitter, netting over his damaged pupil. A smile curved his thin mouth.

"Legatus," Elio greeted.

Cael slid him a slow glance. "High Lord."

Birdsong whistled. A flowery breeze kicked through the estate. Elio could not fathom moving. If he did, he might jolt awake in his bedchamber and the wish he'd made would vanish.

Cael took his hand. His thumb trailed the ridge of every knuckle. "Elio, darling."

"Cael," he whispered.

Elio let out a small, choked breath. His heart felt swollen and too big, as if it had reached through Elio's ribcage and swallowed a missing piece of itself. *You are awake, Elio Henly*, he thought, blissful, ready. *You are awake and alive*. Sunder beamed, wreathing them in newborn light.

"I'm here." Cael Volkov, Keeper of the Basilisk, pressed his forehead to Elio's brow.

And the lion of Aurethia finally, truly smiled. "We're here."

THE
END

PRONUNCIATION GUIDE

The Lux *luh – x* **System**

Sunder *sun – der*

Aurethia *arr – reh – thee – uh*

- Nadhas *nod – haas*
- Atreyu *uh – trey – oo*
- Basset *baas – set*
- Denae *den – eye*
- Yōng *y – ong*
- Thanjō *th – aan – joe*
- Sindra Kimura *sin – dr – ah · kim — oor — uh*
- Melody *mel – uh — dee*
- Innis *in – niss*
- Xander *zan – der*

House Henly *hen – lee*

- Darius Henly *dahr – ee – uhs*
- Lena Henly *lee – nuh*
- Lorelei Henly *lor – eh – lie*
- Orson Henly *oar – sun*
- Elio Henly *eh – lee – oh*
- Alexander Henly *al – lex – an — der*
- Indigo Condon *in – dih – goh · con - duhn*
- Peadar Mahone *pay – daar · mah - hone*

- Ulrich Hutch *ool – rick · huh – tch : hutch*
- Luke *l — oo – k*
- Ciara *see – are — uh*
- Niam *nee – aam*

Draitune *draah – toon*

- Angelina Darvin *an – gel – ee – nuh · darr – vin*
- Ilya Chamber *ill – ee — uh · cham — burr*

Ocury *ock – yew – ree*

Sierra *see – air — uh*

Divinity *div – in — it — tee*

Shepard *shep – ard*

Griea *gree – uh*

- Machina *mock – eh – nuh*
- Goren *gore – en*
- Grabak *grah – bah — ck*

House Volkov *vohl – kahv*

- Marcus Volkov *mar – cuss*
- Constance Volkov *con – stuh — nce*
- Bracken Volkov *br — a – ken*
- Cael Volkov *kay – uhl : kale*
- Harlyn Volkov *har – lin*
- Maxine Caar *max – seen · ca – r : car*
- Vik Endresen *v – ick · en – dreh – sen*
- Kindra Malkin *kin – druh · mahl – kin*
- Kasimir Malkin *kas – sim – eer · mahl – kin*
- Holland Lancaster *haul – land · lan – cast — err*

The Ren *reh – n* **System**

Vandel Prime *van – dell · pr – eye –m : prime*

Lokahn *low – con*

- Rune Makosi *ruhn : rune · mah – kos – ee*

The Mal *ma – hl* **System**

Hük *hee – ook*

- Scarab Muir *scare – uhb · mew – uhr*

Zephus *zeh – fuss*

- Wippler Jye *whip – plur · j – eye*
- Gyana *jee – on – uh*

ABOUT THE AUTHOR

Atlas Laika is the author of *Aurethia Rising*. By day, they work at a non-profit designed to bridge the agricultural gap between sustainable farming and neighborhood access to homegrown food. They've worked with wildlife, practice yoga, enjoy teaching, and even though they're not very handy in the kitchen, they love to cook. They spend their evenings writing about space travel, star dust, sword fights, and smooching.

Made in the USA
Monee, IL
09 May 2025

16962267R10270